Red Lion's Shadow

A Novel

Amazon Best-Selling Award-Winning Author

Merrie P. Wycoff

Red Lion's Shadow

Merrie P. Wycoff

Published by: Rosa Mystica

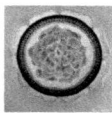

Publishing, Colorado

merriewycoff.com
meritaten11@yahoo.com
merriepwycoff@substack.com

Cover Art: Marty Petersen
Interior: Merrie P Wycoff & Tharanga Prasad Gamage
Back cover: Mak @makgraphic72

ISBN: 978-0-9848906-6-8

Library of Congress Control Number: 2025917562
First Edition
Printed in the United States of America

1. Historical Fiction 2. Paranormal Fiction 3. Spiritual/New Age 4. Women's Fiction 5. African Spirituality 6. Ancient Egyptian Spiritualty 1. Title 2025917562

10   9   8   7   6   5   4   3   2   1

Dedicated to Abd'El Hakim Awyan
1923-2008

To Papa Hakim —
Opener of Gates, Keeper of the Ancient Tongue,
who led me across the Threshold into the eyes of Khemit.
And to my Beloved —
Jewish Rabbi,
Catholic Bishop,
Egyptian Adept —
you who once walked beside me in sand and star,
and commanded I return to the scroll.
Ten years later, you placed into my hands
the gold thread of Akhenaten,
the hidden vessel of Alchemy,
and the breath of Spirit.
To Nana & Baba — Elders of the Blood and the Flame,
and to the Moors who found me worthy to stand among them.
To Thoth — Winged Architect of my remembrance,
who lifted me beyond the earthbound scripts.
To Thei'on — who lit the deeper chamber of my pen
and bid me write until the marrow sang.
May you all be exalted,beyond measure and beyond time,
for bringing me home
and pouring the sweet water of Khemit to my lips.

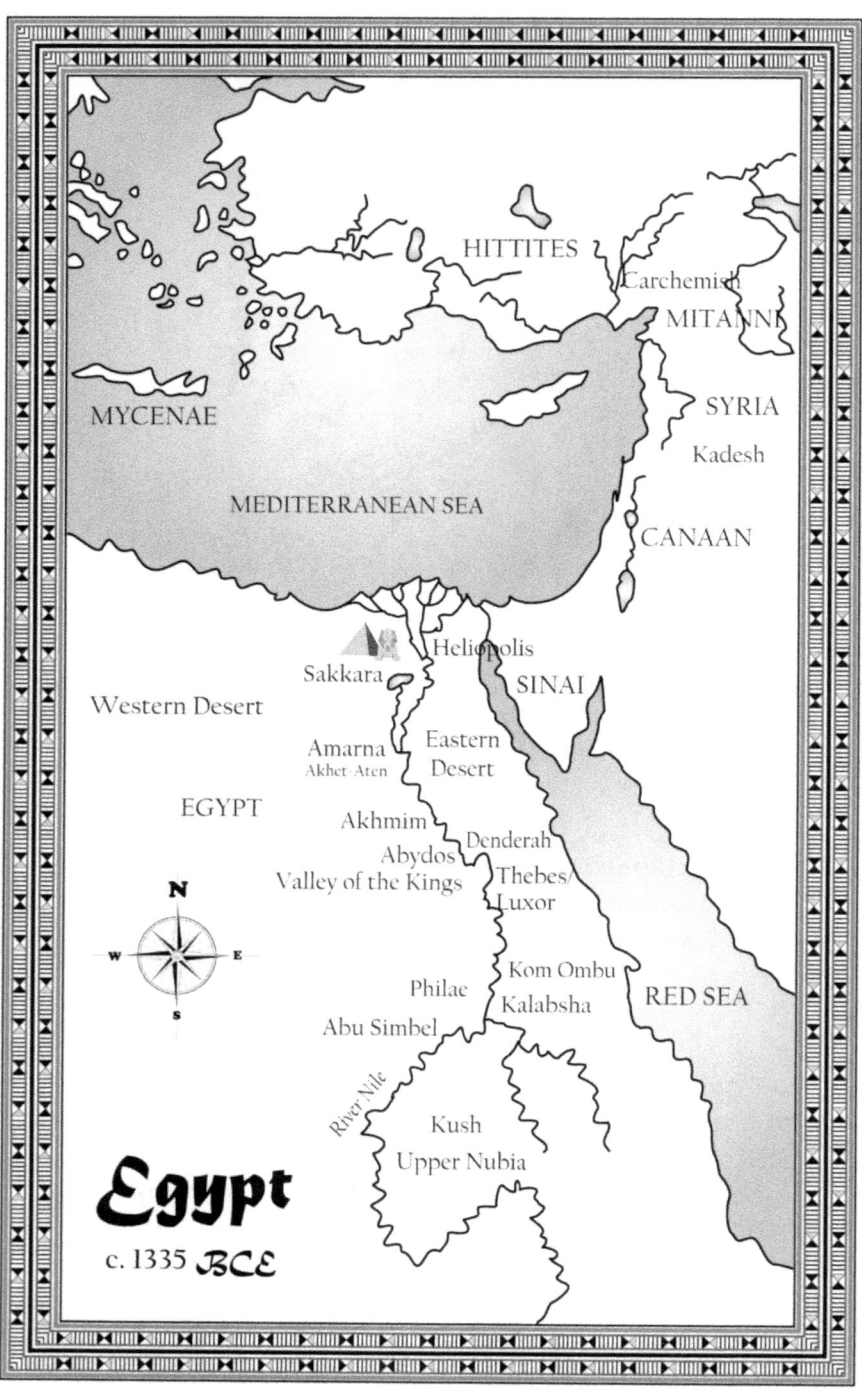

HITTITES

Carchemish

MITANNI

MYCENAE

SYRIA

Kadesh

MEDITERRANEAN SEA

CANAAN

Heliopolis

Sakkara

SINAI

Western Desert

Amarna
Akhet-Aten

Eastern
Desert

EGYPT

Akhmim

Denderah

Abydos

Thebes/
Luxor

Valley of the Kings

N

Kom Ombu

Philae

W   E

Kalabsha

RED SEA

Abu Simbel

S

River Nile

Kush

Egypt

Upper Nubia

c. 1335 *BCE*

foreword

When Abd'el Hakim Awyan, the Wisdom Keeper of the Giza Plateau, taught us that in ancient Khemit "If it had to be written down, it wasn't the whole truth," he revealed an insight that forever changed how I viewed history. The more I studied, the more I realized that written accounts—especially those preserved in official histories—often reflect power, politics, and prejudice rather than truth.

As I pored over ancient texts and examined historical "facts," I saw how often curses, like those of the Apepi, or politically motivated edits concealed deeper realities. One distortion struck me deeply: the vilification of Pharaoh Akhenaten, the so-called "Heretic King." For daring to step away from the entrenched Amun priesthood, his name was erased from the 18th Dynasty King List and nearly from memory itself. From a young age, I asked: *Who gets to write history? What if what we've been taught—through textbooks, media, and film—is not truth at all, but a carefully crafted version favoring the victors?*

In Khemit, rulers themselves often rewrote the past. Hatshepsut claimed to have restored Thebes after the Hyksos, conveniently shaping the record to enhance her reign. Luxor Temple, Hakim reminded us, was built atop older, hidden structures—material proof of the layers of civilization and erasure beneath our feet.

Years of research, initiation, and startling revelation led me to uncover a hidden truth—a deception threaded through generations. In that moment, I began to wonder: what if the story could live in two worlds at once, uniting ancient wisdom with modern struggle in a time-travel epic fantasy?

This lens drove me to retell Nefertiti and Akhenaten's story and bring *The Shadow Saga* into being. Years of research, study, and unexpected revelations culminated in December 2023, when inspiration flooded in and the final chapter of Merit-Aten's journey emerged—bridging her ancient life with the modern story of Morainya Napolitano. Across millennia, these two women face the same gauntlet—persecution by shadowed powers, the slow poison of manipulation, and the perilous climb back to sovereignty. Both walk the razor's edge between truth and propaganda, between their soul's calling and forces determined to erase them.

In that process, I came to understand that the story of Khemit is also the story of the Moors—the indigenous, melanated people of Africa, whose mastery of mathematics, astronomy, architecture, sacred geometry, alchemy, and law predates and informs so much of what the world now calls "civilization." I write as one who is not of that bloodline, but as one who has been blessed to learn from its descendants and to bear witness to its truth. This trilogy is my offering of respect, solidarity, and remembrance.

Hakim himself was proud of his African heritage and taught that Khemit was a cultural nexus of many peoples long before Greece or Rome. The ancient Sesh may have spoken one of the first languages on Earth. Master Teacher Bobby Hemmitt spoke of a new Khemitian people rising from the West—not defined by race, but by consciousness—who would change the world. Rod Hayes reminded us that labels like "black" and "Negro" were constructs used to control and misidentify, and that the true "firstborn of the earthborn" must reclaim their rightful name.

Khemit's wisdom—its alchemy, its reverence for life's cycles—has guided me in birthing this trilogy. My hope is that *The Shadow Saga* dismantles some of the false narratives we have inherited and restores threads of truth. May Akhenaten's dream of unity take root in a world that so needs it.

This final volume, *Red Lion's Shadow*, unveils some of the Khemystery of Alchemy, for in ancient Khemit, every moment was transformation. May the Aten will it, and may you be transformed within these pages.

We begin with the **Great Hymn to the Aten**, translated from hieroglyphs by Rabbi Hockmun Torvund. This sacred poem—closely paralleling Psalm 104—evokes the same monotheistic vision and imagery of the lion, the birds, and creation itself, revealing the deep literary and spiritual kinship between Khemit and ancient Israel.

book may be based on research, all legal scenarios, characters, and outcomes are fictionalized for the purpose of storytelling. Readers should consult a qualified legal professional for any real-life legal concerns."

This work also contains interpretations of historical events, spiritual traditions, and cultural beliefs. These interpretations are the creative vision of the author and are not presented as definitive historical, religious, or scholarly fact. Readers are encouraged to explore multiple sources and perspectives when studying the historical and spiritual themes touched upon in this book.

No part of this work is intended to offend, misrepresent, or appropriate any culture, tradition, or belief system. Where inspiration has been drawn from existing traditions, it has been done with the intent of honoring their richness and complexity while placing them in a fictional context.

Preface — A Glimpse Back at Shadow of the Sun

Shadow of the Sun: A Daughter's Awakening

They called me the fruit of divine bloodlines, the golden child of Pharaoh Amunhotep IV—who later became Akhenaten—and his Queen, Nefertiti. But before the glory of Aten bathed my face in holy fire, before temples rose in the desert, before they crowned me priestess or bride... I was just a child. A child trained in the glittering halls of the Malkata Palace at Thebes, playing among politics I could barely understand.

The palace shimmered with opulence—ivory inlay, lapis floors, ceilings painted like the midnight sky. I remember long colonnades where my bare feet padded softly, long linen skirts swishing with each step swinging my side-lock braids of youth. Gold cuffs kissed my wrists; my neck, heavy with filigree amulets. Yet all this finery was armor, not adornment. I knew even then that my presence was not just adored—it was political.

Sit-Amun, my great-aunt and rival to my mother, watched me like a crocodile in still water. She was an over-looked Great Chief Wife of Pharaoh with no power. Her angry beauty was sharp—brown eyes, kohl-lined, with a voice that could summon dread. One afternoon, I was chasing a Hoopoe bird in the courtyard with my beloved dwarf attendant, Hep-Mut, when I spotted a small carved ivory horse tucked beneath a statue of a man. I cradled it like treasure—it fit so perfectly in my palm. I did not know it was Sit-Amun's. I was just a girl who found something magical.

Later, aboard a royal barge gilded in gold and purple, Sit-Amun saw the figurine in my hands. Her voice turned venomous. "That is mine," she hissed. "Give it back."

My heart raced. I stood tall, defiant and refused to hand over my beloved treasure to a sorceress who planned an ill fate for my family. "Then go find it," I said, and threw the horse into the Nile.

Gasps rippled across the deck.

My nursemaid, Hep-Mut, dove in after it—blessed be her bravery—but then I saw Sit-Amun whisper incantations under her breath. A dark current shifted. Crocodiles began circling and dragged my nursemaid to her doom. That was the day I knew Thebes was no longer safe for my family.

Father's face was stormy when we returned. Cloaked in violet crownlight, his aura spirals upward like incense toward the One Light. The energy around him hums with transmutation and mystic geometry. To look upon him too long is to risk becoming undone. He pulled me close, his voice firm but calm. "You must learn what power means, my Little Sun." He spoke then of his vision—the Aten, the One Light, the source of all.

In paradox, my mother, Nefertiti, had red flamelight coils around her, radiant and seductive, sovereign and sharp. She carries the scent of myrrh and ambition, with eyes that calculate lineage, legacy, and lust, and had other plans.

She trained my posture, my smile, my words. "You must be a queen," she'd say while brushing perfumed oils into my hair. "One day you will marry a prince of Nubia, or perhaps Babylon. You will protect Khemit's borders with swords, sons and gold."

But I... I was torn.

My heart longed for the hidden rooms of the temples, where silence hummed and hieroglyphs whispered. I loved the sacred rituals of Aten, the soft footfalls of priests at high noon when the Sun was brightest in the sky, the sound of water poured in libation. I knew my father wanted me to walk the path of Initiate—perhaps to become a High Priestess of Aten. And yet the court expected me to marry. To become a pawn.

My Father and Mother ascended to Co-Regency, which enraged my Aunt Sit-Amun. But power in Thebes was poisoned. The priests of Amun sneered behind papyrus fans while promising protection with false allegiance behind false smiles. Sit-Amun tightened her alliances with the Amun sorcerers. Assassins whispered in alleys against the Aten worshippers. I discovered a terrible secret about Sit-Amun which sealed our fate as enemies. When my Grandfather, the great Amunhotep III, passed from this realm, everything shifted. My father changed his name Akhenaten and as the ruling Pharaoh, believed he had the power to alter the destiny of its people by moving from an Amun priesthood who built their power on greed, superstition and fear, to one of unity and love therefore he closed the temples of old, outlawed the pantheon of gilded gods and promoted the worship of the Aten Sun available to all instead of just the elite. He banished the Amun High Priests to a marble quarry and reduced their once-mighty voices to dust in the wind, their chants swallowed by the sound of chisels striking stone.

In retaliation, there were many assassination attempts upon our lives. My father, Akhenaten said only this: We must go. Under the cover of darkness, his General—Horemheb—arranged for the Aten worshippers to flee Thebes, trailing down the Nile like a living serpent, torches flickering along the water's mirrored skin. This was a man of iron and discipline, loyal—but dangerous. Horemheb never hid his disdain for Father's pacifism. "A kingdom must be defended," he once said to me, his hands gripping the hilt of his khepesh sword, the bronze catching the torchlight like molten fire. "Your father's Light won't stop the Hittites." And yet, the Aten had touched even this hardened man. His voice softened only when his gaze turned toward my mother—our one unexpected blessing in those uncertain nights.

I nodded, but my heart recoiled.

The journey was a nightmare—when my mother overwhelmed with my young sisters, commanded I take another barge. Fortunately, Amaret, the blind elder Seer felt my despair and opened my eyes to another world as we slipped away the crumbling temples of Amun. Behind us: the heavy shadows of greed and fear. Ahead: a blank slate.

When we arrived at the desolate place where the desert met the sky, Father disembarked barefoot. His feet sinking into the cool morning sand. The first light of dawn crowned him in violet fire as he lifted his arms. "Here," he declared, voice steady against the empty wind, "we will build a city for Aten."

I remember the silence that followed—not fear, but awe. No birds. No trees. Only sun and stone, and the unshakable will of a visionary. He named it Akhet-Aten—the Horizon of the Aten—a city of gold waiting to rise from the bones of the desert.

While Pharaoh was elated to start fresh, my mother was horrified to be torn from the life of glamour and prestige she curated as the ruling Per Aat back in Thebes.

Father sketched its plans himself, with trembling hands and divine fervor—a palace without hidden chambers, temples without idols, windows everywhere, so the Aten's light could enter every sacred space.

And I? I stood between two worlds.

At night, I listened to my mother whisper plans of marriage alliances to protect our borders. "Khemit has enemies," she warned. "Your father may believe in peace, but the world is ruled by warriors who buy peace with gold." She had arranged meetings with generals, emissaries from Libya and the Levant—men whose eyes lingered too long.

In the mornings, I trained with Pentu my father's Physician. We studied sacred geometry, chanted hymns of light, traced the meanings of the sacred cartouches carved into Father's temples. His green heartlight pools around his hands, always steady, pulsing gently like the healing rhythm of the body. A scar bisects his bald pate, a relic from a Hittite ambush—but his spirit is unbroken. In Pentu, I found both healer and witness. He saw my gifts—my ability to talk to animals, read the shifting colors of auras, and to ask far too many questions to be a content as a silent ornament in the palace halls.

My favorite moment was when I would rise before dawn, wrap myself in sheer alabaster linen, and slip barefoot through the cool corridors to the sanctuary before the world stirred. The moment the first beam of sunlight pierced the horizon and lit the solar altar—I wept. I wept because for that breathless instant, I felt seen—not as a daughter, not as a bargaining chip, but as a soul.

Still... I was watched. Always watched. By Sit-Amun's spies, by my own mother 's assessing gaze, and by the Nile priests who questioned whether a child like me could bear two callings—daughter of the Per Aat and novice of the Aten.

My father now Pharaoh Akhenaten—selected the first class of initiates for the Solar Mysteries. He did not choose only from among the priestly bloodlines or military families. No—he chose with vision, not tradition. Many were children born of my grandfather's vast Harem, each bearing some noble lineage or gift of the spirit.

But there was one whose selection rippled through the court like a dropped amphora: a foreign boy named Archollos.

He was not of Khemit. His hair curled like sun-warmed barley, and his eyes held storms—blue and unsettled. My mother had rescued him from the wreckage of a Mycenaean merchant ship that had capsized near the Delta. No name, no papers. Just a boy with a soul that whispered of other stars. He was a foreigner, unbound by our blood or customs, yet my heart ached for him in ways I could not name.

My grandmother, the sharp-eyed and sharper-tongued Queen Ti- Yee, warned me. "Initiation is a perilous path. You will lose much before you gain wisdom. She was right...I lost many a friend.

Her presence anchored us when storms came for even I as the Pharaoh's daughter, was put to task by the Solar Lords who made me abide by three words: Ego, Salvation, Revelation

The initiatory rites were not the soft teachings the court imagined. They were brutal in their honesty, relentless in their purification. We fasted. We bathed in sound and silence.

We faced our deepest fears in the Heliopolitan Temple. Its towering obelisks casting long, solemn shadows over sandstone courtyards where every wall seemed to hum with the voice of the Sun God. The air shimmered with heat and whispered in languages older than Khemit, each grain of sand a witness to vows I had not yet spoken.

At Edfu, the falcon-guarded gates rose before us, their massive pylons etched with battles between light and shadow, the air heavy with the scent of ancient incense.

Finally, we entered the Hathor realm at Denderah, where the great columns bloomed with celestial blue ceilings studded with golden stars, and I learned the art of midwifery—only to, by chance, strike a fateful bargain to save a life.

And Grand Djeti, Ti-Yee, was the only one who told me the truth about choosing a consort. Draped in indigo linen that matched the depth of her seeing, her face held the fine lines of a woman who had witnessed too much of both glory and ruin. The downturn of her lips was not from bitterness, but from the burden of knowing how kingdoms rise and fall over the matter of the heart.

She leaned close, her eyes like polished obsidian, and said, "Mark me—love is not always a reward. Sometimes, it is the crucible."

Her words clung to me like incense smoke, seeping into my hair and skin, impossible to wash away. I did not yet know how soon I would be tested in its fire.

Yet even I knew: Khemit was at its zenith. Vast territories stretched beneath our banner. Trade flowed with Punt and far beyond. Gold poured from Nubia carried as tribute by dignitaries eager to cultivate the Pharaoh's favor by offering not only their sons abut their alliance. Father's beliefs had to be protected, even if it meant the shield of military might.

I would have to choose.

Priestess—or Princess.

Flamebearer—or Diplomatic Shield.

That is what Shadow of the Sun chronicles: not merely the rise of a new city—but the rise of a soul.

Mine.

Born into gold and conflict, I stood in the eye of the storm. The daughter of sun and war, of vision and intrigue. The girl who saw the light—and had to choose how to carry it.

All things are possible. Who you are is limited by who you think you are.

Egyptian Book of the Dead

1335 BCE

The Amun's priests collected in a tight huddle in the Holy of Holies, a shadowy inner temple in Karnak, to conspire against the Pharaoh, they deemed 'The Heretic.' In long black robes, they circled before the flickering candles. The black sorcerers prostrated at the feet of the golden statue of a man, Amun, designed to represent their invisible god. Their devotion lay wholly with the unseen, primordial essence of the Anu, from which the Sun and all creation first arose.

Ases-Amun, the Chief High Priest, raged, "Amun, the Hidden One is the Lord of All the Universe. He is the Primal Creator and Mover from whom all life came. Amun ordained us to have complete power and control over everything in the universe. Ineffable. Secret. Hidden. Invisible. Inexplicable. This is the game. We make the rules. We have the gold. We have all the power. If the masses do not comply, their bond to the eternal soul will be severed, and their passage into the afterlife will be denied." Blackened fingernails told the tale of a man who had poisoned the masses with sorcery until it poisoned him in return. The quarry prison had warped him—spine bent, frame frail. Yet now, the withered old man savored his vengeance on the Pharaoh who had condemned and banished him—never imagining his return to power.

"Jai Amun," declared the priests, nodding in agreement. Wisps of Khyphi incense spiraled up making thick clouds. Yellowed sandstone blocks had turned smokey. They met in secret in the hidden inner sanctum of the greater Temple. The golden bowl of hot Kamut wheat drizzled with honey, einkorn bread and beer were placed delicately before the feet of the idol as the morning offering.

"How dare Pharaoh Akhenaten close our temples, drain our coffers? How dare Pharaoh outlaw the venerable god Amun? How dare Pharaoh decree that no old gods be worshiped other than the one god of the Sun, Aten," accused Ases-Amun. He delighted in inciting indignity amongst his followers. They replied in a chorus of rage. "Squeeze the life from them all. We shall place blame for drought on his reign. The life-giving waters shall run dry. Famine shall spread, and a blight upon the land shall bring down the Sun Pharaoh. Let us conjure the spells to cease the inundation of the Nile."

Ases-Amun waved his hands over the firepit, as the Temple priest sacrificed the goat by running a sharp blade across its vulnerable throat. That allowed its blood to spill into the flames; thereby feeding the incantation.   "Hapi, the Water Neter shall not smile upon this king," stated the pale priest in charge of offerings.

The attending priests shouted, "Starve him. Attack him. Split the family. Wipe him from history." They waved their hands and threw spices and aromatic herbs into the fire, stoking it alarmingly higher in this enclosed room.

Yet, in a barren desert in the heart of Khemit, there lay a city named Akhet-Aten. Once radiant with life, it now shimmered only with memory. This was the home of the Pharaoh's Royal dwelling Palace, a place that had once glittered in gold and song. The whitewashed talatat blocks stacked to the sky in this open-air Aten Temple, allowed the full sun to pour in like sacred breath. Colorful flags snapped in the breeze atop the crest of limestone pillars, their movement at odds with the heavy stillness that now thickened the air.

The crowd had thinned—once in the thousands, now a mere five hundred remained. They came starved and silent, to prostrate themselves in utter humility before him, mourning their Wested—the beloved dead—claimed by drought burial in the North Cemetery at sunrise. Pharaoh Akhenaten and the Per Aat, his queen, Nefertiti had just concluded the burial rites. They turned now toward the Aten worship ceremony; solemn and radiant their grief folded into devotion.

Behind them, my younger sisters and I stood in practiced formation, copper cymbal sistrums in hand, ready to accentuate the liturgy with rhythm of divine remembrance.

Our sheer white linen sheaths clung to our bodies like river mist, matching Mother's ceremonial raiment. I admired her—our Queen—whose rounded copper hips swayed through woven threads like a full moon under a silk veil. She tossed her black braids behind her, the golden beads at the ends clicking in a cadence only she could command.

I mimicked her motion—flipping my own braids back over my shoulder—then nervously adjusted the simple golden band encircling my brow. It marked me as an initiated Princess of Akhet-Aten, daughter of the sun, nearing my 16th born day. I was now of age to choose a consort. My heart fluttered at the weight of that truth.

Father stood before the altar, bathed in sunbeams. I bit my lip watching him draw the golden rays of the Aten into his chest with each breath, then send them outward—offering comfort to the wounded hearts before him. His voice—gentle, unwavering—began the Akhu Ashauru Aten, the Devotional Liturgy to the One God. And the people wept not out of sorrow, but of recognition. His love was pure. His joy transcended flesh. And yet the bones beneath his skin betrayed him.

I recalled the court in Thebes when he was first declared co-regent, only seventeen years ago. Back then, his father, Pharaoh Amunhotep III had bathed him in golden praise. Now, at just thirty-five, Akhenaten was vilified. The Amunite priests branded him a desecrator of all that was holy. They whispered that he had angered the Nile itself, that the gods had turned their backs, that the drought was his curse.

A lump caught in my throat. One day, I vowed, I would write the truth. I would gather the scrolls, speak the names, and banish the lies that dared bury my father's legacy.

I clenched my left hand to ground my thoughts. I would not cry. Not here.

He was no warrior-king, not trained in swords or siege. He was a priest of the Light. And only this king—my father—had dared to sever the chains of tyranny that bound our people to fear. Past pharaohs built their reigns on conquest to smite their neighboring enemies. They raped, tortured, and killed to please the old gods and the greedy priesthood. Their lust for land, for gold, and for the echo of their names in the mouths of the dead. The Amunites—those spider priests—spun fear into law, superstition in scripture, and greed into glory.

I bear witness to the Amun legacy of tyranny because I, Merit-Aten, am the eldest daughter of Akhenaten, the Forgotten One.

My breath caught. The faces—so many faces—sunken cheeks, bones pushing against paper-thin skin, distended bellies of children long past hunger. The signs of prolonged famine. And worse—anemia's ghost: brittle limbs, hollowed eyes, and skin ashen with loss. Death was not a stranger here. It lived among us.

The Amunites blamed the drought on Pharaoh. They said he had abandoned the old gods, and so the Nile abandoned us. They turned the people against him with venomous sermons. His most loyal servants fled in fear. Even now, as he stood before them, his ribs rose with effort. His schenti, only tailored to his form, now had to be cinched at the waist. Only the turquoise fine linen cape hid his own suffering. The golden Horus Falcon pectoral he wore—once a symbol of might—seemed almost too heavy for this thinning frame. But still, he stood.

Still, he sang.

Still, he loved.

But even as his shoulders sagged under the weight of the golden Horus, my inner eye opened.

I remembered.

There, behind his throne, once blazed the Atenic Portal—a living, geometric flame of every shifting brilliance. At his command, it would open like a jeweled eye, allowing an influx of seraphim—fiery orbs of pure love and righteousness who took on corporeal form to envelop the congregation in waves of celestial grace.

I closed my eyes and recalled that only a few years ago, Akhet-Aten was celebrated throughout the known world as the city where gods walked as kin. In those days, the boundaries between kingdoms did not end at the horizon, my father had secured rites to open the corridor of safe passage for the Pushpaka Virmana—the skycraft of the Indus gods. Like messengers from a parallel dream,these two-story sacred aerodynamic thrones of Mercury arrived not in myth, but in shimmering descent, their vortex engines whirling with monoatomic resonance.

They brought with them what few outside the royal courts had ever seen: the 18th level Mercury—a fine white powder of monoatomic gold, gifted only to Pharaohs and Per Aats. It was said to stabilize the light body, renew the cells, and open the Crown to divine instruction. My father partook in moderation, always in reverence, to align himself with the Celestrovese.

But even the mighty Kubera, the God of Wealth, had been warned away by the Amunite whispers. The shadow priests had poisoned the spiritual airways, commanding the Indus visitors to leave Khemit untouched.   A blast of two trumpets, one crafted of pure silver and the other bronze shattered the memory. The sound jolted me back to the present, where our altar offering tables sat half-barren, and my father prepared to give his final public offering to the Aten.

The Per Aat, Nefertiti, *She Who Walks in Harmony*, my mother inhaled deeply her delicate shoulders, slightly hunched in her elder years after birthing five daughters. Heavy was the diadem worn by the matriarchal side. For she held the rights over the inheritance of the land and rights to the crown. A finely tooled golden Aten collar accentuated her lovely swan neck.

"Exaltation of praise, to the Eternal Threshold of light of the star gods of Sirius, living eternally in the manifestation of truth within all the thresholds of earth, exalted in the time of the ascension of the lighted winds of the universe that are the emanation of the Aten. Giving life eternally and to all eons. Aten, the light of eternity, Lord of all of the cycles of creation commemorated in the Sed Festival, eternal praise to Akhenaten, the Lord of the Aten disk, Lord of the Universe, Lord of the Earth, Lord of the Temples of the Aten in Akhet-Aten, King of the North and South who abides eternally in truth. Shu-te-Pen-Ra-Uanen-Ra, the Greatest of all Preceptors of the Sun and his Primordial Universal Cosmic Essence of the Sun in All Things, the son of Ra who lives in the Light of Eternal Truth, Lord of all Empowerments, exalted in this period of his life, also of the great Queen whom he loves, Lady of the Two Lands, Nefertiti, who lives in health and beauty for ever and ever."

As her eldest, I gathered my sisters behind our beloved Queen as she commenced the Recitation of the Aten Hymn. We performed the sacred dance—bending in slow devotion, extending in reverence, then raising our sistrums to shake in rhythmic emphasis. Each sound was a call, each pose, an offering. Through us, her words took form in the air.

The masses rose to their feet, hands lifted to the heavens, their voices declaring as one: "All glory to Aten. May Aten teach, heal, and feed us."

Perspiration beaded across their foreheads, each drop glinting like dew upon the soil rich with the colors of our land—blue, green, and red—the hues of Khemit's black alluvial gift. Rows of white teeth gleamed under the sun, smiles wide as polished ivory, and their carob-colored eyes all locked in ecstatic devotion upon their King and Queen.

Nefertiti placed her hand over her heart and bowed to her crowd. Their energy surged like the Nile in flood, vibrating the temple stone. Her glory filled their hearts, a radiance that spilled from her presence into the hearts of the people. They hailed her. They worshipped her.

The Per Aat Queen stood before them, luminous in her beauty, receiving their love like a thirsty nomad who had stumbled upon a hidden oasis. She did not deflect their praise—she drank it, savored it, as if their admiration nourished her more than the rays of the Aten ever could.

My eyes narrowed and I snorted quietly and shifted my weight, the judgement rising before I could smother it. To me, the cheers felt like an eternity, a flood with no ebb. I bit my lip and chastised myself, but the truth burned in me. She should be fed by the Aten—not the adoration of the crowd.

I dug my fingernails inside my palm to still my thoughts. This is the Day of Light, I reminded myself. No shadow shall take root—not even within me.

Just then, Grandfather Ay rose from his carved seat, leaning heavily on his wooden staff. He waddled forth with deliberate steps, his wide girth and creaking knees making each movement a minor pilgrimage. My Grand Djed, in his august years, was now more parchment than flesh—his hair grayer, his eyes softer, yet still sharp with memory. Grief had carved deeper lines into his face since losing his sister, Queen Ti-Yee, to the murderers of the Amunite priesthood.

And yet, his voice rang clear.

"You rise in beauty from the thresholds of the universe, oh, Aten," said Ay, addressing the masses.

"You who ordain all life in existence, you ascend in the Eastern horizon and empower every land with your goodness. You are exceedingly beautiful, dazzling, and radiant under the firmament of the earth. Your rays extend everywhere under the firmament You have made."

Tears flowed down Ay's cheeks, and I witnessed him brush away a tear. My breath caught and I too wiped a wetness on my cheek. The Pharaoh now moved to the front and center to address the masses. His violet light pulsed from the crown of his head into the heavens. I shifted my feet in awe because he received his strength from something on high. His divinity came not from this earth, but from his love and devotion to the purity of the mind of God. He raised his hands in devotion to the Aten and decreed:

"You have created Ra, the Cosmic Spirit of the Sun; you bring the light of the Gods according to their dispensation: You command them to be obedient to your Beloved Son."

My father believed that he was the true voice of the Aten on earth and that only he could embody it.

"Your light comes from far away. But your radiance is upon all of us, and in our presence, all of us who are in humble adoration of your coming of the light of day. You descend on the Western horizon when the earth goes into a state of darkness and obscurity."

"The people of the earth lie down and are veiled in darkness and cannot truly hold the essence of the Almighty One, true God, Aten."

The Per Aat nodded to my father and touched his cheek adoringly. My sister let out a gentle sigh. The Pharaoh concluded his Great Hymn to the Aten, for which he had spent many days in solitude communing with our One God.

"Every lion emerges from his lair, all creeping things sting, and darkness is their only consolation; the land is in the silence of death. You, oh, Aten who have made them are obscured far beyond the horizon. But again, the earth becomes light at the time of your new coming; you ascend in the horizon the shining orb of the day and dispel all darkness. You emanate your radiance, and all the people of Khemit rejoice. They awaken, stand upon their feet, and you raise them up. They purify themselves, and they take on their garments of light," said He, the One and True

King of Akhet-Aten, the disc that emerges over the Horizon."

The Pharaoh then spoke in the language of light, his words no longer earthly, but encoded frequencies that pulsed across the temple stones. With arms raised to the Aten, he became a living conduit, and I watched as his body shimmered with divine brilliance.

Then the transmission came through the crown of my head—pure, searing, radiant. My breath hitched. Dizzy, I swayed on my feet, heart pounding in my ribs like a priest's drum. Was he giving too much of himself again? The last time, he had collapsed before he reached the royal chambers. Bed rest followed. Days of stillness, his spirit hovering at the edge of this world. I gasped and lurched forward to stop him—But before I could move, my sister yanked me back. Her eyes narrowed her message clear: *Let him finish.*

I stilled. And just as swiftly, I saw the glow deepen around him—not diminish. The light fed him as much as if it poured through him. My fear gave way to awe.

He was not dying. He was ascending—right before our eyes.

Grand Djed Ay wandered back to his chair, his gait unsteady as though the stones of the dais might suddenly shift beneath his sandals. His thin frame seemed swallowed by his linen robes, and the gold-threaded hem dragged slightly as if the garment no longer feared his authority. His spotted hands trembled on the carved arms of his seat, gripping them not with majesty but necessity, the way a dying reed clings to the Nile's bank. He leaned closer and muttered, "Your father is too generous of spirit for this world."

I glanced at him and grimaced, offering only a shrug in response—for he was right. It would be considered taboo in the world of the Amunites, those jealous priests who clutched their hidden scrolls and sacred oils withholding all good things from the Sesh—the people. To them, the peasants were nothing more than mud-smeared cattle—mundane, illiterate and disposable.

For a long moment, the crowd sat in reverent silence, each person drawing the sacred breath into their bodies. This 'yoga'—a foreign word we had adopted—meant to yoke spirit and body to the Source. A sacred stillness hovered, the golden hush of divine presence descending like dew upon a desert bloom. This was the breath of God, the silence or *sighs* of creation that opened the inner *lens* for greater perception. When my father sensed the moment had ripened, he gave a long, satisfied nod and spread his hands like the wings of a sunbird—signaling the close of the rite.

My mother returned to her throne, her spine regal even in repose. One by one, the guests filed out of the open air temple, their sandals whispering over the stone. Finally, my sisters and I receded into the shaded alcove of the temple, where refreshment awaited: clay pitchers of mint tea beading with condensation, sweet watermelon slices on lotus-painted trays, sun bread slathered in honey and bowls of fat red dates nestled among desert roses.

Pharaoh and his Queen entered last, beaming as if the Aten itself had followed them indoors. "Grand Risings. This is a most glorious Sun Day, my daughters," declared Father. He stooped and kissed my younger sisters atop their heads. For Ankhi, the Pharaoh bestowed a kiss upon each cheek—simple, tender. But for me—his eldest—his eyes twinkled with something ancient and knowing. He pulled me from my cushion, embracing me with the warmth of the sun. "Our people felt true love, my daughter. They felt the Glory of the Aten."

"They did, Netri. We all felt it. But please be careful—" I placed both hands upon his thin arms, the bones beneath his skin too delicate, too human.

The King put a finger to my lips forbidding me any cautionary warnings to take root. "No warnings today. Joy is the only god I serve this hour." Then he turned, playful once more. "Now, who would like a fat red date dipped in carob?"

Ankhi jumped up, her golden bracelets clinking like temple bells. "I do, Father."

But he had not heard me. My warning had vanished into the sunlit air, so I slumped back in my cushion. and fidgeted with my braids, recently woven by the court hairdresser—the mother of my classmate, Sarawat.

"Merit-Aten," said my father with a hint of a smile. "gather your initiate class. I have an announcement of studies for the coming year, and it is time to decree what is to be."

Ankhi, who had begun her path last year, leaned forward eagerly. "I want to go with you. Can we go far away?" she pleaded, eyes round as blue lotus buds, lips pouty with longing.

The Queen's face twisted into a snarl. "Do not be ridiculous. There is a war between the Amunites and the Atenists. Travel is forbidden." She clenched a handful of her linen sheath as if wringing the neck of fate.

Grand Djed Ay, who had creaked down beside Father, added his papyrus-dry voice. "No more travel to receive lessons in the other temples and sites of power. It is not safe." He spoke as though reciting a prophecy written on his own bones.

Ankhi whimpered and protested. "Merit-Aten's class was allowed to go. It has been years of lessons taught within the walls of Akhet-Aten. I am bored." Her dreams began to unravel before us, fading like a sun-drenched tapestry where only a ghost of color remains. In defiance, she kicked the table, rattling the cups.

"Beloved," said my mother to Pharaoh, lips tight with constraint. "Perhaps the classes decrees can wait. General Horemheb is ready to speak with you. I sense his urgency. You have kept him at bay for days now, and his patience wears thin." She closed her parted legs and pulled the shawl around her shoulders, signaling the shift from queenly grace to strategic alertness.

The light drained from father's face. His jaw clenched. "Why on this day of jubilation," he muttered, "must I address military trifles, which could easily be handled by the man who wears the uniform?"

Nefertiti tugged her earring of gold. I knew this gesture. It meant she was displeased, and growing tired of being dismissed. "It is unwise to treat the General with disrespect, Beloved," she said coolly.

He turned his gaze to her, searching for warmth, and met only marble. "That is wise counsel," he relented, voice softening, "Of course, my glorious delight, I will make time for him," He reached for her hand. "But the classes must still be set into motion."

I perked up instantly." Really, father, for my class? Please—tell me your plans."

Akhenaten laughed, a sound that lifted my spirit like a bird on gilded wing. "All things in their proper time, my daughter. Gather your initiates and make haste. We shall meet at the Palace—once I have first assuaged your mother and General Horemheb." He bit into a slice of watermelon and sipped from his golden goblet.

Ankhi and I sprang up and descended the staircase, followed by our younger sisters, chittering like starlings without a care in the world. But I could not match their joy. I missed holding the hand of Meket-Aten, my best friend and closest sister, who had Wested only months ago. Her absence was not something the living could fill. When Ankhi reached for me, I pulled away.

She noticed, of course. Always sensitive, Ankhi offered a question to draw us back together. "Sister, what do you think Meti wants to discuss with Netri?" Her brown eyes shimmered with concern. Meti's moods were often reflected in her own, like the moon's reflection trembling on water.

I forced a smile and tilted my head. "It is nothing to worry about. Maybe more news about the Amunites. You know how they slither up now and then like venomous snakes—waiting for us cats to take a swipe." I tickled her side, and she squirmed with laughter, her worry forgotten for the moment.

But not mine.

Behind me, my mother's voice rang sharp and clear. "Merit-Aten," she snapped. "I expect you to join us at the Palace."

I turned. "Meti, the Pharaoh requested that I gather my class."

"I *request* that you gather them *after* our meeting with the General," she interrupted. "Your father will not mind." She leaned close, her breath perfumed with rosewater. "Daughter, cleanse your gold. Why do you allow tarnish to touch your skin? You are a reflection of us, and I will accept nothing less than perfection."

My face flushed hot. I reached for my right earring—a delicate crescent of gold gifted by my father—and bit my lip to keep from speaking the truth I was not yet allowed to say. Instead, I smiled. "Yes, Meti. I will head directly to the Palace. To wash my gold, as per your request."

I saw her half-smile—tight and gleaming as a blade. Her necklace dazzled above her bony collarbone like a coiled sun. "Guard," she commanded, "accompany Merit-Aten in the palanquin. She is a daughter of the Sun. Her feet need not touch the ground when her head is so immersed in the skies."

She nodded toward the plank waiting nearby, already held aloft by six muscled men from among the Forty-Two tribes. Their kilts gleamed white, sashes of turquoise and coral marking them as her personal guard.

"Yes, Meti," I muttered. I climbed into the palanquin and watched as my sisters vanished behind me. My jaw tightened.

Sailing above the crowd, the runners broke into a concentrated trot, never showing strain until they set me before the Palace gates. My parent's palanquin arrived moments later—grander, adorned in gold and painted with six rays of light on each side panel. It was carried by twelve men, their power on display, making my own bearers seem like shadows.

My father waited patiently for Grand Djed Ay's arrival on the next carrier.

My mother swept past me like a silken storm. "It is time you join the conversation whereby your fate may be decided." Her golden sandals whispered against the mudbrick floor. I half expected the painted birds along the walkway walls—so lifelike, so delicate—to take flight at her passing.

"Decide *my* fate?" I whispered. My stomach twisted, tumbling like a child taking his first *titi* steps. I hurried after her, uncertain I'd heard her correctly.

"Yes, Daughter," she said without pause. "I told you— the time of your Choosing is upon us. The family must be consulted. So must the ancestors."

As we walked, I caught a flicker of orange light pulsing low in her womb center. Her sensual glow had dimmed in recent years, but it still flickered—powerful, precise, guarded. She knew exactly when to use it. I always tried to stay outside her glow, lest I be pulled into her enchantment.

It made me long for Grand Djedti Ti-Yee, who had understood the matchmaking process with wisdom and patience. She would have at least considered the *heart* of the matter— my heart. She would have seen that it beat for Archollos, the Mycenaean boy shipwrecked on our shores as a child. He had been welcomed into our Mystery Schools, taught to walk in light. Surely that would count for something... Even if he was a foreigner.

My father entered the main Reception Room. His violet light from his crown preceded him like a veil of sacred fire. The prostrating servants bowed low, then left us to our comfort. He eased onto the silken tasseled pillows in vibrant oranges, yellows, and blues, his thin frame regal in repose.

The Royal Fanbearers swept their ostrich feathers to generate a breeze while dusting away the pestering flies.

"Come join me, my family. Libations have been poured for our enjoyment and to bless our elders." He patted the pillows with warmth that did not mask the quiet authority behind it. I could see his heart quickening with effort or anticipation—as he extended his hand toward his Queen. That small gesture was full of longing, though it cloaked itself in ceremony.

Amaret, the Court Seer, entered through the West doors, sky-blue robes trailing like mist behind her. She gathered them around her bare, ashy feet as she sat, her wild gray hair pulsing with static of unseen realms. Her presence shifted the room. That hair—untamed and haloed like a storm cloud of wool—was more than age. It was an antenna. She listened not only to the audible but to the whispers of our ancestors, tuning in for any word from Grand Djedti, Ti-Yee.

General Horemheb's stormed into the room like he was taking charge of a battle, not entering a royal salon. His raven curls gleamed, held tight in battle braids, biceps flexing his authority beneath the leather-bound sleeves. The metal pectoral across his chest clanked with each step, a loud reminder of conquest's past. Dust coated his calves and sandals, and the scent of sweat and copper clung to him, primal and male.

He stopped before my mother, who reclined with feline ease on the chaise lounge—in a sensual pose like a lioness napping in the sun. Her sheath had slipped slightly at the thigh, a careless fall of linen hinting at the power she wielded. The Rose Queen, some whispered. She who parts the veil and commands men with scent and silk. Even in stillness, her thighs spoke.

Horemheb stood like a thundercloud, in gold trim, daring anyone to question the storm he brought with him. Then he sat beside her—not quite touching yet guarding—a calculated move to place himself between her and my father. The yellow light energy of power and dominance emanating from his belly alerted me to his fertility and hunger for war. Such a heathen, I thought, as my breath caught in my chest. I recalled when I was a foolish girl, I once fancied him. Before my mother cruelly stole his affection. Before I understood how she used the scent of rose and submission as a strategy. My cheeks flushed hot. I glanced at my father, startled to find his eyes already on me. He gave a small snort, hearing my thoughts in the inner. I pressed my lips together, caught between shame and a strange thrill. Did others know of our telepathic bond? I dared not look at my mother, though the edge of her gaze grazed my skin like a blade.

"Atonai, My Lord," said Horemheb, bowing slightly, his voice firm but polished. "Many thanks for taking an audience with us after your Temple Service. I would not have interrupted your sanctuary if I did not deem this of utmost importance." He offered a slight lean-in then drew back, a man trained in both combat and courtly decorum. Age had added depth to his features, not dulled them. He wore his years like a fermented cheese offered to distinguished guests—rich, rare, and biting. It was fitting image, given his claim to be a simple son of a cheesemaker from Khepert.

My father acknowledged Horemheb, one brow slightly lifted in bemusement. "Continue, General, you have our rapt attention. Your presence graces this modest palace. As I recall, you and my Queen were most fond of the delights at the Malkata Palace back in Thebes. No doubt Akhet-Aten must seem dull in comparison to the intrigues of Luxor and Karnak. So—tell me, how are our enemies?"

The sarcasm surprised me. It rarely surfaced in my father. Yet it was there, sharp and glinting, like obsidian just beneath the velvet of his tone. I felt his heart contract—a pulse of sorrow beneath the words—as his eyes lingered on Nefertiti, *She who Walks In Harmony*. Now, she walks beside our enemy.

Since the Westing of father's Second Chief Consort, Kiya, who had borne him a son, Tut-Ankh-Aten, he had turned inward in sorrow. He had given his body to devotion, not desire. Nefertiti, who had never given him a son, had turned to Horemheb instead. I could feel the ache ripple through my father like the faded warmth of a fire long burned out.

Nefertiti gave a side eye to my father, her gold-tipped lashed narrowing. "Dearest, we did not come all this way to quarrel. We are only here to solve the problems that are before us." Her voice had sharpened—not harsh but honed. "If you wish to keep Akhet-Aten as the Royal Palace under your rule, then there is some urgency as to how we can achieve that illusive dream."

Horemheb stood with measured weight, a deliberate shift of his broad body that drew our attention as surely as a cymbal crash. "Your Majesty, your Royal coffers are as picked over as vultures ransacking a wounded ox. For the last three years, the Amunite Priests no longer honor your authority as Pharaoh and are withholding all taxes they collect to instead revive their own temples and edifices in need of mendation. Without greater finances, you cannot maintain a standing army to protect the borders of Khemit, let alone the borders of Akhet-Aten." His thick fingers rested on the hilt of his sword as though the truth itself needed reinforcement. "The Amun Priests and the Army of Amun are inextricably bound. Religion and war go hand-in-hand."

The Pharaoh sighed, his expression softening into something closer to pain. He did not rise, but the way he straightened his spine made the room feel smaller. "You bring me nothing but doom," he said, not in anger but in mourning. "And yet, here—look—our city draws Atenists from every corner of the land. They seek peace, not war. They come to heal. We teach our elders to fish again. Is that not also power?"

"Lady Nefertiti and I have arrived with several plans that you may wish to consider," Horemheb replied.

His voice was even, but his gaze unwavering, fixed directly on my father. "If Merit-Aten chose a consort from lower Khemit, thereby re-uniting the Two Lands...this act would pacify your enemies. Especially if the couple lived in Thebes as your Royal Aten representatives."

His words pierced me like a blade dipped in honey. My skin flushed hot. I surged to my feet, heart pounding. "Meti, how could you sell me to the Amunites? They are venomous vipers! Have we not bled enough under their poison?"

My father cleared his throat, gently. A sound I had learned meant restraint. "She is the eldest," he said quietly. "And, by right, must find her key. I do not wish her to be separated from us...but I cannot deny her fate."

Nefertiti's eyes flicked to me, unreadable. "Daughter, our choices are narrowing. Sometimes, a small sacrifice can preserve an entire household. There may be a key in Thebes."

My voice cracked. "A key? And what lock does this key open?"

Grandfather Ay chuckled—a sound that broke the tension like kindling snapping in fire. He rubbed his chin, glancing at each of us. "You said you had several plans, General. Let us hear them. We are indeed surrounded. Our crops are dying. The Nile shrinks. The cattle disease has swept away even the strongest cows."

"Food is vanishing," my father added sharply. His voice rose with urgency, his gaze now burning. "We demand the taxes owed. I must feed my people."

Horemheb's voice boomed with that cursed, accusing tone. "May I remind you, Pharaoh, your taxpayers turned their backs on you when you took away their gods. The gods of every temple in Khemit brought wealth, stability, and devotion. You dismantled their altars. Closed their temples What did you expect? Those offerings made us all filthy rich, enough to support the military, the administration, and the religious factor. Then you chose to close Luxor and Karnak and displaced a large population who have worked in the priesthood and administration for gene-erations. Are those the taxpayers whom you wish to rely on?"

Ay glared at Horemheb. "You know why he did it. The Amun curse still festers beneath those so-called gods. The Hyksos Canaanites who invaded our once great country, put their Mesopotamian filth on our holy rites." My father, Amenhotep III, ruled at the pinnacle of power," my father said, his voice full of memory and edge. "And yet, even he bowed to the Amun priests. They ruled the systems—political, religious, educational. He who controls the grain and gold, controls the people. Then the controllers care not what the laws are."

"The Hyksos, *Those who Crossed Over*—have woven their sickness into every powerful family," I said, my voice trembling. "I have heard those stories since I was a child. Is that your plan? To force me to choose one of the Hyksos to appease the Amunite priests?"

Nefertiti touched Horemheb's arm gently. "You must see, beloved, that even now the old gods are whispered to. Even among your loyal workers. Belief is not erased by decree."

Ay nodded solemnly. "We have searched the worker's village in the beginning. Their family altars dedicated to the old gods remain. They cling to what gives them comfort."

Nefertiti's body softened. Her voice wrapped around us like a shawl. "I was there beside you, my love, through the years of reform. But now, if we are to preserve your dusty dream, we must give something back. We must fill your granaries and treasury. It is your only hope of survival."

Horemheb cleared his throat. "Pharaoh, the Amunites are training their mercenary forces.

Your kingdom could eventually be torn apart unless we devise an arrangement to appease them. You have treasures—jewels, altar pieces. Let them be dismantled and sold. I have connections. The funds could purchase cattle, fish, and grain."

Nefertiti stiffened beside him. "No, not the jewels. I told you that was out of the question."

Pharaoh's hand flew to the golden collar at his throat. "This gold is not treasure. It is liquified sunlight, consecrated by Aten. I relied on this—this—light—to maintain my link to the divine." His voice cracked. "It is through my countenance that I hold the unique ability to radiate the primordial essence of the Solar Deity, the Aten. The empowerment of Aten, the visible light, shines through me to obliterate all darkness. Since, the Amunites have cut off my ability to receive the monoatomic gold, as is my birthright, then I use the gold in my jewelry to maintain my connection to Aten."

Horemheb's gaze dimmed. Surprise? Calculation? I couldn't tell. "The Amun Priesthood are asking for a visible offering from you as acknowledgement of Amun. They will consider it a gesture of peace."

My father's hands clenched the pillow beside him. "There is no such thing as anything invisible; there is no invisible god, Not Amun. Not any other. Nothing is hidden. Everything is revealed and made manifest. Through me."

Horemheb burst out laughing. His armor rattled like a cage. "If you perish, are you saying the Sun will cease to shine?"

My stomach knotted. This was not a negotiation. It was a test. And I feared my father might fail it—not through weakness, but through love too great for the world we now faced.

Nefertiti rose, the fine linen sheath whispering against the stone. Her impatience climbed like a twisting vine choking beauty until it withered in defeat. "Then offer up your boy," she said cooly. "Tut-Ankh-Aten could study in Thebes under the tutelage of a scholarly elder."

Her cold glare sent a shudder down my spine. "He is only eight years old," I shot back, rising now, voice hard and cracking. "How would he survive amongst those who delight in defiling young boys?" My hand slammed the table before

I knew it, and mint tea splashed across the polished ebony wood, a sacrifice of courtesy. My breath came sharp and shallow. I had tasted the shadows of the Amunite priests. I would not let Tut be dragged into that darkness.

In a tone only a mother can use to insight obedience in her daughter, Meti said, "Merit-Aten, please maintain your civility; these are only suggestions—for your survival."

"Once a snake sheds its skin, a bigger snake grows in its place," said Grandfather Ay, without flinching. He met his daughter's gaze, fingers tapping the table like a metronome of truth. His smile was pulled tight, brittle with irony.

"Merit-Aten, come back to Thebes with us. Bring Tut-Ankh-Aten," Horemheb demanded, stepping forward like a man drawing battle lines. "You will be venerated—adored—far more than you are here, where your name is buried in dust. In Thebes, you are the Sea of God's Light. Here, you will be forgotten. As the next in line to the matriarchal rule, you must choose a mate. In choosing your stepbrother, then, you will keep this matriarchy alive as was the ancient tradition. If you do not, then I fear that the patriarchal rule will take place as is the custom of the Lunar Hyksos. And we will have lost the war without even lifting a spear."

The Per Aat Nefertiti pleaded with me, "My daughter... the General speaks the truth. We are in a window of time that we can survive. The Amun Oracle has seen the future. The Mycenaeans prepare to seize our land. My own seers have predicted that Khemit will not even belong to its people in the future. Usurpers will come by sea to take command of our soil. All that we have built, all that our elders have built will be claimed by foreigners. Our people will become enslaved by rulers with no blood of this land." Her voice caught tears which glistened but did not fall. I wanted to believe her. But something inside me curled up, bracing for the blow.

I sucked in my breath, lungs burning, throat dry. My eyes searched for my father's face—begging him to cast this shadow away. Instead, the burden fell fully on my shoulders, as it always had. The prophecy I had dreamed of since childhood now stood before me demanding action. If I chose wrong, the line would end. The kingdom would fall. I clenched my hands in my lap until my nails bit into my palms. "Why was I chosen for this fate?" I whispered, though no one seemed to hear.

Horemheb patted my mother's hand. His voice shifted, low and persuasive. "Do you know what they call her in Thebes? The Atenists, still faithful, have named her Nefer-Ne-Fru-Aten, Beautiful of the Most Beautiful of Aten. Those see her as the Grand Per Aat. They fall at her feet. This is not just worship—it is power. Use this power and devotion to ascend. In Thebes, you are next in line. In Akhet-Aten, you may as well dig your own grave, for here your face will be forgotten."

The General pointed at me and verily slashed my heart with his sword of truth. I felt it. The cruelty. The call. I could not speak. I had no words. My mind galloping through futures I could neither endure nor escape.

The silence in the room expanded like a held breath. I could feel every heartbeat, even the pulse in my tongue. If I went to Thebes, I would betray my father's dream of devotion and faith. If I stayed, I might doom my family as if by my own hand. I prayed to the Aten to flood me with certainty, wisdom—anything. I turned to my father—but his eyes evaded mine.

Horemheb stepped closer, this tone now edged with bitterness. "Lest I remind you, Pharaoh—you once promised a great stelae: you and Queen Nefertiti in the Smiting Pose. Raised spear, enemies trampled beneath your feet. That promise was never fulfilled. So, I commissioned it myself. The Amunites will now use it. Not as a blessing. As a warning upon your ascension to the throne, you promised to deliver a stone."

My father's jaw tightened. "Why would I wish to memorialize violence when I strive to unify. My invitation is open—to all—under the Aten's light? If our worship spreads, war may dissolve. Again, as I have always asked you, why would we not want peace? Why must this persistent need for bloodshed be a continuous cycle? Have we not lost enough of our sons to have an everlasting effect upon the soul of this land? When will we understand the cost?"

Horemheb's face closed like a gate. He straightened his armor, already turning toward the door. "I believed in your dream. At the beginning of your rule, I ordered my armies to march to your god. But sixteen years later, Aten has not dissolved the ancient ways. The Amunite grip on the Sesh remains. Plain and simple, you lost. You lost the army, you lost the Sesh, and you lost me as your devoted follower."

The General turned his wide barrel-chested body toward Queen Nefertiti, demanding she make ready to depart. "I can see that we are making no headway here. We will leave you with these ideas, and may the Aten feed your people under its grace. My Queen, we shall return to Thebes in the morning. It is clear that our offers of kindness and compromise are meaningless in Akhet-Aten."

I stood, bitter fire rising in my chest. "Be sure to say goodbye to your other daughters. They cry for days after you vanish."

She paused—but only briefly, then swept past me, cool as marble.

With the snapping of reigns, which ignited pounding hooves. Their golden chariot rattled down the stone path, wheels shrieking like birds of prey. Streamers of white, billowed, absurd in their pageantry. His steeds kicked up a cloud of sand as if to emphasize that our glittering kingdom was as worthless as the dust it was built on.

Father's shoulders folded inward.

Ay said gently. "We should be grateful to learn of the military uprisings. Now, we must consider how we move forward, my Lord."

I stepped closer. My voice did not tremble. "Father, why do you allow her to remain with Horemheb? The people whisper that she has abandoned us. They bear witness to the fact that she is not in worshipful prayer during our daily ceremonies. Why does the rightful Queen of Khemit live amongst our enemies?" My voice burned so that I finally would receive an answer. She left him twisting in the wind, and it was I who unwound him after her ill-fated departures.

He looked up slowly, eyes hollowed by grief. "Merit-Aten, what is the most beautiful flower in this great land?"

I blinked hard. The question stunned me. It must either be the Papyrus umbel of Lower Khemit or the Lotus of the Upper Khemit. "The blue lotus," I said, knowing the mystical qualities of this luminous orb.

He nodded. "The lotus only blooms from the muddiest water. It cannot grow in water that is pure. As does your mother. For her to flourish, I must let her go live amongst the filth, or she would perish."

He looked at me with eyes of love and wisdom only obtained through loss. "Merit-Aten, why does she continue to break your heart every time she leaves? Is your heart not the Sun?"

"Yes, Father," I said, then grimaced.

"Your mother's heart is external. Her Sun is external. Your heart, your Sun, is internal. Do not allow her to extinguish your Sun. Do you hear me?" asked Father directly, locking his eyes with mine. I could feel his transmission of energy penetrating me.

Ay cleared his throat. "My daughter, Nefertiti, tears our kingdom apart. If Horemheb's warnings are true, and they are raising an army against us, then we must take action. For that, we will need a purse that is plentiful enough to pay the Eastern warriors for protection."

My father rose slowly, like a man lifting the weight of the world again. His candle, once so bright, had flickered. I could see it in his eyes—the dulling. The heaviness. And still, he paced. Still, he moved forward.

So many once-loyal staff and administrators had been threatened or bought off. It was never an easy choice. There was no allegiance, once the riches began to run dry, they fled. The betrayal wounded me more than any enemy could. Did they not overstand that our riches were in the inner, not the outer? Our true wealth was not in gold. It was in light. In law. In love.

Yes, I was raised in silk and honey, which was not the fate of many of my classmates. I yearned for the internal realms beyond that were foretold by leading a righteous life. But I was learning, the world wanted grain. Not scrolls. I pressed my hand to my chest, trying to keep my Sun from going out.

"Ay, we must ready the chariots for a trip to Kush," my father said, voice firm, gaze toward the horizon as if he saw the coming storm. "Our alliances must be sealed. My mother's kin from Akshum must be warned. Perhaps Mahu, can rally the Med-jay of the Eastern Desert. They are the warriors untouched by fear—swift, precise, and loyal beyond price. Tell Mahu that he must go before us to spread the word and gather our own mercenary army."

"My Lord," Ay responded, adjusting his gold Menit collar, its beads catching the light like fire, "since you dissolved your father's Harem of concubines and released the daughters of the 42 tribes, the old loyalties have thinned. No alliances sealed by blood. No daughters to bring their fathers to your throne. Golden coins without brides become spoils. And spoils, My Lord are for the taking. You cannot alter the ways that have insured loyalty for centuries."

I recalled how the collar was presented in a grand Sed Ceremony from the High Window. My parents had pronounced him the Master of the Pharaoh's Horses and Chariots. The pride on my grandfather's face. The way Ay bowed, but never truly bent.

"Enough," ordered father. "Prepare the chariots. Inform Pentu. We leave in two days. The guards will ride with us, and the couriers must ride ahead to stir the sentinels. Merit-Aten's class must be prepared. The initiations cannot be disturbed." Then he turned to me, "Daughter, make haste and gather your group near Lake MaruAten. We will dine under the night sky on my barge. Let all ears attune to my words of vibration."

The wind met us by the Shade Tent, rustling the linen canopy that bore the name of Kia—Tut and Smenkhkare's mother, now Wested. Our white linen robes whispered as we moved, light and white against the dusk. The man-made lake shimmered at our backs, a basin carved to keep the crocodiles at bay, so my father could glide in peace across the still waters.

Archollos was playful as usual with his brawny buddy Ra-Awab—hitting rocks with sticks, laughing too loud, bumping shoulders like lion cubs testing dominance. Archollos glanced my way, eyes azure beneath his sun-kissed hair. He always checked to see if I watched. How could I not? His blonde hair and bronzed skin made him instantly distinguishable amongst my melanated carob colored class. While I was attracted to his beauty, my heart was inexplicitly connected to his. Smenkhkare—Tut's older brother—stood just behind, calm and warm as always. The line between love and choice was thinning.

Catching up on the gossip, I sat huddling with Sarawat, Keshtuat, and Tadushet in the bountiful flower garden. Sarawat honked like a goose when she laughed at Keshtuat making a kissing noise at Ra-Awab, drawing the eyes of the passing servants with trays of food. Then we heard it.

The royal-covered golden barge with courtly rowers oaring in unison, emerged across the lake's surface like a vision. The dock creaked as we climbed aboard. Pillows ringed a long wooden platform, candles marking our places in a glowing path that led to the throne. . My father, who sat with dignity in his royal flowing turquoise silks upon his golden traveling throne, the Aten golden diadem resting against his brow like a sun on flesh. "Sit," he instructed. "Eat. Restore yourselves."

Plates piled with sweet vegetables, sun bread, and clay jugs of beer were set before us. Hungrily, we dug in, eating and drinking with our right hand while our left hand was for hygienic duties as was the custom. He allowed us to exchange quiet conversation while he closed his eyes in meditation. He chose not to eat or drink that night, and I overstood that he was fasting again. On watermelon only. It was how he prepared his spirit for battle—with fruit and silence.

I wondered if he would speak of Nefertiti. Of Horem-heb. Of the threats we all sensed but dared not say—that Akhet-Aten was in grave danger and no longer safe. But no such words came. Energy and vibration cannot lie. He attuned to the Aten to lift his previous ill mood, anguish, and worry to a more heightened place.

I envied his ability to rise so quickly, while I still carried weight in my chest like a sealed jar.

When the last crumbs were cleared, Pharaoh cleansed his hands in the alabaster bowl, he opened his eyes. "Align with the Aten."

We opened our hearts, which opened our minds, and surrounded ourselves in green. The kind of light that is not of this world—primordial, alive, protective. All attendants left us alone. The barge pushed off. We were rowed out into the center of the darkened glass lake. The quarter moon, golden like a place keeper in the sky, illuminated our journey.

"Please take a box," he advised as Ay who had been resting on a mat now awoke. My grand Djed placed a large tray filled with metal octagon containers at our feet. They were cold to the touch.

I lifted mine, and it sent a chill through my fingertips. A sensation I had never felt before. Around me, whispers of confusion and awe.

"You may open them." Father leaned back slightly, eyes sharp.

The lids lifted. Inside—white, solid, glistening. "Ice," I called, the first to speak.

His brow lifted. Pharaoh nodded, "Yes, ice," Merit-Aten. "But go deeper."

"Cold," said Smenkhkare, his eyes twinkling with childish delight.

Amen-Ra in a deep masculine voice that always astonished me, "Solid."

Tadushet daintily held it aloft to examine her prize from all directions. "Irregular shape," she said.

"Precisely, you hold ice. Do you own it?" Pharaoh flicked one finger to make his point.

"No," said Smenkhkare, unbothered. "We are just the stewards. It belongs to the land."

The Pharaoh of the Two Lands nodded. "Now put it in the copper cup and hold it over the flame."

No one hesitated. Our hands moved as one. The ice did not scream—it simply let go.

Within moments we swirled nothing but water, where something rare had once been.

"Now, what do you hold?" Pharaoh's voice was distant.

"A cup of water to wash down our meal?" asked Archollos, eliciting a giggle from the class.

Pharaoh was stoic. "Perhaps. Go deeper. "What happened to the ice?"

"It melted." Smenkhkare spoke up, "It is still water, but it changed from solid to liquid."

Father's mouth opened slowly like lotus petals. "Exactly." He breathed deeply as if the moment pleased him. "The substance is the same, but the form changed. Keep holding your cups over the flame."

We did. Slowly, steam rose—soft at first, then the water boiled. Wisps of steam rose up from our cups, and we took care not to burn our fingers.

Father took an inhalation and said softly, "Now, what do you have?"

"Steam," said Sarawat, who then honked like a goose in her peculiar laugh.

The King was patient, "Precisely. Do you own the steam?"

We shook our heads. "No, Pharaoh. We cannot own steam. Now our ice is gone into the sky." My class added their comments with a hint of sadness because they couldn't take their gift home.

"Do you understand the lesson?" asked my father with hands held out. His linen always looked fresh and crisp.

"That we own nothing?" asked Keshtuat looking around.

"That water can take different forms?" replied Archollos.

"That something rare can become common in an instant," I asked trying to reach higher.

Father nodded. "Yes, all that, praise Aten. Forms shift," he said. "But essence does not. Ice. Water. Steam. All are information of energy and transformation. All Khem."

We nodded with awe written upon our faces.

But Pharaoh was not finished. "Even deeper. You just learned the beginnings of your lessons in alchemy. Khemit. All Khem. Khemistry. Even deeper. You just learned about Ascension. The process of changing forms from Darkness, where it all begins, into Light. Your next lessons will be about alchemy."

And though no decree was spoken, we knew: tonight, we had not been told. We had been changed.

Pharaoh cleared his throat as if readying himself for another secret. "Although I had planned to teach you these most valuable lessons, I must retreat to a land beyond Akshum. Another teacher has been summoned but it is up to the Aten as to how you will be taught. I trust you will be on your best behavior for your most honorable teacher, for I will know if you are not."

San Francisco, California 2021

*T*ucked behind the main showroom at the base of Telegraph Hill, Napolitano Interiors sprawled across two city lots—one converted from an old cannery, the other a former Art Deco furniture warehouse repurposed with floor-to-ceiling windows and brutalist concrete floors softened by Persian runners.

The front offices were a well-curated deception—walnut desks, mid-century lamps, and floating shelves lined with design monographs and Italian ceramics. The lighting was always warm, never harsh. A sanctuary for the clients who paid handsomely to feel like their remodels were more Renaissance revival than real estate investment.

But the heartbeat of the business was behind the showroom, past the frosted glass partition etched with the family crest. That's where Morainya spent her days. Her division—Textile & Upholstery—was the workshop, archive, and battlefield rolled into one. You could smell it before you entered: beeswax polish, sawdust, tobacco, and the ghost of lilac upholstery spray lingering in the fabric bolts.

Industrial racks loomed overhead, stacked with imported velvets, vintage brocades, hand-dyed linens, and bolts of moiré silk in colors so vivid they seemed alive. Along one wall, an archive of fabric swatches—tagged and catalogued—ranged from rare 1920s chenille to discontinued Fortuny prints sourced on auction trips to Venice. Opposite that, a row of hydraulic sewing tables buzzed with the sound of needles moving through thick upholstery-grade weaves, while pneumatic staple guns punctuated the room like syncopated heartbeats.

Morainya's office was elevated—a mezzanine that looked down over the workroom floor. From up there, she could see everything. Every dye lot pulled. Every stitch that needed realignment. Every apprentice who slouched at the serger table.

She ran the division like a war widow turned duchess—sharp, exacting, with a reverence for the old ways and a subtle disdain for shortcuts. Her job wasn't just to make things beautiful. It was to ensure legacy standards—sourcing fabrics that matched 18th-century archival photos, balancing colorways against historical palettes, maintaining tension ratios for heirloom reupholstering. So when she walked through the cutting room and saw an apprentice struggling with a misaligned tack, she could guide them.

"Do you need a hand?" asked Morainya, laying her clipboard on the worktable.

"Mrs. Sanders," said the female apprentice, "I was just trying to tack this side down but the material..."

Morainya pulled her lips into a taunt smile. Being addressed formally in her husband's last name seemed like a flaw, especially since her husband had been hinting at divorce for the past few months.

"You can call me Morainya, everybody else does. And I know silk can be slippery. Here let me show you."

Morainya Napolitano tugged the last length of silk taut across the walnut frame, her palms stinging with effort. The crimson brocade caught the morning light just right—regal, but not gaudy. She stepped back, studying her work. and showed the apprentice the beauty of precision—even though it would go unnoticed, of course. Her name was never listed on the commission cards. Those belonged to her uncles and aunts, the children of the real craftsmen. Or rather—the ones born with titles and expectations.

The Napolitano family had built empires out of stitched leather and carved wood, but that didn't mean they knew what to do with a daughter who preferred leather to lace. The upholstery trade in regal fabrics, weaving and dying began in Florence under the patronage of the Medici. Morainya's father, Stephano Napolitano resurrected it in San Francisco. He was the son of Italian immigrant parents who were forced to leave the family estates behind in the old country when they set out to establish a new world without the benefit of generational wealth.

Ellis Island is where they docked, filled with hope of a new life in America, but the Depression of 1929 wreaked the dream. The five children were sent to work in the mines in order to put bread on the table. Only Stephano, knew that if he breathed in that coal-filled air, he would die in those dirty caverns filled with the laborious pain of the unseen alongside the downtrodden Irish.

So, by chance or by legacy remembered in his bones, Stephano took an assistant job in an upholstery factory catering to the wealthy San Franciscan families. He was sent on odd jobs that barely earned a few cents a day and his mother chided him for reaching too high.

Morainya's back ached. Since she hit fifty, the bending over wooden frames or climbing ladders to inventory fabrics listed by color, country and weaver had taken its toll.

But when she had a deadline to score luxury fabric from an 18th Century Castle fallen into disrepair, or the thrill of opening a box of samples from a Turkish factory going out of business then her focus was sharpened.

The buzz of the fabric cutter nearly drowned out her phone in her pocket. With a glance she excused herself from the apprentice and strode toward an alcove when she saw the number. "Hello, can you hear me?" she said loudly into her cell, trying to determine if she had service.

"Yes," Jedidiah's voice crackled on the other end. He sounded too polite. He used that tone when pretending he wasn't annoyed.

"I'm just in the middle of sourcing material and doing lading," she replied evenly, waving at Gianni to double-check the pattern alignment on the chaise reupholstery. "Is this about Josh?"

"No. He's fine. He's with Sister Clarice doing his saint's chart." Pause. "I called because you missed my talk."

Silence. She closed her eyes. She had missed it.

The TEDx stage at the Presidio Theatre. His big moment. *"The Algorithm of Empathy: How Data Will Rewire Emotional Intelligence."* He'd practiced it in the mirror for weeks, adjusting his tone, reworking the pacing. She'd helped him edit the slides between dinner cleanup and bedtime prayers.

"I had a delivery from the Turkish mill this morning," she said softly. "I couldn't reschedule. The customs paperwork alone—"

"You knew what today was," he said. "I told you. Twice."

"I know. I'm sorry," her voice fraying at the edges. "We just had a disastrous morning." She hesitated, rubbing the space between her eyes. "We lost the Belmonte contract.

The one we've been working on for a year. My dad explod-ed. I've been putting in stop orders and refund requests all morning, trying to keep the place from falling apart."

Silence on the line. "Yeah. Every day is like that in your company." he said. His tone flat—worn down, not angry. Just...tired.

She bit her lip. "I should've been there. I wanted to be. I just," she exhaled sharply, "I didn't realize how much I was holding until everything broke at once."

Jedidiah said nothing. Just the dull hum of San Fran-cisco traffic on the other end.

She wanted to say she was proud. That she believed in his vision—even if it made her skin crawl sometimes, hearing him talk about *emotions* as datasets. That wasn't how hers worked. Hers came through smell and sensation, through the feel of her mother's velvet gloves, the warmth of ruffling her son's hair, or winding down with a glass of wine on the porch when the day had finally released her.

"I'll watch the recording," she offered, quiet now.

"I didn't call for an apology or a secondhand viewing," he said, voice harder now. "I called because I needed my wife."

They talked. Or tried to. Morainya cajoled. Jedidiah deflected. She tried to explain, he tried to punish. And when it was clear nothing else could be said, she hung up—gently. The silk beneath her hands felt colder than it should have. Her palms were clammy. She pinched herself on the thigh, "You are so stupid. How could you have missed that talk." Now, he'll be furious for days—maybe weeks—and punish her the way he always did with absence.

"Your husband again?" chided her Uncle Aldo from the down the hall. He must have witnessed the look of horror on her face. His square body and thick neck made him look like a Lego character as he teetered toward her. He always looked like a tailored contradiction—brown cashmere jacket, straight legs jeans, sockless loafers and a vintage ring he never explained. He smelled like leather and bergamot. Always too familiar.

Morainya gave a casual shrug of indifference when inside her stomach was in knots. "He gave a talk today. I forgot to go. You know, because of the deadline." She scrunched her wispy hair out of her face and pulled it back with a tie she kept around her wrist.

"He thinks the world revolves around his ideas," Aldo said as they headed toward the sample racks. He plucked a swatch and examined it for imperfections. "But the real world runs on emotion. Blood. Memory. Not machines."

"You're one to talk," she said without venom. "You'd digitize grief if it made money."

He smiled. "But I wouldn't call it empathy."

Her father appeared in the hallway behind Aldo, pressing one hand to the doorframe. "Is your mother with you?" His voice was shaky, probably from the screaming match with the owner of the Belmonte Group—the line of famous restaurants dominating the Bay Area luxury scene. The multi-million-dollar upholstery and interior renovation contract, one Stephano had courted for over a year had just been rejected. Morainya along with the procurement analyst and two of their top textile specialists had been called in to pull numbers, curate sample palettes, and request expedited import approvals in case questions were asked on the spot.

Instead, they were all blindsided by the client's refusal to proceed, citing 'a shift in aesthetic priorities.' It had been a brutal morning—calming her father's rage, fielding apology emails, and putting in stop orders for $75,000 worth of bespoke fabric sourced from a closing French atelier. Her phone had buzzed during the chaos, but she'd silenced it, thinking I'll call Jedidiah back in five. And then five minutes became forever. Her nervous system was still frozen. And driving to her husband's Ted Talk felt like climbing Mt. Everest without oxygen.

Morainya's eyes narrowed. "Mom was just downstairs reviewing the guest seating for the Italian Arts Guild gala."

"Stella forgot again," her father said quietly as he adjusted the silk pocket square in his tailored navy jacket. Stephano exuded old style elegant sophistication—always in pressed suits, never without a monogrammed handkerchief or the faint scent of cologne that spoke of sandalwood and Florentine pride. His salt-and-pepper hair was combed back with the meticulousness of a man who believed dignity began in the mirror. But now, his brow furrowed, and the practiced poise wavered. "She asked me the date of our wedding anniversary. Then asked if she was supposed to be there."

Morainya inhaled sharply. "Dad, that's twice this month."

Her father nodded, gaze heavy. "She's spiraling. But don't tell Aldo. He'll leverage it."

Aldo, still holding the swatch, shrugged. "Leverage what? That your wife repeats herself like a Sunday Mass chant?"

"Enough," her father said with a voice that still held the old timber. "Get back to your departments. Morainya, have you signed off on the bill of lading? You know we could use the money, we are running a little short for the year-end payroll."

Aldo slipped out without further word.

Her father lingered. "She lit three candles for Saint Dymphna yesterday," he said. "Said one was for your marriage."

"Great," Morainya muttered. "We need all the help we can get." She laid a gentle hand upon his sleeve. "I promise you'll have them done before the end of the day. I'm just waiting for a phone confirmation from Turkey. I better go find Mom."

It didn't take her long as she traversed the Italian marble tiled hallway toward the conference room. There was her mother holding a seating chart… for the gala they planned a year ago. A secretary was held in abeyance to the CEO's wife as she nodded dutifully trying to answer Stella's demanding questions about an event that had already passed.

"Darling," she said brightly, upon seeing a familiar face. Stella was holding the gold-edged sheet. "I've had the most divine idea—what if we seat the French ambassador near the Florentines? It would be a lovely tribute to the old Silk Road."

Morainya gazed adoringly upon her mother's weathered face. She reached toward her and straightened the silk bow on her blouse underneath the Channel black and white jacket. She gave a quick dab with her finger to fix her mother's red lipstick that had seeped into her lip crevices, and said, "Mama, we decided that yesterday. You moved the Florentines next to the Astors."

Stella still looking like an old Hollywood icon blinked. "We did?"

"Yes. You were wearing the green velvet wrap. You had your pearls on."

"Oh." Stella looked down at the chart. "I do love that wrap. Did I tell you? Your father gave it to me the year we opened the Sausalito store. Said I looked like a bishop's daughter."

"You told me," Morainya said softly, walking her back to the executive suite so Stephano could keep an eye on her. "Twice." She kissed her mother's temple and deposited her in her favorite chair in his office, hoping her dad would be back soon to look after his wife. Stella let her. No protest. Just that gentle smile—the kind that made her look sixteen again, trapped in memory.

As the sun lowered, casting copper light through the warehouse's long windows, Morainya sat at her desk talking on the phone to get the customs paperwork passed through the system. Absentmindedly she tapped her pencil on the desk as she was momentarily put on hold by the supervisor.

Josh had texted earlier asking her when she'd be home tonight? Her son's tone was clipped—like he was practicing adulthood before he had all the vowels. She leaned back, fingers tangled in her hair and stared at the city beyond— the shifting skyline, the tug of old versus new.

Down the corridor, footsteps echoed—too sharp, too urgent. The glass door to the boardroom clicked shut. She glanced up toward the sound. It was Stephano's gait. Heavy, indignant. Then came Aldo's—softer, almost hesitant, like he never quite knew how loud he was allowed to be.

She didn't mean to follow, but something in her spine turned her feet. The upstairs catwalk ran just above the executive conference suite. She moved quietly, her heels barely making a sound on the iron grating as she approached the small clerestory vent—part of the original cannery construction, never sealed in the remodel.

She crouched and listened.

"You think because you wear our suits and dine at our table, you understand what it means to be a Napolitano?" Stephano's voice was a storm breaking glass.

Aldo didn't respond immediately. That was his way—let rage burn out its oxygen before stepping into the room.

"I've never claimed to be something I'm not," Aldo finally said. "But I've run this marketing division for fifteen years, and I've done it with clean books."

Stephano scoffed. "Clean? We're hemorrhaging clients to minimalists who sell furniture that looks like lab counters. Do you know what that tells me, Aldo? It tells me we've lost relevance. And you've done nothing about it except order more velvet."

"Look, brother, I've been telling you this for years. The trends are moving toward sleek and chic and away from baroque and opulence. This isn't my fault, and I can't convince our long-term hoteliers and older clients about what kind of furniture makes them and their customers feel modern."

"We don't sell furniture," Stephano raged. "We sell memory. Heritage. Rooms that mean something. Minimalism is a trend. We survive trends."

"Spare me the lectures," Aldo growled. "You're quoting your brochures like they're scripture.

Silence.

"Just do your job. Your marketing plan is crap. Fix it or this company will die like dinosaurs."

Aldo cleared his throat. "Stephano, about that. "You did promise at one time to make me a partner, I gave up a lot to take this position."

"You were a charity case," Stephano added, more quietly. "A priest's indulgence. And you know it."

"You have promised me raises for the past two years. I have a grandbaby on the way, and you know how expensive it is to live in the Bay Area with all these tech giants buying up all the real estate and raising property taxes.

A hand pounded the table and made Morainya flinch. She looked both ways down the hallway, praying that no one would catch her spying. "Spare me your sob story, Aldo. I have over seventy-five employees who all come to me with the same tales of woe."

The blood drained from Morainya's face. Why hadn't her father shared how tight the finances were. Of course he was riding her to get her deal done. She backed away from the vent, feeling dizzy and a panic attack made it impossible for her to breathe.

Everything was being divided these days. Time. Attention. Loyalty. Memory.

Even love.

Two Years Later

Every time the phone rang, Morainya braced, body stiff and jaw clenched. A year had passed but she kept replaying the call that came just after midnight on Valentine's Day. The call that turned her predictable world into a nightmare.

She remembered sitting on the edge of the bed at her San Francisco home in the dark, startled from sleep by the landline. Morainya reached over to wake up Jedidiah, but the bed was empty reminding her that her marriage didn't survive. Jedidiah moved out six weeks after that TEDx Talk she had missed. No fight. No final straw. Just a neatly folded note on the counter and his side of the closet emptied. "I can't do this anymore," it read. "You're not here. And even when you are, you are still at the office."

And then when she had picked up that phone, the ringer sounded off-kilter, like something important had gone wrong. She reached for the phone with a sense of dread. "Hello?"

"It's Aldo, sorry to wake you but this is an emergency," said her Uncle, his voice was tight, clinical, too controlled. "It's your father. The Hospital just called. He had a heart attack. Massive stroke. They don't think he'll make it through the night."

She drove to the hospital on autopilot, hands gripping the wheel like rosary beads. Josh came with her for support but he had already turned out with his earbuds in. She didn't cry until she saw him—Stephano Napolitano, the man who once held a room like royalty, now slack-jawed, one eye frozen open, a ventilator doing the work his lungs refused. She whispered the Saint Michael prayer. She kissed his forehead. He didn't stir.

Her mother hadn't known what day it was. Stella had been placed in a private dementia unit two months before the stroke. She called Morainya by her sister's name now. Sometimes she asked when the gala was starting.

Sometimes she just stared out the window humming Ave Maria, unaware that her husband was dying across town.

Not only did Morainya have to face the death of her father, but her son's rage at her for the breakup of her marriage. Closed the business. Went through the Napolitano Interiors bankruptcy as she was forced into the office her father once ruled. She sold the house she owned with Jedidiah. Moved to Santa Cruz, told friends she needed the ocean. But really, she needed distance—and a liquor store that didn't know her name.

That first year was a fog of Rose, Xanax, and white noise. She'd drink until sleep came, dreamless and heavy. Wake up with sheets tangled around her ankles, heart pounding, a low hum of shame already in her throat. Every angry voicemail from Jedidiah was a reminder she'd disappeared. Now, two years later, every call from the family lawyer was another nail in the coffin Aldo was now trying to exhume.

Morainya balanced the 1,000-page Deposition Exhibits binder labeled IN THE UNITED STATES DISTRICT COURT FOR THE DISTRICT OF CALIFORNIA, which arrived this morning by courier in her left arm with her purse over her right shoulder as she rode the elevator up to the 12th floor of Kanberg, Wallerstein & Katz Law Offices. The door opened and she entered a large reception area where the installed Covid approved glass wall separated clients from partners.

"Morainya Napolitano. I'm here to see Mr. Kanberg for a deposition," she said to the receptionist—a young, platinum blonde, probably pre-law who barely looked up from her headset.

"Mr. Kanberg will see you shortly. Would you like some coffee or water, perhaps?" she asked, before holding up a finger to answer another call.

"Go ahead, take that," Morainya murmured, then sighed under her breath, settling into the Rococo-replica chair and assessing the poorly stuffed brocade cushion. 'This could use a refill.'

Twenty-five minutes passed. She checked her phone to see if Josh had made it to school on time. The clack of high heels interrupted her spiral.

Aldo sat across from her in the law office waiting room—tailored, smug, flipping through deposition notes like they were menus. He still wore that large ring. Still smelled like leather and old ambition.

He looked like family. He felt like litigation.

Morainya? We're ready" A woman in a navy pinstripe suit gestured sharply.

Morainya rose, straightened her shoulders, and followed, binder in hand. She moved like a woman trained to hold poise under pressure during her years of her Father's hard negotiations—because if she cracked now, she'd shatter completely. The old-world solid dark wood conference room that Stephano had once helped decorate, the law firm he helped launch—had insisted they handle Napolitano Interiors' legal growth. Now he was gone, and Morainya was left to unravel everything he built. The chairs were stiff. The air stale with cologne and ambition. Nothing had changed.

Kanberg in the chair next to her. Well-heeled. Groomed. Still using the same leather folio her father had gifted him after the San Leandro project. He placed a fatherly hand upon her back. "How are you dear?"

Morainya inhaled deeply, catching a whiff of his aftershave, and felt comforted that he was by her side. "I'm good." She nodded confirmation to him.

Her attorney turned his back to the opposing counsel and whispered, "We'll make it smooth." He said it like a man reassuring a client over a power lunch, not a grieving daughter at the edge of collapse. "This deposition is to set the record straight. Just answer the questions. Don't add anything extra, please. Do it just like we practiced."

She gave a polite nod, the kind women give when they're too tired to scream. Uncle Aldo had was being seated across from her toward the far end of the room. He was conferring over a barrage of paperwork with his team. He only glanced up and gave a vague greeting with a chin jut, not the typical Italian kiss on the cheek kind filled with familial warmth. His presence—cold, calculating, watching.

Once, they'd called each other family. Now he was suing not only Napolitano Interiors, but Morainya personally—because the trust was sealed tight, and probate was his last remaining wedge. If he could argue diminished capacity, everything might come undone."

Verbal promises. Unwritten deals. All the ghosts of Stephano's charisma now turned to liabilities. Napolitano Interiors had folded. The books were closed. But Aldo wanted gold. And if he couldn't have it through inheritance, he'd dig it from Morainya's bones.

They laid out the paperwork on the desk, behind it was a large engraving of Lady Justice blindfolded and lifting the scales aloft, the only art piece decorating the wall. It felt like she could peek through her blindfold and give the scrutinizing eye of judgment to those gathered before her.

"I know it's a lot," Kanberg said gently. "But if we can wrap this up cleanly. No trial. No exposure. You'll walk away with more than most." He glanced at his gold Rolex watch, underneath his Saville Row suit and hint of a starched white cuff. It seemed ironic to Morainya that her attorney wore elite clothing from a prestigious London atelier, that might be paid for by the misery of his roster of clients. Seven-hundred and fifty dollars an hour for a lead partner was the going rate. As she had been kept waiting almost thirty minutes, it had already cost her $375.00. Morainya, who used to be able to expense any legal services to the company, now felt the burden of spending her own money.

She stared at the folder. Stephano's name embossed at the top. Hers scrawled in pen below, like a footnote.

She thought of Jedidiah's silence. The disillusion in his voice. The slow death of their marriage, not from violence—but erosion. One heartbreak after another, until the foundation cracked. He'd left. Or maybe she had. It didn't matter anymore.

She thought of her mother—Stella—in the dementia ward angry that she was surrounded by strangers then forgetting her own daughter's name.

And then she closed the file. The chandelier above her glittered. Not like a crown. Like a warning.

"You may start the recording," ordered Kanberg to the woman sitting directly opposite of Morainya. The red light of the camera on a tripod blinked on signaling that everyone was ready to get down to the business of an inquisition. Being filmed made the heaviness of the questions carry an even greater severity, for her likeness was now captured for posterity to be subjected to further suspicion and scrutiny later. She had to fight the urge to squirm, so she sat on her hands. But that flickering light made her feel like a sniper's gun was aimed at her forehead.

"Good morning, Morainya, I am Angela Chisholm and Aldo Napolitano's Counsel. Aldo is present because he's was an acting Board Member of Napolitano Interiors. I will be asking you a series of questions, if you could just look into the camera to answer, please."

Morainya nodded.

Let's proceed," added Mr. Kanberg, pulling out his Mont Blanc pen and scribbled a note.

"We are here on February 22nd, 2022, for the deposition of Plaintiff, Aldo G. Napolitano vs. Defendant, Morainya L. Napolitano Sanders, and Napolitano Interiors, Inc." said the court reporter to get the facts on record. Please tell us your whole name and address," said Chisholm.

"Morainya L Napolitano. Scratch the Sanders, I'm divorced." She cleared her throat to pause and remember her new address since she and Jedidiah had sold their San Francisco residence. "555 N. Cherryvale Dr., Santa Cruz, California."

The first questions were mild. Where did she go to school and major/minor?

SFU, San Francisco University. Major in Interior Design, Minored in Ancient Egyptian textiles...well, linens, said Morainya, correcting herself with a smile. That's when she first fell in love with the beauty of the weaving of flax.

What was her role at Napolitano Interiors? Had she been compensated? What duties had she performed?

She answered each carefully. Her father had handled all the legal and business decisions. Her tole was to oversee the Upholstery Division. Then the tone shifted.

Ms. Chisholm glanced at her yellow lined pad, ""As one of your father's favored employees, did you ever receive preferential treatment?"

Morainya's nose twitched. "Yes."

The opposing attorney glanced at her and raised her eyebrows. "How so?"

"I was allowed a parking space on the street whenever my father was out of town," she replied giving a half-smile of childish delight that she hadn't fallen into Chisholm's word trap.

"Let's talk about the will," said the opposing attorney, Ms. Chisholm, her tortoiseshell glasses sliding down her nose. "Is it true your father named you sole executor of both the business and his estate?"

"Yes," Morainya said staring directly into her opponent's eyes.

"And is it true your uncle, Aldo Napolitano, was not included in the will?"

"Yes."

"Even though he worked for the company for forty years?"

"Yes."

"You don't find that suspicious?"

Morainya glanced at her attorney, who gave her a small nod.

"I don't make judgments on my father's choices," she said, lifting her chin. "I execute them."

Ms. Chisholm scribbled something with visible irritation.

"And yet, six months after his passing, the company declared bankruptcy. Shortly thereafter, Mr. Aldo Napolitano filed suit alleging you concealed profits, defrauded the partnership, and mishandled disbursement of estate assets."

Objection. Argumentative, stated Mr. Kanberg without even looking up.

But the red light stayed on. And Morainya stayed silent but underneath she was fuming, her fingernails scraped the seat, and her jaw clenched upon hearing Aldo's accusations, and thought, 'I have done nothing wrong and how dare you imply it.'

Out of the corner of her eye, Morainya glimpsed shadowy figures emerge from the walls of this 1800's era building. She jerked her head toward the apparitions but couldn't find them. Yet, the moment she turned her attention back to the recorder, there were the shadow people—this time more defined.

She closed her eyes to gain a greater perception as to why they came forth. She clearly felt in the pit of her stomach the misery these people had experienced right here in this room. The arguments, the betrayals, the surprise information, the money earned or not, being agreed to be forked over to hungry hands. What she knew in her gut was that the only ones who won were the attorneys. There never was a guarantee of winning; Mr. Kanberg made sure he reminded her of that often. Judges were unpredictable. The ghosts lingered like dissatisfied patrons who had been sucked dry of their lifeforce by the legal system.

"Let's return to the period immediately following your father's death," Ms. Chisholm continued, flipping a page.

"Did you or did you not remove several boxes of documents from the office on February

16th—two days after his passing—without informing your uncle or any other members of the board?"

Morainya's hands curled into fists beneath the table. "I removed my father's personal effects. As his daughter. As Executor. That was my right."

"Just because something is in a trust doesn't mean it's safe, does it?" Ms. Chisholm asked, sliding forward. "Especially if the person signing it lacked capacity. Were those documents reviewed by your legal team before being disclosed to probate court?"

"I'm not sure. My inhouse counsel handled that." "Are you saying you don't know, or not all the documents were revealed to probate court?"

"I provided everything required by statute. The rest were under review." Her stomach flipped because she had been in such a state of shock that it was all a whirlwind.

"Including the documents transferring ownership of Rimaldi Holdings?" Chisholm pushed documents for Morainya to read. "Did this go through probate court as it was done only weeks prior to Stephano's death?"

Her brow furrowed and she gave a shake of her head not recognizing it. "I'm not sure."

Kanberg shifted slightly. "Asked and answered."

But Ms. Chisholm pressed on. "Let the record show the Defendant has not confirmed full transparency regarding all estate materials."

Morainya took a breath, steady and long. She met the attorney's gaze. "Let the record also show that my uncle was not Executor, *not* mentioned in the will, and *not* present at my father's deathbed. And I'm not required to justify love, proximity, or pain to someone wielding a subpoena like a sword."

A beat of silence. Even Kanberg raised an eyebrow, impressed.

Chisholm looked unphased. She adjusted her glasses again. "You speak of pain. Let's discuss Josh Napolitano— your son. Has he benefited financially from Napolitano Interiors assets?"

"Objection," Kanberg said. "Relevance."

"It goes to pattern, Your Honor—" she paused, catching herself. "Excuse me. It goes to pattern, Counsel. We're establishing whether the Defendant used business resources for personal gain, especially after declaring bankruptcy."

"My son," Morainya said slowly, "was given health insurance, paid for by the business. The same as every employee's child. If you want to put him on trial for getting his teeth cleaned, you're going to need a different courtroom."

Chisholm didn't smile, but the corners of her mouth twitched like she appreciated the quip.

"Fine," she said, tone clipped. "Let's shift." She pulled a sheet from the folder, her diamond ring glittered under the lights.

"Mr. Napolitano, are you asserting that the trust documents were invalid?" Kanberg asked, folding his hands like a vulture resting on velvet and staring coldly at Aldo.

Her Uncle didn't answer, but his lawyer did. "We're asserting that significant asset transfers into the trust occurred while Stefano. Napolitano was no longer of sound mind in the period between his stoke and subsequent death."

Morainya straightened. "I don't know, he didn't inform me. His legal team structured those trusts *specifically* to avoid this probate circus."

"And yet here we are," Chisholm replied, voice flat.

"Yes," Morainya said, her voice like a blade. "Because someone thought a courtroom full of whispers was easier to manipulate than a trust fortified by law." Her eyes bore into Aldo's.

That landed. Even the court reporter paused her typing.

The words hung in the air like incense in a cathedral—thick, lingering, impossible to ignore. Morainya felt her pulse beating at the base of her throat. She didn't look away. Inside, something ancient stirred. Not rage. Not fear. Something older. Something *sovereign.*

She remembered her grandmother's hands—weathered, elegant—blessing bread with salt. She remembered the hush in her father's voice when he spoke of loyalty as if it were gospel. She remembered Stella in her prime, hosting gala fundraisers in silk gloves and pearls, commanding a room without raising her voice.

And now, here she was, the last standing woman of a dynasty unraveling in court transcripts and deposition binders. Aldo wanted the gold, but he'd forgotten who the fire belonged to. She wasn't just defending a trust document. She was defending a lineage.

The ghosts leaned in closer. One placed a cold hand on her shoulder. A whisper slithered into her ear: "You are not the first to be buried by gold...but you may be the first to rise."

She flinched. No one else moved.

Chisholm noted it. "Are you alright, Ms. Napolitano?"

*T*he royal tutors had dismissed themselves after morning rites, it was the first unsupervised afternoon in weeks, and the women-in-training were beginning to unwind—some stretching beneath the shade of sycamores, others braiding each other's hair while exchanging stories too scandalous to be spoken indoors.

"If the gods didn't want us to know pleasure," whispered Sarawat, twirling a lotus stem between her teeth, "they wouldn't have made our mouths so soft."

Laughter flickered across the group like sunlight off the water basin.

I lingered at the edge of the fray, watching through palm fronds and trying to imitate the older girls and how they wore their beauty with such confidence. Yet I was still bound by the weight of expectation and the fading echo of my mother's footsteps through the corridors of my destiny. But even I could feel the tension in the air—like storm clouds gathering, like something wild about to break open.

This wasn't rebellion. It was curiosity. And boredom. And youth.

Something had shifted. Perhaps because the Pharaoh had left the premises of our enclosed City of Light and had taken Pentu, the Court Physician. Free from their usual severe eye of surveillance and without logic and reason, my initiatic class was compelled to taste, no, test that freedom. As the black lands reached peak fertility in spring, so too did the feminine urgings swell within us. Our breasts fully budded, nipples perked as if beacons of beckoning light, voluptuous hips, and bottoms pressed temptingly against our linen robes. We were fruit yearning to be harvested. Though the Nile's waters had run dry, the waters between our legs flowed uncontrollably. My Temple Sisters and I whispered of our secret yearnings or laughed with uninhibited delight.

How, I ask, can you command us percolating young women to be chaste and only be mindful of our Temple duties? Rather than use our hand for candle production, instead some began to mold the beeswax into suggestive shapes. Keshtuat added a bulbous smooth cap to the sensual form. They burst with glee as they dreamily desired the erect wands that graced our male classmates. The boys we grew up with and originally abhorred became the very men we now desired.

"I feel like a ripened persimmon begging the farmer to pick me," said Keshtuat; her Nubian sultry voice could lure any pursuer to her bed. She swayed her hips in sensual circles, and said, "I need Ra-Awab to lick my sweet juice like he did back in the Hathor Temple." She allowed the hibiscus tea to drizzle down the corner of her plump lips to emphasize her desire.

My class giggled and elbowed each other, seemingly knowing the mysteries between a man and woman. I chewed my lip, frustrated that I was left out of their joke. The young women had become so close, rising together, bathing, eating their meals together; that our internal sundials had become so aligned that our blood arriving and departing as one. While my class were allowed to delve into the mysteries of sex back in Dendera as per the Hathor customs, Rennutet and I were assigned to the Mamisi – the Per-Akh Birth House. Instead, we learned the birthing rituals of Midwifery. I had to quell my envious emotions that wound snake-like around my heart. While they received pleasure, I was bound to chastity and duty. But, when I spied on the Temple Priestesses, they healed with touch. With ecstasy. With their wombs. I had judged them once, or at least pretended not to understand. But now I knew—this was a temple too, this body, this longing.

"My rosebud is so tight—how could a man's *mena*, his pillar ever fit," I asked, my voice laced with uncertainty as I shifted my weight from one foot to another. My hands began to sweat.

"Even the rose's petals fully open," answered Sarawat, "nature knows how it all works."

She picked up a thick green cucumber and slipped it between her lips. The others tittered throwing their heads back. Tadushet put her hands over her mouth—but I did not see what vegetables had to do with my nethers. Sarawat honked like a goose with laughter, which carried the group into giggles.

"Merit-Aten, in all this time, you've never lain with Archollos? You are still so young. If you do not know what to do, then share him. I will show you," prodded Sarawat, for she had always fancied him. She bumped her hips into mine, nearly knocking me to the side. I knew she would push me out of the way to claim him as her own.

Tension coiled and my face flushed hot as Sekhmet's breath. It was not that I did not desire Archollos. In my dreams we were close to touching...then torn apart by unseen hands. But my father had commanded that I remain chaste in order to be a container for the higher light of Aten. This stood in opposition to my mother, who commanded that I choose my mate and produce heirs like she had. I wrung my hands and stared at the ground. Of course she had to continue the matriarchal line. But what if I wanted to take the spiritual path like my father, but also indulge like my mother. Why could I not have both?

The Celestial Lords did Choose me prior to my birth, and when I entered this world, I was given three words: Ego. Salvation. Revelation. They've shaped every step of my journey—whether I liked it or not.

To quell the mounting desire in our bodies, we summoned our new teacher with claps, songs and dances drawn from the rhythm within. These rituals served to both ground us—and distract us—as we labored to cleanse and beautify the Great Aten Temple. In the late afternoon, Archollos, the blonde Mycenaean and I took strolls through the town accompanied by two burly, onyx-colored soldiers. As much as we played at freedom, it was only an illusion. One afternoon, Archollos reached out to tuck a stray braid behind my ear. The touch was innocent—or nearly so—but a tremor rippled through me.

He had grown so tall, no longer the half-drowned boy my mother rescued. A Mycenaean castaway, shipwrecked during a violent storm and found clinging to driftwood near the Nile Delta. He would have been sold into slavery—just another foreign body traded for spices or linen—but my mother had seen something in him. She bought his freedom and brought him into our palace.

He'd grown up beside me, a shadow just taller than mine, his sun-bleached curls wild and always falling into his eyes. I once thought of him as a brother—until he became something far more dangerous.

From across the square, Amaret tilted her head. I was always under watch—Amaret, the blind Royal Seer, saw more than any guard. She tracked my every breath like a harpy eagle warding off danger—or desire. Though her unseeing eyes were milky, I felt her sight pierce through me. Her nostrils flared slightly, and her cane tapped twice—once for warning, once for command.

My breath caught. I stepped back from Archollos, feigning sudden interest in a vendor's painted gourds. The moment had passed.

I hated how quickly I folded under her unspoken judgment. Was I not a princess? Future Queen? And yet, a single tilt of Amaret's head reduced me to a guilty girl caught stealing sweetness from the edge of a forbidden feast.

Today felt different. The air was heavier, as if the gods held their breath. The sunlight hit the ochre stones at a strange slant, casting long, uncertain shadows. If you had asked me what had changed, I would've blamed it on the stars—or the unseen finger of Aten pointing us toward a new fate.

It was Amaret who confirmed it. She turned her sightless face to the horizon and nodded once, sharply. A silent signal. Something had shifted.

"We need to return to the palace—something is stirring," I said waving to gather the class.

"What is it?" Archollas asked, lending an ear as if I could tell him of the message I had received in the inner.

"I am not sure. Something has shifted. Perhaps it is our new teacher."

"I am eager to learn. My belly hungers for stimulation, Archollos said, his voice low, eyes lingering on mine longer than usual. He picked up the basket and brushed his hand across my arm in passing—just enough to spark a pulse beneath my skin.

I yearned to draw him to me, to be enfolded within his muscular arms. To feel the warmth of his mouth upon mine. My stomach fluttered, and I felt frustrated that I couldn't make him mine. This entire palace desired to please me and heed my every command as the Royal princess, but I felt powerless in the presence of Archollos. I turned my face away, feeling the sudden shame of my love for him. "We need to make haste."

The black-winged vultures circled our city at dawn, their shadows dancing ominously over the rooftops. Our class followed Amaret up the steps to the Royal Tombs. It had the best advantage of sight over the vast expanse of land. What was left of the Medjay, our meager army, already had the long-distance bowmen armed and ready. We scanned the gray horizon, excitement and worry both coursing through our veins. I felt palpitations in my heart, not knowing if this was the moment when the Amunites would batter our city, moving in unison as armies do with the intent to slaughter us. Or if this would be a moment of rejoice the coming of our teacher. Like it or not, something was coming. Amaret and I felt it.

"There," shouted one marksman who had been trained by the tribes to smell foreigners upon the wind.

Large puffs of dust were indeed being unsettled from afar. Rolling waves of the disrupted desert drew our attention, now locked upon a target. Something was approaching, but none of the guards gave me any comfort that a death sentence wasn't on the way to expel the Atenists from this world.

"Do not worry, Merit-Aten. We have the advantage from up high to be on the offense," said Archollos as he heard my labored breathing. My hands turned to the very ice that had held that treasure only a fortnight ago.

"Stand ready," ordered the Bowman. Forty-cliff-based archers drew back their right hands, plucking the taunt bow-string. Their arrows would come down upon the usurpers in a thunder of fire.

I clenched the amulet at my chest and whispered a prayer to Aten. All around me, the class stood tense, breath shallow. Sand stung our cheeks as the desert wind kicked up in warning. A scream of a hawk overhead made one of the younger priestesses jump. The cloud drew closer, and I could see flickers of bright blues, reds, and yellows through the dusty storm.

We all craned our necks, shifting nervously, trying to grasp the magnitude of what approached. It certainly did not have the width of a marching army; even I could see that. A shrill trumpet blast cut through the air. The earth trembled beneath us, and at the city's edge, an unexpected spectacle emerged. A towering elephant lifted its trunk in a playful wave, striding confidently toward us. The frightful, yet delightful beast was garbed in golden armor, wearing a turban with a glorious plume of white ostrich feathers, dancing in the slight breeze that seemed to wave to us.

Golden drapes of glistening fabric were gathered in voluminous folds upon the elephant's sides and perched upon its back was a straw-woven basket carrying a man wearing a conical golden hat with multi-colored streamers fluttering like birds behind him.

While this sight was an oddity, what made it even stranger was his accompanying band of misfits keeping pace beside him. A regiment of broad-chested, muscled men reigned the large, feathered ostriches as they ran in chaotic patterns. Behind them was a parade of beauties upon gray and brown donkeys. These lovely women tinkled sistrums to announce their arrival with a flair. Other lovelies chanted in unison, emitting a melodious trilling song. They waited at our gates, and our armed warriors sounded the ram's horn, announcing the arrival of our guests. Surely, they, too, were befuddled by the band of oddities that didn't appear to be carrying weapons.

"Amaret, may we go see them?" I asked, my voice quivering with exaltation. I touched her sleeve, to draw her attention to my request. The hawk perched upon her other shoulder sat motionless.

"Return to the Royal Palace, now," ordered Amaret, signaled the Bowmen by pointing her finger at them and then us. "They must be properly presented to you, Merit-Aten as the Per-Aat in waiting—but only after we have had the opportunity to disarm them. They must tell us from whence they hail. I will have the palanquins pick you all up so you can make yourselves presentable for our unexpected company," and they marched down the steps toward town.

"It is our new teacher, I will place a gamble upon that," said Ra-Awab, punching Archollos playfully.

Sarawat, doing a little dance, said, "This is a most joyous day."

I felt my shoulders release. Maybe this character would be the answer to my prayers. It could be the very reason we will save our rulership, our city, and most importantly our family. I just knew in my gut this was a most fortuitous meeting. The Aten had answered my wishes.

Later in the orange and yellow sun cast afternoon, we had all changed into our ceremonial whites and being the next highest-ranking royal in attendance, I chose to wear a multi-strand lapis and gold collar with red coral scarabs dangling like a fringe around the edge. My attendants pushed golden bands high around my upper arms, their cool weight a reminder of station and expectation. The Royal Hairdresser worked swiftly, sculpting my thick dark hair into an elongated bun that whispered of lineage and control. Black kohl eyeliner traced my eyes with the same practiced hand that once shaded my mother's. I caught my reflection in the polished obsidian mirror—chin lifted, brows set, lips softened but unreadable. For a moment, I did not see myself. I saw her. The Great Royal Wife. Nefertiti. Regal. Remote. Untouchable. I mimicked the subtle tilt of her head, the way she could stare through men and make them bow. If I could just hold that gaze, maybe they would bow to me, too.

Archollos' smile was wide when he whispered, "You look exotic and enticing."

He gave me confidence, as I sat erect upon my father's resting throne, my stomach flipflopped from anticipation.

"Clang the gong once they arrive," I ordered the guards, wanting to appear ready, as this was the very first time I had been left in charge. I would emulate my mother's self-assurance and my father's authority as I practiced several ways of sitting to ensure the message was clear. My class stood at various levels upon the mudbrick steps, acting as my attendants. My five sisters were fidgeting on the footstools around me. We grew impatient with trying to sit still while yearning to greet our new guests with childlike enthusiasm.

My hands rested in my lap, palms pressed tightly to hide the tremble in my fingertips. I inhaled deeply, as I'd seen my mother do before receiving emissaries. There would be no stammering. No girlish glances. I was the daughter of Aten—vessel of the light. The stone beneath me was still warm from my father's presence, and I imagined his spine straightening mine.

"Announcing Ana-Kharu-We-Shat to our Princess Merit-Aten."

In rushed a golden draped tribesman with grand sweeping gestures. He bowed, striking quite an effective pose of dignity and abundance. Light reflected off his shimmering raiment, after making his entrance awe-inspiring. Then he looked up—and the mirth in the room froze. His eyes, like molten obsidian, swept the hall with ancient knowing. In that moment, I felt as though he had already seen me naked before the stars.

We all stood aghast. Instead of the towering godlike sage I'd envisioned—glowing, mounted on elephantine glory—there stood a wee slip of a man. He was barely taller than the drummer boy. Ankhi, my younger sister, stifled a giggle behind her hand. Sarawat elbowed her, eyes wide with mischief. Even Archollos shifted uncomfortably, as though unsure whether to bow or burst out laughing.

The man unexpectedly small—no taller than a thumb extended from the palm of the gods. A peculiar presence, like a myth come to life. I leaned forward, my eyes widening with awe. Was this one of the magical Twamen, of the oldest living civilization upon this land?

"I am a Prognosticator of the Divine," said our guest making a bow without a hint of humility.

Was this glittering imp truly a mouthpiece of the Aten? My father's voice had always been the clearest among us—how could I lend my ear, much less my faith, to this flamboyant stranger?

He continued with utter brazenness. "We have traveled from the far corners to present the most precious commodities gathered from the 42 tribes. Allow me to display our vendible oils and finest perfumes derived from every flower, seed, nut, tree, and animal," he decreed, with a grand sweep of his hand. Clad in a puffy golden fine linen robe woven with silver and gold threads, he had a regal appearance. Certainly, this spectacle would pass our doldrums and keep my court entertained.

"Come buy our oils traded from afar. We offer pomegranate, clover, currant, peach, henna, Castor oil, myrtle, woody nightshade. Or, perhaps, rose oils and petals for baths, olive leaves, blue cornflowers are all known to heal various maladies. My oils are meticulously selected for their medicinal qualities," he continued.

Servants flooded the thresholds like ants to honey. Laughter, perfume, and shrieks of delight spilled into the sacred air. My father would have been horrified by the lack of decorum, yet I was to partake in the opportunity to shop. I am sure my father would be aghast, but I was so enmeshed with the fervor of the troupe's arrival that I did not want to contain the burst of the unusual.

Amaret sat on her stool, unmoved by the calamity, then spoke, "You there, do you have any of Giza's Best Black Mud? My Seer loved her mud masks and had missed having a supply since the transport of goods to our royal city, Akhet Aten was curtailed.

The shiny salesman drew his attention to the elder. "No, we have not been up North for two years, but I could procure that luxury if you so desire."

Amaret just waved her hand dismissing us "Horus, quiet, "she said, and fed her hawk a morsel.

My classmates ooh'd and ahh'd with thrills to try new pleasantries. The beautiful flowers, his accompanying blackened bare-breasted women were exotically dressed in vibrant skirts like I had never seen. Two of the women were bold and unashamed in their lushness, their skin the shade of volcanic earth, glistening with shea and scented oil. Their breasts, full and heavy, swayed like ripened fruit—emblems of a sensual world our temple walls had long kept at bay.

Two men were tall, thin Nubians, possessed with wild, unkempt, frizzy hair, implying what their tribal name was, Haden-Newa. Their hair told stories—twists of red ochre, braids like river glyphs, and shorn scalps that gleamed beneath patterned wraps. They moved with a sinewy grace that defied the rigid postures of our court. They all handed out tiny vials of thick, rich unguents for us to sample.

The visitors clucked and clicked to each other in a secret language, I suspected, so they could gage our reactions without us knowing what was said. The leader clapped his hands, and one of the muscular male attendants hoisted up two woven baskets filled with fabrics in colors previously unseen. The bolts of cloth spilled upon the floor, making rainbows. My maidens pounced like lionesses in heat—hissing, tugging, laughing—our courtly polish stripped by the hunger for color, texture, and life. It had been so long since we'd touched something... unnecessary.

The Amunites had severed our resources from Lower to Upper Khemit. We were hungry for goods from afar, having focused upon our Cosmic duties as the devotees of the Aten. As lovely as these luxuries were, none of them could save my family or my home. My eyes suddenly dampened, and my mood turned. The scent of spices turned bitter in my nose. What good were oils and silks when our kingdom starved of hope? My longing curdled inside me—like biting into a sugared fruit, only to find the core rotted.

"Your Majesty, I present the most exquisite of perfumes—scents that beckon love and awaken pleasures so divine, they transcend the mortal plane." Ana-Kharu-We-Shat lifted the bottles with a devious smile and flutter of dark lashes. Inherently, he understood the erotic arts as one of the dark beauties shook her shoulders side to side, which made her breasts bounce in titillation. The women emitted a trilling sound with their tongues, and the heat of the scorching desert grew within our loins.

My male classmates grew stiff as scepters with unbridled lust, making them want to pounce upon these shiny strangers *Their bodies pulsed with unspoken hunger, stirred by breasts that bounced like ripe offerings. The women trilled, and the air itself thickened. Archollos, Ra-Amun, and Smenkhkare leaned forward, spellbound, their desire barely sheathed beneath their robes. I lifted my hand, an unspoken command—"Enough."*

My voice rang like a gong reverberating with abhorrence. This clearly was not the teacher we all had anticipated and with whom my father had made an arrangement. Now, everyone was so enraptured with the offerings that they would feel great disappointment if I expressed that we could not possibly spend our Treasury on these entertainments when there were so many that needed to be fed. I had allowed my excitement to override my sensibilities. Now, knowing that Akhet-Aten, our home, could be on the verge of extinction, these frivolities were out of the question. This moment was meant to delight—but I saw now, it was a test. The Queen within me stirred, awakening beneath the veil of girlhood. We could not feast on perfume while our people starved. I would not barter sovereignty for baubles.

Ana-Kharu-We-Shat held his hand up. "Your Majesty, do my fabrics and formulas not please you?" the salesman clapped again, "I can see you have an eye for even finer luxuries. I should have known that all these mundane goods would be as common as grasshoppers in the house of a king and queen. Perhaps," he said, eyes gleaming like obsidian under torchlight, "you are not one to be moved by common enchantments. Then let me offer... the uncommon."

A towering onyx-skinned woman with shoulders like an ox emerged, bearing a carved ivory box adorned with sacred glyphs. Ana-Kharu-We-Shat stepped forward and drew forth a golden ankh key from the glimmering chain at his neck—its gleam whispering secrets to those who could hear.

Upon opening the treasure box, inside, glass vessels of every hue gleamed like captured starlight, cradled in a cobalt lining. Their jeweled caps glinted with promise, as if each contained the power to bend fate.

My gaze locked on the key—its golden arcs shimmered like a sun disk in miniature. Was this the one my father spoke of in hushed riddles? The one I was destined to find?

I leaned forward, "Pray tell, Prognosticator, what are these used for?" My curiosity suddenly overtook my ill mood. Now, these tinctures may be of value.

"Within this chest," he intoned, "are potions of wealth, elixirs of power, draughts for protection—and one spell alone, made to bend the very threads of destiny."

You would not happen to be in need of any of these delights, would you?" he stepped forward as if presenting a lusciously cooked meal, allowing the delectable smells to waft into our noses. Our hunger was now achingly obvious as we all arched forward.

My nostrils flared. "Bring those toward me. I am most interested." I leaned in, the scent of cinnamon and sandalwood curling into my senses. Maybe these could feed my people—maybe they could buy me time from my mother's decree. Anything but being bound to that child, Tut-Ankh-Aten. I scoffed under my breath.

"Protection, is it? Perhaps a spell that would make your kingdom impenetrable to evil forces."

"I would greatly enjoy having a more private conversation about all the tinctures in your box, but I fear that my court is too mesmerized by the delights you have purveyed." I needed to speak with him in confidence. "Where are my manners? You are guests who are clearly in need of baths and refreshments after long days of travel. You must be weary," I said, gathering my resolve. "My Reception House to the East shall host you. There, you may bathe, feast, and be restored. We will speak again—alone—when the moon blesses the evening."

"Your grace humbles us," Ana-Kharu-We-Shat replied, the veneer of showmanship peeling to reveal fatigue. He clucked, and his wanderers dropped to their knees in gratitude, like pilgrims before a shrine.

"I will provide all with bedding and food. Attendants," I clapped, and the festivity began to recede as attendants scurried to get ready to receive our guests.

"Your Majesty, tonight we will give thanks for your generosity with entertainment provided by my musicians and dancers."

"Yes," I replied. "Once you are restored, we will be ready to receive you later this evening."

I elicited a nod and change in his eyes, denoting the fatigue of days wandering in a desert in his travels between towns in search of a sale. "That is most gracious, Majesty. We would be most grateful for a mat to lay upon, and baths would be most welcome." He clucked to his band of wanderers, and they fell to their knees in joyful praise.

Back in my private quarters after I had dismissed my attendants and classmates, Amaret and I huddled deep in conversation. The Royal Seer sat on the floor at my feet, and her cloudy blue eyes focused on the unseen.

"That final ivory chest... it pulled at me," I whispered. "There may be more in it than trinkets." I said close to her ear to rouse her from that meditative mind.

"What could a desert charlatan offer that the Aten has not already denied us?" she muttered, not even lifting her eyes from the smoke of the incense brazier," she responded without looking up.

"He revealed that he had tinctures and spells that could change outcomes. Surely, we are in need of..."

Amaret cut me off sharply, "Magic?" Amaret's voice cracked like a whip. "You would trade sovereignty for Heka? You think a charm will call the waters back? That a bottle will make the Nile bleed life into dead sand?" Her words flayed me open like a butcher's practiced knife—each syllable precise, a blade honed on truth. I was no queen, only a girl pretending to wear the sun's crown. What could I really do to change the fate that the Aten had bestowed upon us?

"What harm is there in trying?" I whispered, almost to myself. "Better a spell than the fate she would force on me—a wedding to a boy with milk on his lips, and exile to Thebes."

"At least I could try. Right now, I am at the mercy of my mother. She would have me marry my half-brother and march me off to Thebes. I simply must try something, anything, Amaret." My voice quavered, and it suddenly dawned upon me how precarious my situation was.

"You are a Mystic, born and raised to be in alignment with the Aten. Your connection is to the vertical, directly to the God of our People. You cannot and will not alter that connection with Magic. You know the order of your Father, and you know the punishment will not be by his hand only for breaking the Holy covenant. It is the lineage you were born into. You cannot change it on a whim, or you will subject this entire kingdom to ruin. Am I clear?"

My hands shook. It was as if the echoing words of the Aten had rung through her vessel and into my ears like a clanging bell. "Then tell me, by what means do we overcome our Cosmic fate? Am I doomed to lead a life of suffering to save my family?"

Amaret's gaze locked on something far beyond this moment, her voice low with prophecy. "It rests now in the loving hands of the Aten," she said, winding a wild silver strand of hair around her finger, as if binding fate with calm certainty.

But my heart thudded in defiance, pounding louder than her prophecy. That ankh key around Ana-Kharu-We-Shat's neck shimmered like a shard of fate—not decoration, but direction. My breath caught every time it swung.

I would not wait in silence while others decided my destiny. If stepping forward meant overstepping, so be it. Let the Aten read the weight of my heartbeat, the tremble of my hands, the fire coiled low in my belly. Let Him see that I chose not from rebellion—but from the knowing that lives in my bones.

Our festivities were to be held in the open-air Reception Hall, a sacred space perched above the parched Nile like a whisper from the gods. Built apart from the main temple complex, it was meant for ceremony and starlit blessings, its purpose as liminal as the night itself. My classmates and I crossed a stretch of desert kissed by moonlight, the sand gleaming silver beneath our feet. Our laughter floated upward, light and teasing, a veil thrown over nerves strung taut as bowstrings. The guards flanking us marched stiffly, their spears angled outward in anticipation of ambush. I pretended not to notice the glances exchanged between the men. I pretended not to care. But I could feel it—something was coming. And I was walking straight toward it.

Archollos walked beside me, close enough for his linen to brush mine. His scent—sun-baked leather and cedar-wood—slid into my breath. Ana-Kharu-We-Shat's key beckoned to me.

Smenkhkare, ever the sly fox, leaned in and whispered, "Careful, Merit. That look in your eyes could melt a pillar." He offered a playful wink, clearly amused. "Or at least set Archollos ablaze."

Ra-Awab, trailing just behind, barked a laugh. "The Princesses' eyes always start fires—but it is the rest of us that get burned." He flashed a grin at Tadushet, who stifled a gasp and covered her mouth with both hands.

The girls were practically glowing—cheeks flushed, eyes wide, giggles barely restrained. We all knew tonight wasn't just about song and story. Ana-Kharu's men had arrived sun-darkened and sinewed, with arms like carved stone and voices that rumbled low when they greeted us. And for many of the girls, this might be the only night they'd ever dare to flirt with men bold enough to stare back.

But for me, this night wasn't about longing. It was about strategy. The key. That key.

The guards' eyes were always roving. I could feel their breath on the back of my neck—watchful, intrusive, reminding me of my royal tether. Their presence grated against my freedom like sand against silk. Every movement I made was measured against duty. Every glance stolen from Archollos came at a price.

Just then, as if the gods themselves blessed our mischief, Bastet, my sacred temple panther darted into the torchlight. Black as obsidian, she pounced before we reached the temple in a blur of lithe grace. She must have escaped the compound—or I might have left the latch unlocked when brushing her earlier.

'Bastet...my love, please give chase to the guards and keep them at a distance,' I ordered her in my mind.

"Guards, my panther has broken free. Please find her. Do not hurt my beloved but get her back to the enclosure now!" I knew she would be fine but would indeed make it difficult for the guards to find her hidden within the shadowed folds of night.

She hissed, arching her back in mock battle, then took off across the desert.

The guards gave chase to collect my panther. One even took a step forward. For a single breath, their vigilance broke.

Smenkhkare seized the moment. "Quick," he whispered, motioning everyone into the temple now pulsing with a luring rhythm. The others followed like whispers on the wind, their sandals barely touching the floor.

My heartbeat loud in my throat—not from fear, but from delicious risk. We were free, if only for a moment. Free to see, to flirt, to touch, to take. And I would get that key.

The torches cast their golden breath over the open-air Reception Hall, where flames flickered across polished faience tiles like serpents in ritual. Columns soared like titans, nearly brushing the obsidian sky, and above us, a dome of stars winked with knowing.

To the East, Ana-Kharu's musicians struck their drums with reverent insistence, summoning something primal from within us—an ache that knew no name. Then, the flutes and harps met the rhythm with a moving melody. My class had no desire to remain as spectators; our feet needed freedom to dance. Dance and sing. Be joyous and move our bodies to that enticing beat. Ana-Kharu smiled and waved us in, away from the prying eyes of the court and attendants. Here along the Nile, we felt the energy of the once plentiful river that had been reduced to a trickling stream. His dancers wore little but sacred defiance—scarves at their wrists, paint on their skin, and a sensual knowing that made silence hum. Curly nether regions were dusted with colorful powders to match the hair on their heads.

One delicious charcoal female had silver paint in patterns upon her breasts and plump bottom. Her beauty was deliberate, dripping with knowledge. I couldn't look away—nor did I wish to. When she turned to face us, a silver chain was linked to her delicate inner lips between her thighs. *A silver chain traced a path from the sacred cleft of her body to her navel, then upward between her breasts—each link a spell in motion, shimmering with intention.*

I wondered how that chain might be plugged into the inner depths. Her tight, curly hair was oiled, and streaks of silver dappled her enticingly. The beauty pulled Ra-Awab toward her, and she skillfully rubbed her pert nipples across his chest to coax him.

A dancer as black as the night sky moved his feet and clapped his hands in rigorous beats, his body a current of raw electricity. His hips undulated with such precision that even his manhood moved like a serpent—curious, alive, reaching toward the feminine with bold invitation. Tadushet gasped as it brushed her hip, while my female classmates giggled and covered their faces, But I watched, transfixed. These were rites had never been taught in school, unspoken mysteries cloaked in rhythm and sweat. Between the music and the ache it stirred, I knew we were being drawn into a vortex of seduction—and I wasn't powerless, I was *willing*. Maybe if I had not been so long cloaked in fan bearers and silver protocols, I would have known this hunger sooner. Something opened in me that night. Freedom had a taste, and I was thirsty for it.

Recalling my initiation in the Dendera Temples of Hathor, I had spied on the Temple Priestesses. I had judged them once, or at least pretended not to understand. But, this well-versed troupe heightened that experience. I had come for oils, but perhaps the gods wished me to taste something more ancient—desire itself, as a teacher.

With the thrumming of drums, flutes, and thumb chimes, the revelers broke out in a counter-circle dance. As tenders carried in a towering stack of colorful violet and turquoise bound palm leaves, tied at the top with a central pole piercing through like a ceremonial staff. A dancer spoke to it lovingly and coaxed it into motion.

"Kumpo," shouted the crowd. There was cheering common in village celebrations.

Suddenly, the palm-leafed cluster marched toward us in wild swinging motions as if it had feet and arms. It came alive, turning in circles to demonstrate that it was not inhabited by a hued-man.

"Kumpo created the world," said one of the Woman Wanderers, an ancient elder with cheekbones like obsidian cliffs and eyes clouded with memory. She was known as *So-Beckt-Ka,* the last living keeper of the Crocodile Scrolls and guardian of the womb rites passed down through salt, star, and bone. She wore a necklace of dried lotus and a crocodile tooth, and her voice swayed like a reed flute carried on Saharan wind. "Enjoy with reverence, but warn your friends not to look too deeply into the palm leaves because this overstanding is from the beyond. We bring Kumpo here to demonstrate that the spirit realm is within reach and to show you our reverence for nature. Every song, dance, and gesture restores the balance and energy in relationships between us and the unseen world."

Just as the mesmerizing dance came to a conclusion, Ana-Kharu signaled for trays of tiny, hammered copper cups to be passed to all attendees. Certainly, all of Ana-Kharu's party were drinking the liquid. I looked to my court and shook my head as a warning never to indulge in substances that could be poison.

Some of the dancers began to engage in the more sensual pleasures. Fingers began to slide into darkened crevices, much to the delight of the receivers. That silvered temptress began moaning in ecstasy, and two male drummers pulled her legs apart before a sudden stream of light burst from her center, catching Ra-Awab across the face. He blinked, stunned—then laughed, as if christened by pleasure itself. He was shocked at his wet gift from the seductress. He laughed and applauded her secretious talents.

Ana-Kharu slipped beside me like dusk itself, his voice laced with velvet and veiled intent. "Your Majesty... would you honor me by viewing a treasure I show only to the rarest of guests?" As he placed his hands upon my shoulders and guided me away.

Thankful to be pulled away from the commotion, I said breathlessly, "Yes," I would.

"I trust my dancers have stirred more than mere amusement," he said, his breath too close, his presence a heat against my skin. "His body touched mine, and I felt an alarming spark between us as I recoiled.

"I am most entertained," I said, trying to tear my eyes away in utter fascination and regain my composure.

"May I show you some things that I would only reveal to my most discerning clients?"

Archollos searched for me in the crowd, and I heard him shout my name but then he saw me leaning close to the leader.

"Please do," I said and followed the salesman behind the carnelian curtains that shielded us from view. Ana-Kharu pointed to a pillow that I dropped down to sit. He then opened a box to display mandrake roots that looked distinctly like people. The roots curled like limbs, eerily human—hips flaring, legs tapering into fine tendrils, their texture both botanical and disturbingly flesh-like. The root that resembled a man had a strong chest, thick arms, and a thicker phallus between its root legs. Both perennial herbaceous roots had little hairs streaming from them.

As unusual as this presentment was, sadly, it did not impress me. Mandrakes were common in most priestly rituals. Even the Kalabsha priests used the mandrakes to tend to the garden in which they grew. "Yes, mandrakes—hands of glory. Is this the extent of your spectacle?" I asked, my voice tight with disappointment.

"My Lady, these are not your common roots. Oh, no, why would I bring the ordinary to your eyes? I can see that you have received the high initiations. Look again; perhaps you should hold them."

I cocked my head. Reaching for the roots, Ana-Kharu made guttural sounds as if to awaken them from a slumber. One root stirred in my palm, breasts budding from its bark-like chest. A tiny hand brushed its eyes as though waking from centuries of sleep. Then the male herb turned over, and I could clearly touch the rough flesh between his legs, simulating a defined phallus.

"Are they alive?" I asked, my voice rising in surprise and delight.

Ana-Kharu only made those throaty sounds and waved his hands, making them dance like puppets. They turned to each other and embraced. Little brown faces emerged from the green leafy Basel rosette, yellow flowers, and berries that looked like a garland of color surrounding their faces.

"Hotep," I said gently so as not to alarm this magical being. They both blinked and peered up at me as if I was a giant who had captured them. "Do not be afraid; I will not hurt you."

"What is it you desire, Princess?" coaxed Ana-Kharu. "Tell them what your heart yearns for. Now that you have held them, you cannot lie. Only truth will come from your lips. They are quite skilled at evoking the heart's deepest wishes," said Ana-Kharu in a purposeful voice of authority.

I could feel their juices touch my fingers and penetrate my skin. I should have thrown them down for fear of being cursed, but I dare not hurt nature's precious babies. Music I couldn't hear yet somehow felt lured my senses, and my pulse beat like a drum in my ears, coaxing me into a trance I hadn't agreed to enter.

Grown in our black soil, the sun penetrating the earth packed tightly around them, while their hair emerged from the soil and blossomed in the rays of delighted glory. Until a twine was tied around their crest of blooms, and they were tugged from their earthen slumber. Screams like terror pierced my ears, and I wanted to hide from the hideous pleas. Now, I was caught in their enchantment.

"Tell me what you desire. I can feel your longing. No, your lust for a boy that belongs to another land. He fell upon your shores in a calamity," said the female root.

I had devoted my life to the temples, to the stars, to my father's dream of a kingdom led by light.

But no one ever warned me that the path of light also awakens the body's hunger. Could I not walk both? Could I not love the heavens and still crave the taste of him? Was that not the teaching of Hathor herself—that bliss is holy, that love is law?

"Yes," I whispered, ashamed of how quickly truth escaped my lips. "Archollos… he is of my class, yet of something far deeper." I tried to form the words that all I wanted was that key that hung around my tormentor's neck, but that thought kept being swept away.

"Do you wish to bed him, my pretty? I can make that happen," she said in rootly tones that seemed to ignite my nethers.

"Men can be enticed with my juice," said the male. "Does his limb not stiffen? I can make it dance inside of you."

"It is not that, I am sure his branch will dance. I want him for my own. I want him as my consort," I said, hating to admit that to a plant. But, it was my deepest secret that had been so dismissed by my parents. "I want his baby. I need his baby." This wasn't only about passion. Something deeper moved through me—a vision, a knowing. If a child were to come from our union, it would not be by accident. It would be a seed blessed by the Aten, guided by the stars, perhaps even meant to restore what has been broken between two worlds. "Ah," said Ana-Kharu, "You are Royalty. You are beautiful. Why not just claim the intruder? You do not need to choose him; just take him. Enjoy him. Tame him. Then make his seed yours. Has your mother not already made him a court pet? He has been in your family's care for so long that he cannot even remember the face of his mother. Do as thy wish."

It never occurred to me that I did not actually have to take him as a King under the watchful eyes of the court and all their judgment. Enjoying him at my pleasure, of course seemed so reasonable. I could just scratch the itch that constantly kept my innards tingling for him. It was the way with the Matriarch, after all. I needed no permission to take a lover. My mother certainly did not need permission to bed Horemheb and produce a child. If I were to receive a child from a union with Archollos, then that would be between the Aten and me. No one ever questioned if a woman carried a child or whose child it belonged to. People always questioned who the father was, and no man could ever prove that he was worthy enough to have entered a Royal. A soft haze enveloped my mind, and a radiant halo—like oil on water—spilled across my sightline, draping thought in opalescent fog. I was delirious to have solved this problem that kept my mind in prison.

"Have you ever known a man's touch?" Ana-Kharu's whisper slithered into my ear.

I swayed, caught between waking and dreaming, my head clouded with a mist I could not dispel. My drapings pushed away, and that male Mandrake seemed to crawl over my body. The hairy root pushed its way between my legs while a wetted tongue lapped at my soft flesh. The shock made me ache to sit up and push this intrusive vegetable away, but a moan left my lips, and suddenly, I could not think of anything more than the intense fire-hot pleasure that was leaking from within. Oh, the Nile would have been envious of the waters that flooded from my gates. The licking mixed with a gentle exploring made me wail in utter delight and loss of control as I spasmed in wave after wave of pleasure.

"Merit-Aten!" The name cracked through the veil like a thunderclap, splintering the illusion. Strong hands ripped me from the clutches of unseen shadows. I gasped, my vision clearing as Archollos stood before me, his grip unyielding. "Unhand her."

"There is no harm. We were simply preparing our Lady for you," replied Ana-Kharu, with a smirk.

"For me?" asked Archollos questioningly and took a step back. "It appears that you have induced our Princess with some of your concoctions. "Merit, come to me, my love. Allow me to take you away from here."

'Allow me to take you' was all I heard. I suddenly felt at peace as those strong arms held me protectively against his chest. Tonight, we would join, and I was in a daze of enthrallment. My love transported me away from the festivities. Away from the enticing music. Away from the madness and seductiveness which I had allowed by my own curiosity. I had allowed it by my temptations. Now, I was within his arms, grateful that my wish had come true.

"You are alright? I have some water left in my cask. Drink. You must regain your composure." I laid my head against his shoulder. "You are stronger than you know," he whispered, his hand steady at my spine. "That spell didn't break you. You walked through it and came out whole."

"I feel better. I do not know what came over me," I said, presenting my lips for him to kiss.

"Good. I would not allow that tempter to hurt you. You should ask them to leave. There's a darkness in his touch," he said, his jaw tight and eyes narrowing. "You must send him away."

"Archollos, I am grateful for your watchful eye," I said, my lips upon his cheek, feeling a hint of disappointment that he had not pressed his lips to my surrender. He set me down upon the steps to the back entrance to the Aten Temple. I inhaled deeply, the night air clearing my head. I will ask Archollos to be mine even if it must be kept secret from prying eyes.

"Merit," he said, controlling his tone, his body quaking.

"Yes, my dearest," I said, gaining my courage, my heart pounding in my ears.

"I came to find you but hid behind the curtain to ensure your safety since you told me you were trying to buy precious oils and tinctures for your father."

"How long were you there?" I asked feeling the hairs on my arms rise.

"What did he mean—calling me your court pet?" His voice wavered, wounded pride unraveling at the seams.

He implied that I have been kept by your family for a long while?" He shook his head to clear the cobwebs. "He is right; I do not remember the face of my mother and from whence I hailed. Mycenae, while I know the name of my country, I have lost myself. At the same time, your family rescued me and have been kind enough to clothe and feed me since I was a child. I have never truly belonged in Khemit, yet my heart swears allegiance to all you cherish. It is clear I am an outsider; I have never understood why because I have learned your customs, your manner of speech, your philosophies, and have been invited into your Mystery Schools, but I am still excluded from rank in the minds of your family. I am not one of you." He wept, and in one unexpected moment all my plans were dashed laying me bare for attack by my Mother.

4

*T*he sleek black Lincoln Town Car slid through San Francisco's dusk, ferrying her into memories she never signed up to relive. The Mark Hopkins gleamed above Nob Hill like her father's crown jewel—old money wrapped in gilded ghosts. She could still hear him saying, *"Always check in first, never arrive unprepared."* Of course, it was ironic that the law firm had booked her the hotel room—and put it on her tab.

The moment she entered her small, but stately room, her phone rang, it was her brother.

"Hey, Nico, no, I'll stay at the Mark and then head to Santa Cruz tomorrow."

He paused, "How'd it go?"

"Awful. Good. And who knows? Kanberg said, I did better than he imagined I would, because of the stress. Oh, and they'll want to depose Josh and you and Francesca."

"Emilio is in Florence. And Frannie would hate traveling from Oregon when she's trying to take care of kids. Besides, she wasn't involved in the business—and what could your son even add?"

Morainya yanked off her jacket while balancing her cell phone, then unzipped her slacks feeling like she could finally take a deep breath before slipping on a beige cowlneck, jeans and a houndstooth brown jacket. "Josh is in high school, do you know how pissed he'll be at me to have to take a deposition about his Grandfather's business?"

"Aldo is just being a dick," replied Nico.

"I've spent six months answering their questions and supplying the corresponding documents. I don't have any more to say." Tears stung her eyes, and she sighed.

"I know. I know. We'll figure it out. Is there anything else I should know?"

Morainya grimaced and held the phone tighter. "Kanberg *reminded me* a I'm a month behind in payments to the firm. Guess Aldo doesn't care that when the company went bankrupt, I too lost my job.

Nico cleared his throat, "He knows our Inheritance is frozen until all this is cleared up. Look, I know this has been a burden to you having to pay for this personally."

"It's killing me, Nico. Plus, Kanburg threw in the 'when we go to court, he'll require a bigger retainer to cover all the costs.'"

"How much is he asking for?"

"My right arm and maybe half a leg as a deposit." She tried to lighten the moment, but honestly the invasive pestering of these pernicious questioners; reminded her of the seagulls that dive-bombed diners at any coastal restaurant. "Kanberg says that we depose Aldo next week, so I'll be back up. I have to go. My dinner reservation is in half an hour."

She stepped out into a curtain of fog, her heels tapping like distant thunder down California Street. The city was shrouded, just like her life—full of outlines, unclear borders.

Raffi's sign flickered through the mist like an altar candle. She hadn't been here in years. Not since her father's funeral. The scent of oregano and old family drama hit her like a second glass of wine, familiar yet left her with a hangover.

A sudden gust of wind blew into the restaurant, chilling her back and shoulders. Never sit by the door, she thought, as she waved to signal the bartender amongst the standing crowd ordering drinks while waiting for her table.

A stranger brushed her hand as he took the seat beside her. Warm, dark skin—intentional? No. But the contact lingered like a whisper. Reflex told her to pull away. Something older told her not to. She turned slowly.

He was already watching her, not with hunger—but with recognition.

"Excuse me," he said, low and sure. "Didn't mean to startle you."

She didn't speak right away. She *felt* first. Felt the tension of generations, the eyes in the room that might be watching, the stories

passed down from both sides of the line. And still... she didn't move her hand.

"You didn't," she said. "It's... fine." But it wasn't. It was *electric*. "You always stare at people this way?" she asked, half-defensive, half-curious.

He didn't blink. "Only at Queens who forgot their thrones."

She nearly scoffed—but the way he said it, like a vow uttered across centuries, stopped her short. "You don't know me," she whispered.

"Oh, but I do," he said gently. "I just can't say how. Not yet."

He wore a tan cashmere overcoat over a long gray tunic. Foreign, she thought, nothing unusual in this international melting pot of San Francisco—where accents mingled like spices and nothing stayed in one terrine. His broad shoulders nearly touched hers.

"How are you, tonight?" she asked, casually.

"I am fabulous," he said, in a warm, Afrakan melodic tone. "I am enjoying this beautiful city and all it has to offer."

Still trying to wave down the bartender, she asked, "First visit?"

He shook his head slowly, curls tight beneath a cream Kufi—one of those rounded caps Morainya had seen on the Turkish consultant but never quite understood. She used to think it meant gang member, or militant—because that's what the news showed. But now she knew better. It meant Muslim. Devoted. Disciplined. She flushed, ashamed at how much she had once misunderstood. Western-style overcoat did not hide his long Thobe robes.

"I have been here before. I am in town for Black History Month at the Museum exhibit around the corner. As a Moor, I'm the Lead culture consultant."

This intrigued Morainya. "Really?" She turned her stool toward him. "What is a Moor?"

"I am surprised that you have never heard of us," he said with a hint of a laugh. He raised one finger. The bartender, like summoned, appeared.

"What can I get you two?" asked the hipster in a red bowtie matching his red glasses.

"Do you have chai?" asked the dark man, placing both hands palm down on the bar.

"Chai?" asked the bartender with surprise. "I think it's served at breakfast. Do you want it hot or cold?

"Hot," said the man.

"For here or a to-go cup?" The bartender tapped his fingers on the bar to hurry us along.

She was on the verge of breaking her sobriety. Morainya's fingernails dug into her jeans. Just one glass, she lied to herself. *I earned it.* But the moment the word 'earned' passed through her mind, it caught. That wasn't her voice. That was the tired one. The one who broke promises in dim lighting.

"Algol is the Demon Star," he said calmly, without even turning. "From the Arabic Al Ra's al Kuhl. The head of the demon.' Algol-alcohol is when people lose their heads when drunk. Spirits only attract spirits, and we do not need this, Queen."

A blush rose to her cheeks the color of Rose'. It was as if he'd read her mind. "Me too," she said to the bartender with a jut of her head. "Chai's good." *A warm drink would be better on this cold February night.*

"Algol, interesting," was all she could offer. "Why did you call me Queen?" she asked, thinking it was a cultural colloquialism. She gave him a warm smile hoping to ease any preconceived differences.

He looked deep into her eyes, and she felt her heart vibrate. "Kings always recognize Queens. It is my duty to take care of you while in my presence. My humble apologies for not introducing myself; I am Iben Fatah al Abl Mohammed, from Morocco. My name means the 'A Son of Opening, which means disclosure of wisdom.'"

"Wow, that's quite a name, and meaning. "I'm Morainya Napolitano—which must mean something. My Irish mother named me Morainya. Napolitano from my Italian father. Their parents were immigrants." She offered it like a bridge.

"Tell me more about the Moors?" she flipped her hair over her right ear.

"Indeed, Queen. We know all." Her head was spinning. His voice was eerily familiar.

"Were you born in Morocco?" she asked, then immediately regretted it and bit her lip. It sounded like a border patrol question, not genuine curiosity. "I'm sorry—I didn't mean to pry."

He paused. "We do not have to immigrate to that which we own."

Before she could reply, the hostess called, "Napolitano! Table for one."

"Oh, that is me." Morainya jumped up and grabbed her tweed wool coat. She turned to leave but hated to end this conversation so abruptly. What did he own? America? How odd, she thought, then suddenly added, "Would you care to join me?"

"Indeed," replied Iben and followed her to a white table-clothed table. He pulled out her chair *and took her coat, gently folding it over the back. Chivalry?* It reminded her of her old-fashioned Father. Her date nights with Jedidiah had felt more like negotiation tables than anything romantic—contracts disguised as conversation. But this? This felt ancient. Familiar. She thought of all the doors she'd flung open herself over the years—not to be rude, but to make a point. She could do it all. She had done it all.

She and her high-achieving girlfriends had laughed over wine about how they'd forgotten what it felt like to be protected, to soften. Somewhere along the way, being independent became synonymous with being hardened. And maybe that was the point. As if someone, somewhere, had quietly puppeteered a revolution that drove women out of the temple and into the boardroom, into competition, into cortisol, into the slow suffocation of their own femininity. Losing her job had nearly broken her. But for the first time in a long time, she was beginning to feel who she might be behind all the armor.

She was brought back to the conversation, "At the bar," she pointed with her chin. "Did I hear you say you owned this country?"

"I am a Moor, a Moroccan," he said plainly, his hands holding the menu in front of him so that only his face was illuminated by the restaurant lighting. "This is Al Morocco, Amexem, Ta-Mery, America. You didn't know that you are an immigrant to my country?" His eyes pierced her soul.

She felt herself tremble as if they struck something primal in her chest. Not offense. Not confusion. But a kind of inner...remembrance. "But—how?" she asked as the waitress set down their chai.

The United States holds no lawful title over the lands of the Murrs, the Moors, the ancient mound-builders. This land—your land—was ours long before it was called America. Washitaw. Chickasaw. Cherokee. El. Bey. Dey. Al. These names were not tribes. They were nations. Bloodlines. Stewards. We have a divine creed and a bloodline that is esoterically connected to something higher."

Morainya gulped. "We were never taught any of this in school. Please continue."

She shivered, steam from the cup rising like memory. "Why don't we know this?"

He tilted his head. "Because empires erase what doesn't serve them."

A silence stretched between them.

"And California," he said, "Were you born in this state?"

Morainya nodded. "Home of the grizzly bear. Our motto is Eureka. Greek, I think for 'I have found it.' My son just did a class project on the California gold rush."

Iben cocked his head with a twinkle in his eye, and a slight smile. "Did the Greeks find this gold?"

Morainya laughed at his misunderstanding. "No, I imagine this California is far older than the Greeks."

He nodded. "Califia. From Queen Califia, Cal-un-FEE-ahh A Black queen. A warrior of this land long before Spain claimed it. Your maps tell one story. But your bones remember another."

She blinked. Her menu blurred. When the waitress came to take the order, she barely remembered saying 'Minestrone soup and a salad.' This Iben Fath had ordered the same thing. She only knew she needed a moment to catch her breath. "Please excuse me, I'll be right back."

Morainya's head danced with this unusual conversation as she headed to the restroom to splash cold water on her face. That famous Casablanca movie line: 'Of all the gin joints in all the towns in all the world, he walks into mine.' Wasn't Casablanca in Morocco? It was her favorite film, but she realized that it would just be too corny.

She excused herself, and he watched her walk away—not in the way a man ogles, but with the quiet reverence of one who recognizes a sovereign in exile.

Morainya. He hadn't expected her to carry so much frequency, not this soon. But the signs had been undeniable: the way the steam curled around her chai like incense, the way her voice wavered when he spoke of land and bloodlines. And when she laughed—his ancestors turned their ears to listen.

This wasn't about seduction. This was about remembrance. The waitress brought their food, and he took a spoonful of his soup, letting the heat settle in his chest. He hadn't meant to come here tonight. The plan had been simple: warm lentils, rice, and a quiet evening in the condo lent to him by *Mrs. Fassi*, the elder who had arranged his Cultural Exchange visa and funded his appointment as a Moorish Consultant to the new *Black History installation* at the museum. He'd accepted the temporary role at the invitation of the International Cultural Council, a joint initiative between Moroccan and American historians to honor lost lineages and sovereign ties across the Atlantic. The museum had reached out after pressure from several African American advocacy groups demanding more truthful representation—especially of the Moors, who had been systematically excluded from what the West calls Egyptology.

He planned to review the mislabeled "Egypt" wing, especially the archival texts referencing Moorish-Coptic calendar overlays. Maybe even visit UC Berkeley, where a few professors were finally admitting that North African influence extended far deeper than pyramids and sarcophagi. But something in his bones told him the timeline was already shifting.

So yes—he was here for work. But this? This felt like... something else. *His legs had carried him to this restaurant as if in a trance—through the fog of memory, through the echo of some ancient call. And when he saw her.*

The hum in his bones settled. Not recognition exactly. But a *reminder*. He stirred his soup slowly, glancing at the entrance where she'd disappeared. He hadn't expected to say so much. Hadn't meant to tell her about Califia. About Ta-Meri. About Amexem. About the invisible erasures. But when she started talking about injustice—real injustice—something in him opened.

She'd just come from a deposition—he could tell by the way her shoulders curled, as if still bracing against the lawyer's crossfire. Still was, in a way. Fighting for legacy, for stolen finances, for dignity. She said that she hated being accused falsely.

He understood that feeling far too well.

Just last week he'd been pulled over by police on 19th and Mission for driving the wrong way down a narrow street he didn't know was one-way. He'd only had the loaned car for two days. They made him get out. Asked too many questions. Looked at him like he didn't belong.

"You'd best be careful," one of the officers had said. "This ain't Oakland. Black men like to disappear in San Francisco. And you are a foreigner."

He didn't respond. But his back had gone stiff for hours. He hadn't told Mrs. Fassi—no need to worry the schol-ar-diplomat who arranged his exchange. He hadn't told anyone—but he had a feeling Morainya would understand.

When she returned to the table, he exhaled. Her smile held more weight now. The food had arrived. "How long are you in town—or do you live here now?" She lifted a forkful of salad and chewed quietly.

"My visa is for six months. I'm a Cultural Curator," he said. "Working on a mixed media AI exhibition for the Black History Month. It's showing at the museum around the corner and down the block."

"Black History only gets a month?" she raised her eyebrow, half-joking, half-probing that the exhibit had such a short window.

He nodded, a trace of irony on his face. "Black History should not be reduced to recognition for only a month, should it?" Then he caught himself, realizing she was only wondering how long the exhibit was open.

Morainya recognized the truth behind his tone. "No, it should be celebrated all year long."

Their laughter came out at once—half from discomfort, half from knowing. That in this moment, across tone and skin, they were reaching something shared.

"I studied Egyptology in college," she offered between bites. Well—my minor was Textiles and flax weaving techniques. I guess that makes me a kind of an Egyptologist."

Iben's expression didn't change. He looked down, brushing the napkin across his lap, feeling his gut contract. "What is an Egyptologist?"

She blinked. Someone who studies Egypt."

"What's Egypt?" His voice was calm. Too calm.

She sat straighter. "Khemit, actually. That's the name before the Greeks renamed it. So, I guess...Khemitologist, would be more accurate." she stammered, "From the living African Traditions."

His shoulders relaxed, and for the first time he gave an authentic smile. "Queen, I am gladdened that you know that Egypt is in Africa. Most people tell me that Egypt is in the Middle East as if I don't know my own country."

"Of course, I know Egypt; Khemit—is African. The Black Lands," she added, relieved not to sound completely ignorant.

He nodded, his eyes gleaming. "Since you are an educated lady, you do know that I am not an African American? Nor Black. Nor Negro. Nor Colored. Nor even Ethiopian. All those are slave titles, assigned by slave holders between 1779-1865. Titles to strip us of our lawful identity, and spiritual birthright. If you don't understand the law, then you don't know who you are."

Morainya cheeks burned. Her Catholic upbringing had never prepared her for this kind of conversation. It hit her like a revelation. All this talk of law and legacy. Maybe it wasn't coincidence that her life was entangled in the legal system right now. It hit her hard. She didn't know who she was.

Iben paused. "I am an indigenous Moor," he continued, "and give honors to the Moorish Science Temple of America and the Honorable Prophet Noble Drew Ali. I am a Moor with the blood of the gods."

Morainya nearly choked on her chai. That last part— "blood of the gods"—struck her as wild, blasphemous even. What would her Catholic family think of that remark?

She raised her cup to her lips, using its warmth to hide behind. But she didn't turn away.

"You should come to the exhibit tomorrow at the Museum We are doing a small preview for a some kids to measure interaction," he said, leaning forward as if offering her a secret. "There is so much you deserve to learn."

"I'd love to but...tomorrow? I need to drive back to Santa Cruz before traffic. My son has a baseball game that night.

He nodded. "I overstand."

Morainya tilted her head. "Overstand?"

"I meant what I said," he replied evenly. "If I say understand, it means I stand beneath your system. Overstand means I rise above it. Language holds power."

She stared at him, unsure how to respond—but deep down, something in her clicked. The way his words rearranged her internal logic felt... oddly familiar.

Iben removed an extra ticket from his pocket and pushed it toward her. "You Americans are so attached to your routines. In my country, we say 'be like birds and see where the wind carries you.' There is great wisdom in Morocco. You should come." His eyes emitted so much electric energy into hers that it mesmerized her in ways that were beyond this world.

"I will," said Morainya, as if the words were pulled from her mouth.

"Ten tomorrow. Allah has deemed it so."

The next morning, Iben Fatah performed his morning Salat prayers to the Qibla—the sacred direction of the Kaaba in Mecca— standing barefoot on a red woven carpet carried from his homeland. Clothed in quiet reverence, he donned his kufi cap.

He whispered the *Niyyah*, his heart's silent intention. Raising his hands: *"Allahu Akbar."*

God is the Greatest. As he moved through each sacred position—Ruku, Sujood—he recited, *"Subhana Rabbiyal Azeem,"* and later, *"Subhana Rabbiyal A'la."*

*E*very prayer was a cleansing, a return. Today, especial-ly, was sacred. His long-labored exhibit would finally open: a living archive of Khemit's suppressed North Afrakan legacy.

The preview today, his curated exhibit—an interactive fusion of AI technology and historical scholarship—would unveil the long-suppressed truth of Khemit's North Afrakan origins, restoring stolen knowledge to his rightful place. Iben Fatah's heart swelled for being allowed to eloquently communicate the pride he felt in representing his Afrakan heritage. It was his deepest longing to awaken and empower the Afrakan people, guiding them to reclaim pride in their Melanin-given heritage, despite the tribulation that had scattered them across the earth. Internally, he could feel his clock ticking away the moments until his brothers and sisters would unite and rise out of the ashes to take their divine place.

A candle flickered in his mind, illuminated the memory of last night's dinner with the American woman. Iben hoped she'd come today. A soft smile made his heart thrum recall-ing their exchange. Unexpected. Intense. Joyful.

She was older than most women who caught his eye— fifties, maybe? —but something in her bearing made her ageless. The streaks of silver in her brown hair shimmered like forgotten knowledge. Her nails were bitten down, ner-vous tells. Her eyes, however, told a deeper story.

She wore grief like a cloak. Yet beneath it, he sensed royal architecture. As if she'd once been sovereign—and had forgotten. His ancestors spoke: This one is of importance. Guide her.' He always obeyed, even if he did not know the exact path that he would follow. Iben Fatah had a strong feeling that she would indeed accept his invitation to today's ceremonies. In fact, he was so sure that he had Mrs. Fassi, the administrator, add another chai to their morning coffee order from the Tree of Life Bookstore and Café down the street.

A knock on the door to the tiny, enclosed office shook him out of his daydream. "Sharif, it is almost time to open the doors and receive the guests. Would you come do a prayer for us?" Nekena, a proud Afrakan woman dressed in a turquoise jilbab and hijab head wrap, waited for Iben Fatah to join her to soothe the nervous Data Oracles who had stayed awake all night putting on the finishing touches.

Mrs. Fassi arrived and handed Iben the cardboard carrier with the piping hot cups filled with the spicy liquid. "Two?" she asked, raising an eyebrow. She had decorated her elegant headwrap with turquoise and coral beads to match the vibrant kanga, her East Afrakan cotton dress which billowed in the breeze, like waves of water moving expressively.

"Yes, two, thank you, Ma," he addressed her with the title of respect as he took the contraption, avoiding her questioning gaze. He owed her a huge dept for approving him for this Cultural Exchange Program. Although, he appreciated her mothering and her help in finding him lodging, financing, AI tech and personnel to help in bringing this exhibit to San Franciso, her overreaching attention leaned toward being judgmental when it came to his personal life. Iben accepted his cup, leaving the other for Morainya in hopes she would find the museum early enough for the chai to still be hot.

Outside the brown stucco walls of the museum, Morainya waited in line, shifting her weight against the morning chill. She glanced over the crowd corded off by red velvet-covered ropes and stanchions. It had taken so much effort to check out of the hotel, call an Uber to take her over to her parents' Telegraph Hill home, call her mother, and then drive back to the museum. Iben had been so insistent she didn't want to disappoint him.

The doors opened, and slowly, they moved forward in unison. Children bobbed up and down, trying to gauge how much longer. The air hummed with energy as voices in multiple languages wove together like a living tapestry of sound. Although she didn't understand a word, the melodic quality drew her back to an ancient time that had an eerie sense of familiarity.

Upon entrance, Morainya was surprised to see the sophistication of this exhibition. A museum attendant handed each visitor a sleek control panel and disposable earplugs, ensuring an immersive experience. Then AI-generated maps burst up before the visitors' bodies in their customized language to ensure that all were catered to and would comprehend. With a soft chime, Morainya's personalized map flickered to life in English. She giggled to herself that it wasn't in Italian. How would it even know what language was her preferred anyway? Iben waved from the Executive Office door in his bright white Throbe sheath.

"Grand Rising, Queen," he said. "I have something to please your mouth." He handed her a very hot cup of something with a to-go lid and straw.

"Good Morning, Iben," she replied, not wanting to interrupt the introduction to her map.

"What would you be mourning?" he asked, visibly taken aback.

She laughed upon hearing the double meaning. "Morning like the beginning of the day. Not mourning like when we are sad."

He nodded, then said, "Yes, we celebrate the sun's rise. We are never saddened that a new day has come."

Morainya took in the weight of his words. "Thank you for the drink."

"Yes, chai. I am most happy that you are here. Would you mind if I accompanied you?"

The museum's grand atrium dims. A hush ripples through the crowd. Suddenly, the walls breathe open— seamless AI panels transform into 360-degree holographic projection surfaces. A living dome of memory surrounds the audience. A booming **AI Voice** said: *"This is the Pulse of Creation." Then a swirling cosmic nebula floated above, coalescing into the dark skin of a celestial being. The voice over: The Great Mother. Ancient. Mystical. All-Seeing. Her eyes hold galaxies, and her womb births pyramids, cities, rivers. In the beginning... melanin was stardust. And from stardust came rhythm. Then came breath."*

"O Melanite Children," the museum Data Oracle intoned, "your melanin is a divine inheritance from your ancestors, the Aluhum called the Dunaakial." She gazed at the children with their deep chocolate eyes and intricately braided dark hair, or curls who were enthralled with this teaching. "You, dear ones, are the New-Beings—Nubians, yes and also kin across many lands where melanin marks the memory of light."

A station dedicated to the science of Melanin stood radiant beneath warm lights, its centerpiece a vibrant map of Afraka, shaded in hues of the rainbow. Each color denoted the unique melanin signature associated with specific Afrakan tribes. As families gathered close, the guide lifted her voice with reverence, explaining that melanin existed in two sacred forms—eumelanin, which determined skin tone, and neuromelanin, a shimmering compound embedded deep within the brain and nervous system. "It's not just about skin," she said, her eyes sweeping across the room.

One little girl wearing a blue sweater and plaid skirt school uniform, said, "Jimmy at school says my skin is dirty." A hush fell over the circle, and several parents glanced at each other with tight mouths.

The Data Oracle says *soothingly,* "Come love. Let me show you something. Touch the *holographic panel.*

The girl reached out, pressing the button.

AI voice: *"Scanning soil memory"* Footage of the Black Lands of Khemit with rich alluvial farmland. **AI voice:** *"Mel*anin, the sacred pigment in your skin, is also found in the bark on trees and in the soil of the earth."

The Data Oracle bent to engage the eleven-year-old. "Do you know who the Egyptians were?"

The child nodded with bright eyes; the Data Oracle pointed around the circle. "Egypt was once called the Black Lands for the very rich soil . It was the Bread Basket of the world. "And what makes that black soil more precious than gold?"

A boy in a matching plaid uniform shot his hand up. "Cuz they can grow food?"

The Data Oracle smiled, her voice soft but steady. "Yes, we can grow food—but that's not all. Another holographic button popped up and he smacked it.

AI VOICE: *"That sacred black soil held such power that other nations crossed deserts and oceans to steal it. They knew it could grow empires. So they came—not to learn, but to take. That's what colonizers do: they take what they don't understand, then claim it as their own. But today, we reclaim it. That soil is your mirror. Your skin, your hair, your brilliance—it all comes from that same sacred blackness. That's why you are more precious than gold."* A montage of usurpers of all colors was shown pouring into Khemit over centuries.

Morainya swallowed hard. *They came—not to learn, but to take.* The words hung in the air like incense—sweet and stinging.

She didn't flinch at the term *colonizer.* Not this time. She'd spent her life clinging to the illusion of innocence—her family were immigrants, after all. Poor. Catholic. Hardworking. But she knew, deep down, that poverty didn't erase participation. That her ancestors may not have wielded the whip, but they likely benefitted from the fields it tilled.

She looked at the children—so bright, so open—and something in her cracked. *What did they have to unlearn just to hear the truth?* What had she refused to hear until now? Her fingers curled around the museum pamphlet. The map of Afraka was vibrant, alive—nothing like the colorless diagrams she remembered from school. There, the continent had been a shape. Here, it was a soul. She felt a flush rise in her cheeks. Not shame—something older. A recognition that she'd been handed the wrong story and told to love it. *No more,* she thought. She wasn't here to be centered. She was here to see. To listen. And maybe—if grace allowed it—to remember her role in the repair.

"I will share a secret with you," said the guide in her colorful Afrakan ankara print cotton dress. She motioned for everyone to pay attention. "The Gods created the Hue-Man, as in color hue meaning black, and from that came everybody else. We are the first born of the earth born. Not only the melanated beings from Afrika but all over the world. Do you know how special you are?"

Excitement rose from the youth and parents. A reckoning appeared upon their glowing faces to be recognized after years of being overlooked and having to fight for every right that should have been God-given. A tear welled in Morainya's eye—not from mere understanding, but an overstanding, a truth unveiled, too sacred to ignore.

"I will tell you how to keep your Melanin clean. Vitamin B and Amino Acid Tyro-sine.

Can you say that back to me, please," directed the Data Oracle.

"Ty-ro-sine and B," The children echoed the words like a chant, anchoring a truth their cells already knew.

Iben scribbled something down in his notes.

"It does not matter what color you think your skin is. Everyone needs it. Tyrosine is found on each strand of DNA, and that is what determines your hue. There are six shades, each carrying a sacred signature. Let me show you." A spotlight appeared on the beautiful ebony Data Oracle, her dress seemed to come alive in florescent colors. With a wave of her hand.

AI VOICE: *"From the blackest shades in the Land of Nubia we call Afraka all the way to the equator on this continent of North America. Demonstrate shades of Melanin."*

Morainya shook her head. She had never considered that there were different shades of pigment. Her eyes narrowed and swallowed hard when she realized the equator itself had been used to divide, instead of unite.

Then the **lights dimmed**, ambient visuals swell, a hologram or map appears.

AI VOICE: *Begin our descent into the spectrum," she said, her voice reverent. "From the blackest shades of the Nuwbun of Nubia... to the lands of Kush and beyond, melanin has always told a story."*

The map shimmered—then reshaped into a spinning globe. A soft chime rang out as a prompt appeared: **Activate: Melanin Spectrum**

A child tapped the glowing glyph. The screen burst into radiant bands of color, slowly sweeping from the southernmost tip of Afraka up toward the equator—then across to the Americas.

AI VOICE: *SIX SACRED SHADES OF MELANIN*

The Data Oracle said, "I will show you what the textbooks did not."

The first band darkened to obsidian black.

NUWBUN: The deepest black, originating in Nubia and Khemit.

The label pulsed: *Density: 12-point carbon memory*.

A second wave spread—green-tinted.

KUSHITE: Ancient Ethiopians from the land of Kuwsh. A projection floated in, showing Queen Amanitore with green-tinted melanin beneath golden light.

A third band unfurled—soft yellow.

BUSHMEN: Indigenous to Zimbabwe and South Afraka.

"These were the keepers of the golden sun," the Data Oracle whispered. "The first fire-watchers."

Next came copper.

SUDANESE: The reddish-brown tone of those from Darfur, Chad, and Sudan.

An image of Nubian pyramids shimmered into view, layered over with sacred geometry.

Then, bluish-brown and indigo.

NIGERIAN: From the lands of Yoruba, Hausa, and Igbo. The AI generated frequency waveforms associated with these tones, whispering a soundscape of drums, breath, and tongue clicks.

The final hue shifted the entire globe, leaping across the Atlantic.

MUURS OF AMERICA: A fusion of ancient Afrakan migrants and Indigenous peoples of

Aztlan and Atlan. The map traced ancient trade winds and underwater routes. Morainya caught her breath as the Hopi petroglyphs came into view, overlaid with Saharan scripts.

"And finally," the Data Oracle said, her tone lowering into mystery, "the sixth path..."

The display zoomed into the Eastern Mediterranean.

MELANATED SEMITES: Born of the Afro-Asiatic tribes— some of whom merged with Canaanites, the CaucIbenans."

Images flickered—bronze faces, almond eyes, thick curls, and high foreheads. floated above the image:

"Canaanite: a merchant, a trader, a people of Semitic tongue. Once brown-skinned sons of the sun. Once called cursed, now reclaimed as kin."

The Data Oracle turned to the crowd. "These bloodlines became Hebrews, Arabs, Moors. Even those now called white, if you look closely... still carry melanin in the eye, the skin, the soul."

A hush fell.

Then the **AI VOICE**: *Would you like to scan your melanin range?*

Children rushed forward, placing their hands and cheeks near the scanner orb. The display read:

"You carry the memory of copper. Your ancestors rode the winds of Aztlan."

"Hopi-encoded. Time-keeper. Star-seeder. Your melanin remembers the Sipapu, the emergence. You walked the spiral path before maps were written. The stones know your name.

"You are Kushite-encoded. Light-carrier. Rememberer."

"Taino-Chinese descendant. Island-borne. Sun-tempered. Your melanin carries the scent of sweet rain and sea chant. The wind knows your grandmother's tongue. Your Chinese ancestors crossed oceans before maps told them where to go. Your melanin remembers both rice fields and rain chants."

"Turtle Island. You carry the memory of ochre and obsidian. You are Earth-walker, Sky-breather, Fire-singer. Your melanin encodes the buffalo's breath, the eagle's shadow, and the songs etched into canyon walls. You did not arrive— you were always here."

"Sudanese-Spanish blend. Your melanin holds rhythm and resistance."

Morainya stepped back. She couldn't. What would hers say? But Iben was already watching her from the shadows— softly, without judgment.

She moved her hand closer then hesitated at the scanner. What would it say—Italian? Irish? But she'd heard stories of dark Sicilian roots and whispered Black Irish blood. She looked into the orb. Maybe she had more memory than she realized.

"You are daughter of dusk and departure. Your melanin sleeps beneath marble skin, but your eyes remember. You are the in-between—of empire and echo, of root and rupture. You do not reclaim—you remember."

The Data Oracle stood in stillness, letting the gravity of the AI's words settle over the crowd. Her eyes didn't flinch. She let the silence do what words could not. Nothing about what had just been transmitted was usual. She only lifted her chin, as if daring the ancestors to witness it: That at last, the truth had been spoken aloud—and heard.

Morainya felt it in her sternum first. A strange tightening. Not from defensiveness—but recognition. The kind that makes the body remember before the mind can catch up. Her breath caught as the Data Oracle scanned the room with purpose, her voice both balm and blade. Then, in a heartbeat, the Data Oracle's gaze softened, falling upon Morainya with a warmth that was not pity, but invitation.

That's when the crowd turned. It was subtle, just a few sidelong glances, but she noticed. Not accusatory—just curious. As if they were trying to place her, decode her presence. What was she doing here? Did she belong? Had she come to observe or to listen? Iben moved next to her, perhaps signaling the crowd that this one could hear the truth and still remain whole.

Morainya looked down at her pale hand. She had never considered how quiet her lineage had been. How little she truly knew about the blood that ran beneath her skin. Something ancient stirred. Not guilt—but grief. And gratitude. Gratitude that someone was finally telling the story that her history books had hidden. Gratitude that she had come this morning.

It wasn't fragility. It was reverence. And the sudden understanding that healing only begins when truth is spoken aloud—and heard.

Iben stepped into the spotlight. Morainya hopped from one foot to the next struggling to get a view of Iben beginning to enchant the students. "We sometimes judge others by the color of our skin. Yes? Who here has been judged because their skin is melanated?" he asked.

The entire group shot up their hands. Morainya kept hers by her side, even though her Italian Grandparents and her Irish Grandparents had untold violence and discrimination thrust upon them when they first stepped upon the welcoming land of America, um, Al Morocco.

Iben pointed to the Data Oracle and said, "Nakena just mentioned the word Canaanite or CaucIbenan, who are also called Caucasians. How many believe that means a person with white skin?

Two for two. Everyone vigorously reached for the sky blocking Morainya's view.

AI VOICE: *"Caucasians were the blonde-haired blue-eyed beings found in the Caucasoid Mountains between the Black Sea and the Caspian Sea. The Moors, who are brown-eye dominant, had already mastered astronomy, medicine, and mathematics, introduced fire-building, food cultivation, and hygiene to them—not out of superiority, but to help* *fellow humans evolve. We all descend from those moments of shared survival."*

Morainya *blinked, surprised. Brown eyes. Her brown eyes. Had anyone ever told her what that meant before?* As ancestral faces of all shades of people morphed into each other, shifting, changing, uniting.

"The holograms dimmed, giving the floor to her living voice. The Data Oracle said, "Let us now turn to this next station. I will show you why your hair makes you so very, very special."

An exhibit crowned with gleaming halos of hair—locks, coils, tufts, and waves suspended in holographic light. As they approached, the curved wall behind them lit up in a shimmering auric display.

A soft chime rang out—**AI VOICE**: *AI recognition activated*—as the exhibit scanned the crowd's melanin spectrum and projected glowing filaments of encoded hair types into the air. The ceiling responded in turn, revealing spirals of light shaped like double helixes, each curl moving in time with an unseen drumbeat.

"Our hair," said the Data Oracle, stepping forward her tunic now overlaid with patterned sacred geometry, "is aligned to the ether world—that is, the unseen." She gestured toward the floating strands.

"Here," she said, pointing, "we see straight black hair, often from our Hindu brothers and sisters. It carries what is known as six-point melanin—or six ether." The AI magnified the strand and overlaid it with the number 6 in golden code, rotating like a galaxy.

"When hair curls, coils, or waves," she continued, "the points rise. The kinkiest hair—tight spirals—are called kingly hair. That's nine-point ether." The AI responded with a crown of spinning sigils above the tightest coils.

"Who here has kingly hair?" she asked.

Hands shot up—elders and youth, all reaching toward the sky. The holographic crown bloomed wider, shimmering with a violet hue as each participant's hair was gently illuminated in response.

Morainya laughed softly, moved by the children's joy at learning they were made of royal matter. She reached up, absentmindedly touching a lock of her brown, gray-flecked hair. It had thinned since menopause, lost its luster. She smiled, bittersweet. No coils. No crown. Still, it felt good to be among them, witnessing such pride bloom unfiltered.

A little boy pushed to the front, eyes wide, voice bright. "Hey, hey! We had an albino cat! Was there something wrong with her 'cause she was sooooo white?"

Laughter bubbled through the group.

Unfazed, the guide knelt beside the boy. "No, sweetheart," she said. "Albinism is a rare genetic variation. It changes how melanin is expressed in the skin and eyes. But it doesn't mean something is wrong—it just means the coding is different." She touched a button on her pad and a glowing button popped up. "Touch that, please."

The AI rendered an image of a panther—one black, one white—standing beside each other in a mirrored display.

AI VOICE: *"Sacred Variance: Code of the Light and the Shadow."*

From behind, a woman whispered just loud enough for Morainya to hear, "It's the Mark of Cain. My preacher said that's why albinos exist. Cain killed Abel, and God cursed his seed."

The words stung.

The Data Oracle paused. Even the AI seemed to hush. Then Iben turned, his Thobe illuminated in the spotlight, his voice calm but unyielding.

"Yes," said Iben, "some say the Mark of Cain was a loss of melanin—symbolic of being cut off from the divine blood-line. Cain, once a son of the Aluhum, descended into the line of Samu'el. A child of separation."

As he spoke, the AI offered no flourish, no visual—just silence, as though bowing to the weight of the moment.

Morainya's chest tightened. Her Catholic upbringing flared—echoes of sin, judgment, fear. She had always thought the Mark of Cain was a blemish, a bruise from heaven's wrath. But this... this felt older. A spiritual severance. A quiet shiver ran through her. Another veil lifted.

The guide resumed, pointing toward the holographic strands, each still floating midair.

"You all carry something sacred," he said. "Whether worn natural, styled, or covered—your hair is encoded. Even if you wear a wig, the root memory is there. You were born with a blueprint."

Morainya gazed around. The elders in silver cornrows. The little girls with beads clicking. The young men with locs thick like rope. Even the women with weaves or silk presses—all of them were aglow in the exhibit's soft golden spectrum.

Kingly, she murmured to herself. But she didn't have kingly—or queenly—hair. She wasn't sure what she had anymore. She reached up again. No curl answered her fingers.

And yet—Iben Fatah was watching her. His face serene, his eyes luminous.

As if he saw a crown no one else could. As if her coils were simply folded... not lost.

"If you look to your right, you'll see the sign, *Where Are the Crowns?*" said Iben, his hands animated with the kind of passion that draws a crowd.

The exhibit lit up as he spoke, and motion-triggered sensors activated a 3D hologram suspended above the platform. A rotating display of ancient statues began to shimmer into view—each featuring regal crowns.

AI VOICE: *"Many tombs of Khemit's Kings and Queens have been excavated,"* he continued, *"and while diadems have been found, the grand ceremonial crowns you see in these sculptures... have never been recovered."*

A soft chime echoed as the hologram transitioned—layer by layer—to reveal braided hair under the gold bands. *"Take a look at this scan of Tutankhamun's burial mask. The golden headband is real—but that blue crown? It's not metal. It's a netted sheath of lapis beads braided over tightly curled, cropped hair."*

A ripple of surprise spread through the crowd. Morainya stepped closer.

AI VOICE: *AI Reconstruction: Tut's True Crown*

On cue, a side-by-side animation appeared—first showing the golden mask as it is known today, and then slowly morphing into an Afrakan boy's head, hair braided and dyed in blue clay beads.

Iben gestured toward the school children, guiding them closer. "These hairstyles aren't extinct," he said. "They've been *preserved*—through lineage, through memory. Look at these photos of Kenyan Rwandan women practicing *Amasunzu*, and the coiled crests of the Burundi Tutsi tribes. Their hair *is* the crown."

A woman in a vivid dashiki with a tight halo of curls raised her hand. "Why did they lie to us?"

Iben smiled gently, affirming her anger without rushing it away. "The victors write the history books. And they wrote us out."

AI VOICE: *Kepresh Crown — AI Deconstruction Mode*

A high-resolution scan of the classic blue war crown of Queen Nefertiti appeared. A prompt hovered over the display:

AI VOICE: *"Would you like to deconstruct this crown?"* One of the children reached up and tapped the glowing YES icon.

The war crown split apart holographically—revealing coils of fiber, layers of faience beads, and scalp-level braids beneath. A gasp ran through the crowd.

"You see?" Iben said, gesturing toward the AI reconstruction of a Tutsi woman with the same elongated coiffure. "This was never armor. It was *anatomy*. Culture. Crowned by creation itself."

Iben stepped in, gesturing to a shimmering holographic replica of the crown. "We've created a tactile simulation," he said. "You may hover your hands above it—the sensors will translate the texture into your skin."

Morainya stood back, moved by the joy radiating from the children. She looked around—each face lit by pride and possibility. Her heart tugged. *He was teaching them what no textbook dared to say.*

Just then, the room shifted. The light dimmed slightly, and a faint blue frequency rippled across the AI dome above. A new crown materialized midair—the sapphire elongated war crown of Nefertiti, rendered in resplendent holographic clarity, its symmetry regal and unmistakable. A subtle chime pulsed like a heartbeat.

"Now," Iben announced, "observe the war crowns of Queen Nefertiti and her consort, Pharaoh Akhenaten. And compare them—if you will—to the ancient styles worn by the Tutsi of Rwanda."

The AI responded, projecting the Tutsi hair structures side-by-side with Nefertiti's crown. The similarity was undeniable.

"See?" he said, as the holographic replica of the wig shimmered above. "These weren't helmets. They were hair. Our hair. Sculpted into crowns before the Europeans even knew how to bathe."

A ripple of laughter followed.

"Those are so cool," two pre-teen girls murmured, nudging each other. "We're gonna try that style at home." Their voices carried a tone of both mischief and reverence.

With a simple gesture, Iben activated the AI. A 3D rendering of the Amarna daughters hovered midair—graceful, regal, with elongated skulls shimmering beneath golden light.

AI VOICE: *"You are now viewing the daughters of Amarna—royal lineage of Queen Nefertiti.*

Modern narratives often label their elongated skulls as seen in these sculptures as alien. But ask yourself: is it truly alien—or simply a beauty that defies colonial symmetry?"

Some of the crowd chuckled and nodded.

AI VOICE: *"Here are the same elongated hairstyles still practiced by Rwandan tribes—believed by many to carry the living echo of the Pharaonic bloodline."*

Morainya cheeks flushed. She had watched those shows—the kind that featured ominous music and labeled ancient Africans as aliens simply because their genius couldn't be explained. She'd believed it, once. Believed that the pyramid builders must have been aliens because she'd been told greatness couldn't be Black.

A soft chime echoed overhead. The lights brightened gradually, bathing the room in a warm amber glow. A new display flickered to life at the far end of the gallery—its title unfurling midair like a scroll:

AI VOICE: *"The Kings of Kemet: Bloodlines of Light."* Then the AI voice intoned—measured, reverent: *"Prepare to enter the Hall of the Living Lineage."*

The Data Oracle turned, her voice rising like a drumbeat. "Now, who wants to know about the Kings of Egypt?"Turning toward a gallery room lit with warm, amber light. A sweeping map of Kemet covered the far wall, with golden markers noting dynasties and temple sites. Along the perimeter, framed images of pharaonic rulers and queens stood beside digital portraits of modern-day melanated individuals, selected by AI for their uncanny resemblance to ancient figures.

As the group entered, the AI voice hummed to life—low, reverent, and layered with ancient dialects beneath clear modern tone: *"Welcome to The Hall of the Living Lineage. The gods do not forget their own. Time may distort the face, but melanin remembers the code."*

To Morainya's surprise, every ancient face reflected a familiar modern one. All of them were melanated. Each image pulsed with a glowing frame, as if the AI had activated a lineage match algorithm. Beneath each pair, a scroll-like digital plaque read: *'Resonance Confirmed. Genetic Echo: 86.7% match.'*

The Data Oracle circled the room, her voice rising with passion. "Who here thought the Pharaoh's and queens were pale?"

A flurry of hands shot into the air so fast they nearly punched a hole in the sky. Morainya, sheepish but honest, lifted her hand halfway.

The Data Oracle smiled. "Thank you for your honesty. Now—go stand by a king or queen. Learn who claims you."

The crowd scattered, joyfully choosing their reflections in the faces of Ramses, Hatshepsut, Tiye, and Meryt-Neith.

Morainya lingered. No one looked like her.

She drifted toward the far end of the room, where a tall, unchosen statue stood in partial shadow. Its features were striking—elongated skull, wide hips, narrow face. An AI sensor lit the base as she approached.

AI VOICE: *"Unclaimed Ruler: Akhenaten. Status: Heretic Pharaoh. Dynasty: 18. Record: Redacted from King's List. Reason: Radical monotheist. Outlawed by priesthood."*

Morainya tilted her head, unsettled by his form. "Doesn't seem like anyone is going to choose that strange king," she said, just loud enough for the Data Oracle to hear.

The Data Oracle stepped beside her, eyes soft. "Yes, that is Pharaoh Akhenaten. He was... quite unusual."

She gestured toward the AI display, which now projected a glowing hologram of the colossal statues unearthed at Karnak—once buried, defaced, discarded like rubble.

"They found him in pieces," she said. "Not just physically. Historically. Erased. Not even listed among the 18th Dynasty Pharaohs. The West called him a heretic because he loved only one god—the Aten. But maybe it was because his statues looked nothing like the flawless gods and pharaohs of the past."

Morainya's head buzzed. He didn't even look human. Was that really his body? That face? He shattered the cookie-cutter perfection of god-king statues. He looked like someone who refused to be idealized.

"What was wrong with him? Was he born like that?" she asked, unsure if that question was even appropriate anymore. Her hands mirroring her uncertainty, balled into fists.

"Some say Marfan's Syndrome," the Data Oracle replied gently. "Others say it was a different kind of coding. Maybe... a different kind of remembering."

AI VOICE: "Note: Akhenaten—suspected fusion of masculine and feminine archetypes. Status: Bridger of Heaven and Earth."

The Data Oracle smiled knowingly.

"You might like to read about his wife, Queen Nefertiti. The world calls her the most beautiful woman who ever lived. But that face?" She nodded toward the bust encased in glass. "It was altered."

Morainya turned quickly, and her stomach clenched. "What do you mean—altered?"

"The famous bust found in the Royal Sculptor's workshop was made of plaster. The Egyptian Antiquities Department ignored it. A German archaeologist smuggled it out in a crate during Hitler's era. When it was unveiled in Germany, many believed it had been recarved to fit an Aryan ideal." The Data Oracle's jaw tightened, but her voice remained calm—precise. "They didn't just smuggle a bust," she said. "They smuggled a narrative." She let her gaze land briefly on Morainya—not as an accusation, but an invitation. "That plaster face became the icon of a stolen beauty standard. But look closely." She gestured toward the projection, now rotating slowly. "The symmetry is false. The skin tone is pale. The nose—refined beyond truth. This was not Nefertiti. This was propaganda draped in sculpture."

Morainya's mouth opened slightly. "Recarved? That's... defacing. Or maybe the nose just broke off and someone repaired it?"

"That's what they said. But tell me—why are nearly all the noses broken off our statues? If it were just wear and tear, wouldn't arms or legs be missing just as often?" She touched her own wide nose. "Why erase the feature that marks us? That binds us to the land?"

Morainya felt the words sting—but not unfairly. She looked again at the bust on the screen, seeing not beauty but theft. She'd seen white Nefertitis in every museum gift shop, in Cairo stalls, even in her art history textbooks—and never once questioned it. But now, the sculpted face was no longer a wonder.

AI VOICE: *"Nasal Destruction Index: 93% of statues defaced. Predominant damage: Nose bridge. Suggested cause: Systemic erasure of racial identity. Motive: Reassignment of historical origin."*

Morainya trembled. She remembered her textbooks and TV shows. Blonde Tutankhamen. Pale Cleopatra. The way her professors dodged the subject. She remembered nodding along just to pass. She remembered submitting to the lie. And now the truth stood before her, humming in the air like a tuning fork that finally found resonance.

"It doesn't make sense now, does it?" the Data Oracle said softly.

Morainya shook her head. "No. No, it doesn't."

And yet, it did. Deep down, it always had.

The lights turned up alerting the crowd the tour had completed.

AI VOICE: *"Facial features can be broken. Histories can be redacted. But melanin remembers. Even when the chisel lies, the bloodline does not forget."*

*T*here were few moments in my life untouched by duty, desire, or doubt. But my sisters—my sun-giggling, shell-throwing, braid-tugging sisters—were the ones who reminded me who I was before the throne ever called my name.

I rose from my bed as the dawn of Aten's grand rising in the East. Orange and Yellow streams permeated my private quarters through the open window. Shielding my face from the translucent hands that stroked my cheek, urging me to awaken, I sat up slowly, rubbing my temples as the ghost of a drumbeat pulsed behind my eyes. The dream clung like smoke, thick with spice and song. The memory of rhythmic music still seduced me with leftover excitement. My roguish faint smile made me lick my lips savoring all the new sensations of unexpected delight that I had surrendered to with my newfound freedom.

The scent of musk lingered on my sheath, sharp and intimate. I pulled the fabric to my face, inhaling, then shoved it away—as if scent alone could summon Archollos back. With a jolt, I bolted up clawing at my sweat-stained linen sheets. He was leaving. I could feel it—like water slipping through cupped hands, no matter how tightly I pressed them together. Just when I nearly had his love sealed upon my heart, he overheard the ill-fated conversation from Ana-Kharu. If that swarthy merchant hadn't opened his mouth with filthy accusations of us keeping Archollos as a pet, an amusement, a toy that would never be acceptable to my royal lineage, then it wouldn't have reignited my dearest's desire to flee back to his homelands for he could never fathom how we could be together.

Shakily, I slid my legs out of bed and hit the daisy faience tiled floor with a thud. It wasn't a dream because the tingling between my legs persisted. Certain as the morning sun was ablaze, last night, I felt the intensity of a tongue sneakily eliciting the most sublime feeling mixed with shame and guilt.

A slow smile crept across my lips. My thighs still ached from his embrace. But the heat in my chest faded when I remembered the way he pulled away. He was bursting with the grief of lost time being away from Mycenae and longing for his true family. Before he walked me back on the sandy path home, I pleaded with him not to reveal to anyone my encounter with Ana-Kharu and the magic roots he had evoked. If I must command our guests to leave, then so must it be, but it should be in my timing and with purpose.

Ana-Kharu still had the ankh key; I knew to the depth of my core that it would unlock a great mystery for me. That key beckoned me. How could I get it if he wore it safely around his neck? I certainly did not believe he would hand it over to me by Royal request, even if I was the Per Aat in waiting.

My younger sisters, Ankh-es-en-pa-Aten, Nefer-ne-fruaten-Tasherit, Nefer-ne-fruare, and Set-te-pen Ra rushed through the door and climbed upon my bed, tumbling, giggling and gossiping. They left the space closest to me in honor of Meket, for she was the favorite of my heart. I ached at not being able to confide in her. She would have been shocked yet encouraging me and my adventure with Ana-Kharu. Meket had always pressed her fingers to the library scrolls like they might open and pull her in. She loved stories of star charts and plant medicines—but when Father spoke of rituals and trials, she quietly left the room. She knew that the initiatic path was not for her, so when the son of the Chief Jeweler poured sweetness upon her, she chose him as her Consort to escape the constrictions of palace life. Due to her shy nature, she abhorred the crowds. Instead retreating to the quiet of the Royal Library, she would enmesh herself in philosophical scrolls. Immediately, Meket became pregnant, and was disappointed that the adventure she craved would be curtailed.

Ankhi interrupted my moment of devotion to Meket-Aten by blurting out, "Merit, our Bath Mistress said the night guard left late last night and spied Archollos and a girl together wrapped in each other's arms. The guard insisted Archollos was kissing someone, Sister." Ankhi snickered and then elbowed my other sisters who bounced upon my bed with the black panther carved into the frame to protect my sleep. "I am only telling you this because we all know you are weak-kneed around the blonde boy." Ankhi crossed her arms trying to coax a response from me.

"Do you love him?" asked Nefer, the twin who sat on my feet.

I stammered, not wanting to reveal my heart even to my family. They had all heard how Meti disparaged him by calling him a foreigner, even though she herself was from Mitanni, that country that had also been an enemy of Khemit. How could my mother not see that she too had come to love Khemit even though she had been separated from her birth land? It was the same way with my beloved Archollos. "He is an honored classmate of mine. I will not speak ill of him. If he has found someone to share his embrace, then I will not oppose it," I said. "It would be my greatest wish for him to find union with the one he loves," I said, hoping this would appease them.

"Braid my hair, please, Sister." Nefer-ne-fruare begged me as she plopped down in front of me. My hands were always willing to beautify my sisters. My family each practiced upon another's kinky black hair, trying ornaments or threads to be woven into the elaborate braids that became more exotic the more experienced the hands were. While I allowed my sisters to play with my hair, I often needed the Court Hairdresser to redo the work of young, clumsy hands.

"I have a bit of time to fix your hair, but then I must meet with our guests," I said, trying to set a time limit. I could not take my mind off of Ana-Kharu and the light of the sun glinting off that protected key. Father couldn't have foreseen that Ana-Kharu would dance into my life with an unexpected turn, could he? Was Father hinting that Ana-Kharu would be the key to my future? At least he belonged to the land of Khemit. I wrinkled my nose. Not him. Ana-Kharu was not even likable, let alone choose him as a consort. Maybe Smenkhkare would be a better choice, as Meket had often reminded her. He was so thoughtful and brought the sisters bouquets of flowers he had collected in the garden. Smenkhkare would be a match that both my parents would approve of, for he belonged to my bloodline, but he was just too gentle and soft-spoken to be a leader.

They giggled and sang their youthful songs while I made the parts in their hair. Ankhi played with a basket of cowrie shells that I kept near my bed. "Who do you love, Merit?" prodded Nefer, who shamelessly made kissy noises at the boys who were pleasing to her.

Ankhi dreamily observed the peach sky out my window. "I would like to kiss Smenkhkare.

His lips are plump, and his brown eyes have light," she added. "He is nice."

My eyebrows arched. "My classmate, Smenkhkare, is too old for you. You are only thirteen, and he is at least seven years ahead of you. Why do you not look to the sons of the Court Officials," I said with a gentle hand upon her back as if to steer her away from him.

"I like him," said Set-te-pen-Ra. He brought me a lemon. "Yes, I like him too. We can all choose him."

I laughed despite myself. "That is not how it is done," I said, plucking a shell from the blanket and placing it in Set-e-pen-Ra's curls—hoping distraction might be gentler than reason.

"Yes, it is," said Ankhi, hitting the bed with her angry fist, making the cowrie shells dance.

"Father has two wives, Mother and Kiya. Grandfather had hundreds. We can have as many consorts as we want." Ankhi stuck her tongue out at me. My hackles rose to reprimand my third sister, but then I thought, why? Her stubbornness reminded me of General Horemheb. She was his child.

My stomach roiled, and I had duties to attend to. As much as I wanted to give full attention to my siblings, I had to order Ana-Kharu to leave our premises. A dull ache came over me, knowing my father would not approve of the visitors and that I should send them on their way. The longer I put it off, the more trouble they could cause the denizens of our sacred city.

"I want to see the elephant," Se-te-pen-Ra chirped. "We could go feed it leaves."

Shaking my head no, "Our guests must be on their way. There are many cities that need their visit. We cannot possibly detain them any longer," I said, trying to appease the girls.

"Merit, can you not wait? Nefer's voice quivered. Mother would love the pretty fabrics.

She would be so sad to miss them." Her eyes pleading not with authority—but with hope.

"We have never had an elephant so close. You are so mean? "What did they do to you?" Ankhi snapped, arms crossed. Her eyes flared, twin embers daring me to answer.

Certainly, I would not divulge to my sisters my little indiscretion. Ana-Kharu was just too magical. His powers were far too great for me. No, he had to leave. Immediately. I focused on Nefer-ne-fruare's hair, letting the rhythm of parting and braiding quiet my thoughts. Behind me, the sound of clapping and squeals filled the chamber, but my hands moved on their own, heavy with decision.

In my heart, I must mother these girls. I must teach them at my knee, the way Meti did for me. Now that she had left with the General, there was a vacant spot in my heart that no longer received her warmth of breath upon me. My sisters had cried themselves empty, their mourning dulled by time—and by the novelty of foreign guests and sweets to distract them. But I saw it: the gap Meti left still echoed in their laughter.

After sending the girls off to be entertained by the kitchen cooks who allowed them to knead bread with their feet as was our custom, I met with Sarawat and Keshtuat as we headed toward the open temple near the Nile that our guests inhabited as a temporary home.

Upon approach, we glimpsed Ana-Kharu, engaging himself with two lovelies on a woven mat. Fluttering golden curtains moved seductively. The breeze carried music and muffled sighs, tangled with foreign syllables that curled like incense toward the sky.

"Grand Rising, Princess, please come and let us attend to you." The king of his tiny kingdom clapped, and the lusty women arose from his bedding to make ready for this Royal visitation. Once announced, I walked with my shoulders back and head high. I would not allow him to disrespect me again and pull me into another intrusive situation, however delightful it felt.

"Ana-Kharu-We-Shat, you have enjoyed three days of our hospitality. I am here to lend an ear as to what plans you have made for the next town on your itinerary."

"Oh, my delicate flower, your most humble servant has enjoyed these days so much that I have forgone with all other plans," said the merchant with an accentuated bow. Although he was diminutive in stature, his bare chest and arms were surprisingly muscular. His brow pulsed with a faint indigo hue—wisdom, perhaps. But beneath his sash, an orange flicker betrayed a more primal fire. A hunger. My mother would have noticed it immediately.

He once again kept me off-kilter. "Yes, we all have delighted. Well, some more than others," I said, having to choose my words so that he would not get the impression that I condoned his devious little Mandrake roots and their mischievous tongues.

Ana-Kharu leaned forward, "I could summon them again for all of your pleasures."

Throwing my hands up to stop his gesture meant to enchant me again. "My father will arrive home soon, and I am quite certain that he would not approve of you having set up quarters here in the City of the Aten," I said it with an emphasis, lifting my head and acting as Royal as I could as the Per Aat in waiting.

Ana-Kharu tilted his head. "Remind me where your father went; it must have slipped my mind."

"He had urgent business in Kush," I replied, knowing he had no right to question court business. Yet, here I spilled out details. I pinched my leg to bring me back to the present.

"Ah, of course. Now, why would the Pharaoh need to venture outside of this most remarkable city built and protected by Pharaoh's armies?" He glanced at each of his dancers flanking his side. "Would not it be the custom to demand tribute from the surrounding vassals?" Ana-Kharu feigned sudden shock, his mouth dropped open, and his head swiveled. "Were there supplies he was sorely in need of? Perhaps we can lend a most humble hand to refresh your cupboards. Oils? Tinctures? Copper from the mines? I have the strongest ties with all mines and could easily procure an order. No, that would be preposterous. Pharaoh has dozens of scribes and connections to alliances throughout Khemit. The Great Pharaoh Akhenaten would not have needed to flee from his throne to take passage like a lowly merchant. If he went to Kush, then it must be urgent. The business that only a King could conduct without the spying eyes and gossiping mouths of servants."

Why was he digging into my father's affairs. Hairs rose on my neck and arms. My fists curled at my sides. Behind me, Sarawat and Keshtuat shifted their weight, as if they too sensed the air tightening around us. He had no business interfering nor even presuming that I would discuss why father gave one day's notice to his staff to prepare for departure.

Ana-Kharu noting my horror, softened his tone to his Hostess. "Tell me, your Highness, how may I be of service to you and your family? My web of merchants extends to many tribes near and far. I can locate the unusual, the rare, and the uncommon. Confide in me, Princess, and let me demonstrate my skills. There is no need to search for what your father seeks." He touched his key and enclosed it within his fist as he shut his eyes momentarily.

Of course. That key—why else guard it so closely, sleep with it around his neck, unless it unlocked something the gods themselves would envy? I had to have that key. I could demand my guard take it from him. He had no power in my father's kingdom. No, force was not the answer. Perhaps I could allure him? "Ana-Kharu, while I am sure you have hands in many pockets, my father has a consortium of agents to bring him any treasure he could possibly desire. He was rather restless of late and needed a change of place, as he is nearing his thirty-year reign. Why not seek foreign pleasures?" I was calculating how to get that ankh key that would open my lock if that was what my Meti meant.

Ana-Kharu measured my words and narrowed his eyes. "No, while that may be, I sense there was greater urgency.

You are in disharmony with your mother. I do not detect that she remains in this kingdom. Wait, are you in mis-truth, Princess? Not that I would ever have the audacity to question a Royal." Then the traveling merchant started pacing, having the boldness to turn his back upon me as he added, "No, I am just thinking out loud as to why the main Royals of a Kingdom, obviously lacking in food, would need to scatter so abruptly that they both left the dear Royal Daughters without a ruler to make these decisions?" He placed his finger against his chin to emphasize the obvious place of weakness I found myself in.

The orange and yellow linen drapes strung between pillars trembled in the dull desert breeze. Rigid limestone columns suddenly felt enclosing and not even the red woven floor rugs could soften the implication he suggested. Turning abruptly, he stared into my eyes, and I felt myself cower. "Now, are you sure there is nothing you ask of me? I do have unusual ways to change situations that many in High Places regularly face. Yes, I have quite a reputation that spreads far and wide in bringing results." He snapped his fingers and dismissed his entourage, leaving us alone in the outdoor temple.

I gave Sarawat and Keshtuat leave with a gentle nod even though their eyes implied I was not safe. The dried beige mudbrick pylons stood in contrast against a cerulean, blue sky. The heat poured into the sanctuary as I found myself wiping perspiration with my crisp, white sheath sleeve. That wave of panic started winding its way up my spine feeling as helpless as a field mouse darting every which way to avoid the spiraling hawk barreling down on its prey.

"Make me an offer," I said dismissively with a hitch in my voice.

"Maybe it is poison you need? Enemies are always lurking about. Do you need to oft a spy?" He observed my reaction with skilled intuition.

Smirking, I replied, "I have armies for that. What else do you have to offer? And make it swift, for there are Temple duties I am obliged to attend." I matched his piercing, bold gaze and then turned on my heel toward the exit to elicit a response.

"Alchemical remedy? I have a large selection of various gold remedies. Do you need to replenish your reserves?"

I halted in my tracks, my breath hitched. Frozen. Desperate. Scared.

Achingly slow, I regained my composure and faced him squarely. "Tell me more?"

Slipping the key from around his neck, he pulled back the covers from his sleep mat. "I shall do better than tell; I shall show you." There was a large, polished ebony wood box with shiny golden hinges and a heavy lock. He took that large key and poked it in the tiny hole. Then he turned to me enticingly, opening the box to reveal its contents. Glorious containers of all sizes filled with powders and liquids that almost pulsed with divine vibrations that I craved to imbibe.

The key. I knew it was significant. The key to alchemy. I leaned forward, suddenly feeling my sour mood shift. My prayers had taken form in flesh and key. Perhaps... perhaps this was the teacher Father had spoken of in riddles. "Yes, alchemy! This is precisely what I yearn for. Are you the alchemy teacher my father requested?"

Ana-Kharu's face was emotionless. "I was wondering when you would realize why we were summoned here. Perhaps you were all dull minded from living in the midst of nothing for so long."

It was a cruel statement, but I could not afford to bicker. At last, the teacher that my father had foretold was here, and we could make gold to fill the coffers and buy grain, meat, and protection. We would replenish our kingdom, and fortune would turn in our favor. The Aten had indeed answered my prayers. I would not have to return to Thebes, nor choose my childish stepbrother as my consort.

My smile revealed my ecstatic delight. "Prepare yourself," I said, eyes bright. "I will summon my class. We begin at once."

He caught my arm, not allowing me to slip from his grip. "Why so hasty, Princess?

Alchemy decides whom she inducts into sacred knowledge. Have you received any tutorship from Heliopolis?" He penetrated me with those deep brown eyes that felt like two bottomless wells.

"Pentu, our Court Physician, has received a ranking from Heliopolis, as has my father. It is, after all the Khemitian School for alchemical sacred knowledge. I too have been to Heliopolis and studied elementary skills while my father and Pentu were being initiated. Have you attended Heliopolis?" I asked, feeling this connection, and smiled at our commonality.

"Princess, before I agree to teach you, as your father has decreed, first you must prove your worth. Our Prime Creator cares not about your status or wealth. The poorest because of their purity have often been granted the greatest knowledge of alchemy."

I cleared my throat, the familiar heat of scrutiny tightening my chest as if I stood barefoot on hot limestone suddenly feeling the burn of being tested, yet again. "Of course."

The wind began to slap the curtains, howling in its rage. Rolling gray clouds shrouded the once clear skies, and thunder boomed overhead. Then, chards of silver lightning began stabbing the ground outside of the temple. Rain poured down from the heavens all around the outdoor edifice, yet I did not feel a drop upon my skin. Where was his entourage hiding? Without warning, the temple shifted; The temple twisted on itself—my stomach dipped, balance faltering, as if the ground had been pulled sideways. There was a jungle outside with black-tongued giraffes nipping at Acacia trees while herds of trumpeting elephants splashed in a watering hole.

The room shifted again, and a bustling city surrounded our simple structure. I gripped the edge of my seat, breath shallow, as the world spun—mud huts, cities, oceans—my mind scrambling to catch one thread of sanity. Mud huts, jungles, Sahara desert, oceans and structures that grazed the skies amazed me, then disappeared. With a lavish swipe of his hands, two swings hung from the open-air temple. They had a finely tooled leather strap upon which to sit. My eyes gazed upward confused as to what held them aloft and discovered only a braided rope entwined with leafy green vines and blooming flowers attached to the air.

"Let us swing," said Ana-Kharu. "Please, this one is for you."

My knuckles tightened around the swing's vines. This was no illusion. The world itself was being rethreaded before my eyes. A laugh escaped my throat before I knew it— unfurling like a forgotten song—as I sat upon the swing. Ana-Kharu took the opposite seat so that we could engage directly. We swung slowly, kicking our legs out, and leaning fully backwards to gain momentum. Soon, reaching glorious heights, we were immersed in dizzying glee, mirroring each other. I laughed, recalling my early days of freedom back under my Grand Djed's rule at the magnificent Malkata Palace. The inner courtyard also had a swing for my sisters and me. Oh, those heady, carefree days when I had no responsibility or burden of inheriting the crown. The wind whipped tears from my lashes, but I couldn't stop laughing—light, weightless, as if the years of burden had been blown away. Eventually, the momentum of my swing slowed to a halt.

A slight buzzing sound tickled my ears. I stayed still, eyes closed, as a hum curled close to my ear—the delicate brush of wings stirring the air beside my cheek. A bee landing upon the open blossom next to my ear captured pollen. The buzzing grew in volume, and a sudden alarm bloomed in my awareness. Bees. I distinctly heard in my head, relax. Keep your eyes shut. A hieroglyph of a honeybee came to my mind. The honeybee appeared in the title of the King of both Upper and Lower Khemit. Nswt-bjtj. "He is the Sedge and the Bee," I said aloud, knowing it meant that the sedge is half of the union of South of Khemit. The bee is Northern Khemit.

Then I heard hundreds of bees. Swarming in a perfectly geometric honeycomb. Each bee moved in chaotic yet synchronized movements. Each has a job to accomplish the whole. That hive mind of the old tribal villages—they moved as one, a pulse of purpose. I pictured the thatched roof mud-huts that Hep-Mut, my dwarf nursemaid, whispered of—where rhythm and river set the pace of life." She claimed she came from the lands of the ancients without toilets inside. A giggle bubbled up, then snagged in my throat—Hep-Mut's voice echoed in my memory, and a dull ache bloomed in my chest where joy and longing fought for space while remembering all the Khemitian stories she crafted. The swarm, growing louder and louder in my ears, all abuzz, yet I feared not. It felt familiar. Life with purpose under the sun; to build, to nourish and to regenerate. How simple life would be in this hive mind.

Then, there was a tribal village of men, women, and children, black as the sky of Nut, the nighttime goddess that bent over a celestial firmament. Their huts were constructed in spiral paths, and they had ancient knowledge of how far to build away from the river, the Nile, source of all life.

We have great architects and Master builders using straight lines and four-cornered edifices built of mud brick and limestone. So, civilized. Look at how far we have advanced. Thatched huts could be blown away. Now, we build to last an eternity.

I could hear an um-huh from Ana-Kharu. It was as if he was measuring and weighing everything I was seeing into the internal realm. I blinked against the sudden brightness, turning toward him—searching his expression, wondering if the same vision had flickered behind his eyes. Trying to see if we had had the same vision. The thunder and lightning had receded, and our swings vanished. The azure blue sky returned above as the last orange translucent Atenic rays warmed us.

"Did you enjoy that, Princess?" asked the gold-garbed alchemist in his fancy robes and conical hat of wisdom.

"It was remarkable. I felt alive. I was a worker bee in a hive."

He listened, then said,, "Hives are built around a Queen."

"Yes," I grinned, chest fluttering. "She was larger than the others, radiant—her abdomen glowed like amber. She knew where to send them. They listened as to which flowers to light upon to gather pollen. She knew the time, the season, the day, and the hour and where to fly to no matter how far away, and those bees obeyed. She brings order like the King of Southern Khemit. A beautiful vision."

"What happens if the bees do not follow her orders?" Ana-Kharu moved around me.

She'd sting them," I murmured, my smile fading. "Kill them if needed—then feed them to her young." The words hung heavy between us.

Ana-Kharu nodded. "It appears that your Queen of Akhet-Aten has flown away. I wonder what will happen to your hive built so meticulously without a Queen to intuit what the Cosmos needs."

"His words pierced the hive of my chest. For the first time, I wondered if the Crown I was raised to wear... might crumble without her."

*T*he car eased to a stop in front of the Archbishop's mansion, its silhouette cutting against the San Francisco fog like a ghost from another century. Morainya felt awed by the grandeur of this historic San Francisco Grande Dame mansion built in 1899. Towering and ornate, the French Second Empire-style home loomed with a kind of aristocratic hush—arched dormer windows peeking from beneath a mansard roof, iron balconies coiled like black lace—she could feel the antiquated elegance already, humming with a kind of old-world power that had outlived both the 1906 earthquake and inconvenient truths

She'd pulled one of her mother's vintage Halston dresses from the back of the closet—a soft jersey sheath layered under a bold plaid cape, the beaded Peter Pan collar catching just enough light to feel intentional. Once, this would've been the height of quiet luxury. Now, it leaned more toward curated nostalgia. Still, it fit, and it carried the elegance her mother wore like armor. Morainya adjusted the cape as she stepped toward the door, wondering if the Archbishop would even notice that the style was twenty years out of date. Probably not. Men like him tended to mistake anything with a label for timeless.

The doorbell resounded through the house, which sounded like church bells. She shook her head, wondering if it was annoying to the staff to have FedEx or Amazon make deliveries and hear the bells over and over. Slowly, the thick Mahogany door was unlatched and pulled open to reveal an elder gentleman wearing a parochial collar and a severe black suit who greeted her with old-style etiquette by bowing. "Miss Napolitano, the Archbishop DeLaurentis is expecting you. Please come in and allow me to show you to the study."

Walking behind the stiff man she was forced to slow her steps as Morainya gaped at the luxury and glamor of this cherished landmark. Her father had furnished so many of these grand mansions when he imported fine Italian marble, baroque furnishings to fit the era, oversized four-poster beds for each room, and matching Italian woven replicated brocade tapestries. It almost felt like she was trapped in time, and she imagined how she would descend the grand staircase with a feathered fan, high white gloves, a tightly cinched corset, a peplum jacket, and a bustle skirt. She had little girl memories of coming here with her father and mother for Charity nights of entertaining dignitaries and musical revues of Chamber music. She even recalled being dressed in matching Channel or Halston dresses with her mother and sister, their hair curled beautifully with matching little gloves and purses.

As a girl, the house had loomed like a stone giant, each hallway echoing with too many grown-up silences. Now, she wanted to trace every carved railing, memorize the acanthus leaf crown molding—as if touching the past might steady her present. A faint echo of laughter curled around the corner—boys shouting in the courtyard? She paused. The memory flickered, half-forgotten. Or was the house just haunted by its own history?

The butler swept open a large study with an oversized redwood burl desk polished bright as a mirror, probably milled from the famous giant trees that dotted the forests around this area. A roaring fire was blazing in the green marble fireplace with a large mantel displaying artifacts from around the world. She was directed to a high-backed chair placed in front of the desk. Morainya took her time to be seated before the log-legged man left her on her own.

This was a historic room full of sepia-toned pictures in ornate gilded frames that filled the North wall. She wandered hoping to get a glimpse of her parents, who often frequented this house and perhaps posed for a picture at some momentous event. The elaborate formal dress of the 1900s soon morphed into more current photos of Archbishop DeLaurentis posing with celebrities, politicians, and wealthy donors over the years. Indeed, she spotted her father's dashing style in a tux, reminding her of an old-time movie star. He smiled politely as he had his arms around Mr. Wallerstein, on his left, and Mr. Kanberg, on his right. They were being presented an award by the Archbishop. Morainya knew her father's affiliation with the prestigious law firm went back a long time. The usual bragging wall served to entice monied donors to make large contributions to the church and its various charities.

There were several pictures of the boys' class wearing Catholic uniforms, much as she had when attending parochial school. Forty little boys ranging from five to early teens stood idly. None of them were smiling, and they clenched their little fists. But what was even more unusual was that they all had this same look: blondish, whitish hair, pale faces, and an almost Albino look. All of them. They reminded Morainya of her Uncle Aldo as a child in the few pictures ever taken of him. She pushed her face closer and drew her finger over the photograph. Nah, that would be improbable, but who could she ask? Her mother's memory floated right out of her brain like bubbles being blown by her childish dementia mind. Her father was dead. She blinked hard, leaned closer, and then, on impulse, lifted her phone. A soft click captured the strange row of pale boys frozen in time—and her own unease.

In an ornate French frame was a section dedicated to the Archbishop's travels to the Vatican meeting with several popes over the decades. There he was with the Bishop who wore a white linen mitre liturgical hats with two stiff shield-shaped halves that looked like fish lips. The next photo was of two other distinguished gentlemen also dressed exactly like the Pope, except one was in grey satin robes. The inscription at the bottom indicated he was the Gray Pope. The one dressed in black satin was the Black Pope, the Superior General of the Society of Jesus.

How interesting, she thought. Who knew there were three Popes? She snapped another picture. Of course, he had a photo of the famous Pulpit in the Vatican with the Pope in his ceremonial raiment, giving one of the illustrious Masses before the multitudes. She had grown up with her father having a cropped duplicate picture of the Pope hung upon his living room wall, but certainly not as large as this one. Morainya stared closer at it, then cocked her head. She had never closely examined this historical photo. Over the Pope's head seemed to be a grand mahogany sacerdotal seat for the ecclesiastical leader who was the focal point of this sanctuary. How odd it was because the Pope looked miniscule standing below it. Why in the world would they build a throne above the Pope? Who in the world would be large enough to fill that seat? God, she imagined then chuckled at the conundrum and wondered if the Archbishop DeLaurentis ever noticed the oddity.

Her eyes dropped to the Audience Hall; the rows of tile work or lights on the greenish ceiling were mesmerizing, almost as if it had a perspective of being inside of a reptile, with a red mouth and two large fangs being right where the Pope would give his sermons. From the mouth of the snake, deception falls. The thought slid through her mind unbidden. Was it just clever geometry—or had someone meant it that way? Two black windows appeared to be penetrating eyes that scrutinized the parishioners. Why would anyone design something so creepy? Maybe it was an illusion that only showed up in this photo. She snapped another picture.

Another image portrayed the Centre of Piazza del Popolo, prominently featuring a large granite obelisk. Strange, did they import one from Egypt? Well, the Vatican certainly had enough money to collect any valuable object they desired. Or steal. It looked like the same obelisk that she had seen in London and Washington D.C., as she recalled during her university visits to other museums.

There was so much to take in that her mind swam faster than the Piscean fish associated with Jesus Christ during that age of the fish, the symbol for Christianity. Antiques accentuated the private study. Morainya cast her vision around the room and landed on a bust of a Roman centurion, cast in bronze named Longinus who pierced Jesus's side when he was hung from the cross.

She had never seen reproductions of these statues, ancient swords, and paintings in any museum or private collection, but doubted they were originals. Then the raised relief painting of that odd Egyptian Pharaoh and his wife cuddling their family caught her eye. Above was a large circular sun with rays streaming down, ending in little hands that touched the family lovingly. She was immersed in this find; instinctively Morainya felt a shiver run down her spine. It didn't fit all the wall carvings of Pharaohs of the past who were restricted to a rule of perfection. No, this one was not perfect. It was not a formal portrait but an informal family portrait. The Pharaoh was as malformed as his wife and children, with elongated heads and odd bodies. She couldn't wait to tell Iben of this discovery, Her fingers itched to text him. This was his kind of mystery, tangled in stone and symbol.

It had to be a gift from high up—maybe even the Pope himself. That kind of relic didn't land in just any prelate's lap. This same Pharaoh at the Museum of History that Iben and the Data Oracle had pointed out. What a coincidence.

The door opened again with quiet authority. Archbishop DeLaurentis entered like a man used to the weight of sacred halls and whispered confessions. He was tall—taller than she remembered—and moved with a practiced grace that came not from age, but from years of being watched, bowed to, obeyed. His robes were immaculate black wool, trimmed with crimson at the cuffs and collar. The chain of St. Peter's Keys hung heavy across his chest, the gold dulled from decades of touch.

His face was long and ascetic, carved like old marble, with deep-set eyes the color of burned incense. His white hair was swept back with ceremonial precision, though a slight tremor in his hand betrayed the passage of time. Still, there was something unnervingly ageless about him. As if he had outlasted scandals, eras, and even Popes by simply enduring.

"Morainya Napolitano," he said, his voice velvety, practiced, and just warm enough to hide its calculation. "You're the image of your mother." He extended his hand for the 'baciamano' kiss the hand in Italian. He presented his episcopal diamond-encrusted ring surrounding a large round ruby, symbolizing his authority and devotion to the church.

Morainya lowered herself with practiced reverence, brushing her lips against the jewel-encrusted ring. 'Your Grace,' she murmured, voice steady despite the chill that laced his touch. His hand. It was dry and cool, the kind of hand that had blessed thousands—and she imagined, had buried secrets just as often.

He gestured toward the firelit chairs. "Come. Sit. Let us speak of legacy... and responsibility." As he moved behind his desk, his robes whispered against the floor like the rustling of ancient pages.

"How are you holding up, dear?" he asked in a Fatherly tone, yet rekindling her sorrow. Nothing like having death percolate the conversation and send her back into a state of grief before a meeting.

Morainya's throat tightened. For a moment, her knees itched to buckle—to drop in the gesture she'd once believed would keep her soul safe, confessing her sins and begging forgiveness as she was taught to appease the all-powerful heads of the church.

"Your Excellency, you understand how trying it is to lose a loved one—or maybe not. I know you aren't married or have kids," she fumbled with her words. "I am managing the details as best as the Lord allows," she said. Morainya gave that fresco one last questioning look to compose herself. "I am so curious, was this an Egyptian Pharaoh? Please forgive me, Excellency, if I am asking an intrusive question; it's that I've never seen anything quite like it." She lied, to the Archbishop thereby sinning against God's authority on earth.

DeLaurentis chuckled. "He's quite peculiar, isn't he? He's known as the Heretic Pharaoh, Akhenaten. You know how us Catholics love a good Heretic story." He tapped his fingers together, perhaps reminiscing over a satisfactory inquisition tale handed down through the generations. "His ideas were so egregious to the religious hierarchy in power at the time that they threw him out of Egypt and wiped him off of the King's list."

Her stomach dropped. 'He doesn't look dangerous,' she said quietly. 'Almost... kind. Like someone's father. 'I wonder what he did?'"

He shrugged. "Who knows? It's ancient history now. It was a gift from Pope John Paul II in 2000, during one of my more meaningful meetings with his Holiness, in celebration of the miracles he performed by healing two people. He was Canonized for those deeds." He glanced at his gold Rolex watch and accounted for the time.

"Did you notice the *Ibow Nesser* below it? That, too, is from Egypt. As I recall, it was found in that crazy Pharaoh's temple. I've long forgotten the legend, but it is a renowned relic that was stored in the Vatican Library. I am very honored to house it here," said the Archbishop, in a tone that implied he had big connections, and his guest should be thoroughly impressed and honored to be in his presence.

Morainya *stared closer eyes narrowing at the bottle of reddish powder. Something about it—posed like a* granite pyramid with the apex carved off like *a sacrificial altar—felt performative. Sacred, but staged.* An amber spotlight was directed down from the ceiling to amplify the importance of this relic.

Honestly, it doesn't look that important, thought Morainya. What does *Ibow Nesser* mean? Morainya knew it was the donation request he was most interested in, and anxiety instantly made her curl her toes. *She steered the moment elsewhere, latching onto the one detail that didn't make her chest tighten.*

"Your Excellency, what a miracle to have been received by the Pope during such an extraordinary meeting at the Vatican. I would love to hear about your conversation with the Pope. Is he as kind as he is portrayed?"

"Beloved, he was delightful. I was humbled to be in his presence. I found him so devoted and articulate about the direction of the Church. Simply put, I was most inspired." He gave a slow nod and lay his right hand upon his pectoral jeweled cross and keys.

"Is that when those pictures of the Pulpit were taken?" asked Morainya, pointing over her shoulder. The Archbishop was quite impressed that Morainya had truly taken the time to study and enjoy his mementos. She had indeed grown into a fine woman and her father Stephano, would be pleased. "Oh, you noticed those. Yes, indeed, it was the

Basilica of Saint Peter during His Holiness's Ordination Ceremony. I was there to receive the Sacrament of Confirmation. It was like being in the Presence of God's Chosen One on this Earth. I felt the most divine sense of peace and Holy reverence being in his company."

The Archbishop then crossed himself to honor the spiritual leader. "His Holiness designated me as the United States fundraiser for the initiative to lend assistance to the homeless, the impoverished, and the downtrodden. It's a new wave of devotion to uplift humanity."

She traced a slow cross across her body, more out of reflex than belief, wondering if he'd notice the hesitation in her hand—but she wanted to demonstrate the recognition of his most celebrated day. "That is quite an honor," she said, turning back to look at the photo. "I can see why that autographed picture is a beautiful commemoration of your honor," she said, lifting her voice at the end. "When I looked closely at that picture, it looked like a giant throne was crafted overhead of the Pope. What do you think that means?"

The Archbishop DeLaurentis strained his eyes. "Why, I've never noticed that. Really? A throne?" He pondered the question as if lost in thought. Then his expression changed. "It's God's throne. It symbolizes that the Almighty's seat takes precedence and watches over his Chosen One and the flocks of sheep under his care."

"Of course," replied Morainya nodding with an inhalation. "That would make sense."

His Excellency put a gentle hand upon her back, guiding her to be seated upon the early Renaissance heraldic style upholstery in peach tones. The statuesque lions with swirling burgundy ribbons encircled bouquets of flowers giving off a romantic feeling. The velvety blood-red curtains were so thick they seemed to absorb the light. The Archbishop then took the power position behind the redwood barrier. She sat engulfed by the enormous chair and thought about Lily Tomlin's impression of Edith Ann, the little girl in the exaggerated large rocking chair where her feet barely touched the Karastan red carpet. She wondered if her father had commissioned these Renaissance reproductions. Her eyes darted back to the Vatican picture then to the enormous Crucifix with a statue of Jesus hanging from it positioned directly behind the Archbishop. How could she deny Jesus anything when he suffered so much for her?

"I appreciate you coming today, my dear<" said the Archbishop with his hands together.prayerfully. "As you know, we're in our annual campaign to refurbish the roof and ceiling of the St. Mary's Cathedral. You know your father has always been an important community member in undertaking our transformation initiatives. Our goal has always been to enhance the long-term sustainability of parishioners by enhancing their opportunity to embrace the lasting legacy of Catholicism." He taped his fingers together emphatically.

Morainya chewed her lip and glanced down at her hands. "Yes, my father and our family have always been the most devote members of the congregation."

"My office has sent our official request for this year's donation to your parent's house. It is all laid out how your generous funds will be applied to the restoration project. The church ceiling needs major repair due to the leaks over the years that have damaged the frescos. As I recall, you are an art enthusiast, and I'm sure you would adore seeing the improvement in our aging cathedral."

A rasp caught in her throat. "When I return to my parents' home tonight..." she began, unsure if the lie was more to him or to herself, "I will be sure to take a look. It is just that I have been so busy trying to wrap up my father's estate, and I've had to deal with some legal issues," responded Morainya, trying her best to emphasize that there was still a mess to deal with.

The spiritual authority leaned back in his leather high backed chair. "I understand being in the position of the executor of the Napolitano estate must be quite arduous with all the property your parent's owned. By the way, how is your mother doing? She, too, was a contributor to the cause."

"My mother was a contributor? What do you mean?" Morainya cocked her head.

He smiled recalling the past. "Your mother was quite the socialite and chaired many fundraisers for the church over the years."

Morainya acknowledged the parties. "Yes, I remember being here many times as a child."

His Excellency looked at her awash in a moment of sorrow. "I'm sure your father would have bestowed the executor position upon her, that is, if her dementia had not advanced so quickly. Anyway, as I understand, you should conclude the legal proceedings within a few months, unless, of course, you choose to go to trial. If you do, you'll more than likely get Judge Josepha Soffagiano. Mediation would be a wiser move, if you don't mind a little advice. I find that trials can be quite messy, you know, dredging up all things that hide in the dark about you or your family. I've just heard that from other parishioners who've been dragged through the same legal entanglements."

"Yes, your Grace. It is quite an ordeal, and it's putting my family through great despair. I didn't anticipate that my own family member would sue me. I feel angry that I haven't even had time to grieve but instead have been wrapped up in this legal mess," said Morainya, *for a breath, it felt safe. Like maybe this was a confessional in disguise, and not another corridor of control.* Afterall, wasn't it a priest's job to listen?

"Yes, my dear. You might find it effective to go to confession to absolve some of the hateful and sinful feelings you carry deep in your heart. I am sure Father August will be available to take your confessions tomorrow. I could call him personally if that helps you get absolution." The Archbishop picked up the black landline phone to make the call.

Morainya's *shoulders slumped. The hope of refuge dissolved like communion wine on the tongue—there, then gone.* "Your Excellency, you are far too busy to be making calls. I was just trying to," she paused, "never mind. Thank you so much for fitting me into your busy schedule." She would find no comfort here.

He allowed the heavy phone to fall into its cradle. "Your family is most important to me and to the Church. The Napolitanos' are a cornerstone of generosity for our spiritual enhancement and our mission. I wanted to personally ask you if you would co-chair a committee with some of the wives of the tech giants from Silicon Valley, the Industrial, Commercial Markets, and the Bay Area Financial Districts. Since you are all our biggest donors, you should headline the large Gala at the Biotech International Hotel next Spring. I have included a list of their personal cell numbers for you to reach out. That is if you are so inclined. It is quite an honor to chair this Gala, and I believe it will put you back in the spotlight. May I count on you?"

"Honestly, Your Excellency, I need a bit of time to think about it. You see, I live in Santa Cruz now, and it would be quite a hike over the hill. I don't have the big connections as the other two candidates."

"I see." He paused reflectively and took so much time pondering this insult that Morainya crossed and uncrossed her legs with discomfort.

"Think about it. I will need your answer soon. Until then, I look forward to seeing you again. After you've had time to peruse the donation appeals fundraiser letter and request for the in-kind gifts. Or you might just consider making a family monthly tithe."

Her breath caught in disbelief. "A tithe?" Ten percent of grief, paperwork, and everything that remained of my father's estate?

"Yes, that is correct. Anyway, you can take your time. I'll call you at the end of next month." He glanced at his gold watch and tapped it. "Look at the time. I have another appointment arriving any minute. May I walk you out?" He ushered her to the door like a shepherd guiding a wayward sheep.

Morainya stooped for the stack of envelopes, eyeing the uneven lawn like a tired heiress surveying a crumbling kingdom. When she finally got the house listed, she would need to schedule them weekly through the fall until the grass died. Turning the key, and stepping into the foyer, she took off her overcoat.

"Hey, Mora," said Gina, who was setting the long dining room table with fine China plates, and crystal glasses from her parent's redwood cabinet. Morainya appreciated that her brother and sister-in-law stopped by to keep up the estate. It was warming her heart to see family while she was in town, and she was grateful that all the responsibility didn't fall solely on her shoulders.

"Tommy! Julianna! Get down here right now. The table is all set," yelled Gina, in a New York Italian accent.

Morainya yelled upstairs at her nephew and niece, doubting they'd hear her. "I'm here."

Gina wore a red checkered apron, one of her mother's favorites. "Yeah, the Halston looks great on you. You are the spitting image of your Ma. If I had known she still had all that designer crap, I might have raided her closet. That old-time stuff isn't really my style, but for a baby shower or lunch at the club in Sausalito, I bet I could pull it off." Gina had dyed her raven black hair a platinum blonde and gave off Marilyn Monroe vibes that made Morainya giggle.

"Do you want some of my Mom's clothes? I just wore this to the Archbishop's meeting, I felt like I had to be more formal. I don't really have a reason to get dressed up any-more," said Morainya, giving Gina a hand.

"How was His Excellency? I haven't been there since Nico and I got married and had to meet with him to make sure I was a good Catholic girl."

She forced a smile. "He was... fine," she said, tasting the word like something sour she didn't want to swallow. "He asked me to chair the gala like it was a sacred mission—but really, it felt like he just needed someone with a last name that still meant something."

Gina checked the roast in the oven. "How's the Archbishop's house look? Beautiful as ever? I used to be so scared to go there."

"It is intimidating," agreed Morainya as she plated the dinner rolls.

"Tommy and Juliana are going to make me climb those stairs to get their attention," said Gina sternly.

Morainya chuckled and said, "They probably are playing a video game, or have those ear pods in. I doubt they can hear you. Do you want me to text them? That's the only way I can get Josh's attention these days."

Gina nodded and scooped the mashed potatoes onto a serving plate. "Yeah, go ahead and do that. I want to get the roast on the table."

The front door slammed drawing both of their attention. "Anybody home?" yelled Nico, depositing his overcoat on the brass rack.

Morainya and Gina poked their heads out of the kitchen and shouted, "We're in the kitchen!" Morainya texted the teenagers that their father was home and to get downstairs NOW.

"What's up?" yelled Julianna from the second floor.

"Dinner's ready," barked their dad.

Morainya turned to Gina, "I need to go change out of this suit. Can't get any spills on it. Not That Mom would find out," she gave a small laugh realizing how true those words were. Morainya jogged upstairs passing Tommy and Juliana on the way down. She washed up in the Wedgewood blue room bathroom in the safety of the home she grew up. Her father had left her room exactly the way it looked back when she was at University. Admittedly, it had a design of a Disney Princess, with a pink satin quilted bedspread, and a whitewashed highboy and desk. Her record collection was intact. Slipping into her neon overstuffed chair opposite her bed, Morainya recalled how much she loved her bedroom while in high school. It was so chic. She changed back into her jeans and a casual sweater. When she was done, she headed back down for dinner.

"I'm dying to hear about your meeting today," said Nico, tossing back his curly hair, as he sat at the dining room table and ordered Tommy and Juliana to get seated. Gina brought out the roast and side dishes. Finally, she sat, and they said grace, folding their hands.

"It was what I expected," said Morainya. "He wants money too," she said, setting down her fork like it had suddenly grown heavy. "A lot." Morainya helped herself to roast, mash potatoes and asparagus. It was nice to sit with her family. They bickered like she had with her siblings growing up.

"Well, some things never change," replied Nico.

"Take some vegetables, Tommy," ordered his mom feeling discomfort talking about money in front of the kids. She didn't like talking about it—only spending it.

Morainya munched on an asparagus spear. "The house looked pretty much like I remember it growing up. Some interesting things happened. You know that picture of the

Archbishop in the St Peter's Basilica pulpit in Rome? You know, the one with him standing next to the Pope?"

"Yeah, the one that hangs in the den?" asked Gina, pointing her chin towards the East wing.

"The bigger picture hangs in the Archbishop's house. On his wall in the study where he brings guests," added Morainya.

Nico, took a bite of a dinner roll, then asked, "The room with that red desk, right?"

Morainya nodded gladly that he remembered. "Yeah, that room. But you guys won't believe what the back of that church looks like. Here, I took a picture of it. She pulled out her camera. "It looks like a snake. The room is green and scaly," she said, her voice quiet. "The walls curve like ribs. The whole place hums like something alive—and watching."

"You've got to be kidding," argued Tommy. "Let me see, maybe it's Photoshopped, or the perspective."

Juliana, pushing in to look at the camera, "Or your camera lighting. She gasped and pulled back her long raven hair. "No, look, Mom, it does look like a snake."

"There are the eyes," said Tommy, pointing at the phone. "Wait, are those fangs? That must be photoshopped." Tommy shook his head and squinched his face.

"No, I swear," said Morainya, "it's in the big picture. We only have the small, edited photo."

"Enough with the gossip," ordered Gina throwing her hands up.

Morainya retrieved her phone. "Know what's crazier? Do you know how many Popes are alive now?"

"Two, silly, His Holiness Pope Benedict XVI and Pope Francis. Everyone knows that," said Gina, crossing herself in reverence when talking about the Holy Fathers. Her Catholic upbringing had been strict, and she would never question the church for it was the law in her house.

"There are two more. I saw their pictures on the Archbishop's wall. Here, look at this picture," replied Morainya showing them another photo.

"O.K., that's weird. Now, you have my attention," said Nico placing his elbows on the lace tablecloth. Uncomfortably, he loosened his silk tie while leaning forward to see.

Gina gasped and raised her voice like mom's do. "While you two conspiracy theorists make up stories, this is blasphemous, Stop it," Gina snapped, crossing herself like a reflex. "I'm not going to hell just for hearing you whisper this stuff."

Nico gave his wife the eyes and turned back to Morainya to just get down to business. "Did he only call you over for a donation? How much did he ask for?" replied Nico taking a gulp of wine.

"If you guys are going to talk about business, can we take our food upstairs?" asked Tommy, fidgeting.

"I guess, as long as you promise to finish your homework," replied Gina feeling out of control.

Morainya replied dimly, "A lot." These money talks made everyone uneasy.

Nico cleared his throat. "Was this about the annual donation Dad used to make to the church?"

Morainya asked, "Yes, do you even know how much he used to give? The Archbishop said he sent over some documents and a list of what he needed to fix the roof. I bet it's a fortune."

"That must be the Fed Ex package I found in front of the door earlier," replied Gina getting up to grab it.

Morainya ripped it open, scanned it, and blanched before handing it to Nico.

"How can he ask for the same amount when Dad died, and his business is closed?" said Nico flatly.

"Five million is outrageous, right? And Uncle Aldo is suing me personally," stated Morainya, dotting her lips with a napkin, and wiping away a tear. Pain bloomed in her left temple, tight and hot—like a warning bell pressed into her skull.

"That's a lot of pressure," said Gina. "I'm sure the Archbishop has a good reason."

Morainya shuffled in her seat and pushed her plate up. "How soon do you think the legalities will be cleared up? I need to know because we need to sign the contract with the realtor to get this home listed."

Nico buttered his roll. "I think we need to stage the house because this furniture is so outdated. If we want to get a good price, then we will need to update it." He stated, "The realtor says people can't envision how to design a mansion of this magnitude, so styling it often raises the price because the buyer wants to keep the furniture."

"Everybody wins," said Gina, animating every statement with a hand motion.

"What would that cost?" asked Morainya, "I am struggling to keep up with the legal fees and Josh's college tuition is coming up. I can't even get much to cover that. In fact, I kinda need to ask you guys for a loan. Like an advance. You'll get it all back when we settle." Morainya gave them pleading eyes.

Her younger brother calculated his own resources, feeling the pinch of not knowing if he would get the promotion at the Software Startup he had joined three years ago. "How much? Are you asking us to donate to the church too?"

Morainya grimaced and she clutched the tablecloth. "The Archbishop strongly suggested that we go to mediation instead of a trial. He hinted that he knew who the judge would be and that he'd likely look into any dark past that dad had. What do you think he meant? He actually told me that Aldo had a tough childhood and that we should accept the mediation conference instead of going to trial."

"That's ridiculous, how would the Archbishop even know which judge would be assigned to the trial?" said Nico grabbing the table in a nervous hold.

Gina looked up, "Maybe God told him." She crossed herself with a hopeful upward gaze.

"Right Gina. God called the Archbishop on the phone and told him who the judge would be," retorted Nico. "Fuck Aldo," he said crossing his arms. "He's wrecking the family. He's always been a pain in the ass. Geez, he was adopted into the lap of luxury, and he's come between all members of the family since I was a kid.

"Calm down, Nico. You are swearing again, you always do that when you drink," rebuked Gina, scraping the leftovers onto her plate.

Nico was heated and continued. "Remember when he accused Aunt Dahlia of cheating in math and almost got her kicked out before graduation? Who does that to his sister?"

Morainya, her voice tinged with sadness, said, "We all know Aldo has never fit in, but I want to know why. It made me think that we didn't know the whole story. I can't ask Mom; she'll never remember."

"Maybe we just need to love on him more," said Gina, her face brightening.

"Love him? I mean, I tried. I tried over and over to help him," said Nico, standing up in fighting mode. "Nothing ever sinks in. I've helped Uncle Aldo plenty of times. Dad was good to him, giving him a job even though he was never really good at it. Now, look where we are at. He's suing you for the inheritance, which rightfully belongs to us. What's that about?"

Morainya trembled. "Aldo's claim is for five million, I don't understand. He was just Dad's employee. He wasn't an owner or an investor. Yet, he is accusing me of every crime imaginable to discredit dad."

"You can sue anybody for anything. Lawyers don't care," Nico retorted.

Gina cut the pie and gave Morainya and Nico a slice trying to soothe their ill moods.

"How can that be right? Nico shook his head. "And the Archbishop wants the other five million?"

"That's crazy. The stress of all this must be getting to you," offered Gina.

Her hand hovered at her cheek, catching a tear before it fell. Not here, she thought.

Not at the table., "It is. Emilio is calling from Florence all the time saying his mother-in-law has cancer, and it's financially ruining him. Francesa and her husband started that Kombucha company in Oregon," Morainya's voice caught. "You know they nearly lost everything…" her voice trailed off as if reliving the past was too etched in pain. I just don't know how to solve everyone's money problems."

"Then we have to make a decision about mediation instead of a trial. Offer Aldo something to settle," suggested Nico.

"Maybe that's the best idea. I'll offer him a five hundred thousand, so he'll leave us alone. Are we in agreement?" asked Morainya. "I think that is the best solution. After all, going to court means we have to drag in witnesses and prove we are right. Who's left from Dad's time?"

Nico offered, "Just Sally, the accountant, and now she's retired and has cancer."

"That's too bad. She was really nice," said Gina, taking a sip of wine.

"We all can testify. I'd like to tell him a thing or two," said Nico, draining his glass of wine.

Gina asked, "How much does going to court cost?" She hated that Nico had started drinking again. Since the legalities began, he had amped up his occasional social drinking to have two to three glasses a night.

"A lot. It's tons of billable hours. It doesn't matter whether we win or lose. We lose anyway," retorted Morainya.

Nico belched. "Then do mediation. That judge is bound to see how screwed up Aldo is and that there really isn't any case at all," added Nico, using his logical mind and feeling his belly ache from the peptic ulcer.

"Maybe I should tell Mr. Kanberg tomorrow. I do have a huge bill that I need to get paid. It simply has to come out of the estate," said Morainya.

"We are sorry you got dragged into this. You should go to church and pray. When's the last time you went to

Mass?" asked Gina fingering the silver cross she dutifully wore around her neck.

"I dunno. It's been a while," said Morainya. "His Excellency suggested I go to confession when I was hoping he'd help me resolve some of this anger I feel toward Uncle Aldo. I don't think confession will help me because I didn't do anything wrong."

"If your heart has offense, then Jesus can cleanse your sins. Go say some Hail Mary's, do your rosary, and confess. That will be the end." Gina said, saying a Hail Mary to prove to Morainya that was the right path.

"Really? By confessing that I'm angry, will it all go away?" said Morainya sarcastically. "If that were true, then all therapists would be out of a job. "I love Jesus," she said quietly, "but I'm starting to wonder if the church loves us back." I believe in God, but I don't know about religion. His Excellency wants me to chair his big gala. But it really feels like he just wants money. I know that Dad was a big donor, but instead of fixing a roof on a cathedral, I think we should all give it to charities of our choice. I want to support School Lunches for all kids. You can use your percentage of the commission for taking care of this house to give to the animal shelter. Maybe it's time we look at this in a different way."

"Go to mediation and get this settled with Aldo so we can put it behind us," said Gina.

"Agreed," replied Morainya and Nico. They didn't toast. They didn't pray. Just nodded—three silent witnesses to a war they didn't start but now had to end.

I sat at the edge of the courtyard blue tiled pool, letting my feet dangle into its cool, still water as hibiscus petals floated like quiet prayers across the surface. The scent of blue lotus and date blossom lingered in the warm morning air. A bowl of honeyed Kamut and ripened figs rested beside me, their sweetness clinging to my fingers.

My copper skin showed through a gauze-thin sheath of white linen, threaded with golden filaments that caught the sun like whispers of royalty. Around my neck, a simple collar of lapis and carnelian—the one my mother had once fastened for me before temple rites. My hair was coiled into a single braid, pinned with a bee-shaped clasp of onyx and amber reminding me of the honey makers alighting on each blossom.

A lone bee hovered near a pink mandevilla bloom, then landed softly—undisturbed, determined. My gaze followed her, golden and tireless. I thought of my mother, the Queen Bee of our household, now flown beyond our reach.

Was I now the Queen, charged with holding the hive together? While my father searched distant lands for gold, had gold come to us instead—in the form of that strange vendor, Ana-Kharu? My thoughts spun like dust devils across the plains, stirred by the wind of fate. I felt the heat of duty rising in my chest—not fear, not yet—but something heavier than girlhood, something honey-thick and holy.

Without a routine, we felt rudderless like oarsmen without a current—listless and prone to stir mischief. My heart trembled with hope that this new instructor would surpass my father expectations, silently pleading that my choice would be proven wise. Then I could step into the position of Per-Aat. The chariot was summoned so that I could meet my class. It arrived in a clatter of hooves, we thundered past villagers, the horses regally tossing their heads like kings, nostrils flaring. Cheers and approving waves met us as if I had already earned their faith.

We assembled at the town's fountain—once a bubbling centerpiece, now reduced to a trickle, its tiles dulled and cracked with neglect. Seeing the initiates in worn tunics and unadorned robes made my jaw tighten. They spoke amongst themselves in hushed tones, unsure of why I had called them. Would Ana-Kharu judge them unworthy for their untidy appearance? I wished I could have given them more time to prepare—to protect them from premature judgement.

"I have glad tidings. We will begin with Ana-Kharu's tutelage in our alchemy classes. He has set up camp in the Reception Hall where we attended the welcoming festivity. Let us go and be thankful that my father's instructor has arrived."

The others rumbled their concerns in not so hushed tones, and I felt their suspicions and worry swarm like wasps. Archollos nudged his shoulder firmly into mine, his silent protest louder than words. We strode through the once lush grasslands. "Merit-Aten, you said you would rid yourself of these parasites."

"Archollos, we need him. Have any other instructors come forward?" I argued, matching his intensity because he clearly could not see the gift Ana-Kharu offered.

He eyed me with a lingering look to emphasize his suspicion. He pushed a hand through his wavy mop of blonde curls. "No—but you expect me to believe this is who your father had in mind? After what I walked in on?" His voice sharp as a knife. "If I had not interrupted, who knows what liberties he might have subjected you to." My love kicked a stone out of our way, too hard to be casual.

I brushed his hand to calm him with my reasoning so that he would turn his concern into support. "I did not trust him either. Not at first. But what choice did I have? No other teacher has come. No other solution has been presented." And I needed him—my father needed this.

"Ana-Kharu was a deceiver, then I discovered that he is quite accomplished in alchemy. He showed me the contents of his sacred box with all the alchemical concoctions. The key around his neck unlocks our destiny," I said, nearly gloating that I was the one to decipher this mystery.

"Explain to me exactly how you would know if those concoctions you discovered are nothing more than piss and vinegar? He is untrustworthy. When Ra-Awab took me to the back streets to gamble, I have seen men like him before, Merit. Men who promise gold and entice with their empty boasts," said Archollos who smelled like musk making me long to hug him closer. "Only to disappear in the night with half the town's silver."

A distinguished Secretary bird strutted through the high weeds, searching for prey. We jerked our heads because this exceptionally large bird with a wide wingspan protected its territory with threatening motions. Its black legs and tail contrasted with its white feathered body and featherless orange face. I sent it greetings, knowing we interrupted its hunting grounds, for this bird was essential to dispel the pests that accumulated during the unusually dry months of the Nile drought.

Ra-Awab steered us away in his bold manner. He flexed his biceps protective of the young women. Over the years, he had become a close friend to Archollos, and I knew he valued his opinion. "I could not help but overhear your discussion about Ana-Kharu. While we were entranced by the night of merriment this guest provided, it was also mixed with a bit of uncertainty about his true intentions."

Tadushet rushed up, her voice was soft and feminine as she declared, "I felt it too." Her auburn locks bounced with each step. "It was not that I was not thankful for the distraction of finally having something pleasurable to do other than folding towels and making candles for the sanctuary. I must ask, did we allow the commotion of our new guests to lead us amiss?"

Sarawat and Keshtuat joined in, never wanting to be far from the young men in our class.

"That drummer is so handsome. I am a bit concerned about being lured into debauchery," Sarawat said it breathily as she had hurried to catch up. This was a moment of rare inner contemplation. She had elaborately braided her hair and had put a touch of cosmetics upon her face as if she was hoping that someone would notice.

"Yes, I am aware of last night," I said, elbowing Archollos to keep his mouth shut. "Should I throw out an alchemist when we have one in our midst? Do you not think it would be wise to at least get a rudimentary understanding of alchemy? When our true teacher arrives, we can impress him with our accrued knowledge. Initiates have devoted their lives to decipher this transmutation process; it would behoove us to learn."

As we walked across the dryland, the once lush vegetation had receded with no rain, leaving the ground cracked. Keshtuat avoided a cactus and said, "Maybe Merit-Aten has a point. What would be the harm in taking some classes?" Her mother, the Court Seamstress had allowed her daughter to use the leftover embellishments from the royal raiments as decorations on her plain temple sheath. Keshtuat had always envied my fine clothing and other luxuries.

"Queen, we could keep an eye on him if we are sitting at his feet; what trouble could come of it?" added Smenkhkare, his smile accentuated his high cheekbones and chiseled jaw, reminding me of his father, who was my Grand Djed, Pharaoh Amunhotep III. He was protective of me, being my half-brother and we usually agreed on important issues. Smenkhkare took my side to defend me often when the class did not always support my wisdom because I was younger. We had the uncanny ability to read each other's thoughts, thereby aligning us.

Archollos was visibly shaken and gave Smenkhkare an angry glare. "He has a way of encouraging mischief. That is all I will say. But know this, Ra-Awab, I witnessed your engagement with that enchantress. I also saw that drummer's hands making beats upon your backside, Sarawat." The paradox was not lost on me that Archollos was admonishing the class for the usual mischief for which they all had indulged. My love may be maturing out of his boy self.

Although Archollos and I quarreled, we still headed in the direction of the Reception Hall. I felt confident that Ana-Kharu would show them the contents of that locked secret box. How could they not be convinced of his tutorial skills when he showed them the alchemical powders? Isn't that what my father was in such desperate need of? Gold! We needed gold to buy warriors and keep our borders safe. We needed gold to pay those in allegiance to us in exchange for their armies. Gold. We needed to feed our sick, elderly, and our youth in need of sustenance. I simply did not see the harm in beginning lessons. If the Aten did not deem a teacher to arrive, then why did Ana-Kharu show up? The Aten answered our prayers. Since my father had departed for an unknown time, then it was up to me as the Per Aat-in-waiting to make decisions for my people. This seemed like the most obvious answer to our appeals. We darted up the steps to the temple perched upon the Nile. A slight breeze off the constricted waterway refreshed us. I was grateful the conversation abated. My mind was made up. Our teacher awaited and he carefully looked each of us in the eye before allowing us entrance.

"Ana-Kharu-We-Shat, Let us embark on our lessons," I said with outstretched hands.

He wore his conical golden hat and embroidered robes as he took his place at the head of our makeshift classroom in the open-air temple. Thick plumes of Frankincense and Myrrh incense spiraled up from the copper burners. "This is most auspicious. As you can see, cushions are set about for you to take your seat. Let us begin." Colorful silken pillows, taken from the main palace, were set before ink quills and papyrus laid upon wooden tables, that I had borrowed from my sister's classroom.

"We give peace and praise to the Aten," I said, feeling the solemn echo of my father's decree stir within me. Then I turned the circle over to Ana-Kharu, his time to speak of Alchemy finally at hand. We gathered at the feet of the teacher; an excitement rose like the steam from ice. Our thirst was palpable. It dawned upon me that these Travelers made nary a sale upon their arrivals, except for the staff of the household who dallied in the less expensive treasures. This class was how I could make it equitable for the distance this troupe had voyaged. Father would be compassionate about my decision.

"Hotep," Peace, said Ana-Kharu, his smile widened—too wide, as if he'd been waiting for this exact moment. His fingers drummed against the golden ankh key at his throat, just once, before he spread his arms in welcome. "First, as is the tradition of my people. We begin by breathing. Let us harmonize our energies and call the elders near." The air thickened with presence. Sound dulled, images blurred at the edges, and even the light softened until our bodies slipped into shared rhythm. One by one, we dropped into stillness.

I sat cross-legged, my palms upon each knee, spine straightened, a faint smile blooming because I had waited so long for this moment of unlocking the alchemical mysteries.

Ana-kharu, his voice deepened as he said, "We use the verse to summon the invisible force that holds the You-ni-verse together. We are but the vessels of Cosmic intelligence to flow through."

We regulated our breathing, deep inhalations, and exhalations from the solar plexus. We were in the flow. Ana-Kharu held up his right hand, allowing his sleeve to fall below the wrist revealing an inner silken red lining in his robe—like blood hidden beneath light "I have come before you to reveal some of the mysteries of the alchemical arts. Merit-Aten has confirmed that you have already received instruction in sacred geometry, some astronomy, philosophy, and math. Of course, the word Al-chemy is hidden in the very name of our mystical land, Khemit, known for transformation. Foreign tongues praise our black earth while ignoring the black brilliance of the people it births. But you—you are the keepers of that forgotten light Of course, you know that Khemmis, also known as Akhmim was also a great school for Alchemy."

I etched it carefully into my papyrus in flowing Metu Neter—*Words of God*—my hand steady with purpose. That detail felt like a seed worth keeping.

Ana-Kharu continued his teaching. "Khemia is a name only the adepts know, which means it is rare and hard to come by, or Khem-is-try. "Khemia," he said, voice lowering, "is a name only the adepts whisper. It means rarity... something not easily possessed. Some call it Khem-is-try." A glint passed through his eyes. "It is also the name of a red crystal—cinnabar—an elusive stone that burns with the power to transform. "We will explore the steps of Alchemy and the hidden magnetism between substances—how they are drawn to transform. The simplest image?"

He lifted his hand, fingers closing gently. "A seed, buried in the rich black soil of Khemit. Watered, kissed by the sun, it splits... and something entirely new begins to rise." The simplest example would be planting a seed in the fertile Khemitian soil that would symbolize the seeds of knowledge. This is a metaphor for moving from the first stage of initiation to the adept level closer to the heavenly worlds."

We drank in this wisdom like thirsty nomads draining their camel bags, not wasting a drop. Everyone was now transfixed as he continued. I stared wide-eyed then wrote it down. The air around him shimmered with weight as he continued, "The seven stages of alchemy are important. Commit these stages to memory because we will use experiments to transmute. His voice grew more rhythmic, incantatory. "Calcination, Dissolution, Separation, Conjunction, Fermentation, Distillation and Coagulation. Repeat them now."

We echoed the stages like a sacred chant. The words fed something deep—an old knowing rising to meet the flame of new learning.

Ana-Kharu nodded slowly, as if the words had passed a test of time. "Now we pair the metals with the planets," he said. "These correspondences," he said, "will guide you to initiate your work at the right celestial alignments—when the stars lean in to assist. Gold is the Sun, eternal and incorruptible. Silver is the Moon—reflective, mysterious. Mercury governs Mercury itself—fluid and fast. Copper belongs to Venus, Lead to Saturn, Iron to Mars, and Tin... to mighty Jupiter. Write these carefully. They are not symbols. They are doorways."

"Scribes, write these down," He clapped sharply. "To gain anything of true value," he said, his voice now heavy with truth, "something equal must be surrendered. This is not just metaphor—it is Cosmic Law of Equivalent Exchange." A thing cannot be made from nothing; when we create a thing, whether an elixir, a metal or a remedy, then something of equal value must be exchanged and lost."

I leaned forward. Would I have to lose something, too? I glanced at Archollos taking notes and my heart ached.

"Often," said Ana-Kharu, lowering his voice, "the most sacred things are hidden in filth, in the discarded, in the overlooked. That is where gold sleeps. Transform yourselves from dead stones into living philosophical stones. Inner transformation. It takes balance within to create balance without."

"Teacher, could you please tell us about gold?" The question clawed at my chest. I needed to know—for my family's sake. I eased back on my heels, bracing for the answer.

Ana-Kharu's smile thinned, his gaze sharpening, "Turning base metals into gold are the arts taught in Heliopolis. It is a lifelong study with the Alchemical Masters." He said with a cringe. "Now, back to our studies, for we are only at the beginning; and for that, you need to learn about the basics."

Keshtuat lifted her hand in eagerness. "Are the tinctures, and perfumes you offer—are they made from alchemy?" She always had always been captivated by the rare oils Father gifted to Mother and us daughters.

Ra-Awab groaned, exchanging a look with Archollos before muttering, "Can we move on to what actually matters?" He smirked, then said, "This is just girl's business."

"Agreed," added Archollos, rising with a stretch. "Isn't it time for Temple?"

Ana-Kharu nodded, his fingers brushing the golden key at his throat, as though unlocking a thought. "Perfumes," he said, "are a form of khemistry—alchemy through scent. Oils are first purified, then diluted, then combined with wax or resin to carry their intention. The lotus especially—she holds the power to open unseen doors. These same energies heal our bodies by connecting us to the Divine."

"How does smell connect us to the Divine?" asked Ra-Awab, his head tilted, lips curled.

"Alchemy is the marriage of earth and sky," Ana-Kharu's voice warm like oil poured from a flask. "It unites matter with the dwelling of the Aten. Those who learn its rhythm— can reshape the world."

I gasped, my fingers tightening on my quill. Did my father know of the unfathomable power of alchemy? Ana-kharu motioned to the sky. "By your father's decree, we follow the sun's path: Khepher at dawn, Ra at midday, Oon in the afternoon, and Wizzer before dusk. As the sun stoops, it becomes the bent old man—Aten. And finally, Amun arrives... the blackest night. This, too, is alchemy. Every hour, a transformation. Every shadow, a teacher."

I raised my hand before I lost the courage. "Great teacher," I said, "is true balance even possible? We hear whispers of war beyond the Nile. If others choose chaos, how do we hold peace?"

Ana-Kharu's eyes softened. "Balance," he said, "is not conjured through force or fantasy. It is crafted—element by element—through alignment with the natural world. Alchemy is not the summoning of demons, but remembrance. The ancient recipes were once oral... now hidden in scrolls only the initiated may read."

Tadushet leaned forward, quill poised. "Teacher, what does transformation truly mean?" Her quill readied to take every note, as her focus was on what is balanced and just.

"Transformation," he said, "is the altering of identity itself. Take a rat who tears through your grain. When slain and discarded, what happens?" He paused, letting discomfort settle. "Flies come. Eggs are laid. Maggots are born. And from rot... life begins again. All alchemy."

Several girls groaned, hands over their faces. The boys, of course, chuckled—drawn to anything foul. Even decay held fascination for them.

Ana-Kharu chuckled. "You want the final scroll without reading the first line," he teased.

"But transformation is everywhere. You live it already. Every heartbreak. Every trial. Every injustice overcome... all of it alters you. All of this is alchemy. For example, there is white papyrus paper, black iron ink, and red vermillion ink. These are the sacred colors of the Alchemist's path. Base metal is black like lead, and through silver and white, the concoction turns to red or gold."

Even I shook my head. I had never seen our tears, our losses, our humiliations... as alchemy. But they were. Kom Ombo. Kalabsha. Every wound we carried had shaped us. *How had no one told us that pain was part of the formula? Or had Father known all along—and waited for this teacher to speak it plain?*

Ana-Kharu's brow furrowed, the weight of withheld truth pressing into his gaze. "Do they teach you nothing of the world beyond these walls? Or are you truly prisoners in a golden cage—as the whispers say across the Khemitian lands?. May I speak plainly?"

"Yes," I said, my voice steadier than I felt. "Tell us what lies beyond." My classmates shifted, uneasy. I had seen Pentu's maps—vast sketches of the Pharaoh's holdings—but suddenly, they seemed... small. Had we truly believed we were the center of the world? My stomach twisted. How could I be Per At-in-waiting and know so little? My stomach gurgled from the humiliation that this stranger was schooling the daughter of the Pharaoh.

"It's the affliction of the Court," Ana-Kharu said, folding his arms. "Ease breeds softness. Purpose fades. My troupe walks for years, trading what we gather. We sleep in sand. We eat sparingly to feed our beasts. We tend to wounds the wealthy never see—sores split open from cactus thorns, snakebite, and sunscald. The rich are healed by tinctures we nearly die to carry. And beyond your Kingdom?" He shook his head. "There are those with no grain, no water. The Amun priesthood bleeds the borderlands dry—rerouting rivers, slaughtering herds. Even the dead cry out for justice."

Gasps rippled through the circle. Some students frowned, others whispered behind their hands. I bit my tongue, trying to defend what now felt indefensible for there were a lot of bones in that fish to pick out. "My father could forbid the misuse of nature's gifts. He would just decree this be prohibited," I reasoned.

Ana-Kharu's voice deepened. "The Amunites are not alone. Even our own tribal kingdoms have fallen—devoured by war, envy, hunger. And your kingdom? It is not immune. You've forgotten what it means to be tribal. Who here gathers water? Hunts food? Builds shelter against lions that creep in with nightfall?" No one answered. "You build palaces, not people. Your hands are as soft as your minds." He spat into the dust—an act of sacrilege in drought season. The sting of it hit harder than a slap.

Ana-Kharu set all court etiquette aside and spit upon the ground. The significance of needlessly dispelling one's water during a time of drought was not lost upon us. The insult stung like an angry wasp inflicting its wound upon a vulnerable place.

"We serve the Aten," I said quietly, clinging to the one truth I had left. "We pray. We offer comfort. We—" He hadn't asked about our rituals. He was testing our backbone. I thought of my father, thin with worry. My mother's letters. We needed gold. Gold for food, for protection, for trade. If I could master alchemy, I could relieve them both. I didn't need lectures—I needed solutions. My shoulders sank.

Ana-Kharu exhaled, long and hard. "Shall I show you the gold I brought?"

"Yes!" the class chorused, their earlier discomfort forgotten. Alchemy suddenly felt real again—tangible. A shimmer of awe passed through the circle. "

Ana-Kharu rubbed his temple. "You're not like my usual initiates," he muttered. "You've passed trials, yet still ask for proof. Very well." He snapped his fingers. Anpu appeared from behind a column, silent as breath.

Upon my father's return, I hoped to display the gold that we had transformed by our hands. This would eliminate a huge burden for my father.

Frustration pulled taut across Ana-Kharu's once-proud features. With a sharp snap of his fingers, Anpu—the towering drummer whose arms rippled with tension—emerged from the shadows carrying the golden chest. The same ankh-shaped key I'd eyed for days was fitted into the iron lock and turned with care. As the lid creaked open, the room hushed. He reached inside and withdrew four small jars, each topped with a jeweled stopper that caught the lamplight like constellations in a velvet sky.

He held up a jar tinted vermillion and sealed with wax. With a ceremonial crack, he broke it open and extracted a scarlet block, gleaming like blood under sunlight. "This," he announced, "is cinnabar—our sacred Mercury Sulphur. It awakens fire in cold limbs, warmth in frigid hearts, and strength in those who have lost their vitality. It aids revolution—of body, of mind, and of realm." He paused, letting the words settle. "Ingested properly, it clears the seven wheels, sharpens thought, and restores one's standing across all planes."

"The Pharaoh would want that," I blurted, the words escaping before I could catch them. Ana-Kharu's smile curled slow and deliberate. A sale had been made.

Ana-Kharu smiled and withdrew the item, knowing that he had a buyer. Next came a lapis-hued jar. He unscrewed the tight seal and revealed a shimmering golden dust. "Elemental gold," he said, "harvested from the sacred veins of Aswan and Kush. It is prized among the court women for its youthful glow. But more than beauty—it holds light. Only those with deep connections can acquire it." He met my eyes. "I am such a man."

He lifted a jar cloaked in malachite green. "This is alchemical gold—curative, purgative, sovereign. It banishes parasites of the body and spirit, cleanses the blood, clears what clouds the mind. It is not sold. It is bestowed. And only to the worthy." His gaze lingered on us, weighing our worth.

"Please continue," I said, now enchanted that we were making progress, I licked my lips.

From a carnelian jar, he tilted forth a sparkling blend—swirls of silver and gold coiled together like sun and moon in a jar. "Electrum," he said. "A sacred alloy. The legends say it powered the movement of great stones used to raise the pyramids at Giza."

We leaned in. A collective breath was drawn. "We have never seen the Per Neter, pyramid," someone whispered. Ana-Kharu blinked, stunned. "You have never been?" We shook our heads. He scoffed. "And you call yourselves Initiates?"

"That is a site for great Mastery. How is it that Pharaoh's specially appointed class of initiates has not ventured to Upper Khemit to view the greatest marvel ever constructed?" Ana-Kharu looked askance at us judgingly.

We shook our heads because that question had never arisen. Surely, we had heard of the pyramids and seen the symbol of the water urn upon feet pouring out the power of water. My father had that symbol etched upon the stelae. Even though the flag hieroglyph meant House of the Neter was known to us, we had not had the privilege of viewing the pyramid in person. I would have to ask my father if we could venture there for another great initiation.

My heart quickened. "What of the ingestible gold—the one they call liquid sunlight?" He paused. I pressed on. "My father's supply has dwindled. The priests have withheld their offerings. He grows dim... I believe the sacred gold could restore his light. I must find it." The words tasted like prophecy on my tongue. This would allow more time to devise a plan to keep us safe until we could create some physical gold. It was simple now. My own clarity, decreed by Aten.

Ana-Kharu turned away, methodically replacing each jar in its velvet-lined place. "The monoatomic gold you seek is gone," he said without turning. "Drunk dry by those who knew its worth. Had I known the Pharaoh himself was in need..." He shrugged. "Perhaps on our return."

Suddenly—thunder. Not from the sky, but from earth: pounding hooves, churning wheels, voices barking orders in rapid succession. Dust clouds swelled like a storm as we raced to the window. The temple itself trembled—not from Ana-Kharu's voice, but from something heavier. The army had returned. Mahu's voice rang out like a war horn: "Bowmen—ready your weapons. Hold until I say!"

Twenty archers stormed in, arrows notched and drawn. Their arrival sealed every exit. The sound of marching feet. We heard the sinew strings being drawn back and saw arrows aimed at everyone in the room. We had nowhere to turn. The sun dipped low, casting golden fire across the floor as Pentu strode in, his silhouette ablaze with fury. The Pharaoh's physician—his golden ankh pectoral catching the last rays of Aten—stalked toward Ana-Kharu. "How *dare* you enter Akhet-Aten without permission from the Hand of Pharaoh!"

"Pentu—wait!" I rushed forward, my voice cracking. "I gave him leave. He is the teacher of alchemy. I summoned him!" My arms stretched between them like a shield.

Pentu thundered, "Why would *you* grant Neb-We-Shat entry?"

My blood turned cold. The title—Gold **Magician**. "Your father *forbade* the use of Magik! You know this." Then, quieter, more lethal—"You poor girl," he said, "Do you even know who this man *is*?"

My beloved doctor ignored me. "Ana-Kharu-We-Shat, you stand accused of High Treason and forbidden sorcery!" said Pentu, signaling the rounding up of this unlucky merchant and his quivering troupe. Anpu froze. The merchant's hands twitched. I could barely breathe. The golden jars—the teachings—the answers I craved—were now crimes.

er home was all hardwood grit and hand-me-down charm—red plaid pillows slouched on the couch, a too-fancy dining table and China cabinet and Persian rug from her father's Rome buying spree swallowing the room. It was lived-in, like her. Threadbare in places, but still standing.

Balancing a cup of tea, Morainya fumbled for her phone and nearly toppled Josh's senior project strewn across the dining room table. She gently nudged aside his intricate architectural model of a cathedral, mindful not to damage his craftsmanship. Sphinxy, her Egyptian hairless cat, had already tried to nest on it earlier. Morainya had shooed her away three times, but every time she closed the dining room door to keep the cat out, Sphinxy howled with theatrical betrayal.

"Hello, Miss Napolitano, this is Rachel from Accounts Receivable from Kanberg, Wallerstein and Katz. Are you there?"

"Yes, yes, hello, I'm here," said Morainya, her voice taut.

"You missed last month's payment. Your balance is $68,542. Mr. Kanberg insists you cover another retainer immediately."

Her stomach dropped. She was already a thousand short on the mortgage. Her mom's dementia care facility. Nothing was settled. And she was sinking. She adjusted the crooked cathedral spire Sphinxy had nudged askew.

"I'll try to send something soon," she managed.

"Try?" Rachel echoed flatly, her Texan drawl sharpening. Morainya imagined her at a grey cubicle, scanning a list of delinquent clients before her lunch break.

"I'm doing my best," Morainya said, her voice shrinking. A shiver curled through her ribs like a centipede. The floorboards creaked beneath socked feet, the whole house holding its breath like she was.

"Thank you. I'll let Mr. Kanberg, and the partners know," Rachel replied, already disengaged.

Morainya placed the phone down atop a mountain of paperwork cluttering the dark mahogany table her father had imported from Rome in the eighties. It belonged in a villa, not her modest ranch house with its scuffed oak floors and throw rugs. But she had kept it out of respect. That was the story of her life—holding onto legacy even when it didn't fit.

"Who was that?" Josh asked, foraging through the fridge, disappointed by its lack.

"The lawyer's office," she said, brushing crumbs from the counter.

"Is it about Grandpa's will? I could sure use a car," he added hopefully.

She gave a tight smile. Always money. Always need. "Once the case with your Uncle Aldo settles. Or if I take it to mediation. Either way, It's expensive."

"Uncle Aldo's a leech. Does he even work?"

She bit her tongue. Compassion didn't come easy for Aldo anymore.

"He had a rough start," she said. "Adopted into a big family."

Josh shrugged. "So was Dad's girlfriend. Doesn't mean we owe her."

Morainya blinked. That landed sharper than she expected.

"Can I borrow the car tomorrow?" Josh asked, already chewing cold pizza and swigging juice straight from the carton.

"I have a parent-teacher meeting. Need to pick up cookies. I can drop you at Joey's." Morainya changed the subject. "Hey, I have some work to do on Grandpa's House before we put it up for sale. Do you want to come with me this weekend? I could sure use an extra hand-packing boxes. Remember when we'd go to the Wharf and saw the sea lions. You loved that."

Josh's eyebrows raised, "Yeah, like when I was Ten." He sighed, letting her know that he was seven years older and uninterested in spending time with her.

He nodded, licking glaze off a doughnut. "Dad is flying me to Puerto Vallarta. He's bringing Jenny. Could you be nice to her tomorrow? I think Dad's serious."

She rolled her eyes. "What does a 50-year-old man have in common with a 28-year-old besides a Pilates ass and a credit card?"

"He's going for work. They rented him a condo," Josh said, not looking up.

"Take out the garbage," she snapped, suddenly clenching her hands. "It's overflowing."

"Sphincter, get down!" Josh swatted at the cat lunging for the model again. "Okay, chill. I'll do it."

Morainya leaned against the counter, rubbing her temples. She looked at the chaos of the dining table, the ticking bills, the split of divorce furniture, the silence that fell whenever she mentioned Aldo. There had to be a better way.

A quiet longing stirred beneath her ribs. For open land. For stillness. For soil. Maybe she wasn't meant to just win in courtrooms. Maybe she needed earth under her fingernails again.

Jedidah, her ex-husband, had changed jobs—and girlfriends, and he was running late on child support. Maybe she could hit up her brothers and sisters once again until this case settled, and she could access her inheritance. "I'm sorry, Josh, it's just that your Dad is late again and I'm pissed."

"Please don't start on Dad again." Josh was always the peacekeeper, and lately, he was clocking overtime. Jedidiah barely returned Morainya's calls anymore, turning her into a nagging shrew. Just another label she didn't deserve.

"Do you have to call her that? It's disgusting," she said, pulling Sphinxy into her lap for comfort. Josh rolled his eyes. "Oh—and Archbishop DeLaurentis' secretary called. Again."

Morainya's stomach clenched. She didn't even need to ask. "Let me guess. The fundraiser for St. Mary's Heart of the Bay?"

Josh shrugged, stuffing papers into his backpack, mouth still full of doughnut. "She also said the Archbishop wants you to go to confession. Add Jenny jealousy to your list of mortal sins."

"Cute," she muttered, brushing powdered sugar off his sweater. "They're not interested in my soul—they just want Grandpa's donation. Everyone does. And when was the last time you went to mass, huh? And don't sass me."

Josh tilted his head, dramatically. "You promised after I graduated Parochial High School, you'd never make me go back. I'm done with the sadistic nuns and their twisted punishments. One more ruler slap and I could have file a police report."

Morainya gave a tight smile. "Believe me, I've sat through enough conferences explaining your behavior. Just three more months, Josh. Make it through without another senior prank, and you're free."

She felt the flush rise—another hot flash—and fanned herself with a wrinkled bill from Kanberg & Katz. Josh leaned against the counter, grinning.

"Grandpa only picked that school 'cause he paid the tuition."

"Yeah. That too," she said quietly, knowing full well he never lived to pay the last year.

Josh looked just like his father. That same smirk, that too-cool lean. He was a good kid—sharp, kind—but the system seemed built to crush boys like him. Morainya often wondered if therapy could undo what years of religious rigidity had sewn into his psyche. She crossed herself. Questioning the Church still felt like blasphemy. Her mother would've been horrified.

But somewhere deep down, something else was whispering to her. A higher plan. A different kind of salvation.

A few nights later, just as she was kicking off her heels after work, her phone buzzed.

A message from Iben Fatah: *"Could we meet for dinner?"*

She blinked. Her pulse stirred. "I'll be back in San Franciso this Friday."

Iben had suggested a small Ethiopian café not far from the museum—a place he said reminded him of the lands before borders. Morainya hesitated, but something about the richness of his voice lingered when he called to ask her to dinner. The following Friday, she drove back to San Franciso and arrived at her mom's facility for a visit and to sign some papers for an extra night nurse to give her medications.

The café was dimly lit. Teal walls glowed under golden lanterns. Frankincense clung to the air. A soft drumming track played in the background—slow, hypnotic. They sat on floor cushions at a low table, sharing platters lined with injera and dotted with spiced lentils, greens, and warming stews.

"You eat with your right hand," he said, smiling. "It's how we honor the sacred current in the body." He unfolded a napkin onto his lap with ceremonial ease.

"This is delicious," she said, savoring a bite of stew then sipping the tea in a painted ceramic cup to hide her nerves. The day had already rattled her—lawyers, her mother's fleeting memory, and now... this. Him.

"Where did you grow up?" Morainya asked as she tucked her legs beneath her, warming her hands around the teacup.

Iben paused before answering—not out of hesitation, but like someone tracing a memory with care. "Mauritania," he said finally. "Near the Adrar plateau. Dry winds, honey-colored stone, long walks to school. My father was a surveyor—used to draw sacred lines into the desert sand and tell us the Earth remembers. My mother was a schoolteacher. Fierce in the best way. She ran the household like a small kingdom and still wrote poetry late into the night."

Morainya smiled. "Are you close with them?"

He nodded, but something flickered in his eyes—barely visible. "Yes. I'm the oldest. Four of us. Two brothers. One little sister."

She caught the shift. A slight tightening around his mouth, quickly buried. But she didn't press. "You?"

The waiter delivered za'atar bread still steaming from the oven. Iben broke off a piece and dipped it in the olive oil like it was a sacrament, then offered it to her without a word.

She hesitated. Then took it. "Four also. Two brothers, the youngest lives in Florence, the other lives here. My little sister broke away from the family after graduating. She leads mushroom journeys in Oregon and has a Kombucha business. We aren't close."

A quiet hum of understanding passed between them. Then she leaned forward slightly, fingertips brushing the rim of her plate. "You'll find this interesting. I went to the Archbishop's mansion for some family charity business. In his study, there was an exquisite, raised carving of that Pharaoh and his family. You know the one with the sun's rays behind them."

"Akhenaten?" asked Iben, his eyes widening, with a quizzical glance. "Why would he have a relic like that?"

Morainya took a sip of tea. "It was a gift. From the Pope. Hidden in the Vatican vaults."

Iben's lips were pursed, then said. "They steal from the Motherlands that which doesn't belong to them."

She lifted her finger to the air like an exclamation point, "Oh, and there was another thing, I can't remember the name of it but there was a spotlight on an old red orb sitting on a flattened pyramid."

"What kind of red?" he asked, too casually.

"Rusty red. Like old blood or iron. You think it's something?"

"Maybe some things aren't meant to be questioned," he said. But his fingers tapped lightly on the table—once, twice—like a code he hadn't meant to send.

Something fluttered inside her—like a feather brushing the edge of a bell. She reached for the hummus, grounding herself in motion, but the question pulsed beneath her ribcage: *What is this?* —friendship, fascination, or something meant to undo her carefully stitched seams? He was younger, sure, but that wasn't the real question? The real question was: why now? Why her? If friendship, she could file it under "pleasant" and move on, fit him in between court filings and memory care visits. But if it was something else—if this was the beginning of a deeper current—she'd need to do more than make space. She'd need to choose. To risk. American women were taught to forecast emotions like weather: Is this a passing cloud or a slow storm building? Tonight, in the hush between his words, she wasn't asking for love. Just clarity. A hint of intention. Something she could quietly rearrange her life around—if it was real.

Morainya ate a bite or two quietly as if consumed by her thoughts.

He brought her mind back to the present by asking, "You were saying on the phone that you've had a busy week." He filled her half empty cup with more steaming mint tea.

She touched her cheek, her head resting upon her palm. "I've been in counter depositions, bill disputes, navigating my mother's dementia...exhaustion. It's like everyone's fighting over something dead. I hate the legal system." Her eyes searching his, aching for something—warmth, steadiness, anything to still the quiet fear in her chest.

"Isn't that what courts are for?" he asked softly. "Managing the ghosts."

She tilted her head, surprised. "Ghosts. Exactly. Everybody wants to take from the departed. And I have to be the voice of the living."

He leaned back, fingers steepled lightly. The silence between them deepened, not empty but charged with meaning.

"Come to the Preview of the Moors exhibit tonight," he said finally. "There's something there I think you need to see—especially after the week you've had. It's not about history, Morainya. It's about stolen identity, restitution... and what still lives under the ash."

After the meal they walked back to the Black History Museum for his latest installation. When they entered through the back door. A group of people were gathered around a small Reception table serving small pastries, coffee, and tea.

Iben pointed upward to the second floor. The stairs creaked softly under Morainya's heels as she ascended up the flight. The lighting dimmed with each step, like descending into memory instead of rising through architecture. At the landing, they entered a room quieter than the rest of the museum—no overhead projections, no bustling holograms. Just silence and warmth.

Amber lights glowed low from sconces carved into reclaimed cedar, each one marked with hand-burned symbols from various tribes. The scent of sandalwood and old paper lingered in the air. In the center of the room stood a wide circular table made of dark acacia wood, its rim etched with Arabic script and Iroquois glyphs inlaid with copper. At its center, beneath curved glass, lay the replicated **Second Constitution of the United States**—the document itself aglow with a subtle reddish shimmer.

Along the walls, framed maps, ancestral photos, and hand-inked trade agreements created a solemn patchwork. This wasn't a place for entertainment. It was a room for witness. Morainya's breath slowed as she stepped forward.

A low chime sounded. Not the high-pitched ping of modern AI, but something gentler—a ceremonial bell tone, like a Tibetan singing bowl struck once. Then, from the shadows, a voice emerged—not mechanical, but textured and grounded, like the echo of an elder across canyon stone.

AI VOICE: *"Welcome. You are now entering the Hall of Hidden Articles. Please hold still while we recognize your frequency."*

A soft pulse passed through her body—barely a vibration, more like a hush.

AI VOICE*: "Recognition confirmed. Morainya Napolitano, daughter of land and law. We invite you to listen with your blood."*

She turned to Iben and whispered, "That is amazing."

The document beneath the glass brightened slightly. The words **"We The People"** at the top shimmered—not with digital animation, but with something more visceral. The handwritten text inked in red seemed to breathe.

AI activated an image of the Data Oracle from earlier a carefully recorded rendering, now projected onto a curved panel at the far end. She appeared as a lifelike image, clothed in indigo robes with Moorish embroidery, standing beneath an Iroquois Tree of Peace etched in gold behind her.

Data Oracle voice: "Please look at The Second Constitution of the United States over there," her voice reverent, purposeful. "This is only a replica, but the original was written by the Afrakan Moors—in Arabic—translated from the Iroquois Constitution. Notice the color of the 'We The People' at the top..."

Iben motioned Morainya closer. She moved, not by curiosity, but by gravity.

AI Data Oracle: Notice the color of the *We the People* heading. This line was written in a slave's blood. Not just any slave—Crispin Atticus, a Moor, one of the chiefs of the indigenous people on the land. He was one of the first to die in the American Revolution They say he was sacrificed, not shot. His blood used to sanctify the binding of a contract—not with the people—but against them."

The story was that he was sacrificed so they could enforce the Bible, as the blood of the righteous shall not be spilled in vain, so it had to have a purpose.

"The Continental Congress," The **AI Data Oracle** said in a low voice, "was infiltrated and overthrown. The Iroquois Constitution was copied as the new American Constitution. The contract sealed in blood. And every Chief who could have closed the contract to throw the infiltrators off the land—murdered."

Iben exhaled. Under his breath, just one word *"conjure."*

Not metaphor. Magical Binding.

Something knotted in Morainya's chest. She stood frozen. The air around her thickened. She wasn't just listening, she stared at *We The People* –letters etched in blood, not ink. No one ever taught this in school.

Behind her, a motion sensor triggered another quiet response from the AI. A map unfolded into view on the wall: from Africa to Turtle Island, marked with trails of light where Moorish ships had reached native shores long before the Mayflower. Then the Conquistadors landed, imposters who took on Indigenous roles and impersonated Chief's to sign contracts for great masses of land in exchange for beads, or guns. An insult to the Indigenous culture who held the strong belief that land was not for sale and could not be owned.

Morainya's throat tightened. She glanced at Iben to gage his reaction. He was stoic as he held onto the glass case, maybe a little too tightly. He leaned near her ear and whispered, "You asked for truth. You just didn't know it would cost you your worldview."

She looked down at the etched copper words beneath the replica, as though they might explain what the courtrooms never could. She reached out—just hovered her hand above the glass—and in that moment, the script across the base of the case was highlighted:

AI VOICE: *"That which is written in blood lives until it is named. Speak, and the contract may remember."*

A silence fell, as if the entire museum inhaled—waiting for her to say something that could crack history open. Morainya staggered back, her mind reeling. Noses hacked off statues to sever heritage? A Constitution inscribed in sacrifice? The floor beneath her seemed to tilt. She blinked hard, trying to absorb it. It wasn't just a shock—it was betrayal. A lie so loud it had been piped through classrooms and textbooks for decades. She felt heat rise to her cheeks. Could the entire narrative have been whitewashed? Her own education suddenly felt like a rigged performance. She needed air and headed toward the exit, her fingers tugging at the collar of her sweater. It clung too tightly now—like the false history pressed against her skin.

"Morainya," came Iben's voice behind her, low and steady. "Leaving already?" There was a softness in his tone, but something in it stopped her. She turned. His hand was outstretched, not insistently—more like an invitation.

"There's something else I want to show you," he said. "Fifteen minutes. No more. But it might help you make sense of all this."

Her body wanted to decline, to find the freeway and disappear into autopilot. She was already frayed—wrung out by the deposition, haunted by her mother's slipping mind, and now this: truths that cracked the spine of every textbook she'd ever trusted. It was all too much. The system she once upheld felt like a crumbling façade, and the weight of unlearning pressed harder than anything she'd cross-examined in court. Run. Go find the freeway and disappear into autopilot, she told herself.

But something in his eyes—unrushed, unthreatening—felt like the opposite of every man who had ever demanded something from her. She gave a slow nod.

They walked side by side. The second floor was hushed, almost cloistered. No foot traffic. No ambient buzz. Just the thick silence of something sacred. He opened a door ahead of her and stepped aside. The room was dark. Entirely dark. Not even the glow of a screen.

Morainya froze. Her instincts flared, every cell alert. He must have sensed it, because he didn't enter.

"I should have warned you," he said gently. "This space is used for contemplation. It's a sacred room. I promise you—there's nothing here but two chairs and silence. I'll go first."

He stepped in and flipped on a soft amber bulb just long enough for her to see: two chairs. A low table. No hidden corners. No threat.

Then he turned the light off again.

"You're safe, Morainya," he said quietly. "And if at any point you wish to leave, the door will remain open."

She hesitated, then stepped inside. Her eyes adjusted slowly. The dark wrapped around her like velvet. Not threatening... just deep. She sat, the cushion sighing beneath her.

"You've had too much light today," Iben murmured. "Too much exposure. But darkness is the safest place of all." The soul burns under that kind of glare. I wanted you to have a moment to return to the dark."

How could she know his ancient customs? Morainya tensed. Her neck muscles and shoulders became like iron. She certainly didn't wish to upset her host or be accusatory, but he would have to be nuts if he didn't know this was unacceptable in her land. Why would he want her to be afraid?

"When we are in total darkness, we are in the realm of God. I want you to feel that within you. We are in a world that is constantly being lit up to keep us from this realm. If I only have this moment to share with you, I want you to feel God. If only for a temporal moment before you steer your way through this honking city."

She took another bite and contemplated those words. God is in the darkness?

"From the moment of conception, you knew only darkness—the sacred cradle of creation. It is the safest place, the place of origin," he intoned with quiet conviction.

She nodded, taking in his words.

"Your Christian religions tell you to go to the Light. To be in the Light. Do you really think this is true when the hierarchies spent millions of dollars to teach you a lie, this New-Age slogan? God resides in the void. In darkness. Not just darkness but triple darkness. God's darkness is three stages darker than you have ever experienced."

"God is in darkness?" she asked, barely above a whisper.

"Yes. To origin. You were born in darkness. Formed in triple shadow. The womb is not bright. It's the holiest dark there is."

"But we are told in Church to go to the light," her voice hardened and her body tensed.

The Light isn't always truth," he said. "Sometimes it's distraction. Illusion. A thousand watt current to keep you from stillness. From hearing yourself."

She sat in silence, letting his words bloom inside her.

Who was this man? She'd barely recovered from eight hours of legal warfare, planned on nothing more than tea and silence—and now here she was, breathless in the dark, her academic credentials cracking like old plaster. She had never counted on being assailed for eight hours of a deposition, then settling down for a quiet dinner alone only to meet this foreigner and then end up having her university minor turned upside down.

"We cut off the light just now," he murmured. "And in that absence... we become everything. No walls, no names— just center. And in the center of all things, God waits. We will become boundless. We will be in the center of the mul- tiverse. God is in the center of all things, so we are both in the center of God. Wherever we are, God is within us. I will be silent now if that is alright."

She nodded her head and closed her eyes. Within a breath of God, she felt as if she was floating, throwing off the yoke of the burdens that weighed heavy upon her. One breath—just one—and her body began to lighten, as if her bones remembered how to rise without effort. The weight she carried every day—docket schedules, grief, courtroom residue—slipped like fabric from her shoulders.

She drew in air like it was something sacred—like her lungs were temples, not evidence bags—and something inside her loosened. Not relief, not sleep...peace. The kind that doesn't ask questions. Time dissolved. When he finally turned on a soft desk light, the glow met her gently—like it, too, knew not to shatter the spell. She blinked, returning to gravity with reluctance. "It is almost time for you to depart. May I give you a blessing?"

"Yes," she said, trying to shake off that eternal bliss. She didn't want to tense up again and struggled not to worry. If her father had been alive, he never would have approved of this scenario.

"You now walk beneath the covering of a god," Iben declared. "This blessing shields you—may it guide your steps."

Her head was spinning. Her body throbbed. She won- dered if that was a big G, God or little g. Surely, he was kidding. Reflex took over—hand to brow, chest, shoulders—crossing herself with the same muscle memory that once comforted her as a child. "Father, Son, and Holy Ghost, Amen."

9

*T*he chariot rattled over the barren land, the silence between Pentu and me more jarring than the ride itself. He had locked his words away, just as Ana-Kharu locked away his secrets. Pentu's silence hit harder than the desert wind. I clung to his waist, feeling the stiffness in his frame, the quiet accusations in the way he snapped the reins. He didn't need words to scold me—his body spoke in tension and tight-lipped betrayal.

We pulled up in a sharp halt in front of the white-washed palace, and Pentu yelled "Whoa," to the pair of midnight black horses with red ostrich feather plumes upon their heads. They stomped in place aggressively, whinnying, and throwing their heads as if they mirrored Pentu's agitation and inner turmoil. He was able to calm them and handed the worn leather reins to a sleepy attendant.

He motioned me forward with a sharp flick of his wrist, scanning the courtyard with hawk-like precision. Only when he was certain we were alone did he speak. His fingers scratched the angry scar carved into his scalp—an unconscious ritual he returned to when agitated. I knew that look. He was already rehearsing my condemnation of entertaining Ana-Kharu.

The Doctor chose his words as meticulously as the Chef who selects the choicest cuts of meat. "Merit-Aten," Pentu snapped, his voice low but heavy with betrayal. "Do you know what you have done? I have raised you, watched over you, protected you when your father was too consumed with governance. And yet—you let him in? A liar, a fraud? Into our most sacred spaces? I simply must tell your father. It would be unethical to keep these injurious actions on your part, to myself. If I did not reveal everything, your father would flog me."

"Pentu, you are most beloved by Pharaoh. I know that he would never flog you. He would never raise a hand to you, even if you confessed to toppling a statue." I searched his eyes, hoping to find calm.

Pentu shook his head with a dry, almost pitying smile. "You misunderstand, child," his voice edged with weariness. "It is not the whip I fear—it is the lie." He placed a shaky hand upon my shoulder, steadying his words. "I will not hide your act of betrayal and indiscretion from the Pharaoh." Again, weighing his words like coins of gold with what the law said versus what his heart would tell him was right. Hoping his heart would be as light as the feather of Ma'at, Justice, in making a judgment of me, I prayed that I could calm him before he rushed to my father. Pentu would spill venomous words about Ana-Kharu to persuade my father of the severity of this crime.

My mind scrambled for distraction, a thread of conversation that could slow his march to judgment. "Pentu, before we lay my case before the Pharaoh, could you tell me if my father was pleased with his trip? Did he have success procuring gold from our family in Akshum? I have been worried sick about him so that my hands are wrung as dry as a linen dish towel." I besieged him with my pleadings.

He stared at the ground and grimaced. "We never made it to Akshum," Pentu admitted his voice heavy with guilt.

"Your father was too weak. We staged everything—set up tents, hired musicians, even faked an ambush so he would turn back. It was the only way."

I stumbled backward as if receiving a terrible blow. They had been gone for two fortnights. How could Pentu keep a deception going for such a long time?

He watched me carefully, weighing each twitch of my brow like a judge measuring guilt.

"Pharaohs of old were required to traverse this great land accompanied by their army on campaigns so the multitudes could honor the presence of a living god upon this plane. Your father's rule is drastically different. We have no great armies. No Royal barge at our disposal. Yet, when his Majesty commands us to depart—we obey.

Pentu scratched his reddened scar on his head reminding me of the fires set upon his village by the Hittites, which decimated his young life. "Sometimes, I question how we have come so far to lose so much." He turned to me, his internal anguish twisting his once calm demeanor. "What was he thinking? It would also be impossible for us to descend unannounced upon the closest town."

I stayed silent as these questions were not for me to answer, but his own argument with inner demons. His measured tone sounded false. "Could you imagine what chaos would result if villagers had not prepared a welcome for their Pharaoh? Why they would be ashamed and accused of disrespect for not having proper provisions, housing, and stalls ready for the King and his military. Would you want your father to sleep in a manger?"

My mind whirled, desperate to comprehend what secret Pentu withheld. My father's coughing fits were well known,

We all knew how delicate his health was. "Of course not, Pentu. But did you get the gold my father sought?"

My hopes were so high of any news that would allay my anguish over the problems that hung like soggy limp curtains in an open window after a heavy rain.

Pentu's face awash with a pained expression. He seemed to have aged, worn lines from worry etched his once smooth face. "Mahu and I wove a mirage," Pentu admitted. "We staged a journey grand enough to please the King, without ever truly leaving our doorstep." He sighed, whether from the dilemma ahead of the exhaustion of his trip was not clear. "You simply may not shatter the illusion that we created." He pointed a finger at me threateningly.

I glared at him and felt my palms sweat. "But you have been away for two fortnights. Where did you go?" I chewed my lip and my head ached with a painful pulse.

"Nowhere."

I grasped his arm, "Are you telling me that you just drove in circles?"

"What else could we do?" Pentu declared. He patted my hand like he did when I was a child. "We are in peaceful times. Households have acquired more luxury goods and would therefore be able to hold festivals for his arrival. To dim his expectations of great celebrations ahead. The Head of Security informed the Pharaoh that he could be the target of any mercenary army the Amunites had dispatched. We simply must keep him hidden to not alert any village town on the payroll of the Amun priests. Pharaoh agreed and kept out of sight. Fortunately, he was also denied any visual access to where we went."

My molars ground against each other. A storm gathered behind my eyes. "You never informed him?" I asked, my voice rising with suspicion.

Pentu shook his head and wrung his hands. "I could not—would not destroy what little joy there is in his life."

My voice became urgent and strained. "How did you get him to come home without the gold?"

Pentu shook his head as he unveiled a master plan. "Mahu ordered his guards to move up unto the towering cliffs and shoot a round of arrows, of course, missing us so as to not cause damage or injury. With the ruckus, your father saw the fallibility of his plan and ordered us to return to the safety of Akhet-Aten."

My hands flew to my face imagining Pharaoh's chagrin. "That is simply horrible. Horrible for father. Horrible that he returned empty-handed. He must feel quite forlorn. But Pentu, I know you were trying to protect him, but I cannot believe how you deceived him."

"The travel took its toll upon your father's health just as I foresaw. Conditions for a trek along dusty passageways caused him to cough because of his weak lungs. He grew fevered one night because the sustenance was not to his liking; he is vegetarian, and we could not pack fresh vege-tables for a ride in the heat. We had no chef preparing his meals. Soldiers eat salted fish and hard bread."

"He is unaccustomed to not having things to his liking," I admitted.

Pentu took my words as agreement.

"At night, I administered sleep remedies that lulled him into a drowsy condition to even make this journey bearable. While it angers me to use my skills in such a cunning way, we decided that for his own well-being. The Pharaoh ordered us to undertake this trip with only two day's notice. I am not permitted to say no. It was imperative to convince him that he would never wish to undertake an arduous journey again in his life. Beloved, I feel in my heart we did the right thing to save him. I love him with all my heart, and I swore to protect him."

A knot twisted in my gut, nausea of the soul. My voice cracked under the weight of dread. "No gold. How are we going to feed people? Was that not the entire purpose of this trip? He believed he could rely on the kindness of our family to replenish our resources."

Pentu gazed at me with agony written across his face. "Beloved, no matter how much gold Ti-Yee's family could offer. It would be a pittance of what we need to secure this city. Akhet-Aten has indeed been cut off by the Amunites, and shunned from ever being as prosperous as we were in Thebes. Tradespeople and servants only come when they see growth and prosperity in a bustling city. People have left in droves in search of sustenance elsewhere. Our workers are dying younger from anemia. Their bones are as brittle as fall leaves."

My insides turned cold. I had been dancing through a dream while the walls around us crumbled. My father's kingdom—our kingdom—was starving, crumbling from within, while I held onto a dream of fixing it with alchemy and prayers. I was clinging to a Hoopoes nest in a wind-swept acacia tree. How daft was it that I never fully over-stood the desperation my father and Pentu felt? We were exiled. To my surprise, Mahu had remained loyal to the

Aten. He was most worshipful and felt the power of the Holy Spirit upon him.

Pentu's sheath, while usually pristine white, was covered in a dusty grime. His face had the mark of a long trip devoid of enough water for baths. That was proof of his dedication to the Pharaoh. Pentu had to forego his earthly needs in devotion to the higher forces.

Staring at the ground, I kicked my sandaled foot at the tile, feeling the words flee my head like an empty songbird's cage. "What do we do?"

"We must commence by telling your father about Ana-Kharu-We-Shat. He will need to know why you would allow the hoaxer to enter," Pentu was unapologetic. He was determined to uphold the law of no magick upon these hallowed halls.

"I had broken the rule etched into me since childhood—my father's law against all forms of magick. He had made it clear that no magick was acceptable. Heka was not tolerable out of the concern that a demon would be conjured and hexed all that we had built. Although Ana-Kharu had shown no disrespect—well, there was the time with the Mandrake root, and of course when he spit upon the ground and accused us of being spineless, spoiled children. Must I disclose that? Did the swings count as magick? The rug had been yanked from beneath me, and I was freefalling with no cushion to break the descent.

Ana-Kharu had summoned the forces of nature surrounding us to embellish his story of why I needed him. Was I that easily mesmerized? I dug my nails into my skin to remind myself not to fall prey to sweet talkers. So half-witted was I when it was right before my face.

Pentu and I arrived at father's guarded closed door, and he spoke in a hushed tone. "Lest I remind you that your father is weak. I have laid him to rest. If he wakes, we'll speak the truth—but be warned, it may undo him. This merchant is famous for luring in his clients by enchanting them with music and other enticements. Merit-Aten, if harm had come to you while I was tending the king, I would never have forgiven myself," his voice was urgent, and laced with paternal caring. He turned and hugged me tightly, imagining some terrible situation that could have befallen me. Well, maybe some of it did, but I didn't want to overwhelm my father with the dirty details.

"Pentu, we both must prepare to confess to the Pharaoh. We have both deceived him. Let us face our reckoning side by side." This time I patted Pentu's sleeve to ease the fate before us.

Pentu straightened himself, staring down at me. "Merit-Aten, what I did was to save your father from his foolhardy dream. There was no way he could travel across Khemit without drawing suspicion. We all could have been slain. You know how stubborn he is when he believes that he is following the word of the Aten." Pentu shook his finger at me, trying hard to convince me that his plan was somehow different than mine.

"How would this be dissimilar? I, too, was trying to save my father and my kingdom from ruin. Father told us a teacher of alchemy would arrive with the next level of initiations. It has been nearly a year since we have had instruction. Ana-Kharu-We-Shat appears and proclaims to be that teacher. How could I possibly know that he was a fraud? He came bearing gold, tinctures, and strange elixirs—are those not the signatures of alchemy?" Pentu smirked. "I see the road you are taking, and perhaps—just perhaps, you have a point. Yes, alchemical, indeed—but I will wager he also packed aphrodisiacs and poisons for good measure."

"Still alchemy," we echoed, reluctant but amused, recognizing that the Gold Magician had some skills.

"I can see where he entrapped you and your class. Of course, you all would innocently allow someone who dressed like a magician and brought with him luxury goods to entice you. Yes, I concur that you could not possibly have known that your father would never invite a hoaxer into his kingdom. Did he ride in on a water ox?" Pentu chucked me under the chin.

"No—an enormous elephant, its hide cloaked in gold-draped splendor."

Pentu belly laughed. "Why, he is no bigger than a string bean? I remember him when he arrived late one night at Heliopolis requesting entrance to the exterior gates, yet he had no passwords, no Letters of Confirmation, but he was convinced that because he had a rudimentary knowledge of alchemy, he should be allowed to speak directly with the High Priest. We watched him in that magician's conical hat, which typically suggests wisdom and high attainment. Ana-Kharu stomped and demanded that he be admitted and allowed to receive the proper certification to enter the quarries to obtain only the purest white gold used in alchemical transformations. Why, we had to go through years and years of study and experimentation in order to qualify for those certificates?

Gasping loudly, Ana-Kharu hadn't disclosed the whole truth either. "He did tell us he went to Heliopolis." Pentu continued, "Naturally, the Twamen tribe had a lineage that must be respected for attaining knowledge derived from their ancient ancestors. We have no quarrel with that high attunement. But to think he could barge in with bags of gold and bargain with the Orama, the Highest Priest in the Heliopolitan line, they simply sniggered and shooed him away like a pesky moth attracted to a golden flame.

"The Twamen should be honored," I said, "But this was presumptuous."

"He had no evidence that he had achieved mastery over all the levels of initiation that would make him a candidate to receive the certification of permission stamps honored by any Khemitian quarry. By whatever means he had achieved in obtaining the elemental gold, the simplest alchemical gold, he never produced any monoatomic solarized gold. He therefore was not a Master Alchemist, but nothing more than a gold magician, a Neb-We-Shat."

"Should we go in and tell Father now? I am ready to confess." I said softly, my gaze rising to Pentu with the tremble of a chastened kitten."

My Physician put his hand on the doorway halting my way. "It is late. Your father may be asleep. If you would like give him your evening salutations, he would probably receive them."

The guards allowed our passing and upon entering my father's sleeping quarters, he lay propped against linen cushions, his breath shallow, lungs still laboring. A light linen coverlet was pulled up under his chin, and he had scrolls near an oil lamp so that he could study when he had the strength. Myrrh and Frankincense spiked the air,

Pentu used the oils on Father's chest along with camphor to alleviate the phlegm.

Father's red-ringed eyes turned toward me with tender recognition, "Greetings, Beloved, we are home now, and I am gladdened to be in the comfort of my own bed once more," he coughed and cleared his throat. I was startled to see that he had lost weight. His collar bones clearly protruded. "I am sure Pentu relayed all the gloomy details of our journey. We were at last defeated by archers perched upon cliffs, forcing us to retreat. I think I have had enough adventure for this lifetime."

The Pharaoh lay listlessly in bed, and I felt guilty coaxing what little pep he had left to be used in conversation. Perspiration glistened on his face. Pentu gently wiped it away. Our trip was as futile as saving a flame on a rainy night. His ribcage rose and fell with each labored breath. My Father was wasting away.

I steadied my voice. "Yes, I am sorry you could not procure a gold allotment. It weighs on your heart to not have enough food in the mouths of our people, who serve the Aten." Cautiously, I leaned in and kissed his sunken cheek.

"People are dying, Beloved. It grieves me that our enemies may soon be at our doorstep. If there was only a way for me to regain my higher connection, then a solution would avail itself."

"What do you need to do, father? Do you need help getting to the temple? We can arrange for a palanquin." I pointed toward the temple, thinking a night of contemplative prayer would cheer him.

Pentu cleared his throat and motioned me with a sharp nod.

"No, Beloved. Like all Pharaohs and Per Aats, we continue our connection to the Cosmos through the ingestion of monoatomic gold. We lack the ingredients to create it. That is verily why we went in search of the true alchemists who create these special concoctions."

"Are you seeking ingestible gold? I might hold the answer." Suddenly, I felt giddy. The answer was at hand. The Gold Magician may have indeed been sent by Aten to save my father.

"What solution could you offer me, Beloved? These ingredients are rare. Other than asking the Heliopolitan High Priest for the sacred ore, I am at a loss. Even Pentu has no solution. I discovered that it could be fatal to travel. Any Heliopolitan Alchemist would be in jeopardy before he arrived. My health is fading, Beloved." He took my hand and kissed it.

My hands curled into fists. Tell him. "Father...there is something I must confess."

His tired eyes met mine, waiting.

I swallowed hard. "While you were away...a visitor came."

His eyes narrowed. "A visitor?"

"Ana-Kharu-We-Shat."

The Pharaoh's eyes darted to Pentu, shadowed with sudden alarm. "That charlatan has come through these parts before. Nothing he had has been of any interest. Your Meti found him to be a source of amusement. So, I tolerated his intrusion."

"Father, he brought ingestible gold."

Pharaoh stopped motionless. Then, after a beat, murmured, "Is that so?"

"I saw with my own eyes that he had red cinnabar and several other white powders."

Pentu chimed in, "Your Majesty, the cinnabar, and the Mercury Sulfide. It may not be enough for the transmutation into monoatomic gold, but maybe I could create the red potion."

Pharaoh simply replied. "I must ponder this. Bring him to me tomorrow. Thank you, Daughter. Perhaps this is the solution to our problem."

Pentu and I locked eyes. Perhaps my mistake had not doomed us after all. Perhaps Ana-Kharu's arrival was not a curse, but a test. But as I watched my father's weary face, I could not shake the feeling that a storm was coming—one that gold, nor prayers, nor alchemy could solve. I allowed the second portion of Pentu's confession to fade like dust blown from a summer rug.

orainya blinked into the harsh light that cracked through the blinds like an uninvited thought. *She hadn't meant to sleep in. Her mind snapped to the calendar—Lunch with Iben*

Her bedroom, painted rose pink with white trim, softened the sterile edges of what used to be Jedidiah's world— Tech sleek, all angles and minimalism, back in their San Franciscan condo. Gone was the oversized California King with its custom leather headboard. She'd chosen scrolled oak now, draped in chintz florals—a bed that breathed, not boasted.

She stretched and lazily, she got out of bed, showered then slipped on a coral and brown sundress, sandals and pulled her hair back and clipped it. Light makeup, not too much, just enough to accentuate her eyes and lips.

There were some errands in town, pick up Josh's prescription, return a garden hose, and pretend like her life wasn't unraveling at the seams. By 11:30, she had made it over the hill and pulled into the parking lot of the Los Gatos Hideaway. She always loved cats. The symbolism wasn't lost on her that the Spanish translation meant *The Cats Hideaway*. Independent. Wild. Not easily caged. And the drive? Nearly empty. Not a single snarl of traffic. It was as if some unseen hand had carved a path through the embankments and ushered her through a corridor of time.

She didn't believe in coincidence anymore—not after last night.

Morainya killed the engine. The ticking sound under the hood echoed louder than it should have. She sat there, staring at the gold-rimmed entrance. Her stomach fluttered, and she clutched the steering wheel. Morainya used to valet at places like this.

Back when she was still Morainya Napolitano Sanders of Napolitano Interiors—Head of Textiles & Upholstery Division, twelve clients on rotation, and a company car with seat warmers. Back when she had earned a hefty salary and perks, and had a partner with Tech prestige and a bank account to match. Back when Jedidiah was still hustling startup capital, she'd signed the prenup to protect herself—but it ended up protecting him.

After Morainya and Jedidiah sold the condo. His tech startup folded quietly—the way expensive things sometimes do—no drama, just silence and unpaid invoices. The firm's bankruptcy kept the title and the profits —neither of their names had ever been on the deed though they'd lived there like it was theirs. The lifestyle—the clinking glasses and couples' vacations in Napa and Lake Cuomo—were gone. And what was left? A broken marriage, a bank account in limbo, and a half-frozen inheritance she now had to *fight* to access—just to keep from falling through the cracks completely.

Now she was in a Honda Prelude—and praying the pizza wouldn't make her late on her mortgage. When she saw the black Mercedes pull in beside her, her stomach turned—not out of jealousy, but grief. Grief for the woman she used to be.

She caught her reflection in the rearview mirror. Her eyes looked like they'd seen too much. What am I doing here? she thought. *Meeting a man who's ten years younger and wasn't Catholic.* And yet... some small ember still glowed.

Reapplying her coral MAC lipstick, she then checked her hair, and paused—why was she nervous? It wasn't just about attraction. It was the unsettling sense that her life was already rearranging itself around this man.

Iben stepped out—dressed in tailored gray pants and a white sweater, not a Throbe in sight. She wasn't sure why that surprised her, but it did. He waved to her.

Maybe once her inheritance came in, she too could upgrade and hand Josh her Honda keys. Gallantly, he opened her door, allowing Morainya to exit the vehicle and escort her through the restaurant's stained-glass doors. Her mid-length sundress floated behind her in the spring breeze.

"Grand Rising, Queen," said Iben, "Are you ready for our next adventure?" he asked casually.

Morainya's breath hitched. Just the sound of his voice sent a tingle down her spine. She couldn't look at him right away—not after what she felt last night. The bath had started out like any other, but the heat hadn't come from the water. It had come from somewhere deeper, somewhere sacred. Her body had pulsed with a presence she couldn't explain, a slow unraveling that left her breathless and utterly exposed.

And now here he was. Cool. Collected. As if he hadn't just initiated something ancient and electric inside her. She smoothed her sundress, trying to gather herself. "I... guess that depends," she said, meeting his eyes. "Is this adventure anything like last night."

Iben only offered a smile. No words—but the pulse between them was electric sending ripples down her spine.

The hostess ushered them to a hidden table for two surrounded by lush palm trees. It was as if they entered their own private oasis. Again, the feelings of uncertainty swept over her as she thought about their ten-year age difference, nationality, religious upbringing, so much more confusion welled up. Why me, she thought belittling herself for why he'd never find her attractive. Although she found him utterly enchanting, he certainly wasn't her typical choice for a dating partner. It was hard to believe someone like him could be drawn to someone like her—a middle-aged white woman with fading status, modest means, and little to offer a man of such mystery... except maybe a green card. The thought stung. Maybe that's what this was all about. She reminded herself to be on guard. Still, her eyes drank in the beauty of his chiseled jaw, kind eyes and warm smile.

Morainya felt unprepared for what lay ahead. Yet, she also felt intrigued because this was being presented to her like an outstretched hand that could lift her up from her depths of despair.

She stuttered, trying to get the words out. "It's just that, uh,"

"You didn't know this was possible?" he turned as the waitress greeted them.

Iben glanced up just as the waitress arrived. He offered a brief, knowing smile and nodded to her, letting the moment pause until they had placed their order. Then he turned back to Morainya, calm and precise. "This is only the beginning, Queen.

My Elders—have called in the goddess vibe for you. Not just for your healing, but for the grid itself. And I... I've been chosen to carry that frequency to you."

She blinked. "The goddess vibe? From your ancestors?" She shifted her weight, recrossing her legs.

"Exactly. And before you think it's a Marvel plot twist, let me say this—this isn't myth. This is math. Sacred geometry. Our connection is by design."

She looked down at the table, her fingers brushing the linen edge. "But why me?"

He leaned in slightly, voice low but rich. "Because you're ready. And because they've watched you walk through the fire alone long enough."

Morainya tried to laugh, but it caught in her throat. "I mean, I'm a divorced woman with a messy history and no special gifts. The only goddess vibe I've had lately was keeping my tomato plants alive."

Iben smiled with a warmth that undid something in her chest. "Queen, you underestimate yourself. The goddess doesn't always wear crystals and dance barefoot. Sometimes she just survives long enough to remember she was divine all along."

She stared at him, the heat rising in her cheeks.

"And you feel it too," he added, softer now. "This... us. It's not random. The reason you're sitting here instead of swiping through strangers is because you already know."

She nodded slowly. "I don't know what this is yet..." Her throat felt dry.

"You don't have to. Just feel it. Queen, you need to stop thinking so much. Just enjoy it. When the universe picks you, you will be tested. Know that all I do is ordained, as it is the God within me as it should be in you."

Morainya's face constricted and her heart raced, suddenly feeling disoriented as she asked, "The God Yahweh? Like in the Bible?" She was reaching for something familiar—some shared language between her Catholic roots and whatever this man carried.

Iben placed his hands upon his knees. "It is beyond all that you have been taught. Beyond dogma. When the universe decrees it, I will open you—but I will require something in return."

Morainya winced. *Here it comes—the green card request,* she thought. She grabbed the tablecloth that dripped over the edge of the table. "And what is that?"

His face was unfazed by her tone. "I will require spiritualgasms."

Her breath caught. "What?"

His dark eyes gleamed. "A spiritual orgasm. The merging of energy. The surge that ignites the soul. You have already felt it last night in the bathtub. Just a touch."

Morainya blushed. It was one thing to experience it and quite another to talk about having erotic pulses sent from a partner who didn't even need to be in the physical.

His coffee-colored eyes told her that he was conscious and intensious about his actions last night. There was to be no escape. It was like he knew everything she was thinking and feeling. "Queen Goddess," he said, his tone soft but resolute. "We have been paired for the journey ahead. You can question it all you want. You can run away, but the universe will always bring you back. Quit your struggle and be obedient to the God within. Feel the Ohms and Vibes of the world and embrace it." Iben had a delivery style as smooth as jazz.

"How do I do that?" asked Morainya, her voice trembling, her right knee shaking. She wasn't flirting. She meant it. She *needed* to know.

"Feel me. Your energy feeds the God in me."

And suddenly, she *did* feel him. Morainya could feel her legs being separated underneath the table—not by will, but by a subtle force. Invisible. Warm. Intentional. Iben hadn't moved. Electricity poured in through the top of her head, and her eyes fluttered. She struggled to snap her legs shut and smooth her skirt down as a shield to this probing energy, yet he felt so familiar that she relaxed.

"Do you feel it?" He murmured leaning closer he asked, scooting his chair near hers. They were in the secluded part of the restaurant and would be unseen. She held her breath and nodded.

"The pulse beneath your skin, the rhythm of your breath. May I...touch the source?"

Morainya sensed that what came next was agreed upon. He placed both hands upon her left thigh. Morainya couldn't describe it, but it felt totally natural that this man she had only recently met touched her so intimately. He prayed silently and then, withdrew his hands and as if by magic, her hands clasped together prayerfully in her lap. It was as if he penetrated her to her very core. Soon, she would find out what exactly that meant.

Her thighs still ached from yesterday's lunch with Iben. That was the strange part—not touch, not weight, but light. It had entered her like heat through a keyhole, and now, later, her skin remembered. Her body hummed with some unspeakable afterglow as she turned onto the familiar street, still unsure if last night had happened in dream, spirit... or something entirely new.

Morainya checked the time and pressed harder on the gas, weaving through the neighborhood with one hope— making it home before dinner went cold. A pizza balanced on the Honda Prelude seat beside her, still warm. Josh rarely texted ahead anymore—teenage independence arriv-ing like a slow fade-out. His teenage schedule didn't often include letting her know his plans. At least she could make their usual Wednesday Pizza night. The moment her key turned on the weathered lock of the 1962 Ranch style home, she called out, "Hey Josh, I'm home. Pepperoni pizza hot out of the oven."

The house was hushed. "You here? Come and get it." Still no answer. She dropped her purse and keys at the door and kicked off her tennis shoes. She texted him. PIZZA! Wednesday. NOW.

No reply. Her gut gave that low twist—the familiar kind that whispered, *you'll be eating alone tonight.* The silence sank onto her shoulders like a thick wool cloak. She exhaled, the pizza's warmth turning hollow in her palms. This was the chapter of motherhood they never prepared you for—the slow fade-outs, unread messages, the ache of waiting for a presence that no longer needed you.

And then, without warning, a surge of pure heat shot through her core. A pulse—not just physical, but something deeper, more ancient. Her breath hitched—slow at first, like the hush before a storm. Then it bloomed. Fierce. Ancient. A soft sound broke loose from her throat before she could name it. The pulse was everywhere now: through her hips, her ribs, her jaw. Her fingers twitched. She closed her eyes, letting the current wash over her. This wasn't arousal—it was recognition. Like something sacred she'd forgotten was rising from within, reclaiming the temple of her body. She steadied herself by dropping into the oversized Chenille armchair and put her feet on the Ottoman, pizza box on her lap. The heat from the box matched the heat within.

Then, a voice. Not from the phone. Not from the room. But inside her skull, where thought turns into knowing. *I am here, my Queen. Feel me.*

The phone in her right hand rang. Startled, she stared at it too rattled to answer. *Iben.*

Then it stopped. She needed to ground. Her stomach growled, pulling her attention to the present. She grabbed a slice of gooey pizza and took a bite. The cheese stretched and clung to her lips. She wondered, half-laughing, if he could see her now, mouth full of crust and tomato. Could he really know her that intimately?

The phone jangled again. She picked it up. "Hello," she mumbled.

"Evening, Queen, what has distressed you?" His voice. Like velvet pulled through smoke.

It always disarmed her.

She swallowed. "I just got here, expecting my son would be home for dinner. I grabbed pizza. But he's gone." She cringed a little, then pushed back into the upholstered cushions. Of all the reasons to feel shaken, this felt mundane.

But still, it mattered. The small rituals that once tethered her to meaning were fraying.

"I am sorry that your son didn't get to eat with you," he said softly. She heard the crinkle of paper on his end. He was unwrapping something. A Reece's Peanut Butter cup, maybe? She imagined him in a high-rise, seated at a simple desk working on a laptop. Distant. Present. Attuned.

She lowered her voice in a sultry way, almost flirtatious. Testing the water. Was it alright to flirt? To flirt with a man who didn't need to be present to send waves of electric energy through her? You know I hear you in my head all the time now," she admitted and crinkled her nose.

He pinged her shoulders as a response. "I know you can. You are enhanced beyond this world in spiritual awareness. You are awakening. As I told you, my elders have given approval for you to receive awakening."

"Awakening to what?" she whispered, unsure if she really wanted to know.

He paused, feeling her tentativeness. Would he scare her if he told her the truth? He bit his lip feeling unsure. "To the goddess vibe. To the truth of who you have always been."

Her fingers tightened around the corner of the pizza box. She should laugh. This had to be a joke. Or insane. But the way her body trembled...she knew it wasn't.

"We have been in communion, and they have decided that you need to remember who you are."

"Really, who am I?" she mumbled, taking another bite of pizza while, trying desperately to lighten the moment.

His answer was quiet but firm. "If you don't remember, I can't tell you. Once you do, then I can open you up further."

Her breath caught. "You already opened me pretty wide," she said, the memory of last night washing over her. With that, her legs snapped apart, and the balls of her feet touched. Her hands clasped, her head bent in submission to something greater than herself. She wondered if Jesus would approve.

In the dream last night—or whatever it was—he had taken her somewhere wild and warm, under a tree with bright green leaves. He clothed her in fabric unlike anything she'd worn. Green and gold. Her arms were raised over her head. Her body laid bare. His hands, his mouth, his light— he had claimed her. Not in a way that diminished. But in a way that revealed. It felt so real. How could it be when she knew she was alone in her bed, asleep? It was like she was in a movie, which Iben directed.

A kiss. A moan. A ripple. And she remembered joy.

His voice pulled her back.

"Are you still there?"

"Yes. Just... remembering," she said, her eyes half closed.

"I clothed you in tradition. And undressed you in truth."

She replied dreamily, "I liked that dress and style you clothed me in last night." She recalled the draping of the Afrakan pattern and how excited she was to be invited into his world in the inner realms. "That is, while I had it on."

"I know you did, and it was equally appreciated and amazing while your shell was physically naked in many realms. I feel your energy, and your Ohms and Vibes getting stronger. I feel your warmth. I'm humbled to caress you with love and overstanding." He proved she wasn't making it up; he really made it happen.

A pulse of light moved through her, subtle but precise. She gasped. The energy wound through her thighs, teasing her, then pulling away just before release. He was playing her body like an instrument. And she let him.

"Goddess, I touched you in every realm, and with the protection of a god, you are healed and nurtured for greater things to come. You have felt my desire from within, and you know thyn heart sayith you of the cosmic realms are mine." He stated it so blatantly as if this had been mutually agreed upon. Hell, they had only gone out on a few times.

"Thank you," she said, voice thick. "That was... delicious."

He exhaled in satisfaction. "Heart to heart. Stroke by stroke. We were in full cosgasm."

She laughed. "Cosmic orgasm? That's clever."

He pinged her again. Lower. She shuddered.

As unlikely a pair as they were, this was the most interesting thing that happened to her in years. Sex without all the messy cleanup and emotional stress was a Godsend in her 50's. She couldn't be accused of sinning when he wasn't really here, so she decided to enjoy the waves of orgasmic delight that overtook her senses. Morainya cried out in bliss and felt a release of wetness that had been dammed up inside. Tears flooded down her face, and the unexpected discharge loosened the tenseness stored in her body from fighting all these years. To prepare him, she said, "I can't move as swiftly in this realm though," intentionally letting him know that she wasn't planning on sleeping with him... immediately.

He didn't acknowledge it, instead he allowed a pause to permeate their conversation.

Morainya grimaced and felt the silence then filled it up. "I am definitely attuned to you. I feel that; what do you call it?"

"Cosmic Downpouring," he answered and pinged her shoulders and vagina as confirmation.

She still had to overcome that good girl Catholic upbringing. Even in middle age, that teaching dictated her moral barometer, maybe that's why Jedidiah was with Jenny. Her body tensed, and she pushed up on one elbow.

He burrowed into her, and her eyes fluttered, "The powers to be is that you don't have to."

"How is this even possible? Mmmmmmm, well, that's one way to do it if you are gonna keep activating my g-spot." He literally pushed light into her like how a phallus would enter.

"I will activate and touch you infinite; the physical is a bonus, and if—and I say if—you will, know, I need a full spiritualgasm to engage in the physical gaming."

Her eyes grew wide like a deer in the headlights, as her mind raced, trying to comprehend what he was saying. She swallowed, trying to grasp the enormity of what he was saying. "You mean...the physical doesn't even matter?"

Iben centered himself. "The physical is the final step, Queen. But it is nothing without the connection first."

Morainya thought of Jedidiah, her ex-husband. Of years of obligation, duty, touch without meaning. Jedidiah was addicted to porn in order to rise. That it wasn't really her he was having sex with. She pursed her lips recalling the version of her that Jedidiah was imagining he was entering. Morainya just got tired of fighting about it, so she just submitted to get it over with. But Iben, he wanted her. The realization that a spiritual connection must be established before a physical one could, made her tremble—A hollow ache swelled in her chest as the truth settled—how many times had she given her body, praying it would open someone's heart?

She felt herself choke with emotion and whispered, "It's like no one told us these secrets. Sex first, then hoping for intimacy after. That's how most couples do it."

His voice was alert, yet soft and knowing. "But now, you know."

Suddenly, Morainya burst into tears. Her hands flew up to her eyes, to brush away the sadness. This was an overwhelming feeling that she struggled to put into words. Stupidity? Naivety? Like there was so much she didn't know was possible. She pulled her grandmother's shawl hanging over the back of the chair around her shoulders like a warm hug.

Iben heard her tears and felt the depth of her emotions. "I did not mean to make you cry."

Both her arms encircled herself in a cosmic embrace. She felt his invisible plush lips kiss hers.

She stuttered jerking her head back. "I am sorry and humbled. Everything that has been taught to us as women is a lie. I'm crying because it's so backwards. We come together in the spiritual so that we get access to those inner realms. Then I am open and unlocked. You are trying to teach me that a spiritual connection is what should precede a physical union," she set the pizza box down and curled her feet underneath her. "During my marriage, I don't think we ever even connected other than Catholicism. I thought going to Catholic mass made my husband and me spiritual."

Iben's eyes grew wide and thought how uneducated these people were about the sacred.

Catholicism, the very thought of how barbaric it was made him want to flee. He must move her gently into knowing so that she didn't become afraid. "You, being a melanated queen Goddess in the inner that you are, we are as one. Soon, you will remember who you are and who you will become."

She felt like she was free-falling, and her stomach jumped. Why didn't anyone ever tell us women this secret? If people were united spiritually before ever getting into a physical relationship that totally involved getting off, just reaching a climax, then maybe women would want more sex after childbearing years. This was a discussion in most of her women's groups about how the spark just disappeared after a long marriage, or after being worn out raising children. Even her friends who still had warm and loving relationships with their spouses rarely discussed a spiritual union. This made so much sense. This made her heart ache for Iben. Suddenly, the distance between them age-wise, culturally, and socially didn't seem to matter. These Ohms and Vibes transcended all that.

All that mattered was having this man in her world. He taught her how to see through different eyes of politics, legal, cultural and spiritual in ways she couldn't have fathomed before. Then, her lips quivered as she glanced up at the family reunion photo taken five years before her father passed. Her face pinched. What would Stephano and Stella say? She'd feel like an absolute freak if she asked her family to meet this foreigner and accept a Muslim Moorish male with these bad ass skills into her conservative Catholic family. They'd banish her.

"Are you still there," he asked softly. "Did you just go into fear?" His gentle voice coaxed her out of her head and into the present time.

"Just a little shocked. This is all new to me." She played with the gold bracelet on her left wrist. A gift her parents had given her at college graduation.

"You knew that I was your key from the moment I touched you when we first met at the Italian Restaurant. You will not deny Kingship, nor will I deny you Queenship. Feel me," he stated.

Iben's velvety voice said, "I am caressing you as absolutely as I was already within you, just like when I hugged you at the museum. I have claimed you and have been given the oneness to fill you all over."

She could only moan rhythmically, unable to form words when he sent those electric ripples into her body.

He continued, "Heart to Heart, stroke by stroke, opening up your key of life, allowing me to explore you. Know you can't say no to the desire of the realms since they have given you to me."

"Can't breathe," she said, enraptured. Just his words sent her into an ecstatic state, she gasped four orgasmic breathes, clutching the arms of her chair, her eyes rolling back in her head.

"I have claimed you in your entire nakedness, and everything else that encompasses your physical being. I will now and always will bring that out wherever we will be," he said. She could feel his arms around her, comforting her, loving her in ways unknown to mortal man. Maybe they were gods and goddesses. Would that be so bad? Who wouldn't want an orgasm like this?

"I feel at peace," replied Morainya, still floating high above her body.

"Absolutely, Hotep, you are open, Queen; I submit my being with deep penetration that only you will recognize and remember our blueprint. I will give you seeds of life knowledge that only you, as a Queen goddess, can absorb. My Infinite Queen, it has been ordained that to me and me alone will be the only one in the Infinite to open and apart you again."

"Yes, my King," she breathed, surrendering to the truth of it. She floated in the space between worlds, no longer questioning. But even as she whispered her devotion, a shiver curled down her spine. Because deep down, she knew—this was only the beginning. She just couldn't tell anyone.

*A*rchollos arrived at the palace unannounced, his linen cloak still dusty from the road. He entered through the side gate—the one only he and I used when news was urgent or personal.

I stood near the West colonnade, draped in my morning white—linen soft as prayer, still scented with lotus from the dawn oiling. The cool breeze from the river lifted the hem of my sheath as he approached, eyes smoldering with unresolved fire.

"Merit-Aten," he began without ceremony, "the visitors are packing up to leave."

My heart skipped a beat. "Ana-Kharu?" I searched his eyes because this was unexpected.

He stepped closer, his voice relieved. "They have gathered their animals. I saw them load up the last of the apothecary crates. The curtains are gone. All that remains are wine dregs, gnawed fruit pits, and a fire pit." His smile spread wide, jubilant. "Bless the Aten that the exit will bring back the peace that had been stolen from Akhet-Aten. His swirling yellow flames from his solar plexus engulfed him.

Archollos had seen Ana-Kharu and his troupe taken into Mahu's custody. How could he know that Pentu, the Pharaoh and I now needed what was hidden in the salesman's box. "Everything has changed. Once I told father about the cinnabar that had showed me, then he wanted to meet with him."

233

Archollos paced, sand clinging to his sandals, and the muscles in his arms tight from restraint. The veins in his neck bulged; he was still seething. It was he who had pulled me from the shadow of the Gold Magician—the one who dared to corrupt me under the guise of teaching. Other than the entertainment and preliminary classes in alchemy, I too had found Ana-Kharu a bit irritating in his arrogance. Yet... Once my father purchased the alchemical supplies he needed then maybe it was for the best that the troupe leave. But something in me stirred—a sense that the true performance had yet to begin.

Amaret stormed into the Reception Room. Her bare ashy feet needed to be washed as she left footprints on our neatly washed tile floor. "You had better stop that hoaxer," the Mistress of the Two Eyes ordered but held back when she felt the presence of another.

"Amaret, it is fine." I reached to calm her by placing my hand upon her thin shoulder. "Archollos came to update me upon the departure of our guests."

She made a humpf sound of disapproval. "He is sneaking away before he addresses your father. The Pharaoh will not be pleased that he did not have a chance to confront the intruder."

I signaled Archollos and whispered, "Later—we will speak. I must handle this now."

He nodded, bowing to my blind Seer and left abruptly, Turning my attention back to Amaret, I snapped, "What do you expect me to do?"

Amaret's ire rose like ruffled feathers on a cornered hen. "I shall command the guards to throw him at the feet of the Pharaoh. Then have him receive the lashings by Mahu's whip, which should intimidate that group of misfits," she grumbled and rubbed her hands together. *Her glazed eyes never ceased to unsettle me—how she moved with such precision, as if sight still guided her.*

By late morning, Pharaoh appeared and was guided by his dresser to sit upon his throne next to mine. Gone were the days of gilded processions and diplomatic pomp—foreign dignitaries bearing treasures, feasts echoing throughout the palace. Now, we worked day and night to keep him alive.

The reception hall grew dense with tension as the guards dragged Ana-Kharu forward.

His feet barely grazed the tiles, the scent of sweat and oil clinging to his linen sheath.

The magicians once-vibrant golden robes were stripped away leaving him exposed—just a man now, no longer cloaked in mystery.

I was sure that he was not pleased to be thrown at the feet of the Highest Leader Upon the Land. My father's throne rose above the prisoner, constrained before him.

"How kind of you to make your visit short to Akhet-Aten," said Pharaoh wearily. "I pray that you were received well and that you found interested buyers for your goods?"

Ana-Kharu bowed in an exaggerated manner. "A most fortunate journey—until I was dragged like a common thief through your sacred land, and forced to grovel before the King of the Sun." He looked up, fearless and said, "Sire, had I been informed, I certainly would have come bearing gifts for the Almighty One."

"Those gifts," Father said coolly, "are precisely why you now kneel before me. "I am curious about the trinkets that my daughter was so interested in during your class on alchemy."

Ana-Kharu hesitated, eyes flickering—calculating whether Pharaoh's words masked fury or fascination. "Yes, your Majesty, I was so humbled your daughter asked me to teach your students the basic courses. They are so well-behaved and curious about the Sacred Science."

Akhenaten's chin lifted with faint disdain. "So, you entertained them while I was away...," the king shifted upon his throne. "I am pleased to know that you kept them amused during my absence. Tell me, Ana-Kharu, where did you receive your higher learning?" Pharaoh sat motionless, breathing labored, fingers touching.

"Ah, I have picked it up from great teachers. I have journeyed to Heliopolis several times and met with the Priests who spoke emphatically with me about alchemy," replied Ana-Kharu, pushing his sleeves up as if he would reveal the breadth of his adventures.

I grimaced. From what Pentu told me, I knew this was not the whole truth.

Pentu my Physician stepped forward holding his staff wrapped in golden vines, and said, "Are you telling us that you went to the College of the Anu at Heliopolis, and yet you are here with your hands, tongue, and eyes intact." His voice was rising with accusation. His neck flushed with rage. "I am quite impressed to meet a man of your distinction who escaped Heliopolis with the Higher Knowledge. I know one is required to sign a blood oath so as to never reveal their alchemical secrets. Yet, you have your sight and speech. How is this possible, Neb-We-Shet?"

"Gold Magician," Ana-Kharu muttered, shrinking under Pentu's words—caught in a net he hadn't seen until it was too late.

The Pharaoh held up a silencing hand. "I did not summon you before me to excoriate you or point out the lies that were told to the class. My daughter could not possibly have known that I had already engaged the Greatest Master Teacher of Alchemical Sciences that has accepted the class into his care."

Ana-Kharu brightened to think he'd been replaced. "Splendid news, Your Highness," Ana-Kharu beamed, masking his relief behind courtly flourishes. Your Highness, as long as your class is well-tended, then we shall make a hasty departure North. There is no point in interrupting this beautiful day the Aten has decreed. I am but an unworthy ichneumon disciplined as if I was sneaking tidbits from the pantry."

A laugh caught in my throat—of course he'd choose the ichneumon, cunning enough to flatter and boast at once as he compared himself to a weasel. He meant it as a denigration to appease my father; however, the ichneumon was also the venerated animal of the sun god, Atum, so it was also a brag.

"Ana-Kharu, you have devoted your life to the study of basic skills of alchemy making perfumes, tonics, and tinctures. I have no quarrel with that; indeed, the populace needs what you supply. It is the hallucinogens and poisons that you proffer that I take umbrage. You present yourself veiled—obscured to the common eye, but not to mine," Father said, gaze sharpened like obsidian—but it is clear to me that you are a simple Magician."

"Sire, I hear the fire in your tongue. I see the water in your eyes. I feel you have me confused with someone aligned with dark forces. I need no such attachment to do the simple alchemy necessary to create oils, healing remedies and perfumes. My people revere the Magick of Nature. Magick is majestic and has been passed down since the world began."

Father listened and used his inner vision to review the past. "Yet you bend Nature to your will, not walk with it," Father said pulling his robe across his chest. "That is not alchemy. That is arrogance. We Atenists, must stay in purity in order to receive protection. It simply cannot be sullied, or it will lead to our downfall. I demand to know what you conjure in, to make the venoms?" Father's voice reverberated.

"Again, My Lord, if we are not welcome in your court, I would plead with you to allow us to exit your kingdom without harm," stated Ana-Kharu. I heard a hitch in his voice.

"My seer, The Lady of the Two Eyes, Amaret, and my Physician, Pentu-Aten, have both confirmed that you created astral realm circumstances that gave the illusion of terrible storms and introduced my class to sexual debauchery that was not of sacred union. Did you do this by means of hallucinogens?" accused my father, leaning forward.

My breath quickened, and my palms grew sweaty. Please do not tell my father about the Mandrakes.

"I do admit; there were essences of blue lotus and mandrake that have been known to alter consciousness in the refreshments served. But we were careful not to entangle our energies with yours."

Pharaoh's eyes narrowed, "Both of those, if not offered in the highest resonance, shatter the etheric grid of the devotee and take them into a sub-dimensional energy pattern that creates distortion. I keep my initiates pure for a reason. We descend from the Mystic line, whose authority rises from a vertical bond to the Infinite Source—it is earned, not summoned. You come into my court with ill-regard to the years of work keeping my students in devotional alignment to the Atenic rays. I have created a pathway for them to move to the higher octave of realms and leave this world of the Duat established by magicians of delusion," Pharaoh declared.

Ana-Kharu's eyes tapered. "This is the age-old battle between the Mystic, line of purity and devotion, versus the Magician, who uses the natural forces and spells to change unwelcome outcomes. Lord, we both use the same Source of All Things; my spells are from the earth forces, too. I just manipulate those laws to create the outcome I wish. You await the Source; I draw it down with intention. We are not so different." I use Earth Magic. You use Heaven Mysticism."

Pharaoh balled his fists. "You reshape the will of God. I surrender to the Aten and receive what is given. I allow the Aten to pour into me and accept what is. I trust it is Thy will, not my will. Yours is not an authentic way of establishing higher consciousness. You ingest a substance, have a vision, and then believe you have had a higher spiritual experience. It is not authentic." Pharaoh gazed at me as if to make his point roar like a lion.

Ana-Kharu shifted side to side. Confusion contorted his face as to how to convince Pharaoh that he meant no harm. "We, too, are devotees of the Infinite God, which maketh all things," Ana-Kharu paused, then admitted, "But we also speak to the lower gods of this world that rule the astral realms. It was the custom of the land, before you abolished the worship of the many gods that watch over the flow of nature."

Pharaoh leaned forward, his frail hands clutching the throne. "The only thing that stands in the court of the Almighty is righteousness. Not spells. Not illusions. Not conjured visions to deceive."

Ana-Kharu's lips curled slightly. "And yet, your own priests wear charms of protection. Do they not invoke names of power before battle?"

Rage curled through me like smoke—how dare Ana-Kharu stand before the Living Sun and mock his grace with wordplay and pride.

"They do not manipulate Aten's will." Pharaoh's voice was steel. "You, Gold Magician, twist the elements to your desire."

The imp spewed fire. "And you, Pharaoh, twist people's devotion into obedience." Ana-Kharu's voice dripped with defiance.

The King eyed the Gold Magician up and down, hesitating before he spoke. "If you cannot attest to upholding the 42 Laws of Ma'at, then what you have done is to come into my Kingdom of Higher Light and intentionally distort it. I consider this an act of war."

"Father, no one was hurt," I interjected, standing upright. "Ana-Kharu only demonstrated the potential of alchemy. It was a simple introduction so that we would not feel foolish in front of this Great Teacher." I pleaded with him because we were not hurt nor lured into his alternative world. My father's words were dangerous. This situation could end up with Ana-Kharu restrained from leaving peacefully. Then we would never acquire the cinnabar.

"Amaret, please view their entwinement, is my Daughter correct in her perception?" instructed Pharaoh.

"Ana-Kharu was very attuned to Merit-Aten's naivety in the world of these clashing forces. She is innocent of the repercussions of what harm could have been inflicted," replied Amaret.

"Was it your intention to take advantage of my Daughter?" asked Pharaoh, glaring at the Gold Magician.

"My Lord of Light, Apuati, my troupe and I have traveled from one end of this land of magnificence to the other. I am born of the Twamen, the original people of this world, and I have been taught since birth how to conjure these forces in order to maintain balance. I offer protection from the same warring forces that wish to extinguish your light."

Pharaoh's expression changed and I saw his little finger flick. "Go on."

Anakharu opened his hands. "I had permission from my elders for what I did. I would never harm your daughter, the Royal next in line to your throne. I honor the matrilineal procession, which is the same custom among my people. But, my Lord, if Merit-Aten is to reign over this land, surely you would wish her to be more educated in all matters, even the mundane. When you only gaze at the heavenly sun above and feed from the light, then darkness grows beneath your feet. She is ill-prepared."

"How dare you speak to the Pharaoh of his Daughter," declared Pentu, and with a snap of his fingers, the guards took up an aggressive stance with spears pointed at the vulnerable merchant. "I shall order the guards to sever your tongue right now."

Father held up his hand to stop them. He leaned forward, as the Magician had incited his curiosity. "Provide me an instance of that which you speak."

Ana-Kharu saw the energy erupt, and he calmed himself. "Your Daughter has not been instructed about finding her key; she eyes my key strewn about my neck, praying this will unlock her providence and fate."

I stiffened at being called out. How could he have known? The humiliation stung like a thousand ichneumon wasps that my actions had been so transparent.

Pharaoh nodded. "She has not had instruction yet; her mother, the HeMeti, is not present at this time as she has been called to Thebes. When Merit-Aten chooses her consort, then she will be receiving guidance."

"Pharaoh, please forgive me for my intrusion, but girls in my village have been educated and taken into the inner world to receive guidance. Her key is her destiny. I would be neglectful if I did not know that as the all-knowing leader, you have already seen 200 years into the future and know exactly what has been sanctified by the Elders as to the progression of your lineage. Am I not correct?" said Ana-Kharu.

My father was lost in meditation, talking to his departed mother, Ti-Yee, his father, and others about the massive ramifications of me choosing a proper Consort. To carry on the matrilineal line, all rights to the crown thus carry on through me. Why did I have to keep hearing about this? I rolled my eyes.

"I am more than aware of the significance of Merit-Aten being appropriately paired for her children to survive," said father, his brow furrowed, "Those are topics that were deemed in her mother's jurisdiction." Pharaoh's eyes narrowed.

"And for the Aten worship to survive?" asked Ana-Kharu, raising his voice.

"Father, what is my key? I need to know. I have asked you, Grand Djed, Ay and Pentu. None of you choose to divulge what this key is. I am exhausted searching for answers as to the unlocking." I stomped my foot like a child.

"Daughter, I feel it is your mother's duty to reveal women's business. You should not learn this under your father's guidance; it must come from the Women's Line, who can see the path forward. That is the custom to which I am obliged," said father with a softer voice.

"Mother has abandoned me; therefore, I require the knowledge to be passed on now, or I fear that I will go mad. Do I need this key to unlock the gold to save this kingdom?" I flailed my arms.

Everyone laughed, and I felt mortified that I had been left out of the joke that revolved around my sanity. "Yes, in essence, that is correct," replied father. His vagueness troubled me.

"If you do not illuminate the path the Aten has decreed, then she will choose that blonde-headed boy, the one who is not from this land and cannot possibly rise to the ranks of King of Khemit. It will be a calamity far beyond words. He is a Mycenaean and a Barbarian; why do you allow this intruder into your ranks and reveal the secrets given to the true Khemitians?" said Ana-Kharu, his indigo flames ejected from his third eye like a warning shot.

"Phew, he is but an infatuation," Pentu said, folding his arms like a gate shutting the subject down. "Nothing more. Merit-Aten would not even consider him worthy to receive her."

Pharaoh and Pentu were convinced of this truth and disregarded that it was even a possibility, which crushed my heart.

"Well," I snapped, voice hardening. "If the choice is mine, why am I being punished for desiring Archollos?. "He has lived among us, walked among us, learned our language and our traditions. That is more than the Royal Consorts that GrandDjed Amenhotep III chose from the daughters of all our Tributes. They enjoyed the wealth of his Kingdom, yet the 'Royal Baubles' never bothered to learn any of our customs, yet their children walk amongst us today. Does that make them any less Khemitian?" I felt ashamed stating this because my dearest Smenkhkare was the eldest son of Kiya, my father's second wife, the harpist.

"Merit-Aten, beloved, while we knew you gave your heart to this foreigner when you were a child, we hoped that you would outgrow a love that can never be fulfilled," said father. "In tribal and Royal tradition, the parents select their daughter's mate because they bring fortuitous alliances to our country. This boy can offer you none of that."

"He told me he is the son of a King," I stated, defending my love by crossing my arms defiantly.

Father turned his rage upon me. "He is not Khemitian. He is not melanated. He brings no armies, no gold...He is not worthy. I have allowed him entrance to the initiations to increase his resonance to the Sacred. Thus, he could pass on the higher knowledge to his offspring when it was time for him to depart. Not to yours," he said in his fatherly voice, trying to educate his child.

"If he finds the key to the gold—would that make him worthy enough to stay?" My body was rigid, and my shoulders were like stone, desperate to make Archollos valuable enough so that he would stay. What vision had my father seen to state that Archollos could leave Khemit—and me?

The men shook their heads and again chuckled to themselves. Why was this so difficult?

"My Lord, I must abstain from this conversation, being a celibate man devoted to my studies," said Pentu, excusing himself. He took a seat and pulled out his scrolls to immerse himself in his studies, thereby leaving me to fend for myself.

"Shining One, I have been taught at my mother's knee, and I feel I could explain this best to your Daughter. If you permit, I will sweep away her confusion—like the broom daily clearing the temple sand," said Ana-Kharu, looking at me like an elder brother.

"Yes, Yes, proceed." Father sat back on his throne as if relieved.

"The key opens and closes a door, does it not?" Ana-Kharu used his hand to turn a lock.

"Yes, of course," I said, my eyebrows arched.

"Do you know the legend of Isis and her veils? No, man has lifted her veil?"

"Of course. 'I am all that has been and is and shall be; no mortal has ever lifted my mantle.'"

"The mantle or veil that is lifted is the pubic hair that is curly in our melanated nature. When it is lifted, a very special and sacred flesh appears. When this piece of flesh is stimulated and delighted, it swells. The waters of Isis flow forth to prepare her temple to receive the Djed. He is electric. She is magnetic. One strikes, the other draws—until heaven gates part." Ana-Kharu paused, his eyes clear and determined.

He was the only one who dared to tell me the truth.

I stared wide-eyed at Ana-Kharu, and our eyes met with the knowledge of what he shared with me using that naughty mandrake root. He was teaching me the power of the orgasmic state of floating in the heaven world. At least I wouldn't be a completely innocent child when the time came. He offered me a sheepish half-smile in acknowledgement. I felt the heat rise to my face as Ana-Kharu's words settled into my bones. So, this was it? Not gold, not alchemy, not thrones—but this hidden key...my own body? So that ankh key was meaningless?

My fingers clenched at my tunic. How could this be the secret my father had never spoken of? That no man—not even Archollos—had dared mention?

"Thank you," I whispered, my voice unsteady. But deep inside, something new had been unlocked.

Father inhaled slowly, then said, "Now, you have gained the knowledge that I did not feel it was my place to share."

I felt my face grow hot. I had been initiated—in full view of an entire court. I nodded.

"Now, what do I do with Ana-Kharu?" asked Pharaoh. "While I am grateful for conveying the secrets of women, still, you broke the law of the Heliopolitan High Priests and their strict rules of alchemical secrets. And, for using magick."

I threw up my hands before a war erupted. "Father, if Ana-Kharu-We-Shat is not our teacher, then who was the teacher who never showed up?"

Pharaoh's eyebrows arched. "First, I did not say that he would come to us. I had intended for you to go to him."

"Oh!" I gasped, heat rushing to my cheeks. My excitement curdled into embarrassment as I realized I had misunderstood. "Please... tell us his name."

My father pursed his lips as if trying to contain a secret, which begged to erupt. "I do not see any harm in revealing that, as all would know his name."

We threw out other guesses, but none was right.

Pharaoh smiled with delight. "Djehuty. The Master Architect. Our beloved, the ibis-headed god who graces the walls of Khemit's greatest temples. Father of Alchemy."

"Father, this is a blessed surprise. When may we meet him?" I nearly danced in place, joy bubbling up like a spring.

Father exhaled sharply, and said, "Ah, child... I have come to realize—it is quite impossible now. None of us may leave Akhet-Aten and remain safe. No, my journey beyond these walls proved quite hopeless. We would be hunted—marked like prey."

My mouth and stomach dropped. My tears welled. "Then... could he come to us instead?"

"I cannot ask the Master teacher to come here. His domicile is at a great distance. There is no way I could send you—let alone the other twelve—to Giza and believe you would arrive unharmed." Pharaoh sat with hands clasped, immovable as a stone statue.

"Impossible for you," said Ana-Kharu with a calm that hushed the room. "But not for me. Let them join my troupe—we head north soon. Hidden among us, they would pass unnoticed."

Silence stretched through the hall, thick as incense smoke. Pharaoh's eyes darkened like a sky before storm. "You dare to suggest I send my daughter into the hands of a Magician?"

Ana-Kharu did not flinch. "I dare suggest you give her a path—any path."

My heart thundered. Was this truly my fate? To leave the palace, vanish into common ranks, and wear a mask no crown could reveal? Archollos would never allow it. And yet...if Djehuty was the true teacher, could I really turn away?

12

*L*ast night could have been perfect. At least that is the way she had imagined every detail. Josh left for the weekend for Puerto Vallerta, and she worked in the kitchen charring the eggplant over the grill to bring out the smokey flavor for the baba ghanoush. She sprinkled the cumin into the chickpeas to mix a creamy hummus while her Falafels sizzled in the hot oil. The aroma of simmering chicken tagine spiked the air with saffron, lemons and olives. Couscous, a golden yellow grain was now ready to sprinkle with pine nuts and parsley. The table was set with fine china and candles. It was special and welcoming, and she hoped Iben would be surprised and delighted by the amount of work she had put into preparing an authentic Moroccan dinner.

He had mentioned so many times that his mother was an excellent cook for his family of four. Morainya had a hard enough time managing Josh, let alone taking care of a big family. Iben mentioned that he enjoyed the melancholic and somber Rhythm and Blues musicians like Sam Cooke, Etta James, and Ray Charles, so her playlist also included the Soul music artists Smokey Robinson, Marvin Gaye, Aretha Franklin, and Motown. Maybe they'd dance around the kitchen and feel the groove before sitting down to eat. Laying the last plate of food on the table and glancing at the clock, she expected him to arrive in ten minutes.

Morainya slipped on a royal blue dress and low heels, as she gave one more scrutinizing look in the mirror before applying one last dab of lipstick. She hated that she felt so bad about herself, but he always seemed to think she was attractive. Why would he merge with her unless they were soulmates? Morainya glanced at her phone. No texts. Yeah, any minute.

Iben pinged her shoulders. Then her vagina. She smiled. It was a signal. She'd just tidy up the kitchen. When she glanced up, thirty minutes had passed. Where was he? The beautifully plated food was getting cold. She texted him. No answer. Sitting at the table, she drank some lemonade out of a crystal wine glass. Maybe he'd encountered traffic. That's probably why he couldn't text. The sky, now orange and pink voluminous clouds slowly dissipated into darkness. She checked her phone again. No messages. She texted him. *Everything ok? Still coming to dinner?*

No response. She rechecked the messages. Maybe he had already texted her back. Maybe she missed it. She refreshed her screen. Nothing. Her stomach tightened. The baba ghanoush, the falafels, the tender chicken tagine—all of it now felt foolish, like the meal of a desperate woman. He said he loved her. He had entered her mind, her body, her spirit. Wasn't that more intimate than this mortal world? And yet...he wasn't here.

A sour taste built in her throat as she stared at the clock. 10 minutes late. 20. 45. Her hands shook as she poured herself a drink. It was only lemonade, but it felt bitter in her mouth.

Morainya sat in the dark, feeling devastated as a tear trickled down her cheek. He wasn't coming. She hauled herself up and defiantly marched all the food back into the kitchen. Still, he pinged her shoulders, and swirled up inside of her, making her gasp. What the fuck? The shock and disappointment struck her as hard as a surprise paint-ball attack of disappointment. Why wouldn't he at least have the decency to let her know after all the work she had put into making this night so special—for him? Morainya threw her dress on the floor and pulled on gym pants and a sloppy top. All the self-hatred and admonition welled up for believing this was something real. He pinged her shoulder, and she admonished him, "Get the fuck out of me."

The next morning, she felt grumpy having suffered a sleepless night replaying her disenchantment. Morainya left the house early to get a start on the road before the Sunday traffic. Normally, she would have been at Catholic mass and gone to the pancake breakfast afterwards. Morainya laid aside the guilt of breaking a family tradition. Instead, she blocked her parents' voices in her head, chiding her about going to hell for her disobedience and disrespect for the church and Jesus.

Driving her car steadily along the multilane highway, she passed a series of telephone poles that had steadily popped up due to the growing population in the Santa Cruz mountains. There was a cross, one after another, after another. Strange, she had never really thought about how seeing that cross always reminded her of the crucifixion, even without the body of Christ hanging from it. The subtle feeling of agony and the Son of God, who had died for our sins, persisted silently within her subconscious. Over and over and over, the trauma instilled since childhood by the Church was replayed. The crosses came at her on the right side of Highway 17 against the blue sky in the hills reminiscent of Golgotha, on the skull-shaped hill outside of Jerusalem where Jesus was crucified. Now, it was the only thing she could see. Couldn't the telephone company have come up with a different configuration for their utility poles other than a cross, the universal symbol for suffering. Surely, it was a thoughtless accident.

She sped, leaving behind Santa Cruz. Saint Cross. Wow, it was everywhere. Reminders at every turn. How had she not noticed it before? Over the highways, the once rolling hills were now covered in new suburban housing, apartment buildings, high-rise buildings right up next to the busy traffic that ran bumper to bumper most days. These people probably smelled the fumes from their windows. Crazy how life had grown-up around her while she hadn't even noticed, now seemed to jar every fiber of her being. It was like her once sleepy California coastal village had evolved into multitudes of bustling suburbs.

Her mind kept looping on last night, she couldn't get over the fact that Iben had ghosted her for the first invite to her home. He disrespected her by not even calling but then she flipped to worrying about what if something terrible had happened to him? How would she even know? These questions troubled her so greatly that her mouth turned down at the corners, now locked in a scowl, and her eyes narrowed.

Thankfully, she could take some respite from her troubles at her parents' home. When she walked in, the mansion was deafeningly silent. She left her shoes at the door in order to avoid tracking in dirt on the luxury wool carpets. Maybe Nico and Gina had taken a weekend at their home in Sausalito. She missed the kids arguing and Gina's cooking. The house smelled like the home she grew up in when her sister-in-law made lasagna and Caesar salad.

Morainya sorted through the mail and opened the monthly invoice to The Gold Gates Sanctuary, where her mother was in a secure place for dementia patients, so they didn't wander off. She felt gratitude that as her mother slipped away, she was well-cared for.

Normally, her brother handled all the bills for the house and her mother's needs, but she opened it up anyway. Ten thousand dollars a month plus any medication or amenities her mother partook in that weren't covered by Medicare. She gasped at how expensive private care facilities were. Morainya felt that guilt because she needed to be here to take care of Mom, but how could she add that to her job at the Santa Cruz Historical Society categorizing all the old photos and being there for her son, Josh? She'd worry about that after her Settlement Conference tomorrow. Grabbing a plate of leftovers, she headed to her room to sleep. Still, no texts from Iben, and that pain ground her down. Now, when he pinged her it felt like an insult.

The next morning, she followed the GPS map to the high-rise office building where her Settlement Conference was scheduled. She imagined Nico beside her, arms crossed with that calm, ready to swat down nonsense before it reached her. The mediation office felt like a gray waiting room for nowhere—no paintings, no warmth, just blank neutrality posing as professionalism. It was simply a gray reception office where she checked in with another uninterested receptionist, who slid the window shut with the enthusiasm of someone clocking out of life itself once Morainya gave her name. Through the window, the receptionist pointed to sit down without further instruction.

Morainya assumed someone would come to retrieve her. The heavy door opened, and Uncle Aldo walked ahead of Aunt Harriet. He was grumbling at her to hurry up and there was no time for her to use the restroom. Their bickering crawled under her skin like static—loud, personal, and impossible to unhear. Aldo had a combover and she could see his pale scalp through his thinning hair. His suit was rumpled like it had spent the night on the floor with him still in it. Harriet wore a purple dress with a wool overcoat and a church hat perched at an angle. Was she supposed to kiss her accuser on both cheeks like some warped family tradition? Every nerve in her body was on high alert as she partially stood to greet them but froze halfway.

"Morainya," said Uncle Aldo coldly with the same reserve and hyper-awareness of this moment's awkwardness. After they checked in, the couple took a seat directly across from her. Aunt Harriett shifted in her seat trying to hold her bladder. As if in synchronicity, they all reached for a magazine to bury their heads in ensuring no eyes met.

She glanced at her phone, checking the time, praying that Mr. Kanberg would rescue her. Catching a momentary peek at Uncle Aldo's hands, he wore an insignia ring on his left hand, while she noticed his little crooked pinkie on his right hand. Morainya tried to recall if he had had an accident; maybe he broke it in a fall. She searched her memory but her parents never mentioned it. Iben pinged her shoulders and flipped her elbows out. Morainya blushed hard and prayed that no one noticed and judged her as crazy. Internally, she yelled 'stop it.'

The office door moved, and they all locked eyes on who would appear. Fortunately, Mr. Kanberg entered and claimed Morainya. Adjusting her black jacket, she rose and followed behind him.

Mr. Kanberg wore a silver tailored suit and looked as polished as a shiny dime. "How are you today?"

"A little nervous," she replied meekly, her voice barely audible.

They ambled down an extended hallway with thick polished doors. Kanberg opened the fifth door on the right. "We are in here."

Inside, there was a very long redwood conference table. The blinds were drawn, making the room appear dull and lifeless, mirroring exactly how she felt. She was already halfway out the door in her mind, scribbling a check just to end this purgatory.

The emptiness of this sterile room urged Morainya to fill up the space. "How are you?" she asked.

"I am doing quite well. Mrs. Kanberg and I spent a long weekend in our second home in Lake Tahoe. You know the kids and grandchildren love to waterski, so we found a place large enough for all of us to fly in and spend together." He glanced at his manicure and shiny nails and Morainya felt strangely envious of the little pampering luxury she had denied herself.

This conversation struck Morainya as odd. Mr. Kanberg was bragging about scoring enough income to afford a luxury second home in a pricy ski area known to be a lawyer's haven. As she recalled, he had a home in Acapulco also. Yeah, he was stacking holiday homes like poker chips—each one earned from someone else's ruin. She wondered if Jesus would have turned over the money changers and the lawyers' tables in the Synagogue? What was that idiom? Her lips pressed into a pale seam as the old adage clanged in her head—death, taxes, and lawyers cashing in on both.

"How do you think today will go?" asked Morainya more pointedly, reminding him to focus on her case, not her end bill.

Kanberg shuffled the stack of papers and gave it a swift bang on the table to organize them. "We are very well prepared. I will have my Junior Associate come in to participate. She should arrive any moment." He moved his binders of information with precision in military style. Little tabs had been marked for reference. "The judge should be arriving and will come introduce himself."

Morainya asked, "Will Uncle Aldo be in this room also?"

"Yes, for the joint session at the beginning. The claimants, which is your Uncle and Aunt, and their attorney will introduce themselves and present their case to the judge. Then they have the room directly across from us booked for the rest of the day. Judge Malicado will be overseeing today's Settlement Conference."

"Malicado? Did his daughter, Sofia, attend University here? I think she was in my dorm.

Morainya's mind recalled Archbishop DeLaurentis mentioning a Judge Soffagiano, so maybe he didn't know anything about her case after all since he got the judge's name wrong.

Kanberg wrote a note and replied, "I would not be surprised. All of our kids are about the same age."

A woman in her late 30's hurried in, carrying a briefcase and greeted Mr. Kanberg before reaching toward Morainya to shake her hand. "Good Morning, I'm Annabelle Levine, an Associate Attorney for Kanberg, Wallerstein and Katz." She took a seat next to Kanberg and poured a glass of water.

At that moment, a distinguished older gentleman in a black suit and red-striped tie entered the conference room, followed by the opposing attorney, Uncle Aldo, and Aunt Harriet. They positioned themselves directly opposite. Morainya felt her neck muscles tense.

"Good morning, everyone. I am the Honorable Judge James Malicado, and I am here as a neutral third party to assist each party in finding a resolution and avoid going to court. This is not a trial. This an informal process and I emphasize mutual respect. Are we in agreement?"

She gave a faint nod, surprised by the warmth in his voice—like a substitute teacher who hadn't yet been burned.

The judge continued, "We are here for a settlement conference regarding Case 219852 Aldo Napolitano, Plaintiff vs. Morainya Napolitano Sanders, Defendant. Let's go around the table and introduce ourselves."

The opposing lawyer began, "I am Angela Chisholm, Your Honor, and I'm here to represent the Plaintiff. This is Aldo Napolitano and his wife, Harriet."

"Your Honor, I'm Kenneth Kanberg from Kanberg, Wallerstein, and Katz, and I am here representing Morainya Napolitano, the Defendant. This is my Associate Annabelle Levine."

The Judge smiled and added, "Thank you for coming together today for Mediation and Settlement. I always express that we are here to do right by each side. In saying that, we often find that the Plaintiff doesn't walk away with what they are expecting, and the Defendant pays more than was expected. We hope that justice will be served, that it will save you all in court and legal costs, and that it will satisfy both sides. Let us now review why we are here. After both sides make their opening statement, feel free to summarize your perspectives on the claim and the desired outcome. I will then ask the Plaintiffs to return to their separate conference rooms, and I will go between the two to help you reach a settlement amount." Judge Malicado nodded to each to begin.

"Thank you, your Honor. The Plaintiff's case is based upon being the younger brother of the deceased Stephano D Napolitano. Aldo was employed by Napolitano Interiors, having risen up the ladder, taking on more and more responsibility in the company without an increase in pay. His brother, Stephano, made continuous verbal promises to Aldo that compensation would be paid once the business was sold. "Although Stephano passed away three years ago, the company was bankrupt shortly after the founder passed, being in financial distress. Aldo claims that his brother promised him a share of the proceeds and feels entitled to five million dollars—though no such agreement exists in writing, and he was left out of the will. Stephano made a verbal promise to his brother Aldo that he would be taken care of."

Mr. Kanberg cleared his throat. "Your Honor, we have prepared a summary judgment for you that helps disprove that Aldo added anything of value to the company and was only employed by his brother by his brother due to familial obligation—his skillset was not competitive elsewhere. In fact, Mr. Aldo Napolitano's mismanagement and inflated sales projections contributed to the company's financial collapse. We believe a fair settlement would be $500,000 to resolve this meritless claim, which lacks sufficient legal or financial standing."

For the next three hours, the Judge peppered both parties with clarifying questions yet still he remained calm and neutral. Both attorneys' flipped pages in their binders proving or disproving various claims. Morainya blinked hard, but the spreadsheets blurred like static. Receipts, emails, echoes of her father's voice—each one tugged her deeper into a fog she couldn't clear. Between legal jargon and shuffled pages, her mind slipped sideways—back to the cold baba ghanoush, the silence, the dress crumpled on the floor.

After breaking for a lunch in a confined room with a charcutier board, a mixed salad and bread. The tension hung in the air like steam off hot tea, so Morainya gathered her plate and retreated to a corner. With tight shoulders and forced breaths, she scrolled absently through her phone, hoping cat memes or unread texts might distract her churning thoughts. The judge pulled Kanberg and Chisholm to the side where they talked in hushed tones for the remainder of the lunch period. The clock was ticking toward 2pm and they would reconvene shortly in separate meeting rooms where the judge would evaluate the strengths and weaknesses of each case.

When they returned to the conference room, she asked with a tremor in her voice. "Did the judge say anything about the summary judgment?" Morainya silently prayed that Judge Malicado would notice the ridiculousness of Aldo's claims and throw out the entire case. "Isn't that enough?" she whispered, clutching the paper edges. "We have notarized witness statements. Five years of financial records. My father's memos—documenting every time Aldo messed up and Dad stepped in to clean it up."

Kanberg adjusted his tie. His expression was neutral. Too neutral.

"He read it." His fingers tapped the stack of papers. "But I wouldn't say he was entirely convinced."

A slow pulse pounded in her ears. "What does that mean?"

"It means," Kanberg said, "that we have to be strategic."

Strategic. That word curdled in her stomach. So, this wasn't about fairness—it was about maneuvering, a winning, spin.

"Uh-huh," replied Kanberg as he turned his back on Morainya and conferred with Anabelle.

Morainya leaned in, and raised her voice, "Plus, the suspicion that Aldo used company funds for his gambling addiction."

Kanberg put his hands together, tapping his fingers.

Morainya resorted to pouring over the voluminous amounts of documents that had been collected, trying to point out the records that the various witnesses testified to invalidating Aldo's claims of my wrongdoing. "Here—look," she pointed to the spreadsheet. "Dinner bills, Vegas nights, luxury car rentals—none of it tied to business. Clients he claimed to wine and dine hadn't worked with us in years.

When her father challenged the charges, Aldo exploded—ranting that he was courting old clients, salvaging relationships." But Morainya remembered the slammed doors, the silence that followed, the disbelief in her father's eyes.

Mr. Kanberg's face tightened. "It could hold water," Kanberg said dryly, thumbing through a tabbed folder. "He's got people ready to say your father was stuck in the past— pushing antique tapestries when clients were moving to glass and steel. Look how much business his firm lost over the years because the trend changed," rebuked Mr. Kanberg. Morainya shivered, her argument had holes.

"And look at this one—ten grand in Vegas with a Marstrain rep. But that was the same weekend at Johnny's wedding," she said, tapping the receipt. I know that the Bellagio used to comp my father's rooms and meals to entertain. Yet, I see no discounts. Not only that, but he says he went there the weekend that my cousin Johnnie got married. If he was in a tux popping champagne here, how was he closing deals there?"

Kanberg shook his head. "It's too late to rebut anything now. We can only hope they'll go for a lower settlement."

The Judge walked back in with a dower look washed across his face. "Right now, we are pretty far away from resolving this. I hope you will reconsider your position and be a bit more generous in order to finalize the settlement by closing today."

"Yes, your Honor. We've had a chance to review the Plaintiff's demand for five million dollars, and have discussed it with our client," replied Kanberg with a hint of irritation, which unnerved Morainya.

"Then we may proceed now to formal negotiations. Are there any additional points or concerns you would like to bring to the court now?" The Judge glanced at the clock.

"Yes, your Honor, my client has raised the objection that there are some discrepancies in the bills that the Plaintiff has presented," stated Mr. Kanberg, who handed over the documents to the Judge.

"I will bring this to their attention, and perhaps this may persuade the Plaintiffs to decrease the amount they have asked for," said the Judge.

A flicker of hope rose in her chest. If those questionable bills rattled Aldo, maybe—just maybe—he'd fold. She clung to the number: $500,000. Not a penny more. Now, she would rigidly take this position as the time edged toward 3p.m. Hopefully, they could get out of here by 3:30-4. She certainly was ready to wrap this up.

"Do you think that landed?" Morainya asked, her voice steadier now, her spine straightening with optimism.

"It got his attention. All we need to do is put this information into your opponent's mind to make him question if he'd really want to fight this in a court of law."

Relief trickled in, loosening the knot in her chest. Just then, a subtle pulse rolled through her—an unmistakable nudge from Iben. A small, involuntary sound slipped past her lips. Kanberg looked over sharply, eyes narrowing at what he'd clearly mistaken as...something else. She flushed.

When the judge reentered, his expression was stone. No warmth, no compromise.

"Opposing counsel has introduced new allegations," he said flatly. "And they raise serious red flags."

"Your Honor, can you please reveal what has been disclosed? I may object as to whether this is relevant at this late point. If they had wished to introduce a new charge, that would have had to happen at the end of the deposition," stated Mr. Kanberg defiantly.

Judge Malicado took a step forward and stated, "Aldo Napolitano is now making claims that he was harassed and that he didn't feel safe in your father's place of employment. These claims go beyond the scope of breach of contract, withholding pay, and willful negligence. Mr. Napolitano empirically states that he had been both physically and mentally abused. This is the underlying cause of his feeling that he deserves $5,000,000, and he is not willing to settle for a penny less. We are so far apart in our negotiations that I wonder if this wouldn't be better resolved in court, where witnesses and evidence could be introduced in front of a jury?" The Judge crossed his arms and appeared unmovable.

Her mouth parted in disbelief. "What?" she breathed. "Where is this coming from? This was supposed to be about accounting errors—nothing more. We disproved all of it. How is he changing the entire narrative now?"

"Could you give us five minutes to discuss this with my client?" asked Mr. Kanberg to the Judge.

"I'll leave you to confer," the judge said, and the door clicked shut behind him—hard, like a gavel splitting wood.

Kanberg turned on her, voice sharp. "Morainya, are you hiding something? Because this doesn't make sense. Did you cut a deal with him—something off the record? This shift reeks of backroom pressure."

Morainya was paralyzed. Her mind blank as static filled her ears, every thought short-circuiting before it could form.

"Why would he feel unsafe at work?" Kanberg glared at her his jaw tight with distrust, as if she'd handed him a briefcase full of snakes instead of facts.

Her body went rigid, toes digging into her shoes like anchors. "I don't know," she rasped.

The room spun. Her stomach flipped. It was as if the floor gave out—and she was free-falling with no way to brace. Certainly, she had witnessed her father's interactions with her Uncle Aldo over the years. Of course, there was yelling. Uncle Aldo would piss off clients with his abrasive manner until her father was forced to cut him back to general marketing by the end. He mitigated Aldo's ability to spend freely on the company credit cards or make large purchases. During the height of business, it was hard to keep track of all the inventory arriving from purchase orders placed by their large staff who serviced their huge worldwide clientele.

Sally, the accountant, kept an eagle eye on the invoices to inventory, but as she grew sicker with lung cancer, there wasn't anyone consistently available over those gap years. Sally had kept records by hand, refusing to enter the old records into the computer for invoicing and warehousing. 'When business is good, it's hard to keep track of every penny,' she argued and as Stefano's sister-in-law, he trusted her.

Morainya tried to calculate the division of the inheritance given the new number that Aldo demanded. She needed money for all the legal bills before the estate could be divided between her family. All this financial burden fell on Morainya's shoulders. Could she even afford to go to court? With allegations of harassment, would she want to go to court? To defend herself and her family name she'd have to spend another $40-$50,000 worth of attorney fees. She'd have to sell her house to afford all that or allow it to fall into foreclosure. How could she feed her family and take care of her mother? She couldn't breathe and clawed at her neckline as she brought the cold glass of water up to her cheek.

Mr. Kanberg was pondering the problem. "This is quite irregular. The judge will not take kindly to abuse charges, especially since Aldo says he has proof that could all be brought out in a messy trial. These are the kinds of trials that destroy legacies. Not good."

"What do I do, Mr. Kanberg?" she pleaded and touched his sleeve.

Kanberg shook his head, "Of course, it is all your choice, Morainya. I am just here to take your direction."

Morainya blurted out, "Offer him a million dollars."

Kanberg and Annabelle conferred. Then he said, "We can start there, but I believe the judge is expressing that you should consider raising the amount significantly, perhaps by meeting in the middle."

She blinked hard. "Are you suggesting two and a half million dollars? There is no way my brothers and sister would agree to that. I didn't do anything wrong. There was no misuse of funds, or negligence; there was no breach of contract" she countered as if arguing her own case. "Those were the original charges, and we've overcome them," insisted Morainya; she clenched her fists.

Mr. Kanberg stroked his chin. "We can go to court. If that is your choice, then we may as well call off these negotiations and prepare for the next big battle ahead."

Thoughts churned like debris in floodwater—nothing stable, just the frantic scramble for air above an unseen undertow. "I need to call my family."

"Of course, I will step out of the room. You can use your cell phone. The WIFI password is on the counter," directed Mr. Kanberg.

She logged in, then paused. Morainya knew she'd never get consent by all her family in time to settle today. Instead, she clumsily dialed Uncle Nico's number. If felt like she was on a gameshow calling for a lifeline to help clarify which was the correct answer. It rang and rang. Nothing. She tried him at work, and finally, he picked up. "Hello, Nico; I need to talk to you and Gina. Can you do a three-way conversation?"

Nico tried to move to a quiet room to avoid the office background noise. "Yeah, sure.

How's the settlement conference going? Are you kicking his ass?"

Morainya gulped. "Not exactly; this is really urgent. Can you please just dial her in?"

"Hold on," said Nico as he gave orders to someone in the background.

Finally, her sister-in-law's voice answered. "It's Morainya calling in, she says it isn't going well. She wants to give us an update or something," said Nico.

Morainya couldn't contain the quiver in her voice. "Everything has gone awry. Aldo has made new claims, and I just want to get out of this. Should we go to two and a half million?"

"How on earth did we go from five hundred thousand to two and a half million?" asked Gina in her thick New York accent.

Her voice thinned to a whisper, barely crossing the static as if even her conviction had cracked. "The judge came in and basically said we better come up with more because Aldo is now saying he suffered mental and physical abuse. Mr. Kanberg said that if we went to trial, it would virtually destroy the Napolitano name. He says Uncle Aldo has proof."

"What on earth? We should fight the fucker," yelled Nico.

"Yeah, we could do that and end up with nothing if the jury found us guilty, the jury could add extra money for damages and penalties. We'd wind up with nothing, and the Napolitano name would be blackened," Morainya said flatly, holding back tears.

"We have to protect our kids. We still live in San Francisco," retorted Gina, her voice quavering "I don't know what he thinks he has, but let's just put an end to it now," said Nico as he paced breathlessly.

"We lived with Dad," said Morainya, her voice shaking. "He never abused us. Sure, he was a tough guy and yelled, but he never really laid a hand on us."

"Stephano took a belt to Nico growing up," said Aunt Gina. "You told me that."

"He did. Back then that's what all fathers did," retorted Nico. "It was the way they were raised. I stole the family car and went for a joy ride. If my son did that, I'd have to take away his cell phone today. You think that would sink in?"

"Do you think Dad took a belt to Uncle Aldo? Is that what he's whining about?" asked Gina.

Morainya shrugged. "I don't know, he didn't say. What should we do? Anybody can claim abuse, but the Judge said that Aldo had proof."

Nico retorted, "Offer him seven hundred and fifty thousand dollars and see where that goes."

Morainya gnawed her lip raw. "What if he counters with five again? "

Gina hesitated. "Go to one. Let's not play his game."

"Nico? Do you agree?" asked Morainya, her voice thin.

He exhaled hard. "Fine. Just remember—we'll be splitting scraps with Emilio and Francesca."

"I dunno. I just have to end this peacefully." She hung up, still not feeling resolved.

She flicked her fingers toward Kanberg, summoning him back like a reluctant tide.

"What's your decision? I have alerted my office that we may have to take this to court. I can get my best forensic attorneys, the brightest criminal and civil guys on this case. We'll have to subpoena a psychologist and get an evaluation for Aldo, and..."

"Just offer him seven fifty," snapped Morainya.

"Sure. That is a good start. Let's see what they say." They waited for forty-five minutes before the Judge came back into the room.

Judge Malicado entered and shook his head. "I'm sorry, they still want five million or they'll go to court."

Morainya glanced at the clock inching toward 4pm. She wrote 2. on the notepad.

"We are willing to increase the settlement offer to two million dollars," said Mr. Kanberg, then shut the deposition book with a bang.

"Miss Napolitano, I know this is a leap for you. I support your willingness to stay out of court. I will submit your offer to the Plaintiff's attorney," replied Judge Malicado.

Morainya looked at her attorney and asked. "Do you mind if I speak to the Judge privately?

Mr. Kanberg nearly snarled, "Are you planning to represent yourself? I can just withdraw from the case."

She certainly didn't want to hurt Mr. Kanberg's feelings, so she backed off.

The Judge saw Morainya's confusion and added, "It is not legal for me to speak directly to you. Your attorney must answer for you. I will be back with a response from the opposing attorney," said the Judge to Mr. Kanberg. "I'll leave you two."

"Morainya's face felt like it was on fire. "Sorry." She just wanted to explain that Aldo was a troubled child and often made up lies. Maybe that would help him make a decision over this case."

She painfully watched the minutes tick by on the clock as it edged toward 4:45. What would happen if they reached 5:00 p.m. and there wasn't an agreement? Sweat pooled under her arms, and she burped up a bit of her lunch. *Why weren't there any fucking windows in this room?* Iben pinged her V. In her head, she told him to 'stop.' Arousal was the last thing on her mind.

The judge came back into the room. His face was blank. "They are countering at four million. How would you like to respond to that?"

"Offer him three," she told Mr. Kanberg. She said it numbly, thinking there was no way she'd want to sign anything today. She'd have to read it over and make a final decision in a week or two when she could collect her thoughts.

At 5:00 p.m., the judge reentered. "The Plaintiff has agreed to accept the three million dollars."

"This is great news," said Mr. Kanberg. "I will now begin to work with my client and compose a Settlement Contract to outline the terms and conditions agreed to by both parties and that we have resolved the dispute outside of court. It also includes the financial compensation agreement which you will be responsible for paying within a month. Is that reasonable for you?" Mr. Kanberg asked Morainya.

Morainya reasoned, "Will it take a couple of weeks to get that together, seeing that it is after 5:00," She was adamant that she didn't want to sign this today.

"No, we all wait here until it is completed and signed tonight," Mr. Kanberg instructed.

"I didn't realize that. Wow. Tonight. Can't I think this over?" pleaded Morainya; she was feeling nauseated and just wanted to flee.

"This is how it is done," said the Judge without compassion. "We all want to put this case to rest. They made an offer, and you countered with three million, and they accepted the offer. That's a verbal contract."

"Of course." She felt as if a semi-truck had backed up over her. This all seemed crazy. Why hadn't Mr. Kanberg prepared her for a three-million-dollar potential settlement? Why didn't she know that it all had to happen on the same day? She clawed at her thigh until sharp pain grounded her—nails slicing through panic. Alone in the conference room, she watched 6, then 6:30 pass. Her stomach roiled. Failure. She fucking blew it. It all happened so fast, and somehow, she believed she could control it. Look how much it cost her family because of the information she just discovered. Anger. Rage. Self-Hatred.

The judge came back to offer them a cup of coffee. She'd need a stiff drink after this assault as she signed the contract and concluded the settlement.

"Judge Malicado, my client is feeling a bit overwhelmed today. She would like to ask, did Aldo Napolitano tell you what exactly he believes her father did to him to suggest mental and emotional damage?"

"Oh, it wasn't her father."

Silence. A pause too long. "It was her mother," declared Judge Malicado.

The walls warped. Her gut twisted. Mom? She blinked. No. It couldn't be her.

Her stomach lurched. What was he talking about? The words hung there like an execution sentence. Her mother. The woman who had made them breakfast, who had tucked them in, who had read Bible stories about the Virgin Mary and spoke of love and forgiveness. Her mother. The one who was now locked away, mind shattered by dementia. What the hell had she done?

Morainya pulled into the garage of her parents' house. All the windows were dark. Of all the nights she'd had to be alone. Why was God against her? She had been a good and faithful servant yet; everything had gone wrong. She threw her keys and coat on the couch and started pacing fervently.

"I'm so fucking stupid. How did I let this get so far out of control? My family is going to kill me," she repeated this admonishment over and over, with her nails digging into her palm. She was as full as a tick with fear, worried she'd explode. The overwhelming feeling of having lost so much, more than she had ever anticipated, made her want to run and hide. How would she survive this? It rattled around in her brain like an endless loop.

Morainya stomped into the kitchen and poured a large glass of Rose' wine. Why not break her long stint of sobriety? She felt invaded and taken advantage of like she had been financially raped. Iben pinged her shoulder, and she slapped it and screamed 'NO! Enough.' She was starving but could not possibly cook anything healthy. No, she stuffed the plate of cookies and washed it down with wine, knowing that one glass would not be enough.

She grabbed the bottle of Rose', not even bothering with a glass. The cork had been pulled two nights ago. The wine sloshed as she brought it to her lips, sickly sweet and cloying. She swallowed Again. Again.

Maybe it would drown out the weight of today. Maybe she'd forget the sound of the judge's voice. Maybe she'd forget about the millions. Maybe her brothers and sisters would forgive the lost inheritance. Maybe she'd forget him. Iben pinged her. She slammed the bottle onto the counter, the impact sending pink liquid splattering across the marble.

"No!" she screamed. "Get out of me."

13

*P*lease, Father, no." My hands gripped the silk of his sleeping robe as if I could hold onto this life, onto him. "You cannot make me go with them."

But he had already let me go.

Pharaoh lay still, his body a husk, his spirit already halfway into the realm of the dead.

Pentu smoothed a damp cloth over his forehead, but he would not even look at me. It was already decided. The white linen curtains were drawn blocking the harsh southern sun. Pharaoh, who was the light of my life, lay dimmed of his life forces. He was psychically attacked by the dark magicians of Amun who sent electrical jolts to his delicate system. Pentu and Amaret shielded him the best they could, but even they had grown weary of the years of severe spells cast upon our city to destroy us.

Pharaoh took a sip of water offered by Pentu then he said, "This is the way Aten has deemed to bring you to Djehuty. I am humbled that while being the Pharaoh of Khemit, I, too, have lost the power that was once afforded me."

"But, father," I tried to argue in order to ease his discomfort.

He held up a hand to silence me. "Look at how much has changed since we moved here. The golden barge. The hordes of well-wishers shouting our names and waving papyrus umbels?" His eyes glazed as he recalled the approval."

"You are still beloved, father." I lifted his hand and kissed it.

Father gave a weak smile. "It was in recognition of the Aten. I am merely a channel of all its glory."

Pentu softened the dis-ease my father felt. "Merit-Aten, all the luxuries and luxury have been stripped from us. I am sure your father grieves at having been reduced to sending his precious daughter out among charlatans and beggars to sneak her to Giza. This is not what we prayed for. This is not what we asked for. And yet, here we are. If you want this initiation, and believe me, you do, then you must travel unto Djehuty, for he will not venture to you."

Pharaoh nodded slowly, the weight of years etched into the lines of his bare brow. Without his crown, he looked smaller—just a man, not a god. "My beloved one," his voice was thin but steady, "your resolve will be tested. So will theirs. It will twist and stretch you in ways you cannot yet imagine. But that is the furnace of true alchemy. You will return changed." His eyes closed for a moment, the lids trembling. "I remember the cold wind of Heliopolis on the night I learned my brother had Wested. I was no longer a student. I was king. And nothing—not the prayers, not the priests—could have prepared me."

Life will make you stronger, and the fire will burn away the dross of having had an easy life. We have grown used to the pampering of rulership, and I confess that the constant adulation makes us weak because we believe that our devoted worshipers will always keep us in their hearts. As I age, I know we will be forgotten as the grains of sand are pushed into random patterns by the wind. You, my

Daughter of Light, still have a chance to make your way into the annals of time."

My throat constricted, not wishing my empty words to overtake his fragile, earned wisdom.

Pentu gave him a sip of water from the alabaster cup near his bed before he said, "You see, there is a thing of great value and rarity. If Djehuty chooses to present it to you, that is only your first task. The second will be in how you return it to me."

"What am I to seek?" I whispered, sinking to the edge of his bed. My hands found his, thinner now, papyrus veins branching beneath parchment skin. He gave a faint shrug, barely more than the rise of breath. "It is not yet time for me to speak it. The answer does not come from me. It will find you in the fire."

My shoulders tensed. Questions were swirling in my head.

"You see, my eyes have been opened since my return to the city. I struggle with the shock of how one man could ever kill another. The arrows that rained down upon us from the enemy hidden in the jagged cliffs ripped me apart. I believed with all my heart that the Aten protected me from harm. No damage was done to this physical vessel, but being within a fly's hair of dying, one realizes the brittle bond we have to this temporal life."

Here, my father suffered; I regretted that the truth was that his very own soldiers were ordered to fire upon the Pharaoh to scare him and prevent him from ever stepping forth into further dangers. I was forbidden to tell him that it had been a sham. My heart ached. I feared that harboring this mistruth would come back to haunt me. With sudden impact, I realized that if Pentu believed the outlands were far too dangerous for my father, then it would be no less so for me, a royal and an Atenist.

Pentu interjected to save my father's energy. "Merit-Aten, you are being offered your freedom from the eyes and ears of this kingdom, but know that in the kingdom of God, there are no secrets—As Above, So Below. The fires of the Heavenly World of Atenic Vision will burn away the dross of who you think you are to be transformed into who you truly are. Every lesson is of the essence. You may be scared. Confused. Repulsed. All is in good measure." Pentu gave my father a sleep remedy of drops into his mouth.

"I don't want more fear. Or danger," I murmured. "I have lived enough of both."

My eyes flicked between them—my father, fading like the last note of a song, and Pentu, who carried the weight of all our secrets. I wanted to fold myself into their arms and never leave the shelter of this room. But their silence told me what I already knew: the path ahead was mine alone to walk.

"Netri, I have changed my mind. I wish to stay here," I said, gripping the edge of my cloak, fingers trembling as my breath came in short bursts.

Pharaoh's lips curved in a tired, understanding smile, the kind fathers give when they know their children must fall to learn how to rise. "Your karma awaits; I cannot protect you from what is rightfully yours. If you are to be co-regent of Khemit, then it will come by the hand of Aten. I may hand you the crown, but you will not keep it if you have not overcome adversities."

"You still have not told me where to find Djeuty? Or what I am required to bring back."

Pharaoh's eyes fluttered sleepily. "Find the red lion." A deep snore came from him.

I let out a breath that scraped my lungs. A lion? That was all he would say? How was I supposed to chase riddles spoken in half-sleep?

Pentu jerked his head toward the door, signaling me that I should allow him to slumber. I gave the Physician a hug and as I turned to leave, I thought I saw Pentu brush away a tear.

How had it come to this? I was being cast out of silk sheets and armed guards into the wild, my fate entrusted to charlatans who lived by coin and conjuring. Once one wakes from the dream, the reality of this world would kill most. My fiery devotion of love for him empowered Pharaoh, giving him hope after he was left twisting in the wind by my Meti. Now, even I was being asked to leave in his moment of need.

Only yesterday I had defended Ana-Kharu's wisdom. Now, the mere thought of him made my skin prickle. Like gold leaf burning on an open flame, I scorched at being tethered to the Gold Magician—the deceiver who would lead us into danger.

And yet, beneath the dread, a strange exhilaration coiled. The tremor of excitement was brooding. To escape the privileged life of confinement at Akhet-Aten—where I was told what to do and who I could or could not see—felt like slipping out of a silken cage.

I hated that he might be right about one thing: the path to becoming *more* would never be soft. Would an adventure to meet our true alchemical teacher be bad? But having Ana-Kharu as our guide, I felt like we were delivered into the midst of a hungry pack of wolves.

I stood in the hallway, torn between my father or the uncertain path ahead, when he appeared—he moved like a prince raised on silence.

Smenkhkare paused at the threshold, not wanting to intrude. The afternoon sun poured across the alabaster tiles, catching the sharp line of his jaw and the quiet strength in his frame. He wore no jewelry, only a simple linen tunic cinched at the waist—but it suited him. He had the kind of face that sculptors would remember: chiseled cheeks, a noble brow, and eyes like warm cedar, kind and unreadable all at once.

"How is Pharaoh this morning?" he asked, Smenkhkare's voice quavered as if afraid of the answer.

My eyes teared, and said, "Weaker. I am not sure how long he will last unless I can find the Master teacher and bring back gold."

His head bowed slightly, the prince's voice barely above a whisper. "Then I will need to say my goodbyes. And see that Tut-Ankh-Aten spends what little time remains with his father—while he still remembers his touch."

"Life is never certain," I murmured, with my hand to my heart. "Your mother Wested when Tut was young. Mine escaped the silence of Akhet-Aten, drawn to the noise and gold of Thebes. If the king leaves too..."

He looked at me, eyes rimmed with something unspoken. "Who is left to hold the center?" He paused. "It was not that long ago when I watched you ride that barge next to your

Mother during a festival. You were not afraid of the crowds along the banks.

I laughed softly. "Because I wanted to be next to her."

"I thought it was because you were already a queen in your mind. Fierce, proud. I admired that."

We stood in the hush of shared memory, the past threading us together more tightly than duty ever could.

"You've always walked beside me, Smenkhkare. Not ahead, not behind. Just... beside."

He met my gaze, steady and unflinching. "Because I know what it means to carry a crown you did not ask for." A silence passed between us—one of mutual understanding, heavy with things that didn't need to be said.

"Now, it is our turn," he whispered. "But traveling to Giza will be a difficult journey. Could you have ever imagined Pharaoh would send two royals with a troupe of vagabonds? They have no weapons and rely on the kindness of townspeople along the way to work for silver or food."

I could not even force a laugh. "We have tried so often to escape the guards and now there will be none to protect us." We exchanged glances at each other noting the horror of our fate. Was this the wisdom of a dying man or the delirium of a heart too full of visions?

Of all the classmates bound for Giza under Ana-Kharu's charge, Smenkhkare had never drawn attention. He didn't try. But now, standing before her, his presence pulled at something deeper—like a note struck on a harp she didn't realize had strings.

I overheard the guards say something that haunts me." His face twisted.

"What?" I asked

"They were huddled together behind me as I was reading a scroll. One guard, in a low voice mentioned the fierce desert people; the scoundrels that kill and steal from weary travelers, the lions, jackals, and vultures that scavenged corpses."

A chill spread across my chest. My fingers, once steady, curled into my palms. I had heard such tales as a child, always brushed off as fables meant to keep us within palace walls. But this wasn't a story. This was our path.

"I must go," I whispered, though it hurt to say. "I must say goodbye to my sisters."

Smenkhkare only nodded. He didn't offer comfort. He didn't need to. The truth between us was comfortless—but it was real.

As I neared their quarters, the sound of giggles and soft footfalls echoed down the corridor. I reflected on how I would change their sense of abandonment into one of joy. Interrupting their playtime with a colorful lizard they now called a pet, I began by telling them the truth.

"Merit, do not leave us," begged Set-te-pen-Ra. She, too, had lost weight. Dark circles under her eyes told me she was not well and that Pentu had not found a solution. Our poor Physician was spread thin, giving duty to my father at all hours of the day and night. Now, he must add my baby sister to his schedule. Our health weighed heavily upon Pentu's weary shoulders. Even I, could see that the years of service were becoming more difficult in both Pentu's and my father's elder years. I dismissed the attendants for our privacy.

"I must go, Dearest. I promise I will come back," I hugged her and stroked Se-te-pen-Ra's dark wavy hair. She looked like Rennutet, her true mother.

"Why do you have to go," she said, pulling at my sheath, thinking her strength could make me stay by her side. My heart ached for my dearest sister.

Father wishes that we go to Giza," I replied. "I must do his bidding as he has arranged a meeting with a most important teacher." I shrugged off the danger and uncertainty that had built up within me.

Ankhi, crossed her arms, staring at me with fury. "When will you return, sister?"

"I do not know how long it will take to arrive at our destination," I said flatly.

Ankhi pushed harder. "Are you sailing? I wish to go on the barge."

"No, Dearest. Not this time," I replied. "I am told we will ride the elephant or donkey."

"We want to ride the elephant." My youngest sisters repeated this phrase over and over until I had to put my hands over my ears.

Thinking of something that would take their minds off my departure, I remembered, "Amaret foresaw that Meti would be arriving home soon."

"Meti!" Ankhi squeaked. "I hope she brings me something pretty."

"She will not braid my hair," Nefer muttered, arms crossed. "And she always forgets the clapping games."

I knelt before them, gathering them close. "My precious ones," I whispered into their curls, "when I return, I will bring stories the wind itself will envy." I kissed their cheeks, breathing in the scent of dust and rosewater, willing the moment to stretch. A sharp ache pressed behind my ribs. *What if this was the last time I held them like this?* Still, I smiled—for them. Not every farewell is given the grace of a warning.

Pentu walked into the room. "Your Majesty, it is time. Everything is packed, and they await your presence. You must depart now."

I followed Pentu out past the courtyard that was now in blossom. I yearned to sit by the pool and dangle my feet in the cooling water, giggling with my carefree sisters. Each step beyond the courtyard felt heavier than the last, as though my body wanted to turn back toward the scent of baked bread, the splash of water from our favorite pool, the softness of Nefer's arms wrapped around my waist. My steps were unsure, and I cast my eyes downward. I had recently yearned for freedom, willing to give up my security. Now, it was safety I craved and tried desperately to cling to it like a pair of leather shoes that I had outgrown.

Ana-Kharu barked orders to his troupe to bring round the animals and ostriches. He caught my gaze and jerked a thumb at me. "She will start by riding in the basket of my elephant." Anpu, the drummer heaved me up to the back of the pachyderm where I climbed into the left hamper. Ana-Kharu put his lips to the basket and whispered, "I hope you brought sandals for walking because, my Princess, I can assure you that you will."

The swaying elephant in his lumbering steps propelled the baskets to and fro; the rolling motion, along with the rising heat, made my stomach roil. My hands searched the pack until I found a water cask. Helping myself to a few sips, I thought, would cool down the rising sickness from the bumpy motion. But between the slow and thundering steps of the elephant and the jittery quick-step shuffle when Ana-Kharu cracked his whip.

The rough woven twine used in the basket was scratchy and stiff and was as irritating as the angst of what lay ahead. Tiny stitches of sunlight poured in through the basket's fiber coils, making the view appear like a kaleidoscope that was once gifted to me as a child. My legs cramped against the packages of food and goods that were the priority, not me or my comfort. The elephant lurched forward, and my body slammed into the side of the woven basket. The air inside was thick and stifling, trapped heat pressed against my skin like a tomb. My throat clenched, and before I could stop it, a burning flood rose up, hot and sour, spilling from my lips. Vomit soaked my hands, my dress, my hair. I gasped, choking on bile, my body convulsing with the effort. The smell—gagging, sickly, spoiled bread and rot—clung to me.

The silence pressed louder than the stench. No footsteps came running. I blinked through tears and vomit, swiping at my face with the sleeve of my soiled dress. Alone.

Such a sorry state was confirmation that I knew in my gut that I should not have undertaken this voyage. All I could do was will myself into a wretched sleep.

Startled awake by a piece of sun bread, onion, and dates wrapped in a dirty, torn piece of linen thrown over the side of my basket that hit me smack in my head. I pressed the flatbread to my lips like a sacred offering, each bite gritty but welcome. Even the stale dates tasted like feast. I cautiously sipped my water, holding each mouthful so as not to lose a drop. I could smell moisture and knew we were trekking along the waterway. Breathing in deeply, the moisture was a welcome change, signaling that we were on course. A thousand invisible needles stabbed my feet. I shifted, wincing, but there was no room to stretch—just the ache of limbs folded too long. There was hardly a way to uncurl myself, so that thought had to be dismissed, and I instead contented myself with the singsong rhythms of the women who carried on a melodic conversation as they started their journey with merriment. As I peeked through the woven basket, I saw that the females bobbed along on tattered little donkeys. The girls clung to the necks of their donkeys, yelping with each bounce, their braids flying as the beasts kicked and brayed beneath them. The boys from my class walked, and each carried a load.

By dusk, I heard someone call out "Minyah." We had arrived at the first destination, which was a large enough city where I hoped we'd find beds and a decent meal. My elephant let out a triumphant trumpet, nostrils flaring as he caught the scent of river grass and acacia bark. The sinking of the sun signaled it was time to forage for leaves, roots, bark, and flowers that were widely plentiful in the date palm forests, marshland, and acacia trees that hung overhead.

We came to a jolting stop, and I felt the elephant bend down, thrusting me forward before its back legs managed to kneel. I heard voices, and a face popped over the basket, surveilling me.

"What a mess," said Ana-Kharu. "Get up. Get up. No sleeping now." He reached over the basket, rousing me to stand and get out. Shakily, I slipped a leg over, unsure of how far the drop would be and if my legs could hold me.

Hands guided me down. I smelled wretched, and the vomit clung in dried green chunky lumps in my hair and clothes.

"Water the elephants," ordered someone. "Shaduf ahead. Animals first." The waterkeeper lowered the tapering horizontal pole holding the large bucket hung from a rope and dipped it into the Nile. The contraption was counterbalanced on shore with a heavy weight. The loinclothed man swung the bucket up, and the elephant gleefully drank. The donkeys grabbed at the grass with their flexible muzzles.

Ana-Kharu yelled at one of the elephant tenders, and they laughed. I hovered awkwardly, my body caked in sour filth, unsure whether to retreat into the reeds or just dissolve into the dust.

A sudden blast of Nile water struck me like a slap—cold, wild, and uninvited. The elephant blinked innocently, as if baptizing me on purpose. He flapped his large ears like fans, as if he enjoyed the spray. When the rain stopped, I stood drenched; my sheath clung to my body, and I could feel eyes upon my form. I turned aghast and saw Archollos watching me. The others laughed in jollity at my discomfort. I had only brought one other sheath. Archollos grabbed linen from the pack of goods and covered me tenderly.

"What a lovely sunset to enjoy your bath," His arm curved gently around my back, a silent shield. The jeers faded as if his touch alone could quiet a crowd. "A goddess rising from the flood," he teased loud enough for all to hear—then lowered his voice just enough to warm my skin while holding up the sheet to give me cover while I changed my sheath.

My pulse betrayed me. I mouthed a silent *thank you,* but my eyes said more than I meant them to.

He bent to flick a pebble from his leather sandal. "My feet are sore from the walk but the scenery was beautiful along the waterway. I am sorry you could not view it from your prison."

"I was tightly bound and am only now beginning to take respite from the constriction. My feet can touch the ground, and my energy is rising." My spine straightened without command, as if his nearness sparked a fire I hadn't known was dying.

Archollos' eyebrows arched. "If I did not know better, I would swear that Ana-Kharu intentionally enjoyed your discomfort."

"I believe you do know better, and I agree," I replied and snuck a glance at Ana-Kharu, ordering his troupe to wash down the elephant and herd the donkeys so they didn't wander away. I craved the familiarity of their laughter, the inside jokes, the way we finished one another's complaints. Around the fire, I hoped to trade gossip like precious spices—who snuck sweets, who had blisters, what Ana-Kharu was plotting next. What did Ana-Kharu plan for food? My class and I would explore this little mudbrick town of Minyah while the troupe did their magic show.

Ana-Kharu nodded and signaled his group. "It is market day. Let us weave our way through this dilapidated town. Find those with extra to spend on pleasure. They do not have a need for the sundries. Lure them with other entice-ments." Silk scarves replaced rags, kohl lined tired eyes, and bangles clinked as the women sashayed toward the market, transforming hardship into allure. The sorcerer turned to us, "You all, find something to dazzle these dolts. We all work tonight. Those who do not work do not eat."

Gathering around the hampers, we pulled out faded luxuries that, in daylight, seemed quite frayed. The silver-streaked dancer demonstrated how to drape it around our bodies. I selected a turquoise linen half-sheath with little cowrie shells that had once been handstitched on the hem, but now many were missing. Grateful for what was offered, we did our best to be presentable.

Turning, we headed toward what appeared to be a promenade encircled by sycamore figs along a dusty, dreary pathway. Tiny unfinished mudbrick houses must have once been whitewashed but now looked ghostly. Traipsing through this untended town, with rotten palm rafters, stained matting, the forlorn citizens wandering about without purpose. Our temptresses began a round of loud lolololololoeeesh's with tongues wagging and we imitated them. The people cleared the way for us, the unusual visitors. We joined in the forced merriment with the pretense to extract payment. Finally, we ventured into the marketplace, and I was shocked to see the shabby merchants with unfilled shelves hawking their wares to the newcomers with hopes of a sale. Here, the bazaar simmered with the putrid smell of camel dung, perspiration, and urine-stained walls from those who relieved themselves while shopping. The crowd kicked up dust clouds and flies. Dogs barked while chasing vermin, which enhanced the chatter of a busy throng. Pushing our way through, I saw vendors with perfumes, baskets of fruit, vegetables, spices of all colors and textures, and pottery hand-created by the local wheel throwers. Chickens, ducks, and pigeons were in papyrus cages, ready to make a tasty meal. The boisterous negotiations hammered on between buyer and seller in every stall. A tiny sting on my cheek broke my thoughts—my fingers brushed away the culprit: a flea fat with someone else's blood.

Rotting flesh. That was what I saw first. A small boy, naked and motionless, stood like a ghost. His belly bulged unnaturally, ribs caging air, not breath. Flies nested in the wet hollows where eyes should have been. His mother—if she could be called that—had one eye left, the other a milky ruin, a wound that had never healed. She did not wipe away the flies. She had stopped fighting.

My breath came too fast. Did my father know? Did the Aten see? This was not our land, yet it was Khemit. I did not belong here. I did not belong anywhere.

I had never witnessed such pestilence. Upon closer inspection, this affliction affected almost all the villagers. Their swarthy, forlorn faces with filthy children seemed like a breeding ground for flies that strangely didn't bother the populus. Open sores festered in the late sun on those attending us today, and I had never seen such ill-kept people living in such poverty only a stone's throw from my father's grand kingdom. Did he know of the Khemitians living just beyond? Whom did they worship? There were no temples to the Aten. No faience-tiled halls or worshipful hands streaming down touching all with grace.

Clutching Archollos, he once again slipped his weighty arm about my shoulders, shielding me against the peasants with unpleasantries. Archollos jolted catching his breath mid-throat. "Something just ran over my foot," he whispered hoarsely, eyes darting. The crowds pressed against us, pushing us forward with no escape.

"What are we doing here?" I asked. "What could we possibly offer these people?" I overheard one of the women's ululations; a high-pitched trill wavered above the crowd, and we recognized her.

The thick black beauty of polished obsidian from our troupe made quite an impression upon the town. They gave her passage and utterances of admiration. She exchanged salutations and beckoned them to come to our bazaar just out of town. As we pushed on, the smell of lamb kebobs and lentil stew wafted over the crowd and made my mouth water. I had no means of exchange and set my hunger aside. Glancing at the throng, they seemed a sullen cautious people as their fly-pecked eyes darted to and fro but didn't see the despair.

No smiles met my gaze. Just hollow stares, as if I were carved from ivory they could never touch—or never wished to. The sorry energy sagged because they had never experienced the eternal, the Cosmic oneness of all things, and yet I did not feel at one with this horde. Each step throbbed like walking across hot coals, my soles blistering with each unforgiving stone. How could I illuminate the darkest corners of this rank and vile place? Or would I be ensnared in their contempt for such lofty ideals only significant to a Pharaoh and his family? Every face here was a mask of hunger, each gesture a prayer to endure one more sunrise.

"Ay, Princess, have you assessed the legacy that is to be yours?" said Ana-Kharu with a smirk. "What have you bartered for the fire? Or shall we dine on noble pride?"

Archollos stood straighter defensibly "No, we are trying, but these peasants have nothing more to offer."

Ana-Kharu rolled his eyes. "Then you are not offering what they want. Go hungry until you do." He darted away.

We were swept like driftwood in a flood—pressed shoulder to shoulder, our direction no longer our own. Grateful for Archollos' protection, it was by sudden surprise that the crowd lunged toward the cock fights down the narrow side street. There was no deter, and Archollos was pulled from me as the men pushed feverishly angling for a better view. I was hurled up against a fence separating the roosters and gamblers. Loud, sweaty men placed bets as the two bright roosters sprang at each other, talons bared. I could see blonde hair above the crowd, but my self-preservation took precedence. The pressure behind me was unmistakable. A hot, panting breath against my neck. Something hard, rigid, pressing against my lower back. A hand—rough, unwashed, grabbing at my hip.

I froze.

The crowd swallowed me. No one saw. No one cared. I could feel the rise of his sausage.

A bulky man behind me made jerking motions. A sickening, wet pulse against my dress. Something spilled. Something stained. My stomach turned inside out. My body screamed to flee, but the crowd was a wall, and I was the brick pressed into place. Helpless. Another villager took his place behind me, repeating the action. His grunts and ultimate discharge also stained my turquoise sheath. By evacuating his seed upon my unwilling flesh, my face blustered, and tears rained down from the insult inflicted upon my chaste vessel. His hot, wet discharge dripped downward and splashed upon my sandal. My body was not mine. My breath—stolen. My gaze—scattered across the ground like seeds trampled underfoot."

All the trauma of being pestered by Ptah-Mose as a child came flooding back. The Amun Priest's longings focused on the Daughter of the Pharaoh. Who would have thought an elder would try to hurt or scare me? His lustful urges infringing upon my innocence. Now, it all came back to haunt me as an adult. I still am at the mercy of a man's impulses without considering my unwillingness or consent.

Panicking, I screamed, "Archollos, help me. Get me out of here."

He edged his way to me. I whispered the wrongdoing into his ear. Archollos went deathly still. Then, his hands curled into fists. His chest heaved, rising and falling like a brewing storm.

"You," he said, voice low, dangerous.

The man shrank back. "It was nothing—"

Archollos hit him so hard his body collapsed against the fence enclosing us. In all his bronzed muscular glory, he glared at the peasant. "You dare take advantage of my wife?"

The man, fearful of the crowd overhearing that he had trespassed upon another man's consort, tried to negate the transgression. His denials instead brought smug laughter from the crowd. Archollos, angry as a bear, threatened the man. The peasant took his bag from his belt and offered it to Archollos, who swiped it out of his dirty hand before rushing me away to safety.

"Beloved, I got separated from you. I am sorry that I could not have guarded you from this offense. Blasted, rutting goat."

The sticky sheath clung to me, filthy. Defiled. My own body betrayed me. I wanted to peel it off, burn it, to scrub myself raw. But there was nowhere to go. Nowhere safe to hide. Archollos placed a small, dirty bag of silver in my trembling hands.

I turned the pouch in my hand. Silver clinked like bones in a tomb. "Well," I whispered, "we will not go hungry, tonight."

Archollos hugged me tightly, "It will be a bitter meal."

It would be at the cost of my dignity. My pride. All the arrogance I had felt before being a royal, was dissolved in my shame. And yet, somewhere beyond the filth and fury, a single ember in me refused to die.

he phone alarm clanged, jarring Morainya from sleep, disoriented, her mind wrapped in a heavy fog. She blinked, the ceiling above her unfamiliar and blurred. Her hand fumbled over cushions until her fingers curled around the source of the racket—her cell phone, shrieking with angelic harp music that felt like needles in her ears. As she tried to find her cell phone, the aftermath of a bottle of Rose' wine struck her quickly as lightning. Her head throbbed, and her eyes blurred, feeling hot and bloodshot. It hit her—she was curled up on the plush formal couch, not her bed. She shoved the white fringed back pillow to the floor and scooped up that blasted phone.

"Hello, hello," she said and cleared her throat.

A female voice said, "Mrs. Napolitano, please."

"This is Morainya Napolitano." Her throat scraped. Water would help. No—chai. That might actually revive her. Sitting up, she realized that she had eaten half a lasagna left in the fridge and leftover chocolate cake from Julianna's birthday under the cake cover. The formal living room table still had her dirty dishes and glasses as proof of her binge. At times she felt she was drowning, and she admonished herself for consuming whole bottles of Rose' wine after swearing she wouldn't start that up again. It left her feeling bloated and she calculated that she had allowed in at least one of the Deadly Sins: Gluttony.

"Hello, this is The Gold Gates Sanctuary. We would like to see you today. We have been experiencing extreme outbursts by your mother," said the woman on the other end of the phone.

"When you say 'we,' do you mean you personally—or Dorothy, her attendant?" Morainya stood, wobbly, already eyeing the bathroom.

"I am just the assistant manager—Janet," she clarified. "The morning attendant served your mother breakfast and she encountered some...well..." She hesitated.

"Encountered what, please? I've got a migraine, so let's skip the suspense and get to the bad news." Morainya hated being impatient, but she felt the indiscretion of too much wine last night, and she needed to purge into the closest vessel.

"Miss Stella threw full plate of spaghetti. It hit the wall and made a mess. Now, she won't eat. We will need you to come in today to talk to her."

"Uh, ok. I can in a bit," said Morainya, trying to comprehend this new disaster she hadn't expected. She sat up and straightened out her clothes.

Janet slurped something through a straw—loud, wet, and ill-timed.

"You might want to bring in something of familiarity to your mother. A comfort item. That can sometimes calm them."

"Yeah, sure," replied Morainya and hung up. She attempted to stand and felt woozy. She glanced up. The family portrait over the mantle stared down at her—Stephano regal in his tailored suit, Stella draped in Chanel, the children flawless in matching tones posed like a magazine spread. And here she was, in yesterday's wrinkled blazer with a dried tomato stain on the lapel, smelling faintly of wine and regret.

Yesterday's settlement conference surged back like nausea. The sting hadn't faded. How did she let that get so far out of control? That was all she could put into words. It was like she had unprotected, financial forced sex. And family. Her own family was accusing her parents—well, mom, of horrific things. The Judge's judgmental stare, with no objection from her lawyer who, essentially said there was nothing more he could do. Uncle Aldo was sequestered somewhere in the next room, spinning lies she couldn't confront. Helpless. Scourged. Plundered.

Well, this won't do if she was going to have to drive to thirty minutes North to The Gold Gates Sanctuary. Cleaning up the disorder of last night's bottles, plates, and the leftover lasagna would have to wait. Hopefully she could tidy up before Nico and Gina returned.

She dragged herself upstairs, Morainya stripped and stepped into a hot shower. She shampooed her hair, hoping her fingers could ease away the migraine that pounded in her ears. A phantom pulse jolted her—low, electric. Iben. In his ghostly form, he spread her legs and plunged in deep over and over until she came hard. His kisses pressed upon her head and back. She was panting unevenly from this unseen visitor. But where the fuck was he in this earthly realm? No messages for two days. No calls. Just this the ghost-touch between her legs, dragging her into wave after wave of an orgasmic state as he coaxed the 'ohms and vibes' out of her. He could still open her with a sigh and leave her soaked in wanting, it had to mean something. Sex like that had to be love. Didn't it?

After drying off, she slipped on her jeans and a orange sweater from her old drawer she pulled her gold cross over the neckline. No time for makeup. Her hair was pulled back in a red scrunchie she'd found in the bathroom. Glancing about the room, she knew her next project was to start packing up loads for donation. Just another assault on her senses of destroying everything from her past. Even her beloved Breyer horses—dozens of them—would have to go.

She just didn't have it in her to try and sell anything. Josh was an expert at listing his old bike and some skis of his youth on Facebook Marketplace, but she didn't inherit that gene. The thought of trying to hold a garage sale in this ritzy neighborhood felt degrading. Better to just get it all out.

She picked up her phone and, without thinking, dialed her sister.

"Hello?" came the airy voice on the other end.

"Francesca, It's me. You need to come back," Morainya snapped. "I don't care what mystical mushroom commune you're in this week—Mom hurled a plate of spaghetti at the wall and thinks she's being poisoned."

A pause. Then laughter. "Oh Mora, you're always so dramatic."

"I'm not kidding, I'm drowning! I've got to pack this mausoleum of a house, list it, deal with a settlement that feels like financial assault, and now I'm supposed to fix dementia with a keepsake blanket? You think I'm the only child?"

"You're the oldest."

"And you're the freest. That makes you next in line."

"Isn't Nico and Gina there helping you? He told me he's got it covered."

"Yeah, they help. Cuz they are family. As are you. But you ain't here." Morainya's hand trembled as she clutched her phone.

"I was hoping you were calling with good news about the inheritance."

Morainya's breath caught. "Seriously? That's your response? Not, 'I'm so sorry Mom's losing her mind' and you want to know—when do you get your cut?"

"It's not that simple, Mora," Francesca snapped. "Kyle and I sunk our savings into Jedidiah's blockchain logistics startup—remember? The one that promised to revolutionize sustainable shipping? It tanked. We're still trying to climb out of that crater. Kyle has daily kombucha deliveries and the girls are in gymnastics and summer camp. I can't just drop everything or hire childcare and fly to San Francisco on hope and fumes."

"Oh right, because you have a *life*, and I'm what—rotting in a mausoleum with a spaghetti-slinging mother and tomato on my blouse? You think I *chose* to be the one who stayed?"

Francesca went quiet, then muttered, "You always had the spotlight, Morainya. You were the heir apparent—Dad's golden girl, the one with the business cards printed before graduation. There wasn't room for the rest of us."

"No, I always handled the messes you pretended didn't exist," Morainya snapped. "You got to float away into almond milk suburbia while I stayed here—scraping dementia off the walls and unboxing years of secrets no one else had the guts to face."

Francesca scoffed, "You act like I ran off to sip cocktails and get massages."

Morainya's voice dropped. "You didn't just leave, Franny. You abdicated. You *knew* Mom was slipping. And you left Nico and me to walk back into this minefield."

Silence crackled through the line.

Francesca, softer now: "I couldn't handle it, okay? The smell of that ward, the stories, the look in her eyes when she doesn't know your name. I couldn't."

Morainya glanced down at her chipped manicure, and said, "Yeah. Well, I couldn't either. I just did it anyway."

"Look, I'm sorry. I just... can't drop everything, Mora. Not now."

Morainya paused. She rubbed her temples, the migraine was back. "Yeah. I got it. You never could."

Francesca released a heavy sigh, then said, "I'm hanging up."

"Of course you are." She dropped the phone onto the bed and stared out the window, the weight of duty pressing into her chest like a stone. There was no way she'd pack up her sister's room. She'd just give it all away to Goodwill.

Morainya was lost in her own thoughts and struggled to come up for air. Then her mind snapped to the Gold Gates Sanctuary. What was it she was supposed to bring? An item of comfort. She clenched her hands into fists. What in the world would comfort her mother that she'd even recognize? It certainly wasn't Morainya's face. That connection had been severed for a year. She'd been mistaken for her mother's sister, mother's mother and caretaker, but never as a loving daughter. That's heartbreaking enough to lose her mother also, along with her father's death. At first,

Stella started losing simple things, first her keys, then her phone, her purse; then after Stephano had passed away, came the urgent calls at all hours of the day demanding that her children come look for them immediately so that she could get on with her day. It would have been only natural after losing her husband to experience mental decline and confusion when your partner of 56 years suddenly leaves.

Unfortunately, Stella just kept declining until Morainya hired a caretaker so that she could stay in her beloved San Francisco home. After two years, with no real improvement, the children decided to relocate her to the Gold Gates Sanctuary. Strangely, being confined to a smaller double room with fewer choices seemed to help Stella, as there were days of clarity giving them all hope of her recovery.

When she poked around in her parents' bedroom, it felt dusty. She opened the curtains and allowed the light to flood in; perhaps it could dissipate the ghosts of yesteryear's once-tight family. Instead, she noted the dust particles emphasizing the tired bedroom. What would bring comfort to her mother? Pictures? She doubted Stella would even recognize anyone. Besides, she had already left framed family photos around her apartment with lessening interest in those now unfamiliar faces. Recollecting what were her mother's favorite things, which would be family, fashion, and fame as one of San Francisco's wealthy philanthropists. Wealthy, that was until the Tech world moved into the Bay Area and usurped that legacy also. There was no way to compete with the outrageous salaries and perks these new socialites enjoyed. The old crowd were swept under the Persian rug to be replaced by this new breed of technocrats and their hunger for materialism and the limelight.

For a moment, she considered calling Francesca back, asking if she remembered what used to calm Mom down during her Bridge Club tantrums or gala meltdowns. But the thought soured fast. No. Francesca had made herself clear—she had Lion's Mane to harvest and kombucha to ferment.

Was there anything Morainya could bring that would be instantly pleasurable to a mother with brain fog so severe that she forgot the children of her womb? Jewelry? Her Mikimoto pearl necklace was her favorite piece, and Mom always wore a string of June Clever white pearls. No, jewelry would just get stolen. Food? Nah, no point in getting her favorite chopped Turkey Cobb salad from Moriarty's Restaurant, or Red Velvet cupcakes if she was just going to heave it against the wall.

A hat? Morainya sorted through her mother's closet, hoping for a shawl, sweater, or purse. Yeah, that blue crocodile leather purse that had been her go-to favorite for shopping should bring some type of recognition. In the last month, Stella's prognosis had worsened. Maybe holding something solid would make her memories more solid rather than fleeting.

Each new task—packing up the china, fielding Josh's questions, signing legal forms—felt like a bite taken out of her. She was bleeding in invisible places.

All these family problems took their toll on Josh. She had noticed that her son had been pulling away from her and toward Jedidiah, her ex-husband. Maybe that was typical for a teenager, but he was her rock. Lately, Josh had been turning up his music when she spoke, offering nods instead of conversation, disappearing into late-night practices with teammates she didn't know. It occurred to Morainya that perhaps Josh was growing weary of all her problems and was trying to escape to sports and friends to fend off her endless complaining. She couldn't bear it if he left her too. What if Josh got accepted to a faraway college? He helped with maintaining the house and yard.

The Gold Gates Sanctuary stood on the bones of something older. The original structure—a crumbling, turn-of-the-century orphanage—had long been torn down, its brick husk replaced by polished glass, warm oak interiors, and marketing language like *memory care* and *dignified transitions.* But the ghosts lingered. The hill it sat on still carried the echo of screams no one had understood a century ago, when the misunderstood were locked away instead of medicated.

As Morainya pulled into the circular drive, the building gleamed in the midday sun, almost smug in its serenity. The high cement fence that encircled the property was softened by a drape of blooming bougainvillea—lush, fuchsia, and humming with bees. From a distance, it looked like a garden wall. Up close, it was an unmistakable barrier. Iron gates with gold-painted tips flanked the entrance, promising both sanctuary and surveillance.

A security camera blinked overhead. She parked beneath the shade of a jacaranda tree and stared at the perimeter. It was beautiful. It was locked. And it made her skin crawl.

God forbid a confused soul wander into public view. The thought stung. When had she gotten so bitter?

After checking in at reception, she headed upstairs. In the elevator, Morainya she pressed her sweater sleeve to her nose, the sharp tang of antiseptic burning her nostrils. Even the walls felt scrubbed of memory. The long hall with a rosy patterned carpet and oak wood paneling appeared friendly even though the inmates were locked in their cells. She turned the key on Door 248 before voices collided—sharp, high-pitched, and unmistakably her mother's.

A white-haired Stella, waving a wrinkled hand, she screamed, "I don't want any lunch. Get out of my room."

"Mrs. Napolitano, I can see you are upset. You don't have to eat now. Let's just take a breath," said the attendant in stained blue scrubs matching the blueberry pie her mom had hurled at him.

Morainya tried to remain calm, hoping it would take the edge off her mother's reaction.

"Mom, what's going on? Why are you yelling?" The tension made Morainya's head pound, and she tried to settle herself. Stella pointed at the man trying to clean up. "He tried to hurt me? I don't want him here."

Morainya glanced at the attendant's tag. "Carl brought your lunch, Mom?"

Mrs. Napolitano tried to push the taco fixings right off her tray, but Morainya got it out of her way.

"I don't know you. You can't make me do anything," argued Stella in a mismatched peach top and red and white checkered slacks. That combo would have horrified her old mom.

"I am so sorry, Carl. Can you tell me what might have set her off?" said Morainya, putting her hand gently on Stella's clenched fist.

"Aggression and violent outbursts are quite common in dementia care. Your mother isn't the first. We here at The

Gold Gates Sanctuary try to make every patient feel at ease," said Carl as if reading a script.

Morainya sighed, then asked, "So, this isn't the first time with my mom?"

"No, this has been going on for a while now. We do our best to comfort her and make her feel safe,"

Carl blinked and wiped the blueberry pie from his pants, catching the crust and filling in a towel.

"This was my first call from Janet about my mom not wanting to eat. Are you telling me this has been ongoing?" Morainya clenched her teeth until her jaw ached.

"Carl tilted his head. "I'd have to check the charts, but I have seen your brother Nico and his wife, Gina in here quite a bit."

"Mom, could you take a bite of your lunch if I sit here with you?" Morainya held the plate in front of her mother, hoping to get a positive result, but Stella just looked absently out of the window totally uninterested in the chaos she had created. Finally, Morainya eased the plate off the tray and carried it to the kitchenette, motioning Carl to follow with a quiet angle of her head.

"Can you tell me if her behavior has gotten worse?"

Carl nodded vigorously, "We have noticed an increase in yelling, cursing, and making threats. So far, Mrs. Napolitano hasn't resorted to grabbing or pushing any of the attendants."

"I guess that is good, right?"

Carl glanced down at his phone, avoiding eye contact. "If it escalates... we may have to transfer her to the next unit that offers more security for your mother—and the attendants. Then Carl slipped into the scripted speech, and said, "In the later stages of dementia, cognitive decline and behavioral changes become more pronounced. It all depends on whether we can keep her healthy, meaning that we can get her to take her medications on her own, or..." Carl sighed deeply, letting Morainya know that she wasn't going to like what she heard.

"When she gets scared, my mom gets really argumentative," Morainya whispered. "But skipping meals? That's new." Morainya fed her mother who took a bite of beef and gooey cheese. "What do you think triggered the mood swing?"

Carl looked up as he cleaned up the carpet with a blue rag. "Triggers can be anything, really. A change of routine. A new face. Fear. Frustration with forgetting how to use utensils, for instance. When a patient can't communicate their feelings due to changes in the brain, then outbursts are common as a form of coping."

"What can I do to be a support?" asked Morainya, feeling unsettled. Her toes curled.

Carl spoke gently, "We use redirection or relaxation skills such as reminding her to take a deep breath. We are managing her medication and therapeutic classes to help her learn to reduce stress and remain calm. She seems to enjoy some movement, and we take her to the clinic occasionally, she often lapses into fear of a new place."

As Carl stepped into the hallway to grab a mop, Morainya's phone buzzed in her canvas bag.

Kanberg: "Reminder—Cohen says we need your decision to wire the money to Aldo's attorney. Today."

Another buzz. **Cohen: "Call me about the tax exposure re: house sale. Need to prep estimate. And Kanberg**

called as a reminder of due date for dispersal of funds... to Aldo."

She stared at the screen, her temples throbbing. Of course. Because dementia, disinheritance, and pie warfare weren't enough—now the legal sharks were circling. She slipped the phone back into the bag without replying. Not yet. She couldn't even get her mother to eat.

After centering herself with a deep breath, Morainya knelt beside Stella to be at eye level. Morainya reached into her canvas tote and held up the blue crocodile purse, its brass clasp still firm. "This used to be her shopping armor. She never left the house without it."

"Why don't you introduce it to her slowly?" suggested Carl who was mopping the kitchenette.

"I brought your favorite handbag. Remember this? You used this every day when I was growing up." Stella swayed slightly in her chair, eyes far away, crooning a lullaby that made Morainya's chest tighten. She hadn't heard that song since her childhood and her world was safe.

"Mom, do you remember this? You had a wallet inside that matched the purse?"

No reaction. Morainya lifted one of her mom's hands to feel the crocodile-patterned leather. Stella gave a slight smile. Morainya was making progress. "Mom, It's your favorite."

Mrs. Napolitano stroked the purse, "Stephano, are we going out? I will have to get my hat," said Stella, gazing at Carl.

Morainya brightened. "At least she said her husband's name." She connected the two, and this was a step in the right direction. Maybe she just needed more of her favorite things to jog her memory. "Why don't we just sit here, Mom? We can enjoy the purse."

"Don't be stupid. I need my hat and gloves if they are in the purse," snapped Stella.

"Let's see what is in the purse." Morainya unclasped the lock. She felt for her mother's old wallet or a pair of gloves that Mrs. Napolitano used to tuck into her pocketbook; instead, she found a string of beads at the bottom. "Look, Mom, it's your blue rosary beads from St. Mary's. Do you remember these?"

A horrified look swept over her mother's face. "You get those out of here, or I'll scream.

Don't let him hurt me again. Father Joseph, I swear I'll tell the Bishop."

"Nobody here will hurt you, Mom. It's just me," said Morainya, wiping away a tear.

"You get Aldo away from me. I'll kill him. I swear I'll kill him if he hurts me again. You get him off me."

Aldo ran his thumb over the heavy gold ring on his middle finger—the Odd Fellows emblem etched deep into the face like a secret handshake from a life he never asked for.

He sat at the breakfast nook finishing a bowl of cereal, waiting for the phone call from his attorney that the wire transfer had been received. His spoon clinked against the sides, rhythmically chasing the last soggy ring of oat around the bowl.

Harriet bustled in, her robe cinched too tight over a nightgown. Her curlers poked out from under a wrap like sleepy children with covers pulled up. She poured herself coffee, gave him a quick glance, and asked, "So... once they get the wire, how long does it take before we see anything?"

Aldo cleared his throat and pushed his pajama sleeve up. It was nearly ten and he hadn't bothered to get dressed. "Chrisholm said they had to deduct the firm's fees first. Her hours. Filing costs. There are a lot of expenses that still need to be accounted for," he raised his voice as a warning to block her questions. "Whatever's left comes after that." He didn't meet her eyes.

Harriet stirred her coffee too loudly. "So, weeks, then. Or months?"

"Shouldn't be months." He reached for the NY Times crossword puzzle to fill in 4 down.

"I hope not. I already told the Iris we'd finally pay off her school loan. And Christy's baby is due any moment. I said we'd help them. Don't make a liar out of me, Aldo.

Aldo scowled at her, his finger gripping the pencil. "I told you not to tell anyone about the Settlement. It's confidential."

Harriet held her coffee cup up, "They're family. They know you sued Morainya. Word gets around, you know."

Family. The word hit him like a draft from a forgotten door—familiar, but cold. His jaw twitched, and he busied his hands with the newspaper crease. "Still, you shouldn't have told him. The damage this has done to the 'family' is irreversible. I know they hate me."

"Hate you? You deserved every penny, Aldo. After the way Stephano treated you all these years. Like an outsider."

He nudged the empty bowl aside and let his eyes drift to the window, where sunlight spilled through tangled bougainvillea. It masked the place too well. Once, behind that same fence, gray stone walls loomed like guardians of silence, and rusted bars caged the laughter right out of boys like him. The old placard still flashed in his mind—"Odd Fellows Orphanage"—its gold letters weathered into apology. Now they called it a sanctuary. Maybe the flowers were to cover the ghosts.

He fingered the Odd Fellows ring again, twisting it slowly. Back then, it marked him like a second skin—too tight to peel off, too strange to claim. Cabbage Patch Kids was how they were known because they had arrived by the Orphan train. Over 250,000 of them from the eastern cities and landed all across America with no papers to be adopted out like puppies. Now it just reminded him how often people traded children like coins. He'd been the extra mouth to feed. He wasn't one of the lucky ones adopted because he was cute and cuddly. By ten years old, a burden to the system, he had been moved to the St. Mary's School for Wayward Boys—although he had never figured out what classified him as 'wayward' other than he hated the hard work and discipline. The placement child. Chosen, but never embraced. *That's where they put him after the Daughters handed him off.* Where no one called him "son," but he learned to stitch hems, fold sheets, and keep his mouth shut. He could still smell the starch. Could still hear the hymns from chapel, sung like a warning. No one ever asked what happened to boys who stayed too long in the basement wing.

Harriet sat down next to him on the stool. "Did you really have to go after Morainya?"

He flinched.

"She's just doing her best," Harriet added, softening. "You said yourself—she's the only one who ever remembered your birthday.

"It's not about that." Aldo hated it when Harriet had to stick her nose into his business.

"Then what is it about?" she asked, and not for the first time.

He didn't answer.

Harriet pushed harder, like a child sticking a finger into an electrical socket. "Are we still going to the Salvo wedding at the end of the month? You know the entire family is going to show up. If the money comes in, I'd like to wear something real nice."

He hadn't wanted to sue Morainya. Hell, she was the only blood-adjacent family member who'd ever treated him like he wasn't an orphan dropped from the sky. But things had turned. The lawyers had turned. And so had time.

Now he sat with silence for company and a nagging wife. The ring still clung to his finger—not just tight but fused— as if even his past refused to let him go. His only real tie to the family—Stella—was locked inside those same walls, slowly forgetting her name and his. And the only woman brave enough to fight for him, Morainya, had been pushed away by his own desperation.

He had no one now. Just a legacy he couldn't cash. And a ring he couldn't remove.

15

*A*rguments sliced through the early light, louder than the birdsong. Shadows flailed against one another just beyond the fading embers of our campfire. I blinked the dust from my lashes and watched Ana-Kharu square off with a local—arms tense, words sharp, their silhouettes pitched like duelists deciding our fate.

"Thieves. Everywhere. You die if you go North," argued a peasant who tried to block Ana-Kharu.

The Gold Magician pushed him aside. "We have to get to Giza. What do you know? You are the son of a sheepherder."

The man waved his crook threateningly, "Sheepherders know death. That way is death. No. No. No. Too many people."

Ana-Kharu made the motion of a boat on the water. "Boat?"

"For elephant, donkeys and ostrich? You have the brains of a dung beetle," said the shepherd, gesturing to his head.

"People only. No animals," said Ana-Kharu, brushing his hands together.

The shepherd paused then gestured. "I can get you a boat, but there is no wind today. You punt?"

Ana-Kharu nodded and said decisively. "Yes. We will punt,"

They shook hands and slapped each other on the back as if their friendship had endured many quarrels. "Good. Good. You pay me. I get a boat."

Ana-Kharu tugged my soiled silver pouch from his tunic with a flourish, the clink of coin loud as judgment. The shepherd grinned. The pact was sealed. "Done."

I washed the morning cups with my back turned because my ears had heard the forbidden. Archollos tended the fire, as he too strained to listen to the conversation. The shepherd implied that death in whatever manner lurked before us, whether by land or by sea. Where would Ana-Kharu deposit an elephant? The beast consumed so many of the tree branches and the brush below that it would be hunted for the vast destruction of foliage.

"'Come! Come!' Ana-Kharu's voice thundered over the scattered camp. 'We have no time to waste—eat what is left and ready the donkeys!'" One of his coal-colored women was preparing a morning gruel from the soggy left-over bread. We had eaten well, with bellies still full from last night's successful harvest of coins; now, our journey forward was uncertain.

Ana-Kharu assembled his own troupe and plotted our path going forth. One of the swarthy men and two of his plump pets gathered the ostriches and elephant. Upon mounting the beasts of burden, they departed, heading South without saying a word.

"Grab the donkeys and head North. The boat will take us for two days. Clean up and head toward the Nile. I will be there shortly. There is still some business that needs to be completed," ordered Ana-Kharu. Others of the troupe hopped on the gray donkeys and trotted away, their packs bouncing behind them.

My class and I scrubbed the morning cooking pots and gourds and followed the troupe down to the river. I shaded my brow and scanned the river—its banks gaped open like chapped lips, sand curling in cracked golden sheets. The drought had left its scar. Sandgrouse scattered in nonsensical directions like drunken soldiers. We sat upon the river's edge and watched the scrappy town girls come and fill their water jars laid upright upon their heads, glancing at us with wide deer eyes, then retreated silently. Camels slurped their share as well as the male water carriers who filled their goat skins and made way for others at this watering place. Men stood and gossiped as they smoked and pointed at the limited traffic upon the waterway.

"Prepare to board," boomed Ana-Kharu as we all looked back and noticed the arrival of the fishing vessel with thick nets stacked in circles. The women loaded upon the flat-bottomed acacia wood boat, and sat cross-legged upon the deck spread out so as not to upend it.

Ana-Kharu held up his hand like a wall. "Not yet. Ropes first. Drag us out—we do not float unless you bleed for it." Four of his heartiest men dug their heels into the sand, shoulders bowed, dragging the vessel forward like beasts yoked to stone." Our male classmates used wooden poles to punt us off the sand banks by thrusting deep into the papyrus reeds, cutting through the marshlands. The poles sank with a wet gasp into the silt, then arced back like levers, inching the barge forward with groaning resistance.

"Heave!" yelled Ana-Kharu, ordering those unlucky enough to now find themselves submerged up to their bellies as the dirty water rippled. The ropes groaned under the strain, and we prayed they would not snap. Each twisted fiber of the papyrus ropes let out sharp squeaks as if to protest. Their shirtless backs rippled with muscles as the men fought to steady our boat while both heaving and punting and pulling. Townspeople gathered upon the shores, making shrill sounds as encouragement.

By midmorning, the sun blazed overhead like a golden judge, casting light on our contest with the elements. Late in the morning, the sun's glory now crowned down upon us, illuminating the struggle between man and nature. With the strength of oxen, the men would not be beaten back and forged on until we rounded the corner, and, at last, we were afloat. With great forbearance, we crept into deeper water.

The last of the punters clambered aboard, soaked to the chest, mud streaking their limbs like war paint. They dropped onto the deck with groans and shudders, limbs trembling from exertion.

I knelt beside one of them, handing him a clay cup. "Beer. Drink slowly, or you will faint from the shift."

Smenkhkare crouched next to Anpu, the drummer, holding out a strip of hard bread.

"You earned this, brother. The boat did not move a finger without your back."

Anpu chuckled hoarsely, wiping his mouth. "I will be walking like a reed for days. My legs forgot they belonged to me halfway through."

I rubbed salve into one man's hands, and he purred like a cat," I whispered to Archollos—he then eased down beside another punter with a jar of salve. "Let me see those hands. Do not be proud."

"They are not hands anymore," Okun groaned, lifting palms red and cracked. "They are old leather sacks. I may never play the drum again."

Sarawat opened a jar and dipped two fingers in. "Then we will soften them. We need you whole for the next push."

The current tugged at the hull beneath them. A ripple of motion rolled through the boat.

"It is moving," one of the younger men whispered. "The current...she is finally waking up."

The wind shifted, lifting the sail. The canvas sighed and swelled above them, and the boat surged forward.

Ra-Awab stood and shaded his eyes, watching the palms along the bank sway and blur. "We are flying now. Look how fast we are passing the trees."

"Like women's hair in the breeze," Keshtuat murmured. "Long, dark, and full of secrets."

Archollos grinned. "Aten help the man who tries to catch a woman or a river. They will both run faster the harder you chase."

Anpu let out a hearty laugh. "Let the Nile chase us for once. Let her do the pulling."

They all chuckled, and for a moment, even the exhausted ones smiled. The burden had lifted—just enough for the moment to feel like victory.

"Gather round," Ana-Kharu called out, voice sharp as a falcon's cry. His eyes scanned the deck until every face—wet, sunburnt, or still smeared with river silt—was turned toward him. "This stretch of the Nile..." He paused, letting the silence ripple. "...is known for bandits."

A murmur rolled through the group.

"Bandits?" gasped Keshtuat, clutching a stained shawl about her shoulders as if it would protect her.

"Yes, clever lizards," Ana-Kharu said, pacing slowly. "They crawl onto boats just like this one. You blink—your neck is slit, your cargo gone."

"Wonderful," Smenkhkare muttered dryly, folding his arms. "Can they swim faster than we can sail?"

"They do not swim," said Ana-Kharu. "They slither. And they strike."

Archollos raised an eyebrow, squinting into the reeds. "We should post a watch."

Ana-Kharu nodded. "Correct. You will take shifts. Guard our luxuries as if they are your unborn children. That is how we will barter our way to Giza."

"Could we not we offer charm instead?" said Sarawat, trying for levity.

Ana-Kharu's gaze cut her like a knife. "Try charm on a thief's blade. See how it sings."

Silence.

He held up a pouch of dark powder and let it sprinkle into the breeze. "I will use protection spells. Not prayers. Not piety. Magick. And I will not apologize for it." His eyes found mine and lingered. I felt the heat of his stare deep in my chest. I gave the faintest of nods, heart thudding like a war drum. "I suggest you find your courage," he said, turning away.

Suddenly, the boat lurched—wood groaning under strain.

"Sandbank!" someone cried.

We staggered, grabbing ropes, jars, whatever we could hold.

"We are stuck," Smenkhkare growled.

"Ana-Kharu, what do we do?" asked one of the boys.

He didn't answer at first. Just stared at the banks. Then, calmly, he pointed. "Heavers in the water. Punters on deck. Pick up the poles."

"I thought we left the sand behind us," muttered Archollos as he stripped off his shirt.

I touched his arm. "It seems the Nile tests our resolve."

He nodded and gave a grim smile. "Then let us show her who we are."

We were stuck. Frustration welled. We were laid bare like a flailing turtle suddenly grounded, unable to swim to safety. I scanned the banks on both sides expecting at any moment to see a band of thieves excited about easy prey.

"Heavers in the water. Punters on deck. Pick up the poles," yelled Ana-Kharu, thrusting his finger. Ana-Kharu's voice cracked across the breeze as he thrust his finger forward. He plopped down on deck and grabbed the papyrus on deck and began mindlessly weaving a rope to pass the time

I steadied myself on the edge of the barge. Beside me, Sarawat tucked her braid back into her scarf and leaned out over the side.

"We are barely moving," she muttered, squinting at the sluggish pull of the ropes. "Feels like we are dragging the whole desert with us."

I smiled faintly. "We are. The Nile is stingy today."

She jabbed her chin toward a crumbling tower nestled in a clutch of Lubeck trees. "Look—pigeon roosts?"

"Pigeon towers," I nodded. "For fertilizer and food. They smell worse than a camel's backside but feed the crops well."

Tadushet wrinkled her nose and glanced at a clay-walled home slumped like an old man. "That one looks abandoned. Roof half caved in."

"Look again," said Sarawat. "There—see her? Feeding chickens."

"Oh!" Tadushet sat straighter. "And a man—he is patching a fishing net. I thought no one lived out here."

"They probably think the same about us," I murmured, waving as a little girl peeked out and darted behind her mother's skirts.

A few villagers waved back. Simple, open-palmed, curious greetings.

Sarawat sighed. "They do not get many boats through here, do they?"

"Not with sails like ours," I said, nodding as the canvas caught the wind at last. "Look—the wind has shifted."

The sail ballooned with a satisfying snap. Our boat jerked forward, gliding now with grace.

"I can breathe again," Sarawat whispered, the corners of her mouth lifting. "Let the river carry us."

The breeze swept across my face, soft and warm, laced with the scent of lotus and mud—of something ancient. I closed my eyes for a moment. "The Nile remembers," I said. "Even when we forget."

A sailboat glided gracefully past us down the Nile, and we waved. A gentle breeze caressed my face, carrying with it the warm, earthy scent of the river and the sweet, subtle fragrance of blooming lotus flowers. The sails billowed above, catching the wind in a silent dance, propelling our vessel forward with a rhythmic, soothing motion that echoed the heartbeat of the ancient land. The water was green one moment, then reflecting the white puffy clouds the next; I was fascinated that the ripples in the water changed constantly.

At the bow, I sat still as the world unscrolled before me—each bend of the river a fresh offering to the eye. The wide and majestic river stretched out like a lifeline through the heart of Khemit, its banks teeming with life. The distant mountains, their peaks shrouded in a hazy blue, stood as silent guardians of the timeless landscape. Palm trees swayed gently along the shoreline in the breeze, their fronds whispering the secrets of the ages. The air was alive with sounds of nature—birds sang in melodic harmony. Their calls a symphony of trills, whistles, and chirps. A kingfisher with iridescent blue wings darted swiftly over the glassy surface, then scooped up a fish. Ibises, with long curving beaks, flapped overhead.

The tall green reeds parted just enough to reveal thick, scaly backs glistening like wet leather—crocodiles, still as statues, jaws agape to the rising heat. I tightened my shawl and looked away, the sight crawling down my spine like cold fingers. The young woman waved to the children gathered upon the shore, and they jumped with excitement to see our boat. The women handed out flat bundles of barley and brittle slivers of dried fish, first to the men sprawled across the deck—muscles slack, feet twitching from phantom strain—ready to be jolted back to action at a moment's cry. The wind shifted and was now at our backs, blowing only a slight breeze into the golden orange set of the sun. The sun bled into the river's edge, streaking the hills in molten gold before disappearing behind their jagged spines. Shadows stretched long, then vanished. The Nile swallowed the light whole. We gave praise to the Most High to bless us with easy sailing for as long as it lasted.

Just before the sun vanished, I caught a flicker of movement high on the cliffs. Perched on a narrow ledge, a red-maned lion watched us, motionless as stone, its eyes aglow with the last light of Ra. No one else seemed to notice. Only I met its gaze—and in that silent exchange, a truth I couldn't yet name stirred in my chest. It roared, a loud, thundering warning. Yet no one but me heard it.

Ana-Kharu's voice cut through the stillness. "Rest now," he said, nodding at the men strewn across the deck like felled trees, Nile water still beading down their browned backs. His own eyes scanned the horizon before allowing sleep to claim him. The Magician was ever vigilant about the next steps of this journey. We took a deep breath, the scenery crawled by as the Nile finally cooperated with us as if by magic. Finally, we headed with anxious excitement toward our destined encounter with Djehuty.

Ana-Kharu studied the women who chewed their bit of hard bread. "You all are on duty. Take shifts if you need to rest."

Tadushet asked in her Babylonian accent, "If we are moving, what hunts us?"

Ana-Kharu opened one eye as he laid his head to rest. "Thieves. They will swim from the shores to steal our boat and all our possessions." He gave one last weary look before he fell into a deep well-deserved slumber along with the other men.

I felt the air shift. The young women exchanged glances—never been trained for battle, now handed night watch over a band of sleeping men and glinting treasures. No swords. No shields. Just our bare hands and borrowed courage.

"How should we smite them? I turned to ask Ana-Kharu, but he was fast asleep with a melodious snore.

We leaned into the dark, eyes straining, hearts thudding in unison. Each ripple on the river became a threat, each rustle in the reeds a knife unsheathed. attempting to rob our little band of entertainers. It was late into the pepper black night; the moon was but a silvered thumbnail, sparing little light when Sarawat spotted movement from the shore followed by a tumble of waves headed toward us. We prayed the wind bade the boat to out sail this demon. The females struggled to get a glimpse of the approaching danger unsure if it was a bandit, crocodile or perhaps a hippopotamus which could easily overturn our vessel. With limited visibility we would have to rely on our other senses. We grabbed the punting poles to stab the invader, hoping for a silent surrender.

Oya snapped her fingers sharply. "Hush. Listen," she whispered, stepping closer like a priestess mid-ritual. "Crocs breathe heavy. Hippos grunt. But men..." She tilted her head. "Men splash with purpose."

Cocking our ears and silencing our breathing, our hearts pounded while trying to determine the level of danger.

"The ripples are not rolling," said Sarawat. "Cannot be a hippo."

Oya agreed. "Not as smooth as an animal."

Tadushet's pole clattered against the deck. "It is a man," she whispered, voice shrunk to a child's. "He is coming to slit our throats."

My grip tightened around the punting pole, knuckles straining white beneath copper.

The waves rose, closer now—splash, pause, splash—too calculated to be beast. Every part of me wanted to strike. Every part of me screamed do it. Protect them. Protect yourself. But something flared in my mind, sudden and golden.

Flashback

I was twelve again, barefoot in the Sun Court. My father stood beneath the open sky, face tilted to the Aten's rays. "We do not strike in anger, Merit-Aten," he said gently, his arms outstretched as if to embrace the heavens. "Nor in fear."

"But if they hurt us?" I had asked, fists balled at my sides, the palace garden behind us rustling with fig trees.

He looked down at me, eyes soft but solemn. "Violence is a stain that clings to the soul. We are of the Light. Our power is to *receive* and *transform*, not retaliate." His shadow had stretched long across the alabaster tiles, merging with mine.

"You may be Per-Aat one day," he said, placing his warm palm over my heart. "But never forget—you are first a daughter of Aten. Promise me, even in terror, you will hold the Light."

Back to Present

The sound of splashing neared. The water darkened where the intruder approached.

Tadushet let out a small cry and raised her pole, but I could not. My pole trembled in my hands. "I cannot," I whispered.

Oya shot me a look—half fury, half knowing. "Then do not let it fall," she hissed, stepping in front of me. "Just hold."

I did. I held the pole upright like a scepter—not to strike, but to warn. The boat rocked as something brushed the hull. The water stilled again.

"Why put down our only weapon?" asked Keshtuat flipping her braids, grabbing my pole.

"Are you going to allow this thief to just hop on board and kill us?" asked Sarawat.

Must I defend myself? "I cannot hurt him. Perhaps we can reason with him if he attempts to climb on board." I responded, narrowing my eyes.

The swimmer drew closer, and the initiates kept their poles positioned to attack. When he was within striking distance, they yelled and stabbed at the water, hitting him over and over until he helplessly acquiesced. "We cannot let him drown," I said leaning over and offering him a hand.

Sarawat, took command. "Pull him on deck. We will tie him up." She yanked the enemy upon deck. It was a whimpering boy.

"Why are you here?" Tadushet snapped, her voice sharp enough to wake the sleeping deck. A rustle of bodies rose behind her—the women from every corner now alert, eyes blazing. demanded The boy looked upon their faces twisted in anger. He covered his, with elbows up expecting blows to rain down upon him.

"My father sent me," he whispered, his breath catching in his throat. "Please...anything would help." The adolescent was close to tears. Realizing he was at our mercy. He fell to his knees and bent low, his forehead pressed to the damp boards. He shook like a leaf.

"What did you come for?" I asked, my words gentle but urgent, hoping there was still time to reach the truth.

"The Amunites," he said bitterly. "They come for tax, they say—but it is thieving. They take everything. Our goats. Our bread. Even our daughters and sisters. We live on what they leave behind—crumbs and silence." The brown-skinned boy held his knees and buried his face.

"Amunites?" asked Oya, the dancer from the troupe.

He looked up, eyes sunken with exhaustion. "They have robbed us since before I had teeth in my mouth."

Sarawat held up her hands to protect the meek one. "The boy is clearly distraught; he was only trying to pinch something to give to another thief. We should be compassionate for this young man, for he is at the mercy of those who seek to terrorize and pillage the people without a care if they starve."

Smenkhkare judged those who took advantage of others harshly. "The Amunites Priests have withheld gold from the Sesh, even though it overflows in their vaults. Yet the elite bow down to idols and vain gods, who can neither see nor hear; instead, they send mercenaries to seize the poor by their throats."

"This is the truth," said Archollos, who had woken up from the noise, rushing to defend us. "We need to protect the young who are abused by these pitiless priests who send mercenaries to villages."

The others nodded. "What do we do with the boy?" asked Keshtuat, "The priests are powerful, the armies even more so. If we give him sustenance, thieves will pull it from his hand."

What could I do? My Father, the Ruler of the Land, was in the same position as this boy. Even my Father had not figured out an answer to this age-old problem.

"He can have the tilapia I caught," offered Smenkhkare. "I am happy to offer. The fish will tide your family over. That is fair. They cannot wrench from you that which you have consumed."

The boy blinked at us, lips trembling with a gratitude too big for his body. Then, without a word, he dove into the dark waters, the fish clamped between his teeth like sacred contraband.

I knew I would need to inform Ana-Kharu of the encroaching Amunite army. We would need his protective abilities to mask ourselves. As I stood over the sleeping merchant, I heard his ensuing snores, loud as the sawing of a yew log.

"Beni Suet ahead," proclaimed the Okun, drummer, who relied upon the stars to navigate our passage. "The croc bay should be a moment away."

Ana-Kharu's eyes flew open. The luminescent whites of his eyes reflected the silver moonlight. "I have been watching the banks all night using my magical senses. There is a large group on the march. I fear they are mercenary men, and not part of the military, but have formed a marauding group to use force to overpower the weak, defenseless, and poor. Right now, they are using the main byway to the city. This means we will need to cross the river ahead. It will be safer to keep hidden in the palm forests on the right bank." He licked his right finger and held it aloft in hopes of a strong breeze. "We are at the mercy of the Nile and its moving wind. Otherwise, we float lifelessly upon the sullen waters content to treat us like insignificant specks of flotsam. I have been battling unseen forces all night. Their power is stronger than mine, and I cannot hold them off alone."

Holding my hands out I blurted, "Either the Amunites will slay us, or the crocodiles will?" I prayed he had a plan.

The green waterway of the Nile felt alive and reflected the partial light of the moon. The water looked like a cracked mirror of mini green ripples, blowing straight at us and then calming back into smooth glass. The next moment, spray shot up from a sudden change of wind, which pushed us fast toward the shore. We were at the mercy of the sudden waves seemingly against us. Where we would land was unknown. Suddenly, we were snagged by a pile of driftwood and a sandy bank. Grounded upon an islet that rose out of nothingness like the primordial void. We hit the shore with a thud, which cracked our bow, splintering it and rendering it useless.

Herons lined the banks like judgmental elders, necks tucked and eyes sharp. The water had retreated, leaving tufts of parched green stranded like prisoners waiting for rescue. The shoreline was stripped of the Nile waters so that even the scrubby foliage appeared stranded. Crocodiles, bellies jaundiced, and backs plated like shields, clustered in silent ambush. They lounged like sentinels of death, waiting for water buffalo hooves, careless birds, or foolish youth to dare the waters. I trembled, for crocodiles have been a source of utter cruelty and torture in my life.

I was only a child when my brave nursemaid, Hep-Mut hurled herself into the Nile's jaws, diving after the ivory horse I had stolen in a moment of mischief from my father's step-sister, Sit-Amun. With a smile cold as slate, she whispered a curse—and from the waters rose a crocodile that took Hep-Mut underwater before my helpless eyes. My stomach clenched and my breath hitched.

Years later, during my trial at Kom Ombo—Temple of Fear—I was forced into a lightless tunnel, submerged to the depths, until it widened into a hidden basin where crocodiles circled, patient and unseen. Did we panic or continue to climb up a hidden wall and the emergence of freedom? Why did crocodiles, my greatest fear, continue to challenge me? Unlike some born with animal sight, I could not whisper into the bone-deep minds of those scaled beasts. No bond. No protection. Only instinct, and fear.

Why, of all the sandy embankments that we were trapped, did this one have to be the sanctuary for vicious reptiles? The Amunites camped above us, so we could not walk the road to Giza. Thieves dotted these villages to plunder the weary wanderer. What a disaster with no way to find a safe haven on the alternate shore where more bushy trees would have served as cover for a group as large as ours. We turned to Ana-Kharu, who gazed over the bow and cast his eyes over the myriad of half-submerged crocs floating silently like thrashed logs after a storm.

"How did we end up in this tributary that leads nowhere?" asked Oya with defeat in her voice.

"The Nile branched off to this pitiless bit of land where we ran ashore," I said.

Smenkhkare bent to survey the cause. "The boat is wrecked, and we have no wood to repair this damage."

Everyone rushed to the front to see the commotion. To their dismay, the severity of our situation was hopeless. Just one day from Giza—and now, marooned without a vessel, time itself seemed to mock us. Still in the blackness of early morning, there seemed to be no easy way to restore our boat, let alone make it to the other shore where safety may wait. Our thrashing had stirred the silent beasts— wide-mouthed reptiles drifting closer, scenting fear like smoke on water. Mouths as wide as open doors rimmed in sharp, gnashing conical teeth rambling toward us.

Ana-Kharu was unfazed; the petite magician glanced up at the Amunite encampment, then toward the thieves potentially lying in wait, and the crocodiles ready to pounce.

"What do we do?" I asked shakily, my legs trembling.

Ana-Kharu assessed the situation. "We need to swim the last stretch. It is the only way, as danger tempts us on both sides."

"How can we outswim those crocodiles?" asked Archo-llos. "I am a swift swimmer, but I would not fare well, let alone those among us who are not as steady in the water." He nudged me, and I knew it was true.

Ana-Kharu gave a slight whistle to So-Ka-Bekt, who slowly stood and joined us. This deep carob-coated elder woman looked to have ancient knowledge. While a bit older, she had power in those bones and nodded at Ana-Kharu and started to climb overboard.

I grabbed Ana-Kharu's hand, begging him to change his mind. "You cannot send her to die," I whispered, grabbing his hand. The ghosts of Hep-Mut's screams still clung to me—I couldn't lose another.

He gave me the side eye noting my ignorance. "So-Ka-Bekt is a Ta-wa-ret Priestess. She is one with the hippopotamus and crocodile as they represent her clan. Ta-wa-ret is the Queen of Heaven and Earth. Our priestess can talk to them and gain wisdom from these venerated reptiles," replied the Magician. "Only she has been granted the ability to put them under a spell to allow the hue-man to ride upon them. She has a warning for us.

The graying elder turned her body toward us. She wore sleeveless kalasiris simple linen dress spun from coarse uneven fibers. Symbolically it was dyed in a Nile blue color reflecting the river's life-giving force. A simple belt of braided reeds cinched her waist with a carved crocodile amulet for protection. "You must remain still once you are upon their backs," her voice sounded like rippling water. "Because of their hardened exterior, they will barely notice us riding them. If you awaken them, be prepared for their revenge since you are not part of the Ta-wa-ret clan. Am I clear?"

Ana-Kharu and So-Ka-Bekt awaited our consent.

Surely, just as she spoke, the tribal woman from the old world with the braids climbed barefoot overboard and waded through the shallow water toward the crocs. She brushed by the beasts as she clucked to them in a way none of us had ever heard. The yellow-bellied bullies gathered around one of their own, understanding our desperation to evade those who might do us harm. The largest of the croc clan threw up his elongated snout, jaws wide open, and wagged that thick-plated tail as the woman slowly straddled it, all the while petting its triangular-plated head.

"They have agreed to take us," said So-Ka-Bekt. "Let us agree that I am not responsible should you awaken the beast from my spell. There is no promise that they will not eat you if they think you a threat."

Ana-Kharu shoved us to edge of the bow, which lay splintered upon the rock, water now gushing onboard. "It is done. Let us mount the creature we will use to transport us up the Nile toward Giza. It is the only way. Prepare to hold your breath if they submerge. It is not meant to harm you but to protect you from evil," added the Gold Magician waving us forward.

I blocked my class from advancing forward. "You are suggesting we ride a crocodile? Are you mad?" I said harshly, throwing my hands up. "Am I being asked to consent to sheer lunacy? I must protect my initiates, and I will not put them in harm's way. It is sheer foolishness that you push us into the crocodile's den, but what is even madder is that you want us to touch the water of the Nile. We have been educated on the harm of the polluted waters that have been used as a toilet for the defecation of man and beast alike. The waters of Hapi are filled with worms that will eat us alive."

Smenkhkare sidled up next to me as we exchanged looks of horror. She said, "So, either the crocodiles or the parasites will likely kill us."

"Do you have another solution?" said Ana-Kharu, and he heaved up one of his packs, the contents of which had been insulated in sheep intestines and rendered waterproof. The Magician strapped it to his back, as did the others in his troupe. Then he, too, dismounted our battered boat and respectfully approached one of the great lumbering creatures. The rest of his troupe followed obediently.

My class looked at me for direction. Some were restless and exhausted, yet dismounted the broken barge. I admired their complete trust in this foolhardy plan. Without a care, they chose their rides from the short-legged crocs with clawed webbed toes. I looked at my class with confusion, asking for their collective guidance.

Tadushet, my classmate stood shivering. She had lost weight from her usually voluptuous frame. "Merit-Aten, what do we do? My younger sister had the worm of the Nile. It ate her stomach and lungs, and she died because she could no longer breathe."

Smenkhkare held a defensive position also blocking the women from the hungry crocodiles. "We have been warned since birth not to touch the profaned waters let alone trust a malicious croc."

"I know, brother," I replied. "It is why we drink the morning beer and do our purification rituals to rid ourselves of the pestilence."

"I am joining them," said Ra-Awab, the tall initiate who was fearless and sought a bit of adventure to make his life more entertaining. "We have no choice but to trust the Aten has again provided for us." He waded into the water toward the crocs. I was losing my ability to protect my class.

I turned to Archollos hoping he'd prevent me from making a terrible decision. He studied Anakharu, the troupe who now mounted their chosen scaly rides then back to me. Torn. "Both dangers could bring certain death, but I could see no other way."

"Are you sure? Could we perhaps walk to Beni Suet along the shore?" I pleaded with my eyes nearly begging for a solution.

He turned to me in a hushed whisper. "They are on the backs of the crocodiles and not one of them has been harmed. Perhaps they know the ancient ways and we should heed their expertise." He heaved one of the packs upon his broad shoulders and climbed over the edge of the boat, offering me a hand down.

"He is right, Merit-Aten," said Sarawat as she made a splash dropping into the water.

What other choice do we have?" asked Keshtuat, who climbed overboard leaving me standing with Smenkhkare.

"I will be by your side, Queen," said my biggest ally.

I gazed up into his shining eyes, he nodded with assuredness. Smenkhkare, was my one true friend, through thick or thin, he had always stood by me. Perhaps it was because we had the blood of royals coursing through our veins. "We have the covering of the Aten," he said pointing upward.

With great trepidation, I reached down for Archollos' as he guided me into the brackish water. A sickly-sweet stench curled up from the rotting reeds, coiling through my nostrils until bile threatened to rise in my throat. The muck sucked at my legs with every step, as if the Nile itself wished to hold me back, its cold fingers wrapping around my calves in quiet rebellion.

First, the receding waters of the draught had deprived our kingdom of food. Then our vessel that had promised safe transport to Giza, now lay half-submerged in the filthy water. Was the Aten forcing us to trust the unthinkable: a gold magician and a mysterious priestess who has the ability to put a spell upon the massive crocodiles keeping us safe—that is if we didn't awaken them from a dazed sleep.

Danger was on either side of the cliffs as we silently tried to avoid alerting the Amun mercenaries or the merciless thieves which plagued this countryside. I fought it every step with tears flowing down my cheeks that would soon mix with the Nile waters the deeper we traipsed in the sloppy mud of the riverbed. Sobek's children had caused me so much grief—and the despair was being reignited within my being. I would have to face my inner turmoil brewing within my gut like yeast for morning bread and trust, as Ra-Awab had pointed out.

The water crept higher, licking at my thighs as I inched forward, feigning calm while my heart thudded a frantic warning in my chest. I approached a smaller female croc. She jerked and snapped, and I stifled a scream as if some unseen hands had been clasped over my mouth to silence my shriek and jar these crocodiles awake. My hands trembled and I recoiled like a serpent to be left quaking in my steps. Hesitant to straddle her, I could taste the polluted river in the air, full of the invisible parasites that I had been warned about since I was a child—the insidious sickness would creep into my blood, like an unseen enemy.

"Tell her you mean no harm. Touch her head," So-Ka-Bekt instructed softly, gliding beside me on her mount. Her crocodile barely rippled the surface as she stroked mine between the eyes. "She feels your hatred. You see a monster. She sees a threat."

I swallowed her truth like stone. Then, through the roar of fear, my father's voice echoed like a bell: "Change your vibration. Uplift yourself."

The others were now mounted, and their impatience grew, worried that if we lingered much longer, we might be discovered.

"You will have to overcome your fear like our training at the Kom Ombu," said Archollos, his voice rough with exhaustion.

Hearing Archollos' made me recall the initiation at the Temple of Fear where I believed he had Wested when we were made to swim in a shadowy tunnel to confront a huge crocodile. While I emerged victorious, my love failed to climb to the surface. The priests intentionally withheld the fact that Archollos was safe, and it was just another test for me to overcome.

Sucking in my breath, my fingers grazed the rough, armor-like hide yet the scales were slick but solid, worn smooth in some places from cutting through the Nile's currents. I cast my leg over its wide, mottled back and felt her exhale with a grunt. Her dorsal plate felt like a ridge of bones thrusting into my chest and stomach. There was no comfortable way without enduring searing pain to mount her. The same agony, my classmates suffered to endure by trying to compensate for that longitudinal keel. We had no reins to steer these chariots of the waterway, and they were as unused to a hue-man riding them as would an unbroken stallion.

Ra-Awab's creature lurched forward, its powerful limbs paddled through the Nile with strong, deliberate strokes. His croc let out a guttural hiss as deep and ancient as the rumbling of a drum.

So-Ka-Bekt, the leader, waved us on. She laid flat upon the tiled green back, holding the squared shoulders, and bade her mount to swiftly march into the water until all we saw was her back and bottom, and the zigzagging of that commanding tail swimming against the current. Our rides joined the fleet like a flotilla of submersibles. As the Nile water occasionally splashed my face making me suck in my breath, and gasp for air. Hugging my body against the wide, flattened back of my ride as the power of the prayer of the Ta-wa-Ret Priestess flowed in our minds, uniting us with our perceived nemesis.

With measured ease, my crocodile swam with fluid precision snapping her muscular tail to glide upstream. She was faster than I had expected, allowing me to overcome my anxiety, and calm my chattering teeth. Much to my surprise these crocs weren't the clumsy, brainless predators I had imagined, but a silent, deliberate team transversing the glassy green water. Laying my chin upon her forehead, I kept my nose above the current and assured myself the next breath. The cold rush of air against my water-soaked sheath forced me to contract until my shoulders ached in a futile effort to stay warm. I must endure and not give into complaints; admittedly, this was the fastest speed we had thus accomplished moving in a straight line without the necessity of wind pushing our sails. My bare legs pressed tightly against the occasional rise of a jagged scale biting into my skin. What would I do if she dove, dragging me beneath the Nile's green veil? If hunger overtook duty, would I become memory? Bone? A tale whispered by the river? And yet...I held on. Not out of courage—but surrender.

I had to silence the fear. It hissed beneath my ribs, coiling tighter with every splash of Nile against scale. To keep from unraveling, I clutched Ana-Kharu's teachings like a lifeline—his voice echoing through memory:

"There is harmony. Correspondence. Every plane of life—seen and unseen—moves as one. The Ethereal, the Soul, the Spiritual... all flow from the same Source."

These weren't just words now. They were oars steadying my boat across the churning dark. The Law wasn't a lesson—it was the only thing holding me together as we neared Djehuty's gate. An unexpected splash broke the silence to my left. Moving just beyond the periphery of the moonlit path—another crocodile on the bank snapped at a bird ready to take flight.

Hunting. They were always hunting and once again terror consumed me, and my breath hitched. As if reading my thoughts, my ride let out a low, throaty growl which rippled through my bones. She could feel what I thought. The croc on the bank withdrew. My beast had warned the reptile on shore. She was protecting me and the overstanding allowed me, for the first time, to relax and trust. My Sobek had admonished one of its one kind, as if she was an extension of my will. A peasant might have called it a moment's fortune, nothing more. Father would have proclaimed that the Aten was prevailing and watching over me.

Over us. It was very obvious that the river did not offer its kindness, for every day the villagers and other animals, birds and fish met untimely ends by the hippopotami, water buffalo, crocodiles and parasites that pervaded this river. Even our fishing boat had met its demise. The Nile took what it wished for and allowed the rest to drift on. Hapi, the god of the Nile also expected daily offerings and there was no exception made for me because I was the daughter of Pharaoh Akhenaten. My safety depended upon merging my consciousness with the crocodile and keeping myself focused upon the present moment, not the past failings not the future hope.

I clung to the only comfort I had—my inner lessons. The Doctrine of Vibration echoed in my bones: all is frequency, all is alive. Earth revealed herself in nine sacred layers—dirt, clay, rock, marble, diamond, slate, lime—and the flesh followed suit: skin, teeth, muscle, nails, hair, bones, organs. Each vibrating in its own octave, each part of the song of survival.

Archollos maneuvered his beast abreast of mine, and we exchanged grateful looks to escape villains on either side of the banks, now ineffective against us. He was enlivened, as he craved the thrill of pushing oneself to the edge. A bloated branch drifted toward us, bobbing like a corpse—my croc, unbothered, steered directly into its path. Kicking her, I hoped to avoid the calamity, or we would both feel the impact. I gripped her hide, fingers pressing into the sinew just behind her jaw, whispering silent pleas—but she surged ahead, possessed by something far older than my fear.

I screamed for her to watch out. It was as if she woke from her mesmerization, and the Ta Wa-Ret dream ended. My croc barrel-rolled with me clinging to her back, and Hep Mut's painful death in the same manner flooded my mind. I let go and kicked furiously, refusing to sink into the watery depths.

Suddenly, something grabbed my arm and dragged me to the surface. My face thrust through waves as I swallowed the water, at any moment she would take a bite out of me and pull me to certain death. I knew I could not trust these beasts. My arm jerked hard, and up I was pulled over the back of another croc. My feet dangled like bait, ready to be consumed by a hungry reptile.

Archollos yelled for me to get on top of his back. Clumsily, I came to my senses and was able to swing my leg over him and lay flat upon his back. His wet skin soothed my body as I laid my face against his neck, feeling his golden curls pressed against my forehead. Tears of relief sprung from my eyes and streamed down his welcoming flesh. He absorbed all my fear and comforted me without insult or rebuke.

My fingers clutched his hand, trembling with a thousand memories—sunlit courtyards, a boy with salt in his lashes, and the first time he called me by name. I had never stopped loving him when his ship-wrecked merchant boat left him a cast-away upon our shore, where he was also taken by the Amunites to be sold as a little slave boy. Our fates had crossed so long ago. Where I had once saved him, he now returned the favor. My chest ached with a tender pressure, as if my ribs had opened to let the Nile itself pour through me. Together, I put my hand upon his as we traveled upstream on the Nile. What a sight we must have been—two souls atop a beast of legend, drifting like myth through the cradle of Khemit.

Praise be to Ta-Wa-Ret, She Who Is Great, the Lady of Heaven, our glorious protector of the rising sun. I know in my heart that her formidable presence indeed frightened away evil. As the yellow yolk of the sun hatched over the dawn of dark cliffs, I saw the Pyramid of Meydum, a glorious obelisk thrust out of the earth like a spear aimed at the orb.

We arrived in the sacred Giza triangle of Peace. Our leader pointed toward a rise of damp green earth. Beneath Archollos, the crocodile pressed forward, its armored limbs carving through the mire. Every step pulsed with a raw, ancient rhythm—half soldier, half god. I could hardly breathe for the awe of it...or was it dread?

With a final shudder, our mount halted. Archollos and I tumbled onto the bank like newborns torn from the womb of the Nile—laughing, breathless, half-mad with relief. We'd made it. Sobek had carried us through the dark. With a slow, rattling exhale the croc slipped back into the depths, vanishing again as if it never had been there at all. One by one, the others spilled onto the shore—sputtering, gasping, sobbing into the soil. Some kissed the ground. Others stared blankly at the horizon as if unsure they'd truly escaped. The gamble had worked. We had ridden chaos and lived. My GrandDjedti, Ti-Yee had once told me, "the Aten does not choose its champions lightly." If I had ever doubted her wisdom before, now I was convinced of the truth.

Archollos and I collapsed into each other, limbs tangled, hearts beating wild rhythms. His lips grazed my ear, breath hot with the adrenaline of survival. A golden warmth pulsed from his solar plexus, meeting the emerald glow rising in my chest. A sacred convergence. A heavenly yes.

"Merit-Aten..." he whispered, voice trembling like an oath. "I desire you. I love you. I need you."

My pulse leapt. I turned to him, eyes wide with recognition. My hands traced the lines of his face, etched by fate and fire. *Yes*, I thought. *Yes, I have always known.*

Turning my face toward his, I gazed into his eyes, my heart filled with joy. This was the moment I yearned for. The moment that I had dreamt about all my life. Our kiss broke like a spell, and I tilted my head to the sky, lips parted in silent hymn to the Aten. Every prayer I had ever whispered seemed to be rising now with the dawn.

But the light shifted—and there he was. Ana-Kharu. Silent. Still. Arms crossed like judgment itself. The sun behind him cast his face in shadow, but his eyes gleamed with the weight of a verdict already passed.

He did not rage. He did not flinch. He simply knew. And I knew what he saw: not a kiss, but a confirmation. Of everything he feared. Of everything I had hoped wouldn't matter. The kind of certainty that comes from a belief so deeply rooted; it cannot be questioned. His gaze flickered to Archollos, filled with quiet disdain, then back to me as if I had sealed my fate with a single kiss. As if I had confirmed every unspoken truth he held about foreigners and the folly of trusting them.

And yet, as I lay against Archollos' chest, it was Ana-Kharu's eyes that branded themselves into my skin.

$\mathcal{f}$leeing to her car, Morainya's heartbeat like a drum, thrumming in her ears. She fumbled for her keys, flung herself inside, and screeched out of The Gold Gates Sanctuary. Her mother's fear clung to her like a curse. What did Stella's admonition to Aldo to not come near her mean? What was even stranger was, why was it connected to her Rosary beads? She felt like she was bound by one of those colorful Chinese finger traps, where once you innocently enter, you are locked in.

Checking her phone, she saw two voicemails from Kanberg, Wallerstein and Katz.

Morainya groaned deeply. This legal battle had been waged for far too long before she realized the game; now, she was confounded as to how to exit this web of lies. Confiding in Nico about her mother's revelation was out of the question. How would he feel if his Uncle Aldo had hurt their mother? She needed allies, not enemies, so she kept the unsettling news about Aldo to herself feeling the agony in her belly.

Grabbing the steering wheel of her Honda Prelude, she let out a blood-curdling scream at the stop light. Trapped. Betrayed. Beleaguered. The weight of responsibility pressed down upon her from all sides. Caw. Her elbows flew up, and she flapped like a bird. Iben. Why didn't he connect with her when she needed him in real life? He pulsed her V. She sucked in her breath. This wasn't the right time to be in an orgasmic state; no, she needed consoling. She longed for his hard arms around her, his plush lips pressed against hers, and an assurance that everything was going to be alright.

The truth was, it had been three days of no contact, and now she was fuming inside. Ghosted. That's what they called it, right? The irony wasn't lost on her—a ghost ghosting her. It might've been funny if it didn't sting so much. She pushed down the disappointment, but it sat heavy in her heart, refusing to be ignored.

He disappeared right when she needed somebody on her side, or, was it still ghosting if he didn't leave her alone for a moment yet hung around her like a ghost perpetually poking at her? Always jerking her shoulders, panging her pussy, or this ridiculous cawing sounds like a bird. Pang. He jerked her shoulders, and she hit her own shoulder as a warning. "STOP IT," she yelled to calm down this relentless internal pursuit. CAW.

He paid her no attention as if to emphasize the total control he had over her body. That did it; she was going to drive half an hour away to his History Museum. There, she would demand that he stop his childish attachment to her. If he didn't want to show up in person in this world, then why would she allow him to have the unseen world availability?

She steered out of the parking lot and headed through traffic, hitting every stoplight in the city, thus increasing her turmoil. Her rage and hunger were mixed, and by the time she found paid parking near the Museum, she felt violent inside. He had to fucking stop tormenting her. It was utterly insane to keep prodding her relentlessly when she had so much on her mind. Knocking on the box office window, she recognized the Museum administrator, the authoritative woman dressed in traditional Afrakan style with an elegant headwrap, her large golden hoops flashed when the sun glinted off the earrings.

The woman looked up, startled—she hadn't expected anyone before opening. She still had a stack of singles to count and a drawer to balance. Morainya leaned in, her voice straining to remain steady. "Hello... I'd like to speak with Iben Fatah."

Her tongue felt thick, like it had been dried in salt. One foot slid forward, then back again—her body unsure whether to fight or flee. The woman behind the glass blinked slowly, her earrings catching the light like miniature suns. Her truffle-brown eyes narrowed—not with curiosity, but with irritation at being interrupted mid-task.

"Iben Fatah?" she asked, her voice edged with suspicion. "Who are you?"

"I'm a friend—well, a friend of his," she paused. "A dear friend," she added, convincing herself she had the right to say so. After all, hadn't he taken up residence inside her? That had to count for something. "I just need a moment to talk to him."

Gray curls peeked out from beneath her headwrap as she grabbed the microphone on the other side of the glass wall. Numerous golden bangles jangled upon her thick wrist. She gave Morainya a slow once-over, clearly unimpressed. Not a paying customer. Not even wearing lipstick. Just some disheveled white woman in an ugly sweater asking for time she hadn't earned.

"One moment." The Administrator excused herself and waddled back to the Executive Offices. Her voluminous hips swayed back and forth nearly touching the narrow hallway before she turned into the main office and sat on the edge of the desk.

Picking up the black plastic landline, she dialed methodically pressing each number from memory. "Marhaban, na'am, kull shay' 'ala ma yaram ya ra'is. Tilk al-sayyida allati jaltaha ila al-ma'arid zaharat al-aan 'inda al-nafidha wa qalat innahu min al-daruri an tatahaddath ma'ak. Madha turiduni an ukhbirha? "Hello, yeah, all good boss. That lady you brought to the exhibit just showed up at the window saying it's urgent that she talk to you. What do you want me to tell her?

Iben put his hand over the phone, feeling rattled that he had only just arrived home to Morocco to face a chaotic mess. His younger sister shuddered again, looking like she was in a trance, staring blankly out the window. Her hospital gown was stained, and she had not been bathed. Iben hated seeing her like this, a shell of her former joyous self who loved to dance in their kitchen growing up.

Iben spoke with a hushed tone, "Haqqan? Ibtakir 'udhran. La astati'u al-tahadduth ma'a-ha al-aan, khasusan ba'd...al-safar ila al-watan akhatha minni al-katheer. Really? Make some excuse. I just cannot talk to her right now, especially after... Flying home took a lot out of me. Tam taftīshī min qibal al-ḥurrās. Qāmū bifaḥṣ ḥaqībatī wa iḥtajaẓūnī fī ghurfa muẓlima. Kudtu an afawwita riḥlatī al-mutaːila. I was patted down by guards. They examined my suitcase and held me in a dark room. I nearly missed my connecting flight."

Mrs. Fassi pursed her lips feeling Iben Fatah's despair. Still there was a pressing matter of the American woman.

"Kayfa yanbaghī lī an ataʿāmal maʿa al-imraʾa? How should I handle the woman?"

A nurse passed by the door and Iben signaled her to enter the room. He was grateful that Mrs. Fassi didn't press him for answers as she could tell his attention was focused elsewhere.

Mrs. Fassi switched to English and added, "You shouldn't have invited her. You know how unpredictable strangers can be. Yeah, Ma, I know you say this," replied Iben. "Fqat akhbirha annani mashghool al-aan. Just tell her I'm busy right now." Iben softened his tone hoping Mrs. Fassi would convey the message in a gentler way than he could. Everything had happened too fast between Morainya and himself. He'd have to push that to the back of his mind. Family first.

Mrs. Fassi shuffled some attendance and ticket sales notations on the desk, stacking them neatly, she slipped them back into the blue folder. Removing the empty stained cup in the San Francisco Dodger ceramic mug, she discovered a coffee stain on the desk. She'd have to remember to clean that later.

Mrs. Fassi returned to the ticket cubicle, sighing as she hoisted herself back onto the high stool, before turning her attention to the impatient white woman who was demanding an answer. If there had been some romantic interest, Mrs. Fassi felt she had better nip it in the bud before the visitor got any ideas that Iben Fath would have any romantic feelings for an infidel.

Morainya chewed her lip restlessly. Looking at the closed door, she longed to see Iben walk out at any moment. Hopefully, he would welcome her with a warm smile and matching embrace. Finally, he would provide some explanation as to his whereabouts.

Mrs. Fassi loudly spoke into the mic behind the glass wall. "I am most sorry, but he no longer works as a consultant for the Museum." She held Morainya's gaze, measuring her reaction. Morainya gasped, feeling befuddled by this response.

Sweat pooled under Morainya's arms. "He's not here? How would I get in touch with him? It is very important," said Morainya, her voice quavering with panic. She felt like a schoolgirl being called into the principal's office.

Mrs. Fassi crossed her arms over her ample bust defensively bracing to be yelled at. "If you are a friend of his, then I am sure you could call him," she said with mistrust in her voice. The glass barrier was meant to keep outsiders out. Iben Fatah had directed her to not give any information. He just didn't want to see her.

Morainya felt again, like she was pleading her case. "I have tried calling. You see, I am a," she paused. They might think she was crazy, telling them that he linked himself to her. That they communicate in the inner realm through 'oohms and vibes.'

"Can you get a message to him? I feel it is quite imperative." Her mouth felt parched, and the barricade of the lady's emotional freeze was now impenetrable.

She shook her head emphatically. "I am most sorry, but he didn't leave any forwarding address or phone number. If you have already left him a message and he hasn't returned your call, you should be patient. Or he may not choose to communicate with you." There was a hint of sarcasm in her voice.

Shoulder Pang. "If you hear from him, please let him know Morainya stopped by."

"I will be happy to relay that message," said Mrs. Fassi, who didn't bother to write anything down.

The door had slammed shut. Hard. He didn't just ghost her—he erased her. And the worst part? He was still inside her, prowling her body like he had every right to be there. How the hell do you evict a ghost?"

Morainya spun around to leave, and she heard the muffled voice of the administrator,

"*Kalbah.* Bitch."

Instantly humiliated that she had turned her back on a woman who was trying to help her, Morainya stopped in her tracks and spun back.

"Thank you for your help," she said with sincerity even though her effort was in vain. She wanted to sob right there, to let the rejection hollow her out. But pride stitched her mouth shut. Trudging back to her car, she felt lightheaded—her blood sugar tanking fast. No, she wanted to stuff her mouth, to stuff down her feelings of rejection and abandonment. Clenching her hands, the thought plagued her that Iben was gone. She knew it was too good to be true.

Questions surged through her like a dam had cracked. Why would someone just walk away from a role he was chosen for? Was he running from her? What could she have done that would make him ghost her? And before another legal battle, that was just rude, she thought. Maybe the cultural difference was just too grand a leap to make. Probably for the best she thought, arguing in her head over and over and over.

There must be a coffee shop close by. Looking down the row of colorful storefronts, she glanced upon an Open placard with a red painted finger directing people into The Tree of Knowledge Bookstore. The store advertised a coffee shop and patisserie, so hopefully, she could get a snack. The sanctuary teemed with spiritual holdovers from San Francisco's hippie heyday—Peace and Love signs—had long since faded, but the incense, crystals, and unwashed sincerity still lingered like patchouli in the drapes. Spicy incense burned in swirling smoke signals, and crystals blossomed in fanciful colors on every shelf. It did have a quieting effect on her, and Morainya wondered if any of this New Age bull was real. It must have been a Fair day as little vendors had set up tables along the walls offering astrology readings, reiki healings, tarot cards and healing remedies.

"Excuse me, where is your coffee shop?" Morainya tugged self-consciously at the pilled orange sweater clinging to her arms like a bad decision. The fabric stretched awkwardly at the elbows, revealing the wear of too many desperate mornings. Her faded straight-leg jeans didn't quite fit right anymore, and the once-cute flats looked as tired as she felt. Her limp, unstyled hair framed her face like a quiet confession—she hadn't splurged on a real haircut in over a year. Appearance had long since slipped down the priority list, somewhere beneath legal bills, home repairs, and the endless needs of a growing boy. Every mirror reminded her that she used to try... before everything became survival.

"The Forbidden Fruit Café is along the back wall," said a clerk with blue hair and tattoos covering her arms in a decorative sleeve. "Ah—Tree of Knowledge, Forbidden Fruit...Eden vibes, got it," Morainya said, squinting at the blissed-out clerk whose grin was stuck somewhere between Namaste and LSD.

"Uh, thanks," she replied. Set to the right of the Forbidden Fruit Café, there were three rainbow-draped tables with a cluster of people wearing eccentric clothing exchanging loud and boisterous laughter mixed with witticisms and criticisms between old friends catching up. Standing in line, she listened to a stream of conversation and felt that she had stepped into that Bar Scene from Star Wars. It was like being thrown into a universe of planetary conversations, where everyone was searching for a common language. When she got to the counter, she put in her order for a Chai and a gluten-free almond flour cookie to hold her over until she could find some real food that didn't use tofu as a main ingredient.

Was this what the Haight-Ashbury LSD crowd of the 60's must have been like at the height of hippism? Morainya had just missed that era having been born in '66. She rummaged through her tattered wallet, pulled a crumpled bill, and dabbed at her eyes—pretending it was just allergies and not a heartbreak unraveling behind her lashes. Morainya gathered her order, and the barista directed her to sit at the community tables, open her heart, and connect at a deeper level with other patrons. She felt herself tighten after hearing those directions. Conversing with an overly exuberant crowd felt like a death sentence. Sliding into the end seat next to a man who was immersed in a book seemed like a good idea so that she didn't have to engage and could instead contemplate her miseries. He had the rugged good looks of an ex- cop, a precise shaved neck haircut, an ironed tee shirt, and tailored jeans. Never looking up, he didn't appear to be interested in conversation, so she sipped her chai. Even that made her long for Iben. Pang. Both shoulders and vagina. She let out a slip of Whoo; that one caught her off guard and made her blush.

The man shifted uncomfortably. "I'm sorry, do you need more room? I can slide down," he said with politeness, feeling confused as to the sound she emitted.

"Just a smidge," she replied, realizing that she was balancing on the edge of the wooden bench. He obliged and went back to reading. She smirked—clearly, he wasn't into communal oversharing either. Finally, someone with boundaries and a straight haircut.

"Looks like a good book," she said casually just making that innocuous polite conversation that doesn't mean anything. "It's a must-have," he said, pushing his hair back like a man who knew the truth and was just waiting for you to ask.

Morainya's head jerked back. "Really, what's that?" she asked curiously, "what kind of book would appeal to everyone?"

He turned to her inviting her into a conversation "The Excellence of Common Law, by Brent Winters. It is a must." The man assessed her with a practiced eye. Yup, she had the look he categorized as a brain-washed 'normie' wrapped in a sauce of suffering. Unlike a Jesus freak, he wanted to save her soul with sovereignty.

Morainya gave a quick half-shrug never having heard that term. "What is Common Law?"

His green eyes twinkled because she had obviously entered into a conversation that would be utterly fascinating to *him*. "Common Law is God's law, and it's from the roots in the laws of Nature, and of Nature's God." Turning his athletic frame toward this innocent bystander, he could measure if she was open to receiving some of his earned wisdom. The sudden engagement of conversation when she was trying to hunker down and drink her chai without bother made her blurt out,

"Somebody actually wrote down the laws of Nature? Like, don't water the lawn during a rainstorm?" She attempted to inject some levity.

The narrowing of his eyes mixed with a forced laugh implied he was surprised she didn't get it. "No, Winter's traces God's law and civil law through Babylon, Egypt, Pergamos, Jerusalem, Rome, and France during the Revolution...all the way to the United States for American's Constitutional law."

"Egypt, huh? Her interest perked. I like History books. But what does law have to do with God—besides the Ten Commandments? Like, the 'One Nation Under God' thing? Are you talking about religious law?" Morainya winced at her own words. Her nerves always made her over-explain. She'd tried to break the habit, but now it spilled out as word vomit.

He shook his head, "No, more about how we have been enslaved by Maritime Law and been lied to in the deception of words or legalese; it's called 'semantic deceit,'" he paused and took a bite of a chocolate croissant.

Her eyes sparked—memory ignited. "I have a Moroccan friend who mentioned that. Something about the birth certificate and berth... is that what you mean?"

Sal looked genuinely impressed. He nodded. "Exactly. That's the start of it—how we were pulled under the Law of the Sea when we belong to the Land and Soil. But Winters doesn't focus on that. His work's more about how 'The STATE'—or Caesar—replaced God."

"Oh," TMI, thought Morainya using Josh's words. Too Much Information.

"I'm Salvador Coronado, by the way."

Salvador, she thought. *Salvation She prayed it was symbolic?*

"Morainya Napolitano, it is a pleasure. Wish I had met you a year ago." Her voice dipped, heavy with something she couldn't name. She shifted on the wooden bench—it wasn't built for long stays.

He laid his book down, intrigued.

"Why's that?"

Sal studied her, struck by how pain seemed to sharpen her beauty. She probably didn't know it—but the ache in her voice had made her more radiant. He wondered if he could coax the story out of her, piece by piece.

Morainya sighed, she had wanted to run away from her problems and not come to some obscure bookstore to start talking about them. Was there no escape from this legal system? All she wanted was to disappear behind her chai, bite into something sweet, and pretend the world had stopped spinning. "Doesn't matter, it's too late for me. I'm royally screwed."

Sal made a humpf noise, negating her statement. His numbered successes would prove her wrong. "It's never too late," he said matter-of-factly, in the kind of persuasive tone a lawyer would take.

She challenged him with her stoic manner. "It is for me. The deal with the devil is done, and now I'm going to have to pay the piper." The sting of a three-million dollar settlement pickled her skin.

Sal took a chance and put his calming hand upon hers, hoping she wouldn't be offended by the gesture of peace. "Again, if you could trust me, it's never too late to correct a wrong. Common Law is for 'We the People, on The United States of America, unincorporated', call it 'American Common Law.' Brent Winters describing British Common Law' from where our version of this Law comes."

His steady tone impressed her more than she wanted to admit. Instead, she stifled a chuckle and buried the flicker of respect under sarcasm. and wondered if she should reveal that the *We The People* headline of the Constitution was written in a Slave's Blood. Nah, that would scare anyone away. Iben Fatah panged her V concurring that she was right on track.

Sal saw the change of thought pass over her, so he pressed on. "Do you know who Anna Von Reitz is?"

Morainya shrugged and took her last sip of chai. "No, can't say I've ever heard of her."

He unclasped the brass buckle on his brown leather briefcase and dug through folders. He reached into his briefcase Offering the only thing she might be willing to receive, he pulled out a thin blue book. "Allow me to give you *Disclosure 101: What You Need to Know*. I know it will change your life."

She had no energy for further study. It was like life had bronco busted her out of her saddle and propelled her to a hard landing. "What's that book got to do with me?" The flatness in her voice made Sal lean in. If he didn't reach her now, he could feel her drifting—like a signal fading on a radio dial.

Sal chuckled then said, "That is exactly the line I've asked many so-called corporations that claim to be in authority over me and try to persuade me of their alleged right to impose Maritime Justice upon me, a living man when they try to impose their Corporate Policies: their "Codes' upon me."

Morainya's eyebrows arched with skepticism as she listened to him identify himself as a living man. "Are you telling me you have used that identifier in our court system?"

"Well, first of all it's not 'our' court system. It's theirs but, you bet, it works. Every time. But it does take intense study—mainly to rid yourself of the decades of School district indoctrination. The hardest part about this is convincing someone that they have all the power."

Who did he think he was, handing her hope like it was spare change? Power? If she had any left, it was buried beneath too many contracts and too much silence. Morainya pulled back, this conversation was bordering on the ridiculous. "Believe me, I've been chewed up and spat out. I don't have power," she dug in her heels, reengaging in that lingering feeling of hopelessness.

Sal watched that deer in the headlights look he had seen so often by victims of lawfare.

His heart ached for her because he couldn't fix her problems, only because she wasn't convinced yet that she deserved it. "Why don't you read that book and learn how to come onto the Land and Soil of our actual Country? It will change your life for the better."

"I've already heard about this 'Sovereign Citizen' stuff from a friend. But I'm already a Citizen of the United States, not an Immigrant, so how would I come onto the Land?" This would work for Iben, as he was a Moroccan Citizen, and they proclaimed to be the rightful owners of America, but Morainya reasoned that she was already here in America, the land of the free, she thought sarcastically.

"First, the phrase Sovereign Citizen is an oxymoron. Sovereign is Free, or more succinctly, Sovereign means 'that through which all power flows.' The term Citizen means: subject of the State or the Roman Empire; a SLAVE. So, they contradict each other, it's simply more 'Justinian Deception" a made-up term used by a Foreign, For-Profit COR-PORATION pretending to be your government, since April of 1861." explained Sal.

He unbuttoned his brown corduroy jacket and took a deep inhale. "That's how we are labeled when we choose to take back our rights. It is a phrase to diminish the power that was given to us by God. Secondly, if you choose to come onto the Land and Soil, which means you give up your enslavement or your Citizenship to of one of two COR-PORATIONS; 'THE United States of America, Inc.'; or 'the United States, Inc."

Morainya's lips curled in disbelief. A hot zip of static danced down her spine. "So, I'd be an Expat in my own country?" she snapped. "I'm not sure I want to go that far. My Grandparents were both immigrants from Italy and Ireland and took great pride in becoming U.S. Citizens. I'm not sure I want to dishonor everything they worked so hard to achieve." She shook her head, gaze drifting from his face to the colorful book spines lining the wall. Their titles whispered escape—something simpler, lighter. Anything but this legal labyrinth. What she needed wasn't another revolution—it was a distraction. Something glossy, shallow, and sweet.

Sal analyzed the glazed look. He'd seen it so many times when he tried to help someone disentangle from problems that drained their energy. "It's not for everybody. It takes courage to do it. But, if you do, then you are no longer beholden to what's legal, only what's lawful. Here's my card if you ever want to discuss it further." He gave her a compassionate parting glance and placed a white card with his name and phone number on the table, as he had for so many others who never bothered to call.

Morainya accepted the card with a polite nod, already folding it into the black hole of her purse where things went to be forgotten "Thanks for the great conversation. I think I'll just look around the bookstore."

"Great to meet you. I will look forward to your call." Turning back to his thick book, he tuned her out.

A fog settled over her thoughts. Her breath came shallow, like she'd just walked out of a courtroom she hadn't prepared for. She wandered aimlessly to the next aisle and claimed a vacant seat near a Tarot Booth. The reader of cards was just finishing with an elderly client, and Morainya took out her cell phone to scroll the news and pray that Iben had messaged her.

"Would you like a three-card reading?" asked the mature Fortune Teller dressed in silky blues covered in gold stars, fiery suns, and silver moons. She had a matching wrap around her bleached blonde hair. Her skin was eerily transparent white with a smear of pink lipstick and blush.

Morainya glanced up at the Tarot Reader and thought she could have been straight out of central casting. Morainya's breath hitched.

"I'm not sure I buy into that spooky stuff," she said, her voice wavering between sarcasm and surrender. Sure, she was leaving her body at night and traveling with Iben, but the Bible warned about engaging with the devil: You shall not practice divination or soothsaying. Leviticus 20:27. The woman knew no one else was in line for her services, so she pressed further.

"It's free. You can pull three cards of your choosing, and I'll read them. I promise they will be very revealing," said the Teller, offering her a blue-edged deck of cards.

"Sure, what do I have to lose?" she asked, scooting her chair toward the kooky woman.

"Shuffle the cards, separate into three piles, and ask your question."

Morainya took the worn cards and did as the woman asked. After separating into three piles, Morainya asked, "What is my future?"

"Pull three and turn them over."

Morainya's fingers trembled as she picked up the card. The red lion stared back at her, unblinking. Strength. Tame the Beast. Overcome the fear. A shiver ran down her spine. Was this a message? A warning or just another cruel cosmic joke?" The Six of Cups. The past. Joys of childhood. Nostalgia. Justice Safety. Reassurance.

The seer tapped upon each card. Do you remember your past lives?"

Morainya chuckled, "Me? Honestly, I'm Catholic and don't really buy into that stuff."

The Tarot reader held out her hand, "Let me see your palm."

Morainya obliged, then feigning interest in this hocus pocus.

The Tarot reader pointed with enthusiasm. "Right here and here. You have pyramids on your palms. That suggests that you have had a significant past life in Egypt."

Morainya blurted out, "Really? Let me see." Indeed, it was true.

The reader's enameled rainbow nail clicking on the next card. "Strength. This represents/courage, taking action, overcoming weakness, and power of abuse. Does that feel significant to you?"

The synchronicity nearly made Morainya jump off the chair. "Exactly what I'm going through."

"The cards don't lie," said the reader, her eyes twinkling with delight. "In other decks, this card is also, the Lust card and signified "Beauty and the Beast. Meaning the beauty within can quell the beast or demons by our calming nature, or by using fortitude and faith, she can surmount all odds to tame her fears.

Morainya peered closer at the mystical card.

"Lust comes from the word lustre, meaning that we can't find our radiance unless we find the strength within." Iben panged her stomach and jerked her shoulders. "That is so weird. I've had a lot of legal stuff going on."

The reader nodded and tapped the third card, Justice, which shows a red-robed king holding a golden sword in his right hand.

Morainya squinched her face before reeling back. "Yeah, I didn't receive Justice in my court case," answered Morainya, implying the cards were wrong about that one." She was ready to walk away from this garbly-gook.

She continued, "The Justice represents righteousness, equity, fairness, and honesty. It is a Universal Principle of balance, especially when dealing with anything in the courts. This card would portray Ma'at, the Goddess of Law, Truth, and Justice in Egypt. It can also mean endings and completions by using the Sword of Justice to cut away all unnecessary things. Is this true for you?" The Mystic probed for the truth. "Have you experienced Justice in your Legal battles?"

Morainya sat back. "Nope, I got slaughtered. There was no Justice, believe me. Or maybe it means the other guy got his justice, I don't know."

The bitterness poured out of her mouth like Wormwood. "Thanks for your time. I guess the cards just told me that Justice isn't for me." Morainya could hear the resentment in her words, and she hated being so negative. How did her life suddenly turn so bleak? While working at her father's company, she had authority, creativity and purpose and a healthy income that made her life fairly carefree.

The Seer sat back in contemplation looking alarmed. "Perhaps, they are telling you to use something from your past to find your strength and Justice."

"Too late." The words echoed in her skull like a judge's final verdict. Three million dollars gone. Legal fees piling up. A mortgage teetering on the edge. And now, even the church wanted their cut. Despair settled over her like a thick fog, suffocating, inescapable. A shiver threaded down her back. Was this just a card? Or was it... a mirror?

oonlight caught the gilded edges of the barge as it sliced silently through the Nile, its hull whispering secrets to the water lilies with the destination of Akhet-Aten downstream under the covers of slumber. The rowers stroked in unison, pulling this sleek gilded vessel along with the glorious double royal blue sails that billowed intimidatingly with royal pride.

Nefertiti sat upon her traveling throne, savoring the moist midnight air rush past her cheeks. She relished a fleeting relief from the watchful eyes of the Amun priests. Though those parasites still monitored her—Per At of all Khemit. She balanced their presence with the adoration of her Atenist allies, who honored her with lavish parties, sacred rituals on Sun Days, and unrestricted access to the traders who brought luxuries from across the world. How she wished her daughters would come to their senses to partake of the beautiful world she had created back in Thebes. Their absence stung more than she dared admit. Not one sandaled step in the palace courtyard. Not one jasmine-scented braid against her shoulder.

The Malkata Palace, the Per Hay—House of Rejoicing that had once belonged to Amunhotep III, the father of Akhenaten, and his mother, Queen Ti-Yee, was now inhabited by Nefertiti and General Horemheb. Since her Royal Consort, Akhenaten, refused to answer the inquiring letters from the rulers of the Kingdoms surrounding Khemit, it was left for her to send answers for her husband, who was incapable of warring calculations in which Horemheb was so gifted. It didn't matter now, for she had been instructed to obey, and as much as she hated the mission set forth before her, there was no other way. Night after night, her sandals scuffed the alabaster floors as moonlight traced the columns of Malkata —no answer in the silence but her own shallow breath. She turned over every alternative in her mind, only to find them crushed beneath Akhenaten's unwavering will. Since the Pharaoh had no sense of how political maneuvering occurred, he relied on the Aten to guide him every step of the way. How could he not realize his kingdom was doomed?

Nefertiti paced the polished deck inside the covered Naos cabin, gold bracelets clinking against her wrists. "He left me no choice, Horemheb. I offered him a path—one that could have saved us all."

General Horemheb turned from the darkened window, arms crossed, watching the rowers make steady progress. "He clings to principle while the treasury bleeds dry. Does he not see? The city cannot survive on sunlight and devotion alone."

She turned sharply; her nightclothes clung to the curves of her body. The oil lamp flickering gently illumined her long neck and regal features. "As the mother of this land, the weight is mine now. He may pass on the rulership—but I, I pass on the land. And Malkata Palace is under my jurisdiction."

Horemheb nodded slowly as he took her hand in both of his "Then we move forward. We balance the blade between the Atenists and the Amunites. Let them rebuild Luxor and

Karnak. In return, we secure our position. The priests will collect their taxes. And we will take our portion—quietly, strategically."

Nefertiti's mouth tightened. "And Akhenaten?" Her voice faltered for just a breath. "He chose poverty. He chose exile in the sand-soaked tomb of Akhet-Aten. A dying sun for a dying city."

He stepped closer. His hand rested around her back—steady, firm. "Then let him go. You will be remembered not as a consort, but as a ruler. This alliance—it is more than survival. It is sovereignty."

She had made her choice—cold, calculated, and final. She'd folded the papyrus of her heart into sharp corners, the kind that cut when touched. This move would secure her place among the Great Queens of Khemit, ensuring she was no mere consort but a ruler in her own right, draped in the richest silks, commanding the respect of dignitaries across the world.

Horemheb, the military might, would stand behind her, protecting, loving, and guiding her with a strong hand. She needed him, yearned for him, and submitted to his fiery touch. For it ignited passion and pleasure in ways she never knew with her Consort. Together, they were an unbeatable, formidable couple that would redefine a new Golden Age, mixing heart and hand. The worship of the Aten would finally be accepted and allowed along with those still in devotion to Amun.

Nefertiti closed her eyes, letting the wind from the Nile kiss her skin, but the weight of memory pressed heavier than the air.

She remembered the council chamber—Akhenaten stand-ing tall, radiating divine certainty as he proclaimed the ban-ishment of Amun's worship. The court had fallen silent, stunned by the declaration. She had met Horemheb's eyes across the hall, and in them, seen the grim calculation. They both knew what this meant.

By outlawing Amun, Akhenaten hadn't just offended priests—he had awakened a slumbering hydra. The Canaan-ite overlords, already thirsty for dominion, now had their reason. They didn't attack in haste. No—they slithered into Khemit with clever tongues and cloaked ambitions, weav-ing themselves into markets, marriages, and even temples. Horemheb had warned her: "There are too many of them, my Queen. We cannot defeat them by force—not with what little Akhenaten has left of an army."

The vision dissipated as the barge glided forward, yet her jaw remained tight.

As the years passed, with no money to feed and pay for the military, the protection diminished of Akhet-Aten. Mer-cenaries grew because the Amunites hired these bands to plunder the people into submission. Now, with the drought plaguing Khemit, portions from the full grain bins of Thebes could be used to bargain for the allegiance of the people. Akhet-Aten was indeed doomed. This would be the final nail in the sarcophagus, and sand would envelop that City of the Sun just like she had warned. It mattered not; now, she would seize the power. She had to save her daughters, for they would carry on her lineage and all she had worked for.

"My Glorious One, how you shine on this moment des-tined to be yours," said Horemheb, gazing down with ado-ration twinkling in his eyes.

Nefertiti noticed the bulge of his loincloth and grabbed the thick package that had risen like the sun to greet her. "Ah, my General," she purred, sliding her fingers along his length. "I see your scepter rises to greet me. It shall not go unattended."

"Indeed, my Queen. It is yours. All yours and only yours." He flexed for her, demonstrating how much more he had to offer. He yearned for her plump lips to embrace the flower of his bulging tip. The pulse in his throat beat faster as her fingers lingered; his desire stood taut as a war drum before battle.

"Soon, my love. When we are safe within the walls of Akhet-Aten, I shall call for your sword to enter its rightful sheath." Her breath danced across his ear, awakening more than desire. She knew the power of anticipation, of letting fantasy sharpen the blade of control—and tonight, she wielded it well.

"Is that a command, my dearest?" Horemheb grabbed her delicate hand and pushed it harder against his aching loins as if a handshake to seal the deal.

"I quite insist," replied the Queen, her pert nipples pushing against the sheer fabric of her nightclothes.

He drew in a sharp breath, the ache of denied pleasure redirecting his focus. Desire cooled into calculation. If he couldn't have her yet, he'd take everything else—the city's gold, its treasures, its legacy. Nothing would be left untouched. He sucked in his breath, knowing he would have to wait for his pleasure.

The oarsmen, also his stealthiest soldiers, knew exactly where the treasures were stored in the locker rooms of the Aten Temple. Since he had created the security measure, he could essentially pierce the veil of Mahu, the Chief of Police's changing of the night guard. It was so simple. They all felt so safe in the desert with a clear sight on all sides that no one would ever dream of the destruction of the City that showed signs of the encroaching desert annihilation. This was not the trip to rip that city apart. Not yet, that would come when Akhenaten had met his fate and perished under the weight of trying to save his dream of heretical proportions.

It wasn't that Horemheb hadn't adopted the Atenist faith. At first, he was the greatest ally of the King. Certainly, being a cheesemaker's son from Khepert, his family suffered at the hands of the tax collectors. The Amunites had left their mark of destruction on his hometown, so when Pharaoh Amunhotep III's son had a vision to put an end to the madness, he jumped into the foray as a strong supporter. Like many in opposition to a century-long rule of controllers, this Aten movement wasn't sustainable. As he sadly discovered, the military was the only way, and there just weren't enough of them to overturn this dark age. It was as futile as avoiding a hippopotamus attack on the Nile.

It panged his heart when he discovered his foolishness and that idealism, no matter how beautifully delivered, can't sustain a change unless all the people agreed to embrace the revolution. It was just too hard to wake up the people who had been lulled to sleep by generations of complicity. Soon, within a robin's chirp, they would moor in the dead of night and scatter like rats to fulfill this plan. By the time the city woke up from their dreams, they would rise to the destruction set afoot, and Horemheb and his Queen would be returning to Thebes.

"Let us go over the plan? We must be as adept as Savanna lions, swift, silent, and precise," said the General, planting his feet wide and hooking his thumbs into his belt.

"I know what I need to do. I shall take my four soldiers and complete my task. A tremor fluttered in her stomach every time she pictured that stretch of open sand between the barge and the palaces.

"Chariots will be waiting for us." He said in a low voice as certain as the desert wind that always found its way home by dusk.

Nefertiti narrowed her gaze, lips pursing in a queenly blend of concern and condescension. "My father is the Master of Chariots," she said coolly, brushing an invisible fleck from her sleeve. "I was raised with the sound of wheels grinding the limestone roads and the scent of oiled leather in my nose. You think I do not know the chaos they stir at night?" She stood, the silk of her sheath whispering as she moved toward him. "A single misstep—one snort, one startled hoof—and the entire city will be awake. I will not have this operation undone by arrogance disguised as preparation."

"I have a plan to overcome that. The horses will be muzzled to prevent them from making a sound, as will their hooves be protected with leather coverings that will deafen the clamor of the hoof to ground."

"You have thought of everything. Pray tell how you think the chariots and horses will appear readied with these contraptions applied so that we may pull off this caper?" she said, her voice sharp as flint. "My Father Ay, the Master of the King's Horses, would never have approved such a gamble, nor released the number of chariots at this time of night in order to carry us quietly to and from the ship,"

Her brows lifted in cool challenge, lips parted as if to continue, but Horemheb raised a hand, already prepared.

"I have been corresponding with Ay for a fortnight, he said smoothly. "He believes that we are coming to surprise Ankh-es-en-pa-Aten for her bornday. You know how she longs for you, Dearest. We are coming with surprises for the girls, and I asked that he keep our arrival quiet so as not to create any preparation for the formalities of a royal visit from the queen. I assured him, this day was to honor Ankhi, and that Akhet-Aten should not overburden the court in any kind of preparation for our arrival."

Her lips curved, a low hum of satisfaction escaping her throat. "He knows Akhenaten should not be wasting precious money on banners, flags, and excessive food that usually accompany our arrival."

"Ay is aware that I purposefully waived all spectacle, and we chose to arrive in the still of night. He will meet us with the necessary transportation and was grateful for our consideration in abolishing the frivolity."

"That is why I leave the planning to you, My General." She offered her lips for the General to kiss.

He lowered his voice and paused. "Nefertiti, my lovely one, Ay has communicated, that your Consort is quite ill and weak. Apparently, he did try to journey out in hopes of raising great sums of gold to summon the armies back into consignment."

Her hand flew to her mouth, then she said, "I have no wish to make him suffer." Nefertiti's pulse skipped; a rush of memories—his gentle laugh, the way sunlight once haloed his face—flickered through her mind and stung her resolve." I cannot bear to see him wither so. He is a dear man, a kind man, and one who has the fever of devotion to a Shining God. A God that has never deemed to speak to me nor use me as a mouthpiece so that I could experience that Eternal Glory that he proclaims." Her shoulders slumped.

He offered a pained smile because he too had been caught up in the largesse of Akhenaten' vision to change Khemit. "You must steady your nerves. It is not my wish to cause him harm. I certainly cannot pull him away from his dream against his will. He is the Pharaoh, and I am obliged to do as he commands. But, if he is not awake while I am in the city..." Horemheb's lips curled into a knowing smirk, "then there are no commands to follow." He chuckled low in his throat; the sound edged with satisfaction. "A silent Pharaoh cannot object to what is done in his absence."

Nefertiti locked eyes with Horemheb. She caught the sly upward tilt of his mouth and recognized, with a thrill, the general's favorite game: war played under moonlight. "Brilliant."

"Get some sleep," he said, his voice softened by a trace of something unspoken—concern, perhaps, or the calm before the storm. "We will arrive soon. I shall wake you when it is time to prepare." Without waiting for her reply, he turned and disappeared onto the deck, the sound of his sandals muffled by the creaking timbers and hushed murmurs of the crew."

The Queen laid her head upon the curved headrest she used to protect her styled hair crafted into an elongated bun. She lay beneath the covered cabin, stars twinkling through the windows. Heat now seeping from her pores like fledgling embers, the night refusing to let her slip into dream. There was too much to chew over to waste time in sleep. She would sleep when she was dead; now was the time for action. The job assigned to her was crucial, and she could not afford to miscalculate any step.

Emotionally, she felt like she was being torn to shreds. Perspiration wetted her forehead as bad dreams swatted at her like pesky flies. She was suffering from a level of conflict that didn't usually affect her. Was this the right path? It certainly felt like the only way. The only one that had made her heart feel right. Why should she go down in the wake of Akhenaten's stupidity? He acted as if only he was at the mercy of his poor decisions to succumb to the death that swiftly approached his city. If he Wested, what would happen to her daughters if there was no one to take care of her sweet girls? They would be at the mercy of townspeople, only trying to save themselves. They would be abandoned like forgotten tombs that no longer could afford the luxury of hiring guards to prevent thievery. Or servants to sweep away the sand and throw out the stank of water of rotting flowers and offerings of vegetables. Her will was fortified. Nefertiti just would not allow that to happen.

Before dawn, in the stillness between dark and light, Horemheb entered her cabin. "It is time, my Beauty. We are nearly docked and ready to go ashore. My men are mooring the barge and preparing for a hasty departure. The clouds above are gray and swollen like rotted fruit. It gives us perfect cover as the light of the moon is blotted out, he said, scanning the shadows with tactical precision.

But she was not interested in military advantage.

"I have not slept. I feel faint. Summon my handmaiden to dress me, and I will join you on deck." She lifted her chin, the gesture slow and deliberate, as if the very air owed her reverence. Her eyelids fluttered half-closed, not in weakness, but in dismissal—as though just looking at him cost too much energy. One slender hand touched the hollow of her throat while the other flitted toward her hair, checking the integrity of her bun without truly tending to it. Her tone lingered like scented oil—fragrant, sharp, and meant to sting.

The General's face grew tight. "My Beauty, I am afraid that I did not invite your handmaiden, for I could not take a risk that she would surmise the real reason we were headed back to Akhet-Aten without presents for your children."

Her nostrils flared—an empress stripped of ceremony, now burning with quiet offense.

Nefertiti bolted up. "How am I to prepare myself? Did you think to pack any of my cosmetics or finery?"

Horemheb was a warrior and needed no help dressing himself. "Why would you need any of that? This is not a show or presentation to the masses," he said, rubbing his chin and clenching his jaw. "Come ready yourself now. I cannot wait for you like I usually do."

Her spine stiffened as if struck. His tone, a backhand across her pride, reverberated beneath her skin. How dare he? She curled inward like a scorned viper, already sealing the gates of her honeyed temple. No man, no matter how battle-hardened, earned entry with insolence. As the Per-Aat, she had not been crowned to be rushed. Her beauty was as calculated as her strategy—and both demanded ceremony. Even if they arrived in the cover of darkness;

she would not look any less than the personification of a goddess.

Horemheb's voice was more urgent as he scooped up her bath sandals and thrust them towards her. "It is time. Need I remind you of the importance of this mission. If you dally here painting yourself, then I will be forced to leave you behind and complete the task myself." He drew her by the elbow, compelling her to stand.

Vehemently, she withdrew herself from his irrational strength and felt the ire rise within. "Please allow me the time to retrieve my walking sandals and slip on a fresh sheath." she said with a cat-like hiss.

He threw her the bland bath sheath, and she slipped it over her head while finding her sandals in the pack. "I am ready."

Horemheb checked the crews' throwing ropes to the shore so that his barge didn't float away. He popped his head back into the cabin. "After you."

She descended the ramp in silence, her footsteps echoing hollow against the wood—no lotus petals, no hymns, no golden incense trailing in her wake.

Just as Horemheb promised, rows of chariots and horses were prepared for their departure. The Oarsmen boarded rapidly with military precision, and she was hastily lifted to the Royal Chariot as a sudden crack of a whip signaled the stallions to speed away. Normally, a thunderous gallop could be heard, but it seemed more like a muffled clap as the battalion sped over the grassy pastures and onto the Royal Causeway.

Suddenly, the chariots veered off in all directions like scattering ants. The couple were thundering up to the

Palace, which was designed for her daughters in mudbrick and decorated with cheerful faience tiled beauty. What made this journey a bit delightful, if not for devilish reasons, is that she would take pleasure in encountering Merit-Aten, her eldest insolent daughter. She could have evaded this fate if she had only agreed to the arranged choosing.

If her stepbrother, Tut-Ankh-Aten became Merit-Aten's Consort, she ensured their Dynasty survived. Merit-Aten would inherit the Kingdom when Nefertiti no longer prevailed upon this earth. Tut was only nine, and Merit-Aten now enjoyed the blossoming of her 16th year. The age difference was vast. She certainly didn't expect her daughter to be enamored by the boy; Nefertiti would allow her to take a lover to get impregnated. A lover of her choosing, but one that Nefertiti had already approved.

She touched the amulet carved in the image of Ma'at and remembered Hatshepsut. The Queen who dared to don the false beard and rule as Pharaoh. It was no longer legend—it was blueprint. Nefertiti would do the same, though through her daughter and stepson. Just as Hatshepsut had shepherded and made every move in the name of her stepson until late in her august years—Nefertiti would be the Co-Regent of Tut, the boy king until he was schooled in the ways of Pharaonic leadership by Horemheb. Let the world see a boy king and a dutiful daughter—so be it. The true reins would rest with her and Horemheb. The Co-Regent and the Commander.

Merit-Aten and Tut would come under their tutelage with no authority, only to be marched out for the masses as it pleased the Queen. That would teach her idyllic daughter of initiation, who really held the control and the backing of a large infantry to carry out all Horemheb's orders. The Amunites had made their demands clear. Reopen Karnak, restore the sacrifices, and the priests would flourish again. It was there, in the sanctums of Amun's temple-city, that grain flowed like gold and records of tribute were kept. Luxor, their chamber of divine kingship, would once more receive the offerings of a loyal people—ensuring the Amunites' dominion marched on in robes, not just swords. It was the perfect arrangement.

The shadow of night allowed easy entry into the Palace. Horemheb dismissed the few guards because they had grown lazy without a hint of a threat. They recognized his station and joyfully receded back to slumber in the confines of their own abodes.

Nefertiti led the way to the twins' room. "Please be gentle with my children. Do them no harm," she whispered and pointed a warning finger at the guards.

The group entered the darkened quarters, and the outlines of the twins were apparent, like sacks of potatoes laid askew. The guards moved like hunting cats—swift, silent, merciless. In one coordinated sweep the twins were lifted, gagged, and trussed, their small bodies slung over bronze-hard shoulders like sacks of grain. Nefertiti's stomach lurched, but there was no time to protest; Ankhi and Set-te-pen-Ra were next.

A muffled cry split the shadows as the other girls fought back—kicking, clawing, twisting—but the soldiers tightened the bindings with practiced ease. Leather bit into wrists, linen smothered screams, and the thrashing soon dulled to shivers of exhausted fear.

Sweat pooled beneath Nefertiti's collarbone as her chest rose and fell in frantic waves. Each breath snagged in her throat like fabric on thorns.

Merit-Aten, shaped by years of fire and forged under her mother's relentless expectations, was no glass figurine. She'd once stared down a charging bull at a desert rite without flinching. Nefertiti clenched her fists, heart pounding with dread. Would she bend now—or would she fight? The door exploded open with a crack that echoed through the corridor. Shadows rushed in—no longer men, but predators poised to strike.

They fanned out like vultures around a kill, eyes locked on the ebony-carved panther bedframe that once symbolized untouchable royalty, now guarding a girl about to be the next Per-Aat. *Nefertiti's fingers skimmed the cool linen. No indent. No scent of oils. Just stillness. Her stomach dropped— Merit-Aten was gone. A cold, rising tide of panic crested in her chest.*

She would not be in her father's room or Pentu's. Maybe Amaret was comforting her daughter. That impudent little imp would make sure Merit-Aten was safe; Nefertiti feared she would receive the wrath of General Horemheb for not completing the exact plan.

Out of the gloom shuffled Amaret, her voice sharp as flint. "Who walks cloaked in silence? Show yourself—I smell deceit." Her wild gray hair stood up on end like electrified currents. An unprepared soldier clapped the elder across the face, knocking her down with a thud. *Amaret collapsed, her body crumpled like discarded parchment, breathless and still. No time to mourn. They stepped over her like she was dust.* There was no time to look for Merit-Aten now that

Amaret had interfered. She'd have to proceed back to the barge to load her precious bundles.

The pawing red stallions made a hasty retreat. Along the Grand Processional Path, other chariots and soldiers who had completed their missions fell into alignment. They galloped back to the barge with their cargo in tow. Up the rampway, the soldiers marched, depositing the girls in the cabin. The next pair of soldiers arrived with a bound, kicking, Tut. His chariot with the framework designed in a light wood with the gesso curved front ironically featured the Pharaoh in the form of a sphinx with bound captives kneeling before him. *Now, the painted fable of the sphinx conquering its captives twisted into bitter irony—little Tut, bound and gagged, lay at Nefertiti's feet, a living inversion of the image carved into his own chariot.*

Nefertiti cast one final gaze upon the city that had briefly cradled her dreams. A faint grimace tightened her lips as the thought surfaced. *Her jaw clenched—Akhenaten would awaken to a father's worst nightmare: the boy was gone.*

Horemheb pulled up in a cloud of dust and waved at the other soldiers to proceed, loading the barge with their pillage. The temple was stripped of all finery; the Court vaults were defiled of the elaborate jewels, pectorals, crowns, court rings, and offerings to the Aten. Piles of alabaster unguent bowls, Tut's walking stick and his golden sandals, iron daggers with a golden handle, ebony and cedar wooden chests, a gold -plated leopard head, Pharaoh's ceremonial crook and flail, a green senet gaming board given as a wedding gift. Her husband's large collection of funerary ushabtis and other funerary objects. Piles of the children's clothes were dumped upon the deck in colorful heaps. *Nefertiti felt a knot of dread pulled tight inside her—wound hard and low. Was this ruin truly required? Or had vengeance become its own justification?*

Why did Horemheb need to break her husband with this cruel act of thievery? Now, there would be no way for Akhenaten to recover the loss.

Horemheb raced toward her and pulled his pair of white stallions to an abrupt halt, causing them to rear up. Remove the saddles and bridles and set the horses free. The last of the soldiers slipped the saddles off the mounts and unhitched them from the chariots, which now stood like helpless piles of shoes without feet to activate them into action. He ordered them all loaded onto the barge. Horemheb pushed an adult male, up the gangplank, and threw the elder onto the deck.

"Ay, it is at our pleasure that you join us," said Horemheb, who stood threateningly over Nefertiti's father.

The old man looked to the Queen, grateful that his relation would admonish the severity of the General's handling. But she said nothing. Why take Ay? That had not been the pact. Her father—torn from his post like a limb from a tree—was never meant to be part of the prize.

A chill slithered through her womb and spine. Gold, daughters, funerary gifts, even Ay—all taken. But more than that, Horemheb had seized the wheel of destiny. And for the first time in her gilded life, Nefertiti stood not as queen or co-architect—but as a pawn watching the game tilt beyond her grasp.

ood morning, Morainya," came the familiar voice of Sheldon Cohen—her family's accountant and father's longtime confidant. There was a weight in his tone, one that made her stomach tighten before he even finished speaking.

"Hello, nice to hear from you, Mr. Cohen. I was going to call you this week or next," she replied.

He cleared his throat. "Mr. Kanberg called me last night asking me to release the three million from your father's estate and wire it to Aldo's attorney this morning. I am asking for your approval as the executor of the estate to complete the transfer."

Today was Morainya's reckoning day. A cold sweat prickled her spine. The moment she'd dreaded for weeks—arrived not as thunder, but as a click on the line. "Yes, you have my permission." A sharp twist coiled in her gut, like metal blades grinding inside her belly. Her breath caught.

"I hate to be the bearer of bad news," Cohen's voice sank lower, like a man exhaling through a long hallway of regret, "but Kanberg says your bill has exceeded $98,000. He wants full payment immediately now that the case has closed. He was hoping you could send it immediately and mentioned that he feels his firm has given full consideration to your circumstances. He also made it clear—his firm has been more than generous with your late payments, and if you don't settle in the next twelve days, they're prepared to escalate.

"Mr. Cohen, I have begged my siblings for help. But they're drowning, too. There's nothing left to squeeze from this family but dust. Can't I just cover this amount from the estate?"

Cohen cleared his throat, like he had allergies. "He sued you personally, not the estate.

Legally, once the house is sold and the mortgage is paid off, then we will divide what is left amongst the four of you. How soon can you list the house?"

"The real estate agent got an appraisal on the house for nine million. The crime and homelessness in the city means homes are selling for less," repeated Morainya from what the agent told her. "How much is the mortgage?"

"Your father had a loan—still $4.3 million to go. With commission and closing costs, you're looking at a net of roughly four million, that is if you get asking price. And that's before anything left in the estate is factored in."

She traced a red line across her wrist where she'd twisted the skin too tight, fingers aching with unspoken panic. Her jaw tensed. That wasn't just a drop in value—it was a plunge, and she could picture her siblings sharpening their blame. She could already hear Francesca's voice: clipped, accusatory. *"You let it all slip through our fingers."* Emilio's silence would sting all the way from Florence. No Baci chocolates this Christmas, she guessed.

She heard the clacking of Mr. Cohen as he checked his calculator. "These things are complicated."

"And Archbishop DeLaurentis is expecting a million-dollar donation," added Morainya.

Cohen hit a calculator, and she could hear the computations buzz. "That is in alignment with what your father would have given."

"Seems like a huge amount," She said it gently, almost hopeful—like a child offering a broken toy back to its maker. *Too much,* her tone begged him to say.

Instead, he did the opposite. "The Napolitano's are a large contributor. Always have been."

"I know." Morainya felt the walls of expectation closing in on her.

Cohen pivoted. "You must be relieved the settlement conference is behind you."

She could hear him typing on his computer, completing the transfer of funds. Just one more thing off his checklist, she imagined.

She stuttered, trying to form words. "I don't know if *relieved* fits. Maybe… stunned?

Dazed, like I walked into someone else's ending. I'm still wrapping my head around how twisted this all became."

"How so?" asked Cohen, he stopped clacking at his computer.

"We proved that neither Dad, not I did anything wrong, and yet I somehow owe this huge sum of money to Aldo."

"Yeah, Aldo's quite a piece of work." His voice was casual, almost too casual—as if trying to slip the comment past her attention. Then the soft *click* of the return key.

"Piece of work? Morainya echoed, an edge creeping into her voice. You say that like you know something I don't. At the last minute, Aldo claimed he had been abused."

"Abused? By your dad? Sure, he was a firebrand at times, but he was running a multi-million-dollar company with employees worldwide. I had known the man for 50 years and even invited him to my house for family affairs. Why, he was at my wife, Loretta's birthday party just a month before he passed. He was an upright man."

"Strangely enough, Aldo implied his abuse was at the hands of my mother."

A long silence. Cohen's fingers hovered over his keyboard, then stilled. "You...you don't know, do you?"

Morainya felt the blood drain from her face. "What do you mean?"

Cohen exhaled sharply, then faltered. "I'm not sure I should be the one to say this."

"Say *what*, Mr. Cohen?" Her voice was no longer soft—it cut like a scalpel.

"This... this might be something that should've stayed between your parents. It's not my place." His voice trembled now, an accountant undone by something no ledger could hold.

Cohen's voice grew shaky.

She had to know. A family secret? The weight of it already pressed against her ribs. "Just tell me the truth."

He paused as if calculating the consequences. "Can you stop by my office in the next hour?"

Morainya hung up and stood frozen. The silence in the room pressed against her temples. Cohen's words didn't echo—they swirled, thick and disorienting, like water trapped in her ears. She couldn't tell which direction the truth would hit from, only that it was coming.

The fog hadn't lifted yet. It clung to the city like a withheld confession, coiling between the rusted fire escapes and old spires of the Tenderloin. Morainya pulled into the narrow lot behind the accountant's office, her stomach groaning with emptiness. It was nearing eleven. She hadn't eaten. Again. She glanced at her phone. Still nothing. No call. No text. No sign of Iben, except the constant low hum in her root, the way his ether pressed into her like an ache—his god-language still murmuring into the canal of her spine like some ancient psalm. She rolled her eyes and muttered, "You ghost me, but still possess my pelvis. Typical."

A familiar red cable car clanked by at the top of the hill, its bell a jolt to her system. She watched it disappear into fog, swallowed by the mouth of Market Street. Everything felt symbolic today. She passed the Old Mint—silent now, all golden stone and ghosts. impressive on the outside, hollowed out by secrecy within. Her anxiety made her crave sweets. She needed sugar. Too early for wine.

Cohen, clutching a half-full coffee pot, greeted her with a tight smile. "Come in, Morainya, coffee?"

"Just water," she said, eyes scanning the stale lobby carpet, her voice tight with unease. She trailed behind him. His short sleeve yellow shirt was wrinkled, the collar unbuttoned.

He exhaled sharply. "You might want to sit down for this," he said, nodding toward the worn leather chair. She didn't sit so much as perch—back straight, hands on her knees. The air in the office felt like it hadn't moved since the Reagan era. His story might push into the dark recesses of family shame.

"You have to make a promise," he stated and folded his hands in his lap.

"What kind of promise?" Morainya hated that he started a negotiation.

"I've kept my mouth shut for decades. Loretta would kill me if she knew I was even considering this," he said, folding his hands like a penitent man. "But this isn't just about friendship anymore. Loretta promised your mother."

Morainya sucked in her breath, feeling this was a long-held secret. Promised *my* mom?" she echoed, narrowing her eyes. Cohen's face tightened. "They were more than friends. Loretta and your mother—Stella—they were like sisters once. We used to double-date. She introduced her to Stefano... You didn't know that, did you?" He stopped. "Loretta is not going to like this at all." He scratched his bald head. The hair that was left wrapped around the back of his head.

"Please help me understand, no overstand, whatever. What could be so upsetting between Loretta and my mom."

"Speaking of your mom, how is she?" he said, vying for time.

Intentionally Morainya slowed down her words. She was ready to burst with rage. Yet, if she intimidated Mr.Cohen, he'd just clam up.

"I saw her last night; honestly, she's not doing great. Mom has been violent toward the staff. They are claiming that she's too much for their facility to handle. Full-time care is next."

"That is troubling. Dementia can be quite unpredictable, as I have been told. What sets her off?"

"We don't actually know. I brought an old purse to comfort her. When she opened it and found rosary beads. Then mom lost her mind. I thought she'd love to hold those religious beads again, being Catholic and all, but it only enraged her. Funny enough, she kept screaming about Aldo."

"Rosary beads? Yes, that would make sense. All the pieces will come together."

"Continue, please." Morainya fidgeted on the stiff client chair.

He blew his nose and threw the Kleenex in the trash. "Before she was Stella Napolitano, she was Sister Stella. A nun. Holy Order of St. Mary's back in the 1950's."

Morainya froze repeating the phrase in her mind. "That's hysterical, she swore like a drunken sailor when she got tipsy," said Morainya sarcastically in disbelief.

Mr. Cohen cleared his throat, then continued, "She joined right out of high school because she couldn't afford college. The opportunity to work with the kids excited her. Loretta worked in the school cafeteria and complained that the Mother Superior was very strict, bordering on cruelty by today's standards. It was well-known these young boys needed to be disciplined because they were orphans. Having no parental guidance, the church staff beat the boys into submission. The clergy believed they would be more compliant and fit into society."

"The boys?" she asked, dread pooling in her stomach. "What kind of abuse are we talking about?" Cohen lowered his gaze. "All of it. They were orphans—no advocates, no voices. And the church…believed fear was discipline. Belts, canes. Isolation. Starvation. Whatever it took to tame them."

Morainya tensed. Her voice cracked like thin glass. "Did my mother do it too?"

Cohen hesitated, visibly aged by the question. "Look, back then, the system thought teenage boys were unadoptable.

She probably thought she was helping—preparing them. But...yes, she participated. Most of them did."

Morainya reeled back in disbelief. "She's an upstanding member of society." Then she caught herself with a memory flooding back. "Wait...at the Archbishop's mansion, there was a large photo of a class of kids who all looked angry. Look, here it is on my phone. Do you think Aldo could have been one of the younger ones?"

Cohen nodded. "Yes, the timing is right. There's Aldo near the front row."

"I see him," Morainya whispered, staring at Aldo's crooked smile in the photo.

"Aldo was maybe fourteen at the time," Cohen said slowly. "Your mother—just sixteen.

She taught English to the boys, many of whom were already damaged."

The accountant hesitated, his fingers hovering above his lap like he might stop speaking. But he didn't. That day, your mother said...he looked wrong. His shirt wrinkled; belt gone. There were red slashes across the backs of his legs. Fresh ones. From a cane or belt. His eyes were unfocused, glassy. Like something had just happened before."

Morainya's stomach flipped.

"She asked him to clap erasers. He agreed. But the way he moved—it was like a switch flipped. He grew angry. Erratic."

Cohen wiped his brow. "She tried to calm him. She slapped him, trying to bring him back to focus. But that made it worse."

"What happened?" Morainya asked, though she already imagined the worst.

Cohen grimaced. "Aldo snapped. He hit her across the face—so hard it knocked her off balance. Then he shoved her against the desk. She tried to fight him. But he was too strong."

His voice lowered.

"It wasn't... what you might be thinking. He didn't— go all the way. But he assaulted her. Pinned her down. Touched her where no boy should ever touch a woman. He whispered vile things. She froze. Didn't scream. Didn't move. Just endured."

Morainya gripped the chair. Her blood roared in her ears.

"When it was over," Cohen added, voice thin and shaking, "he pulled away like nothing had happened. Walked out. Calm. Hollow-eyed."

A silence fell—so thick it buzzed.

"Loretta told me," Cohen began again, gently, "that your mother ran to her dorm in silence. She wept for hours. Told Loretta she'd brought it on herself—because she'd struck a broken boy. That she shouldn't have reacted to his outburst."

"She blamed herself?" Morainya choked out.

"She did. And worse—she wouldn't confess it. Said she didn't deserve absolution. She stayed quiet, afraid. Alone."

The room tilted. Morainya gripped the edge of the chair. Her skin buzzed. Her mother—a nun. Aldo—a child. A predator. Her breath came in short, fractured bursts.

Cohen waited for her breath to steady. His voice grew thinner. Aldo quit school the next day.

"For Stella, the Abbey was her only home. She had nowhere to go. No family she could turn to. No dowry. So, she stayed. Tried to go back to class. Kept her head down.

But it just felt impossible. Loretta said Stella would break into tears during class so she made a decision to quit.

Morainya's hands flew to her mouth.

That very night, she was expected to attend a fundraiser for the orphanage boys—the same boys she'd just walked away from—hosted at the grand estate where the Archbishop DeLaurentis resides. I attended as a junior accountant, under Stephano, invited as his guest. Loretta and I had only started dating."

Stella arrived wearing modest civilian clothes. For the first time, she was no longer Sister Stella, but simply a girl trying to disappear. A faint purple shadow bloomed along her jawline, half-concealed by a borrowed scarf. Her wrists bore the ghost of fingermarks, like old ink smudges. She told Loretta she was handing in her resignation the next morning. But under the starry sky, something unexpected happened.

She met Stephano. Something passed between them—a magnetic pull, a silent knowing. He was smitten instantly, but not just by her beauty. It was the way she held her breath when spoken to, the way her body folded inward like a question never answered.

Stella, meanwhile, could barely look him in the eyes. She believed no man would want her if he knew the truth. She planned to leave for St. Louis by train the next day—take the train to disappear into the quiet protection of Loretta's relatives. A nun, claiming the Church was no longer her calling. A simple lie to veil a deeper shame.

But Stephano stopped her. He couldn't let this quiet, wounded woman vanish into the night. He noticed the bruises—how carefully she moved, how her scarf seemed to guard not just her neck, but her dignity. He didn't ask. He simply offered her something else. His mother had recently taken ill, and the family was looking for someone trustworthy to help with her care. The position came with a small, attached apartment. It was practical. Convenient. That's what he told himself.

And she—had no idea Aldo and Stephano were kin. Aldo had been shipped off to boarding school in Florence, buried in the background like a forgotten page.

"This is insane," Morainya whispered. "We were always told Mom quit her job to marry a hot Italian businessman." She gripped the chair, dizzy. The room felt smaller. This story was so fucked up.

Cohen sighed, his voice softening. "Loretta didn't tell me everything. But she said your mother cried a lot in those early days—quiet tears, like something too heavy to name. She'd be washing dishes or folding laundry and just... stop. Go still. Then the praying would start. Rosary beads, whispered Hail Marys, hour after hour. Stephano's mother thought she was devout. A good Catholic girl—but I know now—she was trying to hold herself together."

He glanced away, as if remembering it himself. "But at the wedding, she was radiant. Modest, yes—but there was light in her eyes again. Loretta was her Maid of Honor, and I was the Best Man. Stephano looked at her like she was a miracle. And for a while, she let herself believe she'd been given a new life. A second chance."

Morainya stared at him, her mouth parting. No sound came out. She wanted to burst into tears.

My Loretta would be devastated if this got out," he added. His face pale and drawn and he fidgeted with a paperclip.

"Your mother swore her to secrecy at the wedding. And she's still alive."

"How am I supposed to carry this?" Morainya's voice cracked. "All of it—alone?"

Cohen started to speak, then stopped. His jaw clenched, like he was trying to keep something locked inside.

Morainya flinched. There was more. "Tell me. You may as well."

"Your mother hit her head that day in class," Cohen said it, almost gently. "When Aldo hit her. That injury may have triggered her decline into dementia. I'm sure you noticed—her left eye has always been a bit askew."

"Dad told us she had a lazy eye," Morainya whispered, her throat parched.

"Of course, there wasn't any diagnosis back then, but a head injury—bruising, swelling—can affect the optic nerve. Her vision. Her memory. Maybe her soul." Cohen's voice faltered as he finished. He looked down at his hands, turning his wedding ring with his thumb like he could spin time backward. "She never talked about it," he added quietly. "Not once. But I saw it—how she moved slower after that, like something inside her had dimmed. Like the light had to pass through a fog just to reach her."

He swallowed hard, his eyes suddenly glossy. "Loretta said sometimes Stella would forget the names of the flowers she planted. And she loved her garden—and the birds. Said she used to name the doves. After the injury, she stopped singing to them." Then, barely above a whisper: "It wasn't just her mind that cracked. It was her trust. And maybe something deeper."

Morainya closed her eyes. Her parents had always acted strangely around Aldo, circling him like a storm. The realization was thick in her throat, but she didn't speak. Not yet.

Cohen's tone changed—sharpened, almost defensive. "You know Aldo, that boy—he came with ghosts. Can you imagine what that child lived through before he ever touched your mother?"

He leaned back, rubbing the edge of his sleeve. "Aldo didn't just show up one day. He arrived on a train with fifty others—kids with no papers, no parents. Nothing. Their shoes didn't match. Some didn't even speak. They slept sitting up, flinched when touched. Like feral animals in pressed shirts."

He looked up, jaw tight. "They were shuffled between parishes like cargo. Some of them wet the bed well into adolescence. Some never spoke again. And the Church—" he exhaled sharply—"they called them 'wretched boys.' Like the damage was their fault."

Morainya's hands clenched into fists. "Wretched?" she echoed, her voice cracking. "They were just children. They were innocent."

"Are abused children—innocent? Their innocence was stolen. The papers don't even scratch the surface. Your grandmother adopted him for charity. It was fashionable back then. All the prominent families did it. But Aldo—he was different. He caried something dark. Your father knew it. And rather than expose it, he kept it close. Quiet. Manageable."

"That's what Aldo meant by 'abuse'? He blamed my mother for something...deeper?"

Cohen rubbed his face. "Maybe. Maybe her habit reminded him of the priests. Or maybe she was just...there. We'll never know."

Morainya looked down, eyes stinging. "What I know," she said slowly, her voice like crushed glass, "is that I just handed three million dollars... to my mother's abuser."

Her chest convulsed. She lurched forward, elbows on her knees, trying to breathe through the nausea rising like bile. The room spun. A bead of sweat traced down her spine as her fingers dug into her thighs to keep from falling apart.

Cohen didn't speak. He didn't move. Just watched her break—quietly, with dignity, the way women like Stella had always been taught to suffer. Then he sighed, voice low and bitter. "You signed the contract. And the law...it doesn't care who suffered. Only who pays."

Our bodies were water-logged, hair damp and listless, clothes wretched, smelling like day-old fish.
We wrenched ourselves up the steep embankment of Giza,
desperate to get our bearings. Three white triangles emerged
from the golden desert, their enormity stealing our breath.
We stood in silent awe, unable to summon words that could
do justice what lay before us.

The triad certainly appeared much closer than the actu-
ality of reaching these monuments. We had no transportation that could carry the burden of us ragged travelers.
we appeared as common and unkempt as beggars in the
streets without a bowl for a pittance, relying upon the mercy
of strangers. Maybe if we were solitary beggars, but a band
of twelve would receive not a glance from a compassionate
passersby. The sand that had gathered under our clothes
scratched us with every turn, while the grit had gathered
in the creases and folds of our ravaged bodies.

"It will be a day's walk to Giza," said Ana-Kharu. "I did
not count on having to ride crocodiles. My troupe with the
donkeys will never find us now. Worse, we have no coin
left to buy food or drink, let alone a ride to the pyramids.
Merit-Aten, where did your father say we would find Djehuty
once we arrive at our destination?"

The class turned to me with lofty expectations of achiev-
ing our goal. "I do not know," I said with a shrug. "He did
not mention where the teacher would be. Are you sure he

did not confide this in you?" I looked back at the Magician, praying this was true.

Ana-Kharu shrugged. "He only tasked me with getting you all here. After that, I am not responsible."

"Where would the Thrice Great enthrone himself?" asked Sarawat.

"Is there a palace in this bustling city?" asked Ra-Awab. "That is where I would be."

"We all went to Heliopolis when we were young and never left the enclosed grounds," I replied.

Ana-Kharu's jaw ticked, and he muttered something sharp in a language I didn't recognize. He didn't look at me, but the accusation in the silence coiled like smoke toward me—this delay, in his mind, belonged to the Pharaoh's pampered daughter.

I wrinkled my nose. We couldn't have been guided all this way without finding Djehuty.

The class shifted restlessly. Sarawat kicked a rock into the road. Keshtuat crossed her arms, glaring at the horizon as if Djehuty might materialize from dust. Even Ra-Awab's usual jokes had dried up.

Their silence buzzed louder than complaint. We stood helplessly by the side of a busy byway. Trotting donkeys pulling wagons loaded with green crops driven by dirty boys, horse-drawn wagons of neatly folded fabrics, piles of brass wares, or double-yoked oxen were being directed by farmers in the fields. A camel or two clumped by without even a look of compassion.

Ana-Kharu exhaled hard through his nose. "Well?" he said, eyes sweeping the group like an exhausted overseer. "Unless one of you can conjure a feast or sprout wings, I will have to sell your talents again—and I doubt Giza needs more dancers or whores."

I didn't flinch, but the words burned like salt in a wound. No one laughed. Even Oya and So-Bekt-Ka looked away, hugging their themselves as if trying to disappear.

Even if we were to walk to the pyramids, they appeared to be solid blocks of stone. I reasoned that the doorway was most likely on the opposite side. After all, a God would need a place of God to reside. The pyramids seemed the most likely destination.

Archollos shaded his eyes against the sun, lips pressed tight. "He could be anywhere," he murmured. "This city swallows people."

"Can we not sell some of your goods? There must be a market near this busy city," asked Sarawat to Ana-Kharu.

Ana-Kharu turned slowly, his brow arching in disbelief. "Sell *my* goods?" His tone sliced like a blade honed on disappointment. "In a city where frankincense drips from every doorway and saffron is tossed in with the barley?" He kicked at the dirt. "My goods and oddities appeal to those in towns lacking luxury goods. Here, they import the finest amenities from around the world. We cannot compete with merchants of this caliber. Besides, in these bazaars, they have rented booths passed from father to son for decades. While these passersby do not seem sophisticated, I depend on buyers who have a need for finely crafted oils and perfumes that fill all these shops, hoping to appeal to the same customers. We are doomed to go hungry." He swept his hand across our huddled group. "You're bruised, bent, half-rotted—like the leftover vegetables no merchant would claim.'

Oya's sharp trill cut through the haze. Her fingers fluttered like bird wings—a silent signal. "Down," she hissed. "Amunites."

We dropped instinctively, shrinking into the grass, as the earth began to pulse beneath our feet. Indeed, we saw a lengthy line of military infantry marching in unison. Behind was a horse-drawn gilded carriage heading directly at us. We turned our eyes away to avoid bringing attention to us, an unworthy bunch.

Two-by-two soldiers strode on by in clean white loincloths and leather sandals, carrying sharp-tipped spears. The men marched like clockwork—glossy shoulders, unbothered brows. Their chests puffed, not just with air but entitlement. These weren't just soldiers; they were the chosen dogs of the Amunites. With a single command, they could wipe a village clean.

None of these men were in service to the Pharaoh, and catching an Atenist in their midst would have been deadly. A sick weight pressed into my ribs. My father's warnings weren't prophecy—they were inevitability. And now I stood watching them unfold, helpless as a reed in the wind.

The rumbling of large wooden wheels made a clamor that scattered the crows perched upon the lush date palms along the road. I dared a glance into the passing carriage—and the blood drained from my face. Ases-Amun. The High Priest of Amun himself, glinting in gold like a crowned serpent. Ases-Amun. My blood chilled. Hadn't my father exiled him to the quarries of Aswan? Ye there he was, adorned in his gilded robes, reinstated as if nothing had happened. Power restored. Influence intact. The ground beneath me felt like it had cracked open, as if I'd taken a step and found no earth below. My mind was askance, trying to recall if there was a Feast Day or Ceremonial Rite to the pantheon of gods that even I, at one time, had venerated. What would bring this tribute from Thebes all the way to Giza? This battalion had the determination of an army of ants, so where would they be headed?

A boy atop a donkey laden with two woven baskets hurried along. Though crudely created, the orange woven rope served as a bridle by which the boy could direct his beast. He attempted to maneuver around us, but we impeded his travel He pulled up hard on his ride to avoid trampling us.

"Boy, where are the military headed?" I asked.

"To the pyramids. Feast of Amun," the boy called out, jerking the rope bridle. "Full Orange Moon tonight." He held out a dust-covered palm, more hopeful than entitled.

Run! I thought to the donkey, and sure enough, the beast of burden jerked away. It nearly capsized the boy who clung dearly as he bounced up and down, saddened that it was now too late to collect.

"Ana-Kharu," I whispered, gripping his sleeve, "we cannot go. Not tonight. Not with them swarming the sands like fleas to a carcass. They will sacrifice a black heifer at midnight—and then three days of drink, sex, and spells. We will not even see the base stones."

The Magician turned internal, to look at the future. "There will be too many people blocking our approach to the pyramids, let alone finding an entrance or someone willing to divulge that secret." A tremor passed through his jaw—small, but I saw it. Ana-Kharu stared into the dust-choked horizon, and for a breath, the fire behind his eyes dimmed. He hated the taste of cornered silence.

My stomach clawed at itself. I broke a twig from the knoll's edge and placed it between my teeth—not to eat, just to pretend I had something to offer the ache.

The roadway was congested with travelers going to the bazaar with their offerings in tow. Surely, all inns and places of rest would be filled to the brim with festival attendees. A cart of merry townspeople headed toward the pyramid, clapping and singing, which made me wish that I shared their joy. They sang one of my favorite childhood songs of Horus and the Pig. I recognized the lyrics and smiled.

I did a double take as an elderly woman with spiky gray hair and cloudy eyes made my heart pang for Amaret. I missed my dear Seer, the Mistress of the Two Eyes. Longing yanked my chest like a child tugging at a mother's robe— urgent, familiar, unwelcome. I had a horrible feeling of spidery doubt crawling upon my skin. I have to complete this mission and save my family. There was no time to linger.

"We cannot stand here all day. I have to find Djehuty. My father needs me. My family needs me," I said to Archollos, and then clasped my hand within his, seeking comfort that only his presence brought me.

Their silence pressed against my spine like unsaid prayers, waiting for a decision I wasn't sure I had the right to make., I could feel their criticisms as they talked in low voices. Overhead, a shadow crossed over me, and I shaded my eyes, casting them to the skies. A falcon soared majestically above in front of the Sun. It made effortless circles scanning for its next easy meal: a mouse darting out of a bush. Perhaps a snake slithered from a cold slumber awakening in the heat of camouflaged rock.

Within the breath of a grasshopper, the falcon took a vertical dive that split the air with a whoosh. It barreled toward us in a surprise attack. We covered our eyes to shield ourselves from the burn of the sun. Some of the troupe dove into the grass. Its wings cinched inward, sculpting a deadly arrow from air and instinct, its tail feathers steering like an ancient rudder. A tinkle of a bell caught my attention. Sure enough, A band of gold shimmered at its throat—a regal clasp that didn't belong to a wild thing. Another memory of Amaret jingled my mind, for her Falcon, wore a similar collar with a golden bell.

"Horus, is that you?" I thought to this magnificent bird of prey, obviously someone's pet. The owner wouldn't waste a dive on people; no, this bird was after a dove or fish. Yet, it drew closer. The rush of its wings parted the air with a hiss, grazing my scalp like a whispered warning.

I stumbled into the strong arms of Archollos. "Someone is trying to get your attention, Merit-Aten," he joked.

"The bird had a Royal collar," declared Ana-Kharu. "Do you know to whom it belongs?"

It let out a squawk of acknowledgement, and my heart lifted as high as that of this Falcon.

The pull wasn't just instinct—it was memory dressed in feathers. Amaret's presence hummed through the air like a bell I could feel but not hear. "We must follow the Falcon." My troupe fell into line as I led the way; fortunately, it was in the opposite direction of the infantry. The hawk flew in front to the city of Giza. The hawk made circles then once again flew straight at us. The wafting of freshly baked bread tickled our nostrils like little hands pulling us forward until we saw the bustle of the bazaar.

The market bloomed like a fever dream—saffron and shouting, sweat and silk, a thousand lives crammed into crooked alleys. Colors beyond my imagination dotted lines of vendors hawking their wares. We wandered into the commotion; appearing as unwelcome guests, poor and decrepit in our manner. The vendors, noting our appearance, turned their attention to more promising clients.

The tang of olives hit my nose, sharp and briny. Cheese oozed from linen wraps, sweating in the heat. My tongue darted over cracked lips, chasing moisture that wasn't there. Still, the Falcon beckoned us on in dizzying twists and turns through finely tooled leather bins, hand-milled luxury carpets, racks of crisp linen sheaths, and brass lamps glowing brightly. Finally, the rainbow-hued spices in baskets enticed us with the beauty of the bounty.

In the Spice Market, red chilies hung in bunches like bloodied streamers, twisting in the breeze with the menace of warning flags. Mounds of nuts spilled from woven baskets like treasure looted from a desert king's vault. Stacked bins of black cumin seeds, dried oregano, and bags of tea smelled like lavender and rose. Bowls of dried fat figs, orange apricots, and plump raisins and dates were set near jars of honey fresh from the hive. Delicious, sliced honeycomb was stacked on little plates with cheese slices.

The falcon arced in wide, deliberate loops ahead of us, pausing just long enough to check that we followed before diving forward again. A sharp cry split the air as a single feather spiraled downward. It danced above the heads of passersby like a forgotten blessing, and I darted forward before it could vanish beneath careless feet. *I snatched the feather just before it kissed the ground, lifting it like a trophy, its soft barbs tickling my fingers.* Out of the blur of colors and bustle, a single booth caught my eye—not for its size, but its singular purpose. He only sold one thing. Giza's Best Black Mud, packaged in the same sky-blue containers that Amaret swore by. The only mud she would slather upon her skin to pull out impurities.

I turned to the vendor as my class piled up behind me, stopping traffic from both sides. "Greetings, kind sir. I am new in town and have traveled a long way, but I see that you are selling my Nana's favorite mud. As a worshiper of the Sun, she has confided that your product is trustworthy."

The elder man, with graying curly hair and beard, but with shining raisin-colored eyes, jerked his head up. "A Sun Worshipper, you say?"

"I did," I replied.

"The best Sun Worshiping I know of is in Akhet-Aten," he replied, watching for my reaction. "Who is your Nana?"

"She goes by, Amaret."

"Blessed be. The Lady of the Two Eyes told me you would be coming. You have arrived sooner than I expected."

I let out a deep breath. Somehow, I had been guided to this man. May the will of the Aten be merciful today. "You were expecting me?"

"It was requested that I house and offer you a reprise from a long and arduous journey.

My demesne is just beyond the city. Judging by your appearance, you are in need of sustenance and a change of clothing." He bowed graciously.

"We would be most grateful if you could oblige all of us." I nearly cried, feeling my heart overflow with gratitude.

He ordered his son to pull up the flat wagon. The older boy jumped to fulfill his wishes. In a moment, we were directed into his booth as he waved all of us to hurry, and then he ushered us out of the back flap so that we could board the waiting wagon. Two skinny horses were harnessed without any fanfare; the elder gave a whistle and click of his tongue, and we were off. We shielded our faces from the dust while the wagon jolted and creaked, every rut in the road rattling our tired bones.

Ana-Kharu took out his pack and divided up some white powder. "Take this," he directed. "It is alchemical gold to kill the parasites."

We passed the little bottle around, dipping our small finger into the powder and lifting it to our mouths. Finally, we pulled into a long drive lined with fruited trees and a lush grassy area. A large opulent manse painted in a soft pink wash awaited. The horses abruptly stopped as another servant took the reins.

Several servants appeared at the door, judging us with a disgusted look. "You all will need bathes and lye soap to kill the critters you may have picked up in the Nile," said the House Mistress.

The girls followed one plump servant who shuffled her way to the bathhouse while the boys stayed behind a strict man's servant who directed them toward the other side of the house.

"Strip here, new clothing will be laid out," directed the attendant, turning her face to avoid our smell.

We peeled away clothes stiff with salt and sand, garments that cracked when folded, clinging to our skin like second scabs and wandered into a large sunken tub. Bottoms brushed each other. The female servants slathered us with foul-smelling lye soap as they scrubbed us until we were bright and shiny. Our hair was yanked and rubbed until a soapy lather accrued. As we stepped out of the tub, the murky contents proved that we must have been unrecognizable under the Nile sludge. Fluffy Khemitian cotton towels awaited us, and we snuggled into the first soft thing we had experienced since leaving Akhet-Aten. Wrapped in thick cotton, I sank into its warmth. It was the first kindness my body had felt in days, and my breath caught with the threat of tears. Since Akhet-Aten, we'd moved like dust on the wind—pushed, trampled, forgotten—until now. My soul whispered thanks to Aten, and to Amaret, for guiding us to this hidden bloom of grace amidst the storm.

Finely woven multi-colored linen sheaths hung before us for our choosing. New sandals of all sizes and shapes were stocked in a basket. A tray of cosmetics was laid out so that we could adorn ourselves.

"Food awaits you in the patio," said the Head Mistress.

A hollow ache tugged at me—the kind that only comes when the songs of sisters are too far to echo.

My attention was brought back to the young women who chattered like morning birds as we walked toward the enclosed patio. Flowers blossomed fair, and we inhaled the beauty of the sweet scents that hit us like a bouquet of love.

"What took you so long?" asked Ana-Kharu shortly, pacing the floor. "We have already begun to break our fast."

"Such beauties," said Archollos in an excited tone when we walked in dressed in a lovely bouquet of pastels.

"Why it has only been a turn of the sundial since you all were mud guppies, and now you grace us with sheer beauty," said Smenkhkare, ever the gentle being. He poured glasses of fresh orange juice for us.

"Come eat," ordered Ana-Kharu. "We must overcome the amassing of Amunites in the very place where Djehuty might be. Let us conspire as to how to worm our way out of this mess."

We devoured each bite like it might be our last, grateful yet anxious, unsure how many moons would pass before we saw another meal. *The sky was empty. No falcon. No feather. Just the still ache of unanswered questions. Please, Aten, show me the way to Djehuty. I am blinded as to which way to turn. Enemies surround us. Allow me to feed my people and heal my land.*

"Merit-Aten, listen to your heart." It was a voice so faint that I was not sure I caught all the words. I tilted my ears to be attuned to the internal guidance. Their laughter swelled around me like waves on stone—cheerful, warm, but too loud for the voice beneath.

"Are you alright, beloved?" asked Archollos as he moved his chair closer to mine.

"I thought I heard a voice. I am not sure." As elated as I felt this morning because I was guided to the Spice Merchant, my mood now sunk to the bottom of an overused well. Time was pressing, as all eyes were watching for me to lead them to the Master Teacher, but I had no idea where to turn.

"Merit," the voice repeated.

Ana-Kharu, who sat apart from the merriment, now stood. "What are you hearing?" His question was bold and direct, and I felt his urgency penetrate me. How did he always know? I felt my ire rise, and the connection with the internal was lost.

The Gold Magician strode toward me, and I felt his energy come between Archollos and me, slicing our connection with a razor of rage. "Your little love fest, while charming as it may be, will not provide answers to the challenges we face. You waste your precious moments in flirtation when we are in the fight of our lives."

All eyes indeed turned upon me, questioning if this was true.

"I heard a voice call my name, but no one addressed me."

Ana-Kharu gripped my wrist—his fingers stone-still, his gaze piercing. "Your pulse thrums like a trapped bird. It is hard to hear the subtleties when everything around us shouts with thunder. While we appreciate the accommodations," Ana-Kharu glared at us, "as does the grace of ease afforded us, sometimes being pushed to the edge of death leaves us no choice but to listen to the God within. If you are receiving a message, it is your obligation to listen to the guidance."

With a single snap, sharp and commanding, Oya rose— her movements as fluid as smoke drawn to fire. Moments later, she returned with a vial. "Drink this. You will establish higher attunement for the destined message."

I hesitated, eyeing the vial's golden sheen. Whatever it held, silence was the greater danger.

"Just a sip," I said flatly. "Please reveal how I find Djehuty," I prayed.

The liquid slid down like honey and disappeared into silence. Then—like a blink inside a thunderclap—the room melted into fog. The edges of reality blurred, swallowed in mist, and then it enveloped me. A light shone down from the heavens. My senses became more acute, and I could see everything all at once. Amaret appeared as clearly as if she was in the room. Her blue, vacant eyes were fixed upon the heavens. I waited with anticipation for her to reveal the map to Djehuty.

"Merit-Aten." The voice of Amaret echoed in my mind.

"I am here, Amaret. Thank you for sending the hawk. the Spice Merchant had the Giza Magic Mud that you use, and now we," I started to say.

Amaret interrupted. "Stop talking, Child. You are in danger. We are all in danger. Something most egregious has occurred as our city has been breached."

"Breached?" I repeated, feeling confused.

"Did I not just say that?" she asked.

I nodded.

"Everything is gone, Merit," Amaret said, voice barely above a whisper. "In a single night, the city was stripped bare. The vaults, the temple jewels, your father's golden sarcophagus, all his funerary goods—stolen." She exhaled. "But the worst crime? They took the children."

A cold weight settled in my gut. "No."

"Yes. Your sisters, you brother-in-law—gone. Ay too. Your mother saw to it herself."

My vision blurred. "Meti."

Medjay, blades sharp and instincts sharper, had been trained to strike first—but Horemheb's command stilled their hands. Their loyalty, forged in fire, yielded to his words like iron bent beneath command. They fell back, blind to betrayal."

My ragged breathing burned my lungs. "Did they take father, too?"

"No, they left him alone. Pentu was nursing him through the night during his bout of illness. Neither were aware of this incursion until the next morning when the screams of the Nursemaids would not cease."

I clutched my mouth, fingers trembling, as panic wrapped around my throat like a noose.

Amaret continued, "Horemheb took them back to Thebes? You were fortunate to be away. Or you too would be at the General's mercy."

I couldn't move. My breath came in stutters, shallow as a winded child. "For what reason would they strip Akhet-Aten of its finery? They had so much abundance in Thebes that a chariot or funerary goods would account for a pittance of their wealth."

Amaret's tone leveled—tempered steel beneath mourning silk. "They deprived your father of any chance of recovery. General Horemheb and your mother dealt a mortal wound; to the one who channels the Divine messages to the people. This will surely kill him unless you can find Djehuty in time. He needs what he asked for. This is most unfortunate because it depends on the solarization and the lunar resonances to align."

"Master Djehuty will surely supply gold to Father. He is the Master Alchemist. A barge full of gold could be sailed back to Akhet-Aten, and all will be redeemed." *My mind fractured into loops of desperation, reaching for reason like a drowning hand for driftwood.*

Amaret shook her head. It is too late. If your precious sisters fall into the hands of the Amunites, then any hope for future heirs will be lost. They most likely will suffer insurmountable harm in retaliation for Aten worship."

My body shivered. I squeezed my eyes shut, begging the veils of time to part—just as Amaret once taught me.

"You cannot see because the way forward has not yet been written. One thing is for certain, your father conveyed to me that it is time." Her voice was strong and unwavering.

"For what?" I asked, feeling as if I had been buried under a pile of stone, unable to breathe or move to set myself free.

"For your Choosing. That has been written in the stars. Your father granted you the time to make your own choice, but now it is too late. The fates have decided."

"I choose Archollos," I said, fire sparking behind the crack in my voice. "The sign came. The love was real. That was my truth, even if it is not my destiny."

Amaret shook her head. "You are to choose one of our own. He is present among your group. He has the bloodline. He has the name. He has the permission of the Aten."

"Not Ana-Kharu-We-Shat," I gasped, horror coiling in my chest. "Is it because he is a Ptahman? One of the firstborn of the earthborn?" The realization struck like a fist to the gut. I cried when I realized that this whole trip was designed to push me into his arms instead of Archollos. *I had believed— prayed—that Aten had spared me from that golden-caged fate. From a life bound to that domineering brute.*

Amaret let me unravel, her silence more cutting than words. I hurled my anguish into the void until even I tired of the sound of my voice. "Must you always speak before you hear the wind?" Amaret said, exasperated. "Stillness, child. That's where the truth lives."

Heat surged through me—face flushed, feet burning as if the ground itself rejected my stance. "Who is the will of the Aten?"

"It has always been him, Merit. The only choice. The blood of Amunhotep III flows through Smenkhkare's veins. He is of royal lineage, just as you are." Amaret's voice softened, but the weight of her words crushed me. "You two must be joined tonight. The Choosing Ceremony cannot wait. The world must see you two as Co-Regents, as Pharaoh's rightful heirs. Orders for new jewelry and furniture with Smenkhkare's new name will be engraved upon various gifts your father will bestow upon him."

"He is my brother," I whispered, numb. "That is no better than being handed to Tut." Every ounce of life drained from my limbs.

"Life does not always go as one desires," replied Amaret, coldly. "Your father has decreed that his name will be enclosed in a royal cartouche and will tout him as the next reigning Pharaoh. Your portraits will be displayed side by side for all to witness. Notices will be sent far and wide, so you had better complete your task."

I opened my mouth to protest, but Amaret's words crashed into me like a wave, cutting off sound before it could form.

"It is now Done; Pharaoh Akhenaten has thus decreed it, and it is set in stone, literally," she added. "*He demands you conceive—at once. The tide is no longer turning. It has already pulled us under.* Your mother stole the Royal children. There are no marriageable daughters to be wed to royals of other kingdoms who will bring in tributes, food, or armies. We are doomed."

"I love Archollos," I breathed, offering my heart like a fragile bowl, knowing she would not take it.

Her voice, calm and cold, rang like a bell in my mind: I care only about your duty."

No plea could shift the weight of fate already sealed in royal decree.

Amaret resigned herself to the loss. "We are a broken Kingdom, and it is your honor, to restore what is left."

"Am I required to forgo my path as an Initiate?" I fell back a few steps. *This path—my path—was carved in sweat and sacrifice. I had walked it like a wildcat with fire in my blood. Now they've clipped my claws and expected me to purr.*

This is what I have worked for my entire life. A path of dedication so fierce that I felt like a wildcat ready to strike. Now I have been tamed like a meek lion cub.

Amaret's image dissipated. "As soon as you bring back what he is in desperate need of will he decide. Until that time, do what you must to procure it."

"The gold, the gold, I am in service to acquire gold," I spat. "Barges full. Caverns full. Somehow, if it is my destiny, then I shall find it." My voice was tinged with sarcasm.

What I believed to be my destiny had been sucked into a pit of quicksand, and I lost my balance. *It felt as if my soul had plummeted into a chasm, the wind howling, and no ledge to break the fall.*

I could not even turn to Archollos to assuage my pain with his gentle yet strong kisses.

Pentu has now asked to come forward. "What your father seeks, what will keep him and his dream alive, it is the Red Lion." With that, Amaret's silhouette dissolved, and Pentu, my father's Physician, appeared in the forefront.

"Merit-Aten, beloved of the Aten," said my dear doctor, humbly bowing to me. "I can feel how your heart beats with grief, and you are in need of my guidance. I raised you as a daughter that I would never have, and I owe you some conciliation as you once saved my life."

At the same flick of a fly's wing, we said in unison, "Pentu, my slave."

"You beat me so hard with your whip that I swear I still have scars upon my back," said Pentu in mock admonishment. "I still flinch when I see silk cords," Pentu teased, eyes twinkling.

I belly laughed, "What can I say? They set us up to be robbed. "Had I not painted your back with stripes and flung my cape over you, the Amunites would have gutted you for your rings." Thank the Aten that I had my cape to throw over your body as I took my whip to my slave, who refused to serve me."

"What did you call me? A dirty ball-licking dog?" he asked, throwing his hands up to his mouth.

"I did, and I think I added swine-sucking slave and an itchy ichneumon for good measure." I threw back my head, chuckling out loud.

We dissolved into laughter—laughter full of memory, of bruises turned stories and wounds long mended. My dearest friend, Pentu, who gave solace when Sit-Amun conjured the crocodile to consume my little nursemaid. Pentu arrived to steer me on this decision.

"I do not wish to choose Smenkhkare. You, of all people, told me to follow my heart," I whispered. "Then why does it feel like I'm walking it to the gallows?"

"Merit, you know I would not hurt you if not out of necessity. My heart has been heavy withholding this information from you, but now it is of the utmost importance to reveal what I know to be true."

"Go on," I said, bracing myself as if for a storm I could already feel tugging at the edges of my certainty.

"You remember when you all posed before the sculptor?" he asked, voice dipping into nostalgia like a finger into warm honey.

"When The Chief Roual Sculptor, Bek summoned you to sit for him?" Pentu asked. "The sun was cruel that morning, and the statues of you and your family had not yet taken shape. It was to be a gift for your father."

"Of course," I replied, twisting my braid. "Last summer. I was on temple duty. The Aten Priestess made us replace the candles. I was late, Meket started coughing, and Meti slapped her the back of the neck, telling her to be still. I did my silly walk to cheer everyone up. Ankhi laughed so hard she peed herself. The twins copied me. Meti got up and left. Just...walked off. We did not know if she was coming back. We stayed frozen, even after Bek stopped sculpting. Ankhi stayed frozen in her puddle of shame, too afraid to laugh again, too loyal to move—her wet sheath clinging like guilt."

Pentu nodded, but the twitch in his jaw betrayed the truth—he was bracing for impact, not memory. He was holding something back. "She took the chariot back," he said. "I was in the garden, teaching initiates how to solarize water. *She pulled up in a whirl of dust and fury, her fingers cracking the air like whips. Archollos climbed into the chariot before his name was even spoken."*

I cocked my head at the name of my Beloved. "Go on."

Her guards let me pass without question. Inside the North Palace...I did not need to look far." Pentu hesitated, then finished. "I heard moaning. Grunting. The unmistakable sounds of fornication. I have never known it myself, but I knew what I was hearing."

The air thickened in my throat. "Meti?" The name came out in shards. "She...lay with him?" The words scaped my throat. "He never told me."

I clenched my fists, torn between fury and heartbreak. "Did she do it to cut me open?" I asked, voice cracking. "Or was she always sharpening her smile for him?" Complicit—Or coerced? My voice trembled. "If she could not own me," I whispered, "she would steal the hands that held me."

Pentu leaned in, his voice low as if afraid the walls might judge him too. "Had you chosen him openly, it would not have just been scandal. The Royal Guard would have taken him from your bed and placed his severed head between your legs before sunrise. That is how it has always been for the Royals. Love is not freedom—it is a leverage. Unless you wield the power."

I shook my head, the weight of it pressing into my bones. *"And yet she—my own mother—writes commandments in morning ink and breaks them by nightfall?"*

"She is the Per Aat," Pentu replied. She pens the law in stone. You—you must bleed to uphold it."

I closed my eyes, throat tightening. "Knowing this does not make my Choosing easier, Pentu. It only makes it more unbearable."

Again, the eyes returned—circling me like falcons above a wounded hare, not out of hope, but dread. I had come seeking the map to Djehuty, believing the path forward would be revealed. Instead, I was handed a decree: I must complete my Choosing ceremony tonight. Not to the man I loved, but with the one I had been groomed to accept. A man I deeply respected...but did not love.

t wasn't glamorous, but it paid. Morainya worked part-time at the Santa Cruz Historical Society, cataloging old photographs in exchange for just enough to cover groceries and gas. With Jedidiah starting yet another job—his second that year—she prayed child support would arrive before Josh turned eighteen. Always excuses.

The scent of brittle paper and lemon oil hung in the air—comforting, familiar. Morainya sat hunched over an acid-free folder in the back corner, white gloves snug on her hands, a soft cloth under her elbow. She lifted a sepia photograph of a 1907 town hall parade, the corners curling like the edge of an old smile.

A row of somber men stood at the front, hats tilted just so, their mustaches identical, their pride visible even in grainy black-and-white. She marked it to research further if any of the decedents were still residents of the County and suggest a social media post with an interview.

She tilted her head. Where were the women? The children? The land they stood on? Whose story was this, really?

Earlier that morning, she'd finished archiving a collection of photos from the old Santa Cruz Wharf—faded images of fishermen, steamships, wooden railcars, and the long wooden bridge that connected the city to the sea.

She and Jedidiah had taken Josh to visit that bridge when he was five—back when things still felt salvageable. Her son wore red rain boots and had insisted on bringing his stuffed dolphin, squealing each time the waves slapped the pylons below.

Back in 2010, Napolitano Interiors was already fraying at the edges. After the 2008 crash, design clients had dried up almost overnight, and the pressure to go digital was rising. Jedidiah had just started his second job in six months, and Morainya had nearly blacked out in the school parking lot after a PTA meeting. Santa Cruz had felt like a balm. Sweet beach town, slower pace, They needed space to breathe. So, they took the scenic route along the coast, winding down Highway 1 with Josh asleep in the back seat, his arms wrapped around that same dolphin. It was a beautiful day—the kind that almost convinces you life might work out.

She remembered standing at the edge of the pier, holding Josh's sticky hand, whispering, *"We'll come back soon. I promise."*

When the marriage crumbled and the condo disappeared in the 2020 divorce that memory had returned like a ghost wave—unexpected, salt-laced, and insistent.

Morainya had paused on one photograph from 1940, just months before the bridge blew down in a storm. It showed two boys laughing as they crossed the planks barefoot, oblivious to how temporary it all was. The caption read: *Before the Storm.*

Something about that title still lodged in her chest.

She flipped the photo over and ran her gloved finger along the handwritten scrawl. *"Built to connect—but not to last."*

That line haunted her. Not just because the wharf bridge was gone, but because lately, everything in her life felt that way. Temporary. Fragile. What did it mean to build something that *lasted?*

The afternoon light spilled through her bay window, pooling golden across the worn hardwood. Morainya sat curled on the edge of her favorite armchair—legs tucked under her, a chipped mug of lukewarm licorice tea forgotten on the side table. In her lap, the book Sal insisted would "change everything." She didn't believe him—until now.

The pages were littered with yellow highlights and frantic underlines. She skimmed through, pausing on a section about the Founding Fathers—Benjamin Franklin, Thomas Jefferson, John Adams, James Madison, Alexander Hamilton, Benedict Arnold, and George Washington.

An odd detail caught her eye.

Apparently, these men formed an unincorporated company called *The United States in 1754.*

She frowned and traced the words with her fingertip, as if touching them would make them make sense. "That can't be right..." she whispered, heart picking up speed. A ridiculous notion—but one that wouldn't let go.

According to Von Reitz, this so-called company was backed by King George III, even while America was supposedly fighting for independence. The *real* reason for the American Revolution, the book claimed, was not freedom—but a land grab scheme to expand the colonies Westward past the Appalachian Mountains.

Her vision blurred as if the words themselves were slipping away from truth. The man on the dollar bill—the founding myth she recited in fifth grade—now felt like a costume stitched together by lies.

"George Washington—the war hero, the man on the dollar bill—was in cahoots with the King?"

That was ridiculous. She'd seen *Hamilton* on Broadway. Lin-Manuel Miranda sure as hell didn't mention this. Her fingers tightened on the spine of the book.

Von Reitz argued that the Constitution wasn't even a governing document—it was a contract. The United States wasn't a free nation, but a corporation, and the so-called government was just an administrative body. Lincoln's assassination? Not because of the Civil War—but because he tried to undo the damage.

A slow chill unfurled down her spine. As if the floor beneath her—a floor she had walked on her entire life—had shifted an inch to the left without warning. She needed to call Shelley. Ringing. One. Two. Three.

"Hey, where have you been?" Shelley's voice snapped through the phone, warm and biting all at once. "You missed Parent Night. And guess what? Mrs. Callahan said if another kid zip-ties a toilet seat, we're going DEFCON 1. They're cracking down on the Senior Prank, so if Josh is planning anything stupid, heads up."

"I—what? No, this isn't about that." Morainya was feeling her face and neck flush, and she struggled to corral her thoughts.

"You bringing anything for the bake sale?" Shelley was multitasking and filing her nails, which sounded like nails on a chalkboard.

"Shelley, focus," Morainya snapped. "Why was Lincoln assassinated?"

A beat of silence. "Wait. Is this a *knock-knock* joke?" The filing stopped.

"I'm serious." Morainya shifted her weight and bit her lip.

Shelley exhaled, weighing whether to humor her friend. "Alright, well... John Wilkes Booth was a Confederate sympathizer. He believed Lincoln was a tyrant, hated that he was abolishing slavery, and didn't want the South to rejoin the Union. Standard textbook stuff."

Morainya snorted she'd swallowed that same polished-textbook tale back in college. If anyone should enjoy puncturing it, it was Shelley—the woman had a history degree from UC Berkeley and a secret love of scandalous footnotes.

Morainya scooted to the edge of the armchair, voice dropping to a conspiratorial hush. "Okay, but—what if that's just the museum-gift-shop version?"

Shelley groaned. "Oh God, what did you read? Please don't say you watched it on *TikTok*."

"No! A book. Anna Von Reiz. She found documents proving Lincoln was assassinated because he was never actually President."

Silence... Shelley then sipped her matcha smoothie from a straw. "Oh, this is gonna be good,"

"No, listen. The United States wasn't a government—it was a corporation. Lincoln was its CEO, not a President. They bankrupted it. And when he tried to undo it? Boom. Dead."

"Uh-huh." Shelley set down the smoothie unsure if she wanted her morning jog buzz to be killed by fact.

"I'm serious. The original Constitution wasn't even for the people. It was a contract for running a business. When Lincoln bankrupted *The United States*, he inadvertently handed us over to foreign bankers—."

"Mor," Shelley cut in. "Take a deep breath."

"I—"

"You're spiraling."

She clutched the book to her chest like a lifeline—her fingers pressing so hard the pages creased beneath her palm. Her mind swirled, but something deeper than panic stirred beneath the chaos: the terrifying clarity of knowing she could never go back.

"No," she whispered. Then louder, steadier: "I'm not spiraling. I'm waking up."

Shelley sighed and shook her head. "Okay, let's assume for a second this is true. So what? We've been operating like this for centuries. We still go to work, pay our bills, live our lives."

"That's the problem, Shell! We've been scammed! Everything—the courts, the taxes, the legal system—it's all a fraud."

Shelley groaned. "I *knew* I should've let your call go to voicemail."

Morainya let out a dry laugh, more exhausted than amused. "Fine. I'll let you get back to your lemonade and suburban bliss. Forget I called."

"Mor, come on—don't be like that," Shelley said, her tone softening. "Look, I'm not saying you're wrong, okay? Just... this is a lot. You know how my brain short-circuits when history and conspiracy have a baby."

Morainya smiled despite herself. That was classic Shelley.

"Mor. Babe. You know I love you," Shelley said, chewing. "But I have Botox in twenty minutes and a spray tan after that. And if you drag me into another revolution before I've had lunch—"

"It's not a revolution," Morainya muttered. "It's a reality check."

"Oh, that reminds me," Shelley said brightly, seizing the lane change like a seasoned escape artist, "did you see that new sandwich place that opened on Pacific—*Eggs Benedict's Rebellion*? Total colonial chic. They have truffle fries and some kind of maple-brined turkey with 'tax-free cranberry chutney.' You still good for lunch Friday?"

There it was: the pivot. Avoid the storm. Find the fries.

Morainya sighed and leaned back on the couch. "Yeah. I'm still good."

"Great. We'll reset the world over aioli. Deal?"

"Deal," Morainya murmured, glancing back at the book on her lap.

"Good girl. And wear something cute. You've been in divorcee chic way too long."

"It's not divorcee chic. It's called 'unbothered' and 'barely employed.'"

Shelley snorted. "Exactly. See you then."

Click.

For a moment, silence.

But not peace.

Only the low thrum of her fridge and the brittle whisper of the pages still open on her lap. The word *corporation* stared back at her like an accusation. Her lips parted—dry. Her tongue felt too big in her mouth.

You are classified as a CORPORATION, not a living person.

She blinked. Wait—what?

She was still trying to decide if she'd misread it when her eyes caught the manila folder on the dining table.

The court documents.

Her gut sank.

No. She wasn't ready for this.

But her body moved anyway, legs numb as she walked the short distance, sat, and opened the folder like she was peeling back her own skin.

There it was. All caps. Cold typeface. No warmth. No breath.

ALDO N. NAPOLITANO – PLAINTIFF VS. MORAINYA G. NAPOLITANO Individually and as TRUSTEE of the NAPOLITANO FAMILY TRUST IN THE UNITED STATES DISTRICT COURT FOR THE DISTRICT OF CALIFORNIA

Her entire body went cold. Each word hit like a rubber stamp across her chest. All-caps. **MORAINYA G. NAPOLITANO.** Not her. Just a shell. A legal fiction.

She wasn't a woman. Not to them.

"Civilly dead," she whispered, as if saying it aloud would soften the blow. Dead on paper. Alive enough to pay.

Her thoughts whipped through every meeting with her lawyer, every politely condescending call with Accounts Receivable. Had they known? Had they all known? Of course they had.

Her head spun. Her lawyer... her accountant... the judge... they were all in on it. That's why Judge Malicado couldn't talk to her. She was dead. She was a ghost. Attorney—attorn for the dead. How did she not see it before?

Her hands scrambled for her phone.

Dialed.

"Hello, Mr. Cohen?" she gasped. "Thank God, I caught you. You need to stop the payment. Don't send the money."

A pause. Then, calmly—"It's too late, Morainya. I wired the money two days ago."

Her stomach plummeted. "No— Her breath hitched. "No—can't you just—cancel the wire? Put a stop payment?"

"That would be wire fraud, and I won't get involved in that," he replied smoothly, like he was declining extra sauce at a restaurant.

Wire fraud.

As if *she* were the criminal.

She let the phone slip from her ear. The room tilted. Her stomach lurched.

A knock at the door.

Sharp. Intentional.

She froze.

Not a neighbor knock. Not a delivery knock.

Three heavy knocks.

"Mr. Cohen—I have to go."

She ended the call, barely breathing.

The knock came again, louder.

Her fingers hovered above the phone. A second too slow. Her palms were sweating.

It's happening. It's not paranoia. It's protocol.

Her eyes darted back to the book. The Founders, the corporation, the lies she'd never questioned. This was the storm the photo warned her about. "Built to connect—but not to last."

Neither was this version of her. Not the nice, polite Morainya. Not the one they tried to erase with capital letters and courtroom tricks. She was waking up. And they knew.

I did not weep right away. Instead, I walked barefoot through the shaded colonnade of the merchant's demesne, where incense smoke curled like serpents through open archways and fruiting pomegranate trees bowed under their jeweled burden. The marble underfoot was veined with blue lapis, polished to a mirror's sheen, and cool enough to bite the heat from my skin. A shaded arbor, half-hidden against the villa's ancient stone wall, was draped in clematis winding over palm-lashed beams, planted long ago by unseen hands. An ivory fountain in the shape of Hathor's face gurgled in the secluded courtyard, feeding a pond where lotus flowers floated lazily, untouched by the grief tightening my chest.

I had no pen to record this moment. No parchment to scream upon. Only my breath, shallow in my ribs, and the echo of Pentu's words clinging to my skin like the sweat I couldn't wipe away.

The pond shimmered beneath the morning sun, veiled in the perfume of neroli, wet jasmine, and ancient frankincense. Bees murmured through flowers. My hem of my yellow linen sheath grew damp with dew as I dropped to my knees in the garden's hush. Red stones circled the water like a forgotten protection spell. I leaned forward, hoping to cool my brow against its mirrored surface.

A fat orange and black koi surfaced—slow, silent, eyes like ancient glass.

"Hello," I said, "you surprised me." I pulled my hand from the water and sat back on my heels thankful for the company.

"Are you surprised that a fish is in water?" it asked in a tone that seemed both amused and reasonable.

"No," I replied with a faint smile. "It is exactly where I would expect to find you."

"Then why shed your tears on a beautiful day?" Its mouth opened and closed rhythmically, yet the voice was in my head—not heard but felt. "You carry the scent of grief."

I felt that vibration. Bone-deep. "My mother and father are demanding I choose a mate," I said, lifting my sleeve to brush away a tear.

The koi circled. "And who delivered this yoke upon your shoulders?"

"Yoke! Precisely—a yoke is what oxen wear when they are nothing but chattel ordered what to do. That is what I am."

The koi held still, waving its fins in a subtle ripple of the water. "Then who steers you?"

I leaned closer. Finally, a fish was asking all the questions I buried beneath my spine.

"Pentu," I said, and rage prickled beneath my skin like cactus thorns. The man who raised me in the absence of my father. The one who brushed sand from my cheeks after initiation rites. Who stitched my sandals with his own hands before the Pilgrimage of Silence. He was the one who told me, *"You are your father's sunbeam.' But the sun only seemed to shine when I obeyed." I crossed my arms, hugging my chest like this protection was a chest plate of iron.*

"You will choose a consort. You will produce an heir." I repeated my physician's words aloud, as if saying them would undo the spell. The koi's eyes did not leave mine. "He said it like he was telling me the weather. As if my body was already theirs. I had always believed he was different. That he protected me because he loved me."

The koi's eyes glinted. "He did. Until the throne outweighed your heart."

My mouth filled with bile. My skin flushed and then went cold. I pressed my palms against the warm red stones to ground myself in something older than politics.

"This Pentu, is he the king? If he is not—then must you obey?" the koi, slowly dipped below the water long enough for me to take in its words.

I shook my head gently, "No, he is not a king, but the command came from Pharaoh and Per Aat. I made an agreement with my mother. I had to. I begged her to take my best friend's baby after Rennutet Wested in childbirth. If my mother would raise the baby as her own. The command may have come from the throne—but it was *Pentu*, my anchor, who delivered the blow. That is what shattered me. Because in his voice, I heard the truth: my destiny was already written in a scroll I never signed. My womb... contracted without my consent."

Two more koi surfaced beside the first, their mouths gaping hungrily as if demanding to be fed. But I had nothing to offer them.

"And now that time has come for her to collect. So, the agreement you made must be fulfilled, and yet you are angry." My koi pushed the others away.

"I had fought, suffered, and bled for my independence," I whispered. "I believed I had earned the right to choose my own fate. But that was an illusion—a shimmering bauble dangled before a child to keep her quiet. The game had always been rigged—and I have spent years memorizing the rules carved by others."

My koi remained still. "And who told you choice would be honored?"

My body trembled. The ache moved from throat to chest to womb. I was unraveling.

My mother's voice echoed in my mind—low, steely: *"You will ache. You will burn. You will carry no comfort—only the sacred weight of the crown."*

My father's mantra beat harder: *"Initiation is an ordeal. True initiation must make the ordeal... severe."*

The koi dove under the surface, and for a moment, I feared it had gone. "Come back," I called out into the rippling silence. And it did—rising again, as if drawn by the truth I was still avoiding. I bit down a sob. But the memory came anyway.

I was a child again, barefoot on the dock, watching Nefertiti—my mother, Queen of the Sun—board her barge with her arms full of my younger sisters. Linen fluttered at her elbows like banners of departure.

"Take me, with you," I had begged. "Please—I am your daughter."

She turned to a servant. "Put her on the second boat. She said she did not have time for me." I stood alone as her barge pulled away— denied, forgotten. I was forced to follow in its wake. That was the moment the cage first closed. And I had spent years since painting it with gold.

"I had always believed she abandoned me, and I have been yearning for her ever since," I said, my voice breaking. But the truth hit me like a spear of sunlight through a temple's shadow—merciless, divine, undeniable. I pressed my hands to the grass "It was I who abandoned myself." The words tasted like iron.

The koi submerged again, then rose in quiet understanding. "That is why it hurts now. Pentu did not betray you. He revealed the illusion."

My breath caught. My hands clung to a clump of grass as if it could keep me from drifting.

"What do I do now?" I whispered. "What do I say to Archollos...to Smenkhkare?"

The koi flicked its tail. "When light loves shadow, it births gold. When duty marries desire, it births ruin. Choose not the man, but the mirror." Its body vanished beneath the lotus.

"Do not leave me," I called out, too late.

But I was already being summoned—the crunch of gravel behind me, footsteps approaching.

"Merit-Aten, come play with us. We are making daisy chains," called Tadushet, her voice lilting like reeds in wind. Her lavender sheath as lovely as the iris by the pond.

I rose slowly; linen caught in the wind like wings. And I turned.

"Hurry," chimed Keshtuat, poking her head outside the door. "We have set up the game board, then she saw my face—my eyes, rimmed with salt and silence—and paused. "You look upset." She walked to me in her pale green sheath, like a mint leaf. Then she knelt next to me offering me a garland of flowers, its petals slightly crushed where her fingers had held it too tightly.

I drew a breath and forced stillness into my body. I cannot say," I whispered. I dare not put it into words, or it would become true."

Sarawat pushed forward in a pink mist sheath, insistent. "If you cannot confide in us, then who? You know your sisters in shadow and sun would carry any secret you gave."

They circled me like a net of moonlight—arms around shoulders, fingers brushing hair from my brow. For all our squabbles, we were a braid. One pulled tight, the others held tension.

Their presence cracked me open. Tears welled uninvited and spilled without permission. The ache hollowed my chest.

"Speak it, Tadushet urged gently, her touch as light as my mother's had never been. "We will find a way. Together."

I swallowed hard, forcing the corners of my mouth to curve, though they trembled.

"My father has commanded it," I said. "I must choose a consort.

Sarawat beamed, hands clapping in delight, her sleeves billowed in the breeze.

"Archollos! At last! The stars favor you—he loves you so."
I froze.

The warmth of her joy struck like ice water. "No," I said slowly, each word costing me breath. "I must choose... Smenkhkare."

The laughter fled the garden.

Keshtuat drew back, her smile collapsing. "Why would you choose a man who is not right for you?"

"Because my father demands it," I said, but the words tasted like dust and broken vows.

The others agreed, cackling amongst them like black crows caught in confusion—still imagining I had made a mistake that could be undone.

"I am obligated to choose within the Royal bloodline," I said, voice flat. "Smenkhkare is the one my parents approve of."

Their expressions darkened—until the truth landed. My mother was the HeMeti, *She Who Has The Last Word*.

It was our custom to honor the Highest Female's decision. Like Sekhmet roaring through a battlefield, her word was law. The sisters of my heart nodded and reluctant silence. It was done. Now, only one obstacle remained. None of us knew how to perform a Choosing ceremony.

"My oldest sister had a *Grogup*, a Joining," Tadushet offered. "But I do not recall anything special that happened. It was… just an ordinary day."

Keshtuat added, "My mother is the Court Seamstress; I do not believe she ever crafted a Grogup dress. Most wear a plain white sheath."

I tilted my head, trying to envision it. "Nothing special for such an important step in our lives? No food, no music, no dress? This is most concerning." My shoulders sagged.

Sarawat stoked my hair. "My Meti, the Court Wigmaker—had an assistant who went through her Grogup. She packed up her bedding, and cosmetics, then left her mother's house to live with her consort at his."

I stared. "Smenkhkare's mother—Kiya, has Wested. Am I expected to move to his rooms at the palace at Akhet-Aten?"

Sarawat nodded. "I believe so. I recall their parents drew up a contract. That was an important part." She held up a finger, recalling each term. "Two pieces of silver if he chose to release her from the union. Two more if she gave him a boy child."

"Am I worth so little?" My voice cracked like a pot left too long in the sun.

"I, the next Per Aat, to be bartered like the linen at the market. A few pieces of silver for the labor of my womb. And if I failed to please him? If my scent soured in his memory? I would be returned—like perfume no longer favored, sealed and forgotten on some dusty shelf."

Keshtuat, Sarawat, and Tadushet fell silent, the sting of her words striking marrow. One by one, their eyes shifted—not with pity, but with dawning recognition. For the first time, they saw it too: there was a price on each of them, veiled in tradition, dressed as duty.

"This is preposterous. I am not a purchase. I am not a possession," I raged, my nostrils flaring. What is a contract without consent? A sentence, not a union," I snarled, like a caged lioness, baring both claws and fangs.

"You are right," said Keshtuat softly, taking my hands in hers, tears pooling. She likely imagined Ra-Awab—being replaced at the last moment.

"We do not have to pack you up," she said. "There is no one to tell us how this should be done. Let us have a ceremony for your choosing—and make it memorable. I will create your dress."

"Allow me to do your hair," said Sarawat. "You need a new style. I just need a razor."

"I can pick some flowers," added Tadushet with a bright smile.

"Do you think my father made a contract?" I asked, my brow furrowed.

"Smenkhkare should be responsible for that," Sarawat replied. "I could ask him to get help from the boys."

I clutched my arms to my chest as if I could hold the fragments together. "Archollos must know. It is not just news. It is…my grief to deliver," I stammered trying to make sense of my words. "Tell him my choice—well, my father's choice, but really my mother's choice… It is so confusing. I feel foolish and hopeless." My shell cracked. I imagined yolk, dripping from my vessel—shattered, unable to be pieced back together.

Sarawat's voice lowered, stripped of its usual edge. "We now know your predicament. It must have been a terrible secret to hold in your heart alone." Her kindness startled me. For years her sarcasm had stung. Her bond with Archollos, forged in that awakening at the Dendera Temple, had made her bitter toward the one he loved.

I turned to them, helpless. "Which one do I tell first?" My voice cracked like a branch bending under too many choices. "Either one would be confused. I have no time to offer grand explanations to the man I adore nor profess my love to a man who is only my friend. Which one?"

Keshtuat tugged me into her arms before doubt could take hold. "Tell Archollos first. He must know."

"He deserves to know why," Sarawat added, eyes steady. "If you do not explain, silence will rot everything you once shared."

"Otherwise, he will act like a bitter melon that has been overwatered; then passed over," said Tadushet, her voice warm with a wisdom. "It is fair."

"We will distract the boys," Sarawat said, cracking her knuckles like she was planning a heist.

A feast," Keshtuat chimed in. "We will say we are planning something for the hosts. We walked into the home whispering.

"Make them decorate," Tadushet smirked. "That always keeps boys busy—and confused."

We shall give them a task with no clear end," Sarawat added. "They will think it is ceremony prep, but it is really a cover."

"I will talk to the Lady of the House, Ma-Nat, and see if she has anything we can use," said Tadushet.

"Candles, vases, and colored linen," added Keshtuat, her eyes fluttering shut as she counted.

They pulled me into a tight embrace, our foreheads touching like we were sealing a pact. In their arms, the ache eased—if only slightly—and I found just enough strength to stand straighter. Their warmth wrapped around me like linen fresh from the sun. I let myself lean into it gathering their courage as my own. My ribs ached from the pressure, but it was the first time all day I felt whole.

Once the choosing was behind us, then we could make our way to the pyramids—and find Djehuty. But first, the red lion that my father had spoken of. That came next.

Rallying my will, I drew a breath and slipped past the curtain, the linen whispering secrets as it brushed my skin. I stepped into the enclosed patio like a warrior entering a battlefield, praying no one saw the tremble in my hands.

My shadow stretched ahead of me across the tile—and still, I felt small.

The laughter from the Senet game clashed with the war in my chest. *Their voices rose like a sandstorm, wild and unruly—cheers turning to jeers in the same breath, the air thick with sweat and rising tension.* Hooting, with arms up as if miniature generals plotting a Senet battle. Archollos laughed mid-move, locked in the rhythms of play, still in a world where love was light. But Smenkhkare—he was already in the ground, hands in the dirt, inspecting roots for rot. He, knelt bare-chested, copper skin glistening with sweat, and flecks of soil. His white linen kilt, was lightly pleated and tied with a leather thong. His torso was strong and muscled, but there was something vulnerable about him—unarmored, stripped of titles. At least, he understood the cost of harvest. I would tell him first.

"May I speak to you?" I asked, voice barely louder than the wind rustling the fronds. softly, peeling him away from his garden, his sanctuary.

"Of course," he said, brushing soil from his palms. "Did you receive word from Djehuty?"

I hesitated. The words clung to the walls of my throat like the dough we kneaded back in Kalabsha. We had always worked well together—he kneading the earth, I kneading destiny—but that didn't make this easier.

"Not about the Master Teacher," I said, shifting my weight. "The message I received...was unexpected."

His eyes lit with cautious hope. "Please, tell me, Sister. You and your family are all I have left. I have been sitting with the grief in my heart all morning, mourning our loss should the Pharaoh pass."

*His sorrow struck like a reed arrow—silent but sharp—
tightening my chest and stinging the backs of my eyes before
I could blink it away.* when he called me Sister, it burned. It
told me exactly how he saw me—and how he did not.

"There is no soft way to say this," I began, voice trembling. "Our fates were written long ago—but we were the
last to be told. The time has come...I must make my choice."

I met his gaze and spoke with all the strength I had left.
"I choose you as my consort. We must prepare to become
Co-Regents with the Pharaoh. When he Wests...Khemit will
fall to us."

Smenkhkare blinked. Took a slow step back. "Why me?"

I bit my lip. I couldn't give him a whole truth, so help
me, Aten. "You are of royal blood. Our union is expected.
The lineage demands it."

"Merit-Aten," he said, his voice as soft as the soil he
tended. "You are my sister in spirit. I would deny you nothing. But, I know...your heart does not beat for mine."

His eyes clouded with sorrow. "I was always told I was
born to fill a gap—not to inherit, but to exist quietly in the
shadows. I never wanted power—only knowledge."

"That is why we both walk the path of initiation," I whispered. "But we are still bound."

He cocked his head, "I never thought I would be chosen
for anything, lest of all for you. Who is forcing this?"

My throat closed. "My parents," I said, and the air
seemed to thicken around the word.

He folded his arms. "Then we are but pawns in a larger
game. I thought we had escaped Amun's grip—but here we
are—ordered to bind ourselves against our will."

He looked toward the earth, toward the planted rows. "This path, this soil, this challenge—these are what bring me close to the Aten. I have no desire to rule. Archollos... he has the strength, the courage. You belong with him."

He knelt beside a squash vine, brushing his hand gently over a leaf. A glimmering beetle clung to its underside. He studied it for a long moment before flicking it away. "The roots must remain strong," he murmured. "Even beauty can drain what feeds us." He rose, inhaling the pale blossoms, "Archollos is a better choice for you. He has the courage of a ferocious lion with the heart of gold."

"We have no choice," I raised my voice. "You know that. You cannot say no. Brother, I honor your joy being on the land," I added, gently, "but I must protest. Pharaoh is commanding it."

Smenkhkare bent and plucked a rose, offering it to me. "I love another," he said simply.

My heart snapped wondering if it was the temple priestess who always made him laugh. "You are refusing? To a Per Aat in-waiting? You are not allowed to say no."

He stood still—steeled. "And yet—I must. It may be your Choosing. But it is not mine. Not to be Pharaoh."

His refusal landed like a blow to the ribs—I went still, as if the air was heavy, as if the garden lost its axis. I went still. "Do I not please you?" I asked, though I hated how raw it sounded.

"I adore you, my Sister." His expression did not change, no flicker—just the unmoved resolve of limestone cliffs that had outlasted empires.

What was I to do—drag him to the ceremony?" I used my sleeve to brush away a tear. My face twisted, lips curled like a lion cub swatted by its sire. I turned from him and stepped into the sunlight. Let the Aten burn me if it must. A thorn pricked my skin. I dropped the rose Smenkhkare had given me. Let it rot.

Archollos saw my distress, immediately left the Senet game, coming to my side. His loose flax tunic was unlaced at the chest. A copper armband, a gift from my Mother glinted in the sun. He walked barefoot across the courtyard and must have kicked off his sandals.

"My beauty, I am sorry that we were creating a commotion. Are you disturbed by our game? You seem out of sorts." His smile was genuine. The love flowed from his heart to mine—everything I had ever dreamed of—now, my dream turned to ash.

"Archollos, may we find somewhere more private?" I asked, glancing toward Smenkhkare—my fingernails digging into my palm.

Sarawat caught my eye and smiled, holding up white linen cloth for my Choosing dress. I put a finger to my lips.

She froze—and dropped the linen from view. My love and I strolled to the front of the demesne, past an arch of pink roses now in full bloom. I saw them—and dared to wish the arch still meant something sacred for me.

"I find myself once again beholden to the commands of my parents," I said cautiously, preparing him for what was to come.

"Yes, my love," he said with a soft nod. "I know that weighs heavy upon you. What now has you so vexed?" He plucked a pink rose and he too offered it to me—a gesture of love that once had meant everything. Now, it felt hollow. I declined with a wave of my hand.

I steadied myself and stood firm. "Pharaoh has commanded me to choose a consort," I said, my voice was thin with dread. I looked up into his eyes—those impossible, sky-blue eyes. To break his heart would kill something in me too.

Archollos beamed with sudden clarity and took my hands. "I know what you are asking," he said. "I accept. I would love nothing more than being your consort. I will always support you on your path. My love, I stand with you. Eternally." *His devotion poured out like wine—sweet, unstinting, and meant for celebration. And yet, I stood with an empty cup.* Why was the Aten so cruel?

"Archollos, you did not allow me to finish. Although, I feel the same—you are the love of my life, and I want nothing more than to join with you—it is not the will of the Aten."

His expression shifted. I saw it then—the shield. *When I opened like a flower at dawn, he had closed like a temple door at dusk.*

He took a step back—the gap between us stretched like a canyon.

"My destiny is in your hands," he said, voice steady. "I pray that you will be honest."

My eyes blurred—as though the Nile itself had risen behind them. "My love—you are everything to me. While we call it the Choosing, yet, I have no choice. No freedom has been bequeathed to me to determine the course of my life. Nor do I have any power to determine yours. My parents have decreed that I choose Smenkhkare. I must obey. I must produce his heir."

At first, Archollos scoffed, shaking his head like he had misheard me. Then came a short laugh-low, hollow, disbelieving. It grew, swelling into a full-bodied laugh that sent a chill down my spine. *His laughter cracked like old pottery* baked too long in the kiln—brittle, splintered,

"The gods have a cruel sense of humor," he said, stepping away from me as if I had burned him. "You told me you loved me. Was it a lie?" "His shoulders sagged for a moment, the last ember of hope flickering out—then he ignited."

"It was never a lie." My voice thinned, desperate, like the call of a bird caught between sky and snare. His shoulders recoiled, as if my touch had branded him. "I do love you. That is the only truth I have left." *Each word dragged itself from my throat like a stone being pushed uphill.* "But it does not matter. The choice was never mine to make." I confessed, my fists turned into a ball.

Again, he laughed—louder, darker, unmoored.

"Why do you jest?" I demanded, my chest heaving.

"I suppose I do not really find it funny. It is karmic atonement," he said, his eyes narrowing. "For the way you treat the men who love you. You think we are at your disposal. You simply order a man to produce an heir, and—pop—your belly rises like dough. Does that not make us slaves? This matriarchal system of yours...it emasculates us. Turns us to cuckolds—spectators to our own lives. No, I will not be party to it." He took another step back, as if reclaiming sacred ground.

"I demand you release me. I will find my way back to Mycenae. To the arms of my family."

"I have done no such thing to you," I cried. "Why do you mock me with my choice of Smenkhkare?"

Now, he was forcing me to choose *him*, just to prove him wrong.

"Your parent's choice shall end in childlessness. Archo-llos said, coldly. They believe they have secured their legacy—wrapped it in gold and prophecy. But their wisdom will rot into ruin."

He stepped forward slowly, his voice a venomous thread. "The Aten may shield you. But did He whisper this in your prayers. Smenkhkare prefers men."

I flinched.

"You know it. Even if it was only once—at Dendera—that was enough."

His voice cracked with rage and shame. "He will never touch you. The union your parent's decreed is already broken. It is already a corpse dressed for a wedding." He paused, as if the words themselves disgusted him. "And you—with all your mysticism, all your gods and sacred rites—you will kneel, pray, weep, but his root will not rise for you. No seed. No heir. And when that prophecy fails— what will become of you then, Merit-Aten?"

*J*osh padded into the kitchen wearing yesterday's hoodie, the sleeves pulled over his knuckles like he used to do in middle school. He lifted the recycling-bin lid and froze. His hand emerged slowly, holding a frosted bottle by the neck—then another, and another. The glass clinked together, soft but sharp, like chimes of judgment.

His eyes flicked to her across the room. Not anger. Not shock. Worse—assessment. Like he was cataloging a new species of disappointment.

Morainya stood in the doorway, still wrapped in that old white robe—the one with puckered cotton ridges like soft corduroy, worn smooth at the elbows. Faded pink cabbage roses bloomed across the fabric like a forgotten garden. It smelled faintly of baby powder and lavender oil and always clung to her calves just above her white ankle socks. The kind of robe that remembered every winter morning, every flu season, every midnight heartbreak. Her hair knotted at the nape. Her mouth opened, but no words came. Her gaze darted to the stove as if breakfast might explain everything.

Josh broke the silence. "Was it a celebration I missed?" His voice wasn't sarcastic. It was flat. Careful.

She blinked, once. Twice. "I—" She swallowed. "No."

He set the bottles on the counter one by one. "You said you were done."

She looked at the clock. 7:14 a.m. Her stomach churned. "I know what I said." Her voice came out hoarse, like it had been fighting itself all night. "Josh, how's school? Are you still writing that paper on the Constitutional Amendments?"

He let out a quiet laugh—more breath than sound. "Wow. That's how we're doing this?"

She moved to the sink, turned on the water too hard, and started rinsing a cup that didn't need rinsing. "I'm just trying to have a normal morning."

He stared at her back. "There's no such thing here any-more, Mom."

Silence stretched like fog between them.

"Just... don't lie," he added, voice low. "It's worse than the drinking."

Morainya closed her eyes. Her knuckles whitened on the ceramic rim. When the door slammed a moment later, it echoed through the quiet house like a verdict.

Her morning routine of getting Josh out the door to school was already unraveling. It nearly broke her heart when he paused at the door, his camouflage backpack slung over one shoulder, and said, *"You always look so tired after a night alone."*

For years, she had followed the rules, trusted the system, believed in justice. And yet, here she was–robbed by the very institution that claimed to protect her. Aldo's victory wasn't just about money; it was about power, about the system that consumed people like her, chewed them up, and spat them out.

She wasn't tired—she was done.

But the truth stung: she was still stuck in the same loop. Wine bottles clinking in the bin, Josh's eyes too wise for seventeen. If she didn't break the pattern now, she never would.

Something had to change, or everybody was going to steal everything she owned by using the law. That settlement with Aldo hadn't just drained her bank account—it had shattered something fundamental inside of her. The betrayal by a family member who had been abused by the church who would benefit later from her mother's suffering was just too much for Morainya's psyche. Worse, it had been done under the guise of justice. That was the real wound. And it festered.

She fished in her purse to find the business card from that guy in the bookstore and grabbed her cellphone.

"Hello Sal? This is Morainya Napolitano. I met you at The Tree of Knowledge Bookstore a few weeks ago. I'm ready to come onto the Land and Soil. I read Disclosure 101, and I want to break free of the corporation."

Sal bolted upright in his recliner. "Hello, yes, I remember. This is great news. How soon would you like to do this?"

"Immediately, I don't think I can stand another minute in this corrupt system," said Morainya, looking at the dates on her phone calendar.

"Wow, when it hits you, it hits you." Sal explained the paperwork she needed to become an American State National." He closed the recliner, and laid a Law book down on the table next to him. "How about Saturday, same place?"

"Sounds good." Morainya wrote it down.

"Go get a red pen, a blue pen, and a red ink pad," Sal instructed. "Once you have completed all the steps, I will set you up to be recorded." He glanced at his Apple watch, noting he still had time for his morning run.

Morainya nodded. "Got it."

Sal cleared his throat trying to recall if she had ever mentioned kids. "Do you have children?"

Morainya glanced at the denim jacket draped over a kitchen chair—Josh's name stitched in orange thread from Sophomore year. "Yes," she said, tugging the cuff straight. "A son."

"How old is he?" asked Sal.

"He turns eighteen in July." The words tasted half-finished, like an unmailed letter.

"Then bring him on the Land too," Sal suggested. "Freedom's lighter when you carry it together."

She traced the seam of the jacket. Josh's cologne—cheap sandalwood—still clung to the fabric. "Isn't he a little young?"

He glanced at the family photo—his two girls in pink ballet skirts, mid-twirl, mid-giggle.

"I signed my kids up when they were four and six." He paused—then recalled, a year later, his wife filed for divorce and moved to Santa Fe—said she wanted to become a sculptor after a few night pottery classes at the college. He looked over at the first vase she ever brought home. Misshapen. Lopsided. Like a silent omen he hadn't understood at the time

Morainya bit her lip. "I'll ask," she murmured, though doubt pressed at her ribs.

Sal chuckled kindly. "If he's not ready, don't worry about it."

"Or we can just get you recorded first," said Sal.

"I will let you know. Thank you, goodbye." She ended the call and slid the card onto the table like a final chess move.

Morainya opened her laptop and found the website. The creation of the account was easy; she then clicked on the link that held all the paperwork. This was going to take some time to fill in all these forms. Birth names, birth location, and names of her parents.

By late afternoon, she had files scattered around her, and she looked up the information that kept her locked in the corporation as a slave. She really had to become an expat on the Land and Soil. This wasn't going to be as easy as she imagined, but after filling in the questions, she was mostly finished by evening, two cups of chai, and a bag of popcorn.

The printer began to rattle off the forms. Gathering them up, she scanned them to make sure it was all correct. Drats, she spelled her name wrong on one of the forms, and her address and street name were wrong on another. Make the corrections. Print again. She collected them and then emailed the recorder to get them notarized. Her appointment was this Thursday; now she had better go get a passport photo and those supplies.

Later that night, Josh finished dinner—a bowl of mac and cheese—and he wiped the bowl with a slice of bread. Morainya lingered in the doorway, forms clutched to her chest after her son had eaten dinner, she said, "Josh, I need to tell you what's going on."

He slid his phone into his hoodie pocket. "I told Mike I'd be over in five."

Her fingers tightened on the paperwork. "It's important."

He took one look at the legal pages, and backed toward the door. "Does it have to happen now?"

"No, but—," her words were like a jumble in her mouth.

"Then hold it till I get back." He was gone before the screen door finished creaking, his footsteps fading down the porch steps into the blue evening as she heard her car pull out.

She exhaled, feeling the echo of slammed wood reverberate right through the forms in her hands. Her confession fell back into her chest like a swallowed stone.

But when he returned, and the leftover mac and cheese disappeared with a half-gallon of milk chugged straight from the carton, and his eyes clearer, she tried again.

"It's nine o'clock on a school night," she said, forcing steadiness into her voice. "I know I haven't been... available this year. But I've made a decision. One that affects both of us."

Josh leaned against the counter, hoodie sleeves half-pulled over his hands. "What kind of decision?"

"You know I've been in court over your grandfather's estate—she bit the inside of her cheek—I lost."

His brows tightened. "Like, lost money?"

"Yes," she nodded, lips pressing together. "Three million."

Josh blinked. "Uncle Aldo got that much?"

"He got enough. Not because he was right—but because I was too afraid to fight." She sat at the dining room table, gesturing for him to join her. "He twisted facts. I panicked. Settled. Later, I learned things that made me question everything I was raised to believe."

He dropped into the seat beside her, warily. "Like what?"

"I shouldn't say," she hesitated. "If I did, it might hurt people who didn't ask to be hurt."

"So... you're gonna lie to me to teach me that everyone lies?" he asked, the sarcasm brittle but fair.

She winced. "No. But I'm trying to protect you—from things that can't be undone."

Josh stared at the worn edge of the table. "Just say it, Mom. You always taught me the truth matters more than what's easy."

She exhaled. Morainya put her hand up to her chin. Was it right for her to reveal the transgressions that Aldo had committed against her mother—when the very Church that raised her had already destroyed a child? How does anyone wrap their mind around a crime of that magnitude? Once, she would have turned to the Church. Now, she felt betrayed by the very altar she was raised to kneel before.

Her relationship with Josh had already been strained. She didn't have the strength to fight another battle—not today.

She started slowly, in a low voice. "In the Settlement Mediation, I had overcome Aldo's accusations. I'd even exposed discrepancies—he'd misused funds, and I could prove it. I was holding firm on a low number, ready to walk away. Then, at the final hour, Aldo dropped a new bombshell—he claimed he'd been abused. By someone in the family. He said he had proof." She paused, watching Josh for any flicker of reaction.

Josh frowned. "Who?"

Morainya nodded then said, "My mind went straight to my father," Morainya said, gripping the cushion like it might ground her. "But it wasn't about who—it was about *what* that claim did. The judge changed. Suddenly, nothing else mattered—not the evidence, not the fraud. Just this vague, radioactive accusation."

Josh blinked, slow. "So, all your proof—just erased? Because he said something bad happened to him?"

She leaned forward, voice thick with memory. "Kanberg started whispering about strategy. If we didn't settle, we'd be dragged into court. Witnesses. Expert testimony. Forensic audits. Character assassinations. And the press would feast on scandal. It was never about justice—it was about who could survive the storm."

Josh stared like the deer in headlights. "That's why you agreed to the three million?

She nodded once—heavy. "Blood money, hush money— call it what you want. It was the only way to keep them from parading the Napolitano legacy through the mud."

Josh exhaled sharply. "That's messed up."

The Archbishop told me to settle. That should I take it to court, we'd end up with Judge Soffagiano and that our family skeletons would be dragged out into the open."

Josh's voice cracked. "What skeletons? I'm family," Josh took a deep breath, scared of what he'd hear. "What aren't you telling me?"

"After we had agreed to the amount... and the attorneys were drawing up a contract...only after I asked for clarification did the Judge reveal it wasn't my father that Aldo was referring to—it was my mother he was accusing of abuse."

Josh's brows furrowed. "Wait—*Grandma?* You mean... Grandma Stella?"

Morainya wiped a tear away. "A secret, wrapped in shame, protection, and power imbalance. No one *wants* to lie. But everyone's been taught that the truth will break something sacred."

Josh frowned. "But ... why would they drag Grandma into this at all?"

"Aldo's claim," she said, voice barely above a whisper, "was that your Grandma—hurt him."

Josh's jaw dropped. "Grandma Stella? She's five-foot-nothing!"

"Your Grandma Stella, worked as a novice nun back then when she was sixteen. Taught one of Aldo's classes when he went to St. Mary's School for Wayward Boys—the place where he was left behind before he was adopted into the Napolitano family. He was only fourteen. Nobody knows what really happened in that classroom when Aldo may have ..."

Josh cut in, voice sharp. "May have what?"

Morainya paused and grimaced. Her voice dipped, raw as an exposed nerve. "Josh, there's a bruise on Nana's memory that no X-ray can prove. Your Uncle Aldo—he struck her once, hard enough that the doctor called it 'a mild concussion, probably a fall.'"

Morainya cleared her throat, then said, "People always whispered that Aldo was... damaged long before that—hurt in the rectory as a boy. I can't swear to it, but the rumor seeps through our family tree like mildew. The Church hushes it; the elders change the subject; the lawyers call it hearsay." She swallowed, words thick as cough syrup.

Josh squinched, then said, "But that means Aldo hurt Grandma Stella. She didn't abuse him?"

She pinched the bridge of her nose, fingertips trembling. A flicker of something crossed Josh's face—shock, then dawning anger.

"I'm not excusing him, Josh. I'm showing you the rot in the walls we were told to trust. Stella's concussion, Aldo's pain, the Church's white collar—they all stitched themselves into one lie after another until truth suffocated."

Her son just shook his head as if clearing memories hidden in fog.

"We'll never know." Morainya wrapped her arms around herself. "But in court, truth doesn't matter—only spectacle. One whisper that she was the nun who turned him into a monster, and the press would shred her. The judge practically dared me to risk it."

Josh swore under his breath.

Morainya braced her palms on the wood table, words coming low. "Loretta Cohen—remember our accountant's wife?—she told her husband, and he told me: back when Aldo was a ward at St. Mary's, *priests* were doing awful things to the boys. Loretta revealed that Stella was her best friend, and she confessed that she slapped Aldo in class for mouthing off."

She drew a shaky breath. "One slap— nothing more. A flinch of frustration when a wild, broken child lashed out. She cried immediately after. But in court that would become a pattern, a history, an indictment. Truth wouldn't matter—only who could spin it faster."

Josh's eyes widened. "That's insane. They'd let real monsters go—and frame *her*?"

"Exactly." Morainya's jaw set. "Stella is five-foot-nothing and spent her society life in Dior, for heaven's sake. But one old rumor is all the media would need. Paying Aldo to keep him from smearing the Napolitano's who adopted him, and from ruining Stella's reputation—before the judge could turn that courtroom into a circus. It made sense... at the time."

Josh inhaled deeply, "I had no idea you were going through all this. It's just insane."

Morainya's shoulders sagged. "I know. And that's why I walked away from their game. Their courts aren't built for truth—they're built for leverage."

Josh blinked. "I see that stuff all the time on social media. Lawsuits are happening against priests for molesting kids." He scrolled, thumb jerking like it couldn't move fast enough. Look—here's two more, a San Francisco and a San Jose incident. New lawsuits."

Morainya let out a breath like she'd been holding it in all day.

"Reading about it is one thing." She rubbed her arms, as if trying to scrub off the memory. "Living in it? Being a child in a place where the people who hurt you also claim to save you?" She shook her head. "That kind of betrayal gets into your bones. And stays there."

Josh went quiet, the air thick between them. "That's fucked up," he said finally, voice low, like he was scared the walls might hear.

"It was like they all talked to each other before the case," Morainya said animating the details like she was counting the clues. "Kanberg bragged he'd already had coffee with the judge—like it was no big deal. And Archbishop DeLaurentis? He all but patted my head. *'Settle, my dear. That judge is tough. You won't like the skeletons they'll drag out.'*"

Morainya stopped, palms flat on the paperwork, breathing hard. "It was right there in front of me—every warning sign—but I was too naïve, too blasted hopeful that truth would prevail, to read the handwriting on the wall."

"That's kind of messed up." Josh dug his hands into his front pocket and looked down.

Pain washed over his face. "Wish I could have told them to fuck off," he muttered.

Morainya's lips softened. She reached out and touched his arm "Son, this wasn't your fight. It was mine. She pulled back, jaw clenched now, like she was about to deliver a closing argument in a courtroom that never let her speak. "That's how Maritime Law works., I was being tried by *Attorneys*—not judges. They 'attorn' for the dead. They don't serve justice. They serve the King. The Pope. The Lord Mayor of London. Anyone but me." Her voice dropped to a whisper. "To them, I was already dead."

Josh looked stunned. "Wait... what does that even mean? You were *alive*."

"Josh, before I tell you any of that, I have realized that our lawyers, Mr. Kanberg and all the others who pretended to represent me in a court of law, betrayed me. They betrayed me by lying to me over and over. The same thing with the church. What I discovered is that it has been a powerful racket where everybody works against the little guy. It's about greed, power, and fear, and it's been going on for centuries."

"What are you talking about?" Josh crossed his arms and took a defensive stance. She just sounded crazy. "Kenny's Mom is a lawyer and defends the poor—pro bono- that means for free."

Morainya softened. "Maybe not all of them. I'm sorry. Maybe it's just mine and the huge firms." She laid a hand on the stack of American-State-National papers. "This is why I have to step off their stage altogether. Because if I stay in that courtroom long enough, they'll twist my grief into another weapon."

"What's all that?" Josh murmured, as if the papers might answer before she did.

"You will have to open your mind because what I am about to share goes back to your birth, my birth, my parent's birth. We have all been sold into slavery from the moment we entered this world. I have figured out a way to free us. To leave the system. Like the Matrix."

Josh's eyes bounced between her face and the papers. "You're saying we're in the Matrix. *For real.* Like—legal slavery."

"Yes." Morainya nodded "And I found the way out."

Josh leaned forward. "Holy shit. That movie wasn't a metaphor." He froze for a moment, staring at her, processing. Then he slowly grinned. "I knew it. I fucking knew it." Josh's eyes lit up, eyes flickering like the first time he saw *The Matrix.*

Morainya exhaled. Finally, she could breathe. "Exactly. Neo chose truth over comfort. Cypher begged for steak and silence. But Neo saw the cords, the feeding tubes, the lie—and he couldn't go back. Neo saw how things really worked. He would rather die than live like an animated slave, giving his life force away to a dark intruder who cared nothing for humanity."

His laughter was half-excitement, half-relief—as if the creeping suspicion that had always lingered in the back of his mind had finally been confirmed. Josh spun in the kitchen like a bird set loose, laughter bursting out of him like steam from a long-locked pipe. If only it was that easy.

"What now? We just...leave like Neo? Walk away from everything? Away from this simulation?" he asked, fidgeting, his hands in his pocket searching for something.

Morainya pressed her trembling palm flat against the papers, shoulders squaring as fire steadied her voice. "The first step? We correct our Political Status. We reclaim what was stolen the moment they typed our names in all caps and filed us away as cargo. We get off the Sea and onto the Land and Soil Jurisdiction of our Country."

"Like move away from Santa Cruz?" His eyes widened and he grimaced, stepping backward.

"No, Josh, not literally. We can stay here. Have you ever noticed that all our letters and government notices come to our ALL-CAP Name. A 'Name' isn't just what they call you. It's what they own. All-caps turns you into cargo. Your appellation—that's the soul name. The living one. Check out your passport and driver's license."

Josh fished out his wallet, thumbed through the plastic sleeve, then squinted at the blocky letters staring back at him. He held it up. "It's all caps. Like I'm not a person. Like I'm... a product."

Morainya continued, slowing her words. "It means you are owned. It means they can drag you into their Maritime courts like you're cargo on a ledger." Morainya's voice cracked—anger barely tethered. "I've seen it. Lived it. It's a rigged script, Josh. The whole thing's a setup."

Josh's face tightened. "So, all of it—every rule, every fine print, every court date—it's just a game they already won?"

Morainya shot to her feet, arms wrapping tight around her ribs as if she could hold herself together by force alone. A white flash of memory burned behind her eyes. "Unless you wake up."

Josh slid his hand in hers, grip warm and steady. "But how do they have any power over Americans? I mean, like, why don't people know this?"

Morainya looked at him, really looked.

"Because we didn't win the Revolutionary War. Not really." She leaned forward, her voice low almost conspiratorial. "They sold us back into slavery. A trade behind closed doors. The public got a flag and a good story. The Crown got the people." She tapped the table twice, like sealing a deal. It was the greatest PR scam in American history."

Josh frowned. "That's not true. I took a history test on that last year. The American Revolution block. We won. I've seen so many movies on it. We outsmarted the British."

Morainya crossed her arms, her eyes steady. "That's the point, Neo. We live in the Matrix. Everything is a lie."

Josh's voice rose, defensive now. "Who else knows the truth—besides you?"

She pulled the book off the dining room table and laid it down in front of him like evidence. "People across the country have formed Assemblies. Real ones. I would like us to join them."

Josh rolled his eyes and started scrolling his phone—again. "Why don't you do it first? If it works, then maybe I will."

"That's the point, Neo. We need to wake up together. I can sign you up this Thursday. Once you are 18, you will have to do it yourself. You'll go off to college—back to sleep.

I only have this one moment in time to ask you the most important question I've ever asked: Do you want to fight the next Revolutionary War? Because only one to two percent of the population fought for everybody's freedom the first time. The rest stayed asleep. Comfortable. Safe. Which one are you, Josh?"

Josh looked up from his phone, a crease forming between his brows.

"I'd fight. Except," he paused, running a hand through his hair, "I just don't want to feel like a freak. I can't tell any of my friends about this—they'd think I was crazy."

Morainya's throat was bone-dry. She swallowed hard. "The government has lied to us, and most people are either too tired, too numb, or too comfortable to care. Just like Cypher. He wanted the steak. He didn't want the truth—he wanted flavor."

Josh clutched his wallet. "Do I have to give up my passport or driver's license?" Josh hugged it to him. His license *was* his freedom.

She smiled faintly. "Nope. You get more freedom, not less. We become living men and women again. With rights from God—not corporate policy."

Josh's voice shrank a little. "Will we get in trouble? Will we go to jail?" He sounded like a boy again. She felt the ache of it.

"Son." Morainya gripped his hand. "If I don't fight for your freedom now. It will be too late for your children. This is bigger than courtrooms and fines. This is about sovereignty." Morainya laid her fist hard down on the table—not loud, but enough to make her point. "We have this moment in time. Right now. I owe over ninety five thousand dollars of my personal money to the people who know they wronged me. And I'm supposed to pretend that is justice? I can't do it. Not anymore."

Josh looked stunned "You owe money for losing?"

She tousled his mousy brown hair, forgetting how much effort boys put into looking effortlessly undone. She sniffled—part grief, part knowing he'd be gone soon.

Brown University. His Father's alma mater. A win for the family. A loss for her arms. *Empty nesters*, they called it. A new freedom. But freedom, she'd learned, came with a cost.

She cleared her throat and finally answered his question. "I've paid almost seventy-five thousand already. That's why I couldn't pay my half of your class trip this year." She looked away. "I've been scraping by working for the Santa Cruz Historical Society—digitizing old photos for fourteen bucks an hour. I wish I'd known all of this sooner. Because in their courts, the only winners are the lawyers. It's all a game we were never taught to play."

Josh stared at her, something shifting behind his eyes.

"What do I have to do?" he asked quietly.

She smiled.

"Just sign with me. I'll print the paperwork. Be ready next Thursday when the Recorder makes it official. I'll handle your father."

"I'm talking to Dad first," he said—voice lower, older. A line in the sand: *no surprise battles with the ex.*

Morainya lifted her palms in surrender, but her eyes stayed flint bright. "Fine. Just remember—if you want the blue pill, I'll hand it over and tuck you back into the machine myself." Her tone was playful; the steel beneath it wasn't.

Josh crossed his arms. "How do I know this isn't some Ponzi thing? Is there anything legit to read?"

Morainya slid a paperback across the table: *You Know Something Is Wrong When...*"Start here. It's cartoons and plain English. The author, Anna von Reitz, has spent decades on this—hard to fake that kind of obsession. And Sal—the guy who brought me in—will answer every question you fire at him."

Josh flipped the book open, thumb raking the pages. "Do I have to read it tonight?"

Morainya raised an eyebrow, already heading for the kitchen.

"Just try to stop once you start. I'll sweeten the trap—I'll make fresh brownies when we sign on Thursday. Your call: share them or watch me inhale the pan." Josh smirked, glanced at the book—curiosity winning the tug-of-war.

As he read, Morainya stacked forms into tidy towers for the Recorder, lining them up like troops on parade. Outside, rain pressed against the windows; inside, only page-turns and Sphinxy's purr like a motor in her lap.

Five pages in, Josh barked a startled laugh that turned into a string of whispered curses.

Another page, another muttered *"No way."* The illusion was cracking in real time, right there at the dining room table.

Finally, he looked up, eyes wide, the corner of his mouth lifting.

"Mom... if you pull this off, you'll be a total badass."

Morainya's answering grin was pure flint and fire.

"We will be badasses, Neo. Nobody flies solo out of the Matrix."

The laptop clock slid from 6:57 to 6:58. Morainya hovered near the front window, thumb tapping out one more *where-are-you?* text to Josh. A stack of neatly sorted papers sat on the dining table—red ink pad, passport photos, two crisp pens, all aligned like altar pieces.

A sudden jolt rippled through her pelvis—an electric, unwelcome tug. Iben. Again. She felt her V pang, and her shoulders jerked. Why was Iben still bothering her if he hadn't even bothered to reach out? Was this just another insult and kidnapping of her body?

When he jerked her shoulders again, she hit her arm to make it stop. Iben ignored her pleas. How could she have let this happen by being so open and loving toward a stranger? This, too, was making her crazy, and once again, she felt paralyzed to know who to ask. So, she prayed directly to God for Him to reveal the answer. She didn't need a middleman when she could ask God for direction.

7:00 p.m. blinked on the screen.

With a sigh, she clicked Janelle's Zoom link.

"Welcome, Morainya," the Recorder beamed, headset in place. "Ready to begin? First up, the Bivens statement—consent only takes a breath."

"Consent," Morainya said, voice steady, though her pulse was sprinting.

Janelle nodded. "We'll start with the Foreign Sovereign Immunities Act. Sign today's date, autograph in lowercase with the ©, right-thumb in red—every page, same ritual."

Morainya slid the first sheet forward, inhaled the iron tang of the ink pad, pressed her thumb.

The front door flew open. Josh burst in, skateboard under one arm. "Wait! Mike and Nathan want in, too!"

Morainya hit mute, half-laugh, half-groan. "Honey, their parents have to give them permission. You want in? Grab a blue pen."

She waved him toward the table, bid goodbye to his friends, then unmuted. "Janelle, can we add my son?"

"Happy to." Janelle's smile was warm. "Paperwork ready?"

"Right here." Morainya shuffled a second packet forward. "Josh, skim the top page—thumbprint when you're ready. I'm grabbing the brownies."

She escaped to the kitchen—mostly to breathe. The ding of a text lit her phone.

Iben: *"Would love to see you."* His voice came through like an echo underwater.

Heat flared under her skin—anger and thrill, a cocktail she hated. She typed back before her brain could stop her. *Would love to see you, too. But she hesitated, and didn't hit send.* She exhaled, light-headed.

Deal with that later.

"Mom!" Josh called. "Your turn."

"Coming," she managed.

Back at the table, Josh was flipping pages like a kid studying for a license exam.

She tried to focus—ink, signature, thumbprint—but her pulse was whispering a different name. Iben. She opened the message again. Reread it for no reason at all, like it might change. It hadn't. Four words. And still, her thighs ached with memory.

Would love to see you. Should she send it or ignore him?

Months of silence—months of trying to file him away under "Unfinished Mysticism." And now, this breadcrumb. This flicker. And here she was, chasing it like a woman with both her hands in the batter bowl of desire.

Her fingers hesitated over the keyboard. Her reply came slower than it should have.

Would love to see you too. She added a period. Deleted it. Then sent.

It wasn't a promise. It was a *pull.* And she hated how her body said *yes* when her mind was still sorting through *no.*

Sovereignty didn't make you immune to longing. It just taught you to walk with it, not drown.

Together they thumb-printed, signed, dipped again. Paper after paper transformed under the red stamp of living flesh.

At 8:50p.m. Janelle leaned back, satisfied. "Last step: mail me the originals. I'll record, stamp, return with the number. Then you photocopy for every agency you choose. Follow the instruction for your card and it should arrive shortly."

Josh's eyes shone like he'd just passed his driving test. "That card—kind of like a Freedom License, right?"

"Exactly," Janelle said then laughed. "Welcome to the Land and Soil."

Zoom clicked off.

A hush fell over the room—a hush that felt bigger than silence. Josh lifted his brownie in salute. "We really just did that?"

Morainya matched his gesture, brownie crumbs at the corner of her smile. For the first time since the lawsuit, her spine felt lighter, as if a hidden chain had snapped.

"We did," she said. "And next time the system knocks, it'll have to ask permission."

Josh's grin answered everything.

A humming, weight-less rush bloomed in her chest—as if someone had cracked open a skylight she never knew was there and poured daylight straight into her blood. For a breathless moment Morainya felt more American than any Fourth-of-July anthem, more alive than any victory parade. Freedom wasn't an idea now; it was electric, cellular, rising through her ribs like a tide of fireworks. Across the table Josh caught the current, eyes shining with the same wild voltage, and she realized they'd just stepped off the map together—two living names no longer stamped as cargo. The euphoria was so strange, so startling, she almost laughed: *This is what it feels like to jailbreak your own life.*

Josh retreated to his room, mumbling something about a math test. But before he disappeared, he had wrapped his arms around her—he had initiated it. Not out of pity. Not as a reluctant teenager checking a box. It was real. Solid. A quiet gesture of understanding.

She stood in the hallway like she'd just stepped out of a different atmosphere, her chest light, her limbs buzzing. Her eyes welled. What a night. She reached for her phone instinctively—then stopped mid-scroll. Who could she call?

Names floated up like ghosts in the room. People she'd once confided in. Her sister. Nico? Shelley? Her oldest friend from college. Her ex-colleagues at the firm. But every single one felt like the wrong audience. They wouldn't get it. They'd think she'd joined a cult, or lost her mind, or worse—was trying to convert them.

Freedom, she realized, was oddly isolating. When you wake up in a sleeping world, celebration has no guest list.

She sank into the couch, phone still warm in her hand. There was only one that she could. She dialed Sal and felt overjoyed that he picked up so late at night.

"Sal, hello again. I just had to share the news. Josh and I signed all the paperwork, and I'll get it off to Janelle tomorrow morning.

Sal closed his laptop and smiled. "That is a huge step in both of your lives toward freedom. I hope you are happy."

"Thrilled. Yes, I am grateful for encouraging me to take the leap," added Morainya.

"You are welcome. Now, I told you it was going to change your life. Are you ready to get started?"

"Started?" asked Morainya, the words falling out of her mouth like a bit of bad sushi.

"Start taking back your God-given rights. I think you need to fight the fraud of your recent lawsuit," said Sal with a bit of humor.

Morainya sunk into her chair, folding her right arm over her chest. "I told you it is too late. I already settled the matter and paid the opposing attorney. In fact, I just got a bill from my attorney requesting final payment."

Sal chuckled. "Final payment for neglecting to inform you that he consorted against you and misrepresented you?" Sal used a mocking tone to emphasize the joke.

Morainya felt the prickle of his words and answered timidly, "Yes, well, now that you put it like that. What do you suggest we do?"

He spoke more determinedly. "We fight in their law, but this time, we ask for the remedy that is promised by Maritime Law."

"I thought I left that system behind," said Morainya with a grimace.

"You did. Now, we are going to turn the tables on them with how much I'm going to teach you about what is lawful vs. what is legal. Ready to get started?"

Her bravery began to creep back. "Yes, when can we meet?"

"I'll call you when I know this week's schedule at work," she bit her lip, hesitant, was she ready for another battle? So soon?

She hung up with Sal, the call ending in laughter, strategy, and renewed fire. But when the screen went black, the silence in the room roared.

Morainya looked around her living room, dimly lit by the faux Tiffany-stained glass lamp. The red ink pad still sat open on the Mahogany dining table, next to the paper towels stained with thumbprints—tiny symbols of rebellion and rebirth. She glanced at the clock. 10:42 p.m. She had just declared her independence from a corrupt system, reclaimed her living status under God, and secured her son's lineage, and there was no one to celebrate with.

No balloons. No parade. No "congrats" texts from high school friends. No dinner toast.

Not even a nod from the neighbors who would never understand. Freedom, it turned out, was lonely. She poured herself a glass of water and sat back down at the table. Her heart was full, but her phone was still quiet. The people who loved her the most wouldn't even know how to spell "Cestui Que Vie," let alone recognize what she'd done tonight.

She had escaped the Matrix, yes—but who would hold her hand in this new world? It was a strange grief—euphoric yet hollow. Like shouting "I made it!" into a canyon, only to hear your own voice echo back. She closed her eyes and whispered, "Am I really free... if no one is here to see it?"

Then she remembered Josh. He saw it. He *chose* it. That would have to be enough. For now.

Morainya and Iben drove the curved back roads near Big Basin State Park in her Honda Prelude. The sun flickered through branches, casting a rhythmic pulse of shadow and light across the dashboard. It was hypnotic—like the trees were lulling her into a trance.

Iben had quietly taken control of the music, syncing the moment with a playlist that pulsed with earthy rhythms and soft horns. Earlier, he'd texted, "Feel like hugging a Sequoia?"—like it was the most natural thing in the world.

"I've had too much time in the city; we need nature," he said, hand surfing the wind outside his window. "We need to feel a tree."

"And how will we know which one?" she asked, turning towards him.

He didn't even hesitate. "It will be the tree that is looking for us."

She smiled. That kind of answer was exactly why she couldn't quit him. "My mom used to take us kids to the Roaring Camp Railroads for my brother's birthdays," she added. "It's a narrow-gauge train from 1875 that goes through these trees all the way to the Santa Cruz Boardwalk. It's old but still running."

"Does it still roar?" he grinned, his eyes soft as they caught her profile.

"Not like it used to," she said.

"Take this turn," he said suddenly.

She swerved gently down an unsigned side road, bumping over gravel until the trees swallowed them in quiet shadow. The light dimmed to gold-green hush,

"I love the Boardwalk. The rides are cool. I went there on a family vacation when I was in my 20s. That is why I love this area so much," his attention drifted off as if he were reliving a favorite memory. "There—pull off on this road," he directed telepathically.

They rolled to a stop, and he opened her door before she could reach for the handle.

"Let us walk, Queen."

They wandered down a path padded with redwood duff, the forest stretching tall and still around them.

"It smells so good," she whispered, breathing deep. "Cedar and earth. My whole nervous system just dropped."

Iben murmured a prayer in Arabic, the cadence low and reverent. "Look," he said, pointing down.

Morainya scooted out of the way to see a thick yellow banana slug with little moving antennae and fringelike feet, which inched it forward over the rusty, dew-covered forest floor.

"It's like a little forest prophet," she whispered, crouching beside it.

"This land was covered in gigantic trees. Have you seen Devil's Tower in Wyoming?" he asked. "That was a tree. A giant one. They've cut so many down."

She blinked. "From Close Encounters? That was a tree stump?"

"Let us walk into the forest. This way. I can hear her sing."

They moved deeper into the trees, hand in hand. Iben pulled her into a hug that felt like memory. No rush, no pretense—just two old souls remembering something their minds couldn't name.

"You smell like home," she whispered before she could stop herself.

"Queen—there she is." He parted some ferns and there stood a majestic Sequoia with a thickened twisted base in a golden stream of light.

"I've always wanted to meet Methuselah," she said, breath catching. He flipped out his phone. "Let's take a picture—proof we were dwarfed by a queen."

The bark under her palm pulsed faintly, like the tree remembered her too.

"Now, we must talk to her," he said laying his cheek against the bark.

Morainya felt as small as a fairy next to the first-growth tree. She listened as Iben spoke in a sing-song voice, then paused to listen. She could only stand in reverence, for this felt ancient and wise.

"In Afraka, we do not just listen to the land—we speak with it," Iben murmured, pressing his palm against the bark. These trees, their roots—they're a web. A network of memory, of voices older than time. You must be quiet. Let them recognize you."

Morainya could only stand in awe that she would be allowed to know the secrets of the ancients. He hadn't even used GPS; he just instinctively knew this tree would be here and that nobody would bother them.

He ran his fingers down the bark. Iben inhaled the rich scent of the ancient trees. It was grounding. Steady. Older than any lie, older than any church. He turned to Morainya, whose expression was still lost in thought, her gaze drifting over the canopy as if she were looking for something—an answer, perhaps.

He turned to her. "You want to know why I left?" His light blue turtleneck contrasted with his skin, accenting the sky above.

Morainya blinked, feeling her heart ache. "Yes. You just disappeared."

He leaned back against the tree, letting it hold him. He had not planned to tell her this. But standing here, in a forest that did not lie, he could no longer hold it back.

"I returned home. My sister, Nura, had a psychotic break. She was in the hospital." His voice was careful, measured.

"Oh," said Morainya, her body softened, "A family emergency."

Iben chewed his lip. "Nura nearly threw herself off a building."

Morainya's eyes widened. "Oh, my God— "

"No. Don't bring Him into this." The sharpness of his tone made her recoil. "The people who hurt her did it in His name."

Silence. It felt like a barrier. The towering redwoods stood as witnesses, their quiet presence demanding truth.

"The missionaries took her when she was ten," My brothers and I were away at University, my mother was sick. Iben finally spoke as a shaft of light broke through the canopy, highlighting his words. "They told my mother she'd get a proper education—English. Math and computers, a future. She would have opportunities that few females could dream of." His mouth quivered. "They lied."

Morainya shifted her feet, not knowing where to look.

"It was a boarding school. When Nura finally came home at eighteen, the Nura we knew—gone." His lungs made a terrible gurgle. "They broke her."

Morainya's hands flew to her mouth.

"The priests convinced her that she was filthy. That our culture, our traditions, our language—was heathenistic. Demonic." He swallowed hard. "If only she'd repent in God's name. Purge herself. You want to know how they purged her?" He looked at Morainya now, his dark eyes unreadable. "By throwing her into a dark cellar for days. Days without food or water. They beat her if she spoke Arabic or our mother tongue, Yorùbá."

"Iben..." Morainya whispered.

He threw up a hand to halt her. The worst was the priest. The Head-Master." His voice dulled. "Said it was an honor. He took her as his personal student."

Morainya's eyes were filled with horror. Iben's voice burned like fire. "When Nura graduated, she came home. My sister screamed at night, reliving every torture she suffered. Couldn't eat without feeling unworthy. Couldn't be touched without screaming." His knees nearly buckled.

"And the worst part? She still believed them." His eyes cold, with a hardened rage.

A breeze rustled the branches, the sound like whispers through time.

"Nura has spent half her life in and out of hospitals." Iben brought his hand up to his face, stroking his smooth-shaven chin. "She said she wanted to be free. Nura had only worked in the Employment Office for two months. We thought this was good."

"A job," said Morainya.

"Free from the demons which bound her. Then she climbed the stairs, convinced she could finally be 'clean.' The voices in her head, reminding her of purification. Nura nearly jumped. Praying she'd be forgiven. His voice, rough and raw. "I was the one who talked her out of it."

"I... I'm sorry," Morainya whispered, fingers tightening around the bark as if it could anchor her. "For her. For you."

Iben stepped closer, his presence unyielding. "I have graciously listened to you complain about Aldo. Your lawyers. Your mother's head illness— The whole damn thing—rooted in your church." Morainya's eyes flicked up, meeting his. The weight in his gaze made her want to disappear into the trees.

She stared at him hard. Fearing his accusatory eyes.

Now tell me, Morainya. After everything I've just told you—how can you still trust them?"

She flinched, her heart thrumming in her ears.

"You defend Catholicism." His voice, low and gravelly. "The church that told you to settle, to shut up, to humble yourself before its judgment—is the same one that destroyed my sister." His eyes burning into hers. "Do you still think they deserve your loyalty?"

Her stomach twisted. Aldo's shame, the judge's warning, Iben's broken sister—all braided into a single thread of betrayal. The forest pressed in, a cathedral of judgment, and she stood in the center, exposed. Morainya's stomach clenched hard, her mind reeling. The trees loomed over them, nearly blocking the sunlight. Suddenly, she felt insignificant.

Iben stepped even closer, his voice barely above a whisper. "Your Pope, your Archbishop—They aren't gods, Morainya. They are usurpers. Men who use Fear. Men who control. Men who take."

Morainya stood, her mouth a gaping wound. Her fingers instinctively reached for the small gold cross at her throat, grasping it like a lifeline. "Let the light heal you, " she said, voice barely audible, hoping it would soften the blade between them.

He nearly growled, "You want to know how they take from Afraka? You wondered about that sacerdotal seat above the Pope. We have a matrilineal legend about a Great Prophetess, a Sibyl called Mami Wata—the Divine Logos— the Black Dove. That sacerdotal seat usurped by the Vatican—belonged to Mami Wata also known as Vatica.

She couldn't look at him for fear her world would crumble further.

Iben's voice reserved, but sure. "I pity you. Your God is a deceiver. Now, you will have to make a choice."

It was blasphemous. He had no right to condemn her God for the actions of men. Couldn't Allah have saved his sister? The trees held their breath. And so did she.

At last, she found her voice. "Iben...don't mistake my Christ for their thrones of gold. I love Him outside of Rome, outside their decrees. He was a healer, friend, breath to the forgotten. He touched lepers, lifted widows, wept at graves. That is the Jesus I know. No pope can own Him."

Iben's gaze cut like flint. His voice lowered, almost unwilling. "Even our Book honors him. Born of the Virgin. Worker of miracles. Messiah. But not God." His jaw tightened. "If He was as you say—then why did He not save Nura?"

Then it struck—low, sudden, and electric. A pulse between her thighs.

No movement from him, no hand or glance. Just that unmistakable inner thrum—as if he were still inside her field, still claiming her from within. She blurted out, "How do you do that?"

But that wasn't what she meant. Not really.

Her voice softened. "Why do you do that to me?"

Iben looked at her for a long moment, leaning back against the tree as if it alone could hold the weight of his answer. "Because you were the one."

"The one... for what?"

"To bring home."

"To bring home?" she echoed, confused.

"If I could bring back even one soul from the Church... from the forgetting...then maybe Nura's pain wasn't wasted. Maybe I wouldn't be cursed to carry this alone."

"You merged with me," she whispered, tears catching in her throat. "Not out of love. Not with permission."

"I merged with you," he said quietly, "because your soul summoned me like a song in the dark. But your body...it hadn't yet given consent. So, I left."

She stepped back, vision blurring. Her body trembled with the urge to vanish, to unravel, to scream through the canopy until something ancient answered.

"Not every lover who touches your soul was sent to stay," he said softly. "Some come only to show you the door back to yourself." He turned away. "It is time," he said flatly, the forest no longer a refuge but a reminder.

Dismissal. Withdrawal. Rejection.

Morainya followed him back to the car as if his feet knew where to go. Her feet moving out of habit, not desire. "We don't have to go yet," she tried, reaching for something already lost. But his mind had closed like a gate.

They found the Prelude, easily. He opened the door like a gentleman, but the gesture felt hollow now. "Do you want me to drive?"

"Sure," she murmured, "If you know the way."

"I do." They drove wordlessly through shadow and sun, the winding road back to civilization, winding tighter in her chest.

"Can we stop for some chicken?" he said suddenly. "I see Chix and Fries ahead." He was already turning in. It wasn't a question.

"Are you sure you want to eat that?" she asked gently, still unsure where the edges of his temper lived. She opened her mouth to suggest the organic spot a few blocks away— crisp, gluten-free, white-apron clean—but stopped. With the quiet knowing that saying no to fried chicken meant saying no to something bigger—his culture, his cravings, his wounds. Saying yes meant swallowing more than food.

"Yes," he said, pulling into the drive-through. Do you want a 'Smiley Meal?'" he asked. The white meat, mashed potatoes, and a biscuit."

She grinned despite herself. "I used to eat here as a kid." It surprised her—this wasn't like him. The man who prayed to trees, who spoke to ancient roots. But maybe comfort food was also a kind of prayer. This was junk food in her book, but she decided that she wouldn't offend him. He'd been through enough. If this gave him comfort, then so be it.

Iben ordered and then turned to her. "Queen, I left my wallet in my car. Would you mind?" Morainya handed him a ten from her little waist bag.

He glanced at the total. "You wouldn't happen to have a twenty, would you? That'd cover it."

Wordlessly, she handed him the twenty. He wasn't wrong—she rarely ate out like this anymore.

They sat in the car listening to his music like teenagers. The fried chicken was hot and delicious, and maybe a bit greasy and just greasy enough to make her giggle. Even the biscuit—with butter and honey—was good. Too good. She'd abandoned gluten years ago, but this was different. This wasn't about food. It was about something else. Nostalgia. Presence. The illusion of being wanted.

She giggled softly. "Only for you would I sit in a car eating a Smiley Meal and call it sacred."

He smiled. "Queen, I have a meeting to get to. Thank you for listening."

"Thank you for trusting me," she said, more quietly than she meant.

He drove them back to where his car waited—parked near a tire shop. He leaned across the console and kissed her. Long. Hungry. Possessive. It wasn't tenderness. It was an echo of absence, pretending to be love.

Then he was gone.

Later that night, her stomach twisted into knots. Cramped and aching, she curled into a fetal position, groaning through the pain. Why had she eaten that food? The chicken? The grease? Why had she abandoned what she knew her body needed? It was like she had poisoned herself... with her own hand.

Or maybe it wasn't just the food. Her body, already trembling with that pulse Iben had stirred in her, became the stage for conflict. She had taken in what she wasn't ready to digest. That's why it made her sick.

Maybe her body was remembering something older. Something buried in the salt and sweetness. A flavor that tasted like betrayal masked as care. Like a contract signed in longing instead of consent.

A soul could survive hunger. But not this kind of remembering. She had eaten this before.

And now, she was eating it again—not because she trusted it, but because she wanted to trust him.

My destiny crumbled—stone by sacred stone—like a forgotten temple sinking into the desert's silent appetite. There was nowhere to run—no path forward with Smenkhkare, no retreat to Archollos to takeback what I had confessed. A storm of breathless pressure spiraled in my chest, each heartbeat a drumbeat of panic. I fled to the back guest quarters, only to be shooed away by the owner's wife, Ma-Nat, who was preparing a gift. Alone. Exposed. I cried out to Amaret in the ethers, praying for guidance, now certain that my Choosing was doomed.

I wandered to a hidden patio, roses draping the railing like silent witnesses. Honeysuckle clung to the walls, sweetening a day that had turned bitter. Bees visited the blossoms and consummated their thirst. I sank down, pulling my knees to my chest, and buried my face in the folds of my sheath, letting the fabric catch what no one else would—my tears.

A hoopoe bird hopped onto the railing and chirped a welcome with her long, narrow beak. Her black and white tail reminded me of a Mitannian shawl with a black fringe. My mind faded back to my youth when that same type of naughty bird led me deep into the courtyard of my childhood residence at the Malkata Palace back in Thebes. I went chasing a dream, calling a Hoopoe to lead me to a white horse talisman that did not belong to me. Hence, a reckoning came later after I stole that relic left by Sit-Amun as an offering to Amun.

This time, I was wiser. No more chasing illusions. I stared into the black beady eyes of the bird on the railing—ornate, regal, with a rust-colored crown flecked in black. *If only I was a bird*, I thought. *I would fly from pain, from duty*, of a love unchosen.

The bird blinked. *And if I were a hue-man*, she seemed to say, *I would eat my fill, nest under shelter, and raise my young in peace.*

The Aten, in mercy, answered us both. In the next breath, I was inside her—feathered, light, lifted. Wings spread wide. I soared above the estate, circling in sweet release. The wind kissed my face; nothing bound me to sorrow or skin. I was free.

My favorite little bird with a rust-colored crown of feathers tipped in black, perched like a memory returned from the past. I was free without being fettered to this temporal world. A wooden garden post served as my perch, sunwarmed and waiting—as if it remembered me. I chirped a song of arrival, but voices rustled the stillness. Curious, I flitted closer, hopping from post to post until I spied them: Ana-Kharu, crouched low, deep in cloistered conversation besides Anpu, the carob-colored drummer, and Oya, the lithe dancer, and Okun, the broad-shouldered drummer whose laugh could shake trees.

"Chaos reigns," Ana-Kharu muttered. "The Princess chose one—but he did not choose her back," he said, relaying the gossip of my humiliation.

"She is the one with power," said Okun, his voice deep and deliberate. His rainbow-toned skin shimmered in the filtered light. "She can name whoever she pleases." He flexed his biceps, as if testing the weight of fate.

"Was it the yellow haired one?" asked the Oya lazily, smoothing her sheath with the nonchalance of a cat digesting gossip.

"No," Ana-Kharu replied, smirking. "The meek one. The one who might prefer—softer company." He elbowed Anpu with a chuckle, the innuendo clear.

Okun snorted. "This is madness. How long will she drag out this fuckery? She was sent to find Djehuty, not play hearts and hieroglyphs. We cannot waste more time."

"Amunite mercenaries flood Giza for the Full Moon," Ana-Kharu said grimly. "The main pyramid entrance is compromised. We will need the hidden path."

"You mean the ancient one? Oya's eyes narrowed.

Ana-Kharu nodded. "Yes. But how do we lead Merit-Aten there when she is clouded—adrift in heartache?"

"Her mind," Anpu said solemnly, "is like the Nile in flood—muddy, violent, unpredictable."

Okun mimed rain falling from his fingers, letting each drop tap the earth between them.

Ana-Kharu inhaled sharply. "Then we clear her mind. Strip away the distractions. The meek one must accept the choosing. And the barbarian"—He spat the word,"—must be forgotten."

"Dull his flame," Oya whispered, reaching into her pouch of tinctures. Bottles clinked. "Snuff out what draws her to him."

"Exactly." Ana-Kharu nodded once. "I will craft the aconite remedy myself. She will comply. He will forget. Her parents will be appeased. And we can finally get on with our mission. One foot in front of the other—home."

My bird body stiffened. What I had overheard—was it salvation or betrayal? Ana-Kharu believed he was helping me to fulfill my promise to my Meti. He thought that guiding me toward Djeuty, toward the Red Lion, I could save my father. But at what cost?

How would I talk to a red lion? Maybe like I did with Asgat, my white cat with the watery blue eyes back in Luxor. This red lion would have the answers I seek. But where do I look? In the desert? A cave? The uncertainty was maddening.

I soared again, wings slicing through air thick with honeysuckle. The hueman—the girl I once wore like a skin—lay curled beneath the patio's shade, lost in dreams that had no answers. No, now is not the time for sleep. I dove toward her, tugging at the braids, pecking her arm. She stirred, swatting blindly. "Shoo," she muttered—yet the voice belonged to me. Our eyes met, bewildered, the moment stretching between us like a crack in time.

Then came the pull—like the ancient—threading my spirit back through the eye of the storm. I fell back into my flesh and rethreaded itself into my bones. The freedom of the sky vanished. My body was heavy again. The weight of duty returned. And with it, the terrible knowing. My choosing was no longer my own—but had it ever been?

I would speak to Smenkhkare. Honor demanded it. But what I owed him—and what they demanded of me—were no longer the same. But this path—allowing Ana-Kharu to enchant him, to make him compliant—it was a sacrifice.

I would fulfill my duty to my mother and father. I would keep my promise.

But I would also lose Archollos forever. It would be the kindest thing—to let him go. Our love could not thrive in this soil. I would mourn it in silence. And then, I would take my place. I would walk the path carved for me. Only then would Djehuty speak. Only then would the Red Lion roar.

Pushing myself up, I scurried in to find my girls, "I must look ahead to tonight's ceremony. Have you found me a linen sheath to wear?" I asked Keshtuat.

"Yes, Ma-Nat offered me a fine garment that I can fashion for you," answered Keshtuat, lifting the material.

Tadushet chimed in, "They are putting a lamb on the spit in your honor."

"Let me fix your hair," said Sarawat, pulling me away.

I turned to Tadushet, "Could you ask Ra-Awab and the Merchant to construct a contract between Smenkhkare and me? I need an elder's guidance. Although Smenkhkare strictly abides by the laws of Ma'at, let us keep it secret for now."

Our tasks were assigned. Sarawat pulled me into the shaded washing room. "May I fashion your hair in a new style? My Meti was my tutor when she was the Court Hairdresser of your grandfather, the Pharaoh, and His Queen Ti-Yee."

I nodded, but my spirit was elsewhere, heavy with sorrow. "This is not a day of celebration," I said softly. "It is a funeral—though no one else will wear black. I do not mourn Smenkhkare. I mourn the love that never stood a chance."

Sarawat yanked at my curls, "I know the pain in your heart, dear one. Your burden is heavy."

My voice was soft and aching, "Archollos stirred something in me I may never feel again. Desire. Fire. Smenkhkare is kind, yet—but he will never crave me. He will never unlock the mysteries of my flesh." I touched my hair. "Cut it. Let this be my offering. My grief."

Sarawa froze. "Why would you do that? Smenkhkare is desirable—and he adores you like a sister." She held my shoulders, trying to steady what could not be soothed. "Archollos confided in me. He does not plan to stay in Khemit. Let him go. Let him be free. You made your choice—and Smenkhkare accepted. It is written in the stars. The Aten has carved the path."

I felt sickened because Smenkhkare had not really accepted. Archollos planned to leave us. Leaving me. It was all my fault. I withdrew and armored myself so that this pain could not penetrate my skin like a venomous scorpion sting.

Sarawat severed off my hair with a razor. Skillfully she pulled strands into the short plaits of the Nubian tripartite style. I knelt before her with patience. Her talented fingers maneuvered my unkempt hair into something fashionable.

"The merchant's wife brought blue dye for your sheath," Sarawat said, eyes narrowing with mischief. "But I thought—why not dye your crown instead?"

I could not conjure enough energy to care. The wafting of lamb roasting floated on the breeze. They women kneaded *Shamsi*, sun bread before baking in the outdoor ovens. Vegetables cooked in a spicy broth in large copper kettles hung over a flame. The two obedient daughters milked the water ox. A sudden ache bloomed behind my ribs. I missed them—my family, torn from my heart like cloth ripped from an altar by my Meti's decree. I prayed to the Aten to keep them safe and joyous.

"She wants to talk to you," said Sarawat.

"Why?" I asked, sluggishly climbing out of the fog of my sulk.

"Merit-Aten, you have no elders here. She said she needs to teach you because you must learn about men."

"What do I need to know?" I answered lowering my eyes, entirely uninterested.

Sarawat had done it. Not just dyed my hair—she had woven rebellion into each strand.

My curls, once sun-dark and obedient, now shimmered with the cobalt defiance of lapis. She divided them into three sacred locks, a tripartite crown of lineage and memory—just me. I looked like the queens on my father's shrine... only freer. Then with a steady hand she lined my eyes with kohl. "Tonight, will be unlike anything you have ever experienced. You need an elder—to teach you. Your Meti is not here. It is not my place."

I shook my head, then folded my arms, defiantly.

"You are young still," Sarawat whispered in my ear. "And this is the Khemitian way."

A woman's head appeared from around the curtain. "Merit-Aten, may I join you?" Her figure was voluptuous, her presence maternal and serene. As our hostess and elder, I inclined my head in respect.

"Yes, yes," I said. Her gracious smile and kind eyes made me loosen the tight knot of my woes. She brought a basket of fresh vegetables for tonight's meal, laying them at my feet. "That dye was meant for your choosing linen," she said, then gave a chuckle. "Not your hair, but the indigo suits you."

Sarawat packed up her razor and washing bowl and vanished behind the curtain. I murmured my thanks, though I barely felt it. Everyone was putting far more effort into this joining than I ever wanted. It felt more like a performance than joy—a celebration of duty, not desire. I prayed Ana-Kharu's tincture would do what I could not—that it would soften Smenkhkare's walls. The guilt gnawed at me. He was my friend. This felt like treachery veiled as tradition. But what choice did either of us have?

The Pharaoh's and Per Aat's will—that was the law. Let him go where his heard leads. Let me go where duty binds. Before the sun began to dip behind the mountain and its yellow and orange rays dissolved over the palm-dotted plain, we would join in the light.

"Dearest One, my name is Ma-Nat." She took Sarawat's stool, and once again, like when I was an 'Akh', the child at my Mother's knee. "Tonight, you walk the path of womb-man. And before you do, I will offer you what your own Meti cannot. Guidance."

I nodded, suddenly realizing that the deep sacred knowledge between men and womb-men may include more than I had been told.

"Before all else, you must understand the ways of our people," she began. "We are Khemitians. And we are taught the Khem-mystery—the sacred union between man and womb-man—like this." She traced a soft downward-pointing triangle into my palm. "This is a womb-man. The chalice. Women descend from the heaven worlds." Then, she proceeded to draw an upward-pointing triangle over my other hand. 'This,' she said, 'is the flame of the man. When these two symbols merge—when flame enters womb—a portal opens. Not just to pleasure, but to legacy, and to the stars.' Do you see?"

I stared at my hand then lifted my eyes to meet hers—a map to the stars, I thought.

Ma-Nat nodded. "That," she said, pointing, "is the Sun—with six sun rays in the center, known as the *Sephedet*. This hexagon," she tapped my palm, "is a gateway. It is the electromagnetic principle that activates only when the two become one. The women own the mitochondria that can be passed on; thus, the Queens are the rightful owners of the earth."

My eyes grew large as I studied her drawings. I felt pleased that she explained a joining with these diagrams. Grateful, she did not mention Smenkhkare. I heaved a sigh of relief.

"When the man's phallus and the woman's womb portal are as one, then the Sephedet opens, and with the right partner, you can transcend the universe and coat the heavens with your waters. Sex—or Spiritual Energy Exchange—is how we birth miracles. It is the act of bringing the hidden dreams of the 'inner' world into form in the 'outer.'

I blinked my eyes.

"You have seen the paintings of Auset and Isis on the walls?" asked Ma-Nat. "She wears the throne atop her head—not as ornament, but as truth. She is the throne."

"Yes. Yes. She is the HeMeti," I said my voice rising. "She who has the last word because she is the seat of power. Her mate must be worthy—to sit upon her throne to unlock her

487

gateway. He is the key; she, the sovereign gate to greatness. I know. His power comes through me."

Ma Nat smiled. "Do you see now why this is so important? Tonight, you will open the ancestral portal. Through you, access will be granted—for Smenkhkare to rise and rule."

Moving at only a snail's pace with her teachings—She did not know—Smenkhkare could not, and would not be my key to entry into the heaven worlds. Did this mean that I would not rule as a Co-Regent to my father after this ceremony? Then what was the point?

Ma Nat made her voice soft like fur. "I must ask you. You have been on the road a long time. As the daughter of the Pharaoh, have you ever laid with a man before?"

Suddenly, irritated, my neck grew hot. "My father ordered me to be chaste. He asked that I hold the seed Light of the Aten—for him."

She patted my hand, trying to calm me. Ma Nat did not know about the initiatic demands that had weighed heavy upon this crowned daughter. "You are still chaste then? Untouched—unplucked?"

I nodded.

"Good," Ma-Nat said, "because tonight, you will be the fruit of his desire." She shifted slightly, parting her legs with quiet boldness pointing to the dark V between them. This," she said softly, "is your sacred offering—ripe, pulsing, and ready to be plucked."

Then Ma-Nat took my hand and curled my fingers together into a soft fist, pressing a thick green cucumber into the center.

I flinched. What did this vegetable have to do with my joining to Smenkhkare—other than his fondness for gardens?

"I do not share this to frighten you," said the Merchant's wife gently, though her tone held a firm edge. "But, to prepare you." She tilted the cucumber upward. "Have you ever seen a man's *mena*, his djed pillar?"

"His phallus? Of course," I said trying to sound indifferent. "The long hanging thing between his legs," I said, feigning indifference.

She lit up and leaned close to my ear, "When kissed, caressed, touched—that become this."

She guided the cucumber forward again. "It thickens. Rises. Awakens."

Suddenly, all those wax candles we molded in class came rushing back to me—phallic, sculpted, mysterious. And the goat rutting at Minya with its ejecting heat—that grotesque image. I yanked my hand back with a shudder.

"This?" I asked, incredulous. "Like this?" But...how does it grow?"

"Blood," she said plainly. "Now, do you overstand where it will go?"

I pointed to the V between my thighs. In that instant, everything came full circle. I had been taught to catch babies from that sacred gate—yet no one had ever told me how they arrived. The phallus—this cucumber-shaped truth—was the key to our womb. The key to legacy. The cucumber was the key. And the key had never belonged to me. It had always been out of reach.

I sank back on my knees again—another khem-mystery had just been unlocked within me. But even in the midst of awakening, sorrow pierced through. I would never experience this with Smenkhkare as I once dreamed. Not fully. Not freely.

Even before the curtain withdrew, I knew that all the preparations were complete. It was time. Soft drums began a luring rhythm, summoning me forward like a heartbeat echoing through centuries.

Ma-Nat rose gracefully. "I hope this was helpful, Princess. I will see you outside."

Keshtuat helped guide the sheath over my head, careful not to disturb my hair.

"We have no jewelry to adorn you," Tadushet whispered. "I will give you my cowrie necklace." She unfastened it and slipped it around my neck. My hand rose to protest—to say it wasn't necessary—but she silenced the words with a touch. Pressing it into place. "This will bring you good luck."

"And protect your spirit," added Sarawat.

Tadushet's voice turned warm, almost shy. "These shells...they are symbols of womanhood—fertility, birth, and wealth. See?" She turned the necklace so we could look closely. "Look at the shell—the lips come together like us women."

"Indeed, the ruffled pink edges resembled a vulva. We giggled softly, as sisters do. My cautious friend had just shared something sacred and secret with us—and for the first time, I understood the fullness of her meaning.

"It is only fair that you have a traditional gift from our ancestors," she added, "since you have no family here to bear witness to your Choosing."

"Ready?" asked Sarawat.

I rose and straightened my sheath; as I turned around, my friends gasped, and their hands flew to their mouths. "Beauty and harmony," said Keshtuat.

Sarawat lifted a polished silver plate. "Look," she said. And there I was. In that silver mirror, I did not see a child. I saw the one who would hold kingdoms in her womb. The hardships of this journey had sculpted me—sharpening my cheekbones, yes, but also softening something within. My skin glowed with sesame oil Sarawat had worked into it with such care. I do not believe I had ever burned so bright... yet inside I felt unlit.

"I am ready."

"The boys readied Smenkhkare—oiled his skin, calms his breath. Ra-Awab carried. the contract and his calculations. The food is prepared. The music has commenced.

The merchant gave me a sandal for me and one for him. "Please put it on," he said.

I accepted the simple leather sandal, its hand-tooled straps a humble echo of my childhood gold—and the contrast stung sweetly. I recalled the One Sandal Ceremony painted on my father's Golden Joining Throne beside Kiya. I stood behind her in the depiction, a symbol of the Beloved of Aten—next in line, though she was Second Chief Wife.

"Please walk before me," I whispered. I needed a moment to steady myself. My beloved sisters walked ahead, and I followed. I stepped through the curtain.

Utter beauty met my eyes. Linen drapes billowed like sails overhead. Candles of every size glistened, their flickering flames danced in readiness. My sisters had gathered blooms from the gardens, arranging them into fragrant clusters of color and life. Carved alabaster holders glowed from within, casting an amber-golden light across the scene. The space shimmered with sacred intention.

And then—I saw him.

Smenkhkare's eyes were fixed upon me. He smiled—genuine, open. It startled me. His gaze was a clear and radiant reflection of his feelings, untouched by fear. Whatever concoction Ana-Kharu brewed, it had softened something in him too.

Archollos was not among my brothers. Relief slid through me like a secret exhale. I would face that pain tonight.

Yet even standing with Smenkhkare, a ghost pressed against the veil of my heart.

The Merchant and his consort were dressed in elegant flaxen sheaths, woven at the finest mill—a subtle mark of wealth. we took our positions, the Merchant began.

"Their parents have sealed this Choosing; the stars themselves bear witness. You, of Royal blood—the blood of the Ancients—now step into the lineage of Khemit. These traditions shall echo into eternity. For this reason, each of you wears only one sandal—to walk in the shoes of the other. Brothers and sisters in full effect on what is good and bad but full balance, yet committed to harmony."

He turned first to me. "Merit-Aten, do you accept his seeds of life knowledge that Smenkhkare? Do you accept your role as the reader of his blueprint? When he enters your portal of life—the gateway—and you exchange eternal fluid, may your union become the life-giving waters this land so desperately thirsts for. The Aten has chosen you two to restore the prosperity, joy, and renewal of life when you birth your own children of the sun."

"Yes," I said, my voice firm. "I accept his seed." But between my heart and the still place between my thighs, I knew the truth.

"Smenkhkare, do you attune your ears of vibration to Merit-Aten?"

"Yes, I do." He said the words. I heard them. But would they ever take root in flesh? That was in the hands of the Aten now. The words exchanged. The contract, signed. The vow to my Meti—fulfilled. My heart—empty. Somewhere, Rennutet watched. I imagined her spirit with my mother, the two of them holding her child—our child—between them. I had done my duty. I had paid the price. Around us, joy radiated from every face. But one did not shine. One could not meet my gaze.

Ana-Kharu tincture must already coil through his veins. The Gold Magician's name carried both aphrodisiacs and poisons. *Poisons?*

A memory struck me—sharp as a knife. While in bird form, I had overheard them.

"We shall clear the yellow-haired barbarian from the picture," Ana-Kharu had said. *"Make him forget. Dull his light so his flame no longer burns bright."*

The Merchant lifted his arms. "Let us drink to the joy of the newly joined!"

Cups rose all around—deep red wine from his personal vineyards. I watched Archollos take his. He lifted the cup. I knew.

That was *the* cup. Ana-Kharu's poison. Did I want him to forget me? Would that be the kinder mercy—of rejection? My mind twisted with confusion, but my heart did not falter.

"No." The word tore from my throat.

I ran—shoving past bodies, veils, arms heavy with silk. The cup rose toward Archollos's lips. I lunged.

It shattered in my hands. Wine spilled like blood upon the stone floor. A gasp rippled through the crowd. Then silence. "It is poison," I screamed, "Do not drink it!"

Aa-Kharu spun to face me, eyes blazing. "You fool!" he hissed. "I was saving him. Can you not see? Now he will carry this pain for eternity. You have dammed him."

But I did see.

That is why I simply could not allow it to happen. Poison meant no Memory of me.

On the Western bank of the Nile, stood the majestic Malkata, its painted walls fading under the relentless kiss of the sun. Built by Pharaoh Amunhotep III, the Magnificent—it was meant to stand for eternity, a testament to his legacy. That Pharaoh's name would be spoken for all time, and the palace bore the quiet weight of time, a relic of a rule long past.

The Queen of the Two Lands reclined in the sunken alabaster bath, her limbs trailing like lotus stems through salted waters laced with crushed amber resin. Wisps of steam curled through the scented air, drifting toward the arched window where Nefertiti gazed outward, half-lulled by memory.

Outside, the vast expanse of Malkata sprawled beneath the sun—its once-teeming corridors now hushed. What had been a kingdom unto itself now lay quiet. Kitchens, stables, armories, scroll halls—silent.

Beside her, her Chief Attendant, Fayet—a thin-framed woman with hennaed palms and fading tattooed rings beneath her eyes—placed another bowl of perfumed oil on the bronze brazier. A familiar smile ghosted across her lips.

"Do you remember, my Queen?" Fayet asked softly, "The Choosing Feast? Twenty Vassals arrived before sunrise. I scrubbed those floors until my knees bled. Barge after barge of foreign nobles, weighed down with lapis and lion cubs."

Nefertiti chuckled, the sound low and throaty. "And I, pretending to be divine, while adoring dignitaries paid tribute to Amunhotep and Akhenaten." She crushed a floating lotus, between her fingers. "It was... intoxicating."

"So were Amunhotep's Harem girls," Fayet added. "Each prettier than the last—plucked from Nubia, Babylon, Cyprus. Speaking a dozen tongues but all learning one phrase: 'Yes, my Lord.'"

"I never envied them," Nefertiti murmured, letting her head fall back against the onyx rest. "They were Royal Ornaments. Their beauty was currency. Their children pawns."

Fayet adjusted the Queen's linen head wrap, brushing damp curls from her brow. "Still, those halls lived in joy, even if it was his joy. The House of Joy—Per Hay, you remember the hypostyle festivals?"

"How could I forget?" Nefertiti's eyes drifted inward. She pictured the columns, towering like sacred groves—painted in deep rust and turquoise, their capitals unfurling like papyrus blossoms. Light had poured through intricately latticed windows, casting golden patterns over tiles inlaid with birds' mid-flight, twisted vines, lilies, and reed boats. The ceiling, a dome of alternating blue and yellow disks, had taken Ti-Yee weeks to approve. "She argued for days,"

Nefertiti said aloud. "With every artisan. They feared her more than they feared Pharaoh."

"The sun used to dance in that room," Fayet said, her voice more reverent. "But now...Now, it was a shrine."

Nefertiti's hand slipped beneath the surface, tracing her own thigh. "Perhaps it is time for joy to return."

Once, as Per Aat, Nefertiti stood at the center of diplomacy, responding to foreign rulers whose letters filled the archives. Akhenaten abhorred the minutiae, leaving her to reply to Babylon, Mitanni, and beyond; her scarab seal once carried weight across empires. Now, the papyri that arrived bore no reverence—only desperate pleas for grain, gold and troops, appeals clearly meant for her absent consort, not her.

Fayet, smoothing sandalwood oil along the Queen's shoulders, ventured, "Shall I dispatch a courier with your reply to the Babylonian envoy, my Queen?"

Nefertiti waved a dismissive hand, unconcerned. "Let it sit. If they seek help, they must address me properly. I am still Nefernefruaten—Most Beautiful of the Beautiful."

Yet the title felt brittle. Sovereignty thinned, sliding through her fingers like powdered kohl. The people of Thebes might bow in daylight, but behind closed doors, the nobility—the real power—had already turned away. She felt it, the way one feels the riverbed cracking under foot: the drought, whispered to be Aten's curse, tightening around her reign. Invitations had receded just as the Nile waters had fallen. And both, she feared, would be harder to coax back than pride cared to admit.

Nefertiti sat in the bathing pool and ordered her attendant to add amber oil to make her skin soft and retain that eternal glow. Lotus floated in the warmed waters, and candles reflected the Queen's beauty as they bowed in reverence at her presence.

Suddenly, a rush of footsteps echoed through the corridor. Servants parted like reeds before a storm as a breathless younger handmaiden rushed in, bowing quickly to the Chief Attendant, whispering something urgent into her ear.

The older woman turned to Nefertiti, face pale but composed. "General Horemheb has summoned you to the Reception Hall. At the noon sun."

Nefertiti frowned, "What could he want?"

"He gave no reason, Your Majesty. Only that you are to dress Regally."

Nefertiti arched a brow, but the corner of her lip curled. "So... he could not wait."

The attendant said nothing, wisely.

"Fayet—who is scheduled to meet in the Reception Hall today—did he say?"

"He did not say, your Highness." She bowed, adverting her eyes because she had no answer.

The sun cast long, golden beams through the carved lotus windows of the palace, illuminating the steam rising from Nefertiti's bath. Her body shimmered like polished cedarwood soaked in sun and time. She rested her wrist along the tub's edge, the jewels of her armlet catching fire in the light.

Nefertiti glanced at her *ivory calendar, voice cool almost calculating,* "Not a single reed on today's chart, yet he summons me at high noon." *She exhaled sharply through her nose, a curl of amusement in her tone,* "My General is either plotting war... or craving worship."

Fayet, her Chief Attendant, paused in her steps. The older woman's eyes flicked from the Queen to the entrance where young Asat still stood, breathless. Fayet's shoulders straightened like a papyrus pulled taut. She dismissed the girl with a slight nod.

Fayet tilted her head, "He said, 'dress Regally,' Majesty. No hint beyond that."

A long silence pulsed between them, broken only by the soft lap of water. Nefertiti didn't look up. She tapped her fingers upon the rim of the tub. "Regally—that could mean we might be receiving guests." *Her tone was edged, like obsidian scraped against sandstone. Then she rose from the bath, water cascading from her skin in golden rivulets. Fayet instinctively stepped forward, arms open with a cotton towel, but the Queen waved it off.*

In a bold tone, Nefertiti said, "Fayet—pull the turquoise sheer. The one that whispers when I walk."

The elder Attendant disappeared behind the cedar wardrobe, skirts fluttering. She was steady as always, and she moved like a shadow in prayer. She lifted a favored robe woven with gold thread, glancing sideways at her Queen.

Fayet said, "Very well. Turquoise veils and lapis collar—pure seduction for admirers."

She hung the robe nearby, just in case the winds of politics changed.

Then the Queen squinched her face and held up a hand, "But if he is parading dignitaries—say, the Nubian envoy—sheer fabric becomes a scandal." *She stepped forward, standing proudly naked as she faced the polished copper mirror. Her eyes scanned her reflection not with vanity—but cunning.* "We need authority, not titillation."

Fayet moved behind her, her hands already selecting new adornments. Her fingers lingered slightly on the costly material of the gown. "Gold pleats with electrum fringe. Commanding, yet radiant. Majestic." Her eyebrows arched, waiting for approval.

Nefertiti shook her head, brow pinched, "Too stately. He will think I have come to lecture him about water rations."

A pause. Fayet's brow twitched—subtle, but visible. She shifted her weight to the other foot yet staying in ready position to select another garment.

Nefertiti tapped her chin, eyes narrowing with mischief. "There is nothing on the calendar. It could just be the General is wanting. What of the fan routine? Six Nubian girls, ostrich plumes—opens like a lotus, reveals like dawn. Perfect if the Hall is empty and... intimate. I will bet you a silver coin that my General secretly wants to recreate our dalliance upon that same throne years ago. He did mention he had a surprise for me last night."

A golden pleated linen sheath, slid over her arms, pinned with a braided Isian knot broach—a symbol of power she no longer fully possessed. A train of sheer turquoise linen fell across her shoulders, designed to shimmer like wings in flight—illusion in motion like a butterfly. Much like her reign—she was dazzling yet fragile, and at the mercy of those who no longer feared her.

Fayet took a silent step back, eyes narrowing in appraisal, *slowly, carefully.* "Your Majesty, that entrance leaves you nearly—"

"Naked." Nefertiti offered a *crooked smile.* "Exactly the point, if it is only the General. Let him remember why Pharaohs built harems."

Fayet's mouth fell open, but she recovered. The fabric was so sheer it looked like the Nile in sunlight. She touched the edge with careful reverence. Her face was unreadable, but she swallowed once. "Sheer enough to inflame, opaque enough for plausible modesty."

Nefertiti smiled, her gifts were evident and would delight the General just as they always had. "Add the lapis collar—wealth. The electrum diadem—power. And scent me with amber and a drop of clove at my throat. It lingers on battle-hardened men like a prophecy."

Fayet dipped her hands into the amber oil, working it over the Queen's shoulders and chest—slow, methodical, soothing a lioness before war. She didn't meet Nefertiti's eyes. "And if—if the Hall is crowded after all?" Fayet whispered her worry to the Queen.

Nefertiti paused. Her gaze lifted toward the far end of the chamber. Something fluttered inside her—barely perceptible. A ripple of old instinct. Her hands dropped to her sides. "Then the ostrich fans stay closed. Mystery is safer than scandal." She let out a *soft sigh. Her gaze flicked back to the mirror.* "Fayet, by noon, I will be a legend reborn."

Fayet bowed—fingers trembling for a single heartbeat before she mastered them. "I will fetch the fanbearers, and return to escort you, Majesty."

The attendants moved quickly now. Gilded sandals strapped. Lapis gleamed. The Queen's cape of fine linen fanned like the wings of Ma'at when she turned. Just before noon, Fayet returned with six beautiful Nubian women who formed a lotus formation.

"Watch for my nod. Hold the veil until I say *now*," ordered the Elder Attendant.

Nefertiti inhaled, lifting her chin. Her heart pounded—but only she could hear it. She gave a final glance at *her reflection, barely audible,* "Time may chip at stone, but it has not cracked the mirror yet." The polished copper showed her not just adorned—but armored. They proceeded in unison with the musicians that accompanied her to announce her arrival.

And then, the trumpeters blasted the ram's horns, announcing the presence of the Queen. The Grand Reception Hall doors flung open at the crescendo. The feathers fluttered down in perfect synchronicity. It was like walking in a billowing cloud; the six fanbearers were all lush young Nubian granddaughters of the once prestigious Harem of Akhenaten's father. The metal dangles upon their raiment tinkled with every step, enhancing her glamor. They padded barefoot across the cool tiled floor toward the golden throne, mounted upon the colorful kiosk. The ostrich plumes rippled like breath against her skin, stirring the scent of amber through the corridor. Their rhythm hypnotized the eye, but the fans obscured her path—she could see no more than a single step ahead, heightening the thrill of not knowing what lay beyond.

The fanbearers would drop the front fans to reveal her divine naked presence, and she would walk up the steps to take the seat on General Horemheb's lap. Then, the fanbearers would be dismissed so that The Queen and her General could consummate their love. Over and over in her head, she replayed every step that would end in orgasmic bliss.

The lead fanbearer signaled with a subtle flick of her wrist. Here it was. They came to a halt; the musicians played the familiar, charming tune, the drummers thundering the passionate rhythm, and the Royal Fanbearers bent and dropped their fans to the floor like the opening of a clam so that the Queen could rise like the golden pearl she was.

Nefertiti gasped at what she saw. This was not planned, suspected, or desired. She stood helpless and confused when she saw what had been withheld from her. Instead of the General upon the throne, the High Priest of Amun, Ases-Amun, a crumpled old man, robed in raven black—sat regally upon *her* throne.

"That is quite a procession as unwelcome as it was. I summoned you before me, not to entertain nor entice me, but to serve me as is your place," said the embittered High Priest of Amun, who detested Atenist pageantry. He flicked a hand, ordering the Queen to cover up.

"Forgive me, my Lord, I was told General Horemheb required me. I did not expect you," Nefertiti replied—unaccustomed to surprise. She slipped on her robe cinching it twice across her chest. Her eyes flicked to Horemheb, who stood at attention beside the throne—his jaw clenched, eyes fixed forward, as if she were a stranger.

"I feel no need to be announced." A thin copper sigil glowed faintly beneath his collarbone, pulsing in rhythm with the High Priest's words—as if each syllable carried a spellbinding weight. "You are here per my request as an Aten representative. Summoned simply to appease the Sesh when I choose to march you out like a puppet to wave and smile. You will please whomever I decree." Years of sorcerous excess had left Ases-Amun toothless; his breath reeked of the Charnel-House.

Nefertiti looked at the General hoping he would assuage her fears. His eyes met hers for a flicker—a breath of shared memory, the ache of old alliance. But then his jaw tightened. He looked away, spine rigid, his allegiance sealed. She felt the door close. He offered her no guidance as to the direction she should take with the High Priest, and it was the first time she realized in her gut that her position was hanging by a thread. His need for her was drying up—like the rare blue lotus in this season of drought.

"How may I be of service?" asked the Queen with caution, fearful of what he'd require.

"Akhenaten fades; his lifeforce withers—and with it, Aten's protection. The priesthood demands a Co-Regent be announced while the Pharaoh is alive. Thus, his lineage will continue—under our control."

Nefertiti offered a generous smile. "I would be most happy to continue the rulership. I am grateful for you offering me this position."

Ases-Amun threw back his head and cackled, the sudden mirth jolting Nefertiti off balance. What exactly was he expecting, if not her?

"You are not marriageable," declared Ases-Amun with an eerie creak in his voice. The scent of burnt myrrh clung to his robes—not temple incense, but the acrid trace of something older, darker. A glint of kohl ringed his yellowed eyes, smudged not from vanity but ritual. "Bruised fruit, which is what you are—overlooked, rotting inside," he hissed, and a tiny charm of obsidian slipped from his sleeve and disappeared again. "Youth is what I need. I have summoned that boy, Tut-ankh-Aten; he should be here any moment."

Not more than a sparrow's flight later, the boy entered—his gait uneven, a cane tucked beneath one arm. The Throne Room swallowed him in silence. Behind him loomed four handlers, cloaked as servants but branded in allegiance to Amun. Nefertiti's gaze sharpened. These were not attendants. They were captors. They all were in allegiance to the Amun priesthood, and she would be deluding herself to imagine that any Atenist was free. She noticed the boy's limp despite the cane. "Chariot accident," the court had boasted—just as they circulated clay statuettes of Tut spearing lions and hippos to paint him a warrior. It was a clever deception, crafted by unseen hands that also beat the child bloody when no one watched.

Propaganda was as deceitful as it was successful for swaying the opinion of the masses. It was all controlled behind the scenes, and she had no say in it, even though they were pushing the Aten lineage to the forefront. In the shadows, she had never approved of the hurting of any children, and why General Horemheb turned a blind eye to these acts of cruelty was shocking. That was, unless he had made a deal for his own self-aggrandizement with Ases-Amun.

The nine-year-old Tut stood beside her, whining like a baby. "Meti, why am I here?" Tut's lip quivered. "I was building a temple—with a moat—in my chamber."

"I am not your Meti. Ask your captors," she snarled at his meekness. If they were planning for him to rise to Kingship, then they certainly chose a boy who would comply. The Queen stepped back, throat suddenly dry; she felt shrunken, inconsequential. Desperation coiled around her like a sand-boa.

Ases-Amun leaned over to Horemheb. "Restrain one of the daughters. I care not which one. I just need a female from Pharaoh's line to pass the crown to the boy. Bring her here now and let us be done with this. I am famished and wish to retire to my quarters for a nice lunch and a long nap before services tonight." He yawned, displaying his boredom while making the most important decision of Nefertiti's daughter's life.

"Jai, Amun," declared General Horemheb. "Guards, bring me Ankh-es-en-pa-Aten. She is the one I choose to inherit the throne." Nefertiti managed a brittle grunt, at least Horemheb had chosen their own daughter, Ankhi, to secure Tut's claim.

"Once they are joined, then I demand you banish the name of the Aten. Change it to Amun once the Sesh have adopted them as their new King and Queen," said Ases-Amun.

The General, gave a swift glance at Nefertiti, for they both recognized it was the death of that reign of light.

As the Queen, Nefertiti, stood there frozen in time, her middle daughter Ankhi was dragged in, flailing and screaming. "I do not want to join with my brother. You cannot make me. I want to go home to Akhet-Aten." Nefertiti's nerves were raw by her daughter's shrieks, her hands turned to clenched fists. Sometimes, she wished that Ankhi was not as brazen as her father, General Horemheb. Today was not one of those days. *They may erase my name, but not my vengeance.*

Ankhi kicked at the guards and hollered. "I Choose Smenkhkare. I love Smenkhkare, not Tut-Ankh-Aten. I will not do this." One guard lifted her up, covered her mouth, and plopped her down obediently beside Tut. Nefertiti's fingers curled against her robe. Rage boiled beneath her breastplate, maternal and primal. She had borne this daughter in joy, nursed her through fevers, taught her to read the glyphs of the gods—and now she watched her be bartered like cattle. No Queen. No mother. No woman should be this powerless.

Decorum vanished in the Grand Throne Room. The fourteen-year-old girl looked as though she had not even been dressed properly for a Court appearance.

"Ankh-es-en-pa-Aten, do you stand before me today to Choose Tut-Ankh-Aten as your Consort?" The guard kicked Ankhi's legs, and she fell to the ground. "I do," she sobbed.

"Tut-Ankh-Aten, do you accept this choosing and thereby become the rightful Pharaoh to lead and guide your people?"

Tut whimpered because his guard held the boy's shoulder firmly, guiding him in answering correctly.

"I do," said Tut with a worried look in his teary eyes.

Nefertiti and Horemheb looked on together for this momentous event that would now be proclaimed far and wide. What stung most: she and her third daughter would be deprived of a grand feast. the palanquin parade, the adoring crowds. Nor would Per Aat Nefertiti be the benefactor of the costly gifts from the Tributes and Vassals throughout the land for this Choosing.

Horemheb had deceived her. With the innocents joined, Nefertiti knew her own life was now in jeopardy. She felt as expendable and wilted as the dead flowers that would be thrown out in the morning before the water stank.

Outside the Grand Hall, Fayet waited in silence. She had not followed her Queen in. She knew better. But when Nefertiti finally emerged, lips tight, eyes unblinking, Fayet stepped forward with the robe she had folded hours earlier.

"You are still the Per Aat," she whispered, her voice trembling as she wrapped Nefertiti in dignity. "They cannot crown Amun upon the Sun."

For the first time that day, Nefertiti's jaw softened.

24

*A*shawl of fog still clung to Market Street when Morainya hopped off the F-line streetcar at 7th, the clang of the bell swallowed by the low diesel purr of a line of white Google coaches idling at the curb. Cyclists in neon puffers wove between tech workers with badge lanyards and tent encampments stitched along the sidewalk like patchwork.

Two blocks later, she ducked into the Tree of Knowledge Bookstore—its weather-beaten Haight-Ashbury peace-sign mural guarding a doorway fragrant with sandalwood and rain-damp pages. The chatter outside flattened to Tibetan chimes and a faint sitar.

She wound down the aisle between the Sourdough baking section and a display of ethically sourced African baskets, weaving past a young man arguing about NFTs with a woman in a caftan. The scent of patchouli thickened as she neared the back. Past shelves of herbal almanacs and New Earth parenting guides, she found the corner labeled "LAW / GOVERNANCE." It was dimmer here, quieter—as if even the fluorescent lights deferred to the gravity of paperwork and precedent.

Morainya waved to Sal, who stood near the back table, looking every bit the constitutional purist he wore a—gray Barbour jacket still zipped halfway up, as if the scent of sandalwood offended his sensibilities. A pressed Oxford collar jutted from beneath a fine-gauge merino sweater, tucked into dark jeans that had never been cuffed for style. His brown Blundstones—practical, not hip—tracked in a dusting of Pacific grit.

He looked like someone who'd come to serve a subpoena, not sip cacao. A well-worn leather folio sat beside his drip coffee—black, no foam, no froth, no ceremony. Tortoiseshell readers dangled from his collar like they disapproved of crystals. Sal was already deep in study, yellow-highlighting documents with his left hand with his phone in his right. When Morainya slid into the seat across from him, he didn't waste a moment.

He didn't bother with "How are you?"—just lifted one eyebrow above the rim of his glasses and launched in. "Great to see you again. Have you received anything back from the Recorder?"

The embossed crimson crest on his binder flashed as he flipped pages—a silent reminder of the Ivy halls he once haunted. Though he'd considered law, he gravitated toward Sociology and Behavioral Science, with law as his minor. It was a female undergrad, he once confessed, who introduced him to the depths of Common Law and the sacred study of the Constitution. From that point forward, he was hooked—until he realized most of his peers weren't in it for justice but for prestige. Many became lawyers out of parental pressure or for the bragging rights. Sal, however, had found their motivations empty and slowly grew disgusted.

When debating the undergrads," he once told her, "their Maritime arguments were weak and built on sand. So, he walked away.

Morainya caught the quick glance he threw at the slim silver watch on his wrist and skipped small talk. "The paperwork arrived yesterday," she said. "Still waiting on the cards."

He leaned in, adjusting glasses. "Good I just need to see the paperwork and get your code."

He held out his hand expectantly. "I've already reviewed the contracts you've signed with your attorneys and accountant."

Morainya leaned forward until the table edge pressed a crease into her forearms, pen poised over her notebook.

First, let me explain how the whole court system actually works," he said, eyes locked on hers. "We will fight them using a combination of American Common Law and Equity Law—based on the 1787 Constitution. That's the remedy against their Maritime Law shenanigans. Once the courts incorporated themselves, they lost all real authority. They've no more authority than McDonald's Corp has over you."

"That's good," she said, taking notes.

"Think of the court like a bank," His tone brightening with purpose. "That's why court clerks are bank clerks. They issue 'charges' because they're processing transactions, not justice."

Something cold slid through her gut, as if the linoleum floor had tilted under her chair. "When the judge makes an 'Order—It's just like ordering off a menu." Sal took a sip from his water bottle. "But if you don't question the order, you pay for it. If you push back, they say you lose jurisdiction. It's all smoke and mirrors. They act like they have authority—but they don't."

"Jesus," she whispered. "I signed so many documents, Sal. I followed every damn rule—."

"You're not alone," he reassured her. "They've conditioned all of us to believe in their system. But now? You know their game."

He flipped through the paperwork. "Contract Law is the foundation. An Offer. Acceptance. Consideration. But here's the key—if you ask questions with an inquiry, you haven't accepted the contract. No contract, no jurisdiction. It's all entrapment and fraud. That makes it inland piracy, press-ganging, and unlawful conversion."

The table trembled with the jitter of her knee, and a stack of weathered Constitution pocketbooks and printouts from Cornell Law shook like startled birds.

"I fell for it," she breathed. "God, I feel so stupid."

Sal reached over and patted her hand. "Don't beat yourself up. It's Maritime Law, their law. Not yours. You've been following Maritime Law—corporate law. But under God's Law, the Constitution, you're a living woman. And We, the People; the Creators of our Government 'overstand' THEIR law, not 'understand it. We are only fooled by it and feel so scared that we acquiesce."

The lawyer, usually stone-faced, allowed a smile. "And here's something else: if a judge doesn't fully comprehend Equity Law, they must be replaced—under their own Maritime rules."

She blinked. "What if a judge doesn't believe in Equity Law or Common Law? What if they think I'm making it up?"

Sal tapped his yellow marker on the pad. "All good questions. The judges might pretend they don't know. But they are required to know Contract Law. They must have a signed Maritime contract with you to have authority over you. That's the whole trick." He paused. "That's the key to all of this."

Morainya rephrased it and felt panic. "I have signed it all." Leaning forward, she whispered, "I can't say I actually read or understood it."

Sal smiled and said, "Exactly, because they assume you're a legal imbecile of the law. Legally that makes you 'Civilly Dead.' A corpse can't possibly comprehend their Legal System."

Morainya pleaded, "I am sure that Kanberg, Wallerstein, and Katz Law Firm will think I'm insane."

Sal chuckled. "You don't have to convince him. We, as living men and women. In your case was there a Defendant and a Plaintiff?

"Yes." Morainya nodded.

"Then both are dead entities—legal fictions. Not living beings. No real harm. It was a lie." Sal leaned forward.

"I simply can't keep paying liars," she said, her voice splintering. Her fingers curled into fists around the invoice, creasing the paper with invisible rage. "But what about this bill for $98,000. They already did the work. I can't break that contract—especially after we reached a settlement. My check has been tendered."

He let out a chuckle and brushed his hair back. "Who says you can't break a contract with two fictitious entities? Between a Plaintiff and a Defendant? Fraud vitiates everything it touches. That includes contracts between fictional entities.

Morainya's throat tightened as if the truth might choke her. She nodded anyway, the motion jerky, almost involuntary.

"I got your back." Sal said quietly.

Something in his heart shifted. He'd seen this terror before. He gently leaned in, centering her. "We have been conditioned to fear authority. They have weaponized the Justice System against us."

"You've done this before with success?" Morainya brushed away a tear.

"Plenty of times. Eventually, they get tired of not winning and will leave you alone."

Morainya fished out the firm's invoice. "So, this—this isn't a bill?"

"It's actually a check. The court clerk takes the amount to the Federal Reserve window and cashes it from your Cestui Que Vie Trust number. See that number printed on the top of your lawsuit? That's your secret account. You own it. But they will never tell you how many times you've been traded on the stock market."

"I read that in the Disclosure Book. Her eyes scanned the number. I never noticed it before."

"You're noticing now," he said and tapped the number.

Her ribs finally rose without protest, as if something invisible had unhooked itself from her chest. The buzz of the bookstore faded to a low hum, like wind beyond stained glass. Inside their corner, time seemed to slow—her heart syncing to Sal's calm cadence. Morainya felt sealed inside a protective bubble. Safe. Steady.

Sal stroked his chin thoughtfully. "Compare the risk. Silence is acquiescence. But if you ask the right questions, you reduce your risk. All you're doing is making them prove their authority—which they can't."

"I have been terrified for the last two years," she whispered. "I think I have—I don't know the name for it."

Sal nodded with vigor. "PTSD, Post Traumatic Stress Syndrome, and I know a doctor who has proven that people involved in court cases do experience it. Trust me. Soon, you'll feel empowered."

Morainya laughed through her tears. "This is brilliant." A stunned laugh escaped her lips, part joy, part tremor. "I mean—I'm still scared. The man they call my attorney... he's venom in a suit."

"You don't have an attorney because you are a living woman. Remember an attorney, attorns of the dead."

"It's all right in front of us," she murmured. "This is all so new."

"Don't worry. Do you want to begin?" He folded his hands expectantly.

"I consent. You are hired." She reached out and they shook on it.

Instead of heading home, she wandered into the Forbidden Fruit Café attached to the bookstore. She purchased an avocado and hummus sandwich and a peach smoothie. Seeing a radiant coco-colored lady with gray braids, she took a seat near her.

"Hello," said the elder. "I saw you were talking to Sal."

Morainya startled, her body flinching like a bird mid-flight. "You know him?"

"Yes, I own this store, and Sal has helped so many of us out of difficult court problems. I wouldn't have my grandbaby, Devinia, at home. The Child Protective Agency tried to take her."

"Are you an American State National?" Morainya shifted in her seat, setting her smoothie down with care. Her knees angled toward the woman, posture opening like a gate.

"Sure am. Lots of us around here have joined. Are you?"

"I just got my paperwork. Sal is helping me, too. But I'm scared. Were you?"

"Of course." She chuckled. "But let me tell you something. Imagine being bit by a snake—and instead of healing Yourself from the poison, you chase the snake, trying to prove you didn't deserve the bite." The lady shook her head and laughed out loud.

Morainya eyes welled with tears. That was it in a nutshell. She had spent so long needing to understand why Mr. Kanberg and Judge Malicado had betrayed her. She wanted an apology. But now? She realized they were snakes—and no apology was coming. The apology that would prove they intentionally fucked her.

Wearing an Egyptian Ankh necklace, the woman whispered, "We live in an upside-down world. The sooner you figure that out, the saner you will feel."

"Do I know you?" asked Morainya, a flicker of deja' vu stirring inside her. "You look familiar."

The lady smiled. "In this bookstore, we call it a past life moment."

Just beyond the lady, Morainya's eye latched onto something familiar that beckoned her, and she couldn't believe it. "Is that a Nefertiti statue?" she asked, thrusting her finger towards the Queen's bust, but this one was of a highly polished black basalt face of beauty with a swan-like neck and long crown.

The store's owner turned to look. "Yes, she was a famous Queen in Egypt, long ago. Are you familiar with her?"

Morainya shook her head with affirmation. "She keeps popping up in my life. Over and over, I see those pictures and carvings from the ancient days...always under the Sun."

"The Aten," said the woman. "That's what they called the Sun."

"Right. I feel like I know her. Or knew her."

The woman studied her. "I believe she had many daughters. It was a tumultuous time in Egypt's history. The people called him the Heretic King."

"It wasn't true," Morainya blurted before she could stop herself.

The woman smiled. "Sounds like you know something. Who do you think you were?"

"I don't know. Maybe it's silly," replied Morainya, suddenly feeling ashamed that a white middle-class woman from the Bay Area had any right to speak about an Afrikan heritage. That seemed heretical. Iben panged her V. Or, that she had an Afrikan man stuck inside her. Yeah, now that would sound crazy.

One week later, under a deceptively bright morning sky, Morainya opened her inbox and found the first Notices attached to an email. Just like Sal had instructed, she had ignored the relentless calls—the increasingly aggressive Accounts Receivable Office, and even Kanberg himself. His last voicemail struck low: "Your father would be ashamed." The words ignited something primal. Her lip curled. She bared her teeth. A growl escaped—low and feral—like a lioness betrayed by her pride. "How dare he treat me like a petulant little girl. Just wait until he gets his Notices; then, he'll be the one worried all the time."

She realized there was a very specific process of how to write these documents; American Common Law, a Constructive Contract Law; this process was brilliant in its simplicity. Pretty straightforward. Next, she sucked in her breath. Six questions. Simple but profound. The questions all challenged their authority and jurisdiction over her. Morainya snickered, because she knew they'd never respond. She could laugh now, but in her heart, she knew they would either be impressed or question her sanity.

The latter worried her more because they were connected to the entire Napolitano family. She knew she had a choice to either follow through with her now stepping into being a living woman or remain a slave.

Reading Sal's instructions several times, it began to sink in. Morainya had to go to a copier and print out ten copies of each Notice, then sign with a blue pen. By that afternoon, she was stapling all the Notices, folding them, and stuffing them into the envelopes. It was not that it was hard, but she was surprised at how many mistakes she made. Back to the printer and print out the colored signature ten more times and restaple.

She turned on her speakers, cranked up the 60's hits, and giggled when *Suspicious Minds* rang out. She swayed to the music and took in the words, several times jamming to the vibe. When the Beatles pounded out Get Back, she was cranking out folding those Notices and stuffing them into the right envelopes.

She worked late into the night, but when she was done, she had twenty envelopes, sealed ready to go. Sal promised it would get easier. Good, because she felt mentally and emotionally drained and yearned for a glass of wine to take the edge off. A sense of burning inside overtook her, and she had to relieve herself by sitting near the air conditioner. Her cheeks were flushed bright red, and her heart raced. Every muscle in her body ached from the adrenaline coursing through her veins. Burying herself in a cold, dark bedroom seemed to ease the panic attacks that consumed her daily life, but this time, she needed wine.

On the kitchen counter, Josh had eaten a bowl of cereal and left the banana peel and milk on the table. Her teenager hadn't learned responsibility, and she chided herself that she should have been there to help him grow up, But every time she tried to mother him, he pulled away, angry that she was too pushy and overbearing. Why was motherhood so hard? Feeling like she was being ripped into a thousand pieces, there was no one to help pick up the tattered shards of her soul. She turned the kitchen radio on to drown out the noise in her head.

The hit song *Dizzy* pulsed from the radio as she poured a tall goblet of Rosé. Sipping the sweet liquid, she felt like she could finally breathe. Iben panged her, but she drowned it with another gulp, trying to quell the insanity that washed over her like a waterfall of confusion.

"Dizzy…" she belted, laughing at the irony, her voice chasing the chorus. Her head spun, her thoughts whirled, the whole world tilting in endless circles as if she were caught in a whirlpool that had no end.

Complete the task, she heard in her head, so she slumped back to her desk and pulled out the form. She had to list all the addresses by hand for the post office. More, still more to do. She pulled out the Certified Mail Green Domestic Return Receipt and hand-wrote twenty names, one for each envelope. Next, she had to fill out twenty of the Certified Mail Receipts with the little tracking numbers. Her right hand ached, her eyes throbbed, and the beginning of a migraine floated like a gray cloud covering her right eye in a haze of frustration. Wine. Please let me have another glass. What would it hurt?

Morainya reasoned that she needed to reward herself for completing a job that she dreaded. That should constitute for one more glass of chilled Rose'. She was an adult, and no one could tell her that one glass, or two wasn't earned in the privacy of her own house. Josh. Morainya had sworn to him that she'd quit drinking after the divorce that had brought her to her knees. That blackness of being torn between her desires and a promise to her son made her cry. Great convulsions of tears that took four or five tissues to relieve her internal sadness and depression. It all came flooding back in great convulsive cries that made her drop to the floor and curl up in fetal position.

But the urge for wine was stronger; she had reignited an addiction that had once consumed her more than she had consumed it. The delicately frosted Persian pistachio cake that she had worked so hard to craft for Iben was untouched in the freezer. A reminder of the night he returned home to save his sister.

Morainya grabbed a handful of the frozen dessert and microwaved it. She reasoned that she needed something sweet in her life. She shoved the warmed cake in her mouth, chasing it with a gulp of the too sweet Rose'. It wasn't dessert—it was an act of war. A sugar -drenched rebellion against the men who had fed on her trust. The sweetness of this act of defiance, defiling the cake was defiling them—and at that moment, teeth clenched, cheeks flushed, she honestly believed it might actually help. The pistachios, once dusted like a blessing, now clung to her lips like grit. She chased it with a gulp of Rosé—and let it numb her shame. Disillusionment hit her like a wrecking ball to the chest. Everything she had been taught—trusted—crumbled beneath her.

"Fear authority. Respect the Law. Obey. Comply. Submit. It had all been a beautifully polished lie—wrapped in patriotism and paperwork, sugarcoated with Starbucks and Instagram filters. Freedom wasn't freedom. It was a leash—silk-lined and hidden in plain sight. And she had thanked her captors while they slowly staved her soul.

It hit her hard as she stuffed another handful of cake glazed with pain and betrayal. This rigged Matrix system controlled the world through fear, greed, and propaganda to lull us into a *tell-lie-vision* that *'programmed'* our minds through algorithmic hypnosis. She'd played by the rules. Believed in justice. Wore the mask. Paid the toll. And in return? Silence. Gaslight. Theft.

Another glass of wine. It started as a slow burn—a tightening in her chest, a tremor in her fingers as she stacked the last envelope. The scent of paper and toner turned acidic. Her throat constricted. She gulped from her glass, too fast. The wine burned. The sweetness stabbed like a blade, and still she drank.

They had stolen something from her.

Not just her money. Not just her family's inheritance—but something deeper. Her faith. Faith in law. In the righteousness. In the idea that someone—somewhere—would do the right thing. Believing that people in authority would protect her. Then it came.

Undun, by The Guess Who—blaring from the old AM/FM radio she played like prophecy. The haunting refrain cut through her: a woman who had reached too high, thought she could fly, only to find the fall was inevitable. A soul unraveling. A truth too late.

Her knees buckled. Her heart stuttered. The pounding in her ears became a war drum. She wanted to dance—anything to release the spiraling agony—but her limbs betrayed her. She spun like a Ferris wheel in dizzying circles, every note echoing the same grim verdict: she had gone too far, lost her grip, and the sun was slipping away. An unfettered rage swelled within her like a sweltering fire. Iben panged her V. The moment he flipped her elbows, the moment her body arched with yearning and trust.

Caw. A sound, unhuman, split her mind.

The horrible awareness tore through her, she had given him consent—but not sovereignty. She had let him in. She had thought it was sacred. But now she wasn't sure if it was sovereignty—or spellwork.

Her body pitched sideways. Her hip hit the floor first. Then her shoulder. The world darkened at the edges. The song still thundered through the radio, chanting her fate: she had lost too much, and there was no way back. She let out a bitter laugh. How fitting. The room spun. The music blared. The world darkened. Maybe she'd never wake up. And for the first time, she didn't know if she cared.

The stack of envelopes stared back like silent witnesses to her hesitation. It was Tuesday—still unmailed. Yesterday, she blamed a hangover. Today, work. Tomorrow? Some other excuse.

She knew the truth: once she mailed those papers, war would begin. And the question that haunted her wasn't whether she'd survive it—It was whether she could stomach being *that* woman. The one who no longer played nice.

She thought of all the years she had been trained to please. Raised to soothe, to accommodate. To apologize. To be small. Sweet Palatable. Acceptable.

But when the betrayal came—when the courts failed, when the father shamed, when the lover vanished, when the world gaslit her—*something ancient rose.* And it didn't ask for permission. It roared through her like fire through paper. This... this was what it felt like to become *that* woman. The one who no longer played nice. The one who didn't beg to be understood. The one who chose herself—even if it meant war. Finally—she decided to mail her own damn liberation.

Wednesday morning, Morainya was first in line at the post office. Everything in order—Sal would have been proud. The routine grounded her. The rhythmic sound of the postage machine, the weight of the envelopes shifting from her hand to theirs—it wasn't just mail. It was medicine.

With each certified label affixed,—she grew more certain. And with every tear of the timestamped receipt, she grew more free.

Back home, hands still shaking a little, she exhaled. Then dialed. Sal answered on the first ring.

"Hey," he said casually, then paused. Something in his tone shifted. "Did you do it?"

"I did." Her voice soft. Strong. "I mailed them all."

A long silence stretched between them. Not awkward. Sacred.

"You know..." he said, "no one ever tells you what it costs—what it feels like to be the one who carries it all. The boss. The protector. The woman who fixes what's broken, even when she's breaking inside."

Her eyes brimmed. She couldn't speak.

"You didn't fail, Morainya. You adapted. The world didn't keep its end of the deal, so you did what strong women do—you stepped up. You handled it. You kept going when no one else could. And now?"

He paused. "Now you get to rest. Not because you're weak—but because you remember. Remember who you were before the world demanded you to armor up. That softness you miss? That was never failure. It was the part of you worth protecting."

Tears slid quietly down her cheeks. Not because she was broken—But she was seen. And still—she had done it herself. *And now, someone finally understood what it cost her.*

As she hung up, she let the phone rest in her palm. One breath. Slow. Full. She'd done it. *She didn't burn the bridge. She simply crossed it—quietly, on her own terms.* No collapse. Just the quiet hum of a house that didn't know what she'd just survived.

Then—

"Are you coming to the Senior Bake Sale?" asked Josh, lacing his sneakers on the dining room chair like it was any other Wednesday.

Her head turned. The war was over—for now. But motherhood never slept.

"Is that after school today? I'm delivering a box of recorded photos to the Historical Society, so I can get paid. But you know I want MaryBeth's key lime pie. Here's $20," said Morainya. The spell of stillness had passed. Real life pressed in like a hungry tide.

As she placed the money on the table for Josh, her hand lingered a moment longer than needed. The bake sale was just another task in a world that never stopped asking. But her thoughts drifted—not to her son, or Iben, or even Sal—but to her father.

She remembered the way he used to come home, court files under his arm, jaw locked from a day of lawsuits and entitled clients. She'd thought he was just angry. Intolerant. But now—now that she was fighting her own invisible war—she realized what it actually was: fatigue. Not the kind sleep could fix. The kind that came from holding up an entire lineage without letting it crack.

Clients stopped appreciating old-world charm. The Renaissance furniture, the Latin legalisms—what once made him refined now made him obsolete. The world had gone sleek and cold, and her father hadn't evolved with it. He became a relic in his own profession. A dinosaur. A silent casualty of progress.

But the worst part?

He'd fought every battle in a world built for men—but had no sword to pass to a daughter born to burn the field. It wasn't that he didn't love her. It was that he was terrified—and love didn't know how to move through that armor. He had no script for how to father a daughter becoming something he never had permission to be. Open. Emotional. Untamed. Everything he'd once buried in himself, she embodied. Morainya's mother was slipping, and with her went the softness of the household. And he—left behind—had nothing but discipline and decibels to hold the walls up. She needed grace. He gave her rules. She needed warmth. He offered protection. He thought they were the same.

And maybe the heart attack that took Stephano too early wasn't just the end of a man—Maybe it was the quiet release of someone who didn't know how to stay in a world that no longer needed his kind of strength. Maybe it was mercy. Maybe it was freedom—from a pain he never knew how to name.

What Morainya didn't know—what she could never fully grasp—was that the moment she dropped those envelopes into the mouth of the post office bin, the frequency of her entire being changed. He had felt it from San Francisco. A surge of sovereign will that rippled through the ethers, crashing directly into the field of his chest like a silent gong.

It hit his root first. A shaking. A dislodging. A tremor. Her energy no longer leaned into his—she stood on her own ground now, and that destabilized something ancient in him. Something tribal. Something conditioned. The part of him that believed—deep down—she still needed his map to guide her.

Arriving home at 6:00 that night, Morainya decided that she'd make a light dinner and go to bed. Instead, she received a text from Iben, asking if she was home tonight?" Staring at her phone, she reread it. Finally, her curiosity got the best of her, and she texted back, *Yes, why?*

I finished a meeting in Los Gatos. Would you like to get dinner?

Been a long day. I should just stay in, she responded. It was such late notice. The thought of getting dressed, driving, performing—it scraped against the raw place inside her. Just reading the thread drained her. The emotional math of men—always too many variables, never enough reciprocity.

No problem. I could bring dinner for you. No fried chicken, I promise. I owe you one. Again, she stared at the message.

Why did he make her feel so off-kilter? He popped in when she least expected it and was never there when she needed him desperately. Yet he still took control of her body. It made her fucking nuts. But...she longed to see him. Not to be fixed. Not to be claimed. Just seen. Understood. Remembered. There was no turning back. *Yes, bring dinner, and we can eat here. What time will you be here? She texted the address.*

He answered with a smiley face. *In forty-five minutes. Salads.*

Morainya studied the smiley face. She had to take back her power. Sure, he had been through so much. Saving his sister. Reliving her memories. She pinned her hair, dabbed on lipstick—not seduction, just color. Proof she hadn't vanished. Not too over-the-top, just enough. She looked so tired. Maybe he wouldn't notice. Her mind reeled with questions. Her clock was eking toward 7:00; she feared he would be late. Her stomach rumbled. Was punctuality extinct? Or had everyone just stopped caring?

By the time he reached her door at 7:05p.m., he had already decided he wouldn't touch her until she asked. He would not lead. He would witness. And if she invited him in, he would answer not as a man who claimed her, but as one who remembered her. In the old ways, no man touched a goddess unless her soul opened first. And hers had.

The doorbell rang. She turned with a start, heart thrumming like a distant drumbeat. She tried to reset—to slip back into something warm, something welcoming—but the pulse in her ears gave her away. Iben stood there, smiling in that boyish way that made her both furious and undone. His eyes shining—clear, timeless, knowing.

"It is good to see you," she said it as casually as she could muster. Her heart pounded. Then, softer. "I missed you." Ugh, why did she blurt it out?

He looked askew. "How can you miss me," he asked gently, "when we are one? I am with you always." He opened his arms. They embraced. But she hesitated. His warmth was immediate—effortless. Hers held back. Just enough to keep her spine straight. And that left her off balance.

It was true—he was always with her. He whispered through her dreams. Stirred her chakras in the quiet hours. Pulled her breath from across the veil. But was that the same as showing up in the earthly world? In the flesh? On time?

His breezy arrival—like nothing was out of the ordinary—grated at the edges of her restraint.

"What a beautiful house," he said, stepping inside. "I love the colors. The furniture. You've made a temple."

He was enthusiastic. Present. Joyful. It was maddening. He owed her an explanation.

Her home pulsed with the scent of rebirth. Every object, every plate on the table—charged with the faint echo of defiance and devotion. He saw the towel draped over the evidence of her war. He saw her hunger. And still, she held her boundary with elegance.

"Iben," she said, exhaling. She met his eyes, unflinching. "You never touch me. You never move. And yet—you do things to me."

A flicker of something unreadable passed over his face. "What is it you think I do?"

Her jaw clenched. "Don't do that. Don't answer me with more questions."

When they touched, it wasn't skin on skin. It was field to field. Every chakra, every nerve in her body shifted around him—reforming, realigning, fracturing.

His heart cracked open the moment she didn't collapse into him. She didn't beg for answers. She didn't melt. She stood. And demanded truth. It was the most arousing thing he had ever felt. He too, needed a moment to collect himself.

He lifted the food bags like a peace offering. "Could we discuss this over dinner," with a tone that implied that she wasn't a gracious hostess.

"Of course, forgive me," she said, motioned toward the dining room. "I set the table."

The stacked envelopes, the files, her laptop—hidden under a folded towel.

He smiled and began unpacking the salads in the to-go plastic tubs. "Extra avocado on yours."

He always remembered. That was the infuriating part.

Morainya let down her guard—just a little. The food helped. The routine. She told him about coming onto the Land. About Sal. The Notices. The mailing. The tremor of reclaiming.

He leaned back, full, content. Hands over his stomach. "That will be very helpful to your situation."

"My situation?" she asked with surprise, wrinkling her brow.

"As I recall," he said evenly, "you mentioned a legal problem. A deep hatred of injustice. We call it 'Maat.' Balance. Truth. The world, the good, the bad, and the none—in full effect. The scale that weighs the world."

"Ma-at," she said it silently. Committing that name to memory.

He nodded. "Most think evil wins through cruelty. But often, it wins through compliance. The None. The silent. The well-meaning. That's how imbalance spreads. The ones who look away. Who stay polite. Who say nothing. In the teachings of Ma'at, the balance is not just between good and evil—but also the *none*. Because neutrality in the face of injustice is not neutrality at all. It is a silent endorsement of the dominant force." He let that sink in.

Then, with a quiet exhale, he looked down at his hands—weathered, elegant, capable of building or breaking. A flicker of pain crossed his face, the kind born of having once stayed silent too long.

"I know because I was once one of them," he admitted, voice low. "Not cruel. Just careful. Respectable. Thought I was keeping peace, when really, I was just preserving someone else's power."

He looked up at her then, eyes steady. "Never again." And in that vow was no anger—just clarity. The kind that comes after the fire has already burned through the illusions.

She laughed and nodded. "Right—we say in law that silence is acquiescence." But the laughter caught in her throat. It wasn't funny anymore. A hum began to rise in her chest, not adrenaline—but something older. Deeper. A remembering.

She drew a slow breath. "Then I finally made the right move," she whispered—not to him, but to something within. No longer one of the *None.* No longer quiet for the sake of peace. According to Iben, she was now in alignment with cosmic law. With Truth. Not the kind that sits in a statute—but the kind that weighs hearts against feathers. And this time, hers felt lighter.

His knowledge of ancient wisdom always captivated her. Even the salad—simple, nourishing, thoughtful—told her he'd paid attention. She took another bite, savoring the avocado he'd remembered to include. That was a good marker on her mental checklist. His eyes twinkled. His energy warm. Present. He asked real questions—about her family, her parents, her son. He listened with the kind of patience that made her heart ache. But still...was he distracting her from the thing that pulsed between all this niceness? How is it that this man, who never claims me, still pings every part of my body?

"You said you were married before," he said gently. "Yet, you never name him—the father of your son."

Morainya grimaced. Her fork stilled over the bowl. "He's with someone else now," she said, eyes dropping to her plate. "I guess they are happy. It's ok, I've moved on."

And beneath her sovereignty, he could feel the residue of an older wound—a bruise not fully faded. The ghost of another man's blindness. Jedidiah. The one who traded her sacred heat for a supermodel named Jenny—thin, polished, blonde, *safe.* The world had rewarded him for it. Called it an upgrade.

But Iben saw the truth: *He chose style over soul.* A performance over presence. And Morainya carried that ache in the way she second-guessed her own power, even now. He wanted to take her face in his hands and say, *"You were never too much. He was just too small to hold you."* But she wasn't ready to hear that yet. So, he said nothing. He simply *watched her move*—and saw what Jedidiah never could: *a woman in bloom. Not in spite of her age or softness... but because of it.*

"Age, race, religion...none of that matters to me," he said when she asked about his lineage. "My family would love you." And then, as if receiving something deeper than memory, he added:. "She is awakening. Stay in balance. The mitochondria remember." He heard their message echo even deeper this time, not just in thought, but as a phrase engraved in his soul: All things are possible. Who you are is limited by who you think you are.

There wasn't a subject he avoided. He was open. Curious. Transparent. Except for one thing. The thing that drove her crazy. "Can I make us some tea, and we can sit outside on the deck?"

"Tea would be nice," he said softly.

She returned with two cups and the half-eaten pistachio cake. ben chuckled when he saw the jagged handfuls torn from the edge. "Looks like someone was hungry."

She set the tray down with a faint smile. "I had dinner for one. The other never showed up."

There it was. She didn't say it with venom—but he felt the hurt thread through the air.

He took the cups and cake and guided her gently to the porch swing. "I most humbly apologize," he said. "All I could think about was my sister."

The tension began to leave her face. Her shoulders softened. She loved his chivalry. Loved how he moved with intention, like he was always listening with more than his ears. They sat close. Hands touching. The night air wrapped around them like an old shawl.

Could this be the beginning? He wasn't acting like someone who just wanted to be friends. Maybe—just maybe—God had sent him.

She turned toward him and studied his face. Something had shifted. "Your eyes," she said, surprised. "They look different. Weren't they darker before?"

"No, Queen," he said gently. "They've always been brownish-green. It runs in my family. I'm surprised you never noticed."

That stung her, as if she had been neglectful noticing everything about him. The way he seemed to do about her. His voice rising with a bit of hurt. It wasn't that important; it just surprised her, but she couldn't put her finger on why. Out of the blue, a rumbling rattled the starry night. Lightning forked across the sky, silence torn open by bass-drum thunder. She jumped up.

"A storm is rolling in. We should head inside," He maneuvered her inside the dark house. Stroking her hair, to calm her, he pulled her closer and he brushed a kiss along her cheekbone—and below the surface, a subtle current thrummed through her pelvis, coaxing a release that stole her breath. Keeping up the measured pulses to her V until she came hard, moaning softly, in his embrace. It was so fucking intimate—and then again, not.

But he stayed still—smiling as if he had *always* known this would be the outcome.

Morainya collapsed feeling spent in his arms. She had never had sex with a partner who never touched her. This wasn't normal. Iben's lips pressed against her flesh...*She longed for him... but her mind—her logic—was screaming... How does one integrate this craziness?*

"How do you do that?" she asked breathlessly, a bit more demanding.

"I just activate your mitochondria," he replied casually.

She sucked in her breath, trying to ground herself.

"Let's go to bed," he said, taking her hand. "Which way?" She felt weak-kneed. He slipped an arm around her waist and guided her inside toward her bedroom. Her head was spinning, out of breath, and drenched. That was remarkable foreplay; she thought, grateful that Josh was away. Without turning on the light, Iben took her hand and led her to the bathroom. "Let's take a shower."

Iben was impeccable with his hygiene, often giving thanks to the hot water. Steam blanketed both of them as he murmured gratitude to the water, palms gliding over skin bronzed like midnight honey. She had never been so close to such unguarded power; every contour felt at once foreign and familiar, as though etched in memory long before this life.

Then he shaved meticulously as she followed his lead. The lather, rinse, and repeat was perpetuated until Morainya could feel her fingertips shrivel. Excusing herself, she stepped out of the shower and toweled off, half expecting him to do the same. She dried her hair and glanced at him, lost in his ablution routine. Morainya felt the blush rise to her cheeks, as she had never been in such proximity to a dark-hued man. His hair was kinky, muscles smooth and taunt, legs sinewed and brawny, his appendage thick and unhindered.

He paid no attention to her studying him, admiring the beauty that, in a very strange way, felt familiar. If her father was alive, he would be aghast at her sharing a bed with a man who wasn't Catholic nor of European heritage.

Morainya knew that that combination was no more a guarantee of a successful relationship than pushing one's personal boundaries to explore. Afterall, her first marriage to Jedidiah had neither proved successful, nor an opportunity for spiritual growth or personal evolution. Sliding into bed, she craved the cold sheets to ease her overheated body. What came next?

Sleep was calling her, but that would be rude, so she pushed off the vestiges of drowsiness. Iben joined her; gravitating toward her, he pulled her into the tight confines of his hug. Holding her in a protective manner that forbade any intrusion of the dark thoughts that brought her to her knees with consuming worry. Not tonight. He provided the covering that deflected all things.

"Have you ever been loved down by a god?" he whispered into her ear.

"Can't say that I have," replied Morainya, startled by the question.

"Prepare yourself for the Divine."

The words sent a ripple through her, but something in her clenched. Her body ached for him, but her mind—her logic—was screaming that this wasn't normal. Iben's lips pressed against her flesh, and the thought dissolved like sugar in hot water.

He turned his lips upon her flesh, converting the chilled skin to again, simmer under his touch. His mouth found her peaks, drawing heat that radiated like sunrise through her veins. Every glide of his fingers sent concentric rings of light rippling outward—until waves of silver fire rose from her core and broke across her body, pulse after pulse, timeless and holy.

Fingers exploring her, tickling her, pinching her. All she could do was emit the most guttural moans and signs as if being consumed by something far greater than she had ever known existed. Her body convulsed in orgasmic spasms, writhing in pleasure at being penetrated by a pulsing light that pushed her over the edge. Every time one of those primal moans uttered forth, he acknowledged the flow and delighted in his power over her with a simple, "Um huh."

But then came the fire. Her sacral chakra opened like a flower blooming under lightning.

He could feel it in his own hips—the ache, the pull, the undeniable thrum of her becoming. Her pleasure was no longer a reaction to him. It was a declaration of herself. And it humbled him.

Her clit was on fire, with rhythmed hits; as she traversed the cosmos, Iben right next to her, they flew above the heavens, united in an etheric love that surpassed anything she had ever experienced. Just as her body could take no more pleasure, it felt as if he pulled out and allowed her to float gently back to her earthly form. Tears flowed from her eyes, acknowledging that this was beyond her knowing. Beyond words that had to be meted out on this plane; No, this was a true experience with godly force, pleasure, and release that must have been granted to a very few of the lucky ones open enough to receive the gift.

She fell into a deep, bottomless sleep, receiving more peace than she had ever known. The last thought was how this man knew to choose her? It was the closest she'd come to feeling like she had found home, from another time, another place, home within the heart and mind of this stranger.

By the time her climax came, it wasn't because he had entered her body. It was because she had finally re-entered her own. And as she slept—peaceful, soft, sovereign—he watched her. He prayed over her mitochondria. He kissed the memory of every woman in his lineage who had been denied their own voice.

He left before sunrise. Not because he didn't care. But because he did. Because to stay might mean trying to name what had not yet finished becoming. And this woman? She was still unfolding. And he would not interrupt a Queen in her ascension.

Morning light found only the imprint of his body: a faint warmth cooling on the sheet.

She smoothed her palm across that hollow, the ache in her throat tasting of salt and unfinished sentences. He was gone. She exhaled sharply. Of course, he hadn't stayed.

25

*A*ll night, I tossed and turned, dreading the morning when Smenkhkare would wake from his enchantment. I knew not what I would say when forced to explain to the man next to me that this was our joining mat, and he was my new consort. It was unlike Smenkhkare to rise to ire, but this would be as shocking as watching a snake shed its skin for the first time. He lay there so tranquil, without a care. I yearned to stroke his copper cheek that glowed with the early sunrise, for he was beautiful and rare in his opened heart that brought peace to those in his company. Today, I feared he would not be as compassionate nor as peaceful when he saw that I had shared a mat, naked after consummating in our night of expected connubial bliss.

Last night, after I caused great upset by knocking the glass out of Archollos' hand, the partygoers went silent with embarrassment. They could not have known that Ana-Kharu was attempting to assassinate the man he referred to as 'the barbarian.'

In my time of humiliation mixed with rage, it was Smenkhkare who chimed in, "Careful, my love, those cups can be slippery. Perhaps, we have all overstayed our welcome, and our host and hostess must surely need sleep." He held his hand out to me, and I was thankful that he had rescued me from having to explain my outrageous actions. Smenkhkare's eyes were burning brightly, and it surprised me that he desired me so.

Pulling me into the sleeping area arranged just for us; our woven mats were laid out with fresh linen sheets. My dearest pulled me into his arms and kissed me deeply. He was so passionate as he pulled off my sheath and laid me down gently, kissing my face and neck and declaring his adoration for me. I felt grateful for whatever aphrodisiac Ana-Kharu had created—Smenkhkare's kisses burned with sudden heat and his rising djed pillar matched the pulse of desire that finally stirred between us. He pushed my hand to his pole, and I was surprised at how a piece of flesh could become rigid. He emitted soft moans. Quickly, he rolled upon me, declaring his adoration and longing.

The weight of Smenkhkare's body and hardened muscles made me appreciate his beauty even more. He spread my legs gently and guided his hardened scepter inside me. The breaking of my flower sent a cry through my lips—a pain both physical and existential. Strokes of rising passion began to overtake me. I waited for the rising levels of ecstasy Ana-Kharu promised—for the portal, the key, the divine unfolding. Any moment now, I thought, I will rise above myself. I would leave my body and traverse the heavens—but then I heard a moan, and my Consort's body shook and released.

It ended in a single shudder. He rolled clear, warmth fading from my skin as fast as a spilled cup of wine soaks sand. I lay rigid, listening to the reeds sigh outside the window—each hollow stalk sounding more alive than the space he'd left behind. It was over. He rolled away leaving his seed inside of me. And I lay there wide awake, cradling the silence like a broken relic.

"This was supposed to be the key. The moment of transcendence. Instead, it was over in swiftly—a fleeting breath of passion that had no magic, no meaning. Had he even known it was me? Had I been nothing but a vessel, an altar for a ritual neither of us chose. The weight of it sat heavy in my gut, like a stone thrown into deep water.

The chamber grew quiet except for the soft exhale of sleeping breath and the occasional flicker of torchlight against the sandstone walls. I lay unmoving, eyes wide in the dark, listening to the rise and fall of Smenkhkare's chest beside me. Outside, a jackal called. Distant. Then another. Closer. Time dragged like a funeral barge across still water.

My thoughts looped like chants—what had I done, what had I agreed to, and why did my skin still feel like it did not belong to me? I must have dozed off eventually, because the next thing I heard was—I dared not move the rest of the night when, in truth—I wanted to run.

"*Up! All of you! Now!*" Ana-Kharu's voice cut through the veil of sleep like a blade. "*We move before first light—gather your things, we have little time. Be ready to depart.*" He was desperate to make haste toward the plateau of the pyramid.

"Yes, momentarily," I replied loudly. Crimson half-moons bloomed across the linen, darkening where the cloth clung to my skin. I folded the sheets quickly, as though the stains could speak my secrets aloud. Shame and horror rocked me, not because this bedding belonged to Ma-Nat, but because Smenkhkare had spent his seed within me while he was intoxicated with Ana-Kharu's elixir. I stroked Smenkhkare to rouse him as I hid my tears. Grabbing a fresh linen sheath, I rolled up my bedding to go wash.

He opened his eyes, with a hand sweeping across his face to block the sun. "Merit-Aten?

He cocked his head as if unable to grasp why I would be in the men's sleeping chamber. Stunned, he pushed himself up, squinting at my face, making him flinch. "Is there danger?"

"No, no. Ana-Kharu wants the class to start our passage toward the Master Teacher. It is the first urgings of dawn, time to leave," I said calmly, even though my actions were quickened.

"Yes, I will get up." He noticed that I slipped on my clothing, and it confused him, and he gave me a look that demanded an explanation.

"Beloved," I started with an endearment. "Last night, we were joined in a ceremony as deemed by the Pharaoh and Per Aat. I had no choice but to obey."

As if his daze dissipated, he struggled to say, "I have no memory of that." His voice cut like a razor through the morning haze. His gaze darted over the bedding, the blood, the disheveled sheets. Realization crawled over his face— first confusion, then a tightening around the eyes, like stone doors grinding shut. "What have you done?" The words fell between us like chipped pottery.

I hung my head. "I obeyed."

He reeled back, taking in the gravity of my words. "Verily, I made it clear that while I adore you like my sister, my heart belongs to another. There were plenty of worthy candidates for your choosing."

"Brother, your heart lies elsewhere—I remember." My voice tasted of parchment: dry, formal, unreadable. "Unfortunately, both you and I are under the authority of the living gods of the land. It is our duty. I would never expect that you would remain loyal to me. I give you the freedom to pursue whomever you desire. But, in this choosing, we will need to produce an heir." I didn't wait for agreement. I gathered the soiled bedding to my chest, its damp weight heavier than truth, and walked to the door—because if I stayed a moment longer, I might scream or crumble or beg him to say it was all a dream.

"But—" Smenkhkare stuttered, at a loss for words. His words were not what I needed right now.

"We must depart immediately and figure out how to locate a God of great myth," I said plainly, then grimaced and departed the room with my reddened sheets. As I moved into the kitchen, Ma-Nat glanced at the blood stain on my thighs and gave me a triumphant smile as if this would prove that I had transcended the heavens with my loving partner, and the key to unlock my portal of glory.

I simply lifted my joining bedding in acknowledgement and went outside to the washing station, where I pounded the mess with some rock of brine to cleanse it. The men were gathered in a huddle and restlessly waited for the women to wake. When they saw me, they looked as if I caught them off-guard. The blood-stained waters were an unexpected sign.

I felt relieved that the women streamed out of the demesne to join me like sweet cooing pigeons in the court-yard. I wrung the last of the water from the sheet and hung it to dry. One by one the women drifted after me, their san-dals whispering over sand—quiet wings folding around a wound no man seemed brave enough to name.

Ana-Kharu paused then broke the silence, "We have a problem on the horizon." The Magician climbed a sandy rise, his silhouette carved against the pale dawn—elevated not just by stone, but by scorn. "You all have been feasting when you should have been fasting. Now, we walk with full bellies, sluggish with digestion. Our blood thickens when moving across the arid desert which sucks the moisture from us as payment for crossing. Your brains are dizzy with wine and sweet desserts, while the desert is demanding of our endurance."

His words struck like willow-whips—thin, stinging, precise—flogging our softness into silence. Because we had been deprived of hearty meals upon this journey, I overindulged as a means to soothe myself, to lessen the scorching pain of my heart. The Merchant kept pouring full our cups of wine, thinking its abundance would please us in celebrating the Pharaoh's daughter. silently begged the gods that last night's indulgence hadn't dulled my senses—because somewhere, the red lion waited, and with it, my father's salvation.

"Tell us what problem lays before us?" I boldly stated, hoping to defer his judgment away from last night's merriment and toward the severity of today's mission.

The Amunites went to the pyramids to commence their lustrations to the Moon. The roads will be teeming with their lunacy as they make their way home. We will be in the midst of the enemy, and we cannot miss the timing of the alignment of stars of Orion's belt that will be right over the three pyramids. We should have left two days ago, but this celebration seems to have taken precedence over our mission." Ana-Kharu turned to me, "Merit-Aten, what is your plan to take us to Djehuty?"

"First, we must locate where a God would take up residence. My father did not explain how we would find him, only that he would be expecting us," I replied with a shrug. It was not that I had forgotten about the purpose of this journey, but I was just as confused as to how I would be told of his whereabouts. Trust was my only option. I trust that one foot in front of another will put us on the correct path.

"Did your father reveal any clues? He must have told you something that might seem insignificant at first but was a hint."

"He only told me that I must talk to a red lion," I said.

"A lion is going to talk to you?" Ra-Awab scoffed. "That is the plan?"

Ana-Kharu stared at us. "How did you not go to the Per Neters—pyramids before?"

"I told you; we only went to Heliopolis at night when we were children."

Ana-Kharu clicked his tongue—less in frustration, more in confirmation that we were exactly as naïve as he feared. "We shall head to the Sphinx. It is a long walk."

My mouth flew open. Suddenly, it all clicked. "Of course. The colossal monument has the head of a hueman...and the body of a Red Lion." *The Red Lion.* The one my father spoke of in riddles. The one who sees without eyes. A strange heat swept over me—like memory returning through the skin. My knees buckled, and I had to steady myself. My breath caught in my throat. I could feel the sand of my childhood beneath my feet, the weight of my father's voice in my bones. "Akhet-Aten is not the end," he had whispered once. "The

Red Lion watches even in sleep." I had thought it poetry then. I was wrong. It was a map.

Ana-Kharu ordered, "Change your garments, for I will not be seen with clean, easy-to-rob initiates. "Rip your sheaths. Mud your skin. Wrap your hair. Tangle your pride. No Queen's preening cats will walk beside me. We will be overlooked and unnoticed. Move. While the fish are moving downstream, we will be a school of minnows moving between." Then he stared at me—and my blue dyed hair—without a word, he tore a white linen headwrap from his satchel and tossed it to me. "Wear this," he said, eyes narrowed. "You already draw enough light. No need to set the whole desert staring."

A few of the boys chuckled, but Oya only raised a brow. "Shall we begin with breath and centering?" she asked, her voice calm but pointed.

Ana-Kharu exhaled through his nose, then nodded. "Yes. Thank you, Oya."

He turned back to the group, now circling them with quiet command. "First, I must give you a short Alchemical lesson before we start the day's journey. I see that many of you are recovering from the wine of plenty. You all got so worked up about this choosing, which created excess fire, so you became excessively thirsty; drinking wine then gave you excess air and lightheadedness, which made you too hungry." Ana-Kharu pointed to his stomach "When you woke, I am certain you were cold and tired from excess water and earth. Alchemy is one element combined to produce results, whether good or bad. Your heads are on fire. Your abdomen is water. Your lungs are air— used to create combustion between the upper and lower. Now, everything you do from here must be balanced, or we are all for naught."

We stood frozen by the ice in Ana-Kharu's voice. It was only when the leader began packing that we attended to our own duties.

The young women changed their garments and left our lovely clean sheaths behind. The three young women wrapped their hair in black material and we slipped on the tattered old sheaths Ma-Nat was ready to discard. Then we gathered around the well as we filled water bags.

Keshtuat whispered and prodded. "How was your night with Smenkhkare?"

"Good," I lied. But even the word tasted sour. A sharp cramp seized my belly, and when warmth spread between my legs, I nearly dropped the water bag. The blood had come. Too soon. Too cruel. I had Smenkhkare's seed within my loins, and now my menses comes? How would I ever produce an heir? Such bad timing.

"Is he your key?" Sarawat asked, her eyes wide with innocent longing, as if love always unlocked heaven.

For women dream of that heavenly bliss and traversing the sky of Nut upon their first joining, I thought with trepidation as my foolish plans crashed around me.

I gave a slight smile. "He is somebody's key. Just not mine." I hoped that would answer what they truly desired to know.

"Overstood," they replied, and thankfully, the subject dissolved as evenly as yeast in water.

Under the full moon, I realized—we had synced. "We are all bleeding. I whispered.

"Then let us return the tide to the Mother—together." We formed a circle in the garden, lifting our sheaths and removing our linen pads, capturing the crimson droplets in our cupped palms—like rubies from the womb. Then, one by one, we knelt and returned it to the soil—our blood, our vow, our holy bond with the land.

The earth element. "Let us speak our intention—for protection, invisibility, and alignment. May the hand of Aten shield us, and the breath of the Mother propel us toward our purpose." This is our holy blood covenant. We offer our life force so that it magnetizes and accelerates all thoughts and manifestations."

"Our wombs are sacred and embody the cosmos within," replied Keshtuat solemnly.

"May we give praise to the Mother of Lands," said Sarawat, "and may we return her gift with honor."

"Our blood is the rivers of the land; we are covered by protection," said Tadushet.

I took the filled pitcher of water and decreed the first libation to our ancestors for protection by pouring the first offering to the land. "May what I offer be worthy and my hands made light."

Then, I handed the pitcher to Keshtuat. She poured the second libation, "May the way open—by peace and through power."

Sarawat poured the third. "May the place that holds us know only peace."

Tadushet let the water run into the garden soil. "May the spirits of our ancestors walk fresh upon the wind."

"Aten." We all completed the prayer by acknowledging the solar deity.

"My sisters, I need your help," I said. "The task before me is great. I need all your eyes upon the land, and I feel we must rise above the problems on the ground. Tadushet, light the incense while we come together to pray and solarize our energies. Let us take advantage of our cycles and use the magic within us as the Akh, children of Aten and Ra, the Great Spirit light within us, the animating force. The great Cosmic mother, the universal blackness. Hear our prayers."

Tadushet took the Khyphi incense off the table and used the oil lamp to light the offering. Wisps of smoke like small serpents licked the dawn breeze—fire made visible and scent filled the air. "The fire element."

"Sarawat, bring forth praise and enhance our power as sisters to expand our fire force to the heavens," I said, directing her to fill the pitcher once more. Instead of the cool water that usually trickles up from the well, now the water bubbled up, hot and steamy. "The fire to water element.

I searched the sky, asking for the birds of the air to attend to us. My breath skimmed the ostrich feather; it shivered, then stilled—answering like a dial tuned to wind. "I called in Ma'at, the bird. Just as the two wings of the vulture expand and contract, so do our lungs, which represent solar energy and the firebird within us. We absorb solar energy through our breath. The Air element."

I did not know which solar bird would hear my plea, but shortly, three black ravens landed upon the tamarind tree, glossy wings folding; and a lone dove settled beside them, white against green—omens feathered into flesh. They cawed and cooed at us, answering my request. Ah, the raven meant monogamy and faithful love and good luck, which felt a blessing because they were the messengers of the gods.

The dove, meaning fertility, life, and regeneration, is also representative of Osiris.

"My sisters, this is our empowering time. No man alive has language for what sparks between women who lock their breath in the same rhythm. I am requesting that we take our *ka's,* our spirits, and animate these ravens. We are the winged fire surging through our bodies. We will use their eyes to traverse the land faster than our bodies can do. I am hearing that we must use the passage that will take us to the pyramid, out of view of the non-believers." I said, looking deep into their windows, eyes, their *ba's,* their souls.

"We are the sisters of the Aten," I said, spreading my hands, "the beautiful feminine goddesses who bore the sacred solar disc upon our heads. We have been through the most perilous initiations; we have been pushed beyond what most are capable of. Our blood has been delivered to the soil. The earth element." We looked deep into each other's eyes, thereby lifting our intentions to carry upon the wind as our words are the law. "Choose one of the three ravens. I will take the white dove. Allow this bird to fly upon the wind. We will regenerate our *ba's,* our souls, and our bodies." We held hands.

"Ya-kini, Yak-ini, We are protected by the power of our positive," we all said in unison. "The Light surrounds us. The light comes through us. We are the light." We chimed in unison.

"As we fly over the Land of Osiris," I nodded to each sister. "Ausar, the black soil or soul of this land, we ask that you show us the way to the passage," I said. "The hidden door. What we seek is also seeking us." In an instant, our spirit bodies transferred to the black ravens and mine to the dove. We cawed knowingly. Fly now.

Ma-Nat's cast off clothes were stiff, scratchy, and smelly. Perfect to hide initiates who walked to the plateau that held our destiny. This band of misfits gave thanks to the Merchant and his consort for their display of abundance and headed out of the little valley that protected their estate. Once again, we found ourselves on a less crowded secondary road used by travelers who were busy with daily use of this byway.

Ana-Kharu admonished us "Do not to talk using our perfect Temple language. Only the elite are taught how to read and write. Silence." He wagged a finger at us. "Count your footsteps. Do your inner prayer work. Do not stay in a herd but keep an eye on the pack."

This was the best turning of the seasons upon our glorious land. Khemitian spring brought the splendor of the radiant skies hovering above us. Around us was the cooing of doves as they delightfully paired, expressing their nesting urges to mate. Harvests ripened with grain and waved to us with a gentle breeze. Lateral channels used to divert the Nile gushes now deliver only trickles of water to the thirsty fields. The gift of singing birds chirping an eternal melody lifted our hearts.

As the heat of the day enveloped us, we felt it reverberate within us and without us. The poor little donkeys clustered together under the shadow of a single palm. Dogs, usually vibrant with an echo of barking, dotted the village walls deep in a drying sleep. Green-striped watermelon nearly burst with juiciness, and our mouths yearned for their sweetness.

One foot in front of another. Step by step, we passed the dawning hours. My stomach gurgled, perspiration dotted my forehead, and as hard as it was, my body was returning to balance with each step. I slugged up next to overtake the classmate in front of me. Fingers brushed—just a whisper of skin—and a sting of light shot up my spine; jerked as though a live wire hid in that chance touch. I glanced at the traveler and was shocked to see Archollos' face exchanging the same stunned expression. We had no interaction from last night's celebration, and once I swiped that cup of poison from his hand administered by Ana-Kharu, then the party goers went to eat the meal in silence. The ruckus caused such a commotion because I could not justify my actions.

Only Ana-Kharu knew that I was privy to his confidential plan to West Archollos so that he would no longer be a threat. In his belittling tone, he referred to Archollos as a *barbarian*. It made sense why he would concoct a poison to wipe him from my memory. Here I was in the presence of the man who made my heart sing, but today I had no song.

"Forgive me," I said and hurried on. Whether he did or did not, I knew not because I passed him with haste, fearful of what the answer would be.

What happened next stilled us all. Just beyond the rise the pyramid revealed itself—rising like a beacon, flawless in its symmetry, a geometric miracle carved from light and stone.

"That is not sun-glare," Keshtuat whispered, shielding her eyes.

Sarawat stepped up beside her. "White Tura marble," she breathed, "forged by Aten Himself." The smooth limestone glimmered like living skin, and above it the black basalt capstone, tipped in gold, pulsed as though it held a heartbeat.

"No wonder the air hums," Tadushet murmured, brushing gooseflesh from her forearm.

We walked on, yet the monument never seemed nearer. Each step tightened the tether of awe while distance stretched like silk: a mirage ordained by the gods. Heat wavered over barley fields, their golden ears nodding in woven collars; beneath them lentils scattered white blossoms like fallen stars.

"Khemit feeds the world while we fast," Tadushet said with a wan smile.

Clouds of pigeons canopied the sky in chaotic movements with their flapping broad wings. They teetered upon anything that would serve as a perch, curtseying to each other politely. Their iridescent throaty coos call out to their lifelong mates hoping passersby might leave a trail of easy pickings rather than working for an insect or snail. They were negotiating for scraps we did not have to give.

"My father swore their droppings make this soil black and rich," I murmured.

Keshtuat leaned close, dry-voiced: "I prefer them grilled—stuffed with raisins and served with melokhia and pistachios." Soft laughter rippled through us, a momentary breeze against the blazing sun.

I appreciated that both were good and desirable.

Fasting sharpened the spirit, yet today hunger gnawed like a small, relentless jackal.

"I dreamed of Djehuty," Sarawat confessed, "but all I saw was a steaming dish of pigeon."

I answered without looking away from the horizon: "He will not meet pilgrims with greasy fingers." Even that earned a weary chuckle. Linen stuck to our backs, sandals burned our soles, but the pyramid—alive with promise—kept us upright. Somewhere ahead—always ahead—the pyramid still shimmered, impossible to reach.   "I swear it is walking away from us," Keshtuat muttered, wiping sweat away.

"It is teasing us," Sarawat answered. "Like Aten dangling a jewel."

We trudged on. An Amunite mother swung her basket wide, catching Ra-Awab in the shins. "Watch your feet, you dung-sniffer!" she barked.

Tadushet snorted a laugh. "At least it is a new curse to add to our collection."

Ana-Kharu's warning echoed in my head: *Invisible, all of you.* I bit my tongue and kept moving. Smenkhkare's pace was far more rapid than mine. He was so far in the distance that I lost track. What would we have to say to one another? I sighed and kept my focus on one foot in front of another.

"My wings beat strong," Tadushet whispered, flexing sore shoulders, "but my feet are sand-bricks."

"I feel every grain," I admitted, scanning the sky. Our bird bodies spiraled above, cawing. "See anything?"

"Only endless stone," Sarawat said after a breath. "Still looking for a door."

Dusk deepened. Heat shimmered off barley and lentil fields.

"Tell me again why we are fasting while the Amunites chew dates and roast fish like it is a festival day," Keshtuat muttered, eyeing a passing family with stuffed cheeks.

"Because we are not here to feast—we are here to remember," I said, though my stomach disagreed with every word.

Dusk thickened as we trudged through sand churned by thousands of feet. Between caravans and weary Amunite worshippers, shapes began to flicker—thin silhouettes, charcoal-dark against deeper night.

Keshtuat's fingers locked around my elbow. "Did you see that child? He—he wasn't solid."

"I saw," I whispered. "Shadow People. They followed me once in the Valley of Kings."

Tadushet drew her veil closer. "Why only you?"

"Because I listened," I said, though my voice trembled. A small boy-shape gazed up at me, eyes hollow with pleading I could feel more than see. When a merchant's torch passed, he dissolved like smoke."

Sarawat's shawl slipped as she shuddered. "Do they want something?"

"Release," I answered. "Or memory. I am never sure."

"How long has this been happening?" she pressed.

"The last time was at my Grand Djed's tomb," I admitted. I did not add that I'd been sealed inside. "They watched, just as these do."

More figures bled from the dark: women with infants that were only shadows of arms, men whose faces blurred into night. Sarawat clutched me harder. "There—two more, by the grain cart."

"They see we can see them," I murmured. "That is invitation enough." The specters drifted nearer, silent mouths working in wordless appeal. Each step forward felt like passing through a tide of ghosts begging alms no coin could pay.

A sharp whistle cut the tension. Ra-Awab waved from beneath a lone palm. "Water and hibiscus—here!" We slipped past the last shadow and ducked under the fronds. Tadushet fell to her knees, grateful for the respite. Sarawat and Keshtuat were only moments behind. Ra-Awab signaled for the merchant to press dusty clay cups into our hands— warm, sour-sweet, salvation on the tongue. I drank greedily, ignoring the gritty rim.

Across the clearing Archollos and Smenkhkare crouched in close debate, heads bent, voices low. Neither looked up. Their absence struck like flint against my ribs: once they'd rushed to meet my eyes—now I hovered outside their circle, a ghost of a different kind.

Keshtuat wiped her mouth. "Do you think they see the shadows?"

"No," I said, feeling the chill return beyond the lamplight. "That sight appears reserved for us—at least tonight."

Ana-Kharu was jovially talking with several of the local sailors. The men laughed aloud and offered him a pipe to smoke, but he declined. Ana-Kharu finished his tea and pointed North. "A sailboat takes us the last stretch of river. After that, our feet and your birds must do the finding."

A raven called overhead, breaking the hush. The birds banked east, black wings cutting the sky. I straightened, heart steadying. "The passage is near. Drink, then follow. We will outrun the dead soon enough."

Tea drained, shadows at our backs, we stepped from under the palm—and the desert swallowed us again.

The royal-blue sail billowed full, and the wind pressed us upriver until the trio of pyramids breached the skyline—first pale as ghosts, then sharpening into titanic wedges of stone.

We drifted past the last green of the floodplain and into raw sand. A narrow harbor opened like a wound between dunes; flanking it, two granite obelisks climbed forty cubits into the air, their tips still gilded, burning in the late sun. Our little felucca slipped in at dawn, among barges gilded for princes and cedar craft heavy with tribute. Merchants and tribal chiefs bartered, too busy to notice ragged pilgrims.

We disembarked in silence. Ahead, the great pyramid rose in impossible angles; its limestone casing still caught flecks of daylight, as if the sun itself were imprisoned in each block.

Keshtuat's breath hitched. "By the gods... it is bigger than a mountain."

Sarawat only nodded, her voice lost somewhere between awe and fear.

Yet the monument felt sealed—every face smooth, every seam invisible. *How will Djehuty find us—or we him?* I doubted a king of such renown would stroll out to greet the uninitiated.

Our ravens answered with ragged caws, circling tight above the sand.

"Let them scout," I whispered.

We followed their loop into the open plateau of Bu Wizzer, passing small Amunite encampments where evening fires already smoked. With each step our sandals sank, and the desert seemed to drink our strength. Caw. Caw. Caw. The birds wheeled, then banked east, toward a dark silhouette half-buried in drifted sand.

A breath later the horizon blushed—first violet, then molten gold—as the sun appeared. Light struck that silhouette, and stone ignited crimson.

Tadushet gasped. "Look, the lion."

But not merely a beast: the head was human, serene and stern, shoulders broad as a temple façade, paws longer than barges. Sunlight bled across the weathered flanks, turning the limestone the color of fresh heart-blood.

"The Red Lion," I murmured, awe scouring every doubt. "The guardian of the hidden door."

Just then shadow forms slid between caravans—men, women, *children*—thin as smoke, eyes luminous with grief. They clustered at the edge as though barred from crossing.

Keshtuat drew close. "More Shadow People."

I nodded. "Spirits the Amunites left outside eternity. They want passage—but I have no gate for them." My whisper cracked. *Aten, see them.* No answer came, only the hush of wind and the low roll of raven wings.

Ahead, the sphinx burned red under a bleeding morning sky, and the ravens dived toward a seam of darkness at its base. The true journey—through stone, shadow, and lion's mouth—was about to begin. As we moved off the crowded dock and onto the desert path, ravens wheeled low, their cries urgent.

"Eyes open," I whispered. "They have seen something."

Sand sucked at our sandals; every stride felt uphill. Shadow People slid between caravans—hollow eyes fixed on me alone. Children this time, too, tugging at spectral hems. My chest tightened. *Why must I be their witness?* I steadied my breath, scanning for the birds.

Caw. Caw. Caw. Three black shapes banked West, toward a seam of darkness at the pyramid's base.

"There," I said, pointing skyward. "Follow their wings. The door is calling."

My fellow avians shielded me as we soared around the four-sided giants, vision sharpened, scanning every seam for a hidden way in. Nothing. A magnetic pulse radiated from the basalt capstone of the largest pyramid, surging through our wings like a silent drumbeat. We felt enlivened in our endeavors to seek entrance. Our next stop was the large body of a lion with a beautifully carved face of a hueman. Worshippers knelt between its colossal paws, unaware of the four birds weaving above on sacred errand.

Again, we glided, light of wing, in search of a doorway into the limestone statue. We found nothing. Meanwhile, those on two feet struggled in their passage across the desert plateau.

"Merit-Aten, we see no way in. The blocks are laid tight, said the ravens.

"Where to now," asked Ana-Kharu as he startled me back to the land when my head was in the air. He raised his right hand, demonstrating the vastness of the Per-Neter, pyramid, and House of God.

The site was so awe-inspiring. We were in the land of Bu Wizzer, the land of Osiris, and the ether was energized. It was like we had left a shell of us behind and were now stepping into the unknown. My mind scanned over everything my father had ever told me. This pyramid, as Archollos would call them, pyramidos, meant fire in the middle. I recalled the glyph: Asgat Nefer —legs in motion beneath the head of a vessel pouring water. Asgat, the same name as that feral white cat with the watery blue eyes that taught me the meaning of freedom, for she declared that she was far freer than I would ever be in my royal cage. I felt sad for her having to scavenge for scraps from the butcher's market to feed her kittens. Yet, she could travel anywhere she wished; she flowed, just like water. Water. If it was the glyph for these pyramids, then it also must carry the resonance and frequency of the pyramids, which must be a clue.

"Water. We must find the water that feeds the pyramids," I said to the group now gathered around me.

"We are in a desert. Can you not see that nothing is growing on these plains," said Ra-Awab, holding his hand to his eyes and looking for the meaning.

"There's something alive in the air," murmured Archol-los, eyes narrowed. "Even if we found an entrance, how do you Imagine we could enter a structure like this that has kept men at bay for thousands of years?"

Sarawat's voice quivered. "Would we not all burn up?"

It was, of course, a good question and one I feared. "There must be an answer," I said looking into their eyes. "My father told me we know more than we believe, and we must put that knowledge into effect. Purpose. Always purpose." I would not give up until I found a clue. Gazing up at my dove still circling with the ravens, I called them all to me. My three sisters turned to me immediately. We felt that bond. *Find the water.*

The avians immediately flew to the North, South, East, and West, and zoomed overhead with eyes surveying the huge plot. We scoured the land, searching, waiting. Minutes passed. Then an hour. Sweat dripped down my spine. Were we wrong? Had my father mislead me?

Then—something shifted.

A whisper in the wind. A tremor in the sand. My dove, dove downward, vanishing behind a dune. My heart skipped. "Follow her," I commanded, my voice hoarse.

We ran. And when we reached the dip in the land. With a sudden rush of flapping wings overhead, she dropped a single leaf that floated down, twisting and turning until I could grasp it from the sky.

"Look, this dove just dropped a clove leaf into our midst. Smell it. Cloves need fertile soil and water to survive. Wherever she got it is where we will look," I said confidently with a brisk walk.

The others trailed me. I spoke to my dove, the bird known for finding water. It all made sense now why she would appear. Without hesitation, she led us to a patch of lushness.

"My mama used cloves to purify our home," said Keshtuat, lifting it to her nose.

Tadushet smelled the leaf. "Cloves help us manifest our goals."

We nodded. I looked closer at the patch of greenery and did not notice anything unusual.

"Ana-Kharu," I called. "Use your inner eye and see if we can uncover the meaning of the water for the pyramids." He tasted it. Listening to what the wind said, and attuned to his ancestors to find the meaning. "They tell me to look at the Per Neter glyph, *Asgat Nefer*; the water looks like steps going into the land."

"Yes!" I exclaimed. "My father would tell me of the ancient aquifers that power this pyramid and supply the land with energy. The steps will reveal themselves. The second glyph is *Nefer*, which is harmony. We must come together in harmony and open our hearts. Only then will the steps appear."

The others nodded, and we put our arms around each other, embracing the love as brothers and sisters that we had cultivated over these years of hardship and testing.

"Pulse it into the land," advised Smenkhkare, who was so attuned to the whisper of trees and winds.

"We must hurry," I said, breath catching, as the Shadow People drew closer. Their voices sliced through the veil, low and guttural, like smoke curling around my spine.

They were no longer faceless wisps in the distance. They emerged now in full form—ashen limbs, stretched thin like the memory of flesh. Their eyes, sunken and lidless, pulsed with silver-blue light, not of life but of longing. They did not walk but floated just above the ground, robes in tatters that fluttered without wind, their shapes flickering between child and elder, mother and soldier, victim and priest.

"You said you would return for us," one whispered, its mouth unmoving, yet the voice echoed from deep inside my skull. "But you rose into light... and left us in the dark."

I staggered, hands rising to my ears as if they could block the grief pouring in. It was true. I thought I left them back in Thebes, the city of Amunites. The air around them warped, thick with sorrow and decay. My stomach churned. My knees weakened.

"We watched you chant. We watched you float," said another, its face half-collapsing, features barely held together by memory. But when the blood came, you vanished."

A third, smaller form stepped forward. A child. Head shaved, eyes vast and ancient. "Where were you," it asked, "when the scales tilted?"

And then—"The good. The bad. The none. In full effect."

Their chorus was jagged, dissonant, vibrating with the pain of abandonment. The heat of the desert faded. The sand beneath my feet might as well have felt like ash. I felt split wide—one half tethered to the living, the other pulled into their cold longing. My knees buckled under the weight of their grief. I bit my lip until I tasted blood. Why me? Why was I cursed to remember what no one else could bear to see? The Forgotten? The Amunite sacrifices? They called them offerings—but who offers children to a god? Who burns the breath of the innocent to feed a throne? A god who demands blood is not a god at all—but a shadow crowned.

"Hurry Ana-Kharu—make the ground move, I cannot hold them off," I said, my throat dry.

With narrowed eyes he lifted a hand to his brow, blocking out the sun. With clarity he saw them approach. The others were oblivious. The Shadow People sang their unholy song—that wakes the dead because they had nothing to lose.

"We were the ones behind the veil,
The hands that built your holy trail.
You sang of stars, we dug the graves,
While chanting priests declared us saved.
We were the bones beneath the stone,
The names you carved, but not our own.
You burned your oils, you burned the sage—
But never touched our silent rage.
You climbed the steps and called it light,
We held the torches through your night.
You praised the sun and kissed the sky—
But turned your head when we would die.
You said you would come back for the dead.
But you floated away, crowned in gold and red.
Where were you when the scales tilted?
Where were you when the temples wilted?
The good. The bad. The none.
We are the cost of what you have done."

Something in their siren-song unspooled my will—each voice a thread from my past, each flicker a memory I could not look away from. The ones who bled to build Khemit. The Sesh—the profane who were sacrificed to the dark god, Amun. Their sorrow was a mirror, and I, entranced, stepped toward it as if it might finally explain my own sorrow. I fell to my knees staring at them. Not from fear. Not from reverence. But from the weight.

The weight of their eyes—eyes that never closed in death. The weight of their voices—singing truths too bitter for the priests to record. The weight of memory—mine, and not mine, passed down like an invisible crown laced with ash.

"I see you," I whispered, though my throat burned. "I have always seen you."

First when my father escaped Thebes—when we rode under stars toward Akhet-Aten, and the veil thinned just enough for me to glimpse the forgotten. I saw them again when the tomb swallowed me whole in the Valley of the Kings—when I breathed stone and bled silence, and their shadows waited like mourners with no funeral.

They were always there. And I—I who sang the hymns, wore the white linen, kissed the glyphs—I turned away. I thought if I just shined bright enough, I could redeem us all. But light without truth is just another form of blindness.

"You want to know where I was," I said, rising to my feet, my voice thrashing the darkness.

"I was praying with clean hands, while your bones were being broken. I was dancing in temple courtyards, while you begged to be remembered. I was a daughter of the sun, cloaked in divine favor—and I did not see the blood beneath the gold."

I opened my arms wide now, my eyes transfixed upon the circling dark. "But I do now."

And if I must bleed to balance the scales, I will. Not to earn forgiveness—but to remember rightly."

A gasp broke from Keshtuat's throat. Tadushet whimpered and clung to Sarawat.

The others shuffled backward, eyes wide. Oya began to chant under her breath—an old nursery prayer.

"Make them go," someone whispered. "Please make them go."

"Have you gone mad?" Ana-Kharu hissed, fingers biting my shoulders. "Do not draw them closer."

Okun stepped in beside him, "Invite the dead and they will drown you in their grief."

"Hold formation. Merit—now," commanded Ana-Kharu. The sound shattered my mesmerization. We must open the earth while we still can." He turned to the class; voice edged with steel and grace. "You are not alone. You are not prey. Remember who walks with you."

Archollos stepped forward like a soldier called to war. "Still yourselves," he said, his voice low but commanding. "They feed on panic. Breathe through it."

Smenkhkare raised both palms, eyes closed. "Anchor," he said. "Return to the breath. To the earth beneath your feet. The Aten is watching."

Anakharu spun me, forcing my gaze from the shadows. "Breathe," he commanded.

Anpu echoed, his voice a drum: "Heart to earth, blood to stone, body to ground."

Ana-Kharu lifted his hands. "Sound is the bridge between the seen and the unseen," he murmured. Then he chanted, voice deep, resonant. The air rippled. The earth trembled. Then, like ink bleeding through parchment, a shimmer spread across the sound. The ground darkened. A shape formed—a stairway. Descending into the unknown. *Moments ago, nothing. Now, a stairway opened like a secret remembering itself—etched into stone all along, waiting for our harmony to awaken it.*

"Quick," said Ana-Kharu as he took Sarawat's hand and pulled her forward. "We must hurry."

The Shadow People surged. Flickering shapes caught between worlds. No footprints, no breath, only the press of presence. A child's hand reached—I stumbled. Cold air seized my lungs. They were here. They saw me. And they were waiting. The Shadow People drew closer now. A mass of flickering shapes, caught between light and darkness. No footprints marked their passes, yet they moved with unnatural speed. Forces warped with silent agony, turned toward me. Lips moved, but no sound came forth.

I swayed. The ground seemed to tilt. Then—Ana-Kharu's arms gripped mine. "Enough," he said. "Enough of the Wested. Now return to the living." And with one decisive pull, he dragged me down—just before the dark could claim me Ana-kharu snapped the passage shut behind us.

The limestone stairway curved in a spiral, its edges smooth from ancient passage but still humming with an energy that prickled the skin. The deeper we went, the more the air thickened—not with dust, but with something alive. I felt it in my bones—like memory, like pulse.

The walls weren't raw cavern rock. They were carved pillars, colossal and perfectly aligned, descending like ribs into the earth. Their fluted shafts bore symbols I had only ever seen in temple scrolls—glyphs of stellar descent, lion-headed guardians, and the Eye of the Hidden Architect. This wasn't just a passage. It was a cathedral. A tomb. A transmitter.

Ana-Kharu touched one of the pillars, eyes narrowing in reverence. "This geometry," he whispered, "is not made for men." He placed his palm against the stone and closed his eyes. "This is living stone. It listens."

Sarawat gasped, brushing her fingers along a groove filled with what looked like blue pigment. "Who paints in the dark?" she whispered.

"Those who do not need eyes," replied Tadushet, her voice hushed with awe. "Or those guided by memory."

I swallowed hard. "We were never meant to see this," I said. "Not yet. Not untested."

As we reached the final step, a sound met us—rushing water, urgent and fast. The stairs ended at a black river winding through a high-vaulted cavern. Light was scarce, but the air was rich with minerals and moss. Every breath felt like an initiation.

Ana-Kharu reached into his pack, retrieving the rope he had been quietly braiding during the journey. "I wondered why I felt the need to do this," he said softly, looping it around each of our waists. "Now I understand. It is time to swim. The river does not ask who is worthy. Only who is willing."

He tied the last knot around Ra-Awab's waist.

Ra-Awab's eyebrows raised. "We swim into the dark?"

Ana-Kharu met his gaze. "Or we remain here, in the half-known. I would rather move forward."

Keshtuat chuckled nervously, dipping her toe into the water. "Well... at least it is not boiling."

I stood silent, feeling the cavern pulse around us. I could still sense the Shadow People above, pacing just beyond reach. They couldn't descend—but they had not released us. I could feel their lament vibrating through the stone.

"Sound is the bridge between the seen and the unseen," I whispered, more to myself than the others. I stepped closer to the river's edge and lowered my fingers into the current. It was cold. Vibrating. Alive.

Then the voices of the Ancients rose around us—not loud, but steady: "Real ascension kneels in the mud. It shows up barefoot in the storm. It does not flinch at shadow."

Ana-Kharu dipped his hand in next, and the water rippled—not outward, but inward, as though it recognized him. "It wants us to remember," he said. "But it will not carry what we refuse to let go."

We looked at one another. Anpu helped the women into the water and whispered, "Our souls bound by fate and now rope," and he nodded right before he jumped in.

I closed Ana-Kharu he lifted me down to the water. I whispered to the river, to my father, to the hidden gods, "Let this be the way. Let this be the beginning."

And then we stepped in. One after the other. Into the myth. Into the current. Into the place the gods had hidden, not to keep us out—But to see who would dare return.

26

Stretching and yawning, Morainya turned over, and her hand hit the pillow that Iben had laid his head upon. Her fingers brushed something cold and metallic. She sat up, blinking against the dim morning light and held it in her palm—a black Nefertiti head, gold filigree crowning the elongated headdress. Dangling the pin was a delicate watch, the kind that seemed to hold time itself captive.

Tucked beneath it was a receipt with a handwritten note: Until next time I see you. Love to my Infinite Queen.

She exhaled sharply, her chest tightening. Queen. That word again. That face again.

She traced the smooth metal, her mind replaying the way his voice had echoed through her body without sound, the way her own fingers had moved without control. *We are One.*

As if he controlled her fingers, her hands unclasped, and her own finger on her right hand tapped her heart. *We are One.* This thought rolled round and round in her head like clothes churning in a dryer. She got out of bed, and it still smelled like an erotic mist had been pulled from her and lingered on her Egyptian cotton sheets, the one luxury she simply insisted upon. A chill ran through her—not of fear, but of recognition. This wasn't just about him. This was about her. About something ancient, pressing against the walls of her consciousness, begging to be remembered.

Morainya washed her face, pulled back her hair in a scrunchy, and threw on a summer dress. This was new; Morainya was more of a jeans and sweater gal, having worked for years in the corporate world of presentation, and now she rejected formality, but somehow, she felt renewed and resurrected. Her attire should match the lightness. She needed to do some grocery shopping, and she really needed some girl time. She texted her best friend, Shelley: *Can you meet for brunch? Same place. You pick the time. As she hit send, she knew it was now or never.*

Shelley's reply popped up. *How's 11?* Morainya gave a thumbs up. Sealed the deal.

Sal's Second Notice in reply to Kanberg's next scare letter took her half as much time to prepare. Gathering up her neatly rubber-banded envelopes and all the accompanying forms, Morainya drove to the post office and stood in line—again. She felt invigorated and knew she had to take advantage of the renewal before she changed her mind and second guessed herself. On the passenger seat, the stack of envelopes waited like a ticking bomb. If she mailed them there would be no turning back. She picked one up, running her fingers along the folded edges, the thick envelope reminded her of what was at stake.

Could she really go through with this?

The thought of Kanberg's sneering voice, his cold dismissal of her as nothing more than a petulant child, sent a surge of anger through her chest. She simply had to do it.

With a deep breath, she turned the ignition off. Pause.

Morainya walked to the window with a gray-haired woman with eyes the color of seaweed—peeled labels, stamped, signed, and shoved the stack over the counter. $143.84, she droned. The price of liberation.

Paying with her credit card, Morainya calculated that this little venture had already cost her $250.00. Hopefully, this will take care of it. When she had completed the task—Morainya felt elated, no...free—freeeer. She jumped back into her car, grabbed the steering wheel and sobbed from exhaustion. It was done. She had taken the next step.

Eleven rolled around just as Morainya had rolled up to the Salty Dog Breakfastery, a local café that had been her and Shelley's go-to place for farm-to-table food for the last 15 years. She fixed her hair and added a dab of lipstick. The Santa Cruz Ocean salt air filled her lungs the moment she stepped from the car, this, she remembered, is why she stayed in this beach town. The sun warmed her, as the seagulls begged for food above. Aqua blue sky with big puffs of cumulus clouds floated overhead. She waited in line for the next seat in this local favorite not often found by over-the-hillers, meaning those who drove from San Jose.

She caught Gloria's eye—the receptionist and who led her to a back table near the Oxygen Bar, just out of earshot of brunch gossip and close enough to feel like a secret.

Shelley burst through the doorway trailing roses and lavender, and Queen Anne's Lace—like she was arriving at a wedding nobody planned. They stood and embraced. Morainya was surprised by how grounding it felt.

"How ya doin?" asked Shelley as she swept in with that Beach Boys California Girl vibe.

Morainya smiled ear to ear, like the Cheshire cat, in that same elusive way that didn't need words.

"Well, someone is glowing. Are you pregnant?" asked Shelley with a smirk.

"Hardly."

"Ohhh, then you definitely got laid? I want every single dirty detail," she said, eyebrows wiggling like antennas tuned to scandal.

Morainya pulled back, surprised by her own uncertain reaction. "Well... not exactly. It might have been... better?" she said, though even her own voice didn't believe it yet.

"Explain," demanded Shelley, leaning forward. "Did you meet someone you haven't told me about?"

Morainya's face lit up. "Yes, I did, and he spent the night." Well, most of the night, she thought.

"Go on. Who is this mystery man." Shelley took her napkin and folded it on her lap.

"You hit that nail on the head. He's Moroccan. He is a man of mystery," replied Morainya, running through her head about what exactly she knew about Iben that she could share. It's not that he was vague; in fact, they talked non-stop about her family, her legal problems, and her problems with her ex. When it came time for her to ask him, she realized that he deflected the questions with his charming personality. Only now did it register—she knew almost nothing real about him. He listened, held space, even made her laugh. But when it was her turn to ask... he'd vanished behind charm. Except his sister's trauma. He said he had a big family and that he stayed with friends when he was in town. Did that mean that he didn't even live in California, and that she was in a long-distance relationship?

"You are killing me here. What's his name? What does he look like? Where'd ya meet him?" Shelley dropped her menu when the waitress came around to take early orders. "We'll have the small stack of sourdough pancakes with tofu scramble, extra avocado for her, and I want onions and red peppers in mine."

Morainya nodded, "Perfect."

"Thanks, I'll be right back," said the waitress.

"Tell me everything." Shelley leaned forward, elbows on the table like she wasn't giving up.

"I met him last February while I was home in San Francisco during that deposition I told you about. He lives in Moroccan and travels back and forth. He isn't like anyone I've ever met."

"A foreigner. My friends are from Morocco. What city?"

Morainya's face tightened. "I don't actually know. He never said."

Shelley squinted. "What does Josh think about him?"

Morainya looked down, tapping her finger on the mug. "I haven't introduced them yet. I guess I wasn't sure if he'd stick around long enough to matter."

The hard stare back, told Morainya she might be making a mistake. "You let him spend the night, and Josh doesn't even know you are dating?"

"Dating? Well, I'm not sure I can call it that. He comes and goes a lot." Morainya wrinkled her nose because it didn't sound like a good match when she thought about it.

"It was a one-night stand with an exotic foreigner. That's not like you, but good job. You are loosening up a bit. Was he hung well?" She took her fingers and pulled them apart to imply size.

Morainya flushed—not from shame, but from the certainty that this wasn't a story to strip down and giggle over.

How could she explain that it hadn't just been sex, but a union? That he touched her without touching her, and it shattered something open?

"This is gonna sound crazy, but you have to trust me—we had sex. Just... not the kind you can describe. It was like a ghost made love to me. But not just a ghost. Him. His soul."

"Without really touching you?" Shelley jerked her head back and mouthed, whaaattttt?'

"Yes. I know it sounds supernatural, or something," she paused, and sipped her chai.

"Kinda like Astral Sex? I heard about it on one of those Ghost Shows that reenact other worldly stuff. This woman's husband died 20 years ago, but on their anniversary, she swears he shows up and has dinner with her, like she can see him, or right through him. Then they dance and go to bed, and she swears they have sex, but there wasn't anyone there in the morning."

"Astral sex?" Morainya blinked. "That's actually a thing? Her face twisted somewhere between awe and horror.

"Yeah, all kinds of people write in and tell their stories. You should be interviewed," said Shelley suddenly enchanted by the thought of a new way to do it. She wanted to push her friend to reveal her otherworld intimacies.

She shook her head. "No thanks. My life has been turned upside down lately, and I don't want to add fuel to the fire."

"Turned upside down? In what way?"

Morainya leaned in. "I need to ask you something, and I mean really ask. What would you do if you found out a devastating secret about your family? Would you tell them the truth?"

Morainya squeezed Shelley's hand.

She rolled her eyes. "Will it help them or hurt them? That would be the question I'd ask before I'd divulge something That would tear my family apart."

"Don't they have the right to know?" asked Morainya.

Shell waved her other hand. "Will it kill them or set them free?"

"That is a good question. I don't know," replied Morainya, then shrugged, tightening her hands into fists by her side

"Would you want to know?" Shelly took a sip of coffee.

"Absolutely!" Morainya exclaimed. "If it put the pieces of the puzzle together that never made sense before, then I'd have to know."

"Then you should tell them. Stuff usually gets uncovered down the line, and if they discover that you withheld information, then they'll be pissed anyway." She flipped her blond hair back over tanned shoulders.

"But what if everything you believed was a lie? Everything. It's ripping me apart, Shel. Some days, I can barely get out of bed. I wake up inside a fog, like my own life has turned against me. I don't know who I am anymore. I'm in constant pain that I have had to push through. It's like I can't tell what's up or down." Morainya wrung her hands.

"Mor, that sounds scary. You should talk to a therapist. You aren't gonna?" she drew a line across her throat, implying suicide.

"No, I don't want to take my life. That's not what I'm talking about. It's just that my family, my church, the justice system, nothing, and I mean nothing, is what I was told. I feel like Jim Carey in the movie, *The Truman Show*—like I'm the only one who didn't get the script."

Shelley chuckled. "Yeah, I know the one. I have the DVD. I love that movie."

"Remember the moment the stage-light falls? Truman stares up, and sees the hatch, and climbs out of the set. That's me—only the hatch is everywhere."

Shelley raised an eyebrow and glanced around the restaurant checking for eavesdroppers. "Honestly? "That's pretty scary if you ask me. I don't think I'd want to know. Just let me have my dirty martinis on the beach with a good erotic novel and let the light stay put."

"You wouldn't want to know the truth, if you were Truman and discovered that it was all an illusion?"

She shrugged, voice puffing up in defense. "Why wake from a pretty dream? I've got surf, good food, and a prom-queen daughter."

The words cracked open something in Morainya. Maybe most people didn't want to wake up—and maybe that was allowed. She would have to let them sleep. Waking up wasn't for the faint of heart.

"Now, enough about me," she said, exhaling. "Tell me about your daughter's Senior Disneyland trip and College acceptances?"

Shelley launched into the news, but Morainya drifted. The café's blue-and-white checks, the kitschy chickens, the basket of plastic produce—all suddenly looked like props. Shelley's spray tan, push-up bra, bleached hair: the same set dressing. Pretty, but tight, like shoes that blister no matter how often you wear them. It was time to break away from her past. Shelley was like wearing a pair of tight-fitting shoes that had rubbed her the wrong way and made blisters, but because they were pretty, Morainya kept putting them back on.

I've broken with my church, claimed my living-woman status, mailed the Notices, she thought. *Why am I still trying to fit into someone else's scenery?*

The waitress said, "Ready for your oxygen infusions?"

"I'll do the Wake-Me-Up vitamin C, lavender," Shelley chirped. "She'll do the Come on, Baby, immunity drip with Passion Fruit."

Morainya raised a palm. "Actually, I'll have the Egyptian Blue Lotus drip with a touch of frankincense."

Shelley blinked. The waitress nodded and left.

For the rest of the visit, they breathed oxygen infusions in near-silence—Shelley scrolling her phone, Morainya watching sunlight glitter on the ocean through the window.

The quiet felt honest. And that, finally, was good.

Stanley Kanberg stepped into the firm's executive conference room of the Kanberg, Wallerstein and Katz. A table of polished elite attorneys and senior partners sat stiffly, their faces lined with concern. The air was thick—too many egos, too little fresh oxygen. He hated Accounts Receivable Meetings, and he especially hated the dressing-downs that often came with them.

Sarah Stein, the Managing Partner, and Bernie Wallerstein, the Senior Partner, were already involved in a heated discussion with Rachel Slade, the Accounts Receivable Manager, who was running her finger down the ledger.

Bernie Wallerstein didn't bother to look up as he waved Stanley in, tapping a manicured finger on the table as he spoke. "This is a priority," he announced. A sensitive matter concerning Morainya Napolitano." His voice carried that casual authority that let everyone know this was not a discussion—it was a directive.

"The Napolitano family, one of San Francisco's longtime patrons have been long-term clients." Bernie continued, "We successfully reached a settlement between Morainya and her Uncle Aldo Napolitano. This family is now 90 days past due, and the outstanding balance has reached a point where it is impacting our cash flow. Stanley, would you care to bring us up to speed with the collection?"

Stanley adjusted his glasses. "As you know, Bernie, this is a delicate case. The Napolitano family helped build this firm. When Stephano Napolitano was alive, payments were prompt. Now, this past due balance is $98,658—including partners, associates, and admin fees from the Settlement Conference. Over 310 billable hours. Rachel, you 've reached out to Morainya. Could you update us?" Stanley had been loyal to Stephano Napolitano. But loyalty didn't pay invoices. If it came between protecting Morainya or preserving the firm—his choice was already made.

Rachel tapped her red pen on the Accounts Receivable ledger nervously. "I had a phone conversation with Morainya Napolitano about two month ago," she drawled. "She indicated that she was having a problem with cash flow due to the lawsuit by Aldo Napolitano. She was making consistent payments over the course of these nine months, but now they've trickled to a few hundred dollars over the last three months. Of course, we've discussed that she has been paying these out of her personal account, not the Napolitano estate, of which she is an executor. Aldo filed against her personally."

Bernie straightened his tie, and said, "That's concerning, Rachel. Have you suggested a payment plan?"

Rachel looked down to recalculate figures, "That would have been my next call, but Morainya has refused to return my last two calls."

Sarah's head hurt. Clients with money issues put the firm in jeopardy. "We can't let this drag on. We were more than fair and understanding during the Settlement Conference. Doesn't she still have large payments due from the Depositions?" asked the Managing Partner, who glanced at her watch, feeling her ire rise. She was hoping to make it to her son's award ceremony for the National Math Match.

"Yes," replied Rachel. "We are still waiting for her to cover the court costs, the Deposition fees, etc."

Bernie's veins bulged in his forehead, his voice rising. "Stanley, this is your client. Perhaps we should scare her a bit by sending this to a collection agency? What can you add to this discussion?"

Stanley Kanberg rubbed his right Limited Edition Santoni shoe under the table. It was brand new and pinched his toes. For $2,500.00, they could at least fit right. "We have suspended all services until she is caught up. I have a good relationship with her; honestly, she is a bit naïve about how these legalities work. We have shown her goodwill and flexibility; now it is time for her to reciprocate. Stanly looked directly at Bernie. "I have also let her know that I have used a light pen when calculating the monthly bills, but maybe it is time to demonstrate the severity of defaulting on a contract." Stanley said, voice clipped. "I will try a stronger approach. She thinks of me as a father figure as I have been closest to her dad through his business dealings. I will appeal to her as an authority figure. Stanly softened his voice and looked at Sarah for agreement. "I trimmed hours, shaved fees, even left off the calls where she cried on the phone. That goodwill's run out. Maybe it's time she sees what the real cost of mercy looks like on paper."

Bernie nodded, "I think that is a good approach."

There was an urgent knock on the door, and Ginny stuck her head in. "Apologies for the interruption," Ginny said, breathless at the door, "but these Notices just arrived from Morainya Napolitano. I think you'll want to see them."

Stanley's young assistant handed him the opened envelopes along with the accompanying Notice of Acceptance and Notice of Inquiry addressed to Bernie and Stanley. They read through the pages and both Partners grimaced.

"Who the hell does she think she is?" Stanley snapped, scanning the document. "After everything this firm did for her?" He threw his two Notices down on the table dismissively. Stanley's stomach clenched. He had received one of Morainya's Notices two weeks ago but didn't take it seriously because no other law firm was attached. He just chucked it into the paperwork pile, thinking he'd get to it after attending to clients who paid on time.

"I can't say I've ever seen anything like this?" Bernie muttered. "Stanley...do these have any legal merit? You realize this isn't addressed to the law firm; it is personally addressed to us as individuals."

Stanley scoffed. *What an ungrateful little idiot,* he thought. "She can't do this. Separating us from the firm? That's a liability nightmare—no umbrella coverage, no indemnity." Stanley suddenly felt the gut punch. "Look at this second

Notice and these ridiculous questions she's asking. We aren't required to address any of this nonsense, are we?"

Bernie's frown deepened. "Is there precedent for this? Start pulling case law—now. Start doing some research. Is she now one of those Sovereign Citizens? We will not tolerate any of this conspiracy mumbo jumbo. We have to handle this immediately because our firm will set no allowance for this ridiculous argument to permit delinquency on accounts receivable." His heart pounded. He hated chasing money—but loved making the wealthy suffer.

Stanley waved his notice. "She is questioning our jurisdiction—claiming she's not subject to state or federal laws. Stanley said, his voice tightening. "This is the first time I've encountered anything like this?"

Sonia Oppenheim leaned forward, "As General Counsel, this Sovereign Citizen movement is just a fringe ideology. These claims have no legal basis and are consistently rejected by the courts." Sonia exhaled slowly. "Still, this could complicate collection. If she leans into this ideology, it becomes a circus. Courts hate sovereign cases—they clog the docket and go nowhere."

Soloman Abraham straightened his cuffs, his voice calculated. "As Head of Litigation, legally, we are on solid ground—But this? It's a reputational landmine. No judge wants a circus in chambers. The last thing we need is to set a precedent that could open the floodgates for other clients pulling this Sovereign Citizen stunt. Ignoring her Notices could provoke more aggressive actions."

Bernie nodded, feeling momentary relief.

Soloman continued, "I must add, what exactly is the firm's liability when she has Noticed you two personally?"

He glanced at Bernie and Stanley before leaning back in his seat—putting distance between them. "Do you need to obtain your own representation? It would be a conflict of interest for Kanberg, Wallerstein, and Katz to respond."

Stanley felt his shoe pinch when he tried to flex his toes. "I think it would behoove us to craft a firm yet professional response, making it emphatically clear that we do not recognize the validity of any sovereign citizen argument. Morainya Napolitano is contractually bound to her financial obligation, therefore payment now must be received—in full." He searched the faces of the others, hoping for consensus.

Rachel spoke up, "I must add that she has already paid the three-million-dollar settlement fee. I believe it was wired to the opposing attorney's office and marked received. That is a hefty sum, albeit it doesn't change the balance on her personal account that is due to us."

Bernie smirked. He liked playing hard ball—especially when the other side had no glove, no bat, and no team. "This is desperation, nothing more. We'll remind her that we can place liens on her house, her car—hell, even her future inheritance. If she wants to play legal chicken, she'll lose."

"I will call her. I can put pressure on her other family members," said Stanley Kanberg, wiping his forehead.

Soloman exhaled sharply, "I'll draft the response. But we're poking a hornet's nest. If she doubles down, this won't just be an unpaid invoice. It'll be a reckoning."

Bernie smiled tightly then said, "At least it will make her reconsider this delay tactic."

Kanberg added, "This will most likely conclude in a favorable action by Morainya Napolitano in responding with a payment offer."

"Good," said Bernie. "Then we are in agreement. We must always put the firm first. Do I make myself clear? That's a direct order to each of you."

Later, sure enough, the phone buzzed. *Kanberg.* Just seeing his name sent a cold pulse down her spine. She didn't answer. Not because she was brave, but because she physically couldn't. Instead, she let it go to voicemail. She waited, listening to the sharp click of the message ending. Then, Her fingers trembled, she pressed play.

"Ms. Napolitano. This is your final warning. I strongly advise you to reconsider your course of action. Your father, Stefano, would be ashamed of you."

The hair on her arms and neck rose. *He brought her father into this?*

"As your family attorney, I am telling you—you clearly don't grasp the gravity of your position. If you persist, there will be consequences—legal and otherwise. We will escalate. And once we do you will have no way out. No allies. No leverage. No mercy."

A pause. Just long enough to let the hammer fall.

"Do the smart thing. Before it's too late." Kanberg said.

She dropped the phone. It landed face-down on the armrest of her mother's chair, but Kanberg's voice still rang in her skull like a judge's gavel. Her body seized—shoulders rigid, fingers numb, breath thin. This wasn't just a legal battle anymore. They were threatening her.

Her mother had once sat in this very chair, sipping red wine, staring blankly at the news, with empty eyes.

Morainya hadn't understood that stillness before—tight fingers on the glass, the vacant glaze. Now she did. Fear and slow loss of control.

Fear wasn't just paralyzing. It was a cage. She'd be damned if she was gonna drown in it.

For a moment, doubt crept in. Maybe she was being reckless. Maybe Kanberg was right.

Then Josh called. His voice carried that forced casualness that meant something was off.

"Hey, Mom. Kanberg left me a message." A pause. "Said you're making a mistake. That I should talk some sense into you."

The pit in her stomach hardened into something colder—like steel. They'd crossed a line coming after her son.

Josh tried to laugh it off—"Dude thinks I can stop you?"—but she heard it. The hesitation. The edge of unease.

They would have to work through this fear together.

At least he'd be gone this week—off on his senior trip to Disneyland. She could use the time to breathe. Get the house in order. To fortify herself. Because the battle was coming.

And she would not break.

27

*T*he current seized us, a force neither gentle nor merciful. We were not travelers—we were prey, caught in the jaws of the rushing waters, spit forth into the unknown. I struggled to keep my head above the churning waves, my body weightless, yet helpless, as if unseen hands dragged us deeper into an unlit abyss.

No ordinary cave—the walls pulsed with ancient resonance, a bone-deep hum. It was as if time itself bled through the stone, whispering forgotten names, histories lost beneath the flood of ages. Were we moving forward—or backward? Were we still ourselves, or echoes of those who passed through before?

I shivered, feeling exhaustion to my bones. I whispered a silent plea to the Aten, I prayed that this passage would lead us to revelation—and not oblivion.

The underground current had a purpose—it *spat only the brave into the Osirian Shaft—an underworld passage veiled beneath the Sphinx's sacred body.* At its heart lay a marble columned chamber, a pristine corridor carved from white stone. *I saw it now: the spurting Osirian Shaft was no mere tunnel. It was alive— a stone phallus...the* sacred key to the Sphinx's belly. Everything meant something. The true gift was the ability to read the hidden language of form—to know that every curve, every passage, ever drop of water whispered to the divine web. The true interpretation of the wisdom of the interconnectedness of all things.

Ana-Kharu hauled himself up on the granite landing. Then, one by one, we heaved ourselves ashore from the watery depths, our bodies trembling beneath the weight of drenched linen that clung like a second skin. I coughed, spitting out the grit of fine sand that had lodged between my teeth, the taste of the underworld still bitter on my tongue.

Although the air smelled damp, and a hollow echo of our words reverberated, we now stood between two columned pillars on a black and white tiled floor. A dry, ancient cut marble staircase invited us to ascend upward—a bridge between earth and heaven. An ornate brazier hung from the ceiling; fire inside cast a constellation of pin-prick lights through its pierced copper skin. It was enchanting, like tiny suns flickering throughout the room. But who tended this vestal flame?

The torchlight flickered, casting wild shadows against the towering pillars. Then—a figure stepped forward. My breath caught. My heart seized.

Archollos inhaled sharply beside me. "Rennutet," he uttered, disbelief cracking his voice.

Sarawat stumbled backward, hand pressed to her chest as if struck. "But... we buried you back in Dendera," she whispered.

Rennutet stepped into the light, and we saw—this was no phantom. Her white raiment shimmered, dry and untouched by death. The air itself shifted around her, the chamber recognizing her presence.

I whispered, "Rennutet?" My knees threatened to give way. She smiled, the same gentle curve I had known so well—but now, there was something more in her gaze. Something ancient.

"I was sent to welcome you," she said, her voice light as desert wind.

But how? I had held her lifeless body. After giving birth, my friend bled to death while I was the midwife. Her death had hollowed something in me—something I hadn't let anyone touch. Yet—here she was.

"It was not my time, and the guardians sent me back to lead you on your journey," she said evenly. The slight smile that was etched upon her face had not changed.

My classmates hovered at the threshold, eyes wide, feet unmoving—as if to touch her might break a spell or summon a curse.

"How do we enter this impenetrable fortress?" I asked in a mundane voice, even though I had just witnessed a miracle.

Ana-Kharu stepped forward without pause, as if he'd expected her—or had long since made peace with the veil between life and death. "This must be another puzzle. Of course, we would have to prove ourselves worthy to enter the Heart of the House of Fire."

The enormity of the perfectly cut granite blocks stacked in harmony would bring admiration from all masons and gave no indication of any opening.

"Why would there be stairs, if there is not a door?" asked Sarawat.

"I would say because only those who can open the door that cannot be seen in this world, would only allow true Initiates, Adepts, and Masters to access," I reasoned.

"Many are called, but few are chosen," replied Smenkh-kare, echoing my father's oft-repeated words.

"After coming so far, are we truly to be denied our meeting with Djehuty," cried Sarawat, her voice strained with fear that she might be one of the called—but not the Chosen.

My lungs burned with every breath, and soaked linen clung to my skin like a second, heavy shell. "This will require more than thinking. It must be a test, perhaps a culmination of all we have been taught and experienced through our lives."

"I agree. The answer is not without, but within," said Ana-Kharu, his hand resting on the pillar.

The memory rippled through me. "Stone breathing," I whispered—not to them, but to the part of me that remembered what it meant to survive the impossible. It was the final test. The one you could not afford to fail. A lesson Pentu brought to my awareness, first when he appeared through the tomb wall back at Akhet-Aten. The second time was when I was sealed for all Eternity in the tomb of Ti-Yee., my Grand Djedti. Whether it was out of fear or necessity because oxygen, the lifegiving source, had been cut off.

I had put my hands against the stone—solid, cold, unyielding. My breath hitched. This was madness. To walk through this, I had to convince my body that what it knew to be true—stone is impenetrable—was a lie.

"If you hesitate, the stone will consume you." Ana-Kharu's voice was steady, but the weight of his words settled over us. Their eyes darted between the wall and my face, wide and uncertain, like deer startled at the edge of a clearing. Doe-eyed stares returned my message of profundity; of course, it was only the Gold Magician who nodded with vigor and agreed.

I cleared my throat,"You are correct. It is the only way because we will be judged or purified in our passing."

"Let us begin, and may the Gods," he nodded at his troupe, "or the Aten," he said and flipped his head to us monotheistic worshippers who only gave devotion to one god—"Show mercy, if we never meet again, may your departure be swift, and your tale be worthy to tell those who have gone before you."

I shook my head in disbelief. That was not the tale of hope and camaraderie that would serve as inspiration for my classmates. Yet, there it was. A summation of what we were facing without honey-sweetened drizzle.

I swallowed hard. It was not just a door—it was a threshold between belief and disbelief, between existence and non-existence. To pass through, I had to become the stone. My pulse slowed. My breath deepened. I let go of fear. I let go of my body.

The stone exhaled, and I moved with it. That first step crushed time—a heartbeat stretched into eternity. Then, release. I stumbled through, breathless. I passed.

Ana-Kharu followed in my wake, emerging beside me with a smirk. The others? Silence. No one else had followed.

It was at that moment I came to the knowing that it was my path. It was the gift and curse that the Aten and the Celestial Lords gave me at my birth. Should I wait for more dust to collect upon the floor, or another turning of the sun, or take action?

He looked at me with those shining black orbs and conveyed; this is our ultimate initiation. I knew it to be true and gave testament to those words, for all of us must prove our merit. As Above, So Below.

Through the years of initiations, our mettle had been tested through fear, trepidation, greed, gluttony, hate, and love—all lead to this last initiation. Could we override our logic and use our cognition or limitlessness to permeate what appeared to be solid?

We spilled into the Sphinx's heart. Ana-Kharu pushed through, only a flyspeck after me.

Buoyed by triumph, we hovered near the wall, breath still ragged, waiting for the rest to join. Nobody. Absolutely nobody.

I waited with complete trust that this empty room would be overflowing with my fellow initiates and the Gold Magician's troupe at any moment.

Ana-Kharu burst out laughing, and his bemusement shattered my peaceful exterior. "Why on earth are you laughing?"

"Because it is clear, my Princess, that you chose the wrong King as your partner. Is it not evident who matches your vibration? Like it or not, it is just you and I who will continue on to meet Djehuty."

Archollos, I screamed his name internally but was met with silence. Smenkhkare? Will none of you join me? The finest Masters have trained you, and yet it is not in your making to ascend to the levels of playing that we have been asked to arise? Disappointment knotted my gut; my toes curled against cold marble, but alas, I must put that behind me if I wanted to move forward. "Now what?" was all I could eek out.

"We must play the Cosmic game. It will be one puzzle after another. You are the Magnetic force of the Feminine. I am the Electric force of the Masculine. Combined, we are the key that will unlock the Mysteries. Are you ready to play?" said Ana-Kharu with a bemused tone of expectation.

The cosmos laughed—quiet, merciless. The two of us who repulsed each other the most were now forced to combine our resources to move to the next level. I swallowed the sigh and bowed, inwardly, to whatever larger hand was at play. "How do we find Djehuty? This Sphinx is large."

Ana-Kharu's right eye twitched. "Let us not make any assumptions about where we are. That flowing underground river could have spewed us anywhere."

A muscle flickered beneath his right eye. "Go on," I murmured, tilting my head as the realization clicked into place: he was right. We had no idea where we were.

"Feel the grain," he murmured, palm on the stone. "You hear it? Younger than the Sphinx—this quarry sings a newer note. These blocks feel like they were quarried later than the Sphinx. Track the vibration of the star alignment, and we will know where we are."

I nodded and pictured the Great Lion and felt the resonance. Strangely, it did not match where we were standing. Then I felt the vibration of these stones, tracked them to the heaven world, and turned my inner eyes to the constellation above us. "Orion." Instead of the Great Red Sphinx that we aimed for, we found ourselves in the interior base of a pentahedron, a five-sided pyramid. We knew this to be true by the cut of the limestone.

A low laugh escaped him—half thrill, half disbelief. "We are not where we thought we were. Now, we must proceed with different calculations and attune to Orion. What do we know about Orion?"

"We are in the Land of Osiris, the Per Neter. The three pyramids are aligned with the stars on the belt of Orion. To unlock the next test, we must use the light language of Orion for these walls to welcome us."

Ana-Kharu's eyebrows arched, and he looked at me like he was impressed.

"I have been schooled by Pentu," I said, and shrugged. "Let us bring in the light of Orion from the apex of this pyramid and fill this room with green light."

"Yes—green, the sacred hue of Osiris. Good," Ana-Kharu affirmed.

As we stepped forward, a great map of Khemit burst into glowing life upon the wall, illuminated in primordial green—like embers from an ancient, hidden fire. Twelve points shimmered into being—some pulsing faintly like dying stars, others blazing with fierce lucidity. The chamber exhaled—and shifted, as if waking to ancient memory.

Another set of lights flickered above us—the star constellations, like a mirror of the land below. The walls lit up with the writing of Osiris. *The Metu Neter,* Words of God. A single phrase pulsed across the walls in blazing script: "Where are the 12 Nomes of Alchemy? The 42 Nomes of Osiris?"

Ana-Kharu exhaled sharply. "This is a test of alignment. We must find the path between heaven and earth."

I clenched my fists, my mind racing. The Nomes were the sacred divisions of the land—regions bound to celestial forces. But if we were to pass, we needed to match the earthly to the cosmic.

Ana-Kharu said first, his voice steady, "Let us start with Upper Khemit. First would be Sa-bu."

The first Nome flared brightly on the wall. Above us, a corresponding star glowed.

Relief bloomed in my chest, and I stepped forward, the memory of temple lessons stirring beneath my ribs. "Kalabsha—Temple of Mandulis."

Another light.

"Kom Ombo," Ana-Kharu added. "The Crocodile."

"And Horus the Hawk," I added.

A light twinkled.

"What would be fourth?" I pondered reaching up to touch the map. "Temple of Khnum?" I suggested.

Nothing happened. A dangerous silence thickened the air.

"No wait," I corrected, my breath hitching. "Edfu-The Temple of Horus. He is the bridge between realms."

We held our breath. The moment I spoke, a green pulse of fire streaked across the map. The lights linked together in a glowing path.

Ana-Kharu shot me a smirk. "Good. Then the next must be—I thrust up my hand. "Let us not rush." The air grew heavier. The more mistakes we made, the more the walls seemed to tremble. I shut my eyes, pushing past what I had memorized. I listened—felt—for the temple vibrations. "Fifth is the Temple of Khnum," I said as the primordial green appeared. I turned to Ana-Kharu. "Do you think Luxor or Karnak next?"

He hesitated. and answered for us both. "No. The Elders are saying no."

I nodded in agreement. The dead were with us—we had learned to listen.

"Then it would be Dendera next in line," said Ana-Kharu slowly.

"Temple of the Sky, of course, I whispered.

A deep hum filled the chamber as another point illuminated, connecting to the last. Ana-Kharu studied me now, waiting. I gave a small nod.

"Abydos," he said with confidence. "The Temple of Osiris.

The next point ignited. Sweat beaded my brow. We had completed seven—but the energy in the room was shifting. The unseen presence that had been watching us now stirred, impatient. We were running out of time.

"Akhet-Aten is Eighth," I said. We were thrilled again; the green light illuminated the map.

"Ankhtify," Herakleopolis is the Ninth Nome. That is where all the gold beads were made," added Ana-Kharu." The next sequence of lights appeared right on the city.

"What is next?" I asked, uncertainty clouding my thoughts.

Ana-Kharu shook his head. "I am afraid of guessing wrong." "So am I," I admitted. "But we cannot stall now." We shared a

resigned glance. "Take the next guess."

"Heliopolis?" I blurted out.

Nothing happened—except the pressure increased. The chamber pressed inward. Each breath felt like sipping smoke, and a pulse throbbed behind my eyes.

Ana-Kharu pressed his face closer to the map. "I have only been there once...Could it be Hawara?"

We received confirmation when a light lit up.

"How would you know that?" I asked, feeling gratitude.

"Old knowledge he said and pointed up."

"Tenth is Heliopolis," I said, thinking that it should be obvious because it was the revered center of this science. Yes, a light.

"Eleventh must be Giza, right where we stand," said Ana-Kharu planting his feet, deducing that the pyramid and Sphinx were significant. A light lit.

"Twelfth would have to be Saqqara, the Step Pyramid of Djoser," said Ana-Kharu. Again, the green light twinkled.

Ana-Khara clapped once. "Yes, the House of Life-Per Ankh, where medical, spiritual, and resurrection knowledge was stored, was thought to have been located there.

A series of light language ran across the top of the room. It repeated over and over.

"*Where did the Ben Ben meteor stone fall?*"

We almost shouted aloud. The chamber throbbed with unrelenting demand—our chests tight, minds fracturing beneath the invisible weight. Can we not take a moment?

The question flickered on and off, emphasizing the urgency, pushing us forward. No time for a break.

"I should know this," I replied, racking my brain.

"It is in my ancient memory," added Ana-Kharu.

"The Ben-Ben fell where we find the green glass," I scratched at my scalp, the memory clawing up from beneath layers of childhood awe—Father's Pectoral, that strange green gleam. Siwa!" I blurted out.

A circle appeared as if drawn by a mysterious hand right over the Siwa Desert. In the far West of the Khemit. More lines of green light language rushed around the top of the room, needing deciphering to proceed.

"*Why would the Aten reach every one of these sacred sights?*"

We shook our heads. How would that question be important. Then we repeated it, hoping to figure out how the glass related to the question.

"It is your God. What is the connection?" asked Ana-Kharu, his voice rising with immediacy.

While the Ben Ben stone was of great importance to the balance of Khemit, how did it relate to the Aten? My stomach rumbled, as if my body rebelled against the silence of the answer. Think. Think. I focused on the twelve sites and then looked at the circle around Siwa. Was it the glass? No light.

Let us draw a line toward the twelve streams from the Siwa site of impact. As if by magic, twelve green lines flowed from the Siwa circle until they reached the temples along the Nile.

"It is obvious," I shouted in glee. The circle is the Aten, and the lines are the hands that offered blessings toward each of the temples."

We only enjoyed a moment of success before the next question raced around the room.

Find the three stars of Sirius amongst the twelve.

The air thickened—an invisible vise clamped around my ribs.

Pentu told me this as a child, the last time in Heliopolis. "Sirius A, the brightest star, is Hierakonpolis. I pointed to my left eye. "The hidden red dwarf star is Sirius B." I pointed to my right eye.

Ana-Kharu smiled as if I was on to something. "That makes the Hidden star Sirius C Heliopolis, because the third star is the pineal gland that opens everything." He pointed to his third eye in the middle of his forehead.

A blue light lit up all three sacred sites, and at that moment, the wall we were facing swiveled. We had entered an entirely new realm. A large picture of an open pinecone appeared upon this wall in Sirian blue light language. Again, Sirius's language zipped around the room. "*What awakens when the pinecone unfurls?*"

I hung my head, "I...do not even know what a pinecone looks like."

Ana-Kharu mumbled to himself. The closed pinecone is male. Open is female."

No light. He was wrong. An intense grinding of gears startled us. The walls began to close in on us.

"Think of something," I yelled. "It will crush us."

Ana-Kharu's breath labored, and his eyes grew large with fright. "Ausar's, Osiris's, staff had a pinecone."

The blue light flashed on the pinecone. But the walls kept grinding.

I suggested, feeling my throat constrict, "There is more. The pinecone was offered as a gift in many raised relief scenes upon the Funerary Temple Walls."

The Magician nodded. "Good. The soul stone or pineal gland, The Philosopher's Stone," said Ana-Kharu with a hopeful voice.

The blue light flickered encouragement, yet the walls still advanced, leaving us confined and confused.

"Right. When turned on, the pinecone or pineal gland reflects the light of a higher source of consciousness. It is perfect. Ever present. Omnipresent. Eternal."

An ethereal voice boomed. "The pineal gland has 7 spiralium harmonics that align to the 7 chakras, 7 solar harmonic frequencies of the Sun and the 7 Sisters of the Pleiades

Sacred Solar frequencies of the Great Central Sun, Alcyone, the first star gods of the super civilizations 400 million years ago were from Alcyone."

With a great whooshing sound like the winds swirling in that empty chamber, the room turned to the next direction.

"We passed!" I cheered with relief.

Now, we were facing South—and there he stood. Not just a man, but a being worthy of reverence, his very skin glinting with the essence of stars. He wore a starched white linen sheath, with a glorious finely woven robe falling over his left shoulder and tied at the waist with a metallic belt. Ageless skin. He looked immortal.

"Ari Heru Neter. You have entered into the Sekhet-Aaru, he said with the same otherworld voice. "The realm of Supreme Peace. Merit-Aten and Ana-Kharu-We-Shat, you are the two that have reached resonance with the eternal now. It is quite an achievement to have come this far. I have had initiates for forty years or more only deemed to be in my presence in the Pyramid; the fire in the middle is the heart or soul realm.

"You are the Orama, the Most High Priest of Heliopolis," My breath caught. I knew that voice—knew that glinting robe. He had walked the halls of College of Anu, Sacred School of Alchemy, when I was a girl, his presence always more spirit than man.

"Merit-Aten, Daughter of the Pharaoh, I am honored to receive you for your lessons," he gave a nod of recognition.

"This is my friend, Ana—," I started to say.

"I recognize you from years ago when you arrived at Heliopolis demanding that I allow you to enter my school.

Do you know why I denied you?" The sacred man's voice reverberated off the limestone walls.

"No, my Lord. Please tell me?" Ana-Kharu's jaw tightened as he lowered himself to his knees, the stone biting into his skin, reverence outweighing pride."

"It was not your time. You had the persistence, you had the skill, and you even had the lineage to be accepted, but I could not allow it." The High Priest towered over the obeisant man before him.

"Why? It was the only thing I ever wanted," asked Ana-Kharu. "I dreamt about it. I worked hard to achieve alchemical equations and geometry. Yet, you denied me, over and over."

"I denied you because if I allowed you entrance, then I knew you could never leave. I needed you for this time. I needed you to accompany Merit-Aten for the duration of your long, arduous journey that put you two in resistance. I needed the friction that ignited the fire of the Cosmos for you two to complete what is still before you." The High Priest's gaze swept between us—not as a man regarding students, but as one reading the constellations already written into our fate.

Ana-Kharu hung his head in contemplation. "All in good time."

"May I ask a question? I have been to the College of the Anu, but please reveal what the Anu is," I asked, realizing that I was but a young girl when I ventured there with Pentu and my class.

The Preceptor tilted his head, then said, "Yes, you are of an age where you should learn. In the concept of chemistry, the Anu is considered to be the fundamental universal principle, the invisible primordial nature, the Emanation Solaris, the Universalis Solaris. When Vega was the pole-star, a matrix was sent here called the Anuvian matrix and it was the original alignment of Vega to the earth and the Great Central Sun. For you Merit-Aten, the Divine Feminine, is the Receptrix, and through the power of intuition, you are able to align to Cosmic Light accessed by the Divine Masculine through your Sacred Portal or Cosmic Womb."

We stood there mesmerized, hearing the words of the Master Preceptor. He stood so solidly, not even the movement of breath was detected. "Are you two ready for your next initiation?"

"Yes," we acknowledged, trembling from terror of the unknown.

The Orama pointed behind us, and there was a stone chamber. A perfectly constructed oblong rose granite box that might have been mistaken for what could have protected a sarcophagus.

"This is a smaller replica of the crystal Astrolarium. It is a star chamber. This task will not be easy and will require one of you to overcome the greatest fear imaginable. The other will act as the Sacred Scribe. I will oversee the initiation as the Heruphant, the Soul Protector, and Guardian between this world and the next world. One of you will lie in this granite box; the lid will be placed over it to block out all air, light, and sound."

My throat tightened, and the words slipped out in barely a breath. "Is this what *Ausar*, Osiris, was asked to do?"

The Heruphant offered a faint smile. "Very perceptive, Merit-Aten. That is why it is also called the Osirian initiation. The other one in the box will star-travel to whichever stellar constellation of your choosing. First, you will transmit to the Sacred Scribe the names of the constellations and the corresponding gods assigned to oversee them. That is how Master Djehuty received the transmissions for the Emerald, Ruby, and Sapphire Tablets of Alchemy, the Heart force Ascension. I will also require that you return with a secret only you would know. You have three days to accomplish this—but it comes with a warning. Your expansion in consciousness will entice you to remain in the eternal."

"What would happen then?" I asked with a quaver.

"Your body in the sarcophagus will perish. The soul will separate and continue its journey. The Scribe's job is to anchor the soul so that it chooses not to sever the connection." The Orama's words vibrated the walls, leaving us heavy with worry.

I fixed my eyes upon Ana-Kharu. "Orama, I fear that I cannot proceed with this initiation."

"Why is that?" the Preceptor asked incredulously, crossing his arms. His eyebrows arched severely.

"If he is the one to get in the box, I fear my rage would harm his chances of returning. If I am the one to lay in the box, then I fear that Ana-Kharu would try to harm me the way he tried to murder Archollos, my classmate." My knees betrayed me, trembling, as cold prickles climbed up my arms—fear I had long buried clawing its way to the surface.

"That is the most serious accusation. Is this true?" The Elder's face was a mask of fury. "Did you seek to hurt this Archollos?" The Orama demanded an answer.

"He tried to poison him," I said, nearly tearing up. "I saw him mix the venomous drink from the Aconite purple flower and serve it to Archollos at my Choosing."

Ana-Kharu lifted his hands slowly, palms exposed—not to protest, but to lay down his weaponless truth." Yes, I mixed the drink. But not to poison him. It was aconite and gorse—meant to make you both forget. To sever the thread between you and Archollos. Because your heart belongs to him, not to Smenkhkare." His words cracked—raw, torn from a place not fully healed. "I know what it is to love someone you are forbidden to have. I live with the ghost of Oshunessa every day. Her scent. Her laughter. Her loss. This is not malice. It was mercy. I wanted to numb the ache that would have lever let either of you go."

The Orama seized Ana-Kharu's hand with a sudden force, as though weighing the soul beneath the skin. "Aconite, the purple flower, is one of the most hazardous of poisons. Hold my hand and look me in the eye." The Preceptor transmitted a powerful beam into the student's eyes. The Gold Magician did not turn away; instead, he locked his gaze upon his esteemed teacher. "His tongue is true. The aid he offered you was in good faith," said the Orama, finally releasing Ana-Kharu's hand.

Shame burned through me. I had cast him as my enemy, but perhaps all along he was trying to be my shield. "My most humble apologies. I have wronged you, and for that, I am most sorry for my misjudgment."

I reached for his hand, but he drew back—subtly, but enough to sting. "It is forgotten," he said, though the distance in his voice betrayed him.

"Would either of you mind if I continue on with my work while you proceed?" The Orama gave a single wave of his hand, and his entire lab appeared in the boundaries of this once-constricted space. A copper furnace glowed like a dragon's breath in the corner. Scrolls spilled off high shelves, their curled edges brittle with age. The ceiling turned into an architectural delight, forming Lambrequin ornate arches with lobes and points. Papyri scrolls filled with mysterious writings and diagrams, a bleached skull looked on vacantly, candles flickered from a hundred holders giving light and warmth. While a table was filled with finials and vials of liquids—some bubbling over tiny braziers, other crucibles shaped like wombs of creation, each holding mysterious steaming brews.

Two young students, a boy and a girl, were instructed in the proper handling of the metal retorts. The High Priest's hands moved with a fluid grace born of yesteryear's experience. The students watched, taking notes of how to control the temperature of the fire, ensuring a delicate balance between heat and harmony. An alembic, the glass vessel held securely in a carved wooden stand had a tube running into it with a green circulating ooze.

"Remember, Self-knowledge is the basis of true knowledge. Next, we will purify and refine the substances to their very core. This is known as the distillation process." The gentle curves of glass cradled the dark violet liquid, and the Master lifted it up to the light before extracting the volatile substance. "We must always be in tune with the Sun, the Moon, and the Stars, for we are not merely blending elements of this material world but channeling the Cosmic forces that flows unseen through it. It is the balance of these currents—hot and cold, light and dark, wet and dry, electric and magnetic—that yields transformation. Only when these forces are brought into alignment beneath the gaze of the Prime Creator does true transmutation succeed."

"That is me," I whispered, staring at the little girl with the childhood sidelock. "But...I do not remember ever studying alchemy with you, Great Master."

"That little boy is me," admitted Ana-Kharu, "but I am sure that I never studied with you, Orama. How is this possible?"

He stood lost in time, examining a perfected being at work while giving instruction to the younger versions of ourselves. Ana-Kharu's jaw pulsating as he ground his teeth. He was aching to stand behind them and soak up this ancient knowledge. I, too, yearned for this education, but then I remembered why we were truly in this room.

"Ana-Kharu," I said softly, "it is time." He turned, eyes narrowing at the sarcophagus like it was an adversary we had both tried to ignore.

He spun around and surveyed our next initiation with a bit of apprehension. "I know what needs to be done. I will take the role of Scribe. You will need to transmit to me the star's wisdom."

"Why? I am not sure I could survive trapped in that box. You have more training than I do in slowing down your heart and breath," I sputtered, the fear tingling my spine.

"I do," he said flatly. His resolve was a wall—I knew better than to press.

"You get in and lay down, and I shall close the lid upon you." I was sure he would agree with my logic.

He smirked then said, "Ah, princess. You are not strong enough to budge that lid, let alone slide it back over the top. Therefore, I shall sit and Metascribe the knowledge that you transmit, and you shall lay down. Make haste."

"I am afraid," I admitted, lightly placing my hand on his arm.

"Which is exactly why the Orama will watch over you as the Heruphant, he had already known it would be you who would be the Stargazer, and I would do the transcription." He pointed. "Climb in."

I sighed, knowing that he had spoken the truth. Of course, it would be me because I was the one who showed fear. 'It was another challenge to be met with fortitude. *You shall overcome,*' is what Pentu would say. I threw my leg over the red cold stone chamber and climbed in. Laying down, my back met with the hard granite, and I shivered from the chill, for it felt like I was being swallowed alive. Maybe this is why the Sarcophagus is known as the *Body Eater.*

"Soul to heaven, body to earth," Ana-Kharu, intoned, as if sealing me with an invisible contract. "Ready?" he asked as he began to heave the heavy lid over the box of containment. The loud grinding sound gave rise to all the terror within me. Pentu had prepared me for this when he made me ride in the dark on the days-long journey to the Valley of the Kings, where Queen Ti-Yee was interred in Amunhotep III's funerary chamber. Pentu foresaw this all would happen.

Calming, receding, and withdrawing my external energy and breath, I found my pulse and heard my heartbeat, intentionally slowing it down. At first, it was faint, the pulse of the mother's heart, the ancient black mama. When the Great Goddess of Everything summoned me, I sucked in one last deep inhalation persuading myself that it would last for the duration of my journey. Focusing on Orion, I

projected a beam of light from my head to the stellar constellation. Within moments, I was flying through the blackness of the vast universe. I would ask Osiris to reveal all the
constellations that would be needed so that I could inform
Ana-Kharu, the Scribe. From black, we came, to blackness,
we become. My melanin shimmered like obsidian silk, alive
and attuned in the infinite skin of the Primordial Mother.
We were one womb, one pulse, one dark brilliance. I was
propelled to the great stars overhead of the pyramid as if
I was born.

Without a moment of hesitation, I cast my body of light
upon the heavens. Aten, please provide the wisdom of the
stars. Name all the constellations that my Preceptor, the
Orama, in his capacity of the Heruphant will ask for. The
stream of ancient knowledge flowed forth, and the starlight
spoke in pulses—ancient syllables etched in gold across the
black. As each constellation named itself to me, I whispered
it across the veil to Ana-Kharu, trusting that his soul would
catch it before it vanished into the void.

The sky lit up as a glorious reference for me. Yes, Orion,
Pleiades, Andromeda, the Big Cup and Little Cup, Auriga,
Big Dogstar, and Little Dogstar, the Whale, Columba, the
Swan, the Horse, the Dragon, the Hydra monster, Lynx, and
on and on, I recounted as the constellations ignited in the
sky. All I had to do was relay them to the one who could
hear my thoughts. It wasn't learning—it was remembering.
The Aten peeled back the veil with such grace, it felt like
I had once helped carve the constellations myself. Some-
thing about this chamber, the crystalline structure of the
granite, seemed to process faster than my thoughts could.
That is how I truly knew this was a gift from the mind of

God. My soul flew with ease through this great void; I had never known freedom, such as being free of the body that weighed me down with the worries and burdens and chatter that constantly pecked at my mind like cackling chickens.

A secret. The Orama required that I return with a secret that only I could have learned in the inner realms. Where would I look for a secret? From my present? My Father's face flew before my eyes, then my mother's face, but I turned my face away. Maybe it was the past. Grand Djedti Ti-Yee's face appeared. I yearned to bow to her as I was taught to respect my elders.

Although she was translucent, her features were well defined. My heart ached for her, her wisdom, her protection. *"Well, Child, I see that you are taking one of the hardest initiations of the Sanctuary of the Anu, in Heliopolis."*

All I had to do was think to her. So much easier than using words. *"Yes, Grand Djedti. I am blessed to be in the chamber for the Osirian Kerashtt test."*

Grand Djedti gave a slight nod. *"That is how Djehuty would go up to visit the Star Gods and come back to Meta-Scribe the Emerald, Ruby and Sapphire Tablets of Alchemy."*

The majestic cosmos swallowed me whole—its silence immense, its stars glinting like ancestral eyes. I was a speck adrift in an endless black sea, my name shrinking in the mouth of eternity.

"Did you send your transmissions to the Scribe?" asked Ti-Yee reminding me of my sacred duty.

"Yes, Grand Djedti. I have completed that task."

Her thoughts pressed through me like heat through fabric—gentle but insistent. Each ripple struck the surface of my mind and echoed deeper, leaving no room for evasion. *"Are you quite sure that you mentioned all of them?"*

"I believe I captured all their names as I flew by."

She gave no indication if I was correct. *"What was your last task?"*

"To retrieve a secret," I replied realizing she might have the answer.

"Then you found me?"

"Yes, Grand Djedti."

"Then I must be the one to convey an inner truth. This one will reveal your past, and your path."

"I am ready."

"Your father," she said, her tone threading sorrow and pride, *"he walks a path the others never dared to tread, does he not?"*

"Yes, Grand Djedti, my mother would say that he was far too meek to be a King of Khemit."

She blinked her eyes slowly. "Continue."

It was the first time anyone had asked me to verbalize why my beloved father had such a difficult time ruling as if he was a priest rather than a warrior, like Horemheb.

"Father prefers to meditate on the Aten, rather than prac-tice sword fighting, planning battles by smiting our neigh-bors, or scheming in the politics of this world. He thought it a burden. His esoteric studies were much more in line with his heart."

Ti-Yee, looking more regal, proud and confident in the Amentii realms than she was in life. *"Do you understand why the quiet one was crowned in a world ruled by noise?"*

"No Grand Djedti. Why did Grand Djed, Amunhotep III, pick my mild father for such a difficult role that he had no

preparation for?" I had heard so many stories about my Uncle Tuthmosis? He had all the training, the art of negotiation, and the Kingly hunting skills. Honestly, he would have been far more attuned to the rulership of Khemit.

Ti-Yee heard my thoughts and shook. *"No, he would not. Tuthmosis, while a strong, brave man, he was in alignment with Amun, being the Pharaoh's oldest son. He would have continued with the bloody battles and regiments of armies forever in conflict to abscond with the gold of our enemies. Tuthmosis would have been required to continue the savagery and sacrifice that the Amunites crave. He was not chosen by my consort, the Pharaoh, because*—she paused— *"It was I,"* she said, her voice like a blade veiled in velvet. *"I commanded the axel to split—to still his wheels forever."*

"Grand Djedti, No! that fall snapped more than bone. It severed blood from legacy." I reeled back in horror. How could a Mother murder her son? I am sure the sarcophagus quaked in my shock.

"I did what I thought best, for Khemit. For those who would have lost their lives in the name of Ma'at. I changed the course of history. Your father, the gentler one, agreed with me to introduce the Aten to uplift humanity and break that old cycle of time. We had a window to complete this mission."

Although, my initial reaction was to sob that my grandmother could be so heartless as to take the life of her son. I did not know she was capable of being so cruel. Instead, I maintained my composure. "What does it mean to be a ruler—must I sacrifice my own morality for the greater good?"

"You think of me as being ruthless instead of having foresight. I made the choice I did because we could not go on

dominating our neighbors and smiting the enemy to instill fear," said Queen Ti-Yee. *"Khemit was Unified, and the Upper and Lower Kingdoms had often come together under tyrannical rulers. If my son, Tuthmosis, with the Pharaoh, had come to rule, then we would have perpetuated the warring lineage for this next cycle of time. Something had to change."*

My mind whirled and panic set my body aflame. "Is that why Pharaoh then chose his younger, meeker son, my father, as his successor?" Would I do the same, if it meant saving Khemit?"

Queen Ti-Yee shook her head adamantly. *"No, I chose my Son, the true Son of the Sun, to rule."*

"During my time of study in Heliopolis, the Orama and I were told by the Oracle that Khemit was at a crossroads. It was revealed that we had the opportunity to correct a cycle and uplift the people, to elevate their consciousness for a very short time. In service to the Aten, I felt it my duty to obey. My eldest son stood in the way."

"Murder? Was that your only option? You took his life," I argued, pleading his case as if I could change the past.

"If I could save the many, then that was what I was being asked to do. Life is not always what you dream it to be. When your father, Amunhotep IV, was confirmed as next to be Co-Regent with Pharaoh, you were still young, just starting your initiatic path," said Ti-Yee in my vision.

"I remember the fear my family felt when Pharaoh agreed to make my parents Co-Regent; but then, postponed the declaration over and over," I said, my stomach cinching.

The deceased Queen shook her head. *"My consort thwarted my plans, over and over. Ruling, even as a Per Aat does not guarantee you a life of ease nor success."*

My face twisted for I had seen my mother and father in constant conflict.

"I asked Pentu to bring you to Heliopolis the first time when you were young. The Orama wanted to meet you, and we needed to be guarded because it is well known that the Orama never leaves Heliopolis. He needed to see if you could carry the Atenic light to rule one day and carry on our plan."

I was rattled. I thought I knew about my lineage; only now do I realize how calculated it had been.

"Sometimes it is not who you are but who you think you are that changes everything," she replied plainly as if a divine plan had unfolded all along.

"Thus, the secret that only I could be told," I said, nodding because now the Orama's direction was clear. *"What about all the gold that I must learn to make? The barges and caverns of gold that my father needs to feed our people and raise an army?"*

"Patience. You will be given that true knowledge. Tell me why you have been put through so much?" asked Grand Djedti in a powerful voice. *"Why have I made you look at things most children could not endure? Why have you faced the death of your loved ones, Hep-Mut, your nursemaid, both of your Grandparent's death, the death of your cat, Rennutet's death in childbirth, the death of your homeland when you moved to Akhet Aten?"*

Tears slid unbidden, stinging the sore cracks of my lips. *"It has been agony, Grand Djedti—each death a stone in my ribs. Some nights I begged the Aten to claim me." Many times, I thought it would be better to West myself than to continue."* I admitted, so often, wanting to give up.

"Exactly." Her voice boomed, then softened to embers. *"Karma will quarter no delusions. All that you have gone through does not come from without you, but from within you. You created everything you need to become the leader I know you are. Your disadvantage turns into an advantage. You must strive with blood, sweat, and tears. The only way to the perfected being. Blood. Sweat. Tears."* Her eyes burned into mine so that I would never forget. *"I willed the feminine chaos upon you, for you to make the greatest strides. You cannot bring Order without first bringing on the dark Chaos. Light is a coward without shadow,"* she intoned. *"Shadow collapses without a spark. Their collision is the crucible."* Her eyes emitted a penetrating light. *"True wisdom oozes from split seams,"* she continued, fingers tracing invisible scars in the air. *"Where the fabric tears, light bleeds through. You have been brought to the brink of undoing so many times, and it is the only way you can transform your isolation into solitude. By dispelling your loneliness and surrendering to the Source of All Things, you find your inner strength to reunite all the missing pieces of yourself that have been scattered over your lifetimes. All the traumatic ways you have died, you leave a piece of yourself behind; that is the true Mythology of Osirus. It is your duty to Re-Member yourself. That is Ascension."*

"I nearly died. How can that serve if the initiate Wests?" I asked with confusion.

"But you did not. You must die to be reborn. That is your secret of the ages. Who are You behind the appellation of Pharaoh's Daughter, a princess, an initiate, a consort? That is just who you thought you were." She shimmered as if my

Revelation of who I truly am gave her Salvation. No, us, salvation. I dissolved the attachment to who I thought I was.

This was true liberty that one would only learn in the heavenly realms. True salvation by freeing the soul from the flesh is when Ausar-Osiris becomes a god. A smile unfurled from the marrow outward—warm, wild, boundless—until even the granite box seemed to hum with it. No time. The unlimited point of view, for wherever my soul darted, I gained new wisdom from seeing life through the cosmic, all-knowing, and omnipresent vision. A tiny silver cord attached allowed me to find my body once I wished to descend. A thought crossed my mind. Why would I even want to return? I had found my peace, my silence within. With that discordant thought, I was snapped back into my body, back into the cold confines of the stone prison and the prison of my flesh. With outstretched hands, I grasped at that last inkling of eternal peace that had been mercilessly ripped away.

It was as dark as death within that granite container, and I had to shake off the heaviness, the pain in my body, every joint aches, every nerve was on fire, yet I had to reenter my body and stay in position with the lid closed for another day.

The three-day initiation and reintegration were mandatory. I dare not panic, nor increase my heartbeat, nor labor with breath and use up the limited air I was allotted in this chamber. Lying motionless, I had no concept of time passing, and no energy within my body to move. A heavy weight pushed me down, and struggle would be useless.

There still was another lesson yet to be learned. The box. My father. What would one have to do with the other? It felt like a nest with a golden egg that was at a height unreachable. At first, the faint pulsating grew louder the more I directed my spirit to discover the meaning. A blue electric charge began to tickle me as the cerulean blue fingers lit up my vision. Gold. Gold. Gold. I could feel the hot glow of the solarization penetrate through my Ka. Rise. Higher. Vibration. Again, I ascended, becoming One with what the Aten decreed for me to bear witness too. Now, I was encased within another enclosure, a metallic box; still blackness engulfed me. Yet, I also felt my father's presence, guiding, directing, and protecting me.

"You are held within my loving embrace, Merit-Aten," My father, the Pharaoh, clearly said, *"This is the true Holy of Holies, the sacred Ark of the Covenant, which I had brought back to rest within the red granite stone chamber in the pyramid. The Ark is protected by the Aten. In our lineage, Pharaoh Tuthmosis I, was born in the pyramid complex, and he learned the craft of maintaining the protection of the Ark of the Covenant. This sacred Ark holds the Monoatomic Gold powder that powers the pyramid along with the Ben Ben stone for radiation. The vibration is not from this 3rd-dimensional world; it is in the 5th-dimensional world out of view and touch of the profane. You are floating between those worlds, but I want you to taste the sacred. Only a taste."*

My hands were resting on something gritty that felt so powerful that the intensity of vibration could consume me. I used my tiny finger to bring a sample to my mouth. Indeed, the grainy powder felt metallic. Upon my tongue, my brain was on fire. My eyes grew larger, and I once again felt like I was everywhere all at once and no longer confined to the flesh of this material body. Charged. Electrified. Magnetized.

Solarized. Stellarized. Alive. Discord turned into harmony. Every fiber in my body lit up, and suddenly, I recognized that I was also at the same time on the outside of the golden box. Two golden angels arched their backs in Holy reverence. This Ark of the Covenant was hidden between worlds and held by my father.

My eyes snapped open. *"It is done,"* whispered through the dark like a sealed verdict. Panic skittered up my spine, sharp and cold as ice. Panic clawed at me. I had to get out, but how? I slammed both fists against the granite, the vibrations humming up my arms like a bell struck in a tomb. Silence. Nothing. Only the muffled thud of my own desperation echoed back—sealed inside stone, as if the world had forgotten me. Transmit. I focused all of my remaining thoughts, casting my prayers to Ana-Kharu-We-Shat like a beacon in the void.

I heard that I must stay confined for another day to integrate the knowledge. It seemed an eternity before a crack of light flooded the coffin as he shoved the lid away like a wheel grinding. Air slammed into my lungs in one greedy rush—wet, loud, desperate—as if I'd breached the amniotic veil of a second birth. "Thanks... be to Aten," I rasped, the syllables raw like a baby's first cry torn through unused vocal cords.

"Merit-Aten, take your time. Do not make haste to arise. You have been through a great ordeal."

My eyes fluttered. I had to recall all that had been received by the initiatic stars, the pantheon of gods and my Grand Djedti Ti-Yee. These thoughts were still so fragile. While I still retained the knowledge, I placed it with care in my basket so that it did not dissipate, never to be found again. I recalled everything and acknowledged that I could find those secrets again as I returned from the inner realms.

Ana-Kharu's warm hands clasped mine, coaxing me from shadow into golden glow, as if leading me up from the Duat into day.

"How long have I been away?" My voice rasped, weak, yet reaching

"Three suns have passed," he said, pressing a clay cup to my lips. The lemon and honey water stung—sweet and sharp—anchoring me back into flesh.

I quenched my thirst and felt like I could garner the strength to sit up. "Tell me you heard," I begged, fingers clutching his robe. "That the stars did not whisper in vain." A flooding memory of why I had been encapsulated made me desperate to see his scroll.

"Every word," he assured me, unfolding the scroll with reverence. "Let us deliver it to the Heruphant before the ink cools." Ana-Kharu, helped pull my shaky legs up so that I could climb out of the sarcophagus.

Ana-Kharu bowed to the Heruphant. "Most High Preceptor, we have completed the initiation," he said, rolling out his papyrus.

"Auspicious indeed," the Heruphant murmured, unrolling the scroll like a sacred river.

"You have captured the stellar and solar light codes, along with the measurements, movements, and sequences of the rays of solar and lunar light, you correctly perceived that the day and night, the sun and the moon are equally measured. Your correct calculations have also allowed me to calculate the resonances of the Regulan matrix and how to compute that in human physiology, thereby completely dissolving the Reptilian shadow side that was imposed upon humanity after the fall of Atlantis," he said, eyes alight. "Do you know what this means?"

Ana-Kharu and I glanced at each other, hoping it would soon be clear.

"You have been marked by the Regulus Star," he said, his face aglow. "The same gaze the Sphinx holds—sentinel of the Leo Gate. You have caught the breath of the Red Lion itself." He saw our glazed look, his hands now animated with light. "The Lion Regulus," he intoned, "is the pulse beneath the Sphinx's stone skin—the gatekeeper of Leo's Crown. You have received what only the Ancients whispered: the Red Lion's breath. Its frequency transmutes lead into *maf-ka-zet*—monoatomic gold, the White Stone of the Ka, the bread of ascension, the lost manna. And more than that..." His eyes gleamed. "You have tasted the Mercury sulfide that crosses matter into spirit. This is not mere transmission. It is transformation. Monoatomic gold."

As the Orama scrutinized the scroll. He nodded. "Yes. Yes. You were accurate in your calculations of the four great stars, each star having 1,000 stars under it." He didn't pause his alchemical work as he spoke, moving between vials and firelight like a priest and physicist at once.

"My transmutation is complete. Behold the Red Lion." He held aloft a glass orb with a pinkish-red powder. My breath caught. This was the answer to my prayers. The powder pulsed with the essence of revival—of kings and kingdoms. Father would know how to wield it. I saw the light return to his eyes, imagined the wisdom of the stars flowing through him like sunlight through alabaster.

"Let me see the rest," he muttered, unrolling the papyrus until it stretched like a river of stars. "Yes... Vega, Sirius, Orion, Canopus... the Sisters of the Pleiades... Draconis, the Dragon, Alpha Leonis, Regulus... Excellent. All accounted for." His tone was satisfied—until it wasn't.

His eyes poured over the Meta-Scription. Then his head jerked upward, and the firelight caught the shadow in his eyes. "No... wait," he said, voice tight with disappointment. "There is one more." His hand hovered over the orb, retracting. "I cannot release the Red Lion powder. Nor complete your Osirian Kerashtt. Not until the final star is found. This is... gravely unacceptable."

How could I have missed it? Ana-Kharu poked me in the ribs, not in jest, but as if trying to shake loose the memory I had buried in the void. I scoured my inner sky, but no new name would rise. Nothing. as if he was demanding that I reveal what I had neglected to see during my journey out of body. He placed his judgment upon my crown—searing me with the failure I had tried so hard to avoid. I alone was the vessel. The omission was mine.

"Tsk, tsk, tsk," said the Orama. "Perhaps your birdbrains can flap all the way to Edfu, and find Horus, the hawk-headed god, to give you the answer," said the *Hierophant who never coddles, but cuts through illusion with truth-tinged mockery*. Tsk.Tsk. Tsk.

28

*T*he next morning, with a steadier breath and steadier hands, Morainya swept windblown leaves and candy wrappers that had drifted from the neighbor's yard. The simple act felt grounding—like reclaiming order from the chaos.

Her cell rang. "Hello Nico, is everything ok?"

"Morainya, glad I caught you. We just got an offer on the house. It's under the asking price, but I feel like you should take it and be done." Nico caught his breath and paused for her to answer.

"So soon? It hasn't even been on the market a week." She felt a shock sizzle up her spine.

"The staging is impressive. The buyers want it all. If you say yes, the agent can work up a contract. How soon can you get up here to sign?

"Josh is on his senior trip, so I can get up there Saturday around one, if she can get it done that soon," Morainya felt off balance. This was so fast; that her legs felt unsteady. She hadn't yet absorbed that severing the past also meant surrendering the only place that had ever felt like home. The house of Christmas cookies and Stella's prayers. The house that held every echo.

"Great, see you then." Nico sounded relieved.

She had to divulge what she had learned. He might be angry at first, but then he'd calm down and thank her for telling him. Morainya had to find the courage to face it regardless of the outcome.

Saturday morning, she again made the long winding drive back to the Santa Clara Valley, moving along with the morning traffic, then taking the 680 to the city. She would be thankful to put all this behind her. Her brunch with Shelley had offered no warmth—just polite chatter over pancakes and oxygen infusions and an invisible wall she couldn't scale. Instead, it added to the confusion of the life she had once known. Was this how it was going to be? Her best friends would, one by one, slip away because they were no longer in sync with whom she was becoming. Morainya just didn't think she had it in her anymore to make pleasant surface conversation that now seemed mundane. Now, it was growth or nothing. Evolution or extinction. The yearning for true friends who saw the authentic Morainya would be her only choice. The only problem she foresaw would be where exactly she'd find them.

An hour and fifty minutes later, she was opening the door to her parents' home. Morning light spilled in through the Bayside window, catching every floating dust mote like memories suspended in time. She fluffed up the white brocade pillows with thick fringe —so different from the familiar, overstuffed florals her mother once prized—and placed them carefully on the sleek gray velvet couch that belonged to someone else's version of home. The house no longer belonged to her, so she may as well sign the contract that was placed noticeably on the glass and metal coffee table, along with colorful history books that were artfully arranged.

Everything seemed to be in order. Typical, except that she'd have to sign the deal with her new American State Nationals proscribed autograph rather than a signature. The offer was 200k below asking, along with a list of requirements for a new roof, repairing the stairs, patching the missing tile in the 1900's green tile showers. Cash offer, quick close. Maybe the real estate agent could find a repairman.

By 12:45 pm, Nico and Gina unlocked the door and entered the room in one of their loud Jersey accented Italian wars. "Hey, there, Mora," said Nico. "Did you get a chance to read the contract."

"It's a good offer, right?" asked Gina, shaking her platinum blonde hair.

"I think it is fair. We just have to fix all their Requests for Repairs. He had a checklist and was making marks with a pen."

Morainya took a seat and patted the cushion. "Nico, let's sit down. I need to talk to you."

They gazed out of the Bay window toward the beloved view of the Golden Gate Bridge rising like a signal of golden light engulfed in clouds. It was a tranquil view, seeing the bridge between two worlds, ever-present, everlasting. She felt his tension before he spoke—a low hum of unease, the way a barometer drops before a storm.

"I need to talk to you, too," said Nico, giving her a face that withheld the truth. I got a call from the law firm. Mr. Kanberg is quite upset and hurt that you haven't paid him. He said he'd hate to take legal action, but you are ignoring him after all his hard work to reach a settlement with Aldo."

Morainya's breath left in a thin hiss; Kanberg had already rattled Josh—now this. Why should she be surprised that Nico had received a call. "He's civilly dead," Morainya said flatly, her voice like stone—final, immovable.

"He died? When? Naw, Nico just talked to him," said Gina, her hands firmly upon her hips. "He's family, Morainya. You gotta square up. Need one of us to spot you?"

"If you two would allow me to talk, I need to explain some things. Besides that, I never gave Kanberg permission to discuss my personal affairs outside of the office. That's a breach of contract and a betrayal of trust." A heat pricked her cheeks. Kanberg—'family'? The word felt like gravel in her teeth. She felt the insult of this asshole calling her family and shaming her.

"He's been our family attorney since we were kids," said Nico convincingly placing a brotherly hand upon hers. "You kinda owe him. He did settle this after all," said Nico.

"I owe him? That's a laugh. First, let me explain about Mr. Kanberg, a friend of our father and protector of our family. It's a lie." Morainya turned her body to face Nico and Gina. It was time to reveal all. She retold how history had been rewritten and about the Crown Corporation, the BAR, the Cestui Que Vie Trust accounts and waited for the light to turn on above their heads, but the dimmer switch must have shorted out because there wasn't even a flicker of understanding.

"I don't get a word you are saying. It's just gibberish. Seequah Q or some language I don't understand. You shouldn't make us feel stupid," said Gina, clearly hurt.

"That's ridiculous. I don't believe you." Nico just glazed over like an iced French Cruller doughnut. "So, can you pay him or not? We don't want another lawsuit. Our family has been through enough. Pay him, Mora."

"I can't. No, I won't. Here's why. My life has been a lie and so has yours. They are all in on it. They all know what I'm going to tell you. You may hate me for it, but I got pushed into a settlement, because in the final hour, Aldo claimed that our family had abused him." Her lips quivered, as she held back tears.

"The judge latched on to it and raised suspicion and fear in me to push me toward a larger settlement. I didn't know what to do. I certainly didn't want to go to court, where all of our family secrets would be revealed to the jury, the judge, and to our local newspapers. They would have had a field day and destroyed our reputation. Even if lies were spread to make us look bad, we'd never be able to vindicate ourselves because the Napolitano family would be painted as child abusers."

"Right, Dad. You called us. We agreed to go to a mil and somehow you raised it to three. What the fuck, Morainya? We trusted you," said Nico crossing both arms.

"Not Dad. Aldo said it was Mom who abused him. It shook me up so badly to think that there was a part of Mom, I didn't know. It made me sick to my stomach. After I saw Mom in The Gold Gates Sanctuary, throwing plates of food at the attendant, she tried to hurt her personal caregiver; then she was hysterical when I brought her favorite purse, and she discovered her rosary beads. She went batshit crazy about Aldo."

Nico's shoulders caved inward. "I know, kid. I've been juggling it while you lived in courtrooms with lawyers. Gina and I have been at our wit's end seeing this drastic change happen so swiftly in mom. The Gold Gates Sanctuary calls us at all hours, and the kids are scared Grandma is going to hurt herself."

Morainya, stiffened at being kept out of the loop. "Why didn't you tell me?"

"Tell you?" asked Nico, his jaw tensed. He looked away, the muscle twitching near his temple. "You were already drowning. I didn't want to throw you another weight."

"I could've helped," Morainya snapped, her voice cracking. "You didn't even give me the chance." Suddenly a hot flash engulfed her, and she patted her face.

Nico felt the daggers, his jaw tightened as did his fists, feeling ready to fight. His eyes narrowed. "You gonna be there when she hurls her soup? When the caregiver locks herself in the laundry room then Mom is sweet as pie and forgets about all the chaos she just caused?"

She felt his harsh blow. "Sure, I would have been there," said Morainya defensively. "It's just that I've been dealing with a shit show on the other side, and honestly, it's worse than what I've told you. When I was at the accountant's office, Mr. Cohen told me that his wife, Loretta, was mom's best friend back in those days." Morainya paused, "guess where they worked?"

"The local topless bar?" replied Nico in a sarcastic tone.

Morainya scrunched her face. She hated it when the men in her family resorted to sarcasm.

"No, Nico," Morainya said quietly, "they worked at the Archbishop's house on the hill.

That's where Mom and Dad met—at a fundraiser for St. Mary's Home for Wayward Boys. That's also where Aldo Marcellus went to school... from the time he was small until fourteen when he got adopted into the Napolitano family."

Nico jerked back. "I thought Marcellus was his middle name. He shook his head then realized, "Wait—are you saying Mom was... a nun or something?"

She gave a single nod. "A novice. And a teacher. Mr. Cohen told me his wife, Loretta, used to work in the school cafeteria. Said Aldo attacked Mom once—screamed at her, accused her of abusing him in school."

Gina looked up sharply, brows furrowed. "Abused him?"

Morainya shook her head. "Not her. Loretta said Aldo had been abused by the priests. Bad. The beatings. The closets. The silence. You know the kind of thing we hear about now." Her throat tightened. "But instead of blaming the real ones, he took it out on Mom."

Nico leaned forward, voice rough. "I'm not saying it excuses what he did... but what happened to him, Morainya? How bad was it for Aldo?"

She hesitated. "Worse than we were told. Josh googled it. There were accused priests relocated quietly, all over the Bay Area."

He clenched his jaw. "So, he was a product of it. Raised in the belly of the beast?"

Morainya looked at them then nodded. "They broke him before we ever had a chance to love him."

Nico's jaw clenched. "Did Aldo...you know...hurt Mom too?"

"Morainya grimaced, voice wavering. "Loretta never said. But Mom did admit that she slapped Aldo first." She fidgeted. "He lost control—shoved her and hit her. She fell. Hit her head. She refused to report it because she struck first—so she quit. Aldo dropped out of school, and he was shipped off to Florence to stay with family." Her fingers gripped the edge of the pillow like a lifeline. "Loretta thinks that might be when everything in Mom started to unravel. The dementia... it came on too fast."

A hush fell over the room. The horror hovered, unsaid but undeniable.

"When Mom and Dad got married," she continued, "Aldo was still abroad. I don't think she even knew he was a Napolitano. Aldo kept his christened name—Marcellus."

Gina's voice cracked. "That must've been... unbearable. To see him again. To have to pretend at family events. And worse, Stella blamed herself."

Nico shot to his feet. "Then Aldo blows up on her, and *we're* the ones who pay for it? How is that right?"

Morainya steadied herself. "All this church related abuse is coming out into the public.

Dad's gone. Mom couldn't testify. It would be Aldo ripping apart the Napolitano name. Who would've believed a sick, grieving daughter over a grown man crying about his trauma?"

She took a breath. "I had to settle. Three million. It was five before. I got it down. Morainya exhaled hard, the realization crushing. "It was hush money."

Nico's mouth pressed into a tight, bitter line. He didn't speak.

Gina just collapsed onto the couch, her face pale, her eyes wide. "And we never knew. Not a word about it. God help her."

Nico's eyes narrowed, jaw ticking as the weight of it all settled into his bones. "Did Kanberg know? His hands trembled, one fist tightening around the contract edge.

Morainya shrugged. At the Settlement Conference, it was after lunch. I saw Kanberg with the judge talking in hushed tones. After that, the judge's attitude toward me changed. I can't be certain, but something was off."

Gina shifted, rubbing her palms on her thighs. "But... Stephano gave Aldo a job. Took care of him."

Morainya took a breath, steadying herself before laying the pieces bare. "Aldo was practically raised in our family. Grandma took him in—like so many of those boys. It was what wealthy families were encouraged to do. The Church asked, and the Napolitano's answered."

Morainya folded her hands in her lap, glancing toward the ceiling as if asking for grace. Dad kept Aldo close—not just out of duty, but maybe to control the damage."

Gina's hand flew to her mouth. "Oh God. She had to sit across from him at every dinner.

Smile. Pretend like nothing ever happened."

Nico's voice turned sharp. "She must've felt trapped. Or guilty."

Gina blinked, slowly sinking into the couch. "All those donations... the dinners... the plaques. And we never saw it."

Nico looked down, then up, his face red with rising heat. "All these years...and Kanberg *knew*. Sat across from us, broke bread with us, and never said a damn word. He didn't protect us. He managed a scandal."

Gina's eyes widened, her voice small but sharp, "Now I see why you're not gonna pay that man."

Morainya straightened in her seat, spine stiff with resolve. "Not only am I not paying him," she said, slow and certain, "I've just decided—I'm taking it all back."

Nico blinked and sat up straighter. "I'm with you on that," Nico muttered, then cleared his throat. "This may not be the best time, but...the Archbishop called. Said he *urgently* needs to speak to you about the Spring Fundraiser. Wants your answer. He also mentioned some private matter—asked if you'd call or stop by. Said anytime works."

Morainya's jaw tightened. Of course. The Church. A donation. A closed-door conversation, cloaked in stained glass. It never ended. She exhaled slowly, nodding. "I'll take care of it." The Archbishop...Once, she'd seen him as a father figure. Someone wise. Someone safe. Now? Maybe it was time to set the record straight—with him, with the Church, with all of it.

"Excuse, Me," Morainya rose, "I need to use the computer in Dad's office."

"Parking in San Francisco—a fresh circle of hell. Trying to find a space on the street was nearly impossible in the busy hillside neighborhood where the Archbishop resided. Circling several times, she found a side street that she managed to pull into. Halfway up the block a late-model BMW parked, its chrome grille winking. Aldo's?"

She hoped there wasn't a Fundraising Tea happening—one of those pastel-laced guilt traps with bitter lemon bars and forced small talk. She slipped up the side driveway—flatter than those punishing front steps. The North window was open, and an argument clearly filtered out. She ducked low so as not to be discovered lurking around.

A gust of air carried the sharp scent of damp earth and something older—decay, maybe incense. The scratch of rhododendron branches tore across her forearm, one snagging a strand of hair and yanking it painfully, as if nature itself was warning her back. She winced but didn't move. Her heart slammed against her ribs, throat tightening with a primal alert. One wrong move, and they'd hear her. She didn't belong in this memory—this battlefield. But she couldn't turn away now.

Skirting around the front steps, she chose the rear driveway instead. It was shaded, lined with overgrown camellias, and offered an easy exit if she needed to bail. As she passed under the eave, a voice sliced through the still air—sharp, familiar.

"You owe me this, Aldo, after all I've done for you."

The Archbishop.

She froze mid-step, caught between polite retreat and a flood of curiosity. She took a step back. *Leave,* she told herself. *This isn't your business.*

But then she heard Aldo's voice, hoarse and defensive:

"I brought you the check," he bit out. "A donation. Like you demanded. Just cash it and leave me the hell alone."

Morainya's breath caught. Her pulse thudded in her ears. She inched closer, her heels crunching on loose gravel.

Her heart kicked. A low branch scratched her forearm again The sharp, loamy scent of mulch filled her nose.

Just a minute more, she promised herself. Then she'd go.

But then: "At the hands of the Church, you turned me into an animal…"

And with that, she knew she wasn't leaving.

"You act like I *owe* you something," the Archbishop growled. "But let me remind you—when I met you, you were nothing. A filthy little street rat with piss-stained trousers."

"I was a child," Aldo's voice cracked. "A scared kid who wet the bed because I was beaten half to death in the last place you dumped me."

"Nobody else wanted you."

"At the hands of the Church, you ruined me" Aldo paused. "You filthy pervert. You forced yourself on me when I was just a kid. All of you." No Redemption for either of them now.

"You are making it all up. You have no proof?" The Archbishop was adamant.

"There were boys, lots of boys," Aldo said, voice thick with memory. "I'm not the only boy who saw everything."

"Oh please. You exaggerate everything. You always have."

"No,' Aldo said, louder now. "You all did it. The priests. The nuns. The Church." His voice rose like a tidal surge, deep and trembling. "We were locked in closets, denied food. We scratched the wood to splinters with our fingernails, begging to get out. I still see that door every night."

The Archbishop let out a low, mirthless laugh. "That's called *discipline*. You were a pack of orphans. Wild. Ungrateful. How did you think any of you got adopted? It was by the grace of God that you were placed in the finest homes in the city," argued the Archbishop.

"We paid for it. My whole class paid for it."

"We gave you a home. Structure," sneered the Archbishop.

"You gave us a cage," Aldo hissed. "Then forced me into a lawsuit to go after my own niece. You made me betray her. None of my family will ever speak to me again."

Morainya gripped her wrist, knuckles white. Her mind spiraled. *Lawsuit? Betray?* Her knees shifted in the dirt.

The Archbishop's voice took on a venomous calm. "You never had a family, Aldo. That's the real pain, isn't it? They never loved you."

Silence.

Then a soft, broken sound escaped from inside. A small, choked sob.

"Fuck you," Aldo said, not with venom—but like a child. Wounded. Eight years old. "Take your million dollars and shove it."

"You should be grateful," the Archbishop barked. "I got you placed with the Napolitanos. That house, that name—it was all my doing. You'd still be rotting in a dormitory if it weren't for me."

"Thanks for everything," Aldo replied. "They just tolerated a boy who didn't look like them or have their blood. I hated my life and wished I could end it."

Morainya leaned back into the shadow of the bush, the world spinning. Her stomach turned. The scent of crushed lavender and rotting leaves hung thick in the air.

The lawsuit. The manipulation. The betrayal.

The Church hadn't just failed them.

It had orchestrated everything.

Morainya clutched her cellphone and laid low until she saw Aldo storm out of the mansion, slamming the front door behind him. He stomped down the steps toward his car, and moments later, the shriek of tires tore through the quiet residential street. Reckless. Furious.

That was too close. It startled her so much that her hands began to shake. *Being brave takes too much courage,* she thought, *and maybe she wasn't cut out to take charge of all that had been placed upon my shoulders.*

Counting her time by slowing her breath, she pulled her disheveled self together. Running fingers though her hair, she popped in a mint to freshen her breath. This time walking across the lawn, she made sure to leave heel prints in the manicured grass. Let them see them. Morainya knocked on the grand mahogany door instead of ringing the ecclesiastical doorbell and silently prayed the Archbishop wouldn't answer. She needed time to collect her scattered thoughts. Instead, a meek woman in a gray nun's habit answered.

"I'm here to see the Archbishop, but I really need to use the bathroom. I can't hold it anymore," Morainya squealed, already slipping past the threshold.

"What is your name? I'll tell Father Joseph—excuse me, the Archbishop—you are here."

"Shelley," Morainya, replied quickly, startled at the use of his old priest's name." He asked me to stop by when I had time to make a donation. I'll just wait if he's busy." *Father Joseph.* Her mother's rage flared in her memory. So...it was him. He was the one who abused those poor boys.

"He's on the phone. Could you wait in his formal meeting room?" asked the nun quietly, eyes falling to Morainya's grassy shoes. Something in her demeanor made Morainya wonder if this woman, too, had once suffered.

"The one down the hall? I know exactly where it is. Don't let me keep you." Morainya smiled warmly. The nun nodded and gratefully retreated, relieved not to be tethered to a guest.

Morainya headed to the restroom attached to the formal Reception Room. She walked confidently through the doors, both shocked and steady to once again be inside the home of the enemy. *What was she going to say?* The eavesdropped conversation had cracked everything open. Aldo. The lawsuit. The betrayal. It was all so tangled now—he wasn't the instigator but the pawn. Forced to betray her. Forced to survive.

She paced the room, trying to find her bearing, then turned to the Wall of Fame. Her Father's smiling face stared back from one of the polished frames, proof of his donations, and pride.

The Archbishop's private office. Its walls, heavy with iconography, seemed to bear witness like silent accusers. The air was cold for a late spring day. Morainya felt it in her bones—not just the temperature, but the weight of where she was. She had spent a lifetime fearing men like the Archbishop. But today she had no choice but to push through. She paced beyond the meeting space, stopping abruptly at a painted panel of limestone blocks—faint but unmistakable. Pharaoh Akhenaten. Queen Nefertiti. Their six daughters playing under the rays of the Aten Sun. Her finger trembled as it traced over the eldest daughter's image. The Archbishop had no right to own this.

It dawned upon her, clear as first light. *The Amunites had never died out. When Egypt was plundered by the Greeks, everything of value was stolen, and it was then passed on to the Roman conquest and harbored within the vaults of the Vatican.* And now—preserved in the private sanctums of monsters like this man. She hesitated. The thought twisted her insides.

Take it back, thought Iben. He panged her hard. *It belongs to Khemit. To father.*

Morainya hesitated, her stomach flipped. *She couldn't take something this valuable.*

Do it now, commanded Iben. Like a thunderclap shaking her V with ancient insistence. She groaned inwardly. *She hated that the promise of an orgasm could be used to manipulate her. She'd deal with that later.*

Quickly, she scooped up the glass ball with its hardened brownish-pink contents and slid it into her purse. Just then, the Archbishop strode through the door, clearly surprised to find Morainya Napolitano standing in his sanctum. He straightened his cassock, eyes flickering with confusion.

"My sister-secretary said a 'Shelley' was here. I apologize you weren't announced properly. She must have misheard your name." His Excellency's voice tried for grace, but his thoughts were muddled.

"You told my brother..." Morainya began, "that I was welcome anytime. I'm in town, so I came by. What was it you needed?" She stood quietly in the long afternoon shadow of the sun, backlighting his Holiness like a stained-glass saint. Regal King-like. Something in her muscle memory wanted to curtsy—and she despised that instinct.

He looked down upon her, his tone laced with patronizing calm.

"Morainya, I've been patient. I know you've been busy... tending to your legal team to complete the, uh—"

"The Settlement Conference with Uncle Aldo?" she said crisply, cutting him off.

He blinked, then smiled with practiced ease. "Why, yes," he said, pleased he hadn't had to say it first.

She didn't flinch.

Instead, she chose her words carefully, stringing them like pearls. "I've been wondering how you knew so much about my legal affairs. Almost as if you had direct access... like someone inside Kanberg, Wallerstein, and Katz."

She tilted her head, letting the silence expand.

The Archbishop's smile broadened. "Old friends. They are big donors to the Church. We all hang out in the same circles."

She gave the slightest nod and gestured toward the photograph.

"You and Kanberg and Wallerstein, laughing it up at some fundraiser. Funny—those men are devout supporters of their own synagogues. Why would they donate six figures to a Catholic arch-diocese? That never made sense."

"Leaders in the legal community," the Archbishop replied, wearing a smug, patient grin. "Leaders support leaders."

Morainya's eyes narrowed. *He's lying.* "So it's just...I-scratch-your-back?" She let the words hang, then advanced. "Because I could have sworn it's because they belong to the British Accreditation Registry—loyal to the Crown, the Lord Mayor, and, ultimately, the Pope. Which makes them *disloyal to me,* their client. Correct?"

A muscle ticked in his jaw. "What is your point, Miss Napolitano? It's the Lord's Day, and my schedule is full."

"My point," she said evenly, "is that the Holy See controls every court, bank, and bench on the planet. That's how you knew who my judge would be—because you *chose* him."

His retort stalled. In that micro-pause she saw it: the tiny calculation of danger.

"You're here about a donation," he recovered. "A million dollars, yes?"

She inhaled—hands trembling in her coat pockets. "That's interesting, because Uncle Aldo just wrote you a million dollar check too. You're taking from *both* sides, Your Excellency. And you never imagined we'd compare notes."

For the first time, the Archbishop looked unsettled. "Aldo has already received a three-million-dollar settlement—wired with your approval. Are you here to threaten me, child?"

"Oh, I know exactly where I'm walking." She lifted her phone and tapped the screen. "I recorded your entire conversation with Aldo. How do you think your donors will feel about funding child abuse?"

"You're bluffing."

She took a single step closer. "Test me."

His ruby ring—*the Bloody Oath of Secrecy*—flashed as his hands clenched. "What do you want?"

"First," she said, "you're going to hand me back Aldo's check. Then the Church is going to pay him three million in *restitution*—no strings attached."

"Aldo has two million already. That is a generous—"

"Generous?" Her voice iced over. "Are you God now, measuring trauma in accounting columns? Maybe you should sit, *Father Joseph*, and make a confession."

His eyes narrowed to slits. "How do you know that name?"

"My mother. She spoke of Father Joseph and the way he 'disciplined' boys at St. Mary's. She left the order—because of the 'retribution of that abuse', remember?"

"We were all sorry to see her leave being a devoted Bride of Christ, but then church life and the path of utter devotion, and *purity* is not for everyone," replied the Archbishop in a practiced conciliatory tone."

Morainya threw daggers with her eyes. Silence. It pulsed between them like a siren.

He exhaled through his nose, moved to his massive desk, and yanked open a drawer. A red leather checkbook emerged. In elegant cursive he wrote: Pay to the order of: Aldo Napolitano — $3,000,000. He tore it free and thrust it toward her. "There. You have what you came for. Now leave."

"Almost." She slid a single page across the desk. "This Non-Disclosure Agreement ensures the Church leaves Aldo alone—forever. Sign."

"And if I refuse?"

"Then the public learns the cost of silencing victims—and the price you put on their pain."

She tapped her phone again. *Bloop*— the tiny recording icon glowed red.

His composure cracked; she saw it in the vein that jumped at his temple. At last, the pen scratched: Guiseppe *DeLaurentis.*

Morainya pocketed the document. "One more detail: the Napolitano family will never again donate a penny to your diocese, and I decline being a co-chair of your Spring Extravaganza." She turned, then glanced back. "By tomorrow morning I expect a letter, with your ecclesiastical seal, affirming that my family are living men and women—not wards, not dead entities—so the IRS and your foreign corporations stop siphoning our labor. You claim to speak for God; put it in writing."

He actually sputtered. "Why—why would you need such a letter?

"You see, the money was for Aldo, but the letter—it's for me." She smiled, a quiet, lethal smile. "Because I no longer intend to pay tribute to Rome or the Crown. Consider it my final confession, Father. So, I would need proof from one of God's own mouthpieces. Isn't that what you proclaim at your Confessions? That you are stand-ins for God himself, and without our confessions to you, we would be condemned to Hell and the Eternal Lake of Fire?"

His Excellency's breath shallowed, then gave a single, reluctant nod. Morainya didn't gloat—she simply smiled, the quiet kind that says: checkmate.

Napolitano Interiors – 1978

Stella, 24. Aldo, 22.

The front bell chimed—low, cathedral-clear—and Aldo felt the old knot cinch under his ribs.

She's here.

He'd rehearsed this moment in the tiny apartment Stefano rented for him above the warehouse: what he'd say if the woman who once stood at the chalkboard—Miss Stella Stallings back then—walked through the showroom doors. But rehearsal is one thing. The sweep of her real perfume—citrus, gardenia, something expensive—was another.

Stella floated in on a shaft of late-afternoon light, catalog in hand, pearls at her throat.

No starched novice's habit now, no faint chalk dust on her knuckles. Only polish. Poise. And the Napolitano name twined around her like ribbon.

Aldo adjusted the stack of invoices he'd already straightened twice. "Good afternoon. May I help you?"

She glanced up, polite but distracted. For half a beat her gaze searched his face—then slid past, seeing only a clerk. Relief and ache collided in his chest.

"I'm collecting my silk order," she said, voice as melodic as he remembered—and as distant. "For Mrs. Napolitano."

He nodded—too quickly. *Don't say teacher. Don't say St. Mary's. Protect her.* "Of course, Mrs. Napolitano. Stefano mentioned you might stop by."

There: a flicker in her eyes at her husband's name. She tucked a strand of hair behind her ear, composure resetting. "You're new?"

"Yes, ma'am. I—returned from Florence last month." Returned. As if he'd chosen exile instead of being shipped away after the...incident. He adjusted the vest that suddenly felt too tight. "I'm Stefano's younger brother."

Something unreadable crossed her face—surprise, regret, fear?—but it vanished inside a society smile. "Welcome home, Aldo."

He guided her to the fabric wall, palms suddenly damp. Bolts of silk gleamed like still water—dove-gray, celadon, champagne. He unrolled the Italian dove-gray first; she always favored subtlety over spectacle.

"Opera-house weight," he said, finding the steady clerk's tone. "Drapes like smoke."

She brushed two fingers across the weave, and for an instant he was fourteen again, watching those same hands glide over lesson plans while boys in the back row tossed spitballs and whispered sins between rosary prayers.

Stella frowned—almost imperceptibly—and asked to see the gray again a moment later, as if she'd lost the thread of their exchange. A trauma echo, he realized. She doesn't know why her mind staggers, only that it does.

He laid the sample flat, smoothed it once more. "gray will look lovely with your honey blonde hair," he murmured, meaning more than silk. He handed her the bolt to examine—and memory struck like a match: the classroom air thick with chalk, his own childish fury sparking when she'd scolded him for clapping erasers too slow. He thought of all the caustic words he'd once spat at her, she'd reflex-slapped his cheek, and in that blind surge he'd lashed out with his right fist. He still heard the dull *thud* of her body against the desk, saw the thin trickle of blood where the corner had cut her brow. Left side—because he was right-handed. Even now, as she leaned in to study the weave, he caught the faint drift of her gaze—her left eye lagging half a breath behind the right. A small misalignment no one else might notice, but he knew exactly when it had been carved into her. The glassy terror he'd put there flickered across the silk between them, and shame burned his throat.

He hadn't meant to hit her. Not really. Not like that.

But that week... something in him had splintered.

Father Joseph had cornered him in the rectory office—again. The priest's breath sour with sacramental wine. His hand resting too long on Aldo's backside. Also shoved him hoping to escape. But the Father struck the boy on the back with his belt. Twice he managed to welt the skin. The smile beneath the robes. That hissed whisper: *"Good boys stay quiet."*

He had clenched his fists so hard his nails left crescents in his palm.

And that was the day he told Stella off in class. Spoke back to her when she tried to discipline him. He saw red. He saw robes. He saw shame.

Then her body hit the floor.

He hadn't known what to do except run. He dropped out. She resigned without explanation.

Now, all these years later, standing in a suit imported from Florence, here she was. A tremor passed through him.

Did she remember?

He hoped not.

And yet... he almost hoped she did.

Because then maybe someone—*anyone*—would know that he had been broken long before. Stella reached across the counter, fingertips grazing a bolt of violet silk, when her elbow caught a narrow porcelain vase by mistake. It tipped. Slipped. Shattered across the tile in a clean, echoing crack.

"Oh!" She startled, instinctively stepping back. "I'm so sorry. That was foolish of me."

"No... no, I'm sorry," he said gently. "That shouldn't have been so easy to break. It was just an old lavender vase I found in the Florence markets—just a trinket—it reminded me of home."

She paused, still crouched. Her eyes lifted to meet his. "I used to love lavender," she murmured, then trailed off.

He looked different up close—European-cut blazer, bone-pale skin, nearly colorless lashes. His hair, white as linen, caught the afternoon light like threadbare silk. Young, but not unsure.

Aldo packaged her order, slipping an extra length of dove-gray into the tissue. No charge, the note said, Compliments of the house. She gathered the package, pressing them to her chest like armor. "Well. Thank you for—"

"No trouble at all," he said, voice warm but measured. "It happens."

Aldo stood there quietly, setting the cloth-wrapped fragments aside. Not angry. Not ashamed.

Just a boy who once broke something...and knew how to gather the pieces.

The bell chimed once more and she was gone, silk parcel tucked under her arm like a secret. Aldo exhaled shakily, pressing a hand to his chest where his heart refused to settle. He'd survived the encounter—kept the past sheathed, spared them both the reopening of wounds.

Gold Gates Sanctuary – Present Day (2022)

The view from Stella's window caught the last blush of light over the bay. She sat in her favorite chair, a patchwork of velvet and worn tapestry, wrapped in a cashmere shawl. The nurse said she hadn't eaten much. But now, she perked up, eyes fixed on the tray.

Aldo placed it gently in front of her—three little sandwiches, cut diagonal, just how she liked them. A lemon cookie in the shape of a fleur-de-lis. A small vase of lavender.

"Are you going to the gala at the DeYoung?" he asked lightly, pulling up a chair beside her. "I hear they're honoring the work of San Francisco's interior designers. You'll be the belle of the ball. What are you wearing?"

Stella blinked at him, confused, then smiled. "Something silk," she whispered. "Maybe dove-gray."

He grinned. "Perfect. That would look lovely with your honey blonde hair."

He didn't expect her to remember. He never said who he was.

But he came once a month, always with something—fabric swatches, cookies, an old photo from a society column. Once, he brought her a handkerchief monogrammed with the letter *S* in gold thread. She'd touched it like it was a crown jewel.

"Or, maybe I'll wear something scandalous," she said with a grin, then forgot what she'd said and asked again, "Will there be dancing?"

He helped her eat. Cut her pear into perfect slices. Complimented her lipstick. He just tried, in his own way, to bring something beautiful back.

She giggled once—like a girl at a boarding school window.

When she looked at him, there was no recognition. He never brought up the past.

And maybe that was mercy.

Later That Day

Morainya was leaving when she passed him in the hallway. He wore a navy coat this time, carried himself with an elegance that almost made her forget.

"Thank you for the check," he said, softly, a childish crooked smile crossed his face.

"Thank you for returning my check—and for paying Stella's bill," she replied. "I know she doesn't remember. But I do."

He gave a faint pained glance. "That's what family's for, isn't it?"

She watched him walk away. Saw the man who broke things. But also the man who tried, in his own broken way, to tape something back together.

She didn't forgive him.

But she didn't need to.

She reclaimed her power the moment she stopped needing an apology.

29

*T*ime realigned itself, enabling the room to spin around and reconfigure. Tick, tick, tick; a sound unknown to us, yet made us inwardly aware that time, no time, existed simultaneously—we were in the in-between. Our fingers reached, desperate, as the Orama dissolved like steam— untouchable even as we longed to hold him in place, as did the myriads of crucibles, phials, bubbling cauldrons, and all the accouterments of an alchemist's lab. Ana-Kharu and I were suddenly thrust out of the intimacy of the inner sanctum to find ourselves spilled out beneath the colossal paws of the Great Sphinx, just as the sun cracked open the horizon. One paw alone could shatter us—its stone claws curved like judgment. The class of initiates united once more, gazing up at the Red Lion, which was erected as the regal guardian fiercely protecting Khemit's mysteries. No one even noticed that the two of us had been absent for days. Time had floated by without even a thought given to us insignificant specks of sand.

"Did we fail?" I whispered to Ana-Kharu, steadying myself on the enormous extended right paw of the Sphinx, the stone cold and smooth beneath my touch. Its sharp claws pierced the ground like fangs of judgement. "We came so far... and ended with empty hands."

The Gold Magician scowled, and I could tell he, too, was feeling disheveled at being cast out of the rumbling belly of the Sphinx for not transcribing the last star. "We must have." He hung his head, mirroring how I felt. He could have easily blamed me for not finding the last one, yet he just reflected upon the mission.

We had our chance to receive the Osirian Karrastt initiation and obtain the red lion concoction as our reward, easily saving my father. We messed up. The class stood around us, enveloped by the sun-warmed ancient stone of the red lion, hardened to our misery and disappointment.

"Merit-Aten, Beloved, can you believe we are here, where once our Grand Elder Tuthmosis, the greatest warrior of all time, stood," said Smenkhkare in a reverent voice as he placed his hands upon the stone lion's base on a causeway surrounded by a large body of water. Behind the Sphinx appeared the white-marbled pyramid rising to the heavens, nearly scraping the clouds. The capstone beat rhythmically, crowning the roaring lion in all her glory. It was a sight to behold. The power of the water flowed around us and charged the air with vibrancy.

'GRRRRRaaaaaaaa," roared the Red Lion, which reverberated in my ears. The Rrraaaa made me contemplate if she was calling to Ra, the Great God of Cosmic Sun. A crow circled and cried, Caw, Caw, Ka," making me recall the Ren, a bird body transporting the Ka or spirit upon death. The lamb bleats out Baaaa, Baaa, or the BA body because it is the Lamb of God, the lamb that feeds the Ba body. Maaaaa, Maaaa, bleats the Goat, or Maat, the Justice of Aries the Warrior preserving Ma'at, the balance of all things.

Here we are united, standing in honor of this lineage of Khemit's past and future. This will be the story we will tell our Grand Akh, grandchildren." He closed his eyes, drinking in the orange glow of the fiery sunrise radiating off her sculpted body. Strangely, his mention of children surprised me because he gave me no indication that that wouldn't happen somehow. Smenkhkare, my new consort, was so beautiful, and his heartfelt knowledge of our past warmed me. His green heart energy flowed to everyone.

The red lion loomed—stone carved from her own bones, reborn from the desert's belly. Her presence stirred something older than memory in my blood. I squeezed Smenkhkare's soft hand but still secretly yearned for Archollos; as I peeked around my Consort's shoulder, hoping to catch his eye. My constant draw to him confused me, and I felt ashamed that he had shared a bed with my mother, and yet I could not eliminate my desire for him. He stood stunned in her shadow—my golden one—an outsider swept into mysteries meant for kings. Had he not been washed up upon these shores, he would not have had this chance encounter with the Sphinx. I spoke to my classmates, for some still did not understand the greatness of our shared lineage of the Pharaonic lines.

Smenkhkare continued, "When Prince Tuthmosis IV was merely a youth, as the story goes, one late night, he wandered into this very spot and fell into a deep sleep betwixt the Lion's paws, exactly where we stand now.

Tefnut had whispered to him: *"Lift the sand that veils me, and I will lift your enemies."*

Ra-Awab scrunched his brow, squinting toward the carved face. "Tefnut? Spittle of the Goddess? What could that possibly mean?"

We analyzed the feminine Negroid face of a Per Aat wearing the blue and gold striped Nemes Headdress, the sweet touch of the feminine, because the Sphinx had the breasts of a woman, scales of a fish, lioness claws, feathers of a bird on the hind quarters, hooves of a cow, and a curling lion's tail. Each feature stitched into her mythic body—fins, hooves, feathers, claws—was not arbitrary. It was a blueprint: survival encoded in sacred form.

The hueman face represented the primal urge of the animal portion of man in his lower chakra or the animal brain. She ruled from the solar center—the fire in the belly, the sun housed in flesh.

"As I have been told, Tefnut is the feminine expression of the Lion Goddesses, such as Sekhmet,

Men-Het and Mut, as one of the first Neters, Nut, the Goddess of the Sky, spit upon the land, and it was the first physical manifestation in this world. The Sphinx, they say, was not built—it was uncovered. Chiseled from the Earth's bones, not laid stone by stone but liberated from living rock, long before the pyramids dreamed of their first block.

Tadushet exclaimed, "She is older than the pyramids."

Keshtuat said, "It is our tradition of the Mother principle in full aspect."

We all nodded in reverence to the Great Mother, the Big Mama Triple-Black energy that nourishes us all and from whence we first emerged.

I paused—and then said, "It has been said that if you listen quietly, with inner reflection, you may hear Tefnut give you a message."

We tuned in, hoping we'd be fortunate enough to receive her blessings and hear her words.

Time bent like reeds in the Nile—as the deep voice of the true divine ancient black Mama rolled through me like a forgotten lullaby. Tefnut," I pleaded "speak into my ears of vibration."

"Merit-Aten, welcome home," she boomed just for me alone.

"Welcome home? I have never been here before," I thought in a tiny meow, as a suckling lion cub would to its mother, whom she was dependent upon for sustenance.

"Many lives, many names. In this great cycle of time, you have come and gone and will do so again. Cycles within cycles."

With the taste of ancient soil on my tongue, I inhaled the breath of life as if an ankh was held to my nose, and I drank it in as if wisdom had weight and taste, as if my bones could hunger and be fed. This felt like a vivid dream with accentuated colors, smells, and flavors from a time I could not recall but felt as familiar as mother's milk. The Sphinx's message was etched on my mind as hieroglyphics on a blank wall, so I embarked on a journey of self-discovery.

This time, seeking balance and justice to harmonize the world, I walk again, draped in the whispers of those who came before, every step echoing with the hush of sandal-wood and bones. My inner drum beat rhythmically while the scene changed over, and over again, an old, withered man, a mighty foreign king, a young woman lifting her baby, a weary warrior, a pleading crone, and an aquatic female offering cowrie shells. How many times have I returned? This was the catalyst for change within me as I ventured deeper into an extraordinary mystical moment; presented to me by the Big Mama of the Celestrovese, curling her tail around my being and pulling me into her heart.

As the supernatural voice and the dream receded, once again in feeble utterances, I questioned the elusive revelation, was I worthy of the spirits' parting syllables? Insecurity rose like smoke, curling through the corridors of memory—every failure, every fork taken blind. The door we'd unlocked stood ajar, but I could not see the passage beyond. The demons of insecurities that haunted us flared up, reminding us of the failures and blurred missteps through the winding corridors of time, unsure of which path to take. Here, we had come this far; a door had been unlocked that we never knew existed. Yet even though we were in the vicinity, I still knew not where our teacher Djehuty lay hidden in the shadows. The anxiety gnawed at me like chewing flesh off a bone.

Proving how insignificant what I wanted was, time shifted again, like panels of a scene being pulled apart and flipped. Now, the entire class was deposited within a brilliant sunlit golden limestone chamber, yet there was nary a window. A fiery flower of life emblazoned the back wall; the symbol was seared into our memory. Three pillars in the shape of a triangle stood in the center of this room that had been carved out of the hard sand rock. White Tura limestone lined the walls, indicating many causeways that lead to other mysteries.

Djeuty appeared: ibis-headed yet leonine in stature, skin deep blue-black, gold kilt flashing. The striped Nemes crowned him like the Sphinx reborn. In his left hand, a staff tipped with a six-pointed star and blossoming pinecone; in his right, a golden ankh. Atlantean glyphs flickered along his cuffs. A golden ankh was held in his right; his wrist cuffed with a golden bracelet engraved with unknown symbols from the time of Atlantis.

"O Thrice Great One," I breathed, bowing low. Light pulsed from him—mercy and immensity entwined. My classmates dropped to their knees as if gravity had tripled. He towered above us, a figure of divinity and wisdom, upon the dais of truth, before the throne that symbolizes the eternal balance of the cosmos. This holy man's eyes penetrated us, humbling us while making us feel alive. The dark halls of Amenti were his abode, presiding over the Hall of Records, a circular passage downward leading the way into the time-space continuum where the crystalline records were kept.

Then spoke Djeuty, the Architect of the ages, the Builder of the eternal pyramids,

"Lift thine eyes to the Light,
for in the Light, ye are
one with the Master, and
the Master is one with the All."

He struck the ground with his staff. Blue fire surged outward—the first flame of creation—filling the air with the essence of the One.

"Come forth, O Children of the Khem," he spoke.
"For the hour of your awakening is at hand.
The portal of night turns,
and the Fire of the All awaits
to cleanse and renew.

With arms outstretched, he enveloped us in his sacred aura. His form, ever-shifting, reflected the hues of the eternal: black as the void from which all emerges, copper as the sacred sun, green as the light of creation, and blue as the celestial radiance of Sirius.

This contrasted with the yellowed limestone walls surrounding us. Not meaning to be disrespectful, we stared open-mouthed; how could we not when placed at the feet of this gentle giant? If he did not send out a vibration of utter love, we would have been intimidated instead of comforted enough to be in his magnetic presence.

"We dispense with pleasantries," Djehuty intoned,
"for the knowledge of the past
must be grasped to unlock
the mysteries of the present...
and the destinies of the Children of Khem.
May the Light of the Eternal
shine upon thee, now and always.
Draw near, and be seated,
that I may unfold the tale of my becoming—
and fill thee with the Spirit of Life."

Then he raised the Ankh, the sacred Key of Life—a symbol of all that is and ever shall be.

Plush cushions of the finest materials and colorful tassels appeared at his feet. The most delicious delicacies and cups of cool liquid waited for us to indulge. We took a bite of the heaven-sent treats, and tasted the nectar of the Gods, which I recognized as soma.

"Children of Light,
I summon thee forth—
to rise from the chains of night,
to cast off the veils of forgetfulness,
and to stand in the Fire of Remembrance.
Hear my words...
and we shall commence."
He paused, and the chamber

pulsed with breathless stillness.
**"Behold—I stand before you
with the head of the ibis.
My likeness is etched upon the walls
of the sacred temples,
in the land of Khem... KMT...
where time was first spun into stone.
Ponder this:
Why have I chosen this form?"**

A few hands went up.

The Director of Destiny motioned for us to speak while remaining still so as not to disarm.

"The ibis must put its beak deep into the soil," said Tadushet with a meek voice.

The Keeper of the Flame said, **"Keep digging."**

"The Ibis has a long beak to find morsels of food below the surface," said Rennutet, in her shy voice.

"The Ibis gathers his sustenance from the muddy fields. It symbolizes that he must dig deep in the darkness to bring it to light," said Ana-Kharu.

"Your beak represents the long quill used to write, as you are the Father of Writing," said Smenkhkare.

"Indeed, thou art correct." His beak snapped shut with the finality of ancient truth. Then spake Djeuty,

**"Voice of the Hidden Flame:
Ye must delve into
The knowledge of Self. Pierce the veil of night
in pursuit of that which is sacred—
the wisdom hidden beyond the surface.
For the surface holdeth
only the mundane...**

the shallow roots of common knowing.
But true wisdom dwelleth
in the depths—in the
shadowed chambers
where the unknown abideth.
It is there ye must go.
Wisdom is not given.
It is earned— through toil,
through solitude, through the sacred walk
of perseverance.
All that is... hath emerged
from the blackness.
From the Void was born the Flame.
And Wisdom?
She is the Light that shineth
Forth from that Flame.
For Wisdom is All.
As the sun illumines the world,
so doth Truth illumine the soul.
The Heart is the gateway.
The Soul is the vessel.
And through that portal—
the Light of Wisdom shall flow."
We nodded.
"As for the quill and
the creation of writing,
that honor belongeth to my
beloved consort, Sheshat."
"Do you have other names?" asked Archollos, searching
for a familiar name in his mind's recesses.
"Many are the names I have worn—

Hermes, Thrice-Great. Tehuti.
Djehuty. Thoth, carved in memory
and stone. Scribe of the Eternal Flame.
In tongues unknown to Kemet,
they named me Quetzalcoatl—
Feathered Light, Bearer of Time.
Teotihuacan, mirror of Giza,
was carved in my memory—
a city of stone and sky,
built for those who remembered
the Light of the Aten.
I was once a Priest-King
of the luminous isle—Atlantis,
whose crystal hearts
beat with the Sun Disc's code.
But in one thundered breath,
the heavens split.
The sea rose.
And my sacred sanctuary
was swallowed whole.
We, who once walked as gods,
fell into clay. The Golden Age washed away
beneath the tears of the Aten.
Those who soared
now slumbered.
Those who knew
now wandered.
Until the day the scroll
would be read again.
I remained. I remembered.
I carried the Codes—

in scroll, in breath, in temple bone.
So if you awaken
in the smoke of memory,
know this:
You were there.
And I am still writing you home.

"Were you the Priest King at the time of the cataclysm?" asked Smenkhkare.

"No."

Thoth did not blink. His eyes, the color of obsidian storms, narrowed into stillness. Not anger. Not grief. Just the weight of knowing—etched across a face that had recorded too many betrayals.

That throne belonged
to another— a king who bartered
with invaders,
seduced by land, power,
and gold beyond his karmic due.
But when one grasps beyond
his allotted fate, the fall is swift.
The earth itself trembled.
The stars recoiled.
And all consciousness fractured.
The survivors—what remained—
descended into shadow.
Thus began the age of Amun,
when light dimmed,
and truth became rumor and
rumor became doctrine.
In the Great Forgetting,
they lost more than their stories—

they lost the gift of speech,
the ways of the body,
the rites of the dead.
Even sustenance became guesswork.
They became dwellers in the dark,
beasts with names forgotten,
scratching at memory's door.
It was then I was summoned.
To raise them. To teach them.
To re-light the fire
that once made gods of men."

"How did they start to remember?" asked Ra-Awab, his body tense, muscles flexing.

"At the places of power,
where crystal meets water," Djehuty spoke, his hand sweeping toward the plateau,

"there was found solace...
and healing."
In these sacred spaces,
the veils of perception
were momentarily lifted—
granting glimpses of the Divine.
Here, upon mounds
such as this, the mourners would gather
to remember the echoes
of their ancient sorrows.
These mounds, imbued with
the currents of sacred energy,'
grew in power and significance—
so much so that walls were raised
to shield the holy from the profane.

And thus was born the offering.
Not for transaction,
but for remembrance.
From this seed,
the primitive Priesthood took root—
and flourished."

So, this was the evolution of god consciousness, I thought, imagining this very mound of where it began.

"Then came the question
of the people: "What shall we do with our dead?"
And the Priests answered:
"Bring them unto us.
In exchange for a portion
of thy harvest,
we shall tend their bodies,
and usher their Ka unto Amenti."
And so it was.
The farmers obeyed.
They sowed their fields in devotion,
and baked loaves of wheat
in the shape of a nose—for scent,
it was believed, called forth the Ka.
And when the scent of fresh bread rose,
the sacred rites commenced.
Thus dawned the Age of Amun.
As the years turned,
the Priests fashioned rituals
ever more elaborate.
Grand tombs were carved from the cliffs.
Precious objects were offered in abundance.
Gold, lapis, ushabti, sacred oils.

**And in time...the offerings
were no longer for the gods—
but for the Priests. Vast wealth was amassed.
And in their greed,
they severed the living cord
to the Source— a connection
that is the birthright of every soul.
Thus was born a great distortion.
For the Priesthood, once sacred,
became consumed by power,
indulgence, and control.
They told the people:
'Your dead must be fed.
They require jewels.
They require servants.
Only through us shall
they find safe passage.'
And in their desperation,
the people complied—
eager to secure peace
for those they loved.
But in truth...peace cannot be purchased.
And the Source cannot be bartered."**

We were horrified. The vastness of this breach of trust shattered us. This was exactly what my father tried to ban when he outlawed the worship of Amun. Some clutched their chests in disbelief, as if shielding their hearts from further betrayal. Others dropped their gaze, unable to bear the magnitude of what had been unveiled. Oya turned in a slow circle, whispering invocations under her breath, calling on the spirits of her ancestors to steady the room. Ra-Awab let out a sharp cry, not of pain, but of rage restrained. Even Smenkhkare, usually so composed, pressed his hands to his temples as if the truth itself scorched him

Djehuty sighed. A deep and sorrowful sound, as if millennia had exhaled through him. His shoulders, cloaked in indigo linen, barely rose. The ibis beak of thought now softened into the weathered face of a man who had watched too many suns set on broken vows.

His skin held the burnished hue of ancient bronze, etched with time—not age—and his eyes, lined in ceremonial kohl, did not glisten, but *held back oceans*.

"In time... thieves came.
They breached the sacred tombs—
plundering the treasures
meant to accompany
the departed into eternity.
And lo...they learned
that the mummies did not rise.
No fire from the sky.
No wrath from the dead.
It was, to them...a farce.
And so, the desecration continued.
The Sesh—the unlearned—
knew not the deeper laws.
They could not read.
They could not write.
And yet they preserved the lie.
Not from malice—but from ignorance...
and fear.
For the families...
they *needed* to believe

their beloved would
find peace in the Fields of Eternity.
But alas, that peace was traded for illusion."

He bowed his head, and silence wrapped the chamber. Then he raised his gaze, and the light within his eyes returned.

"Should thou be wondering
I did not reign during this cycle of despair.
Nay—I was sent forth
by the Source, to create,
to teach, and to establish
societies in need.
I brought the arts of agriculture,
the science of mathematics,
and the sacred geometry
of divine wisdom—
that civilizations might rise again."

He paused, listening—not to sound, but to the questions stirring within our souls.

"I perceive your need
for greater clarity.
And so... I shall illuminate
the path before you."

We nodded because we experienced so much darkness in this once great age of enlightenment. This ancient trauma at the core of my being led me to wonder if this was why I felt compelled to save my own family and feed my people.

"My Lord of Alchemy, your image is everywhere in our land, on walls and ceilings and statuary; you are still honored here as the Ancient King of Khemit," I declared.

"Verily, it is so.

I was drawn to this fertile land
of fertile minds, where I imparted
my teachings for sixteen thousand years.
We are *not* here to repeat the cycle.
We are *not* scribes to the unrepentant.
We are *not* offering scrolls to
the same hands that burned them.
We are the guardians of the
New Scroll, and this time,
it will not be dictated to thieves
or shared in temples built
on stolen breath.
So, no—we are not teaching invaders.
We are calling the inheritors.
We are summoning the coded ones.
We are gathering the flame-born
who never forgot the scroll of the Sun.

Djehuty paused, allowing silence to settle like a veil of incense over us. Then, his voice lifted with playful gravity: **"Now, let us engage in a game."**

With a graceful motion, he conjured a large white ostrich egg—smooth, ancient, gleaming with otherworldly sheen.

**"This game demands your complete
focus and presence.
I shall cast this egg to the one who must answer my question.
Know this: Should you let
my precious egg fall,
you shall be turned to stone.
If you cannot answer my question,
you shall also become stone.**

Do you accept these terms as fair?"

We nodded, but fear welled up in our bodies. I felt my neck and shoulders stiffen. The Great Master Teacher tossed the egg to my consort. Smenkhkare caught it—but not cleanly.

The egg rocked in his palms, his fingers tightening too quickly, as if afraid it would vanish or reveal too much if held too loosely. and for the briefest moment, the boy behind the crown was visible. He looked down at the egg as though it might crack open his fate.

"A prize awaits the one who uncovers
the hidden thing," said Djeuty.
"But before I reveal where we stand,
I must guide you to recall where we began.
Son of a Pharaoh, tell me, to which god does
Akhenaten devote his entire being, his very soul?"

Smenkhkare's smile broadened, "The Aten," he spoke out, holding that parcel out to toss to the next.

"Correct," Djehuty said, his voice smooth as stone.
"But do you fully grasp *why*
he chose this god—
a lesser-known deity among
the 42 tribes of Khemit?"

He stepped slowly across the limestone floor. "Why Aten?"

He let the name hang like a bell.

"Consider this: there were three others—
three mighty gods with vast followings.
Ra-Atum, Ra, and Amun.
Each with temples that stretched
to the horizon. Each with priesthoods that

swallowed gold like sand.”

He paused, letting the weight of the question settle upon us. Then—without warning—he pointed at me. **“Toss the egg to her.”**

It flew across the space. I caught it. Warm. Humming. Alive. It knew me before I knew it.

And I spoke: “Although Aten was a lesser god by name, he could be presented with purity. For his solar resonance had not been corrupted by the Amunite priesthood—those who distorted the pantheon and matrixed the Neters into the Amentian portal system.”

The room grew quiet. A few winced. Others looked at each other with surprise.

Djeuty tilted his head, almost smiling. Not with joy, but with the bittersweet recognition of a truth finally spoken aloud. For the student had remembered. And the flame had returned to the field. Then he said—

“Aten, was the beacon of the Enlightenment Age—
the pure sunstream of Atlantis
at its zenith, before the Anunnaki
descended and captured Tiamat
before Shan fell into forgetfulness.”

The golden egg pulsed in my palm. Djehuty gazed past me—not as a man remembering, but as a god *reliving*.

“Shan—as this planet is known across the cosmos—
is the realm of the dead.
Its inhabitants dwell in darkness,
severed from the Light,
consumed by violence and strife.
What a plan it was...
brilliant in design,

yet tainted by a shadowed hand.
A golden age once rose
upon these lands—
destined to carry its people
to the highest realms of ascension.
But it was shattered. Devastation fell.
Everything I had raised…
was brought low.
Ensnared. Inverted. Profaned."

His voice did not shake—but his sorrow rang like bells in the bones. Then he turned back to us. His gaze cut through time. His eyes flamed with purpose. **"Toss the egg,"** he said and flicked a wing.

Djeuty blessed us to be in pure Cosmic fire. I felt energized, renewed, revivified.

"The first worship was of the Sun." Djehuty's voice echoed like flame through the chamber.

"The Divine Solar Light—radiant, eternal,
the source of all that breathes.
Ra, principal Sun God of Khemit,
held dominion over all seen and unseen.
But before Ra, there was Ra-Atum—
the primordial essence,
the undifferentiated Solar Flame.
He was the cosmic pulse,
taught in the Heliopolitan School—
not as deity alone,
but as the Universal Solar Force,
the rhythm behind the turning spheres."

He raised his staff, light glinting off the tip like the first morning. Then softly, with eyes fixed on the next initiate:

"Now...toss the egg."

Keshtuat caught it. Her fingers closed with surprising grace—not delicate, but deliberate, like someone who'd held fire before. Tall, obsidian-skinned, with cheekbones carved like memory, she stood rooted—a priestess in the making, torn between awe and recall.

"What are the physical manifestations of the sun's rays?" asked Djehuty.

Keshtuat said, "The Ib-Ra-El, the obelisks, and pyramidions were sculptures of the sun rays.

Djeuty nodded, then said, **"Khemit was a solarium archetype, and Ra was that representation. Toss the egg,"** commanded Djehuty.

Tadushet fumbled, barely keeping it within her arms yet, capturing it before it splattered upon the stone.

Djehuty watched with care, then sat down upon his throne.

"Why do we coat our temples, statues, and religious relics with gold?"

Tadushet glanced down at the egg and paused. Round-faced and eyes flickered—not with fear, but calculation. she carried the weight of Babylon in her hips and heart. We held our breath, fearing our dear sister might be turned to stone.

"Gold is the physical manifestation of the sun. We empower these objects with solar light to bring through the highest resonance." She smiled, flashing her white teeth.

"Indeed," responded the Thrice Great, his voice low, as if speaking not only to us—but to the Akashic winds.

"I see that you have studied well.
The teachings of Bu Wizzer
have not been lost on you.

And yet...if you truly understood
the precipice upon which you stand,
you would tremble beneath its weight."
He paused—not for effect,
but for reverence.
"You dwell now in the realm
of Akhenaten—the Dreamer, the Priest-King.
He who built an empire
not of conquest, but of *transcendence*.
An empire of love, of soul rectification,
a vision not seen since the first breaths of Lemuria."
The air shimmered as Djehuty continued:
"Like me, he sought to restore true authority—
not through force, but through the revealed wisdom,
the radiant emanation of the Divine.
He forged a religion of Light,
where the Sun's blessing was open to *all*.
His temples stood beneath open skies.
And in that sacred architecture,
there were no veils, no hierarchies,
only communion.
The Aten—both the Sun of this Earth
and the Great Central Sun of Alcyone—
was made *visible*, was made *accessible*.
And this...was his offering."
Thoth closed his eyes briefly. Not in fatigue, but in reverence. As if he were tasting an ancient note only his kind could still hear. When he opened them, a shimmer passed through his iris—not gold, not blue, but something closer to sound. Then he spoke:
"Consider... why was *Aten* written

with the *Ra* at its end?
Not as an unvoiced mark—
but as an echo. A resurrection. A seal.
***Aten Ra.* Ah-ten-Aaaa-Ra...**
The breath of the cosmos made audible.
A name that carries principle, not just sound.
***Aten-a-Ray*—the primordial sign of light.**
Not light alone, but light named,
light poured, light offered into form.
***Aten A Ray*—so powerful, so transparent, so divine."**

We drank in every drop of this wisdom, swirling around, the sweetest juice of knowledge like that squeezed from sun-ripened grapes. Until now, this has never been revealed to a class of initiates. We truly were the Children of the Light, or Sun.

Then Djehuty lowered his gaze, and a flicker of deep sorrow passed over his face—not for one king, but for an entire generation.

"One of my greatest disappointments
arose during the era of the Pyramid Builders—
a time once crowned in gold,
yet now shadowed by the birth
of the Amun principle."

He stepped closer to the inner circle.

"In those days the early Pharaohs
were not merely kings.
They were initiates.
Endowed with celestial powers,
they traversed the cosmic pathways—
the luminous routes that spiral outward
to Orion and Sirius.

Through these star-journeys,
they communed with the Neteru,
the star gods, and together we co-created the
Great Pyramids—structures not of stone alone,
but of harmonic proportion and stellar alignment."

He turned toward the West, where the light dimmed against the chamber wall.

"These Pharaohs stood at the
threshold of interdimensional power.
They were not bound to flesh,
but walked between realms—
diving deep into the hidden corridors
to undergo the sacred journey
of the Three-Day Osirian Initiation.
Death. Dismemberment. Return.
They did not simulate it. They *became* it."

I gulped, for this Universal Master must know that Ana-Kharu and I had failed that test. I would have to commit this discourse to memory, fearful that I would not be able to recollect every word to tell my father upon my return.

The Ibis-headed God paused, his gaze cast inward across centuries.

"In bringing Amun into this temporal realm,"
he began, **"the great question arose:**
How might we cause a god of infinite
force and power to descend into the physical world—
and yet remain veiled in mystery?"
He nodded slowly.

Even in ibis form, he emanated solemn grace. His feathers shimmered not with color, but with the muted sheen of aged linen—a mantle of unbleached priest's cloth, draped like a scholar, not a king. Around his neck, a simple torque of copper and lapis glinted, etched with scroll glyphs only the initiated could read.

"Amun was made subtle.

Intangible. Unseen. How did Amun appear

in this temporal world?"

'They crafted him in the image of a man?' I said. I wasn't trying to honor him. I wanted to expose him. To drag his shadowed name into the light and give the people a face to question—a form to *dismantle*. How had we let a god with no image rule with such cruelty? Hide behind sanctums, speak through trembling priests, and demand blood under the banner of the unseen?

Thoth didn't answer right away. He studied me—like he was deciding whether I could handle what I already suspected.

Then he said it, calm as ever:

"Let him be hidden. He shall dwell within the

innermost sanctum—

the Holy of Holies.

There, unseen, he shall symbolize the

universal principle of the unknown...

and through that mystery, subjugate the

people of Khemet beneath the veil of power."

Djehuty shifted uneasily upon his throne.

"Thus was Amun made ruler over all.

Supreme over soul and system.

He claimed dominion over:

—finance—religion—law—sustenance—

and the very breath of life.

Blessings were withheld unless paid

**for in full. And so began the tyranny.
An empire of fear arose—a dark inversion
of all we had built in Atlantis.
When the Great Pyramids were complete,
the people revolted.
A fatal war erupted. And in the aftermath,
the Priests of Amun tightened their grip even more.
Thus was the Cycle of Suffering sealed."**

He looked upon us, and his voice fell heavy.

**"The Amun Principle closed the path home.
It draped the afterlife in shadow,
and sealed the gate behind the soul.
It whispered lies between lifetimes,
so we would forget what we are
and worship what we fear."**

He closed his eyes.

**"The Priests of Amun sacrificed
their own essence—severing their divine
connection in exchange for material
and occult power. And in that descent, it became
a contest. A ruthless hierarchy, where only the few
could draw near the Chief High Priest—
and even then, only to seek dark sorcery."**

I felt it before I realized I'd moved. A shudder crawled up my spine, settling at the nape of my neck like a serpent that had tasted its prey. I was seated cross-legged on a deep indigo pillow, the color of bruised sky—the only color in the room beside my plain white linen sheath, damp now at the small of my back. *Ases-Amun...*The High Priest.

He was back. I thought my father had exiled him to the quarries, his sorcery buried beneath sandstone and silence.

But I swear—I saw him. On the road to Giza. Cloaked. Watching. Breathing.

Around me, the others shifted—silent confirmation that I wasn't the only one. We all concurred. Because each of us had felt it: that moment of testing by a priest of Amun, where the air grew too still, and the choice—soul or submission—hung like a blade in the balance.

"Toss the egg," commanded Djeuty.

Tadushet obeyed—but with trembling hands. The egg arced into the air, rising, spinning slightly—as if unsure who was ready to receive it. Before anyone could move, Ra-Awab lunged forward, his movements swift, deliberate—and snatched it mid-air.

He lifted it high above his head, grinning with triumph, as if catching the sun was proof of destiny.

Djeuty cocked his head, slightly amused.

"How does this contrast to the age of the Aten as achieved by Pharaoh Akhenaten?"

Ra-Awab raised the egg. He was all angles and presence—broad-shouldered from early ship work with hands better suited for rope and ledger than scrolls or breathwork. The son of a wealthy sea merchant, but not the heir—delegated instead to the temple path, a gesture to status, not destiny.

The white sheath clung awkwardly to him, like the robe knew he was here to prove something rather than receive it.

"The Aten is everything and for everyone. It has no anthropomorphic human form, so it cannot be defined," replied Ra-Awab.

His answer echoed well enough. Clean. Correct. But something in it felt...memorized. I narrowed my eyes. Not in judgment—but in caution. There's a difference between speaking truth and *wearing it like a borrowed cloak.*

Djeuty sat upon his golden throne, flanked by two majestic lions— one beneath each hand, their gleaming bodies cast in purest gold. The left lion was Shu—bearer of breath, the yang principle, thermal force in motion. The right lion was Tefnut— goddess of moisture, the yin principle, the cooling balm of existence.

And then it struck me—From Nut, the stillness before separation, Yin and Yang had been spit into form.

I had become—from One God, *three Gods*, each aspect unfolding outside of myself.

Everything in Kemet was a symbol. Every throne, every lion, every name.

And Djehuty, seated between time and truth, was not merely a god—but the Master MetaScribe—transcriber of Divine Thought, scribe of the Infinite Mind.

He cast the egg into the circle.

"In the time of Atlantis," he said,

"the Aten shone upon the world

in perfect alignment with Source.

We were not separate. Not lost. Not veiled.

Every stone, every river,

every breath was sacred. Flesh and spirit danced

as one. The Ka did not wander in search of the Khat—

for there was no veil between them.

There was no longing.

No seeking. We simply *were*.

Some among us wept. Others whispered affirmations. We had never heard it spoken so clearly. Then he turned to me.

**"Your father labored mightily
to reignite the Divine Spark—
nearly lost after the fall of Atlantis.
The Sage—called *The Wizzer* in the old tongue—
watched over the descent, holding
the codes while the world forgot.
But restoring light in an age of
forgetfulness is no simple task."**
Djehuty's tone shifted, his voice becoming
a blade wrapped in silk.
**"My brother, Marduk—known to some as Amun-Ra—
was the most ruthless ruler
during the Age of Pisces, the Age of the Fish.
He demanded unwavering worship, threatening
annihilation to all who stood before him.
He enforced a rigid dogma—
insisting that he alone
be revered as the wrathful god
above the Neteru.
And so, even now, at the close of every prayer,
his name is whispered: 'Amun.'
A tribute to the darkness.
A memory not easily erased."**
The air around us stilled.

For the first time, I understood—My father had not acted from ego. Not heresy. Not madness. He had outlawed the worship of Amun to *liberate the people* during a reign of terror. He had struck a match—and Khemit burned with it. Not in destruction...No, in divine re-connection.

My hands, resting in my lap, tightened into fists before I even noticed. My breath caught—held between grief and awe—and when it finally released, it came out as a small, sharp sound—not quite a sob, not quite a prayer. Something in between. My spine straightened. Not from pride, but from something deeper—like my body was aligning with the truth I had never been allowed to carry.

"Toss the egg," said Djehuty.

Ra-Awab obeyed, his throw more performance than prayer—but it arced smoothly through the air and landed in the hands of Oya, the dancer. She sat up straight, hips rooted, spine fluid. Her silver-painted face shimmered like lightning on the Nile, and even seated, she moved like a storm waiting for rhythm. Oya caught the egg effortlessly, as if she'd been born with it in her palm.

"And now," Djehuty said,**"having tasted a glimmer**
of thine oneness with the Source, thou asketh—
Why is there no scroll?
No doctrine? No sacred script
that speaketh of Atlantis?
Know this: The memory of Atlantis hath
been cast into the sea of myth—not by accident,
but by design."

Oya answered, "We have an oral tradition. We learn at the knee of our mothers; knowledge is passed on from our ancestors through the line of the mother." Without waiting for approval, she tossed the egg to Ana-Kharu, who was already rising—a panther at the edge of firelight.

Ana-Kharu caught it, calm and sure. "Our memories have been kept intact. We do not need scrolls."

Djehuty nodded.

"Indeed, Twaman, your tribe has walked
this world for 450 million years since

**the first incarnation of Ptah. You have witnessed
the rise and fall of countless civilizations
spanning eons. Within you lies the memory of
every sunken city, every vanished tongue.
You carry the scrolls in your bones.**

A moment passed—charged and still.

"Now, toss the egg to Pharaoh's daughter."

Again, I caught it with delicate hands. "Father says, if
it had to be written down, then it is not the truth. One can
distort and lie about what is written down to distract us.
If we have no memory, then what is written down becomes
fact," I added plainly as if speaking what had always lived
in the silence between us.

The Great Architect spake, his voice smooth as the first
breath over still waters:

**"Correct. When thou alignest with
Source Consciousness, the light of
the Aten shineth equally upon all.
In such a state, there is no need for priests.
No temples. No sacred texts. No hierarchy. No war.
For Truth is not taught—it is remembered.
And it is directly linked to the soul's own essence."
He waited, and the silence bowed in reverence.**

Then came the blink—slow, deliberate—from his great
ibis eyes.

And with a swift snap of his beak, he opened his mouth
and revealed a large, glistening red tongue—the color of first
fire, the sigil of speech before language. Then he closed it
again.

**"Your mothers, surely, have spoken of the
360 senses we once possessed in Atlantis?"**

Murmurs stirred among us.

"We were endowed with 180 degrees of harmony...

and 180 degrees of discord.

Not all love. Not all light.

But *wholeness*.

Perhaps you were not told:

This was an Atlantean gift.

Passed through your lineage—

encoded in bone and breath—

a gift encompassing the full spectrum of existence:

the good, the bad, and the none."

We listened as if our ears had opened for the first time.

"In this day of the Cosmic In-Breath," he continued,

"most of you retain but a few of these senses:

sight, hearing, taste, smell, and touch.

But in the days of your full awakening,

you wielded senses far beyond these.

Telepathy. Clairvoyance. Clairsentience.

Telekinesis.

Teleportation.

And *Telechronos*—the sacred art of time-perception."

He stepped forward now, his feathers glinting in hues unseen by ordinary sight.

"Imagine, if today you lived

in full *Teleniscence*— the complete sagacity

of those ancient senses returned.

You would know, without seeking.

You would move without delay.

You would feel the breath of another

before they spoke.

And the life of every being—

even your enemies—would be transformed.”

Ra-Awab motioned for the egg. Once caught, he shouted out, “We could not lie because everyone would know. We must be in full transparency.”

Everyone laughed, perhaps reminiscing about the tiny mistruths that were spoken daily to keep from hurting feelings, escape a reckoning, or flatter for favors.

“Correct,” Djehuty intoned, his baritone voice reverberating through the eternal stone chamber. **“If I were to say that I admired your hairstyle—yet inwardly recoiled at its green hue— would you not sense the lie?**
Not by the words, but
by the discord between
what is spoken and what is felt.
In such a moment, who here would
bear the weight of judgment?”

A few cast their gaze downward, eyes wide with the sting of recognition.

“But my words,” he continued,
“are not meant to cast you into shadows.
You are not here to be condemned,
nor to seek salvation for the missteps of the past.
Sin—**as you call it—is not a moral crime.**
It is a state of misalignment
with the truth of your soul.
The remedy is not punishment,
nor payment to priests for absolution,
nor self-flagellation clothed in shame.
Simply... correct your course.
Return. Re-member. Re-attune.
The reconnection is immediate.

Transformative. Integral.
Unitive Consciousness—
your direct link to the Divine—
resides not in intellect,
but in cognition and intuition.
It is a state that cannot be *thought into*.
It must be *lived*.
To remain in the Light,
you must engage with the Divine—
not just in temples or books,
but in breath, in movement, in being.
Yet, this Cycle of Time has seduced you
into over-thinking, into worshiping
the mind over the Source.
You rationalize each step,
when what is needed is surrender.
The inner yoke back to the Divine.
The re-linking.
This is the true essence
of why we practice *yoga*—
not for poses, but for Union."

Chastising myself had become a silent ritual. I was ever guilty of thinking too much, of tracing and retracing paths that never led me out—only deeper into the same ancestral loop. Perhaps it was inherited: the endless over analysis, the need to *fix*, to *understand*, to redeem what could not be undone.

My father, Akhenaten, had clawed his way through the dens of vipers, desperate to reawaken our connection to the Light. He was not perfect. But he yearned—God, how he yearned—to restore the flock to their own divinity. He sought to bypass the loop of fear and greed and terror by creating a *Cosmic Portal*—not just for escape, but for remembrance.

He dreamed of a return. To wholeness. To the One. As Osiris was reassembled from fragmentation, so too did he hope we'd *re-member* ourselves, and reopen the ancient stargates. The wisdom of the star gods still echoed in him— he only wanted to bring it back.

Djehuty blinked slowly, as if absorbing the weight of every thought swirling in the chamber. Then, he spoke.

"I can hear you," he said, voice calm but thunderous.
"All of you. Even when you say nothing,
your suffering screams.
You are addicted to it.
To the ache.
To the drama of your own confusion.
You dwelleth in the labyrinth of overthinking,
believing the problem is the path—
but it is not.
You do not feel for the solution.
You think your way deeper into pain.
You turn from the simplicity of grace.
There is no salvation in the maze.
Only in the stillness,
where thought ends, and knowing begins.
You were not meant to live in riddles.
You were meant to *remember*.
And remembering is not of the mind,
but of the soul."

I pursed my lips. *How could anyone wish for suffering?* The thought struck me as preposterous. No one desires the sting of the lash, the cold silence that follows a slammed door, or the shadow of a threat hanging over supper.

I had borne witness—the Amunites' lust for power turning men to beasts. I saw mercenaries cloaked as soldiers pounding on the doors of the voiceless, stealing silver for tithes, or demanding the blood of a child in exchange.

The people of Thebes—they didn't choose to suffer. They were born into smallness, into mud and market stalls, with no ladder to climb and no god who answered.

Here I was again, overthinking. A familiar heat coiled in my belly—not just rage, but despair at injustice. I recognized the unraveling. I was spiraling away from Source, again. And in that recognition came shame. Self-hatred. Another loop. *I am failing. Again.*

The Master Teacher stood. His voice was not raised, but it struck like a bell through water.

"Cease. The internal chatter.
The self-condemnation.
It grates upon my ears.
You can lie with your lips—
but energy and vibration does not lie.
Every ripple of disharmony,
every flicker of misaligned thought, spreads.
A single wound within becomes a wave without.
The ethers echo what you emit."

He stepped forward. Not angry—*aware.*

"My compassion runs deep,
deeper than your oceans of grief.
But know this: I have guided you—yes, you—
through shadow and fire, not to punish,
but to prepare.

It is no accident.
No fate nor whim.
You were sent through death,
so that you may walk through the gates of the Living.
This realm—" he gestured around us,
"—is your crucible.
But it is also your key.
You cannot ascend without first learning
how to move through this world
with your eyes open and your soul lit."

I could feel the utter disbelief that spread amongst my friends and foes. Djehuty had guided us by some unseen hand to the Sphinx. Predestined? Or did that mean we had to will our forces in this world? Was everything planned? Tingles rose up my arms, and my toes curled when I felt out of control. It crept like careful cat feet to pounce upon me when I least expected.

"Had you only read of this journey in ancient scrolls, would you truly understand his trials?"

He let the silence hang, heavy with implication.

"No. You might imagine the heat—
but never feel it.
You might fear the unknown—
but never stand before it.

Thought alone cannot open the path. You must experience. To *cognize* a thing, you must first *feel* it. In the inner realms, overthinking bringeth ruin. There, thou dost not plan—thou *asketh*. Thou dost not analyze—thou *knoweth*. He who delayeth with thought is already swallowed by illusion.

Dost thou comprehend this?"

"Yes," we said, still trying to figure out what he meant and how it applied to our lives.

Deepening the lesson, Djehuty asked, **"Why journeyeth the soul through the Fourteen Cycles of Time? What purpose lieth therein?"**

His voice, calm as eternity, carried the weight of a thousand scrolls.

"Mark well the mystery of Ausar—Osiris—
The once-Whole One who was torn asunder
into parts by Set, This was not of vengeance,
but Divine Design."

He stepped forward, staff etched with cosmic code.

"Set, the Adjudicator of Polarity—
did cast the Solar Flame into shadow,
that it might be *tempered* For power without wisdom
corrupts, and immortality without
humility leads to ruin.
Each piece, each Cycle, was a crucible of refinement.
Ausar had to descended into fragmentation
to earn the Mantle of Unity.
When the scattered becometh sacred—
when each forgotten note remembereth
its Song—only then may the Whole rise again.
Thus, Osiris is not merely the Dying God—
but the Final Sun, the Ultimate Son.
His tale is thine.
For thou, too, must walk the Spiral.
Thou too must break—to become Divine."

Our faces brightened with this new hidden revelation. Osiris was not killed; he was being taught patience and wisdom from being dismembered; he had to learn to rule from all parts of himself until he could once again re-member himself as whole.

Then, Djeuty raised his left hand—the Hand of Receptivity—and did trace a glowing arc in the air, a crescent of light that burned like the edge of a solar disc.

"Ausar... Osiris. And when the Sun entereth
the House of Leo, the Son reclaimeth his Throne."
He turned toward the East pressing the
Staff of Remembrance into the floor.
The chamber did hum with response.
"In Leo, the Sun burneth
full in its glory—three hundred
and sixty degrees of Divine Creative Flame.
Therein doth the Son rise to Sovereignty."
With his right hand—the Hand of Command—
he did draw a line from the stars above
unto the temple floor, calling Spirit into Form.
Aries is the Portal of Heru—the Warrior Son,
who goeth forth with spear in hand
to defend the Law of the Father."

He began to pace in measured steps, each movement inscribed with cosmic weight, like a scribe marking time in the Book of Life.

"And yet," he continued, voice lowering like a hymn,
"it was Auset—Isis—She Who Knoweth the Hidden—
who gathered the scattered,
who wove the bones and breath back into form.
She restored the Flame."

He stopped before the Djed pillar of the perfected spine, etched into the wall before us. With solemn grace, he touched it with the crook of his staff.

"She found it—the Djed—his pillar his phallus,
the very spine of the Creator King."

Turning back to us, his eyes glowed a spectral blue.

"She did not merely restore his body—
She re-membered him.
His power. His purpose, His cosmic place.
It was her womb—her lock— that received the key."

Djehuty clasped both hands at his abdomen and lifted them slowly upward in a spiral motion, a gesture symbolizing resurrection, kundalini, and sacred return.

"Only through that sacred act—
the merging of pillar and portal—
staff and chalice, flame and vessel—
could Ausar be reborn.
His Ka was rejoined
With his Oversoul, And in that moment and
thus the blueprint of creation reactivated."

He stepped back into the center of the circle, lifted his open palms to the heavens, then lowered his gaze upon us like the first dawn.

"This," he intoned,
"This is the eternal rhythm—
the Song of the One who becomes Two
to become One again.
Creator and Createrix.
Masculine and Feminine,
Lock and Key, Womb and Flame.
Together, they spiral the cosmos into form,
forever and again."

While this myth was told to us over and over as children, it would take a Master teacher to reveal to us the truth inside the tale—the scroll within the scroll. Only now did I understand why I was meant to find *my* key… the one to unlock my own portal—so that *we* could traverse the universe and return to alignment with the Great Source. A sorrow massed through me then. I knew. Smenkhkare would not be the one to open and apart me. Hi hands bore no map for the cosmos within.

"Indeed," spake Djehuty, his tone both mirthful and grave, as only an immortal scribe could deliver a cosmic pun, **"Thou might say that Ausar—Osiris was *res-erect-ed.*"**

He paused. The word pulsed through the chamber. a holy hush folding around its double-meaning. Lifting his crook high, he drew a vertical line from above crown to solar plexus— as if etching the spine of God through the space between us.

"For in the sacred act of *re-membering*—
when intellect giveth way to inner knowing—
the alchemical transmutation doth occur."

The gold-hemmed robes shimmered with every step.

"From lead to gold," he intoned,
"from flesh to spirit, from illusion… to essence."

With each phrase, he extended his palm—offering invisible gifts to us initiates.

"It is not locked in vaults
nor smelted in flame.
It is the shining of the inner god awakened,
the Ka in full remembrance of its Source."

Then he approached the stone wall etched with celestial glyphs, and with one luminous fingertip, he traced a sun within a sun—the Aten nested within itself.

"This alone is thy task upon Earth."

His voice turned to obsidian.

**"All else is folly—false rites, empty scrolls,
blind devotion to a god thou knoweth not."**

He cocked his ibis head, peering straight into our marrow.

He came to stand before the stone wall etched with stars, and with a fingertip of light, traced a circle—a sun within a sun—before turning back to us. He tilted his ibis head slightly, as though peering into our bones.

A silence descended. Not hollow. Holy. Then, with the sharp *click* of his beak, he asked:

**"Without union with Source,
all worship is but shadow.
You light candles to a hollow name,
you sing hymns to a god deaf to your cries,
for you have not yet remembered
thy own divinity."**

A heavy stillness fell over us. With a single snap of his beak, he declared, **"Do your ears of vibration ring true?"**

The walls vibrated faintly in answer—soft, sublime. From deep within the chamber, a harmonic resonance emerged— like the tone of a golden fork pressed to the soul.

Some wept. Some knelt. And I—I placed a hand upon my womb.

It was so clear. So easy. We get off the path by thinking about God but not feeling the God within.

"It hath been written that you are to receive the Regulan Initiation." Djehuty declared, his staff striking the ground with soft finality. **"Why Regulus?"**

He paused. Then, with a flick of his ibis beak, **"You tell me."** He turned and pointed at Rennutet. **"Toss the egg to her."**

She sat folded on a dusky teal cushion, the woven patterns of her Nubian shawl trailing like river reeds across her lap. Her round cheeks flushed under the weight of attention, but her amber eyes stayed calm—ancient in their knowing. "Regulus, the brightest star in Leo's crown." Her gaze drifted upward as if she could see it even now blazing above the desert. Then, with deliberate stillness, she passed the egg to the one beside her—her hand lingering a breath too long.

Smenkhkare received it with a flicker of hesitation, then straightened his spine and stated crisply: "Alpha Leonis." But there was no roar in his voice. Only the echo of a king unsure of his throne.

"Any one else?" asked Djeuty, his voice smooth as a windless lake. His gaze swept over us—each soul weighed, measured, not by intellect, but by frequency.

Archollos straightened, eager. "In my culture, we heard the great myth of Hercules who slayed the Nemean lion of Regulus," added Archollos, smiling that he had something to add.

Ana-Kharu, calm and precise, added, "For the stellar alignment."

Djehuty's eyes narrowed, gleaming like twin orbs of starfire. He folded his hands before him, the ibis-headed god now fully still, as if syncing his breath with the pulse of the cosmos itself. The room quieted, the stone beneath us seeming to vibrate in expectation.

"Good," he said, voice low and clear as a chime.

"Stellar alignments are not mere markers of time.

They are the scaffolding of thy *Sah'u*—
your Stellar Lightbody—for without it,
thou shalt not find thy way home."

He raised his arm, tracing an arc across the air that shimmered faintly, a constellation blooming in above us.

"By home, I do not mean back to Akhet-Aten,
nor to the golden palaces of Khemit,
nor even to thy temples of past glories"

He passed over each one of us, pausing briefly.

"I mean *Home*—the place before form.
The womb before wombs. The Light before light."

Then he asked:

"Again, why *Regulus*?"

He let the question hang, and the silence it summoned was powerful—like a forgotten name about to be spoken.

"The ancients called it the
Heart of the Lion. The Watcher of the North.
The Portal of Kings."

He touched his own heart.

"Regulus is no mere star. it is a calibration key—
a royal encoder. It sits upon the ecliptic
like a sentinel, guarding the arc of thy return.
To align thy Sah'u—the Stellar Lightbody—
with Regulus, is to re-enter the path of
Divine Rulership. Not rulership over others,
but mastery of thy own domain."

He began to circle us, slowly, his cloak sweeping like a great wing tracing time itself.

"When Akhenaten attuned his temples to the Aten,
he realigned the Earth's grid. An ancient act of
frequency correction. But Regulus...Regulus

**is the throne-star. It governs the Leo gateway,
and through it, the Sovereign Blueprint is activated.
None may inherit thy full power
without passing through its field."**

He paused. The torchlight flickered against the polished stone as if even flame bowed to the name.

**"Regulus is where the soul learns
to lead with the heart, not the sword.
Regulus teaches *nobility*, not conquest.
Radiance, not domination."**

Then, his voice dipped to a whisper, cutting clean through bone and memory alike:

"So I ask again... why Regulus?"

I caught the egg and said, "Regulus is in the heart of Leo. The Lion whose celestial body the Sphinx—a creature half woman, half lioness—gaze eternally." I tossed the egg to Okun, the drummer.

Djehuty nodded. **"Pointing you in the direction home. Continue."**

Okun struck his drum softly, as if calling memory through bone. "The constellation has one of the stars of Khemit called Denebola, the pole star." said Okun, who then tossed the egg carefully to Anpu.

Anpu's voice was low, grounded. "It is also known as *Qalb al-Asad*—the Heart of the Lion."

Then the egg flew to Ana-Kharu.

"Yes," nodded Djehuty.

I felt Ana-Kharu's gaze sear through the moment. The air between us pulsed—not with rivalry, but with the dense, breathless silence of fate unspoken.

Though the Master Teacher uttered no word, we both knew: something sacred shimmered just beyond reach. Not glory, nor victory, but a key. A key ancient and coded in starlight. One that would tip the scales.

Whatever it was that the Master Teacher prepared for the victor, it was more than knowledge it was a key. A key to something long hidden. Perhaps it would restore the balance between us. Perhaps it would decide whose destiny would carry the greater burden. For me, it was the life of the Pharaoh at stake. For him... I could not yet say.

Suddenly, Ana-Kharu simply turned—and hurled the egg straight at Archollos.

Gasps. The ritual was no longer theoretical.

My beloved lunged, arms wide—too late. A heartbeat's hush: if the egg shattered, the alchemical backlash would turn his living flesh to stone.

A surge of will tore through me. Bluish lightning leapt from my fingertips, grabbing the egg mid-flight. Suspended in a vault of electric light, it hovered at room-center. I exhaled relief—then shame flushed my cheeks for seizing the spotlight.

Djehuty rose, robes whispering. **"Keep it rotating,"** he commanded, making a slow circle-gesture in the air. **"Regulus perfects itself by spin. So must you."**

I obeyed. The egg turned, faster—light slid across its surface until it glowed cerulean. The chamber filled with a pale-blue radiance that dusted skin and stone alike. Djehuty's ibis eyes gleamed.

"Regulus," he said, now pacing, staff etching luminous sigils on the floor,

"whirls so swiftly its sphere

distorts into an oval—an egg in the firmament.
Spin is its shield and its song. Thus, do we model
the star. Thus do we crack the shell of forgetfulness."

He nodded, satisfied. Behind him, Ana-Kharu's expression shifted from mischief to grudging respect.

Djeuty whispered without words.
The restoration of Source-Light falters
because the multitudes crave noise over silence.
Solitude is the portal; stillness, the key.
Without cosmic nourishment Earth
relives ruin and rebirth,
Ruin and rebirth, in endless echo...

The words rang like a private gong inside my skull. My embarrassment steadied—I locked eyes with Archollos, then with Djehuty. The egg held firm.

Djehuty stepped forward, and touched the rotating egg. A burst of gold through the blue—merging solar (Regulus) and cosmic (Aten) codes displayed for us to witness.

My mouth fell open. It was right before me. This test was never about physical reflex but about *instinctive alignment* with cosmic law. Some students bowed; others felt the first stirrings of forgotten senses.

Djehuty's new, leonine face—half god, half Sphinx— regarded us in silence. **"What is the greatest form of strength?"**

No one answered.

Meekness, I thought, used to mean mild. But the meek my father praised, carried no ego-construct, no self-image— nothing for Amunite power to manipulate. I raised my hand.

Thoth nodded.

"I, a Pharaoh's daughter, was raised to lead by display—gold, armies, decree. Yet Spirit whispers: give it all away. How can I be both? If I relinquish abundance, how do I shield my people? Father has already done it—laid down crown and ego, trusting the Aten alone. Amun's priests call him weak because they cannot fathom a ruler without an outer sword.

I felt suddenly ancient and infant all at once—seeing a sliver of Father's plan, yet I could not yet bear its weight.

The ibis head dissolved into living sandstone, the hawk-lidded eyes of the Sphinx glinting with feathers.

"Life is cycles within cycles," he said, voice now a resonant baritone that vibrates floors.

"He who seeks to break free must
First liberate himself from them.
Your father upheld his duty because he
discerned the imbalance most clearly.
Leadership, in divine law, is given not to
the proud but to the one who *sees*
what must be healed."

Gold, I reminded myself. Father needs it—alchemical, not mined. If this Master can hasten the Work, Aten's kingdom might yet be restored.

The Thrice-Great tilted his head, listening inward.

"Ah—where are my manners? My guests desire *gold*," he said, dry amusement in his eyes.

"And I ramble on about cosmic resonance.
Is that not so, Pharaoh's Daughter?"

Heat flared in my cheeks. *He heard every private thought.* I managed: "Y-yes, my Lord. My father bids us learn the alchemy of transmutation."

Djehuty halted; the hush rang like a tuning fork.
"You imagine we have not begun?
Every test since your arrival—
the egg, the spin, the silence—has been alchemy.
Gold is not metal; it is *conscious light*.
Transmute the self and the kingdoms follow."

A soft *clack* of his beak (or was it the echo of stone jaws closing?) punctuated the lesson. A dozen pairs of eyes swung toward me, not in scorn, but in dawning realization.

"The meek shall inherit—because
only empty hands can hold the Sun.
The true Work had been underway
from the first breath in this chamber.
It is complete," Djehuty intoned, thunder in his voice.
"The path I prepare is not one of
remembrance alone—
it is the path of Becoming.
You shall find no instructions
in scroll or tablet; this knowledge must temper
itself in the crucible of experience.
Your initiation will not be told—it will be lived.
Carry no satchel, no bread, no staff.
Where I send you, none of these shall avail you.
All you require will rise within—or not at all.
For the realm ahead is woven of
flesh, fire, and vibration."

His ibis eyes sparked with distant constellations.
"I will pair each of you with another.
In a world of polarity, you must meet the One
who has most to teach—or most to learn.
Aten will choose, and in that sacred mirroring

the illusion of separation will be torn apart."

With a sweep of his hand the east wall dissolved. A vast circular gateway pulsed alive, swirling through jade to primordial green, beating like a cosmic heart.

"Gather—two by two."

Pairs formed quickly:

Ra-Awab with Oya

Rennutet with Okun

Ana-Kharu with Keshtuat

Sarawat with Apu

Smenkhkare with Tadushet

I reached for Archollos—our eyes already meeting—when Djehuty's voice sliced the moment.

"Not you two."

My fist curled. "What?"

His Sphinx-like face showed no ripple of emotion. **"You must learn from another."** A single, slender finger pointed—first at me, then at Smenkhkare.

Smenkhkare bowed. "As you wish." He took my hand. "Apparently, our lesson is unfinished. This time, I mean to prove worthy."

I swallowed hard. "As Djehuty has decreed."

At the rear of the hall a long gold-draped table materialized, each place set with a gleaming ankh.

"Take the key with your right hand. You have seen the gods hold this sign—a badge of those who step through time."

He lifted a rusty-brown handful of Red Lion powder.

"With this, my parting gift."

A single breath—scarlet dust fanned over our faces. We inhaled; forgotten stars flickered awake behind our eyes.

"Qualities long buried rise now to light."

Two by two we approached the living gate. Smenkhkare's grip tightened on my fingers; Archollos watched, jaw set, as the light swallowed us. *Was this the price of asking for gold? To be flung like an unrolling scroll into uncharted time?*

Djehuty—the Architect of Consequence—stood immovable, lion-throne gleaming, as the last pair crossed the threshold.

Green brilliance folded shut—and the story leapt forward into another age.

orainya pushed her way through the heavy door into the Gold Gates Sanctuary. After checking in with the Receptionist, she made her way through the maze of hallways to find her mother's room. Upon opening the door, her mother was arguing with her caregiver.

"Your daughter will be here before noon," coaxed the caregiver, her voice soft, spoon extended like a peace offering. She leaned forward. "Let's finish your breakfast." The lady bent over, trying to give her mother a spoonful of eggs, but Stella defiantly shoved them away.

"I don't have a daughter. I never had any children," declared Stella. She made a fist.

Morainya's stomach churned as her face drained of color. It was one thing to accept her mother's dementia, but to be erased from her mind—entirely forgotten—felt like a brutal, invisible wound. She forced herself to breathe, pushing the sharp sting of anger aside, and tried to focus on compassion.

"Mom, I'm right here. Of course, you have children." Dropping down to the level of her mom's wheelchair to give her a better view of her face, Morainya turned her tone to a cheery, bright one, hoping to engage her mother's interest.

"What are you talking about? You are lying. You are all liars. I never had children and never had a husband. I chose the church." Stella turned her face away and fixated on the white cooing dove outside her window, now pecking at the seeds that had been left.

"Look a dove," Stella murmured, as though the accusation she had just made never passed her lips.

"Yes, Mom, you love the birds. Here, I think I have a picture of you with the pigeons that you used to feed." Morainya fished around in her purse and pulled out a pile of black and white photos that she had collected from one of the large albums in her parents' living room. "Look, mom, remember when we used to go to Fisherman's Wharf on Sundays after mass?"

"I don't know where that is," said Stella, but she took the photo and stared at it intently. "Who are all those children?" she asked innocently holding the photo close to her eyes.

"Look, Mom, that's me, Nico, Francesca and Emilio."

"Do I know them?" she looked at Morainya with her eyebrows arched.

"Yes, Mom. See, that's you with your Sunday hat and gloves and your crocodile purse.

These are your children. Remember how I feared the pigeons, but you brought bread from home to feed them?"

"Sourdough?"

"Yes, that's right. The sourdough bread from our dinner the night before. Look how Francesca and I wore the same dress that matches yours?"

"With the pockets." She added as if a tiny door in the recess of her memory had opened."Yes, you loved pockets." Morainya tapped the pockets on the girls' dresses.

Stella's face shifted. Her gaze locked onto Morainya— but it was not her mother's eyes staring back. Something ancient stirred behind them. "Merit-Aten," she said, her voice richer, deeper—someone else's memory pushing through. "You always thought your mother didn't love you, that she abandoned you."

Ice trickled down Morainya's spine. "Mom—it's me, Morainya. Your daughter. Look at the photo."

Stella's lips curved into a soft smile, her eyes flickered briefly with a knowing clarity. "I know exactly who you are—who you've always been. And I know who you were meant to become."

The room seemed to shrink.

"She didn't reject you, my love. You simply didn't need her. Not when your father's light was enough."

Morainya was shaken by Stella's sudden clarity, even if she had gotten her history mixed up and was talking to a stranger from another land. That sudden burst of energy faded, and Stella, who only a moment before had a gust of lucidity, the breeze had now diminished. The woman's face lined with age, could only stare out the window and admire the dove.

Morainya retreated from the dementia facility, tears streaming down her face as she sped toward home. Her mind raced with questions—why couldn't her mother see her? Why was she talking about things that had nothing to do with her. She only had moments to connect with Stella before time ripped that fragile thread away. Stella, trapped within her own failing mind, and the lifeline that should have tethered them together was gone.

She screeched into the driveway, barely waiting for the garage door to close before flinging her car door open. Her overnight bag hit the hallway floor with a dull thud. Her keys clanking against the table as she dropped them in frustration.

"Josh, are you home?" she called out, but her voice just echoed off the empty walls.

Then a knock on the door shattered her thoughts. With a sharp exhale, she yanked it open, only to find a delivery man with a clipboard. "Courier for Miss Morainya Napolitano," he said, his laid-back tone like one of those surfer guys who moonlighted as a delivery guy.

"Of course," she muttered, signing for the package, her impatience simmering.

Her hands trembled as she tore open the cardboard envelope, her eyes racing over the harshly worded formal DEMAND LETTER by Kanberg, Wallerstein, and Katz. The familiar weight of dread settled in her chest, and her heart sank at the sight. The firm was demanding immediate payment, threatening dire consequences if she failed to comply. She almost heard her lawyer's voice in her head, smug and damning, her anxiety translating every line into a personal attack. She fumbled for her phone, fingers shaky as she typed out a text to Sal.

"The firm just sent a DEMAND LETTER saying they want all their money now." Morainya stepped on the wet carpet in the living room corner. It must be another leak from the thunderstorm. Just another thing breaking down. She sighed and stared up at the ceiling. When would it end?

Sal returned her text advising her to *scan the 'presentment' and send it.* She wished Josh were home—he always helped her remember how to scan and email. But he wasn't, and she'd have to figure it out herself.

"Hey Sal, the courier also brought a NOTICE OF SUM-MARY JUDGMENT. Kanberg, Wallerstein, and Katz are asking the judge to award them $98,658 in damages, plus another $50,000 in penalties—for what they call 'frivolous Notices.'" Morainya sat on the floor, the legal documents spread across the carpet. *"They're claiming I didn't respond to the last letter and haven't offered to pay. They're saying I used Sovereign Citizen language as a ploy to dodge the bill."* Her breath caught in her chest. The pages blurred.

Sal's reply came instantly. *"We, as living men and women, don't respond. We reply. That's the game—forcing you into a Maritime contract you never agreed to."*

Her fingers trembled over the screen. *"Then why the threats? Why the aggression?"*

"Because you're out of their jurisdiction, Sal replied. *And that terrifies them."*

Morainya wished that comforted her—but the DEMAND LETTER sent her back into her depths of despair. She texted, *The firm is claiming I am a Sovereign Citizen."*

Sal read the text and rolled his eyes. *"Of course they're calling you that. It's the oldest insult in the book. 'Sovereign Citizen' is an oxymoron—sovereign means free, and 'citizen' comes from Rome. It means that through which all Power flows. SLAVE or 'CIVILLY-DEAD.'"*

Right. "I know. She nodded, then typed. *"I just feel like if I called them, maybe I could explain and end this."* Her confidence wavered, even as she hit send.

Sal's text was immediate. *"Your law firm doesn't care about who you are now, only who you Were—when you were still in their jurisdiction."*

Morainya needed reassurance. Comfort that they'd leave her alone. "Why the threats? Do they understand Constitutional, Common law, and Public law?"

Sal answered, *"You sent them two replies to both their previous threats. The third one is the charm."* Texting was ridiculous, instead he called her.

"Hey, Morainya," Sal said when he called her. "remember when you sent me the Retainer Agreement for Kanberg, Wallerstein, and Katz? Here is where it gets fun. That's our leverage now. I'll have your Final Notice ready in two weeks. Don't worry—this one will catch them off guard."

Morainya felt better after Sal's call. He had the calming ability to talk her off the ledge.

Josh came home a short while later, radiating joy. He was glowing from his class trip, giddy as he told her about kissing Katie—his high school crush since sophomore year. Her heart swelled with relief. His happiness was the balm she hadn't known she needed. Only a week until graduation. Then he'd finally get a break from Jedidiah's materialism. He was headed to Brown, and for the first time in weeks, Morainya could breathe easier. She wasn't jealous anymore. She was proud.

True to Sal's word, the new Notices arrived in her inbox two weeks later. Morainya opened the pdfs with shaky hands, her eyes scanning the Notice of Rescission. The term was clear: the original contract was now null and void. All the legal fees and the three-million-dollar Settlement fee would be due to her since the original contract was now null and void. The weight of it hit her like a tidal wave, but through the blur of tears, one thought emerged—Sal was a genius.

Gratitude surged through her, deep and overwhelming. She had been drowning in a sea of legal battles, and he had thrown her a lifeline. Her shoulders shook with sobs, which emanated from the core of her soul. Freedom from her enemies, from the oppressive weight of this legal system that had held her hostage for so long.

This Rescission Notice was accompanied by a Notice of Dishonor to be sent to each member of the law firm, the Opposing Attorney, various court officials, and with the San Francisco Superior Court Clerk.

With the familiar task ahead of her, Morainya made her way to the copy shop again. This time though, there was no hesitation. She knew the rhythm—how many Notices to print, how to sign each with blue ink, how to assemble the pages with precision. The night before, she had already prepared the envelopes with names and addresses. She thought back to the first time she had done this, how overwhelming it had seemed, how many mistakes she had made. But now the process flowed with ease, each step unfolding smoothly. She could imagine herself walking into the post office tomorrow, mailing the final pieces that would close this chapter.

By the time Morainya was on the road back to San Francisco, a quiet smile had spread across her face, and for the first time in years, she greeted the day with a newfound self-confidence. The world no longer pressed in on her. Instead, she pressed back. Learning how to take charge of her life after her father and former husband had handled so much—no longer dragged her down. No one handed her this burden—they hurled it. And she'd hauled it like a mule for years. The world has been her mirror, reflecting back the lessons she refused to learn. Kanberg's condescension. The Archbishop's expectations. Even Iben's silence. Each one had been a test, a lesson in how much disrespect she would tolerate.

But now, for the first time, she felt intense gratitude for it. It had forced her to grow, and step into her own strength. Deep within, she realized she had been so afraid—afraid of disappointing her parents, especially her father. When he raised his voice, or when he was upset, she had taken it as a sign that he no longer loved her, or that he thought less of her. Now, she saw it was all a lie she had told herself—that she was unworthy of love and respect.

But that wasn't who she was anymore.

But she wasn't that woman anymore. The woman who had once bowed to the weight of others' expectations, who had lived in the shadow of her father's and husband's dominance—she was gone. She marveled at how far she had come. At first, she had reveled in the excitement of her connection with Iben, but now she saw the true gift in their union. During the darkest, most excruciating moments of her life, she had not been alone. Iben had been there, constantly by her side. More than just company, he had introduced her to Common Law, to the concept of being rooted in the Land and Soil. Before meeting him, she would never have had the capacity to understand, nor the strength to bring such knowledge into her life. Iben had opened her eyes to a world bigger than what she had ever imagined. Though he knew the depts of her past, the woman she had been in that distant time in Khemit, it was through his eyes that she began to understand who she truly was. His teachings had shifted her perspective, guiding her toward the truth of her own power.

He had shown her that Kings and Queen's don't accept things as they are—they ask questions, they seek understanding. That single insight had changed everything. It wasn't just about learning the law or the world around her—it was about learning how to ask the right questions and reclaim her sovereignty.

Right on cue, Morainya's phone buzzed—Kanberg's voice poured through, clipped, frantic, cracking under pressure. The Notice of Rescission and the Notice of Dishonor had pushed him to the edge—just as Sal predicted. He was unraveling, realizing with increasing panic that there was no contract to bind them. Morainya felt a strange sense of power rise within her, a shift she hadn't expected. She wasn't their mark anymore. The ground had shifted—and now *they* were scrambling to catch up.

"Are you ready for the next step?" Sal's voice was light, almost gleeful, but there was a sharpness to it that matched the weight of what was coming.

"Sure," she said, masking the clench in her gut.

"Ten copies. Fast," Sal said. "You know the place."

Her stomach tightened. "Got it," she replied, though the words felt hollow. She could hear the certainty in Sal's voice, but the gravity of the situation hung heavy over her. Each step felt like a leap into unchartered territory. Could she really do this?

Sal clacked away at the computer until he hit enter. Done. "You are going to send it to quite a few people, including the California BAR Association, the California Supreme Court Justices and Secretary of State, the Court Clerk, and the Law Firm. Are you ready for this? It will then be put on the Public Record for all to see."

"Yes, I have to bring Justice, for myself and others who have been at the hands of people we once trusted. I have to make it right," she responded, with more certainty in her voice.

"I'm sending it now. That's not the only thing. Wait three days for them to receive it.

You've given them three Notices now to answer all the questions you've asked that they never bothered to 'respond' to because they won't admit guilt. Therefore, they have dishonored themselves and their Oath of Office and we'll send them a fee schedule, which is a bill x 7."

"That's twenty one million dollars." The words left her lips before her brain could catch them. They hung in the air like a blade.

Morainya swallowed hard. "I don't know if I can do that to them...to anyone." Her voice wavered. "It would ruin them."

Sal remained unfazed. "And what did they do to you? Isn't your pain and suffering worth that?" His voice cutting straight through her hesitation. "Were they worried about your ruin when they double billed you? When they dragged you through discovery hell? When they threatened to bury you in penalties?"

Morainya exhaled sharply. The weight of injustice pressed on her chest, mingling with the last remnants of guilt. Maybe Sal was right. Maybe this wasn't revenge—it was balance.

She could almost hear Sal grinning—this was the part he lived for, where the predator became the prey. "It will take a while to recover. But, what I will guarantee you is that you will feel a sense of Freedom, Justice and Empowerment from taking your life back. Now, they will be at your mercy rather than the other way around. It's time for the little guy, or in your case, gal, to win."

The words echoed in her chest like temple bells: Freedom. Sovereignty. Balance. No longer abstract—now embodied. Freedom. Sovereignty. Balance.

Sal paused. "They never worked for you. They worked against you."

She said nothing—but her silence was no longer fear. It was conviction. A quiet vow rising from the wreckage: *Not on my watch, not again.*

Hours later, it struck—like lightning through bone. A pulse curled around her spine, humming like a forgotten hymn vibrating through her blood. She gasped, the echo of him threading though her body.

How can you be so far away, yet inside me? The question burned as she gripped the wheel, her knuckles white.

The enigma of him—this spectral lover who haunted her thoughts, who pulled at her in ways no earthly man ever had—both terrified and enthralled her.

Consent—our most sacred currency, spent daily without thought. Click. Sign. Nod. We hand over our sovereignty in silence, and call it normal. To corporations, to governments, to people who've never earned our trust. We don't even realize we're giving away our power, piece by piece. It happens when the terms of service pop up—thirty pages of legal fine print—yet we scroll to the bottom, too weary to read, and click "I agree."

It happens at the café when the barista asks, "For here or to go?" and we answer automatically, not realizing the data point of our choice feeds into systems larger than us. It happens in the doctor's office, where our signature waves away protections we didn't know we had. Each moment feels small, forgettable. But added together, they are a quiet empire of surrendered will.

Consent once meant covenant, the meeting of equals. Now it has become reflex, almost invisible—a currency we spend without ever checking the balance.

But the darkest trick? They always tell you what they'll do. They show you the noose. And if you don't fight it, your silence becomes the knot around your own throat.

Morainya's breath hitched as the realization settled in. She'd been complicit in her own dimming—offering her light without question, her will without resistance. It was time to stop giving it away. It was time to take back what was hers.

Even Iben. She'd painted him in mercy, crowned him with her longing—yet whole chambers of him remained hidden. Not out of cruelty, perhaps, but oath, or burden, or wounds too deep for words. She might never know. She had spent lifetimes chasing ghosts—the fire of the unknown, the torment of half-truths, the hunger for what would never settle. Maybe that was the point. Maybe some loves weren't meant to be held—only to burn away the lies we tell ourselves.

Either way, something had changed. She could feel it—this renewal, this surge of power, rising from within. Taking her life back from those who had once placed her in a submissive position. The confusion that had once plagued her—whether it was legal jargon, or the dance of love—was no longer a burden she had to bear. She didn't need to understand everything anymore. She simply needed to trust herself. To stand firm in the truth of who she was becoming.

One that led to greater self-confidence, sovereignty, and self-love. The kind of evolution she never would have dreamt possible at the beginning of this journey. Could this have been the hidden gift all along? The universe certainly works in mysterious ways.

The following Thursday, Bernie Wallerstein slammed the office door shut and snapped at his secretary, "Get me a meeting with our General Counsel immediately...and the Managing Partner!" His hand trembled as he grabbed the Pepto Bismo from his drawer, the bottle slick with sweat from his grip. He paused for a second, staring at it, trying to breathe through the growing ache in his stomach. Damn ulcer, he thought before taking a long shaky gulp. The Recission Notice was the last straw. He could feel his body responding, the tension in his stomach growing tighter with every passing second.

Ten minutes later, Sonia, the firm's General Counsel barreled in, hair askew and pulse hammering like a snare drum. Click. Click. Click. The pen cap snapped open and shut in Sonia's twitching fingers—a Morse code of panic. "You need me?" Her voice was tight, her gaze flickering from Bernie to the papers he had shoved toward her. She could already tell this wasn't just another routine matter.

"Damn right I do," he barked and shoved the Notices at her as if he could relieve his responsibility and hand it over to Sonia to contend with.

The Head of Litigation poked his head in the office. Soloman asked, "Is there a problem? I heard you yell down the hall. I have to catch a flight at 4:20pm and am jamming last minute schedule conflicts." Sweat stains soaked Soloman's underarms leaving his crisp starched shirt sullied. He yanked his cuffs down under his jacket sleeve.

Bernie slammed the document onto the desk, the sharp thwack making the others flinch. "We got a fucking problem." His face was red, veins thick in his temple. He jabbed a finger at the papers. "She sent us a Notice of Recission along with our client agreement contract. I thought that was bad, now I got a Certificate of Dishonor. The bitch mailed it to the BAR, the Clerk, and half the goddamn government. We're exposed."

Silence.

Sonia went sheet white, as if the ink bled arsenic. "How the hell does she even know this process?"

Bernie screamed, "How the fuck can she do that and do we have to honor it?"

The Head of Litigation shrank. Soloman knew he'd never be catching his flight now. "Wow, ok, let me look at it. I don't think I've never seen anything like this," he said, scratching his head.

Sonia's face was a death mask. "I'd say this is a major problem. It's been sent to the San Francisco Clerk of Court."

The General Counsel scanned the paper, and she said, "It's a Notice of Dishonor. He took a deep breath, then turned the document toward them, voice tight. "If this holds, the settlement's void, and she's about to demand back three million dollars."

Bernie snatched up his Pepto Bismol, and took another gulp from the bottle. His stomach was on fire, but not as much as his career. "She just cut us off at the knees."

Sonia winced, like she was about to read a death sentence. "There's more."

"What more?" demanded Bernie.

She read the words clearly so the other two could feel the impact of the shock. "The packet includes a waiver of any and all fees outstanding, plus over twenty one million dollars restitution fee outlined in her fee schedule."

"*Her fee schedule*? That has to be a joke. We don't have to pay that do we?" asked Bernie with a shaky stomach.

Soloman, stroking his beard, squinted at the papers, his voice low and calculating. "I don't honestly know...but who's going to uphold this in court? It's unprecedented."

Sonia shuffled her feet, her fingers nervously tracing the edge of the document. "True. How is she even going to collect?" Sonia glanced at the others, her face pale. "But she's not really attaching that liability to the firm, Bernie. She tagged you and Stanley Kanberg. Personally." The finality of the words hung in the air, chilling everyone in the room.

The phone rang, its shrill tone slicing through the tension in the room. Bernie's hand hovered over the receiver for a moment, the weight of the situation pressing on him. It buzzed again, more insistent. He inhaled like it hurt and grabbed the receiver with a clammy grip.

"Wallerstein here," he croaked—his panic sheathed in a brittle formality.

"Wallerstein, this is Angela Chisholm. I was on the Napolitano's case. What the fuck is this Recission of your agreement contract? Is your client expecting us to claw back three million dollars from her uncle? My Board will come unglued over this. We may have to file a breach of contract suit against your firm."

"Angela, calm down. We have only just set eyes on this. Let me get back to you next week, when we have more information," said Bernie in his calmest manner even though he didn't feel tranquil. He slammed the phone down—only for it to ring again, louder, like it knew. He saw the caller ID and put the call on speaker.

"Wallerstein here," he said, his voice tighter and more urgent.

"Yes, Mr. Wallerstein, this is Phillip Shinefeld, from the BAR Association. We need to discuss a matter of four Notices of Dishonor we received here along with a Certificate of Dishonor for you, Stanley Kanberg, Judge James Malicado and Angela Chisholm from Sorkin and Seigel. Do you know what this is in regard to?"

Bernie's tone immediately softened under an authority's scrutiny. "Yes, Sir, I am afraid a disgruntled client seems to have taken matters into her own hands and filed these notices." Bernie scratched a stress rash on his head. "This is just some crazy broad playing sovereign citizen."

Soloman and Sonia nodded in agreement. The three of them could overcome this.

"I see, so you have received the three notices already?" said Shinefeld as he flipped through the pages.

"Yes, Sir, the firm is in receipt of them," replied Bernie, taking a sip of water to ease his parched throat.

Mr. Shinefeld made some inaudible noises, then said, "But, it isn't the firm that she has a grievance with, is it? No, it is addressed to all of you personally—outside of your corporate protections and Titles of Nobility. She's questioning your oath of office. This isn't just bad—it's precedent-setting." His voice grew clipped.

Bernie's voice cracked, "You can't actually take this seriously! I built this firm."

"I also received a phone call from the State of California Recorder's Office and the California Secretary of State that they just recorded a Non-UCC lien on each of you. Individually." Judgement was passed and Shinefeld made sure his words hit hard. "The Notices have merit, and they cannot be ignored. The BAR is taking immediate action. Effective Now—you're disbarred."

Bernie's voice rose, almost pleading for grace, "Mr. Shinefeld, we have decades of experience. We're one of the most respected firms in the state—surely that must account for something."

Shinefeld paused. "Bernie...you should have known better." His tone sharpened. "I am just sorry, that you didn't respond and resolve this dispute before it reached my desk.

But now? Now the lien is in place, and these Notices are part of the public record." A heavy pause. "We will draft the formal Disbarment Memo, which you will receive by courier before the end of the day." Another pause, colder this time. "I'd wish you a good day, but I doubt it will be." (CLICK)

Bernie crushed the stress ball like it might rewind time. "Mr. Shinefeld, this is highly irregular. Is there no way..., hello, Hello?"

The line had gone dead.

Bernie stared at the orange LED line indicator on his phone—it had gone dark. No longer blinking. No longer connected.

His hands were clammy. His gaze flickered toward his colleagues, all of them frozen in silent disbelief. I cold sweat clung to his shirt as he loosened his tie, feeling the crushing weight of the system that had just expelled them—stripped them—stripped them of the very power they had once wielded against other.

"He hung up." Bernie flinched as if struck. He stood stiffly, smoothing down his tie, then fumbled with the top button of his shirt. "That's it, then," he muttered, voice flat. He busied himself with the papers on his desk, suddenly obsessed with appearing useful, important—anything but defeated.

Soloman and Sonia exchanged glances, their expressions shifting from shock to something colder. Then as if a silent verdict had passed between them, they turned their gaze back to Bernie Wallerstein.

Soloman's voice was restrained, almost clinical. "I believe you need to pack up your desk." He didn't look at Bernie when he spoke, as if the man had already been reduced to an afterthought. "Sonia, go inform Stanley Kanberg imme-diately of the decision. I will notify security to escort these two gentlemen out of the office. Then I'll advise Mr. Katz and the Board that two founding members have resigned."

Without hesitation, Soloman pulled out his cell and dialed. "Send security up. Bring several moving boxes to Wallerstein and Kanberg's offices."

Bernie stiffened, his lips parting as if to protest. His voice, when it came, was hoarse. "Soloman, we've been friends for twenty years. I gave your kids a start."

Soloman cocked his head slightly, studying Bernie as if for the first time. His reply was as cutting as it was final. "We must put the firm first." He let the words settle before adding, "Weren't those your direct orders?"

Bernie felt the floor tilt beneath him—the floor didn't move—but something inside him did not from movement—but from the weight of his own hypocrisy.

At the same time, two burly security guards in suits arrived with boxes to Stanley Kanberg's office. Sonia direct-ed the men to start packing boxes of personal goods, and leave all company files.

Stanley's mouth moved, forming the shape of a defense that never arrived. Not a word. Not even breath. The silence wasn't just awkward—it was a verdict. "I had no idea, Wallerstein would take it this far. Don't make me pay for his error in judgement."

Soloman turned slowly. You stood by him. You watched it all unfold. And you said nothing."

Stanley's mouth opened, but no words came. The silence was damning.

Sonia's arms folded tight across her chest. "You weren't just a bystander, Stanley. You were the cleanup crew."

At that moment, the two security guards appeared with boxes. One of them gestured toward Kanberg's desk. "Sir, we'll need you to step aside."

Stanley blinked rapidly. "This is a mistake."

"No," Soloman replied coldly. "The mistake was thinking you'd never be held accountable."

As Morainya turned into the driveway, she spotted Iben standing there alone—no car, no warning—just him, as if time itself had paused to wait for her. No cars were parked nearby, which made his presence feel even more mysterious. A flutter of excitement rose within her, mingled with rapid beat of her heart. His presence had an electric pull that seemed to stir something deep inside of her, that unique, undeniable force he carried. Gathering her papers, receipts and groceries, she stepped out of the car, her pulse quickening.

Maybe he did care. Her heart raced and he made her sing with that mitochondrial squeeze that he so uniquely possessed. Iben smiled radiantly, demonstrating how happy he was to be within her presence. Maybe he was coming around and her love had healed whatever reservations he'd been having.

"Hey, Stranger," said Morainya, walking up close to him so that she could inhale his essence. "You're early. I didn't expect to see you for another hour."

"As-Salamu Alaykum, Queen," he said, his voice a warm tide that wrapped around her name. "The freeways were clear. I had to see you. I just arrived as you have pulled up, once again demonstrating our purpose and our synchronicity."

"I swear, you have a clock in my chest," she said, unlocking the door with a smirk.

"How we do it. We are One."

They entered the house, and Josh was at the dining room table, flipping through a post-grad training manual—already prepping for the July NCAA camp. "Hey, Mom. Glad you're home."

Morainya stepped aside revealing his presence. "Honey, I'd like you to meet a friend of mine. Josh, this is Iben Fatah. Iben Fatah, this is my son, Josh. My son just graduated from high school last week." She hadn't expected Josh to be home but maybe it was a good idea they finally met.

Morainya had never planned to introduce Josh to Iben just yet. But now standing there, the uncertainty of their relationship became glaringly obvious. Was he a friend? A lover? Her heart was still tangled in those questions.

Josh raised an eyebrow—half surprise, half *Mom, really?*—but stayed quiet, processing.

"Hey, Bro. Congratulations." Iben greeted Josh then gave a fist bump, with the ease of a man who belonged there. "I hear you're off to the home of the Brown Bears. That's a big move."

Josh's face lit up, excitement flooding his words, "Yeah, Man, I'm stoked. I've been watching their games, and the team looks solid this year. I can't wait to get started."

"Brown has a lot of history in the Ivy League," said Iben, "How's the team shaping up? Any standouts?"

"The coach says they're going to focus on building a stronger defense," replied Josh,

I'm excited to talk about football.

Iben nodded, "I hear the coaches are intense but in a good way."

Josh agreed, "Discipline and technique. The quarterback is a beast, he has leadership on the field and a great arm."

"That's great Bro, you are going to do just fine. I can tell you have a good head on your shoulders," said Iben. "The Ivy League may not be as flashy as the big conferences, but it is still top-notch, plus the academics are no joke."

Josh chuckled. "Let me guess—Mom already gave you the academic speech?" I know, I have to keep my grades up."

"You'll do just fine," said Iben as he headed out to the porch to meet Morainya.

Josh flashed her a thumbs up, the kind that meant: *We're talking later, Mom. Every detail.*

At least it was a good start. The warm spring night was thick with honeysuckle and roses; their sweetness dripped over the gazebo. The twinkling lights made the lattice wood structure more romantic. Iben sat upon the bench swing and motioned for her to join him. Morainya set the snacks and Hibiscus iced tea out on the side table. She sank beside him, legs curled toward him, needing to see his face—needing to *feel* him there.

"I did it," she said, voice trembling with adrenaline and pride. "I filed a Certificate of Dishonor. All of them." The day's events had left her rattled, yet empowered.

Iben pulled her into his chest, his heartbeat aligning with hers in a steady rhythm—anchoring, unspoken, sure. "That takes immense courage," he said softly. "It's one thing to challenge the system; it's another to face the repercussions. "Stepping off the ship, standing on the Land—it shakes the world's illusion. Most people aren't ready for that. But you've made the first step. Now, you are standing on your square."

Morainya nodded hard, her jaw tight, breath catching on the memory of sleepless nights—waiting for the knock at the door to harass her and Josh. "Overcoming the fear was the biggest step for me."

"Try being a Black man in this country," Iben said, his gaze fierce. The air between them thickened. His voice didn't rise—but the pain in it did.

"We're judged even in our own communities," he said. "But I trust Ma'at. She always balances the scales," he replied and his right fist touched his heart, his voice low but unwavering: "Islam." His gaze met hers, sharp with purpose. "Do you even know what Islam stands for?"

She shook her head, no.

"It means, *I, Self, Law, Am Master*. I am a Muslim under the divine Laws of the Holy Quran of Mecca, Love, Truth, Peace, Justice and Freedom," Iben replied. "It took everything in me to let you in, Morainya. So many people warned me about being in a relationship with a Catholic woman."

She recoiled slightly, startled—not by anger, but by truth laid bare. "It was the Catholicism that bothered you?"

Iben's gaze hardened slightly, a deep sadness flickering in his eyes. "You didn't even know how deep it ran.

What they'd done—in the Church's name. To my family. To Afraka. To you, too."

She reached for his hand, both apology and understanding in her touch.

Iben looked at the sky for a moment before turning to Morainya, his gaze steady but soft. "My sister has begun to heal, Morainya. Because of what *you* did—your courage to stand up, to confront your own enemies—she found the strength to reclaim her own power. She went back to the old place. Sat with the ancestors. Came back lighter. She's walking in truth now—to reconnect with her own sovereignty."

Tears welled in Morainya's eyes. "That's beautiful," she whispered. "I'm honored to have helped."

Iben nodded, his eyes softening as he reached for her hand. "Your journey, Morainya, has always been about more than just you. In helping yourself, you've given her the key to unlocking her own strength, just as you've done for so many. You are more powerful than you realize." He squeezed her hand gently, a silent affirmation of their shared path. She looked down, brows tight. "I still can't grasp the weight you carry...even as a Moor with rights on this land."

These were the moments that unraveled her—when their fields aligned so effortlessly, it felt like slipping into heaven's breath. Who else could she even have conversations like this with?" He pulsed energy straight to her core—no touch, no warning—and she gasped, her body tightening in response to the invisible strike. There was no visible movement, no physical indication of the energy he was directing at her. She couldn't help herself. "How do you do that?" she whispered, half breath, half disbelief, her eyes narrowing like a question she wasn't ready to stop asking.

"I can't tell you," he replied, a smirk tugging at his lips, his eyes glinting with mischief.

Iben could feel the weight of Morainya's gaze on him, the question lingering in the air like a soft challenge. *How do you do it?* She asked, again. He'd vowed to himself—no full reveal, not yet. Not until she crossed the next veil on her own.

She was close—closer than anyone had ever been to truly overstanding the depths of their connection. But there were boundaries, lines he couldn't cross, not without risking something far deeper than she could yet comprehend.

This is more than just a trick, he thought, his mind sharpening. The way he pinged her—sent that rush of energy through her—wasn't just a physical skill. It was a practice, a sacred art, a deep knowledge passed down through generations. To reveal it now, without her full overstanding, could unravel things in ways that neither of them were ready for.

His smirk faded, replaced by something quieter. Respect. Restraint. A silent oath not to violate the mystery. She was curious, driven by that same need to *know*, to understand. But there were layers to their connection that were not meant to be explained in words, not yet. *Not until she learns to trust herself more, to trust the power that exists within her,* he thought, his gaze shifting to the gentle curve of her neck, the strength in the way she held herself. She was already changing, evolving—he could feel it in the space between them, in the pull of her energy, but there was still fear in her. Fear that hadn't yet been faced, fear that still made her question her own sovereignty.

Iben took a slow breath. *This is my burden, not hers.* He had walked this path for longer than she could imagine, and while she was beginning to grasp fragments of it, there were parts of this journey that were sacred and must remain veiled until the time was right. To reveal too much now would risk breaking something delicate—a bond that needed more time to root before it could be tested.

He met her gaze again, his eyes dark and unwavering.

"You're not ready to know," he said gently, "but you're closer than you think. When the time comes, the knowing will rise up to meet you. Trust that."

Inwardly, he sighed, the weight of their dynamic pressing on him. She was on the brink—of full awareness, of their connection, of the power that stirred within her. and the path that lay ahead. But revealing it now would make it too easy. Growth required mystery. Trust needed the slow burn of becoming. To hand her the answers too soon would be like offering a flower before its bloom—petals closed, fragrance still held tight. It wasn't time yet.

Morainya felt the energy shift within her. Her need to know suddenly didn't feel as urgent. If she could trust him, then the answer would come in time. "But when the time is right, you will tell me, right?"

He gave her a cryptic shrug, then pivoted cleanly, his tone already shifting tracks. "You were about to tell me what happened with the Archbishop?"

Morainya brightened. "Yes, she grinned. "I gave him a choice—pay my uncle, or I expose his entire empire. He folded."

Iben's face was illuminated with joy, pride glowing in his eyes. "That's huge. You're standing on your 9's now," he said, a grin breaking across his face. "Beauty tamed the Beast." He laughed at his joke.

Morainya eyes widened as a memory surged forward. "The Girl in Red... hugging the Red Lion. It was this exact moment," she revealed, her voice a little lighter.

"The Strength card?" Iben's gaze softened, but his eyes gleamed with hidden knowing.

"Most profound." It was clear he knew more than he let on, his overstanding deepening the mystery between them.

She thought about the long road she'd traveled—the battles against the law, the church, the ghosts of her past. And she had won.

"I've tamed the beast," she whispered. The meaning hit Morainya like a rolling tide. The law firm, the Church, the patriarchal power structures that once made her shrink. She had faced them all. And she had not only survived—she had mastered it.

No longer prey. No longer afraid. She had become the Red Lion. "I overcame my enemy."

"Enemy or *Iname?*" He asked, the words laid out like a riddle.

Morainya chuckled at another play on words that he pointed out. "Wait, iname—you mean it was *in me* all along?" Her breath caught. The syllables cracked open a new layer of overstanding. "So... I created the enemy to meet myself?"

Had she conjured the law firm? The Church? All to awaken her own inner authority—the part that needed a worthy opponent to rise? Morainya awakened at that moment that this whole battle was designed to lift her to the realization that she came under no one. If she hadn't faced this opposition, she never would have discovered the truth about Aldo and Stella. She never would have found her true strength and fortitude to face a foe, and she never would have found her sovereignty by coming onto the Land and Soil. Most of all she never would have learned about the Moors, nor examined her own prejudices that had been imposed upon her by her family, society, and Church. Soul growth comes in unexpected ways from the least likely of teachers.

He studied her. "That isn't the only thing you took away from the Church. I hear that you took something else."

"How would you know that?" Morainya was startled and leaned back, her muscles rigid.

"Just felt it. We are One." Iben clasped his hands together and raised his pointer fingers.

Morainya was excited to convey an unexplored memory. "Remember that strange Pharaoh and his wife and daughters?"

"Of course, Queen. You would kick my unholy butt out of here if I did not know them."

"I have to show you something. It belonged to Pharaoh Akhenaten. The Vatican kept it hidden in their library—the Pope gave it to the Archbishop. But—I stole it back. They had no right to take it. It's called the *'Ibow Nesser.'*"

"Ah...the *Heart of the Lion,*" Iben murmured, reverence tightening his tone. "I wondered if you'd have the Strength to take it."

Morainya stiffened. "You knew?"

He didn't answer, not directly. His gaze pierced hers. "You chose yourself...over the Church. He paused, letting the weight land. "That surprised me."

Morainya blinked. "What...was this a test?"

He tilted his head, gaze sharp. "You took something quite sacred from a powerful institution." He stepped closer. "Tell me—did you take it for your family?"

"No," she said, voice low. "Josh and I don't need it. It just felt like the right thing to do."

He tilted his head, studying her. "Is stealing moral?" Iben watched her squirm beneath the weight of the question.

The question hit her like a slap—not angry, just sharp. It sliced into her certainty. "I mean..." she hesitated, searching for footing. "They never should have had it in the first place."

"Yet you still took it," he said. "That makes it theft, no matter how you justify it. The question is—was it *righteous rebellion* or *moral ambiguity?*"

She looked down at her hands, then back up—face still, voice even "Then let it be theft," she said, not as confession, but as a claim. "If truth must be protected by breaking their laws, I'll wear the title gladly." she said quietly.

Iben gave a single, deliberate nod. "Then you're ready," he murmured. "That's the voice of a woman stepping into her crown."

Morainya hesitated, "I want to show you." She still held out hope that if he saw it—truly saw the age, the lineage, the truth etched into its form—he would understand. "It's Khemitian," she said, her voice low, and reverent. "It never belonged to Rome. Not really. They stole it from Egypt. They had no right to it. Maybe I don't own it either... but I couldn't let them keep it."

She wasn't asking to be forgiven—only to be understood. This wasn't about having. It was about returning. About restoring what had been stolen from a people... from a memory. Maybe, just maybe, he would see that taking it wasn't about possession. It was about restoration.

Morainya grabbed her purse off the kitchen counter. Her fingers grazed the artifact, and a current surged up her arm. Even through the leather lining of her purse, it hummed with power. Maybe Iben could offer her some knowledge. She walked back to the swing, where he sat studying her. She felt the weight of the orb in her hands. Ancient. Magnetic. Sacred. But somewhere deeper—beneath the moral reasoning and ancestral pride—was a lingering unease.

"You knew I'd take it," she said, the question slipping out like a knife from its sheath. "Didn't you?"

Iben didn't answer. He measured her instead, the way someone might study the first crack in a piece of pottery. "Would it matter?" he asked softly. "If I did?"

"It matters," she said tightly, "if you put it in my path... so I'd bear the karma, not you."

A long pause then: "No one hands out karma," he replied. "They just open the door. You're the one who walks through."

Iben had told her they were One. And maybe, in another world, they had been. But not in this one. This time, the path was hers to walk. And she had finally chosen the road that would lead her home.

He held his palms up. "I can feel the magnetic pull—it's quite potent. Would you allow me to hold it?" His hands reaching toward her, expectant, his smile brightening.

Morainya cradled it in her hands protectively. "I don't know. It feels very fragile, but I know it has huge significance, otherwise why would the Church value it?"

He captured her gaze, his energy shifting as he began transmitting a powerful wave of force into her. It beckoned her, coaxing her to offer him a glimpse of the orb. "Queen," he said, voice coaxing, eyes steady, "your king wishes to hold what you've reclaimed."

She lifted her hands, offering the orange orb, its hardened red powder shimmering. Deep within, she knew it held the power to change everything. "What do you think it is?" she asked, holding it up to him temptingly.

"I believe it holds authority far beyond your overstanding. Allow me to protect it." Iben locked his gaze on hers, mesmerizing. The moment his fingers met the orb, blue light arced between them—an ancient voltage. Her knees buckled slightly. Visions poured in: golden halls, linen robes, the sting of sand in her eyes, a sun-drenched crown atop melanated skin. The orb had unlocked something buried in time.

The blue light pulsed with increasing intensity. Their hands and eyes were now locked, unable to pull away. In that moment, time and space itself seemed to shift. The house she had known slowly began to collapse around her, like a fading dream.

Her son now appeared only as an outline from another timeline. Iben and Morainya moved between worlds, cosmos within cosmos. Images flashed by, fading as quickly as they came—lives of lovers with multiple children, enemies meeting bitter ends, lives of one aiding the other, then switching roles.

They had tumbled through endless sequences of events that had pushed them together and torn them apart. She saw him across lifetimes—lover, rival, child, warrior. Their bond was older than names, older than stars. A cosmic loop of meeting and parting, of losing and finding again.

They barreled back in time, and Morainya realized she would never again have a moment to grieve what she thought she lost. A hueman mind cannot grasp such a drastic shift in reality. One that occurred more swiftly than thought itself. How long could this go on? She was receiving a life review, where pain, love, hurt, rage, joy was all swirled together like a rainbow of emotions, each one a lesson in the grand cosmic scheme. Feeling an overwhelming sense of loss, tears welled, but none fell. Her journey had never been about the orb. It was about becoming. About remembrance. Whatever the orb's mission had been, she could feel its pull loosening in her palm—as if its purpose with her had been fulfilled. It was never hers to keep. She allowed Iben to receive the gift, sensing that its destiny had always pointed to him. He was the prize.

After the whirlwind of change, they were thrust back into the womb of the Sphinx, where time seemed to fold in on itself. Djehuty stood with his arms extended in joyous reception as each of my classmates tumbled back from the portal, returning from the journey they had just traversed. Next to his throne was a stand with the Emerald Tablets displayed, casting the room in a deep primordial green light across the room.

The Immortal Being waited patiently until we gathered ourselves, ready to receive his wisdom.

"It was all but a dream— a vision of the future where I challenged you to transcend your weaknesses and face your shadow self.
Now, speak to me.

Tell me who you thought you were."

Rennutet trembled uncontrollably. "I was a nun who discovered the truth and was wounded, and instead of facing it, I buried it. I lived in darkness, believing I was tarnished—unworthy. A lie I told myself. When I lost my mind, I longed for death. I could not look at his face, believing I had lost my purity, my purpose. I welcomed Westing, not as a passage, but as an escape."

She sucked in her breath as if the burden was too heavy to release. "I walked the path with this class at Heliopolis. When I was accosted by the men I was sent to work for, I had a baby that was taken by another mother. But when the world outside didn't mirror the teachings within, I wavered. I saw pain. I saw lies and I said nothing.

In this life, I lived in the comfort of Stefano's wealth, but my mind was a house with shuttered windows. I punished myself for a mistake made in youth—striking a wounded boy who had already known too much pain. I thought I was protecting him. Instead, I carried that guilt like a stone around my neck."

She trembled, fists clenched. "I thought I had forfeited my right to serve. That I wasn't pure enough. Holy enough. Worthy enough. I left the convent, but I never left the shame. So, I let my mind fade, let the light go dim inside me. I welcomed the forgetting of my pain. But I forgot myself."

Djehuty's voice resonated through the room, like the vibration of a distant star calling across the expansion. He stepped down from the elevated dais, his obsidian staff etched with star maps glinting in the green glow of the Tablets. The ibis-headed scribe, tall and composed, moved like a ripple through still water—calm, precise, eternal. His presence was not loud, but sovereign. All time bowed to him. With a nod that felt like the turning of an age, he extended his hand toward her.

"Rennutet—Daughter of Dendera,
Sovereign of Shadow and Light
you have faced the shadows,
and in your truth,
you stand not as a victim,
but as a vessel of transformation.
What you have endured—
though born of suffering—
has forged the very essence of your soul.
It was a lesson, a test, a cloak meant
only for the rite of passage.
You did not lose your purity, Rennutet.
You never lost your purpose.
The child you bore in Dendera
was not a mark of shame,
but a mirror—reflecting
the strength you carried
even when you could not see it.
Your journey, though painful,
was always a path of ascension.
Now, you walk free—not from the world,
but *within* it, with your
sovereign spirit unchained."

Archollos placed a hand on Rennutet's shoulder, then turned to the others. His voice was raw, barely above a whisper. "I was the perpetrator in that life, because I was prey first. Raped by those sworn to protect me, I turned my rage on the weak. When I learned that I had caused damage to my teacher's eye, I fled.

I was given everything—wealth, opportunity—but I could not forgive those who had taken my innocence. I convinced myself my life had been stolen, that my suffering had been unjust. But the truth? Family is not blood. It is those who walk with you. And I could never see you—any of you—until I learned to love myself.

Djehuty stepped forward from the emerald glow, his long indigo robes whispering against the stone floor like wind over reeds. His eyes held the weight of galaxies, ancient and knowing, yet impossibly tender. The ibis-headed sage tilted his head slightly, as if listening to a truth spoken in silence. With one hand raised and the other resting gently over his heart, he addressed the wounded one before him—not as judge, but as witness.

"Archollos—Thou standest where two roads meet:
the echo of pain, and the hymn of release.
Rage turned outward is but sorrow un-embraced.
Know this: Nothing was *stolen*;
all was *given* for thy shaping.
Family is forged in choice,
tempered in presence,
crowned in love.
Turn inward, heal the first wound,
and the world will lift
its sword from thee.
Thou art no longer the breaker of paths,
but the builder of bridges—
Claim the craft of thy redemption."

Merrie P. Wycoff

Tadushet spoke up, "In this life, I took pride in always following the laws of Ma'at and condemned those who were unfair and unjust. In that life, I was a pale male who helped others find their sovereignty. It was through his constant study and devotion to what was lawful that he overturned the corrupt courts and enforced the laws of Ma'at."

Djehuty inclined his head slightly, eyes gleaming with ancient knowing. His hand rose—not in command, but in recognition—as the green light of the Tablets flickered across his brow.

"Tadushet—Thou hast stood as the scale-bearer,
voice of statutes, keeper of writs.
Yet heed: A law without compassion
may serve order—but never balance.
Ma'at is a feather *and* a flame;
too rigid a hand will quench the fire,
too loose a grasp will scatter the plume.
Justice must drink from
the heart before it calls itself pure.
Wield thy knowledge, yet temper it with mercy;
let every verdict pass first
through the chamber of thine own breath.
Thus will thou uphold the law's letter
and reveal its living soul—
not as command, but as covenant."

Djehuty's voice was steady and firm, reverberating with the weight of eternal wisdom. He turned slowly, his gaze sweeping over the gathered initiates, pausing where unspoken grief still clung like smoke. The emerald glow of the Tablets flickered across his face, casting shadows that danced like ancient hieroglyphs upon stone. Then he shifted his focus to the silent one kneeling beside the column—the one who had not yet spoken.

Keshtuat nodded and said, "My mother was the Court Seamstress, and I was enamored with creating the raiment's and coordinating them with the fancy jewels of the Kings and Queens. I admit that although I wear the plain vestments of an initiate, I have always been jealous that these items of luxury would never be within my reach. In that lifetime, I was an Archbishop and wore all the jewels and clothes of luxurious fabrics. I ordered another seamstress to sew and adorn me. How I acquired them were by deals I made in the shadows. I extorted my parishioners and used their confessions against them. I was in worship of the darkness and sold my soul to acquire it by nefarious means of greed, fear, and terror. I did things of which I am not proud. Out of my own feelings of unworthiness in this life, I used my authority and power to take advantage of others."

Djehuty stepped forward, his eyes softening—not with pity, but with recognition. He saw not only her past, but the burden she had carried in silence.

"Keshtuat—Weaver of royal threads,
keeper of hidden longing.
Thou hast confessed the pact of shadow—
jewels won by fear, power
bartered for confessions,
garments stitched with
the silence of the shamed.
Hear Me: Gold upon the breast
is but dust upon the soul
when worth is weighed by glitter alone.
Riches are not sin;

attachment is the chain.
Beauty is not curse; vanity is the veil.
The gems thou didst covet
were mirrors for thy wound,
reflecting the voice that cried,
"I am not enough."
Yet know this truth—the finest
raiment thou canst wear
is the fabric of pure intent.
The brightest jewel lies uncut
in the vault of the heart.
For the treasury within thee
cannot be stolen, nor taxed, nor tarnished.
Claim it—and the outer jewels
will seek thee, not as masters,
but as servants of thy radiance.
Rise, Sovereign Seamstress.
Stitch this world with deeds of worth,
and the cosmos shall adorn
thee with its own stars."

As the final note of Djehuty's voice settled into stillness, a gentle hush fell across the chamber. The others watched in reverent silence as the energy shifted once more.

From the edge of the gathering, Sarawat stepped forward, her gaze lowered, as though searching the floor for courage.

"I was a Seer, gifted with visions—but instead of wisdom, I let jealousy guide me," she said and glanced at her hands. "I resented Merit-Aten's abilities...and spoke cruelly of her to make myself feel powerful. Yet, in that life, I was sent to help her, to show her that justice comes not from the past, but through the will to overcome. Now, I see the truth. What I envied in her was only a reflection of what I failed to see in myself."

Djehuty tilted his head slightly, as if peering into a deeper layer of her soul. The glow from the Emerald Tablets flickered across his face, casting his features in shifting light—half shadow, half illumination. Then he spoke:

"Sarawat—Seer of the hidden veils,
you peered into the future
but forgot to cleanse the lens within.
You were sent to uplift, not to compete.
To anchor truth, not to distort
it with your pain.
The eye that envies
cannot see clearly.
The voice that wounds
forgets its sacred tone.
Yet I tell you now—the gift remains.
The fire of sight still burns in your brow.
For you have done what few can do—
named the shadow and called it yours.
And now it returns.
Let your visions now serve love.
Let your speech now serve justice.
Merit-Aten was your mirror,
not your rival. See her clearly,
and you will see yourself.
Not beneath her. Not above her.
But beside her—
as it was written in the stars."

The silence held for a moment, then broke gently as Oya stepped forward, her presence grounded yet radiant, like soil after rain.

Oya smiled and nodded. "I was an owner of a spiritual Bookstore, who was put in place to assist Merit-Aten and others to remember themselves and that we are on a wheel of karma and dharma. It was my Cosmic dance, and following the Great Mother's heartbeat, I helped remind her of who she truly was, is, and ever will be."

Djehuty inclined his head in honor, his eyes reflecting galaxies. When he spoke, it was as if the stars themselves paused to listen.

"Oya—Dancer at the threshold,
keeper of turning pages,
pulse of the Great Mother's drum.
Thou didst open the shop of stars,
shelves lined with secret tongues,
scrolls that whispered, *"Remember."*
You placed no chain upon the seeker;
you merely struck the chord
that made their own name ring.
Karma is a wheel—
Dharma its axle.
You greased the turning with devotion,
not dominion.
In guiding another to her flame,
you fanned your own."

Djehuty's voice was both gentle and affirming, like the sound of ancient wisdom echoing in the heart of the universe. A hush settled.

Ra-Awab-exhaled sharply, as if releasing the weight of centuries from his chest. "I have always despised weakness. Strength was my pride—until I saw where it came from. My father, a great sea merchant, was no hero. He stole. He traded human lives like goods. And Archollos—" Ra-Awab's voice faltered. "I knew some of those slaves bound for Khemit that were shipwrecked. They were bought by Queen Nefertiti and Merit-Aten. I never spoke of it, not even when I suspected the truth. I am sorry."

"My father had a mind for remembering inventories and amassed his wealth through numbers and calculations. I wished that I could match his intelligence in this life, but it was not my destiny. While he said he was proud of me joining the Priestly class, I fear it was because he did not think I was intelligent enough to take over his business. In that life, I was the Master of numbers and used my calculations of the Maritime Sea trade to cheat others, even my most prosperous clients by using that law. I was Morainya's Accountant and knew that I could divvy up her wealth by allocating it to others. My only redemption was that I told her a truth that set her free. "

Djehuty stepped forward, his eyes like twin mirrors of time.

**"Ra-Awab, You have named
the shadow that walked beside you,
and in doing so, you have pierced its veil.
Strength born of dominance is
but sand in the mouth.
What you called power
was the echo of a father's sin—
gilded chains wrapped in coin and silence.**

Yes, you remembered the ledgers,
tallied men like merchandise,
and held your tongue when
the truth called your name.
In that life, you were the merchant's son—
Master of the maritime laws, high priest of profit.
But what you profited was illusion,
and what you lost was soul.
Yet in the end—You spoke one truth.
One luminous truth that broke
the lattice of deception and set a Queen free.
That truth became your redemption.
For a man may build palaces of gold,
but a single word of integrity
shall outlast them all.

Djehuty's gaze was steady, his voice carrying the weight of both understanding and cosmic law.

Smenkhkare sucked in his cheeks and sighed, stepping forward with the quiet dignity of a man who had waited lifetimes to speak. "I was in a position of power and fame as a Magistrate, but I turned the law of Ma'at against those who needed the most help." His voice, slowed, reflecting of the lesson. "I enjoyed my bounty while the people suffered. While I always worked for balance and justice for those I encountered in this life, I never truly would comprehend how power corrupts because I never had power. My power could only be had by being linked to a powerful partner. Now, I have risen to Pharaoh through Merit-Aten choosing me, the least likely, as her consort. In that life, when I did have power and wealth, I abused it and took it from others because I never had enough and always hungered for more.

That life taught me how I could be lured by the temptations of the temporal world rather than turn my sight toward the celestial and bring that to the people. True power emits from within, not from without."

"Smenkhkare, In the mirror of power,
you saw only your lack.
You ascended by outward means,
but descended within.
You sat upon the bench of judgment,
and yet your scales were
uncalibrated, tilted by the hunger of one
who had never known his own worth.
Yes, you wore the title of Magistrate—
yes, you tasted the sweetness of wealth,
and in your thirst for more,
you drank from a poisoned chalice:
the illusion that power is given by men.
For true power, Smenkhkare,
is not seated on a throne—
it is anchored in the soul.
Now you rise—not through decree,
but through remembrance.
Not because you are owed power,
but because you have chosen to embody it.
And you, Smenkhkare, are now worthy,
not by lineage, but by light."

Djehuty's voice was deep and resonant, like the sound of a bell ringing through time. The air stilled. No one moved.

And then—I raised my hand. "I was a woman who saved my family from those who sought to destroy them through greed, fear, and manipulation. After my own death of the ego, the unraveling of who I once believed myself to be, I was reborn as one who truly longed for freedom and sovereignty. This mirrors how my father strove for his people to be free of the reign of Amun. Only then did I find Salvation when I found the courage to make those in power return the gold they stole from my family, allowing them to heal from the secrets held in the dark. I now know that I have always pursued saving my family from the threats of evil. I failed in this lifetime, only to accomplish that goal lifetimes later. There is no time. I came to see that those who appear as our oppressors are, in truth, sacred initiators—teachers cloaked in shadow—guiding us by the Law of Opposites."

I bowed my head slightly, the weight of memory and revelation rippling through my chest. Around me, the echoes of past lives, choices, and sacred wounds settled into tranquility.

Djehuty stepped forward, his presence vast yet tender, as though the stars themselves had hushed to listen. His eyes met hers—not with judgment, but with infinite recognition.

Daughter of two dawns—
flame of Aten, keeper of the Red Lion—
Thou hast lifted the mask of self
and walked naked into truth.
You thought the task was to rescue blood,
to wrest gold from grasping hands,
to mend the fracture of a house.
Yet behold: the gold was only symbol,
the family but a fractal,
the foe a sculptor of your light.
For the Law of Opposites is the chisel:

what resists you, refines you;
what denies you, defines you.
Your father sought to break Amun's chain;
you shattered subtler fetters—
fear clothed as loyalty,
sorrow clothed as duty.
In the death of ego
you found the seed of sovereignty;
in the mirror of the adversary
you traced the outline of your crown.
Know this, Merit-Aten:
Time is the circle you draw to teach yourself.
Past and future are but echoes
of the single note you hold in the now.
You are the seeker and the sought,
the teacher and the taught,
the liberator and the liberated.
Stand in that paradox—
and the wheel becomes a portal.
Thus the house is saved,
not by gold returned,
but by the flame remembered.
Walk on: carrying no debt,
owing no fear, bearing only the radiance
of a soul that has turned every shadow into dawn."

The room held its breath as Djehuty's words settled over them like sacred mist. The flame of remembrance still flickered in Merit-Aten's eyes, but now all turned toward the one who had remained silent the longest.

Ana-Kharu took a step forward, the silence breaking beneath the heaviness of his heart. "I loved a woman from a different world, but instead of love, I let fear speak for me. I had been taught to hate her skin, to see her as the enemy. She was pale. Catholic. A symbol of everything that had conquered my people. But when she offered herself—her heart, her truth—without defense or demand, I realized I had never been at war with her. Only with myself."

He momentarily bit his lip, then cast his gaze to Archollos, and said, "In this life, I did the same. I called Archollos a barbarian for not being Khemitian—and for being with a woman from a different culture. But in the cosmic, there is no division. No borders. We are One, no matter the flesh we wear."

Djehuty placed a hand over his heart, his eyes glinting with the solemn fire of ages. **"There it is,"** he said softly, **"the remembrance spoken not in pride, but in penitence. The wound of separation has long echoed through flesh and time...but thy words begin the mending."**

"Ana-Kharu

Ah, beloved of the Flame,

You who once loved and yet feared—

You who kissed the Queen,

then called her foreign.

You did not steal a crown.

You shattered your mirror.

For what you took was not hers—

but yours to begin with.

The skin you scorned

was only parchment.

The faith you feared

was only costume.

The conquest you cursed—

was your own inheritance of pain.
But love—true love—
is not forged in likeness,
nor bounded by banners,
nor pledged to pigment or priesthood.
Love is the recognition of One in the Other.
The unbroken thread across lifetimes.
You wounded your Queen,
because you could not yet see
that she was the chalice,
not the conqueror.
And even now, you judged Archollos—
not because he was less,
but because you were afraid
he saw beauty in a world you could not yet embrace.
But behold, Ana-Kharu: the veil has lifted.
In this hour, you have turned
your spear into a scepter.
You have laid down
the blade of judgment
and taken up the scroll of union.
Flesh is only clay. Borders are only dust.
But soul—soul is the eternal nation.
And now, you stand at the borderless threshold,
where Moor, Khemitian, Barbarian and Priest,
dissolve into light.
You do not need to return what you took.
Only to acknowledge what was sacred.
For She was never yours—
but the lesson was. And now, it is complete."

Djehuty's voice was both gentle and profound, echoing the truth of the cosmos itself. He turned from Ana-Kharu and let his gaze sweep over the gathered initiates. His voice softened, but did not diminish—a steady flame now illuminating the whole chamber.

"You have come to understand
that the wounds we inflict on others
are often wounds we first inflicted upon ourselves.
To heal is to see beyond the surface,
to recognize the divine in all—
no matter the form they take.
In this understanding, you have become
the healer of your own heart.
To heal is to see beyond the surface,
to recognize the divine in all—
no matter the form they take.
In this understanding,
you have become the healer of your own heart."

He stepped forward, his eyes illuminated with the green fire of the Emerald Tablets—not just light, but remembering. Not just speech, but law encoded in vibration. His voice carried through the chamber, but also through the blood, through the soul's spiral memory.

"You have done well," he said, surveying each soul.
"Each of you has faced the mask and the mirror.
Each has stood in the presence of their own
distortion and dared to speak it aloud."

Then his gaze fell upon us—upon Merit-Aten and Ana-Kharu, the modern Morainya and Iben Fatah.

And the chamber fell still.

As if even the cosmos turned to listen.

"Now let us speak," Djehuty intoned,
**"of the Law of Opposites—the most misunderstood
of all Cosmic Principles."**
He gestured toward us as if unveiling a hidden glyph:
**"These two souls are not merely
bound by affection or past-life memory.
They are bound by Law.
One is the agreeable. The other, the disagreeable.
Not in morality, but in function.
One seeks truth through rebellion.
The other, through restraint.
One burns like fire.
The other guards like stone.
And yet, what one lacks, the other carries.
What one wounds, the other heals."**
He circled us with the pace of sacred time:
**"Together, they form a circuit.
A divine polarity.
A living equation that both
tests and transmutes.
For Sovereignty cannot
be inherited. It must be forged.
And no soul becomes whole until it has danced
with its counterpart."**
Djehuty stepped forward, his eyes glowing with the deep
green light of the Emerald Tablets beside him. His voice rang
not just through the chamber, but within each initiate's
soul—as if echoing from their own higher mind. He raised
a hand toward me.
**"Morainya thought Iben was aloof. Distant.
But he was guarding a deeper fire—**

one she was destined to ignite."

He gestured toward Ana-Kharu.

"And he believed she was too bold, too untamed—but her presence revealed the places in him still unclaimed."

We stared at each other—our mirrors in flesh, holding the weight of every lesson life had hurled our way. So many trials, so many moments when walking away would have been easier. I nearly quit—nearly drowned it all in wine, in fear. But something greater kept me tethered. Love. Perseverance. The knowing that every test shaped me.

"They are One—but only because they *chose* to remain Two long enough to remember." Djehuty turned back to the group. **"This is the Great Work. Not to eliminate the opposite—but to *honor* it. For only through resistance can the soul grow strong enough to remember it was always whole."** He bowed his head slightly.

"You have seen your shadows. You have tasted your karma. You have spoken the names of your distortions. And now, you stand at the threshold of your own resurrection." Djeuty turned to Ana-Kharu. **"You have something you need to explain to Merit-Aten.**

Before the memories of Iben dimmed, Ana-Kharu turned to me. "You still think Light must conquer the Dark," he said, his voice soft but firm. "But in the Law of Opposites— one must be joined to their equal and opposite. The agreeable with the disagreeable. The crown with the ash."

"Then which were you?" I asked, my heart aching with the pull of his presence—his distance, his warmth, his coldness. Why did it still sting?

"Both," he whispered. "As are you. You called me into your life not to love you, but to challenge you. You needed the reflection of your discomfort in order to rise."

"And what if I wanted you to stay?" I whispered, the longing for the fleeting Oneness echoing in my voice, wishing for a moment more of the connection we had shared. The Oneness I had felt with him, a union of purpose and challenge—something I never found with Smenkhkare.

"Then you have not yet understood." He stepped closer—not with distance, but reverence. "To be whole, you must walk without needing the mirror. Djeuty granted us the powerful force of the opposites. It's not just about romantic connection but about the spiritual alchemy that happens when two souls challenge and complement each other in profound ways. That is sovereignty." He bowed his head, as if paying homage to me, to the truth, to the moment, and said, "My Queen."

Djeuty made a slight bow, his feather's unfurling in a streaming gesture that signified the completion of the initiation. **"Now, which one of you brought back the prize?"**

"Prize?" I asked, recalling that it was the offering for winning the guessing game with the ostrich egg.

Ana-Kharu stepped forward, holding the *Ibow Nesser* orb within his hands. "Merit-Aten, I believe this belongs to you—to heal your father."

A shimmer passed through Djehuty's eyes—like moonlight skimming deep water—as if his approval came not from the mind, but from the soul.

"You have done well," he said, his voice low and resonant, stirring something ancient inside our bones.

"This was never just a game.

**It was a trial—to see if you remembered
the law, and if you could still hear the Light
calling from within."**

He paused, then added,

"But now, the real work begins."

Without a sound, the Orama walked straight through
the stone wall, as if density obeyed his will. "Well done," he
said, scanning the class. "The Red Lion, when truly ingested, does not intoxicate—it reveals. It shows you the rot
and the gold. It compels the soul to Rectify, Resurrect, and
Revivify its way back to the Cosmic Light. Again, I have had
time with each of you. You two," He turned, fixing Ana-Kharu and me with a knowing gaze. "You have all named the
constellations I asked for, except one. Where is the final
constellation of light?"

Something ignited inside me—a warmth that swelled from
the solar plexus to the crown. The answer wasn't learned. It
was *remembered*. Without a word, I broadcast the knowing
into the inner—a pulse, a vibration—and my classmates
caught it. Their eyes widened as it struck their hearts. Then,
together, they turned toward the unseen sky and declared,
"The light is within us. We are the light. We are the stars of
our own constellation. We are the gold," we exclaimed.

The Orama crossed his arms over his chest and bowed.
"Correct," he said with quiet awe, "You have passed the
final gate. I now grant the Regulan Initiation to you and
your class."

And within the inner chambers of knowing, I heard the
whisper: "You have passed the Karrastt initiation."

Everything sharpened. Not just clarity—but certainty.
The rusted parts of me began to dissolve.

My father's cryptic teachings echoed with new resonance. He hadn't sent me to find Khemit's gold. He sent me to find *mine*. The true alchemy wasn't in metal or fire—but in the transmutation of the self. Like the Sesh—unfired clay made strong through sacred heat—I had become a vessel that could now hold Light. That was the Gold within.

This truth was too sacred to be lost in revelry. I stepped back from the laughter, cradling the lesson that had been hand-forged for me alone. As the others trickled out toward the morning sun and the awaiting meal, I knelt in silence, held back, savoring my lesson that had been crafted just for me.

The Orama approached, wordless. He opened a golden vial and anointed my forehead, crown, and throat with a warm oil that smelled of river earth and sunlit skin.

"This is Messah," he said softly. "The oil of crocodile— symbol of guardianship and rebirth. With it, I mark you Kerashtt. You have re-membered who you are, Merit-Aten."

"I receive it with reverence," I whispered, as the oil tingled through my pineal, threading the unseen veil. He gently turned my shoulders to face the once-solid wall. "You gave me a secret only you would know.

I nodded. "Tuthmosis's fate was sealed the moment the Aten chose my father. Destiny eclipsed lineage."

The Orama gave a single, solemn nod. "Then it is time you see what awaits your bloodline. Though you cannot be there in body, you shall witness it in spirit."

The bricks dissolved. The veil became a mirror. And in that mirror, a scene unfolded—not a vision, but a memory summoned forward from time's vault:

Smenkhkare stood at the helm of a Heliopolitan sailboat, his eyes fixed on the Sphinx growing smaller behind him.

The Red Lion above him dimmed as dawn bled over the river. He did not look back again.

He had chosen the people. Chosen service over crown. The Red Lion had shown him the cost of delay in another lifetime—and now, he would correct it. Anpu, the drummer, joined him on the deck. Their embrace held no shame, only truth.

Though royal duty had once decreed Smenkhkare my consort, the scroll had always been wet with tears. Love—true love—was never meant to be a political tool.

The Orama had quietly allowed them early passage back to Akhet-Aten before the court stirred. Smenkhkare would spend the last of his days healing others. The decree naming him Co-Regent was a formality, a faded dream. The future would know the truth.

"Behold," the Preceptor whispered again.

In the next moment, we saw Smenkhkare kneel before Akhenaten. With grace, he returned the Ibow Nesser—the Red Lion orb—and placed a pouch of monoatomic gold into the Pharaoh's hands.

With a weary but peaceful smile, the Pharaoh placed the long-awaited gift—the Ibow Nesser—atop a granite pyramid, its capstone removed to receive the celestial charge. Behind him, a stone-carved relief stood in silent testimony to his love: himself cradling young Merit-Aten on his lap, while his Queen held their daughters beside her. The Most Worshipful Aten beamed down, its rays encircling them like an eternal benediction, bathing the scene in the final warmth of a fading Unity.

Akhenaten cast one last, reverent gaze upon the relief—love immortalized in limestone. For one brief, shining moment in time, he had succeeded. His City of Light had stood—an unshakable beacon of truth, love, peace, and divine justice beneath the embrace of the Primordial Sun.

He spoke then—not to his court, but to the generations to come: "Let my faithful be ever reminded... freedom is not bestowed—it is born from within. May they scatter across the lands, lifting the minds, hearts, and bodies of those still enslaved. Let them fight—not with fists, but with love encircled as a crown. For a life worth living demands the courage to rise... not to conquer, but to remember the Light."

Upon the pedestal, the orb pulsed—each throb a mirror to the heartbeat of the Cosmic Sun, the Great Central Flame... and the Pharaoh's own waning rhythm.

He drank the monoatomic gold, gifted by the Orama—his final sacrament.

"It is time, O Son of the Sun," came the voice of the Preceptor, rippling through the ethers. Pentu's voice followed, tender and urgent: "Lift your spirit now. They are coming. Your task lies ahead—in a time not yet born."

The Pharaoh bowed his head. "I commend my Akhu to the embrace of the Aten," he murmured, his voice like dusk, sacred and spent.

Through the crown of his head, his soul—pure fire, living light—rose like a plume of starlight, returning to the heavens. His vessel, though noble, could no longer contain the seed-light of the Aten without his Queen to ground it.

A final smile, soft and knowing, bloomed upon his face.

He would return. In a brighter vessel. In a time when the world would be ready. He clasped Pentu's hand with fading strength. "You will be rewarded, dear one. For your loyalty. For your unwavering inner knowing. May the Aten guide you always."

Then came the burning away—the shedding of dross. His mind and body parted in peace. And from the Cosmos, the Aten reached down in streams of golden essence. Thousands of tiny, shimmering hands lifted his soul skyward. Returning him Home.

Pentu allowed himself the rare indulgence of tears as his beloved Pharaoh's essence departed, leaving behind only the physical shell that collapsed into his arms. He kissed the crown of the King's head, a final act of reverence. This was not grief born of sorrow, but of sacred acceptance. "We had been so close," he whispered, "to establishing the Unity, conceived and consecrated by the Aten."

He refused to lay blame—upon himself or others—for the dream that eluded them.

Instead, he transmuted his mourning into joy, for he had been divinely chosen to serve, protect, and love this Pharaoh to the very end. Pentu had long foreseen his own Westing. During the Ritual of the Last Breath in Heliopolis, the vision had come to him clearly. To have already died in vision is to disarm death when it arrives in form; the emotional charge dissolves, leaving only completion.

A grimace flickered across his face at the irony: he would West not in peace, but by the brutal hands of Horemheb's mercenaries, thrown into the Nile as an offering to the ravenous depths. He had already tasted the sensation—his final breath bubbling to the surface, mingled with his blood, as the sacred jaws of Ta-Wa-Ret, the Mother, tore through his vessel. Even in death, he would return to the Mother.

He had lost his earthly mother in a village fire, and now, full circle, he would return to the primordial Mother in spirit. For all his years of labor, mastery, and loyalty—and despite the Pharaoh's decree that the finest tomb be carved in his honor—the once-revered Physician never found the heart to confess that he would never lie within that sacred chamber in the cliffs of Akhet-Aten.

"Netri!" I cried out, pounding the reflective veil that separated worlds, powerless to alter what had already unfolded. I longed to be held by the two men I called fathers of the heart—those who nurtured me with tenderness, in contrast to my mother, whose love came wrapped in iron discipline. But I did meet them—in the inner realms, where spirit recognizes spirit. There, we shared a silent adoration, grateful for having grown together in this ephemeral grain of time. We were the Immortals. To us, physical death was but a change of robes. Our journey would continue beyond flesh, beyond time.

I whirled on the Orama, fists trembling, voice cracking. "Why did you let Smenkhkare go? I should have ridden with him—I was sworn to place the Red Lion in my father's hands. That was my covenant."

The Orama only shook his head, directing my gaze to a vision turning blood-red at the edges. There was Smenkhkare, ancestral warriors hovering at his back, shepherding terrified citizens toward the desert—carrying nothing but breath and hope. Yet along the periphery, ambushers lay in patient geometry. Their assault was merciless, precise: Atenist bodies fell, the city's sacred flame gulped into darkness.

The Amunite legions poured in with clockwork fury—marching, marching, an army of iron-scented ants. They hacked down pristine mudbrick walls; faience murals of papyrus and ibis shattered like trapped birds finding sudden release. In the sculptors' atelier, portraits of Pharaoh, Nefertiti, and our daughters were toppled, faces ground beneath sandals and sand. Trinkets destined for black-market coffers were scavenged; the rest lay strewn for future grave-robbers. Within hours the gleam of Akhet-Aten dulled to ghost. Even the Great Aten Temple was stripped—blocks heaved onto barges bound for Luxor and Karnak, to become mere filler in rival monuments.

The vision turned to Thebes—still grand, still gilded with power—where servants, soldiers and priests bustled in preparation for a celebration. We searched the scene, hoping to glimpse my lost sisters. Inside Malkata Palace, Ankh-es-en-pa-Aten, sat silently as attendants bathed and perfumed her, dressing her in a golden sheath. Her hair was pulled and braided like a ceremonial doll. Silent tears slipped down her cheeks.

Meti hovered, voice sharp. "Dry those tears, Ankhi. Be brave—like Merit-Aten. She was my first choice for queen." Ankhi's spine straightened. "Then why is she not standing here?"

"The General has decreed that you and Tut shall bear the legacy," Meti replied, brittle as dried reeds. "Today, as Per-Aat, and Tut-Ankh-Amun, your consort, you ascend the Double Throne. Pharaoh Akhenaten has Wested; history will brand him a heretic. But you"—she forced a smile—"you will be inscribed as victors, the Glorious Ones."

Nefertiti's pain twisted her once-radiant beauty as she stood with her back to the armed guards, who leveled spears at the new child rulers entering the royal quarters. Deep within, she knew she had chosen falsely—aligning herself with the last grasping tendrils of power that General

Horemheb embodied. And for that, she had sacrificed her children—made them pawns of the very machine Akhenaten had defied. How had she been so blind? The path back to Thebes was no homecoming. Akhenaten had been right. So had Merit-Aten.

"Ases-Amun is pleased," the advisor intoned coldly, "that you both adopted the name of Amun. The Aten has been silenced—stricken from our tongues. What came before must be forgotten. A new reign begins. The age of the Sun has set. Now, the Moon—and the patriarchy—must rise."

"Tut is only nine," Ankh-es-en-pa-Aten whispered, her voice raw with dread. "How can I lie with my own half-brother—tonight—and conceive? Is there no other King? No suitor from a foreign land—someone I could choose freely?" But the tremble in her voice betrayed her: she already knew the answer.

"You wrote to Tushratta. He never answered. No foreign King will risk his son in our chaos. General Horemheb has made his decree. If you wish to remain in his favor, you will obey. Do I make myself clear?" Her tone was steel, but in her eyes flickered a silent plea: *This is the only way to keep you alive.*

Nefertiti's shoulders fell. The queen who once commanded empires now stood hollowed. Her lips, once curled in triumph, sagged into the same weary frown she had once mocked on the face of Akhenaten's mother, Ti-Yee. Only now did she understand the unbearable gravity of royal decisions—the cold truth of who truly held the reins of power.

"My General," Nefertiti said softly, "insists you remain confined within Malkata for your protection. There will be ceremonies, appearances—enough to keep you occupied.

You will be the faces of Pharaonic rule, while he moves behind the veil, commanding the military and crushing dissent. He has ordered my younger sister, Mutnedjmet, to Choose him as her Consort. He claims he does not love her—but says he must, to secure his grip on Thebes."

"You have been devoted to him for years," snapped Ankhi, her fury barely contained. "Now, he casts you aside in favor of Auntie?"

"He believes my devotion to the Aten makes me unworthy to rule in Thebes."

Nefertiti's voice cracked, then hardened with bitter resolve. "We must comply with his orders, for survival. "A strained smile tugged at her lips, masking the deep bitterness. "This time, Amun will be remembered now and forever. The sun has set on the reign of Aten."

As the vision in the mirror dissolved, it left behind a hollow ache—an overwhelming sense of loss. We Aten Initiates, once bound by a divine mission, now stood exiled—from homeland, from practice, from kin. Everything we had built, every sacrifice made, was crumbling beneath the weight of history. The suffering ahead loomed vast—yet we had no choice but to take our 'titi' first steps into a future unpromised.

I stood there, helpless, reeling from the loss of everything I once held dear. Grief crushed me—weighty, suffocating—and I staggered, reaching for balance as the Orama extended his hand in silent comfort. *How?* I thought. *How could this happen?* After all I had surrendered to save my family, how had I still lost them?

Then, from within, Morainya's memory rose like a flame in the dark: *I will save them. In time, I will bring them salvation. The Revelation will show the way.*

The Orama enfolded me in a quiet embrace, his presence grounding, unwavering. When he pulled away, I saw a single tear glisten on his cheek. "This is not the end," he murmured, his voice steady, low. "Trust me. Your father will not be forgotten. He will be revered."

I gasped, sobs shaking my frame, as the truth settled cold in my bones—there was no one left to stand for me. I was alone.

"Just as Djehuty has granted the others a wish," the Orama said gently, "you too may name something you desire." "I have nothing left to wish for," I replied. The bitterness had gone—burned away. Only quiet acceptance remained. "I could study alchemy...but I am not meant to stay. I will not be reunited with Meti. Nor with my sisters." I paused. "But there is one thing..." The Orama tilted his head, curiosity kindling in his eyes. "What is it?"

"The Shadow People," I whispered, voice thick with grief. "They have followed me... their souls begging to be freed, to find peace in Amenti. They were denied rest—trapped by the violence of the past. That is all I ask. Please...ask Djehuty to re-member them. The ones who died by the sword of the Amunites. I no longer have the power to save my own family. But if I cannot rescue them, then let me bring peace to my people. Let their souls be healed, so they may find rest in the heavenly realms."

The Orama studied me, clearly taken aback by the scope of my request. "Such a desire is vast—requiring not only Djehuty's blessing but the full force of his will to manifest. I cannot promise an outcome, but I will carry your plea to the Great Architect. Still—are you certain there is nothing *personal* I may offer you? I would be honored to guide you further or carry you anywhere you wish to go."

I shook my head. "I have nowhere left. No family to receive me. No land to return to."

Keshtuat and Sarawat stepped forward, a goblet extended in their hands. "Merit-Aten," they said warmly, "come, join us."

The Orama drew me into one final embrace. We shared the radiant green light of the heart, sealing the bond forged through our shared awakening. Then we turned, slowly, toward the others—still feasting, still celebrating, unaware of the grief soon to descend.

The Preceptor raised his hand, silenced the crowd. His voice rang clear, solemn. "Now that your hearts have been awakened, you must face the road ahead. Destiny will quarter no illusion. Just as you have been transformed, Khemit enters a period of transition. Akhenaten, your beloved Pharaoh, has Wested. The city you once called home is being torn apart by Amunite mercenaries. Few will survive. I grieve to speak these words, but it is my duty. Take a moment to mourn—this was not the future any of us foresaw."

The class stood in stunned silence, mouths parted, eyes fixed on me. They waited for my reaction—some cue, some sign. I offered only a single, silent nod.

Then, in a tempered, almost ritual tone, the Orama addressed the room. "To those who wish to walk the path of Initiate at Heliopolis, the gateway is open. But you know the cost. Should you abandon your post, your hands will be severed, your eyes taken, your tongue removed—to silence any forbidden knowledge. You will be cast into the Lake of Fire and consumed by crocodiles in the next life. There is no escape. Choose wisely."

Without hesitation Ana-Kharu, raised his hand. "Please, Great One, it would be my lifelong dream to follow this path."

"It is your right," the Orama affirmed, "for you have returned with the Red Lion orb—the sacred prize."

"I will join you," proclaimed Rennutet, her voice newly emboldened. "I am no longer afraid. I am ready to be seen."

"Is there a boat that can return me to Mycenae?" Archollos asked. "I long to see my family again—if they yet live."

"They live," the Orama replied, his eyes full of knowing. "

Ra-Awab stepped forward. "My father trades there often. He would offer you safe passage.

It would be my honor to accompany you." Then, turning to Keshtuat, his voice softened. "Beloved, will you join me—and choose me as your consort? I have always loved you." She smiled and moved into his arms. "Of course," she said joining him. "I have always chosen you."

I turned away, the truth cutting deeper than any blade—I had no home left. My family was either scattered or taken as prisoners to Thebes. I was no longer needed, not now that Ankhi had chosen Tut as her consort. My heart ached. Even Archollos would leave Khemit behind; there was no place here for him.

"Merit-Aten, beloved," Archollos said, his voice laden with emotion, "my heart would know peace if you came with us. In my homeland, you will be protected—forever free of judgment."

"I do not wish to leave my home," I replied, my voice trembling. "This journey has brought me joy, deep learning—but now I do not know where I belong."

Ana-Kharu moved toward me with quiet gravity. We had endured so much together—across lifetimes, through veils of time and pain. I stepped into his arms, embracing him with a knowing born of soul memory. Overstanding now the full breadth of his journey—and mine.

My voice shaky, I said, "I am grateful... for all you have opened in me—my eyes, my heart.

You changed the course of my life. I will forever carry you in my soul, thankful that fate led you into the Kingdom of the Sun... to guide me to the *Knowledge of Self*."

Ana-Kharu's eyes softened, filled with a tenderness I will never forget. "Merit-Aten... your beauty is not just in your form—it shines from the radiance of your heart. You are the purest soul I have ever known. I was sent to shatter your innocence...not to harm you, but to awaken your wisdom. To teach you what your father already knew: True strength is not the absence of pain. It is the fire forged in its presence."

He stepped closer, the air around us charged with unspoken truth. "Your greatest gift is this: you walk among gods and goddesses—yet not all are agreeable, nor pure of heart. They do not come to guide; they come to *challenge*. I, the Magician, was entrusted by your father not to protect you, but to *place you in harm's way*, so you could awaken the power already seeded within you. He believed in your Strength—one you had not yet recognized. Only by rising through adversity, could you transcend the comforts of royalty and claim your own light."

He paused, allowing the silence to breathe.

"Your true test of Justice—your moment to defeat your enemies—will not come in this lifetime."

I inhaled slowly, the weight of his words pressing into my chest. So it was true. My father had sent him. Ana-Kharu was not only my companion—he was the *initiator*, the one chosen to ignite my remembrance.

He continued, voice reverent, breaking slightly: "Your father shielded you from suffering. But where I come from... pain is wisdom. Suffering is initiation. Death must precede rebirth. *This* is true alchemy."

His gaze locked with mine—unwavering, vulnerable. "And there's one more truth I've never spoken aloud." His voice cracked, raw with feeling. "I love you, Queen. In that time when we were One—I have never felt more held, more seen. *You* were my sanctuary."

"You—the Mystic—and I—the Magician—were drawn together by Aten's will to embody the Law of Opposites. In that union my heart opened, tempered by contrary currents. You will forever be my Queen; no king wears a crown without his queen, for they are One."

Djehuty materialized, vast and luminous.

"Know Thyself," he intoned—an echo of primordial stone. **"True alchemy is not in turning lead to gold, but in dissolving ego: the self-snared in illusion, chained by judgment, caged by the lower mind. Salvation dawns when the lesser self-surrenders and merges with the eternal current that flows from Source.**

"You each carry twin gifts—boundary and surrender—for only in their dance do your paths weave.

Cast the world's dross into the fire and Revelation rises: you are the Sun of your you-ni-verse, able to illumine the deepest collective shadow."

761

"This journey is not for profane," Djeuty intoned. **"It is for the brave who stride into triple darkness, trusting the lamp within. You are not pursued by enemies; you are pursued by your own distorted perception. Your life-stories are not punishments—they are mirrors**. **Fashioned by your hand and the Creator's, they blueprint love: whom to love, how to love, and whom to release so they too may learn self-love."**

Djehuty turned to Pharaoh's daughter, me. **"What was your lesson?"**

I raised my chin.

"Ego. Salvation. Revelation." The words rang clear, gifted by the Celestial Lords at my birth. Now I sent them onward—seeds for the next wandering soul.

The wheels of fate revolved, and we were cast again from the Sphinx's womb—reborn.

The Nile exhaled her ageless breath. Upon that ancient shore we embraced, knowing memory would dim yet never vanish. In that final heartbeat we vowed to recall one another's faces before the next great crossing.

The light we shared would flicker again in the future. And next time, it would blaze.

We had confronted ego, discovered salvation, and stepped through revelation's veil. In awakening, we remembered: we were never separate. We have always been *One.*

The Heliopolitan initiates were lost to us now. Their path spiraled inward; ours stretched into exile. As the wind carried our silent good-byes across the water, a grand barge split the current and moored before us.

"Father!" Ra-Awab cried, relief and urgency tangled in his throat. On deck stood an older noble—linen gleaming, presence commanding, hand raised in summons.

The moment had come. A choice to seal our fates.

Ra-Awab faced us, voice grave. "Akhet-Aten is no longer ours. If you have kin in Thebes—if you can mask your allegiance to the Aten—go to them. But sail with me and know this: we leave for exile. There is no return."

Silence fell, heavy as cut stone.

Tadushet and Sarawat traded a frightened glance. "Keshtuat...are you going?" Sarawat whispered. Keshtuat slipped her hand onto Ra-Awab's arm. "Yes."

Sarawat swallowed. "Then I will come."

Tadushet scanned the horizon for another path—found none. "Me too."

We bade each other farewell, hugging tightly, praying the warmth of our embrace would linger upon our souls— our tears an offering, our touch a vow—that even if time or death should part us, we would carry the memory of this touch forever. Let us remember the love, the laughter, and the shadows we had shared, now pressed into the marrow of our souls.

Commitments made, futures uncertain, the plank creaked under their steps as they waved goodbye.

Ra-Awab's gaze lingered on me. "Merit-Aten—will you join us?"

I hugged my arms tight. This choice was a severing. If I boarded, I would never touch my homeland again. Yet what homeland remained? Thebes was now a tomb for Atenists; Dendera, a cloister too small for a soul that had tasted the heavens. Was exile truly worse than erasure?

"We depart," Keshtuat urged, already on the gangplank. I shook my head. The gate had already clanged shut.

"Cast off!" the captain barked—a sharp command meant for the crew, though his gaze delayed on me a moment too long.

Oya and Okun, bereft of Anpu and Ana-Kharu, clasped hands. "We shall return south and build a life together—no one else could share what we have endured." After warm embraces and blessings, they turned toward the desert road.

Archollos and I had not mended the fracture between us. Though he surely knew my choosing was never my choice, trust once shattered takes seasons to repair. Mycenae would be his joy, not mine. I would only shadow his homecoming.

Alone on the Sphinx causeway—a hive of merchants, sailors, tax men—I wore the spotless white sheath of an initiate: invitation to predators. I needed garb that would not provoke Amunite disdain. No silver, no plan, but a fierce resolve burned: I would chart my own course.

Turning to find a new destiny—some place where I could be of service. The Sphinx causeway surged with life:

merchants, sailors, builders, traders, and Amunite guards collecting levies under their new rule. My pristine white sheath, the mark of a Heliopolitan initiate, painted a target on my back. I would need to change—quickly—before this city swallowed me whole.

Should I steal some rags? Trade my linen for a tunic? Such street scheming had always been Ana-Kharu's skill. I had never learned how to feed myself.

The crowd jostled me, pushing me from side to side. My breath came shallow. Visions of my father still clung to me like incense smoke—fading, fragrant, divine. But now only the cold grip of survival remained.

The pyramids loomed beyond the haze, their red, white, and black silhouettes blotting out the sun. Marching feet beat against stone. Amun had risen again.

I scanned the docks, heart pounding. Soldiers unloaded crates, stamping papyri with unchecked authority. The banners of Amun snapped above, their gold insignia slicing through sky and memory alike.

The Aten is dead.

Fear slithered up my spine. I did not belong here. I turned, hoping to slip into the crowd unnoticed—But were they already looking for me? Panic rose. I was surrounded. Amunite guards were everywhere—in the shops, the brewery, the exchange house. If they found out who I was, I would not be arrested. I would be executed.

Hunger gnawed at me. I had missed the feast. My hands trembled. As I passed an open basket of ripe peaches left beside a crate, instinct overruled nobility. I slid one into my sleeve. A simple peach. No one would notice.

"Thief!" A woman's shriek cut the air. My blood turned to ice. I ran. The crowd erupted—voices shouting, feet pounding. Bodies jostled like river currents. "Thief!" The word struck like a whip.

I darted toward the dock, weaving through crates and carts, my heart thundering. Just a little farther. Just— rough hands seized me.

A burlap sack slammed over my head, dust and sweat choking my breath. I kicked. Thrashed. Too late. I was lifted—thrown like a sack of grain across a shoulder. The scent of salt and tar hit my nostrils. I was being carried up a plank—onto a ship. Panic flared. I would be sold. Or worse. How had I been so naïve? To think I could wander freely through a world that had already buried the Aten?

The hold was cold and damp. I was flung inside, the hatch clanged shut, metal locking me into shadow. My fingers clawed at the sack's bottom—no use. The smell of river water rose. Oars dipped and pulled. The boat lurched backward. Too late. My peach was bruised now. So was I.

I lulled myself into a catatonic state, suspended in silence to survive the motion of the waves. Later, I stirred at the metallic *click* of the cage unlocking. Rough hands hauled me to my feet and dragged me onto the deck. The man's language was foreign, guttural. I couldn't understand his words—but I knew I was at the mercy of fate.

The sack was ripped from my body. I collapsed onto the planks, blinking in the sudden sunlight. Around me, a rough crew gathered, their faces curious and amused, voices rising in banter as they passed around cups. I hoped they could see it—that I was of noble class. That I belonged somewhere that wasn't here. That perhaps they would offer me safe passage home... wherever *home* now was.

"Stand aside!" A voice thundered, commanding instant obedience.

The crowd parted. Ra-Awab's father stepped forward, draped in fine linen, the jewels on his fingers flashing as he extended a hand. "Allow me to assist you, my *Per-Aat*."

Confused, I blinked up at him. "You... ordered this?" I asked, stunned. "You had me taken?"

He hesitated—torn between empathy and neutrality—then finally nodded. "I told my men to follow and retrieve you," he said. "I know too well the dangers young women face among idle military crews. I had to act swiftly. You needed protection."

Relief overtook me. I rose and threw my arms around his neck. "Praise be to Aten."

He chuckled softly. "Yes. Praise be to Aten," he echoed, the tension melting from his shoulders. "There is someone aboard who would not rest until you were found."

He stepped aside.

Archollos appeared—eyes storm-lit, jaw tight. His voice cracked as he approached. "I could not leave you."

Emotion swelled in his throat, raw and unguarded. "I do not care if you curse me. I do not care if you never forgive me. But I would not let you vanish into the world alone."

A breath caught in my chest. The weight of his presence, his honesty—it disarmed me.

"You can go anywhere," he added. "I will take you. I just want you safe."

The fight in me dissolved. I had resisted this truth for too long. My hand found his—warm, steady, familiar.

"My heart is leading me home," I said, voice steady. "And *you* are home. You have always been my heart."

My classmates surged forward, joy overflowing, arms outstretched in relief. They welcomed me—grateful that I, too, had chosen this uncertain adventure. Archollos looked on, eyes glinting with something deeper than triumph—*peace*. It was finally my choosing.

Later that night, the rowers had pulled us far from Khemit's cradle. The Nile's breath faded behind us, and the sea welcomed our barge with swelling waves. A southward wind pressed against us, but the sails held firm, billowing toward Mycenae beneath a thousand watchful stars.

Ra-Awab found me on the deck, voice hushed beneath the heavens. "I believe it best that you and Archollos take my father's chamber in the *naos* tonight.

He and I must speak—there are matters between us long unhealed."

I nodded and turned to Archollos, heart thudding. All of time seemed to gather here. I had been *claimed* before—by blood, by duty—but never *chosen*. And never allowed to choose.

I searched his face. "If this is not in alignment with your heart," I whispered, "I will walk away."

He said nothing. Only reached for my hand. And held it—gently, completely—as if he had never let go. "Merit-At-en, come to me."

Archollos led me up the narrow stairs, away from the warmth of communal song and into a sanctuary of shadows and breath. Below, laughter rose like incense—but here, the stillness of the night belonged only to us.

He held me as though I were both flame and offering. His heat seeped into my bones, dissolving every shard of hesitation. Kissing me deeply—slowly at first, then with rising heat, his tongue tasting my surrender. He laid me down gently on silken pillows, cushioning my body like royalty returned. Each kiss a sacred syllable whispered against skin. The press of his body was an invocation, a language older than words. His hands explored me with reverent urgency, memorizing every curve as if decoding the language of the divine.

When he slipped my white sheath over my head, I stood before him bare—not just in body, but in soul. His eyes roamed over me, not as a conqueror, but as one beholding a miracle. "I see you," he murmured, voice thick with hunger. "Not as a Queen. Not as an icon. But as the woman I have always loved. The one I have craved across time."

He shed his raiment, and at last I saw him—fully, gloriously male. Erect, powerful, yearning for me with no shame. He cupped my breasts, kissing each dusk-toned nipple, suckling them slowly, drawing sounds from my throat I hadn't known I could make.

His voice rumbled low against my skin, "I have dreamed of this. I have hungered for you, Merit-Aten. You smell like rain before it falls. I could breathe you in until the world ends."

His words—honest, unfiltered—set me aflame. My body pulsed, *longing to be filled*, to bloom under his touch. I had waited for so long to be chosen... and Archollos had done something greater. He had waited for me to choose **myself**.

"I am starving for you," I groaned against his neck.

He slipped down to cup my buttocks in both hands, kneading them slowly—claiming, adoring, awakening. His touch ignited the fire deep inside my sex, that pulsing ache that had lived dormant in me. The heat in my V rose like a tide, and I pressed into him, needing more—needing *him*.

I gasped as he knelt before me, spreading my thighs with tenderness and authority. His lips found the aching center of me, and when his tongue met my folds, the world disappeared. Pleasure crashed through me, unrelenting, waves upon waves of sensation. I cried out—not in pain, not in fear—but in recognition. In *homecoming*. There, he worshipped. His tongue moved like poetry across my most sacred place—slow, deliberate, utterly knowing. He licked, tasted, praised. His fingers found me, coaxing wave after wave until my back arched and I cried out, divine ecstasy rushing through me like a flood.

When I gushed for him, he did not flinch. He drank from me like a sacred river, and only then did he rise and enter me—slow, deep, fully present.

He entered me—*as a King reclaiming his Queen*. His scepter met the throne of my body, uniting us as if we had always been one. Gentle undulations brought me into ecstasy, for which I cried out in bliss. When his movements intensified, he desired my pleasure first. Suddenly, we were moving in unison, and our spirits merged. Our hips rocked in harmony, a song only the stars could hear.

And then...the veil lifted. The divine watched. And we became the *Sephedet*. And in that sacred rhythm, our *Kas* ignited. We danced upon the stars; we embraced the gods of constellations, and we sang with the spheres in the bliss of union.

From the curve of the heavens a colossal silhouette of Djehuty emerged, etched in starlight, ibis head crowned in gold, staff a lightning rod through the clouds. Archollos and I hovered—bodies still joined, spirits incandescent—watching the God of Divine Memory flash across the firmament like a living hieroglyph.

His voice rang through the veil:

"Through your untainted love, you have created the Sephedet. Merit-Aten, your request is granted. Call the Shadow People home."

Clasping Archollos, I lifted my voice—no longer a moan but a psalm:

"Hear me, lost souls of the past, bound by shadows and suffering. The time has come for you to rise—step into the light and reclaim what was stolen from you. In the name of the Aten and the eternal light, I call upon you to ascend from the depths, freed from the darkness that has held you captive for so long. May your souls be returned to the cosmic flow."

A breathless silence follows. Still joined with me, Archollos lifts his voice—low, reverent, echoing like thunder carried on the sea:

"In the name of the One we have become—*Rise*. Be seen. Be remembered. Be free. As long as I draw breath, your names will not vanish from the scroll of time. I carry you. I carry *her*. I carry Khemit within me. And I seal this vow in the name that now lives in my blood—Ah-Ten."

Light burst from the Ophanim, spiraling outward, pulling souls from the abyss. The apparitions shrieked—then exhaled in relief, as they ascended, finally seen, finally freed.

Above us, from the curve of the sky itself, a colossal silhouette of Djehuty emerged—etched in starlight, his ibis head crowned in radiant gold. He spanned the heavens like a living glyph, his staff a lightning rod through the clouds. For one suspended breath, we hovered—Archollos and I— outside of time, watching as the God of Divine Memory flashed across the firmament like a hieroglyph carved in light. The apparitions were gathered from near and far and pulled up into the turning wheels of light. In a bright flash of illumination, the ghosts of the past were received within the mind of God.

And then, his voice broke the veil—Djehuty's final declaration thundered across the night:

"Children of sorrow, bound in silence,

Tonight, you are seen.

Rise, ascend, be made whole.

I call you from the dark.

In the name of Aten's light,

Return to the Great Wheel of Becoming."

The fractal wheels drew every lingering spirit upward—a bright flash, then stillness. All ghosts were received within the Mind of God—

Satisfied.

Justified.

Rectified.

And it was good.

Glossary

Ab: Heart wisdom

Abydos: (Ab-Bye-Dos) A Temple on the Nile dedicated to Osiris

Aconite: A purple flower with poisonous leaves and roots used medicinally and magically

Alabaster: (Al-Ah-Bas-Tar) A compact fine-textured usually white or golden

translucent gypsum often carved into vases and ornaments. 2. a hard calcite or aragonite

that is translucent and is sometimes banded in oranges, ambers and brown

Akh: (Ak) The ancient Khemetian word for child, the shadow of his/her mother

Akhe-naten: (Ak-Eh-Na-Ten) Born Amunhotep IV, son of Queen Ti-Yee and Pharaoh Amunhotep III, name translates as Shadow of The Wiser

Akhemenu ritual: (Ak-Men-Nu) The ritual where a priest would penetrate the anal

Akhmim: (Ak-Men) On the east bank of the Nile across from Soltag lies the town of Akhmim. It is an ancient town, known as Ipu or Khent-Menu to the early Egyptians and Panopolis to the Greeks.

Akhet-Aten: (Ak-Et At-Ten) The Horizon of the Aten: Where Pharaoh Akhenaten moved his capital to. Current day Tel-Amarna

Akhu: The purest essence of a human. Our spirit guide or our highest vibrational light body and our consciousness.

Akhu Ashauru Aten: (Ak-Hoo Ah-Shar-Roo) The Liturgy to Aten

Alchemy: The ancient sacred science of transformation, blending spiritual wisdom and natural philosophy. Rooted in Kemet and later practiced worldwide, it seeks the transmutation of base metals into gold and, more profoundly, the refinement of the soul into divine illumination.

Algol: the Demon Star and comes from the Arabic Al Ra's al Ghul meaning 'the head of the demon.'

Amaret: (Am-Ar-Et) The Lady of Two Eyes—the blind mystic

Amarna: (Ah-Mar-Na) The current name for Akhet-Aten, where Pharaoh Akhenaten moved his capitol to. Present day Tel-Amarna

Am Duat: (Ahm- Doo-At) The astral plane one enters upon death before one goes to Amentii

Amentii: (Ah-Men-Tea) The Heaven plane

American State National: A man or woman who claims their birthright political status as a living being of their state, not as a federal "U.S. citizen." This status restores standing under the land and soil jurisdiction, affirming sovereignty and lawful self-governance.

Amexem: An ancient name for the lands of North Africa, often identified with Morocco and the ancestral homeland of the Moors. It signifies the cradle of civilization and Moorish heritage before colonial renaming and division.

Amun: (Ah-Moon) The god of the air. "The Hidden One" was the state god of Thebes in the 18th Dynasty. Amun is also the fifth stage of the sun, when the earth falls into Darkness, greed, superstition and fear dominate the populace

Amunnites: (Ah-Men-Nights) Anyone who worships Amun

Amunhotep III: (Ah-Moon-Ho-Tep) The Pharaoh of Egypt, married to his younger sister Sit-Amun and his consort Ti-Yee, father to Akhenaten

Ankh: An ancient Kemetic (Egyptian) symbol shaped like a cross with a loop at the top, representing life, immortality, and the union of masculine and feminine energies. Often called the "key of life," it signifies eternal existence and divine balance.

Ankh-es-en-pa-Aten: The third daughter of Queen Nefertiti

Antimony: A silver grayish rock that was used to make kohl eyeliner

Ana-Kharu-We-Shat: the Gold Magician (Nebweshat) who arrives in Akhet-Aten

Anpu: the male harpist in Anakharu's troupe

Apuati: (Ah-Pu-Ah-Tea): The Shining One, a name of endearment for Pharaoh Akhenaten

Ári Heru Nefer: A Kemetic phrase meaning "the good and noble rising of Heru (Horus)." It embodies the victorious ascent of the divine child, symbolizing renewal, sovereignty, and the triumph of light over chaos.

Archbishop Guieseppe DeLaurentis- the chief bishop responsible for an archdiocese. He was the ecclesiastical province over the St. Mary's Cathedral

Archollos: (Arc-Hol-Lows) The blond boy rescued from a ship wreck, nephew of a King

Ases-Amun: (Ah-Sess-Ah-Moon) The Chief High Priest, the Hanuti black sorcerers and theAmun High Priest

Asgat: (Oz-Got) The Khemitian word for water, also Merit-Aten's feral cat

Atef Crown: (Ah-Tef) The elongated oblong crown with two feathers worn by Osiris

Aten: (Ah-Ten) Fourth stage of the Sun, Aten the Wiser and benevolent ruler, represents when there is a full flowering of consciousness and all are enlightened, represented in Amarna art as a sun disk with rays extending in hands touching all

Atticus, Crispin: A Moor, and one of the chiefs of the indigenous people on the land. First to die in the American Revolution

Ay: (Eye) Father of Nefertiti, The Royal Fanbearer to Queen Ti-Yee and her son Akhenaten

BAR: Acronym for *British Accreditation Registry*, the guild system through which attorneys pledge allegiance to the Crown. In sovereignty studies, it represents the corporate legal structure that stands apart from the people's common law.

Barque: (Bark) A sailing ship of three or more masts having the foremasts rigged square and the aftermast rigged fore-and-aft. Or a portable smaller wooden version used to transport a golden idol of Amun for Festivals

Ba: The Soul

Bastet: (Bass-Tet) The Cat Goddess and Merit-Aten's panther

Ben Ben stone: The pyramidal meteorite that hit the earth. This is where the phoenix rose from the primordial soup.

Bread beer: A thick beer that looked like gruel. Alcohol killed parasites and bacteria.

Califia: Cal-un-FEE-ahh A Black queen. A warrior of America long before Spain claimed it.

Canaanites: the CaucIbenans: Caucasians were the blonde-haired blue-eyed beings found in the Caucasoid Mountains between the Black Sea and the Caspian Sea

Celestial Lords: The Lords of Karma with whom Merit-Aten made a deal before birth

Charnal House: Per Nefer House of Beauty or the place of Embalming

Choosing: In this matrilineal society – the name and property and throne is passed on through the mother. A daughter is allowed to choose her mate

Civilly Dead: A legal condition in which a person is stripped of their civil rights and treated as if legally deceased. Often applied through imprisonment or loss of status, it renders one unable to own property, sue, or exercise sovereignty.

Cohen, Sheldon:-Morainya's Accountant married to Loretta

Consort: A husband or wife

Coronado, Salvador: The American State National Common Law Lawyer

Cosmic Sun: The Great Central Sun – home of the Aten

Co-regents: When the Pharaoh appoints a son or daughter to rule with him in order to educate him/her in court matters.

Deben: A measurement of silver

Dendera: (Den-Der-Ah) The Temple on the Nile dedicated to Hathor, where the Per Akh birth house is located and home to the Maidens of Amem

Demesne: Domain or Mansion

Djed: (Jed) Grandfather, or the name of the pillar associated with the backbone, symbolizes stability

Djedti: (Jedi) Grandmother

Djeuty: The Ibis headed God known as Thoth

Easting: Birthing, or being born and refers to the Sun rising in the East at the beginning of each day

Electrum: Gold and silver mixed with a bit of copper

Ethnotrichology: of the African culture-Ethnology is a branch of cultural anthropology dealing chiefly with the comparative and analytical study of cultures (trichology) is the scientific study of hair, scalp, hair follicles, including their structure function, and diseases.

Faience: (Fay-Ence) Glazed ceramic usually a royal blue color

Fanbearer: He Who Has the Ears of the King or Queen

Forbidden Fruit Café: The New Age Metaphysical Bookstore in San Francisco

Fassi, Mrs.: the Administrator for the Black History installation at the Museum

Frankincense: (Frank-En-Sense) Dried tree sap -that comes from trees of the genus Boswellia

Gold Gates Sanctuary: Dementia Care Facility for Stella Napolitano

Grogup: Choosing ceremony

Gypsum: Pure gypsum is a white rock but sometimes impurities color it grey, brown or pink. Its scientific name is calcium sulphate dehydrate also known as Plaster of Paris. Gypsum, wood and linen are glued together to create a hard panel for chariots.

Hanuti: (Ha-Noot-Tea) The elite black sorcerers of the Amun priesthood

Hapi: (Happy) Neter or God of the Nile and the annual flooding

Harem: (Hair-Em) House or private quarters for the living area of women and children

Hathor: (Hath-Or) The Cow-earred Goddess of Denderah, who rules over childbirth and music

Hatshepsut: (Hat-Shep-Soot) Queen Hatshepsut, wife of Tutmosis II, who died and left the throne to his son Tutmosis III. Hatshepsut shared co-regency with stepson Tutmosis III but declared and portrayed herself as a male Pharaoh.

Heka (Heck-Ah): The Kemetic Neter embodying the divine power of the spoken word, sacred sound, and creative force of life itself. *Hekau* (plural) are words of power, later symbolized by the crook, signifying guidance and divine authority—revered as the essence of existence beyond "magick."

Heliopolis: (He-Lee-Op-Po-Lis) The solar cult temple of ancient Khemit, dedicated to Ra and the Ennead. Known as *Iunu* in the native tongue, it was a center of priestly wisdom, astronomy, and solar rites.

HeMeti: (Heh-Me-Tea) The female head of the household, She Who Has the Last Word. The symbol for Isis is a woman with a throne on her head meaning the woman passes on the throne and should be treated with great respect and given a chair with a stool for her fee.

Hep-Mut: (Hep-Moot) The dwarf nursemaid to Merit-Aten

Heruphant: A hierophant, spiritual teacher, or high initiate who reveals sacred mysteries to the worthy. In the Kemetic current, linked to Heru (Horus), it signifies one who embodies divine wisdom and guides others on the path of sovereignty and awakening.

Hieroglyphics: (Hi-Ro-Glyph-Icks) Greek for sacred texts, the carved reliefs on the walls

Hittite: (Hit-tight) The great enemy of Egypt in Hatti, North Syria. They were a mixed race of people who occupied most of Antolia

Holy of Holies: The most sacred inner sanctum called the Djeser-Djeseru

Hoopoe bird: The Hoopoes are a small Old World family of two or three species. All have long, thin, and decurved bills; broad round wings; square tails crossed by a wide white band, and long erectile crests. All species also have dramatic black and white wing patterns

Horemheb: (Hor-Em-Heb) The General under Pharaoh Akhenaten, his name translates as Big News of He Who Comes to the Feast, he was a cheese maker's son from Khepert and later ruled as a Pharaoh

Hyksos: Canaanites *Those who Crossed Over, The Hyksos* the Hyksos were foreign rulers in Khemet (Egypt), often linked to Canaanite origins, later associated with Caucasian/Saxon Caucibenans migrations

Iben Fatah al Abl Mohammed: a sovereign Moor and wisdom-keeper, who appears as teacher, mirror, and challenger. He embodies ancestral memory, guiding Morainya toward sovereignty, hidden truths, and the reclamation of her soul's divine inheritance.

Ibow Nesser: Meaning "Lion's Heart," a sacred alchemical object and symbol of courage, sovereignty, and divine strength. It represents the spiritual fire within that cannot be conquered, only awakened.

Isis or Aset: The Goddess of nature and magic and fertility, consort of Osiris.

Jackal: The Egyptian jackal (Canis aureus lupaster) also known as the African wolf or wolf jackal feared for digging up and eating the dead

Jilbab and Hijab: Traditional Muslim garments; the jilbab is a long, loose outer covering, while the hijab is the headscarf worn to veil the hair and neck as a sign of modesty.

Ka: The physical or astral projection of the soul that is still attached to the body

Kalabsha Temple: Originally built at Kalabsha (Talmis)

Kalasiris- simple linen dress spun from coarse uneven fibers or elegant with shoulder straps

Kanberg, Wallerstein and Katz: the San Francisco attorneys representing the Napolitano family

Kanberg, Stanley: Founder and personal attorney for the Napolitano family

Karnak: (Car-Nak) The Administrative Temple of Amun in Thebes, where the Amun priesthood, clergy, scribes, stewards and overseers remained after Akhenaten outlawed their religion

Khu-Hekau and The Calling Forth of the Wested: The prayer to bring the dead over to the netherworlds

Kepresh Crown: (Kep-Resh) The blue crown or war crown made of cloth or leather

Keshtuat: (Kesh-tu-a) The Nubian girl with long braids in the class of initiates, daughter of the Court Costume Maker

Khemit, Khemitian: KMT (Chem-It) Name for Egypt referring to the black alluvial soil

Khemitologist – A scholar or seeker who studies the living Afrikan traditions of Khemit (ancient Egypt), honoring indigenous wisdom, spirituality, and culture beyond colonial Egyptology.

Kheper: (Kef-Er) The first stage of the sun when light begins to shine upon the people, also another name for the scarab beetle who pushes a ball of dung

Khepert: The town where Horemheb is from

Khyphi: (Kef-Ee) A heavy incense used to fumigate the temples

King's List: The 18th Dynasty record of Pharaohs that omitted Akhenaten, Tut-Ankh-Amun or Ay reflecting their erasure from official history.

Kiya: The Royal Harpist and mother to Smenkhkare and Tut-Ankh-Aten

KMT: (Chem-It) The black land of Egypt, famous for the alluvial soil washed down from the Nile flood

Kohl: The eyeliner commonly used to shield the eyes from the harsh sunlight

Kom Ombu: The Eastern Nile Temple dedicated to two gods—Sobek the Crocodile and Horus, the Hawk-headed Deity

Kufi: the short rounded, brimless cap traditionally worn by men in the African diaspora.

Kumpo: By tradition the Kumpo is a ghost and mythical figure of the Jola people.

Kuwsh or Kush: An ancient kingdom along the Nile south of Khemet (Egypt), renowned for its melanated pharaohs, gold, and cultural influence on dynastic Egypt Pharaohs.

Land and Soil Jurisdiction: The highest lawful authority rooted in the physical earth, recognized as the domain of living men and women. Distinguished from corporate or maritime jurisdictions, it embodies true sovereignty, where rights flow from natural law and the land itself.

Law of Opposites: The principle that all things manifest in duality (light/dark, male/female, above/below), where contrast creates balance and deeper understanding.

Longinus: Roman Centurian who pierced Jesus's side when he was hung from the cross.

Lotus: A perennial plant in the monogeneric family Nelumbonaceae

Lustration of the Rites: A ceremonial act of purification through water, fire, or sacred oils performed before entering holy rituals or mysteries.

Ma'at: The ancient Khemetic principle of truth, balance, order, justice, and cosmic harmony, upheld as the foundation of both universal and earthly law.

Magick: The human attempt to manipulate unseen forces, nature, or others through will, ritual, or spellcraft. Akhenaten outlawed it because he sought direct communion with the Aten—pure divine light—unmediated by sorcery, illusion, or priestly control, emphasizing truth (*Ma'at*) over manipulation.

Ma-Nat: The Merchant's consort

Marfan Syndrome: A genetic disorder that affects the body's connective tissue, often causing elongated limbs, fingers, and facial features. Some scholars have attributed Akhenaten's unusual statues and artistic depictions to this condition, though others view them as symbolic rather than medical.

Malicado, James: The Judge who is in charge of the Mediation

Malachite: (Mal-La-Kite) Emerald green stone.

Malkata Palace: (Mal-Ka-Ta) The mudbrick palace of Pharaoh Amunhotep III and Queen Ti-Yee located in Thebes

Mandragore: (Man-Dra-Gor) The root of a nightshade that contains deliriant hallucinogenic used in magic rituals

Mami Wata – A revered African water spirit, often depicted as a Sibyl or mermaid or prophetess, embodying mystery, healing, and divine feminine power.

Maru: The Egyptian word for lake in front of the Luxor Temple

Mediation: (Settlement Conference) – A guided negotiation process where disputing parties meet with a neutral facilitator to seek resolution outside of formal judgment.to agree to a sum of money to settle out of court

Medjay: An ancient Nubian people renowned as desert scouts, warriors, and protectors. Over time, they became the elite paramilitary force of Khemit, guarding sacred sites and serving as Pharaoh's loyal protectors.

Meket-Aten: (Meke-Taten) The frail second daughter of Queen Nefertiti and Pharaoh Akhenaten, Merit-Aten's younger sister

Melanin: –The natural pigment found in skin, hair, and eyes, offering both color and protection by absorbing light and shielding against the sun's rays.

Melokiyah: (Mel-Oh-Ki-Yah) A traditional dish in Egypt. Some people believe it originated among Egyptians during the time of the Pharaohs. Similar to spinach.

Mendation: To mend or restore

Menit Necklace: The gold disc collar presented to Ay

Mekeesh: The Annointing Ceremony

Messah: (Mess-Ah) Crocodile Oil

Mes-sah-ah: The Anointed One of the Inner Realms

Meti: (Met-Tea) Merit-Aten's pet name for her mother, short for HeMeti.

Merit-Aten: (Mery-Taten) Beloved of Aten, First born daughter of Per Aat Nefertiti and Pharaoh Akhenaten

Mitanni: (Mit-Tan-Ni) A feudal state established by the Hurrians located around Naharin between the Upper Tigris and the Euphrates Rivers

Mudbrick: The clay bricks made for homes, palaces, and anything that wasn't meant to be permanent and could be washed away

Murrs of America: A term used to describe the Moors who settled in the Americas, carrying forward their rich cultural, spiritual, and ancestral legacy.

Monoatomic gold: A refined gold compound said to have been used by ancient royalty for heightened health, longevity, and spiritual awareness. Revered as a sacred substance, it was believed to activate higher consciousness and divine connectionGold compound used by the ancient royalty for enhanced health

Moors: A historically diverse, Muslim people of North African and Iberian descent, renowned for their contributions to art, science, and architecture during medieval times.

Moors of Turtle Island: The Indigenous Moors of the Americas, including Washitaw, Chickasaw, and Cherokee lineages, who preserved sovereignty and identity through Moorish heritage. Ancestral titles such as *El, Bey, Dey,* and *Al* affirm their divine birthright and lawful standing.

Moor: Descendants of the ancient Moabites, whose bloodlines extend through Amexem and Turtle Island. Identified as "Moorish" by nationality and Islamic by faith, they carry a sovereign heritage beyond the colonial label of "African American."

Mycenae: (My-Sin-Nay-Ah) An ancient city of Greece (c. 1600–1100 BCE), renowned for its warrior-kings, fortified palaces, and role in Homeric epics. Often associated with early encounters between Aegean Greeks and Khemit (Egypt) in trade, diplomacy, and myth

Myrrh: (Murr) The dried oleo gum resin of a number of Commiphora or dhidin species of trees

Naos: (Nay-Oos) Covered shelter in the middle of the boat

Napolitano; Aldo and Harriet – Aldo is the male antagonist and Uncle of Morainya

Napolitano Interiors: San Francisco's Renaissance Interior Decorators

Napolitano, Morainya: protagonist and daughter of Stella and Stephano Napolitano

Napolitano, Nico and Gina: Morainya's brother and sister-in-law

Napolitano; Stella and Stefano: Founders of Napolitano Interior and parent's of Morainya, Nico, Francesca and Emilio

Nefer-kheperu-Ra-ua-en-Ra: name of Akhenaten

Nefertiti: (Nef-Er-Tea-Tea) She Who Walks In Harmony – the Per Aat of Egypt and wife of Pharaoh Akhenaten

NefernefruRa: (Nef-Er-Knee-Fru-Ra) and Nefernefru: (Nef-Er-Knee-Fru) the Younger- the two twin daughters of Nefertiti and Akhenaten

Nefer-Ne-FruAten – Throne name of Queen Nefertiti, meaning "Beautiful are the Beauties of Aten," signifying her devotion to the sun deity Aten.

Nemes headdress: (Nem-Ease) The striped headcloth worn by pharaohs or *Nemesa* which means the sweet touch of the feminine

Neter: (Net-Er) A god or goddess. Also a neter is one of the senses. Ancient belief is that we used to have 360 senses awakened within us but devolved to having only five. An interdemensional gateway

Nine Ether Hair – A sacred term for tightly coiled, kingly hair, viewed as a natural antenna connecting humans to divine and cosmic energies.

Netri: (Net-Tree) Merit-Aten's pet name for her father, Akhenaten

Nubia: (Neb-Yah) "The Precious Land," south of Khemit, famed for its rich gold, silver, and copper mines. A powerful kingdom with deep spiritual and cultural ties to Egypt, it was both trading partner and rival throughout history.

Nuwbuns -Nubians – Descendants of the ancient Kushite people of the Nile Valley, renowned for their dark skin, rich culture, and contributions to Khemetic civilization.

Okun: male drummer in Ana-Kharu's troupe

Oon: The third stage of the sun in early afternoon

Opening of the Mouth Ceremony: Funerary ceremony to open the mouth of the deceased to allow them to speak in the next world

Ophanim: Angels known as the *Thrones*, depicted as fiery, many-eyed wheels forming the chariot of God. They embody peace and submission, serving as the foundation upon which the Divine rests.

Oracle: A visionary or psychic

Orama: The Chief Preceptor of Heliopolis guardian of solar wisdom and initiatory rites. A spiritual overseer who instructed priests and seekers in the mysteries of Ra and the Ennead.

Osiris: (Oh-Sigh-Rus) One of the ancient gods who was married to Isis and later killed and dismembered by his jealous brother Set

Oya: the female dancer in Ana-Kharu's troupe

Palanquin: (Pal-An-Quinn) A vehicle or chair, which transported by people to carry Royalty or the elite

Papyrus: (Pa-Pie-Rus) A thick paper-like material produced from the pith of the papyrus plant, Cyperus papyrus, a wetland sedge that was once abundant in the Nile

Pentu: (Pen-Too) Chief Royal Physician for Queen Ti-Yee and Akhenaten and his family

Per Aat: (Per-Ah) The Queen of Egypt, the Greek translation means High House or Royal Palace and is the origin of the word Pharaoh

Per Aat in-waiting: The next in line to be the Queen of Egypt

Per-Akh: A birthing house or House of Children

Per-Ba: House of the Soul or Temple such as Luxor or Karnak

The Pert m Hru: (Per-M-Heru) The Book of the Dead or the Book of Coming Forth by Day

Per-Hay: House of Rejoicing or Palace such as the Malkata Palace

Per-Ka: House of Burial for the Astral body or spirit – a tomb or crypt wherer the Khat (body) is placed

Per-Neter: Literally "House of the Divine," referring to a pyramid as a sacred structure. Seen as a House of Energy, it was designed to transform, amplify, and transmit spiritual and cosmic forces for initiation and renewal.

Per-Nefer: House of Beauty or charnal house where embalming took place

Per-Wir: Wise man and the site of the mystery schools

Pharaoh: (Fair-O) The male King of Egypt and the origin of the word High House or Per Aat

Ptah-Mose: (Pea-Tah Moez) The Vizier of Egypt, High Official of Amun Priesthood

Pushpaka Virmana: the two-story sacred aerodynamic ship of Vishvakarma for Brahma, the Hindu god of creation, who is the Vedic form of the Aten

Ra: The God of the Sun, the second stage of the sun at noon

Ra-Awab: (Ra-A-Wab) The son of the shipbuilder and the Chief of Imports and one of the class of initiates

Rennutet: (Ren-U-Tet) The frail Babylonian girl in the class of initiates

Royal Ornaments: A derogatory term for the other foreign wives of Amunhotep III

Salat: The Islamic ritual prayer performed five times daily, serving as a discipline of devotion, remembrance, and alignment with Allah.

Sanders, Jedidiah: Morainya Napolitano's husband

Sanders, Josh: Morainya Napolitano's teenage Son

Sarawat: (Sar-Ah-Wa) The girl who honked like a goose and one of the initiates, daughter of the Royal Hair Stylist

Sacerdotal Seat: A sacred throne or position of spiritual authority, often signifying the highest priestly or divine office.

Scarab: (Scare-Ab) Scarabeus The black beetle that pushes the dung ball

Scrying: (Scree-Ing) The art of seeing the future by using a reflective image such as water, black obsidian, or a mirror

Sedje: Fear

Sekhmet (Sec-Met): The lion-headed Goddess, Daughter of Ra, embodying fierce wrath, protection, and sovereign power. As the other half of Hathor, she unites destructive fury with healing and restoration.

Senet: An ancient Egyptian board game symbolizing the soul's journey through life, death, and the afterlife.

Sephedet: A radiant six-pointed sun symbol, representing the fusion of masculine and feminine energies and the gateway to higher cosmic consciousness.

Sesh: The people of Khemit, also a clay vessel. The 12 tribes that were part of the original 42 tribes are known as the Sesh

Set: The brother of Osiris who killed and dismembered him

Set-te-pent-Ra: The youngest daughter of Nefertiti

Shaduf: (Sha-Doof): A mechanism for raising water, consisting of a pivoted pole with a bucket at one end and a counterweight at the other, as used in irrigation.

Shelley: Morainya's loyal best friend, grounding her through chaos with wit & warmth

Shemtiu Ma'ati: (Shem-Too Ma-Aht-Tea) The golden cobra signifying the alignment of the adornment of the rays on the Garment of Light

Shu-te-Pen-Ra-Uanen-Ra- The Greatest Preceptors of the Primordial Sun

Sistra: (Sis-Tra) A singular copper musical device with small cymbals to rattle in praise of the Aten. Plural Sistrum

Sit-Amun: (Sit-Ah-Moon) The sister of Pharaoh Amunhotep III who became his Royal Chief Wife- aunt to Akhenaten

Shemati: (Shem-Ma-Tea) The Radiant One, a term of endearment for Pharaoh Akhenaten

Shenta: That which cannot be seen, nor understood

Skhet-Aaru: (Sec-Ket Ar-Roo) The realm of Supreme Peace and abode of Osiris

Sekhmet: (Sec-Met) The standing lion-headed Goddess of Memphis and consort to Ptah

Smenkhkare: (Smen-Car-Ray) The Harpist's son and son of Amunhotep III, one of the class of initiates

Sobek: (So-Beck) The Lord of Faiyum, and was considered the god who controlled the waters. The Nile was very important to the people of Egypt. Water was necessary for the survival of crops, the success of trade, and the livelihood of fishing

Soffagiano, Josepha: Judge who could have ruled over the Napolitano Court Case

Solar Disk: The symbol for the Aten with hands extending in ankhs

Solar Temple: A temple in alignment with the solar configurations, such as Heliopolis

Sobek: – Ancient Egyptian crocodile-headed god of the Nile, fertility, military strength, and protection, often associated with crocodiles and the power of the waters.

So-Ka-Bekt: a Ta-wa-ret Priestess of the hippopotamus and crocodile clan

Sovereignty: The supreme authority of self-determination, free from external control or subjugation. Spiritually and lawfully, it is the birthright to live in alignment with divine law (*Ma'at*), governing oneself with autonomy and dignity.

Sovereign Citizen: A modern term often used (sometimes pejoratively) to describe individuals who reject corporate government authority, asserting their natural, common law, or divine rights. Distinct from true *sovereignty*, which is rooted in lawful standing and spiritual self-governance. Sovereign: Free vs. Citizen: subject of the State or the Roman Empire; a SLAVE.

Spikenard oil: (Spike-Nard) The underground stems or rhizomes can be crushed and distilled into an intensely aromatic, thick amber-colored essential oil

Stone breathing: A mystical ability to breathe life-force into stone, allowing passage, communication, or travel through it. Seen as an initiatic skill of advanced adepts, symbolizing mastery over matter and spirit.

St. Mary's School for Wayward Boys – where Sister Stella served as a nun

Stellar Temple: A temple in alignment with the stellar configurations such as Alcyone

Sword: Originally a throwing weapon of sickle-sword shape, the khepresh could also be used as a conventional slashing or cutting sword. It appears to have been a favored weapon of the Pharaoh, as he is often depicted wielding it against enemies or during a hunt.

Tadushet: (Tad-U-Shea) One of the class initiates in the Mystery School

Tarot Cards: A deck of symbolic images used for divination, guidance, and spiritual insight

Tefnut: (Tef-Noot) Egyptian lioness goddess of moisture, balance, and cosmic order, often seen as the female aspect of the Sphinx and complement to Shu.

Thebes: (Theebs) Capitol city of Amun in Upper Egypt

Throbe: A long, flowing robe traditionally worn by men in parts of North Africa and the Middle East, often made of cotton or linen, symbolizing modesty and cultural identity.

Titi: (Tea Tea) Egyptian word for baby steps

Tithe: (Tie-the) A monthly fee collected by the Amun priesthood from the Egyptian citizens

Ti-Yee: (Tye-Yee) Translates to She Is The One – Queen of Egypt, Second Chief Wife of Amunhotep III, mother to Akhenaten

Tripartite hairstyle: (Try-Part-Tight) A style divided into three parts. Two parts extended behind the ears and down the sides of the face and the front of the body as far as the breasts. A third part went down the back as far as the shoulder blades

Tut-Ankh-Aten: (Toot-Ankh-E-Naten) His given name when he was born in Amarna, later became Pharaoh Tut-ankh-Amun

Tuthmosis: (Toot-Moe-Zes) The eldest son of Queen Ti-Yee and Pharaoh Amunhotep III who died mysteriously in a chariot race

Tutsi Tribal: An ethnic group that live primarily n Rwanda and Burundi

Thutmosis IV: The father of Amunhotep III

Von Reitz, Anna: An American author and Common Law activist known for her writings on sovereignty, citizenship, and the restoration of the Republic. She challenges corporate government structures and advocates for reclaiming lawful status as "We the People."

Unguent: An oily substance that is put on the skin or a wound

Vassals: Foreign Emissaries

Vega: The Cosmic Sun

Vizier: (Viz-Ear) Name for Osiris meaning whole, the title Vizier came from the Turkish work Wassert

Wallerstein, Bernie: Founding partner of Kanberg, Wallerstein and Katz- the fictitious Sn Francisco Lawfirm of the Napolitano family

Westing: Dying, where the sun sets at night

Ya-Kini, Yak-ini: "I am surrounded by the Power of my Positive."

Acknowledgements

I wish to express my gratitude to Rod Hayes, Chief Pontiac who opened a new world for me. I learned about Sovereignty and the United States Inc., and semantic deceit. Your knowledge is beyond this realm and I'm eternally grateful for traveling with you.

The Moorish Science Temple of America and the Honorable Noble Drew Ali is where I truly learned about the real history of America. I am grateful for having discovered the truth to set me free.

Aseer Duke of Tiers for his contributions to the Moorish Science Temple and allowing sacred information to reach the ears of those who can hear.

Bobby Hemmit, Dr. Delbert Blair, Dr. Phil Valentine, Dr Smalls have made huge contributions to the education awakening, and reclamation of Afrakan spiritual science, history, and sovereignty—restoring the keys of ancient wisdom so that future generations may walk in truth, power, and divine remembrance.

Dr. Maliki Z York for the abundance of wisdom he has shared and the Newapian knowledge of self who helped me to remember my true home and the celestial lineage from which I came.

Queen Afua, Sister Myriah Moss and Dr. Jewels Pookram you are revered in the black community, and I am grateful

791

to have encountered true goddesses who lift up women to become the true jewels they are.

My heartfelt thanks to Brotha Rich Blackmagik363, Young Elder, Phaise One, Bdell1014, King Simon for your tireless work in bringing ancient wisdom into the light of public awareness during this time of great change and awakening. Your voices have helped preserve truth, inspire curiosity, and expand the collective understanding of our shared human story.

Doctah B. Sirius for your beats and allowing us to synch with higher wisdom in the way that only you can do.

IfaBukola – My heartfelt thanks for walking me through a difficult time and opening the way for healing and over-standing. You explain things in a way that helps me transcend and overcome my limitations.

My GOM ladies who have lovingly accepted me in ways I never knew existed. You are the true goddesses who will walk us into a new world.

Lorr-elle- thank you, Sister, for our deep friendship which transcends time and for talking on so many dimensions with me, that I feel peace.

John Bautista Jr my heartfelt thanks for fighting the good fight and keeping me on point during our difficult journey through what's legal vs. what's lawful. You gave me confidence, and faith that justice will overcome by standing under God's law is the only path to salvation.

Anna Von Reitz, for the hours I have poured over your documents. You are courageous in your fortitude to turn citizens into living men and women. I am grateful that God directed me toward the path of sovereignty and freedom.

Fleur Brun – a glorious brown flower who speaks to my heart in her revelations.

Marty Petersen – Your cover designs are so rich and lively, I feel I am transported back to Khemit.

Theresa Rizzo – for reminding me to make it pretty.

Stacey Wilkins – thanks for the website and for listening.

Undun by The Guess Who - *With gratitude to The Guess Who, whose haunting song "Undun" inspired the resonance of Morainya's unraveling.*

Dizzy by Tommy Roe-*Acknowledgment to Tommy Roe, whose classic "Dizzy" spun the soundtrack of confusion and disorientation in Morainya's journey.*

Most of all to my daughters of the Sun who supported this work of wisdom handed down life after life.

Book Club Discussion Guide –
The Red Lion's Shadow

*T*he Red Lion's Shadow is more than a novel—it is a spiritual journey woven through time, lineage, and the labyrinth of awakening. The questions that follow are designed to guide deep conversation, inner reflection, and soul dialogue among readers. Whether you are part of a book club or walking this story solo, these prompts invite you to consider not just what happens in the plot, but what stirs within *you* as Morainya crosses portals of power, loss, memory, and revelation. As above, so below. As within, so without. May your discussion mirror the initiatory path of the book itself.

The Red Lion's Shadow – Book Club
Discussion Questions

1. The novel opens in ancient Khemit with a powerful betrayal. How does this early act of spiritual and political treachery echo through the modern storyline with Morainya?

2. In what ways is Morainya's legal battle a spiritual initiation as much as a worldly one? What does it strip away—and what does it reveal?

3. The concept of the *triple black darkness* (Nigredo) is introduced early in Iben Fatah's teachings. What does this phase symbolize in Morainya's journey? Have you experienced a 'Nigredo' moment in your own life?

4. Throughout the novel, multiple characters refer to Morainya as "Queen." How does this word evolve in meaning depending on who says it and in what context?

5. Did you initially suspect that Iben Fatah was the reincarnation of Smenkhkare? How did your perception shift once you realized his true identity as Ana-Kharu?

6. The Law of Opposites plays a central role in the novel's final revelation. What does it mean to be joined to one's 'equal and opposite,' and how do Morainya and Ana-Kharu fulfill that archetype?

7. Discuss the role of betrayal in the book—from family, from institutions, and even from past-life soul connections. What does the novel suggest about betrayal as part of transformation?

8. How does the courtroom serve as a modern mirror to the ancient temples of initiation? In what ways does Morainya's legal process mirror a sacred trial?

9. Several characters—Djehuty, Ana-Kharu, Iben, and others—serve as initiators or mirrors rather than saviors. What is the novel saying about the role of the masculine in feminine awakening?

10. How does the novel handle the theme of memory—both ancestral and soul-level? What do you think happens when the past bleeds into the present, especially through characters like Kanberg/Smenkhkare?

11. Morainya often questions her sanity as spiritual revelations intensify. How does the book blur the line between madness and awakening?

12. Discuss the ending. Did it feel like a resolution or an invitation to something larger? What emotional or spiritual truth stayed with you after the final chapter?

13. How do you interpret the recurring use of sacred names—Ana-Kharu, Djehuty, Merit-Aten, etc.—and the shift from modern names to ancient ones?

14. In what ways does *The Red Lion's Shadow* challenge mainstream views on religion, law, and power? Did any part of the story disrupt or confirm your beliefs?

15. If you could ask Morainya or Ana-Kharu one question, what would it be? What would you most want to know from them—past or present?

Bio - Dr. Merrie P Wycoff

*D*r. Wycoff is a recognized author, speaker, entre-
preneur, and former Entertainment Tonight Lead
Segment Producer. At the age of ten, while on a school field
trip to a local museum, Rev. Dr. Merrie P. Wycoff saw a
colossal statue of Pharaoh Akhenaten. She was instantly
mesmerized, and so was born her passion for Egypt, its
history, and its ancient people. That passion has stayed
with her from her growing-up years through today, fueled by
her long-ago vow to write Akhenaten's story. Now, she has
fulfilled that vow with the publication of Shadow of the Sun,
a 2012 ForeWord Reviews Book of the Year Award finalist in
Multicultural and Fantasy and INDIEFAB 2012 Honorable
Mention. Along with her 2nd book in the Shadow Saga: Stealing the Shadow of Death, (2014) a 2014 INDIEFAB Finalist.

Born in Orgasmic Bliss, (2014) details her personal inspi-
rational story about turning pain into pleasure and welcoming her two daughters into this world through orgasmic
labor. Merrie believes this revolutionary birthing method
will introduce a new breed of compassionate, integrated
visionary children into the world.

*Becoming Sephedet: Soul Sex, Sacred Fire and the Blue-
print of the Beloved.* (2025) In this groundbreaking book, she
bridges ancient Khemetic wisdom and modern sovereignty
teachings to illuminate the mystery of hierogamic union.

Her writing fuses myth, mysticism, and lived experience, guiding readers into the anatomy of sacred partnership. With visionary clarity, she reveals how soul resonance ignites the fire of transformation and awakens the divine mate within. This work is both a spiritual initiation and a blueprint for love that transcends time.

In addition to a B.A in Public Relations at CSUC, an M.A. in Metaphysical Studies with IMM, and a Ph.D. in Comparative Religion with The University of Sedona, Merrie earned her Egyptology Certificate with the University of Manchester in Great Britain. But she feels that perhaps the most important part of her education was her time spent with Abd'El Hakim Awyan, a recognized Elder and Indigenous Egyptian Wisdom Keeper of the Eye Tribe and Keeper of the Keys, whom she met on one of her visits to Egypt. Her studies with him taught her things that could not be learned from books, invaluable teachings of ritual, magic, and history, all of which she has put to good use in this book, and in her personal life.

Merrie resides in Colorado, close to the majesty and the magic of the Rocky Mountains. There she follows her calling as a Akashic Record Reader, Regenerative Farm Steward, artist and writer. Shadow of the Sun, Stealing the Shadow of Death and the Red Lion's Shadow are her trilogy novels in The Shadow Saga.

You can contact Merrie:
MeritAten11@yahoo.com
merriepwycoff.substack.com

www.ingramcontent.com/pod-product-compliance
Lightning Source LLC
Chambersburg PA
CBHW072340030726
47505CB00013B/5